And I heard my voice say 'I killed a boy, in Bohemia.'

The horrors we voiced – and they were not a few, once l'Angars started us on that road. A hundred bad men have a tale of sins it would be hard for any other hundred to match; and men told stories to the darkness that I would hesitate to recount even now, and I hoped that they were lying. And the voices went on, so that it was possible to grow tired of listening to the atrocities we had committed – this one for the English, that one for the king of France, or the Holy Roman Emperor.

Eventually, our voices trailed off, and we returned to silence, and I prayed. I prayed fervently; I imagined myself at the very cradle of the newborn child, and I imagined myself as a man-at-arms of the Wise Men, as I often did. The world of the Gospels was so *imminent* in the Holy Land, it made my meditations somehow practical; I could now imagine a stable, horses, the colour of the earth and the shape of the buildings in the Holy Land.

Christian Cameron is a writer and military historian. He participates in re-enacting and experimental archaeology, teaches armoured fighting and historical swordsmanship, and takes his vacations with his family visiting battlefields, castles and cathedrals. He lives in Toronto and is busy writing his next novel.

Also by Christian Cameron

The Chivalry Series
The Ill-Made Knight
The Long Sword

The Tyrant Series
Tyrant
Tyrant: Storm of Arrows
Tyrant: Funeral Games
Tyrant: King of the Bosporus
Tyrant: Destroyer of Cities
Tyrant: Force of Kings

The Long War Series
Killer of Men
Marathon
Poseidon's Spear
The Great King
Salamis
Rage of Ares

Tom Swan and the Head of St George Parts One–Six

Tom Swan and the Siege of Belgrade Parts One–Seven

Tom Swan and the Last Spartans Parts One–Five

Other Novels
Washington and Caesar
Alexander: God of War

Writing as Miles Cameron

The Traitor Son Cycle
The Red Knight
The Fell Sword
The Dread Wyrm
A Plague of Swords
The Fall of Dragons

THE GREEN COUNT

CHRISTIAN CAMERON

ORION

First published in Great Britain in 2017 by Orion Books.
This paperback edition published in 2018 by Orion Books,
an imprint of The Orion Publishing Group Ltd
Carmelite House, 50 Victoria Embankment
London EC4Y 0DZ

An Hachette UK Company

1 3 5 7 9 10 8 6 4 2

A CIP catalogue record for this book
is available from the British Library.

ISBN (Mass Market Paperback) 978 1 4091 7280 2
ISBN (eBook) 978 1 4091 6525 5

Typeset by Deltatype Ltd, Birkenhead, Merseyside

Printed in Great Britain by CPI Group (UK) Ltd,
Croydon, CR0 4YY

www.orionbooks.co.uk

For all the people who put together the amazing 'Torneo Del Cigno Bianco' in Verona, Italy; for all the chivalrous knights and clever ladies who make it so magical, and most especially for Simone Morbioli, Beatrice Morbioli, Giulia Grigoli, Maurizio Oliboni and finally for Sabina Cattazzo, the most elegant of cooks …

GLOSSARY

Arming sword – A single-handed sword, thirty inches or so long, with a simple cross guard and a heavy pommel, usually double-edged and pointed.

Arming coat – A doublet either stuffed, padded, or cut from multiple layers of linen or canvas to be worn under armour.

Alderman – One of the officers or magistrates of a town or *commune.*

Bailli – A French royal officer much like an English sheriff; or the commander of a '*langue*' in the Knights of Saint John.

Basilard – A dagger with a hilt like a capital I, with a broad cross both under and over the hand. Possibly the predecessor of the rondel dagger, it was a sort of symbol of chivalric status in the late fourteenth century. Some of them look so much like Etruscan weapons of the bronze and early iron age that I wonder about influences …

Basinet – A form of helmet that evolved during the late middle ages, the basinet was a helmet that came down to the nape of the neck everywhere but over the face, which was left unprotected. It was almost always worn with an *aventail* made of *maille*, which fell from the helmet like a short cloak over the shoulders. By 1350, the basinet had begun to develop a moveable visor, although it was some time before the technology was perfected and made able to lock.

Brigands – A period term for foot soldiers that has made it into our lexicon as a form of bandit – brigands.

Burgher – A member of the town council, or sometimes, just a prosperous townsman.

Commune – In the period, powerful towns and cities were called communes and had the power of a great feudal lord over their own people, and over trade.

Coat-of-plates – In the period, the plate armour breast and back plate were just beginning appear on European by the time of P due to adva which a steel to be

Because large pieces of steel were comparatively rare at the beginning of William Gold's career, most soldiers wore a coat of small plates – varying from a breastplate made of six or seven carefully formed plates, to a jacket made up of hundeds of very small plates riveted to a leather or linen canvas backing. The protection offered was superb, but the garment is heavy and the junctions of the plates were not resistant to a strong thrust, which had a major impact on the sword styles of the day.

Cote – In the novel, I use the period term *cote* to describe what might then have been called a gown – a man's over-garment worn atop shirt and *doublet* or *pourpoint* or *jupon*, sometimes furred, fitting tightly across the shoulders and then dropping away like a large bell. They could go all the way to the floor with buttons all the way, or only to the middle of the thigh. They were sometimes worn with fur, and were warm and practical.

Demesne – The central holdings of a lord – his actual lands, as opposed to lands to which he may have political rights but not taxation rights or where he does not control the peasantry.

Donjon – The word from which we get dungeon.

Doublet – A small garment worn over the shirt, very much like a modern vest, that held up the hose and sometimes to which armour was attached. Almost every man would have one. Name comes from the requirement of the Paris Tailor's guild that the doublet be made – at the very least – of a piece of linen doubled – thus, heavy enough to hold the grommets and thus to hold the strain of the laced-on hose.

Gauntlets – Covering for the hands was essential for combat. Men wore *maille* or scale gauntlets or even very heavy leather gloves, but by William Gold's time, the richest men wore articulated steel gauntlets with fingers.

Gown – An over-garment worn in Northern Europe (at least) over the *kirtle*, it might have dagged or magnificently pointed sleeves and a very high collar and could be worn belted, or open to daringly reveal the *kirtle*, or simply, to be warm. Sometimes lined in fur, often made of wool.

Haubergeon – Derived from *hauberk*, the *haubergeon* is a small, comparatively light *maille* shirt. It does not go down past the thighs, nor does it usually have long sleeves, and may sometimes have had leather reinforcement at the hems.

Helm or haum – The great helm had become smaller and slimmer since the thirteenth century, but continued to be very popular, especially in Italy, where a full helm that covered the face and head was part of most harnesses until the armet took over in the early fifteenth century. Edward III and the Black Prince both seem to have worn helms. Late in the period, helms began to have moveable visors like *basinets*.

Hobilar – A non-knightly man-at-arms in England.

Horses – Horses were a mainstay of medieval society, and they were expensive, even the worst of them. A good horse cost many days' wages for a poor man; a warhorse cost almost a year's income for a knight, and the loss of a warhorse was so serious that most mercenary companies specified in their contracts (or *condottas*) that the employer would replace the horse. A second level of horse was the lady's palfrey – often smaller and finer, but the medieval warhorse was *not* a giant farm horse, but a solid beast like a modern Hanoverian. Also, *ronceys* which are generally inferior smaller horses ridden by archers.

Hours – The medieval day was divided – at least in most parts of Europe – by the canonical periods observed in churches and religious houses. The day started with *matins* very early,

past *nonnes* in the middle of the day, and came around to *vespers* towards evening. This is a vast simplification, but I have tried to keep to the flavor of medieval time by avoiding minutes and seconds.

Jupon – A close fitting garment, in this period often laced, and sometimes used to support other garments. As far as I can tell, the term is almost interchangeable with *doublet* and with *pourpoint*. As fashion moved from loose garments based on simply cut squares and rectangles to the skintight, fitted clothes of the mid-to-late fourteenth century, it became necessary for men to lace their hose (stockings) to their upper garment – to hold them up! The simplest *doublet* (the term comes from the guild requirement that they be made of two thicknesses of linen or more, thus 'doubled') was a skintight vest worn over a shirt, with lacing holes for 'points' that tied up the hose. The *pourpoint* (literally, For Points) started as the same garment. The *pourpoint* became quite elaborate, as you can see by looking at the original that belonged to Charles of Blois online. A *jupon* could also be worn as a padded garment to support armour (still with lacing holes, to which armour attach) or even over armour, as a tight-fitting garment over the breastplate or *coat-of-plates*, sometimes bearing the owner's arms.

Kirtle – A women's equivalent of the *doublet* or *pourpoint*. In Italy, young women might wear one daringly as an outer garment. It is skintight from neck to hips, and then falls into a skirt. Fancy ones were buttoned or laced from the navel. Moralists decried them.

Langue – One of the sub-organizations of the Order of the Knights of Saint John, commonly called the Hospitallers. The *langues* did not always make sense, as they crossed the growing national bounds of Europe, so that, for example, Scots knights were in the English Langue, Catalans in the Spanish Langue. But it allowed men to eat and drink with others who spoke the same tongue, or nearer to it. To the best of my understanding, however, every man, however lowly, and every serving man and woman, had to know Latin, which seems to have been the order's lingua franca. That's more a guess than something I *know*.

Leman – A lover.

Longsword – One of the period's most important military innovations, a double-edged sword almost forty-five inches long, with a sharp, armour-piercing point and a simple cross guard and heavy pommel. The cross guard and pommel could be swung like an axe, holding the blade – some men only sharpened the last foot or so for cutting. But the main use was the point of the weapon, which, with skill, could puncture *maille* or even *coats-of-plates*.

Maille – I use the somewhat period term *maille* to avoid confusion. I mean what most people call chain mail or ring mail. The manufacturing process was very labour intensive, as real mail has to have each link either welded closed or riveted. A fully armoured man-at-arms would have a *haubergeon* and *aventail* of *maille*. Riveted *maille* was almost proof against the cutting power of most weapons – although concussive damage could still occur! And even the most strongly made maille is ineffective against powerful archery, spears, or well-thrust swords in the period.

Malle – Easy to confuse with *maille*, *malle* is a word found in Chaucer and other sources for a leather bag worn across the back of a horse's saddle – possibly like a round-ended portmanteau, as we see these for hundreds of years in English art. Any person travelling, be he or she pilgrim or soldier or monk, needed a way to carry clothing and other necessities. Like a piece of luggage, for horse travel.

Partisan – A spear or light glaive, for thrusting but with the ability to cut. My favorite, and Fiore's, was one with heavy side-lugs like spikes, called in Italian a *ghiavarina*. There's quite a pretty video on YouTube of me demonstrating this weapon ...

Pater Noster – A set of beads, often with a tassle at one end and a cross at the other – much like a modern rosary, but straight rather than in a circle.

Pauldron or Spaulder – Shoulder armour.

Prickers – Outriders and scouts.

Rondel Dagger – A dagger designed with flat round plates of iron or brass (rondels) as the guard and the pommel, so that, when used by a man wearing a gauntlet, the rondels close the space around the fingers and make the hand invulnerable. By the late fourteenth century, it was not just a murderous weapon for prying a knight out of plate armour, it was a status symbol – perhaps because it is such a very useless knife for anything like cutting string or eating ...

Sabatons – The 'steel shoes' worn by a man-at-arms in full harness, or full armour. They were articulated, something like a lobster tail, and allow a full range of foot movement. They are also very light, as no fighter would expect a heavy, aimed blow at his feet. They also helped a knight avoid foot injury in a close press of mounted mêlée – merely from other horses and other mounted men crushing against him.

Sele – Happiness or fortune. The *sele* of the day is the saint's blessing.

Shift – A woman's innermost layer, like a tight-fitting linen shirt at least down to the knees, worn under the *kirtle*. Women had support garments, like bras, as well.

Tow – The second stage of turning flax into linen, *tow* is a fibrous, dry mass that can be used in most of the ways we now use paper towels, rags – and toilet paper. Biodegradable, as well.

Yeoman – A prosperous countryman. Yeoman families had the wealth to make their sons knights or squires in some cases, but most yeoman's sons served as archers, and their prosperity and leisure time to practise gave rise to the dreaded English archery. Only a modestly well-to-do family could afford a six foot yew bow, forty or so cloth yard shafts with steel heads, as well as a *haubergeon*, a sword, and helmet and perhaps even a couple of horses – all required for military service.

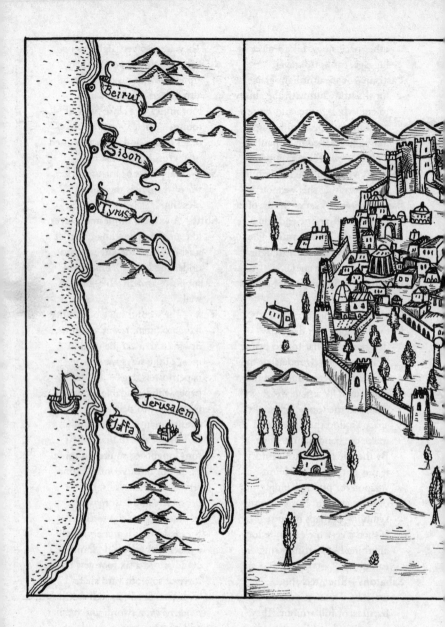

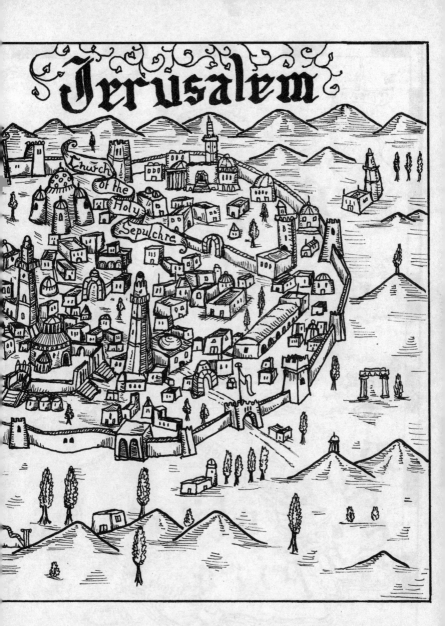

Jerusalem

Church of the Holy Sepulchre

Bulgaria
✠ ✠
Constantinople
1366-7

Black Sea

Constantinople

Marmara

PROLOGUE

Calais, June 1381

Chaucer smiled. 'You are quite the hidden man, William. I had no idea you held a barony on Cyprus.' He raised his cup to Gold. 'That was a fine tale. I think I even believe parts of it. Did you go to Jerusalem?'

Gold nodded. 'We did. But you know Sabraham, so you've heard all this before,' he said.

Chaucer laughed. 'I don't need your word on it to know that a crusade manned with the same mercenaries who burned France would come to a bad end,' he said. He set his wine cup down with a click. 'But you haven't made it to the Green Count's crusade or the Italian Wedding yet, much less to being the Captain of Venice.'

'By God's grace, Master Chaucer! Why not regale us with your own Spanish war? You spin words at least as well as Messire Froissart. And you were, I think, with the prince in Spain?'

Chaucer nodded. 'Aye, William. We know all of each other's secrets.'

Sir William laughed. 'Not all, I think, Geoffrey.'

Froissart finished his wine. 'I would very much like to hear of the tournament at Prince Lionel's wedding – from a participant. But please tell me of Jerusalem!'

Sir William nodded. 'Oh, the Italian Wedding ... the lists there were murderous. And it was worse behind the tapestries.' He laughed.

Froissart looked dismayed.

Chaucer guffawed. 'Now there's a tale!'

Morning came with the crowing of cocks and the rattle of dishes. The inn had remained busy until late, as a famous knight had told his tales of war in the Holy Land, and men had come: men from the castle, men from the garrison, men of the sword and men of the pen. Calais was a busy town, full of both soldiers and merchants, and a good tale was worth the cost of some beer.

But when morning came, there were hard heads and unfinished works, and crockery that had been left on the trestle tables being cleared away; bits of muttons stuck to the pewter, and the lees of wine dried like old blood in the cups. The inn's servants, most of them young women, moved briskly, picking up dishes and dropping them into steaming coppers of sudsy water. The youngest girls swept the unwanted food into wooden buckets: bread trenchers full of meat juice, and small dishes of peas and turnip which had to be scraped with your fingers into the bucket and then stacked, because Mistress was *this* particular. And the buckets of food-slop went to the pigs. Nothing was wasted except the youths of a dozen young women.

William Gold sat in a corner and watched them while he tied his points. Some of them didn't even know he was there; others avoided him the way mice move around a sleeping cat. The innkeeper's daughter brought him a cup of small beer and he raised it to her, silently, and went back to his points.

The next time the knight looked up, his former companion Chaucer was seated at his table.

'By the Trinity, messire, you move too silently for an honest man,' Gold said.

Chaucer wrinkled his lip and sat heavily. 'I'm not sure I've ever claimed to be an honest man,' the courtier replied. 'Have we received passports? And what on earth are you doing awake at this ungodly hour? We were only just abed!'

Gold leaned back and drank off his small beer. 'You are awake yourself,' he said. 'Nothing from the castle. Nor will there be. It's Sunday, messire. We should all be on our knees to our saviour.'

Chaucer winced. 'You do not mean to spend the whole of the day on your knees,' he said.

Gold shook his head. 'I have a great deal for which to be thankful,' he said. His eyes happened to cross with Aemilie's, the innkeeper's daughter. She flushed.

Chaucer shook his head and snarled, 'You pious hypocrite!'

Gold looked at him as if he smelled something foul. 'Whatever prompted that, messire, it was ill said.'

Chaucer looked meaningfully at the young woman.

Gold raised an eyebrow. '*Honi soit qui mal y pense,*' he said. 'I am off to Mass. Aemilie, would you run an errand for my old legs?'

'Old?' Chaucer asked. 'Have you crossed forty yet?'

'Yes, My Lord,' she said with a curtsy. In fact, most of her attention was on a younger woman working a stain in one of the oak tables.

'My book of hours is on my bed,' Gold said.

Aemilie bobbed again and vanished towards the stairs.

'Do you really imagine I'm tupping servant girls?' Gold growled.

'You certainly have in the past,' Chaucer replied.

'On Sunday?' Gold asked.

'Are you really so naive as to imagine that God, if there is a god, counts the days?' Chaucer asked.

Gold stood with his hands on his hips, his right hand very close to his dagger hilt. Chaucer sat at the table, apparently unmoved by the threat of the big, red-headed knight.

Slowly, Gold's body relaxed. 'By the saviour,' he said, 'I forget how you are, Geoffrey.'

Chaucer managed a slow smile. 'I forget how *easy* you are to sting.'

Aemilie appeared, bounced down the stairs, and handed over the knight's book of hours. It was very plain: a simple red leather cover, a few vellum pages with a pretty little painting of the Annunciation of the Virgin, and the rest paper; plain as plain, it might have belonged to any housewife in Calais. The cover had shield-shaped rivets bearing Gold's arms and a clasp.

Chaucer took the book of hours, opened the latch, and flipped through it.

'By the rood,' he said with a smile. 'You copied it yourself.'

'So I did,' Gold admitted. 'My clerking is not so bad.'

'All your letters lean like drunken men,' Chaucer announced.

Gold, stung, drew himself up. 'I do not make letters for my living,' he said.

Chaucer smiled. 'And I do – no doubt there is something witty to be said about the pen being mightier. Let us, for all love, go off to Mass instead.'

Aemilie's father came out to see his two famous guests out of the courtyard, and then he came back in, the smile wiped off his face, to glare at his daughter.

'Do not flirt with Sir William,' he said. 'Men like Sir William are … very dangerous. And not suitable … company.'

Aemilie put her shoulders back and turned her head slightly away.

'I can handle myself, *mon pere*. And he is a true knight —'

'A true knight who has sent more souls to Satan than the Plague,' her father said, and then ruffled her hair. 'I'm sorry. I was rankled by Master Chaucer's ... words.'

Aemilie nodded. 'Why are they so friendly to each other? If they hate each other?'

Her father smoothed his houpland and pulled the liripipe on his hood carefully through the belt that held his purse. 'I don't think they hate each other,' he said carefully.

'Master Chaucer speaks to injure Sir William,' Aemilie said.

'Hmm,' her father said. 'Yes. But perhaps ... Sweeting, men are odd cattle, and these two have seen many things together. I think that they ...' He paused, looking into the kitchen, Whatever fatherly wisdom he was going to impart was lost in a crash of crockery and the sound of pewter flagons bouncing off stone and tile, and enough blasphemy to fill the circles of Hell so lovingly described by Chaucer's hero, Dante.

Three hours later, Sir William returned, accompanied not just by Chaucer but by his own squire and a dozen of his pages and men-at-arms and archers as well. If they were all nursing the results of the night before, none of them showed any sign. Aemilie directed her dozen women in serving wine and loaves of good bread and wedges of thick English cheese. Men who'd been to Mass had not eaten.

Sir William met her eyes. 'And you, mam'selle?' he asked. 'When do you go to Mass?'

'Which I've been,' she said with a curtsy.

Chaucer nodded. 'She's been up an hour before we were, William. Probably heard Matins.'

'And I say my own hours,' she put in. And then curtsied, as she had spoken out of turn, but she was not willing that Master Chaucer would believe her a light of love.

Chaucer smiled at her. 'You have a book of hours, lass?' he asked.

She went behind the inn's low bar and emerged with her book, which was long and narrow and conscientiously made. It had more decorations than Gold's.

'Flemish?' Chaucer asked.

Aemilie nodded. 'My pater brought it to me. For Christmas,' she said.

Chaucer nodded. 'Would you like a new prayer, Aemilie?' he asked.

'Oh,' she said. 'Are you a priest?' She didn't think he looked like a priest, but a woman could never tell.

'Just a clerk, lady. But I write prayers. Here – how do you feel about Saint Mary Magdalene?' he asked.

Aemilie frowned. 'I wonder ...'

Chaucer's eyes sparkled with his particular and wicked merriment. He took a pen case off his hip and paused. 'Perhaps not the right saint for an attractive young woman. Saint Catherine of Alexandria?'

'The Blessed Virgin, if you please,' she said, bobbing.

Chaucer flipped through her book. He paused, took out his own, the most elaborate of the three on the table, and opened it to a pretty picture of the Annunciation.

'Damn me, that is fine,' Gold said.

'You know where I got this,' Chaucer said. He looked up from his pens.

'By the sweet Saviour of man,' Gold said. He weighed it in his hand as if it was made of gold and he found it wanting. 'Hers?' he asked, and his tone invested *hers* with a great deal of meaning.

'Oh, yes,' Chaucer said.

He began to copy his prayer to the Virgin into the young woman's book. His script was perfect: neat and fine and dark.

Even the innkeeper stopped to watch him write.

'Beautiful,' he said.

Chaucer smiled. He was concentrating; his mouth was slightly open, and Gold smiled to see it.

Chaucer came to the mid-point in the prayer and breathed before writing *domini*.

'Will you tell Froissart about Jerusalem?' he asked.

'Of course. It's wet outside – the lads like a story and so do the lasses.' Gold looked out of the narrow windows and shrugged. 'Will you tell them about the Italian Wedding?'

Chaucer frowned. 'No. You may, if you like. I ...' He took a breath and finished the prayer. 'I still see it.'

Gold knew that Chaucer meant 'I still see her. Dead.'

He reached out and put a hand on Chaucer's shoulder.

An hour later, the common room was full again. Gold sat back to tell his tale. Froissart had a pen in his hand today, and so did Chaucer.

5

But Chaucer was copying prayers for Aemilie, and filling her little book. Froissart was copying down what Sir William Gold had to say.

FAMAGUSTA

November 1365 – January 1366

There are many advantages to word fame, and not the least that men will more readily follow you if they've heard your name.

There were many men on Rhodes and Cyprus in the autumn of the year of our Lord 1365 who knew my name. I was not famous, but I had been knighted by an imperial knight on a famous field of battle and now I had played a small role in a crusade.

So when I made it known that my friends and I planned to take an armed party to Jerusalem, there was no lack of volunteers.

If you've been listening, you have heard all that I have to say about Alexandria. What happened there is still black to me, and just telling it seems like a lash upon my soul. I won't tell it again. But I will say that as the gentle weather of that autumn kissed the streets of Rhodes, many men had time to repent the sins they'd committed in the streets of Alexandria, and to think that they'd best spend some of the loot they'd gained by visiting the holiest city in the world, the scene of Christ's passion, the centre of the middlerealm, as the old monks would have it.

Many of the routiers left for Italy as soon as the Venetians and the Genoese turned their ships for home, but many stayed, because the king of Cyprus said, or at least he said at first, that he would launch a second attack immediately. But from Rhodes, the capital of my Order and Christendom's greatest fortress, we heard that the king had sunk into a lethargy. He had reason: his people were restless, he'd mortgaged his kingdom's future on his crusade, and his wife, *so men said*, had been both unfaithful in body and unfaithful as a vassal, stirring treason. Although I was now a baron of Cyprus, I was not tempted to remain and be a courtier at *that* court.

Not even a little.

Besides, my friends – my surviving friends, Fiore dei Liberi, a knight of Udine, and Nerio Acciaioli, a Florentine knight, and Miles Stapleton, who was knighted on the beach of Alexandria with Steven Scrope – you know that name, don't you, Chaucer? Of course you do … At any rate, my friends had sworn on our brother Juan's tomb to go to Jerusalem. And I had promised my lady, Emile d'Herblay.

We had originally thought that it would just be a few of us. In fact, when we first broached the idea on Rhodes, the older Hospitallers told us to go unarmed, as pilgrims. The Hospital is, in part, a business, and maintains hospices, inns, and hospitals across Europe for pilgrims going to any of the great sites: Padua, Rome, Compostela, Constantinople or Athens or Corinth or Jerusalem, holy of holies. In Outremer, they arrange letters of credit and travel passes with the local Islamic rulers. And let me just add, as a man of the world, that it was said on Rhodes by the oldest knights that the Holy Land was safer and easier for pilgrims under the Mamluks than it had ever been under Frankish rule.

I suspect I'll have a great deal to say tonight about the Mamluks and the Turks and their ways. I'll let that be, for now.

So we laid our plans, and then, perhaps a month after Alexandria and less than a week before we were due to board a Venetian great galley for the short dash to Jaffa, Nicholas Sabraham appeared as if out of the aether, as he usually did, and we sat in the courtyard of the English inn. The sunlight of the Mediterranean is still brilliant in October, and there were old sails from the Order's fighting galleys rigged in most courtyards so that tired old soldiers could sit and tell lies in comfort.

By the Cross, friends, I thought I was old that autumn. Old, wise, and tired.

Sabraham was a favourite with my archer, John the Turk. They swapped some greeting in Turkish, and John fetched Sabraham a cup of wine, which he seldom did for me. John was a warrior and not a servant. As I have mentioned before, he would clean armour all day and his care of horses was divinely inspired, but laying out clothes and serving wine was generally beneath him. I should add for those new to the story that John was not a Turk at all, but a Kipchak, and he'd been sold as a Mamluk, taken by the Turks, forced to convert to Islam, and then taken by me and forced to convert to Christianity. I'm also sad to say, even now, that he was a better Christian than I.

Except on the battlefield.

Sabraham was another odd one, an Englishman who was a veteran of the East. Some said his family were Jews; that's possible, as the Hospitallers generally aided English Jews and still do. Sabraham spoke ten local languages and had lived in Aleppo, Damascus and Cairo and he knew more about the East than any Englishman I ever met, even in Venice. He generally led any *exploratio* of the infidels, and often went by himself. He was friends with Nerio's uncle, the great knight Niccolò Acciaioli. Did I not say that I myself enjoyed some little word fame? Sabraham was widely regarded as one of the best knights, in council or in a fight, to adorn the Order in many years.

There he sat, in the bright sunlight of Outremer, dressed in a dreadful fustian arming coat that had been new when Caesar commanded armies in Gaul and padded arming hose so grimy with dirt and oil that they were somewhere between grey and black.

'You are going to the Holy Land?' he asked, when his wine was in his hand.

I waved vaguely at the Grand Master's palace. 'I have our passports,' I said. 'Quite a sheaf of letters and several pounds of seals.'

Sabraham drank wine. 'Good for nothing but starting fires, unless they can be scraped clean,' he said.

'What?' I sputtered, or something equally nice. I'd spent the better part of two weeks walking from one office to another, arranging for all the parchment to get us to Jerusalem.

Sabraham sat back and fingered his beard. A pair of squires came into the yard with swords, saw us, and went somewhere else. My young scapegrace, Marc-Antonio, appeared and poured wine and muttered apologies.

'Oh, go and train, you worthless boy' I snapped. He was late to rise because he was fornicating. I didn't give a whit what he did in his late hours, but as I was chaste and he was not, I resented him. I didn't know the girl, but barracks rumour had it that she was Genoese and pretty and well-born, which suggested that there might be trouble.

Sabraham raised his bushy eyebrows. 'You are not usually so surly, Sir William,' he said.

'Your pardon, my friend,' I muttered. I wanted to be going to Jerusalem for a wide variety of reasons, a few spiritual, and most of them petty and even venal. My lady would not hear of a wedding, or anything beyond a chaste kiss, until we had been to Jerusalem.

Given the passion of her welcome to me on my return from the crusade, I had expected more.

Ah, yes, the endless ability of men to layer sin on sin. Fornication, adultery, impiety ...

I was distracted by my thoughts.

Sabraham cleared his throat so I started, and then nodded, as if accepting my apology. 'I am sorry if I bear bad tidings, William,' he said. 'But Mamluk rule on the coasts of the Holy Land has collapsed. The sultan has recalled almost all of his soldiers. There is no military governor in Jerusalem, even if he would accept a letter from a hostile power, which we are, just now. Does the Grand Master think that we can sack Alexandria and then casually return to the *status quo ante bellum*?' Sabraham finished his wine in two great gulps.

'I am not alone in surliness, I find,' I said, in a friendly voice. One does not want to be mistaken with a man as deadly as Sabraham.

He waved a hand in the air, dismissing my remark. 'Would you consider going armed?' he asked.

I suspect my smile split my face. To go armed to Jerusalem ... that would be a great *empris*. Or so I thought then. Age and wisdom and a little reading have forced me to acknowledge that my Saviour had little time for weapons and armour and those who wore them, and might have preferred that I go with humility.

Humility has never been my strongest attribute, I fear.

I knew that Sabraham had his own reasons. He had been to Jerusalem enough times to have a wife there, or so men said, and, while he was not a knight of the Order, men would follow him.

'How many?' I asked him.

'As many armed men as we can raise,' Sabraham said. 'I have just seen Fra Peter. If he is recovered, he will captain the *empris*. He would like you as his lieutenant.' He made an odd face. 'And I would take it as a favour if you would fetch Acciaioli. I have ... news for him.'

I had last seen Fra Peter in a bed in the great hospital of Famagusta, still recovering from three wounds taken in one fight at Alexandria's stone bridge.

After a few enquiries as to Fra Peter's health and recovery, I left Sabraham with a pitcher of wine and ran up into the inn to find Nerio and Miles Stapleton. Fiore, I knew, was off at the 'sand pits' as we called them, training squires to be knights.

Nerio was dressing. His new Genoese squire was Achille, a tall man with a broken nose, a former oarsman who had also apprenticed as a tailor. He had washed up on Rhodes like driftwood, and Nerio had just lost his squire Davide at Alexandria.

'Move the button, there's a good fellow. I'll wait,' Acciaioli said with his charming smile. 'Ah, Ser William?'

'Sabraham says we may go to Jerusalem *armed*,' I said. I was elated. So much for cynicism. 'And he wants to see you,' I said more seriously.

'A letter from home, perhaps?' Nerio said. Sabraham moved around more quickly than most men. We knew he had returned to Cyprus, at least.

Through this, Nerio was looking at himself.

Nerio had a small, round mirror of silver set in ebony. He was the only man I knew who owned a mirror. It was hung over his washbasin – we had monks' cells. He must have taken down the wooden crucifix to put the mirror up, and that says all you need to know.

He looked at himself in the mirror, took a long look, and smiled, satisfied by what he saw. Only then did he turn, smile broadening.

'Marvellous,' he said. 'Wonderful. How glad Juan would be.'

We embraced.

'Sabraham wants me to raise routiers for the trip,' I said.

'Money?' Nerio asked. He generally funded us. He was very rich, and we were not.

I no longer fought against his riches. I shrugged. 'Not yet. Surely men will go to Jerusalem for their souls,' I said.

We exchanged a look, and I sighed.

Nerio was the vainest of my close friends, and had the worst temper, the worst habits of body, the most waste and the least energy. Despite which, he and I were probably the most alike. Nerio had a low opinion of men in general.

He was seldom disappointed.

'Or not,' he muttered.

Miles Stapleton was the very opposite of Nerio in almost every way. He boiled with energy at all times. He was modest and humble, never putting himself forward. If he had a vice, I never saw it – he didn't chase girls or boys, he drank little, he didn't experiment with any of the vices of the Levant ... Did I mention Sabraham and Acciaioli playing the devil with hasheesh?

Miles could be dull though, and Nerio was never dull. There's a sad comment there on the condition of knighthood, because while Miles was certainly destined for eternal paradise, he wasn't always much company for an evening. Nerio seemed to care little for his immortal soul, but he was witty, even brilliant, and his loyalty and generosity trumped his other sins.

I do no justice to Miles. He was not so much a prig; he never commented on the rest of us except to praise us, and he was loyal, faithful to a fault. And he leaped on the Jerusalem *empris* like a dog on a marrowbone. But he could be too easy to tease; if one of Nerio's ladies exposed two inches of her breasts, Miles would flush and turn his head away, which would only egg us all on, if you take my meaning. And then pretend to indignation with humour.

Word spread rapidly. Indeed, Miles borrowed a pen, ink, and parchment from Ser William de Midelton, the turcopolier and head of the English *langue*, and we all three scribbled as best we could, writing handbills. Even Sabraham took a turn, and there we were. Most of the 'Crusaders' who remained on Rhodes were at their own expense, and in the style of Venice, the Hospitallers thought it best to keep them outside the walls. They had a camp, comfortable enough in late summer but now, I'd guess, a little chilly as the autumn winds began to blow from Thrace.

Sabraham took Acciaioli aside. They spoke for a while, and Nerio stood straighter. Finally they both returned to the table at which we were writing.

'Ser Niccolò is dead,' Nerio said without preamble.

I must digress again. The Acciaioli are incredibly famous in Italy – Florentines, bankers, and lords, too. There is no one in England quite like them. Niccolò, whom I had met, had risen from errand boy to great lord, the Grand Seneschal of Naples, no less, as well as one of the finest jousters of his day and a lord of Achaea in Frankish Greece. He had told me that Nerio was his son; in public, they were uncle and nephew, at least at times, and I confess that Niccolò had a wider variety of ... relationships ... than most men. Some said he had been the lover of the Empress Catherine; many claimed that the Prince of Achaea was actually his son.

Nerio, who was never anything but amused (or angry), was … shattered. He was pale, and he actually swayed at the news that his father was dead.

I rose and threw my arms around him. 'He was a great man,' I said, and some other twaddle. He was a great man, and no mistake, but I'd only known him a few days.

I was once no great hand at comforting man or woman, but I have learned that a hug cures a great deal. Miles was even better; whatever he murmured, it was deeply felt, immediate, and Nerio burst into tears, which was an epochal event. Miles just held him, which tells you who Miles was, too.

It was such a shock to have Nerio in tears that when Fiore came in, he paused in the entrance way, frozen in surprise. Even when he started to move, his face was still registering surprise.

'He's crying,' Fiore said, or something equally obvious. The day-to-day life of mere human beings puzzled Fiore, unless they had weapons in their hands. He walked around us, watching us the way a cat watches a mouse hole, until Nerio broke out of Stapleton's embrace.

'I wasn't even there,' Nerio said bitterly.

'Why is he crying?' Fiore asked.

Sabraham caught his shoulder and pulled him away. 'Someone close to him died,' he said.

I poured Nerio a cup of wine and handed him a square of linen that I kept in my purse for cleaning my sword. He blew his nose, drank the wine, and frowned at Liberi.

Fiore raised both eyebrows. 'Ah!' he said. 'Of course!' He stepped forward and threw his arms around Nerio as if we all embraced each other every day.

Nerio grinned, wept again, and his hands feebly pounded Fiore's back.

The young recover quickly. In an hour we had a dozen handbills written out, and all of us went down to the camp of the crusaders, where we paid a pair of *ribauds*, masterless men with threadbare cotes and hose worn to having no feet, to walk the camp and cry our 'wares'.

And the next day, as soon as the inn opened its heavy, iron-bound doors, a succession of men came into the yard to sign for Jerusalem.

They were quite a collection. There were knights, and men-at-arms, and men who claimed to be men-at-arms, and men who claimed to be squires or archers, and a couple of actual archers, and even the two *ribauds* we'd paid to do our recruiting. All told, there were nearly a hundred men, and most of them were soldiers of one stamp or another.

It's a funny thing, the word 'routier.' I'll note that to this day, it is a word men always use about someone else and never about themselves. Of course it is an unkind word, and conjures brigands and thieves and rapists, which, to be fair, most of our new recruits were. Arsonists too, I suspect. But every man of them considered himself a soldier of Christ. It was the other men who were false crusaders.

And did not my beloved Father Pierre Thomas always used to say 'My church is full of sinners'?

Sabraham stood with me, his thumbs in his belt, and watched them as they came to our table and placed their names on a roll. The men who claimed to be archers were sent with John. The rest were served some watered wine and asked to wait.

Fiore had rigged a brand-new pell in the courtyard. He stood by it with a heavy wooden waster, a wood sword, in his hand. Nerio would summon men forward by name, and they'd be asked to swing at the pell.

A few were like antic jesters, and one man was somehow afraid of the pell, or of the opinion of his fellows; he handed the wooden sword back to Fiore and fled the yard. Some took a few hacks at the wooden pole and gave over; some seemed bent on cutting it in half, and a few demonstrated style and skill, fencing with the inanimate wood as if it was a living man.

I was still at the table as the soldiers started demonstrating their skills, dealing with a trio of latecomers, all Gascons. The smallest was a surly lout.

'What's the pay?' he asked.

'Perhaps you save your soul,' I said.

'Fuck that,' he said. 'Pay me in coin or I walk.'

'Walk,' I said.

Several men looked at me. I shrugged. 'We'll do our best to keep you fed,' I said, 'but this is a pilgrimage and not a military adventure. No one will be paid.'

More than a dozen men agreed with the Gascon and left. On the other hand, more were arriving every minute, and men on their way out paused to mock those coming in. The turcopolier looked into the yard and shook his head.

We told every man that we'd summon them when the *empris* was ready. Some were satisfied, and some clearly felt that this was all wind.

The next morning, Sabraham woke me. It was still dark.

'I am ordered to return to Cyprus. There will be a delay.' I rose and embraced him, and he was gone into the darkness with his men, George and Maurice, at his shoulder like falcons on a fist.

Rhodes is a great fortress. It is also a small community of knights and monks and priests with a handful of nobly born women, most of whom are outbound or returning from pilgrimage.

The gossip is virulent, and constant. Hence, I seldom saw Emile, and she was wise to fear it, as events proved, but the separation was killing me. It is curious, and probably a dreadful comment on man, that when she refused to acknowledge my love, and demanded her favour returned to her, I bore the knowledge that she was close by with equanimity. Now that we were all but betrothed, I missed her, and I was jealous, I confess it. She went riding with Nerio or Fiore, but not with me, and she attended a different church. She had a supper with the Grand Master and a dozen senior knights; no great matter, and an honour usually accorded to noble pilgrims, but I was jealous. Of fourteen men all old enough to be my father.

So much for the virtues of chivalry and courtly love.

But on Sundays, we usually arranged to attend High Mass together, and my friends would mix with her knights. Jean-François and Bernard had not gone to Alexandria, and we reassured them that they hadn't missed anything but horror. Ser Jason had gone with the count, as a volunteer, and when I saw him the first Sunday he was tight-lipped and angry, although he grew more resigned to what he had seen, as you will hear.

At any rate, it was the first Sunday in Advent, I expect. We met outside her lodgings, near the French *langue,* and I knelt to her, and she smiled, and all my jealousy fell away as it always did.

Her knights all bowed, and Bernard, the smallest and yet the most debonair, saluted each of us and fell in with Fiore, Jason with Nerio, and Jean-François with Miles. We were well matched, and our squires and servants filled out our little train. Emile wore something blue – I remember the hue but not the garment.

'I hear that we are going to Jerusalem in earnest,' Emile said, putting her hand on mine. Oh, the touch of her fingers! I would trade my slim hopes of Heaven for another touch of her, my friends.

I nodded, trying not to snatch at her hand or act the boor. 'Madame,' I said, all correct. 'It may be that we will go to Jerusalem armed. Monsieur Sabraham reports that the Egyptian government have withdrawn their soldiers.' I looked back at Monsieur Jason. 'It could be quite dangerous,' I said.

Ordinarily, he'd have met my comment with a quip. He was a different man since Alexandria, and he shrugged and looked at Nerio.

'Will you escort pilgrims?' she asked, and she was eager, and my heart soared.

'Madame, in truth, it will not be my expedition. I am merely recruiting routiers and crusaders who wish to fulfil their vows. But Monsieur Sabraham has given me to understand that – perhaps – we might escort pilgrims.'

She nodded. Our time together was already almost at an end. The cathedral's doors were yawning like the gates of Heaven and hundreds of priests and soldiers were entering, but Emile was one of perhaps five women and most men looked at her. And why not? She was beautiful – in the full growth of womanhood, my age or a little older, with her children walking behind her, dressed in blue velvet, and a great lady from her plucked forehead to her dark red leather shoes. Her light brown hair was neatly coiled atop her head and covered in her sheer linen veil. She looked like a portrait of the Queen of Heaven.

And every eye that was not on her was on me.

And tongues would wag. I knew, in my head, that this is why she avoided me the rest of the week. To give them no reason for poison. But it irked me.

'I will have to go to Famagusta soon,' I said. 'May I send word when I know about pilgrims?'

She favoured me with a discreet smile that still had a hint of something, a promise, around the corners of her lips ...

The life of arms can be terrifying, exhilarating, or ferociously boring. Sadly, the next two weeks were the latter. After Sabraham's initial admonition and our enthusiasm, nothing happened. There was no summons from the Grand Master, although I caught him looking at me one day in the tiltyard when I was playing against Fiore – swords on horseback.

I have to say that Fiore loved Rhodes, a place where there was nothing to do but practise at arms, and where such practice was much praised and encouraged. I think he might have been better fulfilled had he taken the vows and become a knight.

At any rate, I had the Grand Master's attention, but he didn't say anything; and I asked about, and no one had heard of such an expedition except from us. Sabraham was gone again – back to Famagusta, he had said, without a word of explanation.

As an aside, I remember that I spent the next weeks scribing with some of the brother sergeants and a handful of knights. My hand wasn't good enough to copy manuscripts, but I sat with the turcopolier and his officers and made copies of accounts, and I took notes on meetings, and signed a contract with a small company of crossbowmen out from Genoa. The Order hired the best men at a fair wage, but no mercenary got rich fighting for the Order; mostly they defended fortresses, with little opportunity for plunder. It was good to feel a pen in my hand, and it was then that I started the book of hours you mocked, Master Chaucer. I began by copying out prayers to Saint Michael, and then the Pater Noster ...

It passed the time.

I practised at arms, my body and my mind healed from the brutality of Alexandria, and most evenings I sat in the English inn with a dozen other Englishmen – often with Jean-François and Jason de Bruges or Bernard le Hardi, sometimes with Nerio. It was not a hard life, but we were all waiting, and it quickly palled.

I learned a great deal about the way cards fell. Cards were new then; some men say that Franciscans brought the idea back from India – cards with printed scenes from the Gospels. They were meant to educate illiterates. Soldiers found a way to gamble with them. I doubt it took a pair of routiers an hour to work out a game.

Bah. I have missed my mark again.

On Christmas Eve, Sabraham returned, daring winter storms in an Order galley. He came in after we'd all been to vespers. The English keep Christmas with a little more boisterousness than most, although the Germans have some quaint customs of their own, as I'll share in time. But we were drinking some carefully hoarded good English ale and eating a fine game pie and laughing when Sabraham came in out of the cold.

Everyone in the common room fell silent.

'It is good to be home,' he said. We welcomed him, and he drank off a tall tankard of ale, and we all toasted King Edward. Even John.

At midnight we walked across the town to hear Mass. And then back to our inn to feast. I love Christmas.

And indeed, Emile sent me a message, which said nothing save '*amor vincit omnia*' in fine Gothic letters. I daresay my limbs trembled. And Sabraham, as his Christmas gift, brought a pass from the king of Cyprus to make a passage to Jerusalem.

'The king despairs that he will ever move his army to attack the enemy again, but there are some new lords lately come with fresh soldiers,' he said. 'Some names I had not heard before, who come too late for Alexandria and now press the king to fresh adventures.' Sabraham shrugged.

The turcopolier, William de Midelton, sat back. 'He must have drained his treasury and then some,' he said.

'They say in Famagusta that he has mortgaged the next seven years of incomes,' Sabraham said. He looked at me. 'Father Pierre Thomas is very sick,' he said.

That struck me like a hammer.

'I could not even get to his bedside. Your Fra Peter Mortimer is there, and a dozen other prelates. Even the Orthodox bishop is praying for him.' Sabraham looked sober. 'I did not see him, but rumour is that he is in a very bad way. And speaking of rumour ... I heard your name mentioned several times at court,' he said.

'Oh?' I asked, prepared to be flattered, and desperately worried about Father Pierre Thomas, the papal legate of the Crusade and the finest human being I have ever known.

'There's a Gascon knight recently come, and he claims to know that you murdered a Savoyard noble during the sack. He's very forward about it.' Sabraham's eyes fell on me, and his gaze bored into me. Quietly he added, 'A certain lady's name is mixed into this ugly story.'

I froze.

'At court?' I asked.

'Often, and loudly,' Sabraham said. 'That rumour will come here, soon enough.'

I looked at Nerio, who was close enough to overhear.

He just laughed. 'Someone says you killed d'Herblay?' he asked. 'There are twenty knights of the Order who know you did not. Who cares, any road?' He gave an elaborate, Italianate shrug. 'He died like a dog. Someone had to put him down.'

I knew perfectly well whose butt-spike had killed d'Herblay in the fire-lit rubble of an Alexandria night. When I found his corpse, it had a diamond-shaped puncture wound in the forehead, a neat thrust through heavy bone with a long sword.

'Gossip like that can do a great deal of damage to reputations,' Sabraham said. 'Little men care nothing for the truth. And you, my young friend, have climbed high, and quickly, and there are a good many men who do not like you or your success.'

'Who is this Gascon?' I asked.

'Florimont de Lesparre,' Sabraham said. 'He claims to be a friend of the dead Comte d'Herblay. He certainly knows the Count de Turenne.'

It didn't seem that dire to me. 'Oh, Turenne,' I said, or something equally banal. After all, the count, for all his pretensions, had not been a paladin in the assault, and had been one of the first to advocate that the Crusade withdraw. I thought of him as a man of no consequence.

I forgot that he had mighty relations. I forgot the Savoyards, and their Green Count.

We virtually had to raise our little crusade again; in the three weeks since we'd held our review in the inn yard, a third of the men we'd engaged had wandered off to other work, or sailed for home, or gone to take service with the king of Cyprus, who was rebuilding his garrisons on the Turkish Main. But with one more effort we passed a hundred men, and before we'd digested our Christmas beef, we paraded them all outside the walls and mustered them, examining armour and weapons. Few of them had horses, and their armour needed a great deal of work, but Emile gave me money, and so did Nerio. And we had some money; John and Marc-Antonio had not hesitated to loot at Alexandria, and so I was probably richer than I'd ever been, at least in coin.

We had permission to use the Order's armourers, and we proceeded to spend a week training a hundred men. Most of them, almost eighty, were men-at-arms. Ten of them were knights, and, with the Grand Master's permission, we added Emile's knights and retainers. The Savoyard knights had better armour and better training than almost anyone else.

By the fourth day of Christmas, we had as many men as we were likely to have, armed well enough. The Order was sending six knights and twenty brother sergeants as a 'caravan'. We sailed in four Order galleys, with a Genoese round ship carrying some horses and almost two hundred pilgrims.

Despite the time of year, we made fair time, had only one bad night at sea, and landed four days later at Famagusta. The king and his court were at Nicosia, and we already had his licence. It didn't occur to me to go and attend the king in person, especially as Lord Grey, nicely recovered, was there on the beach to embrace me and tell the news. Which was a mix; he had another dozen knights, mostly Englishmen, who wanted to go to Jerusalem, and he'd raised as many men as we had ourselves, including a few old friends whose presence delighted me: Ewan the Scot, Ned Cooper, Rob Stone, all archers, and two dozen more like them. Added to the twenty archers that John the Turk had approved, we had as fine a body of archers as Hawkwood had in Italy; although some were Scots or Welsh or Irish, and two were Flemings and one an Italian. And one Kipchak, of course. Archery, like swordsmanship, is an international language.

But there was a note from Fra Peter, ordering me to attend him. I stayed only to see Gawain unloaded from the round ship, to catch the eye of my lady and bow to her, and then I took a riding horse and galloped for Fra Peter. Because he said that Father Pierre Thomas was *dying*.

'I am not dying,' Father Pierre Thomas said. He was lying in a fine bed, dressed in a wretched leather vest over a hair shirt and scapular. He was thinner than I had ever seen him, but his voice was strong.

Philippe de Mézzières was there, booted and spurred as if for travel. 'I came as quickly as I heard,' he said.

'Your role, my friend, is to prepare the letters to go to the Holy Father,' Father Pierre Thomas said. 'I will be ready to travel on Tuesday, I promise.'

Fra Peter Mortimer, the knight who, with Father Pierre Thomas, saved me from both death and a life of pure sin, coughed into his hand and looked at me. 'When I found him on Saturday,' he said, 'he was barefoot in the rain and cold.'

'I was doing penance for my sins,' Father Pierre Thomas said. I swear he sounded pettish – he, who was always patient. That was the first indication I had that he really was sick, and in pain.

'What sins?' I said. I hadn't meant to speak, but the words blurted out of me.

Father Pierre Thomas's eyes seemed to catch fire – not with anger, though, but with amusement. 'Ah, William Gold, I have sins. I may not wear them on my sleeve as you do, but they are there, and every one of them petty, venal, foolish, and human. Even now I feel anger that none of you will leave me in peace to say prayers that need to be said, for my soul, my own peace of mind, and all the souls of all the poor devils who died at Alexandria.'

De Mézzières frowned. 'They were crusaders,' he said. 'They died in the army of Christ.'

'Many souls were riven from bodies that were not crusaders,' Father Pierre Thomas said gently. 'Men, women, children; Jews and gentiles and Moslems. All dead now.' He voice caught. 'And I led you there,' he said, softly but clearly.

I knew what he meant, even if de Mézzières was too much a creature of the Cypriote court to allow that Arabs and Jews had souls and were men. Fra Peter glanced at me and his eyes bid me hold my tongue.

It was, for me, the beginning of a ... change. A gulf that opened gradually, between me and many of my brothers in arms, about what we do and how we do it. Perhaps I'll speak of it later, and perhaps I will not. But there, on that bed, lay a man whose every word and action I respected, even loved, and he had never carried a sword. He accepted responsibility on his own soul for all the horror of Alexandria, and it was killing him, or so it seemed to me, and indeed, seems to me still. Plague was running through Famagusta, and was reputed to be worse in Genoa and Constantinople that winter. But Father Pierre Thomas didn't have the Plague. He had a conscience, and it smote him to the ground.

A grim thought. The routiers who raped Alexandria went back to Italy without a backward glance, their ships laden with booty and slaves. The legate was, in the eyes of the pope and most of Christendom, the commander of the crusade.

I knew that if anyone was in command, it was King Peter of Cyprus. And I knew that he had done none of the crimes, and made every effort at restraint. And yet, to be the commander or a king was to bear the responsibility.

All this in a few beats of my heart. Father Pierre Thomas blessed us, and we three withdrew. There were other dignitaries there: the Chancellor of the city, the Orthodox bishop, and a rabbi. Outside, in the main chamber of the abbey, was King Peter's admiral, Jean de Sur. He spoke a few sentences to de Mézzières and shrugged.

De Mézzières wouldn't meet my eye.

'Is he dying, though?' he asked Fra Peter.

The English knight frowned. 'Ask his physicians,' he said. 'He is heartsick, and all this talk of renewing the war is no help, I promise you.'

De Mézzières furrowed his brow. 'Are you so easily defeated?' he asked. 'The Egyptians are beaten. Their peace offers show how weak they are, and indeed, they are emptying the Holy Land to defend Cairo.'

Fra Peter said nothing.

De Mézzières glanced at me, as if I was disfigured.

'You will find no welcome from the king,' he said.

I shrugged. 'I expect none, as I have no intention of returning to court. I am going with Fra Peter to Jerusalem.'

De Mézzières started. 'You ... ' He paused. 'Did you kill the Count d'Herblay?' he asked.

'No,' I said. 'I wish I had. But it was the act of another.'

'A Christian knight, slain by another?' he asked.

I all but spat. So did Fra Peter. 'A rapist, an arsonist, a murderer,' I said. 'Bent on the massacre of women and children, whom I was sworn to protect. I dropped him when he refused my order. But I didn't kill him.'

Fra Peter frowned. 'Twenty men of the Order saw what happened,' he said. 'De Mézzières, this is an incident that can only bring shame on us all. Father Pierre Thomas was protecting the innocent, and d'Herblay was ... like some demon from Hell.'

De Mézzières sighed. 'I know how men can be in a sack,' he said. 'And there were some bad men among us.' He looked away. 'But d'Herblay's people are making a loud noise at court. The Count of Turenne says there are witnesses that you killed him in cold blood. They say ...' He looked at me. 'They say you committed adultery with his wife, and then murdered him, and that you must be prevented from marrying her.'

'I saved the king's life on the beach at Alexandria,' I said. My voice was soft, but my anger possessed me utterly. 'I saved his life again in the fight at the bridge. Half the Order of Saint John saw what d'Herblay attempted to do. These accusations are—'

De Mézzières nodded. 'They are very real, and they could cost you your Order of the Sword and your lands held of the king. You must come with me and defend yourself.' He looked contrite. 'I am sorry I allowed myself to listen.'

Fra Peter flexed his sword hand, a tic I'd noted in him a few times, when he was really angry. 'Sir William is charged to join me in taking several hundred pilgrims to Jerusalem,' he said. 'That is his duty to our Order. He has done his duty to your king, and been excused. This talk is poison – pure foolishness, the sort of malicious drivel that makes men fear to visit Cyprus or your king's court.'

'Unsay that!' de Mézzières said.

'You know I speak the truth,' Fra Peter said. 'This Florimont de Lesparre and his people are the king's new favourites. They have his ear, they are kin to d'Herblay and Turenne. Tell the king to stop listening to such stuff and have a care for his own reputation.'

'What are you saying?' de Mézzières asked, and he touched his sword hilt.

I stepped between them. Think of me as a peace maker ... The image should make you laugh. But it was not funny at the time, I promise you – two men I respected, ready to fight.

Of course, I'd not been on Cyprus. I had no idea what had been happening.

'*Gentilhommes!*' I said.

Father Pierre Thomas had risen from his bed at the sound and tottered to his door. It was his apparition at the door and no word of mine that brought them both up short.

'My friends,' Father Pierre Thomas said.

They both looked sheepish. I looked sheepish too. Monks scurried away from us.

De Mézzières bowed low. 'My Lord,' he said.

'I am no man's lord,' Father Pierre Thomas said. 'Why are you, two of the very pillars of the temple of the church, arguing like shrill fishmongers in Avignon?'

Neither man wanted to speak. It is surprising how quickly the greatest cause can become a petty squabble when you have to relate it to a third party, especially one whom you love.

'Fra Peter. Your voice was loudest. Speak,' Father Pierre Thomas said. He could be quite fierce.

Fra Peter nodded at me. 'Newcomers at King Peter's court are slandering young William,' he said. 'The king is behaving erratically—'

'That is almost treason to say,' hissed de Mézzières.

'No, it is not,' Fra Peter said.

'Silence,' Father Pierre Thomas said.

I had seldom heard him speak so forcibly. He was pale, but the skin close to his lips was pinched and white. 'The king remains the head of our crusade and the general of our cause.'

Fra Peter shook, visibly, with the effort to repress something he wished to say.

I got down on my knees, in front of Fra Peter, de Mézzières, and a dozen monks, a Greek Orthodox priest and a rabbi. 'Father,' I said. 'I will confess my sins, but I did not kill d'Herblay.'

Father Pierre Thomas shuffled over to me and put his hand on my head. 'Bless you, my boy. I know who killed d'Herblay. He has confessed it. Nor was his sin so very dark, in that level of hell to which we went.' He went to de Mézzières. 'Tell the king that he should be more moderate,' he said simply.

De Mézzières now took a turn hanging his head. 'I have told him. The result is that I am to accompany you to Venice and I am not welcome at court. Pardon me, Ser Peter. My only desire was to save this young man from the loss of his lands and Order. The rest was unbridled anger.'

Father Pierre Thomas smiled, blessed us, and made his way back into his chamber. He sighed, like a father at his children, and we heard the planks creak as his weight settled into the bed.

'I'm sorry,' Fra Peter said, extending his hand.

'As am I,' de Mézzières said. 'Sir William and I are fated to mis-understand each other.' He took my hand as well.

'My Lord, when I am back from Jerusalem, I will come to court.' I bowed.

De Mézzières shook his head. 'Does the countess accompany you to Jerusalem?' he asked.

Fra Peter nodded.

De Mézzières looked away. 'Then the damage will be done. Listen – they mean to disinherit her. To charge her with adultery in front of her liege, the Count of Savoy, when he comes here.'

I have been hit in the head a few times, but I can see through a plot when I have to. 'Of course!' I said. 'She holds all the lands, not her husband. He held them only for his lifetime. Is there a brother?'

De Mézzières shook his head. 'I don't know. I do not listen at keyholes,' he said proudly, 'even when it would be to my benefit.' He sighed. 'But the admiral might know, or any of the king's inner circle. You really should go and face these charges now. In a month or two, the king will have made up his mind.'

'The Green Count is coming here?' I asked.

'So we're told,' de Mézzières said.

'Do you know the Bishop of Cambrai?' I asked.

'I know the name. Robert of Geneva.' He glanced at me. 'Yes, he is reported to accompany his cousin the count.'

I did not pray. I cursed, and a dozen religious men flinched.

Robert of Geneva, coming to Cyprus.

Perfect.

The next few days, the first of *Anno Domini* 1366, were spent in training and mustering two hundred soldiers. None of us liked the number – John the Turk summed it up.

'Too many for sneak, too few for fight,' he said.

But we had almost three hundred pilgrims. In addition, we had many 'volunteers' who could not be turned away; the chance to ride armed to Jerusalem was too good to be missed.

My friends, I feel I need to talk about Chivalry. Here, a little more wine, lass.

I have spoken ere this of my deep respect for Geoffrey de Charny. And in his *Livre de Chivalrie*, he suggested a sort of hierarchy of chivalric effort. He says, '*Qui plus fait mieux vault,*' or, 'He who does most is worth most.'

And he was quite specific about what 'doing most' meant. Fighting in a tournament is better than not fighting; travelling to fight in a tournament is better than fighting at home. Fighting in war for your lord is better than any tournament; fighting far away from home is better. Best of all is fighting for God, in the Holy Land. De Charny, whom I helped kill, didn't invent these ideas. He codified them for all of us – for the fighting class, the *ordo* of chivalry.

I mention all this because when you offer a knight the chance to go to Jerusalem and *fight*, you offer him the chance to *do more.* So a great many young men came to us in the new year – so many that we had to turn some away.

So I suppose it wasn't just my name. Or my name at all.

At any rate, we jousted and fought on foot, and the archers lofted shaft after shaft, and Lord Grey shook his head at me.

'We're taking these louts to Jerusalem, and we just turned away knights.' He was watching Fiore humiliate half a dozen mongrel routiers. It was not that Fiore meant to humiliate them. It was just his usual mixture of arrogance and impatience. Bah, not really arrogance. He was everything he thought he was.

At any rate, they looked like six urchins playing blind man's buff against a man with two good eyes.

I nodded.

'We're taking Scrope,' Lord Grey said decidedly.

One of the delightful issues facing me in Cyprus was one of authority. Fra Peter had told me that I was to be his lieutenant. But he had five other knights of the Order who outranked me absolutely, and Lord Grey was sure that he, as the legate's gonfalonier, outranked me, and then some of the richer English knights, like Scrope, were also sure that they outranked me socially – even though Scrope had just been knighted.

This is where reputation becomes like hard coin in a buyer's market.

'Not my decision,' I said mildly. 'You need to speak to Sir Peter.'

Lord Grey turned the family grey eyes on me, grey as England's skies. 'Why don't you ask him?' Lord Grey said. Being a great lord, Grey didn't fancy being told 'no'.

And I couldn't very well plead that I couldn't stand the arrogant Scrope.

'Of course,' I said, mildly.

It's not in Vegetius, but this *is* part of the art of war.

Ah, Vegetius! I remember when I was laid up before the jousts at Calais – when du Guesclin took me in '58 or '59. I was lodged with Gaucher de Châtillon, the Captain of Reims, and a gentler nor better knight you'll never meet. He had a Vegetius. *De Rei Militiaire.* I read it while I recovered from wounds. Really, I think I lay in bed and waited for visits from Emile, and learned to love Machaut. But I did read Vegetius.

I bring this up because the second day in Famagusta, I found an old Genoese selling some small jewels, several devotional paintings and half a dozen volumes. One of them was Vegetius, in a fine hand, and bound in was Llull's *Book of Chivalry* in French, which I could read slowly. The Latin Vegetius was beyond me, but I was surrounded by churchmen and I had a hankering to learn Latin. Or rather, to improve my Latin.

He was a cheerful old codger, and my Italian pleased him. He bought me a cup of the local drink, a warm mixture full of sugar. Sugar cane is one of the principal exports of Cyprus, of course. Anyway, we sat together in his stall, while Marc-Antonio looked over the market like the Venetian he was.

He was shocked that I wanted the book. That amused me. He showed me other wares, sending his boys running for gloves, a jewelled dagger, an ostrich plume, a whole narwhal's horn, which he claimed was from a unicorn. As I was born in London and not yesterday, I scoffed at the horn, derided the construction of the dagger, asked the price of the plume, and then returned to the book.

I flipped it open. It was written in a fine hand, as I said, in two columns. I could make out the chapter heads well enough. I'd read it in French. 'How much?' I asked.

He leaned back on his stool and sipped his sugar between his teeth. 'It is a fine copy,' he said.

I shrugged. 'I can read the hand well enough,' I said.

'A man offered me sixty florins just yesterday,' he said.

'You should take that,' I said. I rose to my feet. 'It's an excellent offer, and better than I can afford.'

He sipped his drink again. 'Ah,' he said. 'Perhaps sixty florins and I add in the plume, which is worth five florins anyway.'

I rose to my feet and sketched a small bow. 'Too much for me, messire. I give you good day.'

I smiled to show I was not offended, nor meaning to give offence, and strode off before he could stop me.

That night, a great many of us gathered to share dinner in one of the town's excellent inns. I won't say there was a festive atmosphere; there were many factions on Cyprus, and the Genoese and Venetians not the least, but the profession of arms does like a good tavern, and there were a great many of us who'd just visited Hell together.

We were sitting, well fed on octopus, drinking a heavy red wine, when Scrope leaned back in his chair and spoke to his companion, a Gascon knight named Gaspar something. He pointed at me, fairly obviously, and I heard the name 'd'Herblay' said aloud.

'She's more than a little soiled, is she not?' the Gascon said. 'Didn't the king fuck her in Venice?'

He laughed when he said it, and Scrope laughed with him.

I might have killed them both on the spot. But whatever I heard, Fra Peter heard more, as he was a seat closer to them than I, and he placed a heavy hand on my right arm.

Scrope looked at me, and I realised I wasn't overhearing a conversation.

I was being baited.

I took a deep breath.

It is one thing for Father Pierre Thomas to preach to you that you must turn the other cheek. I know what my Saviour preached. It is another thing to live in the world of men, and soldiers, where, from time to time, some churl tests your manhood just to see if you are all that men say you are, or because he himself is lacking something and wants to see that you might lack it too. I say this in the fullness of age, but I was not utterly a fool at twenty-five.

I let the breath go, and counted to five in my head.

'Of course, Monsieur Florimont says she has always been thus, and is quite ... mad,' Scrope said, his eyes on me. 'Mad with lust. Perhaps I will have a turn,' he added with a smile.

Fra Peter had had enough, and leaned across the table. 'Wherever you were trained, apparently your master forgot to tell you never to mention a lady at table except to praise her.'

Scrope shrugged. 'I imagine that I was trained better than many a knight here,' he said. 'By noblemen, not by hedge knights and routiers.'

'I beg to differ,' Fra Peter said.

'I suppose it is easy to be rude, when you are protected by your cross and sacred calling,' Scrope said.

I laughed aloud. It was … antic. Mad, foolish, and it made me laugh, that this sprig was rude to Fra Peter. I laughed, and I made sure he knew I laughed at him.

'Tell me what is so funny, Sir William,' he said.

'Only that Lord Grey asked me earlier to beg a boon of Ser Peter, here, to let you come with us to Jerusalem,' I said.

His face closed, and all the smug importance fled.

Fra Peter rose. 'I do not think I wish to have Sir Steven at my side on the road to Jerusalem,' he said.

I nodded. 'Lord Grey wishes it greatly,' I said.

Fra Peter pushed back his chair, angry and a little surprised to have been so insulted. I put a hand on his arm, and he shook it off, and then looked at me. For once our roles were reversed. He managed a smile, turned, and left the inn.

I had Nerio across the table and he had, of course, heard the whole exchange. Miles Stapleton was too far to have heard a word. Fiore was already on his feet beside me.

I had had ten deep breaths to steady myself. I tapped Fiore, got his attention, and made him sit. I poured wine with a steady hand. Then I let my eyes come up, and fix on Scrope. I leaned over, so he could not mistake my words.

'Scrope, you are very young. The next time you decide to make an arse of yourself, don't involve a lady, eh? Or trouble a great knight with your blather.' I'm proud to say my smile was gentle, and it did not waver, although my heart was pounding and ready to fight. 'If you want to fight, you have only to say so,' I added, as if it was an afterthought.

Silence fell while I spoke. Most of the men at my end of the table heard me reprimand him like a wayward squire.

He shot to his feet. 'You ill-born bastard! I'll—'

I stood too. 'You'll challenge me?' I asked. My inference was plain.

'You're a killer,' Scrope said. 'You murdered d'Herblay. We all know what you are, Gold. I'll not give you an excuse to murder *me*.'

Now the table was utterly silent.

Nerio laughed. 'Let me understand,' he said. 'English is not my first language. You say that you can insult Ser William all you like, and then refuse to fight him, because he has killed men and you have not? Or is it because you are a great coward?' Nerio smiled. 'In Italy, we would call this cowardice.' He shrugged. 'England may have different ways.'

Scrope looked at me. He was afraid. He was young, and he had trapped himself into an impossible position. He had no friends at that table or in the inn – that is, even the Gascon was appalled by the last exchange.

I was still standing. 'I cannot challenge you,' I said, looking down the table at where the other knight of the Order was sitting. He nodded. He approved of my actions, and I was beginning to see merit in the Order's strictures. I *liked* controlling my anger. But I allowed myself a bit of a sneer. 'So you are safe, unless you choose to challenge me. And I will not call you a coward. You are young. You have insulted a lady and a great knight. I recommend you apologise.'

He stood there, his nostrils white with anger and fear, and I thought, *damn, I have been you, my lad*. But he couldn't do it. He couldn't apologise. Or even come up with a witticism. He turned, spat, and all but ran from the inn.

The next day saw us training our mercenaries and trying to jolly our crusaders to participate – always a thankless job. The weather was increasingly bad; there was a hard wind blowing off Africa to the south, with sand in it, and the waves off the port looked murderous. We had cold rain intermittently; enough that I have a memory of standing at a pell, my gambeson soaked all the way through under my maille and my harness, and the leather of my brigantine so wet that I feared the leather would stretch and distort and the iron would rust under it.

But the rain and the cold were unifying elements, and Fra Peter used them to hammer our little army into a cohesive thing in just a week or so. I won't say we were a band of brothers, but two days of hacking at pells and practising a few fairly simple manoeuvres on horse and foot; dismounting and passing our reins to pages, or advancing in a tight, ordered line by having every man in the file grab the knight's lance, as we did in Italy; these manoeuvres, executed in pouring rain, helped us grumble together. I noticed that Lord Grey was distant with me, but I was too busy and too tired to take much note.

Our third or fourth day in Famagusta I was summoned by Father Pierre Thomas. In truth, I had given him little thought, or rather, when I thought of him, it was mostly to congratulate myself on my mildness in the matter of young Scrope. I looked forward to seeing the legate; I thought perhaps that he might praise me.

It was the end of the day, and forty of us were sitting in the straw of a well-thatched barn attached to the Cistercian monastery, drying and polishing our armour and toasting our sodden gambesons and jupons over a courtyard fire. It was not unpleasant; wine was flowing, and squires and pages and knights were working together, another sign that Fra Peter's methods were succeeding.

I left Marc-Antonio and John to finish the work and pulled on a dry wool cote and a sodden cloak and went across the yard and down a single street to visit the legate.

I cannot remember what I was thinking. I can only remember my shock at discovering that he was pale and trembling in his bed, and a dozen religious men and doctors clustered close around.

Sister Marie was there. She was the legate's Latin secretary, a brilliant mind in a small frame. Despite small stature and eyes weak enough to need spectacles to read, she was a fine sword hand and a pleasant enough companion, if a trifle judgemental. I had never seen her swear or blaspheme, nor indulge in wine, nor make even the gentlest lewd comment. Her entire and fiercest joy was in the disputation of theology, and her second joy was in swords, and the two seemed close allies, at least in my mind.

She caught the hem of my loose cote and kept me from entering the legate's bedchamber.

'He's made his will,' she said solemnly. 'I think he's dying, William.'

Sister Marie and I had a great deal in common. First and foremost, we shared a love of Father Pierre Thomas. And, in a way, he had made us. Sister Marie was tolerated in a world almost entirely inhabited by men because Father Pierre Thomas had the stature to have a woman as his Latin secretary. And Father Pierre Thomas had taken me from a life of brigandage and horror to be something like a knight by that same stature.

She told me that he'd got much worse in the day or so since I'd last seen him, and that his breathing was very bad. 'But the worst of it is,' she said, 'that I think he … I think Alexandria is killing him.'

Now I know, friends, that you are gathered to hear tales of chivalry and deeds of arms, and not to hear of the life of one old priest, no matter how saintly. But I need you to understand, because everything that happened in the next two years sprang from that moment, that Father Pierre Thomas was not a warrior. He always questioned the use of violence for any purpose, most especially as a chastisement of the infidel. Ser Peter and I had both heard him openly question the utility of crusade, and we had both seen him offer his own body in the forefront of violence, when he himself went unarmed and un-armoured.

Father Pierre Thomas was born a serf in a peaceful part of France. He had no training for war and little experience of violence. Even I, a knight, a trained man, a veteran of three campaigns by the English in France and years as a routier – even I found Alexandria a terrible shock. Even now, my friends, when I think of that city, my mind glances around some things I saw there, like water passing rocks in a mountain stream and leaving deep and complex eddies.

But Father Pierre Thomas had no armour in his mind. He experienced Alexandria as a Christian. He had not the armour of training, the cult of chivalry, even the love of prowess and victory.

I think Sister Marie was right. I think that Alexandria was like a disease. He could not get it out of his heart.

But by then, I had already spoken to young soldiers; Miles Stapleton had come to me for guidance after the sack. 'Let me talk to Father Pierre Thomas,' I said. I meant it. What I lacked in years and mature wisdom, I might have in experience of war.

She looked at the crowd of religious men. 'They will not leave him,' she said bitterly. 'They give him neither air nor rest. He is a living saint, and each wishes to claim a little of his spirit for themselves.'

'I could scatter them like Jesus and the moneychangers,' I said. I was almost serious.

Sister Marie gave me half a smile. 'You would, too,' she said.

But we underestimated Father Pierre Thomas's stamina and inner strength. While she told me about how little he was eating, Father Pierre Thomas was sending the learned men forth with an admon-ition to find other, worthier men and women to serve. I went into his chamber with Sister Marie and a copper pot of chicken broth, and he smiled when he saw me.

But he was very low. I was shocked all over again. His skin was almost transparent.

'Have you slept at all, Pater?' I asked.

He smiled. 'For my sins,' he said, 'every time I close my eyes, I see the sack of Alexandria.' And yet his smile was genuine.

'Oh, Father,' Sister Marie said.

He said a prayer. Then he said, 'Do not weep for me. Many truths have been revealed to me since this affliction began, and I have hope that through these afflictions, I atone for my sins and I will go bright and new to my maker.'

I sat by him and held his hand. It was cold, colder, it seemed, than the outside air. Yet his eyes were bright.

'We should send for Ser Peter,' I said.

Sister Marie went out for a moment.

I would never have another chance. 'Father,' I said.

'Yes, my son?' he answered.

'Father, the sack of Alexandria was not your fault,' I said.

He smiled. His smile was not grim or bitter; it was merely distant and a little sad. 'Was it not?' he asked.

Somehow, none of the platitudes of the warrior came to me in dealing with this man. I could not say, *These things happen* or *You must break some eggs to make an omelette*. Nor yet *Sometimes good men do bad things*.

'We killed an entire city, like Florence,' Father Pierre Thomas said. 'For nothing. No gain to Christendom, no higher spiritual goal, nor even an advantage of trade. And I was the preacher of this *empris*.'

I ran my fingers through my beard. 'Father,' I said, 'When we were in Venice, did you not tell me that it was God's will, not our will, whether the Crusade happened or not?'

I felt I had handed him a good argument, and I sat back, and was appalled to find that tears were running silently down his face into his beard. 'Oh, William,' he said, his voice untouched by his own tears. 'God gave us free will in the hope that we would do good, not evil.'

Sister Marie returned. I confess that Father Pierre Thomas was making me uncomfortable. My own defences against the horrors of the sack rested on foundations about our role and Father Pierre

Thomas's sermons. To see him undone was to threaten my own peace of mind; or rather, as I knew no peace, to threaten the truce my mind had made.

Sister Marie knelt by the bed and took his free hand, and the three of us said some prayers until Ser Peter came, and then he prayed with Father Pierre Thomas. We watched for some hours, and long after full darkness, Father Pierre Thomas called for his own confessor and changed into clean vestments.

After he changed he was much better, and he fell asleep. Sister Marie found me a pallet in the Abbey, and disoriented me by throwing her arms around me and bursting suddenly into tears. It was, if anything, worse than Nerio's tears. I knew Nerio concealed his emotions behind a carefully worked facade of courtliness, but Sister Marie seemed made of iron. I let her cry and thought of my sister, who was a nun in the Order of the Hospital. I wondered how many friends she had lost in treating the Plague, which had become her speciality, and indeed, both of us were salted against it in youth, when our parents died and we did not. I hadn't thought much of my sister in months, but now, with Sister Marie's slight weight in my arms, I thought of her.

She straightened up, clearly embarrassed to have shown weakness. So I made myself smile at her.

'You need sleep more than I,' I said.

She shrugged. 'I will keep vigil over him.'

This made me feel weak. But I could also tell she had other things on her mind. I can be perceptive, when I put my mind to it. Fie on you, Chaucer. You always think I'm a dolt.

Bah.

She had never entered into my cell, which was fully against the rules of her convent – no nun could enter a man's cell. But now, in a burst, she pushed past me and closed the door softly. She leaned against it as if gathering strength.

'Do you know Queen Elanor?' she asked very quietly. 'Can I trust you, William?' she breathed.

I bowed very deeply. I remember that especially. There was something about the good sister that deserved my special attention. I bowed the way I would have for the Black Prince. The bow that promises service.

She pursed her lips. She was no beauty, but a hard-faced woman

34

who had made her way in a man's world. This is unfair; she had the most gracious smile, when she troubled to display it.

In sorrow, she looked like the Queen of Heaven. Not the beauty, but the dignity.

Or so I imagine.

She waved her hand and said nothing.

'What is it?' I asked, or something equally useless.

She shook her head. 'The queen needs help,' she said. 'I don't even know why I'm telling you this. She doesn't need a sword. She needs ...' She frowned. 'God's help.'

Having just come from my own spiritual guide's bedside, I was feeling puissant. 'Sometimes we are God's tools,' I said. Was I self-important?

Always, I fear.

The nun looked at me with her level stare, judging me. 'Do you know what this serpent's nest of gossip is saying about the queen?' she asked.

Well, men only talk about queens to call them shrews or whores. Men are depressingly regular in this regard. But I wasn't likely to say so. 'No,' I said. 'I have been on Rhodes. Thank God.'

She took a deep breath. 'I do not think she is blameless, but I think someone is ... trapping her. Like some wild thing. Someone is killing the king's love for his wife. A-purpose. Or so I believe. And so she believes.'

I shook my head in pure fatigue. I was too tired, and, I confess it, too wrapped in Father Pierre Thomas's illness, to care much for a queen I'd never met. But I managed to say the right thing.

'How can I help?' I asked.

Sister Marie shook her head. 'Honestly, William, I have no idea.' She managed a flash of smile. 'It is just better to tell someone. Promise you will keep this to yourself.'

I nodded. 'I swear,' I said. 'Although I may ask about the court. If I am permitted into the king's presence. And de Mézzières?' I asked.

Sister Marie shrugged and looked at the floor in unaccustomed hesitation. Finally she said, 'De Mézzières got me involved, hoping all the queen needed was a ...' She paused a long time.

'A friend,' I asked.

Sister Marie met my eye and in the dark cell, for a moment, we were close as lovers, eye to eye. 'I was born a peasant, like my good Father Pierre Thomas. No queen needs me as a friend. But I am known to have "good sense". Sometimes, this is more a burden than a virtue.'

She nodded to me, as if we had met on the street, and passed out of my cell.

And then I fell on the monk's pallet and slept.

I was awakened for Matins. I rose and dressed, fumbling with my laces in the darkness, and I made my way down an unlit stair to discover that Father Pierre Thomas was dead. It was an odd moment, not as horrible as it might have been. I had had a dream in which he was dead – glorified, even. I do not claim this was a dream from God, or any such nonsense – it was a normal enough dream to have when you fear your friend and counsellor is dying.

But I did have it.

And there were no men about except Fra Peter and de Mézzières. Both were in shock, virtually clinging to each other, and I had never seen either man so utterly incoherent.

Sister Marie and a large group of faithful women did everything. Sister Marie took charge, calmly, betraying none of her own grief, merely helping move the body. They washed him and anointed him, and then laid his body in the Carmelite church.

I was not needed by the women. It is interesting to me that in some crises, women exclude men as thoroughly as men exclude women in others. I would have washed his body. Indeed, I cried enough tears to have washed anyone. I would have given my life to save him.

But the doors were shut. And then, when they had laid him out in the church, and the doors were opened, the three of us went in, and we were the only men in a church of women; perhaps two hundred women weeping, and three men. And it was strangely as if we had been called to the vigil of a knight; we knelt, and we waited, and none of us knew what we waited for.

It was a long night, and a long morning. I remember none of it. I will not pretend. It passed in black grief, and I felt as if my life was of no worth.

At some point, others came. I may even have been asleep, although I pray it is not so, but merely prayer and meditation and sorrow; but what I do remember is that a woman gave a great cry, and there we were. I had been somewhere else, and then I was there, in my body, with my knees feeling as if the flames of Hell were rising round me and my back afire too.

I was there, when his body seemed to glow.

Say what you will.

I was there.

He was the greatest man I ever knew. And I saw his skin take on a golden glow, so that in the darkness of a church before sunrise, I could see the faces of a thousand men and women. And they were all the people of Famagusta, not the court; there were Orthodox priests and women in black shawls, and Moslem women and men in their long clothes; there were Jews. There were monks and nuns and knights and merchants and all the people, so many that it was almost impossible to move, packed like seabirds pack together in a bad storm.

And I could see them. I could see Emile. I could see Marc-Antonio and Nerio and Fiore.

Sister Marie took a cloth of cotton and went to the bier and wiped his face.

Bah. I can't go on.

His death delayed our pilgrimage and sent all of us into a different whirl of preparations. He was the papal legate of crusade; he was also a prince of the Church, the Latin Patriarch of Jerusalem and the Archbishop of Cyprus, too. He would have hated his own burial, and all the ceremony that attended it. The cloth of gold, the frankincense, the wax candles and the golden goblets at communion; all of them served to remind me of the day he had shown me the archbishop's ring on his finger and told me that all he saw when he looked at it was the value of food and lodging for twenty poor women for a year.

But the impact of his death was deeper. Many of us, especially his Englishmen, as we called ourselves, suspected that with his death the whole mechanism of crusade would break. He had been in the process of travelling to Venice with King Peter's admiral and de Mézzières to negotiate the strategy of the next campaign. I confess, on the one hand, that this very planning may have been the pressure that killed him; physically and spiritually exhausted, the reality of military planning and the reality of the horror of the sack may have undermined his health terribly. But without him … There was no one to plead in the west for the next reinforcement, which was almost certainly going to include another army of routiers under the Archpriest and the Green Count of Savoy.

And without him, a great many of us lost heart and interest in the great *empris*. He had a great heart and he was, until the sack, indefatigable. No care, no worry, no hesitation in his innermost heart would keep him from giving us his advice and his spirit. His passion carried us, even after the horror.

The king came from Nicosia for the services. I was a baron of Cyprus and entitled to a place in the king's court and procession, but I chose instead to walk with the Knights of Saint John around the bier. Nerio and Fiore and Miles were with me, and Ser Peter, and I had no friends among the Cypriotes or the Frenchmen who now surrounded the king.

After the service, the king sent for me. I went immediately, attended by Nerio, and, I confess it, fearful. I was standing in the dooryard of our inn, waiting for John to bring me a horse, when Sister Marie appeared as a stench of wet wool and a huge enveloping cloak.

She smiled shyly, the only woman in an inn full of men. 'William, I must beg a boon of you,' she said in Latin.

'Anything for you,' I said, my eye on the stables.

'I want to come to Jerusalem,' she said.

I didn't choke. It was, in many ways, a perfectly reasonable request. She was a woman, a nun, who could defend herself. A good companion.

'I will speak to Fra Peter,' I said. 'I'm fairly sure I can find you a berth.'

'Bless you,' she said. 'And on the other matter ...' She looked both ways.

Let me say that Sister Marie was the worst conspirator imaginable, because she was so very honest, and because she was in the throes of a deep grief.

But John came with my horse, and she vanished.

I was still thinking of our small expedition to Jerusalem when I rode into the abbey courtyard. The abbey was hosting the king; the court filled every cell, and the king's wife, Queen Elanor of Aragon, was at the nunnery on the far side of the main square with another hundred knights and ladies. Remember, Famagusta is not Venice or

Genoa or even London; there are fewer than six hundred good houses in the town, for all of its fame, and the court filled it to overflowing.

The king was holding court in the abbey's hall. It was a fine building that might have been in London or Rome: heavy stone, with timber in the upper storeys, and a fine colonnade. The king sat on a raised dais, surrounded by his intimate friends – in this case, Florimont de Lesparre, whom I knew because he was pointed out to me by Nerio, and de Mézzières, and several of the knights of the sword.

A hush fell over the men and women in the hall as I entered, and every head turned to look at us. My chest was tight. Scrope stood by Lesparre, and I had to expect that what was coming would be bad.

Nonetheless, I bowed deeply at the base of the dais, and then knelt in a reverence and waited to be recognised. Scrope turned his back on me; Lesparre made a great show of looking me over, and the king quite genuinely seemed deep in mourning and inattentive rather than gratuitously rude. He was speaking to de Mézzières, who wore all black. De Mézzières could see me, and kept indicating, with small motions of his head, that the king should look in my direction.

Odd thoughts go through a man's head. Should I be enraged? Was the king humiliating me, or simply oblivious to my presence?

A woman said something behind me and a man laughed. That laugh was like a blow.

And yet, I was sure that Father Pierre Thomas would have said that I was only humiliated if I chose to be humiliated. I confess that this is the sort of thing that wise old men say and that doesn't always apply to someone following the life of arms, but the more I watched the king, the less likely it was to me that this was done apurpose. And yet . . .

With the miracle I had just witnessed fresh in my blood, I had no need of anger.

Someone else laughed.

The Order does a great deal of kneeling. Much of it is done in armour. The articulations in your knee harness can eat away at your knees. In fact, I was kneeling on a good Turkish rug in a comfortable pair of wool hose, and I used the petty anger at all the laughter to stiffen my spine. I had been awake almost all the night before, and spent a good deal of it on my knees. I determined to show nothing – neither anger nor resentment – but to kneel and wait.

More laughter.

It was beginning to seem unlikely that the king really didn't know I was there.

It began to seem possible, if you were losing your temper, that the king was instead trying to fool de Mézzières, who would not usually tolerate such behaviour from his king.

Florimont de Lesparre grinned at me.

I have relived all this a dozen times. It was happenstance that I had already decided on a course that was both proper and honourable; happenstance, and perhaps a final gift from Father Pierre Thomas, or rather, a final lesson.

Luckily, I am stubborn.

Luckily, I had some time to collect myself, because I thought the king merely in grief, as I was myself. I'm sure, had I knelt and understood immediately that the king *meant* to humiliate me, that I'd have reacted in anger.

I continued to kneel.

Nerio had not knelt, and he stood at my back. I know now that he stood with his left hand on his long sword, and his head thrown back like a Roman emperor. Of course he did. I smile just thinking about him.

More time passed. My knees burned, and the muscles at the base of my spine began a mild, dull ache. I had done this half the night.

I had never done the vigil of a knight. I had been knighted on a battlefield. But I had kept vigil with Juan, who had died at Alexandria, and he had knelt for almost twelve hours. In armour. I had managed to kneel without complaint at Father Pierre Thomas's bier.

I set my face as best I could, and began to pray. I did not pray because I was so very good, or holy, but because I had learned that the meditation of prayer could calm me even in the moments before a fight – a valuable weapon.

Nerio muttered something. I considered whether to answer or not, and by the time I thought of answering, the moment had passed. I would kneel in silence.

Around me, the laughter gave way to a brittle chatter. People were on edge; men laughed too loudly, and the jape was going on too long. I no longer had a shred of belief that the king did not mean this. I had set myself to endure, and I began to contemplate the Nativity of Jesus.

It was just Twelfth Night; my favourite meditation, and the first that Fra Peter had taught me when I was just a routier. I still meditate on it; the three Magi, and a dozen courtiers and some knights and pages, all gathered at the entry to a stable, looking at the Queen of Heaven and the newborn child. I recall that in my meditation, the Queen of Heaven was Emile and the child glowed with the golden rosiness that I had seen in Father Pierre Thomas's face.

I won't say that I was unaware of the hall or my knees or the increasing pains in my back. I will only say that, like fear and rage, these things were further away, viewed as it were from a distance, and I managed to stay in my prayer for so long …

'William!' hissed Nerio.

I came out of my dream of the Nativity to find that my back was a scream of outraged muscle and my knees were almost without feeling.

The king's chair was empty. The door behind him closed.

De Mézzières looked terrible. He was standing by the empty chair. De Lesparre was also gone, and Scrope stood with his hands in his sleeves. Scrope did not look best pleased.

It is interesting what you miss, when you allow yourself to give way to rage. Had I been enraged, I would have missed that Scrope looked … devastated. I am not saying he was any friend of mine; merely that whatever 'this' was, it was not his intention. It was writ in his face, and I, in my calm shell and bodily pain, began to wonder what was going on.

Most of the men and women in the hall were on their knees, or just rising. Of course, they'd all made their reverences as the king left, and if I knew him, he'd left in a single motion of discontent. I had lived with him for six or seven months.

I remained on my knees.

One by one, the rest of the hall rose and moved away. They were silent; there were a few whispers.

I tried to control my breathing, because my back *hurt*. But I was damned if I would give an inch. I knelt, and knelt and knelt, and the knowledge that Compline must be close was more wearing than otherwise.

Eventually the bells rang. I rose cautiously to my feet. I stumbled, and without Nerio I would have fallen, but the relief to my back muscles was almost miraculous. My feet were odd and felt as if they were attached to someone else's body, and I walked perhaps twenty steps like an old man or a leper.

But by the time we crossed the threshold of the hall, my stride was better. We went to the Carmelite church and heard the service. I didn't kneel, I promise you. But we sang the hymns, free of the court, and rode back to the inn.

We were in the yard when Nerio laughed. 'We are very different,' he said. 'I want to kill every one of them, just because they laughed.'

I remember looking up and seeing stars. I wasn't sure just what I felt.

'I thought that at one point,' I said. 'Perhaps I will again.'

'Lesparre will think you are ... light,' Nerio said.

I'd like to say I said something wise, like *I cannot be responsible for what Lesparre thinks* or manly and full of *preux*, like *Lesparre will learn better in time*. But what I really said was banal.

'Weather's changing,' I said. 'The wind is fair.'

It was odd that I didn't care. Lesparre was nothing to me.

It took the church eleven days to prepare to bury Father Pierre Thomas. We could not leave; even fully trained and prepared, with a fair wind for the coast of Syria and our holds filled with food and water, we could not leave. It was as if the world held its breath. Even the court – and I will not shock either of you gentlemen if I say that I think King Peter was already descending into madness – even that court of fools was in deep mourning, though I noted that of the whole court, only the queen came to the Carmelite church.

I can't remember how many days passed without incident. But perhaps the third or fourth day, I was at vigil with Fiore in the Carmelite church, and when I was done – and by Saint Peter, my knees were not my friends – we rose when Fra Peter and Nerio came in, swords drawn, and knelt in our places. And we both creaked like old men as we made our way slowly from the bier to the colonnade and with one accord slouched against pillars and began to do little exercises to relieve the pain.

There were a dozen women there, kneeling quietly in the privacy of the side chapels.

One of them was Sister Marie. It was odd to see her with other women; somehow, I'd never associated her with them. And one of the women was obviously the queen of Cyprus. She wore a superb headdress and veils that were worth more than my warhorse. She was not particularly tall, but slim and dignified and younger than I would have imagined.

This is not a comic story, but you have to imagine that Fiore and I thought we were alone until our eyes adjusted, and so, like mimes or acrobats, we were posturing, grunting, and stretching …

I suspect I blushed.

The queen looked at me a moment, and then leaned forward and spoke to Sister Marie.

She nodded. Fiore caught my eye and we gathered the scabbarded swords we'd laid against the pillars, the hilts lodged securely in the stonework, but before we could slip away, Sister Marie was there.

She caught my hand and squeezed it.

'William,' she said.

I nodded.

She led me to a door – the sacristy, I think – and I realised that the queen was there to see me. It was not happenstance. And indeed, she came in with two ladies and Sister Marie, while Fiore stood outside with his sword drawn.

I knelt. She raised me.

'My Lord,' she said in her Occitan French. 'I must first apologise for my husband's treatment of you.'

There is absolutely nothing a loyal knight and vassal can say in such a circumstance. So I said nothing.

'I must ask you a terrible question,' she said. 'It is not what these good women brought me here to ask—'

'Your Grace!' Sister Marie said in protest.

'But I would trade my immortal soul for a clear answer. Has the Countess d'Herblay shared my husband's bed?'

'Madame!' spat Sister Marie, clearly furious.

Calm is a gift. Perhaps, I agree, I was merely numb at the death of a man I nearly worshipped. Perhaps I was numb again at the ingratitude of King Peter.

But in truth, I think that I read her question in her first glance. She cared little for saving herself. What she cared about was her husband. I will forestall my story and say that although in the end I thought her as mad as he, in this she was noble.

43

At any rate, thanks to prayer and fasting and Father Pierre Thomas, I did not give her the answer she deserved. Instead I bent my head.

'Never,' I said.

'Oh, God,' the queen said, and burst into tears.

I should perhaps have seen an astrologer that month – King Peter had several excellent ones, wise men with great ability. And perhaps they would have warned me that people would fall into my arms in tears. Nothing could have prepared me for Nerio; Sister Marie was an easier experience, as, despite her armour, she was a woman and a close friend.

The queen of Cyprus was another creature entirely, and she fell into my arms and wailed, and clung to me like a limpet. Sister Marie looked as if she'd been struck; the other two ladies turned away in pure embarrassment.

She was a queen; she collected herself as fast as she collapsed. Indeed, she might have given Nerio lessons; the moment she was out of my arms, she was upright, and very much a queen.

'I need your help,' she said simply. 'Men seek to destroy me.'

I know that digressions spoil a tale, but I have to pause here. Twenty years on, and many weeping women and some weeping men later, I suspect now that I was played from beginning to end. Oh, the queen *certes* wanted to know if Emile was the king's mistress – that was genuine enough. And she needed me. But the tears?

A very effective recruiting tool.

I was just learning to master my temper, but I had not yet even begun to learn to master my reaction to women, especially beautiful ones in tears.

So I knelt and asked her to command me.

And God, who works in mysterious ways, chose that afternoon at the Carmelite priory for my Emile to be on the steps when I emerged with Fiore, blinking in the sun. The sight of her affected me, and I almost gave us away on the steps. I wanted to throw my arms around her, or kneel at her feet. And I confess even now that her smile of obvious pleasure at seeing me was restorative, so that only then did I know how black my world was becoming. Juan, Alexandria, Father Pierre Thomas.

I needed her.

She passed me, and Jean-François gave me a greeting and we clasped hands, as Bernard did with Fiore, and in that moment, the queen of Cyprus came out of the central doors. She paused, two steps above Emile.

And then she smiled, and stepped towards Emile and extended her hand in greeting.

I saw Emile's hesitation and knew, in that single heartbeat, that there had been jealousy and bad blood. Being away from the court meant I had seen none of it; of course, Emile had been back at court the last sennight.

And then she, in turn, smiled, and the two women clasped hands.

I was going to look a fool if I stood and watched.

Fiore's eyes slid off them – two of the handsomest women you might ever see, dressed like portraits in a book of hours, both beaming with happiness.

'I have been thinking about crossings with the sword,' he said happily, 'all the time that we were kneeling, and I have come to the conclusion that, while every crossing is its own self, nonetheless they can be classified three ways. May I show you?'

I laughed at him. But later that afternoon, there I was in the inn yard, trying to get to a cross that would allow me to enter for a grapple by following his direction and his categorisation.

This was life with Fiore; I think he loved Father Pierre Thomas, but he loved his weapons more, and nothing stopped him from considering these things. I can only compare him to two very different walks of men: fishermen, and astrologers. I have known Cypriote fishermen to stare at the water for hours with a line out, and still be instantly attentive in the moment the great tunny strikes the hook. That was Fiore. And, on the other hand, the very wise astrologers who study the heavens every night and react with delight to a shooting star and rapture to the hint of a new comet . . . That is also Fiore.

Fra Peter watched us for a while and then picked up a stave and joined in. He was the most devastated of all of us, and in truth, except for de Mézzières, Fra Peter Mortimer was the most stricken of all the men I knew. I think that, had he not had the passage to Jerusalem to command, he would perhaps have been in a very bad way, and even as it was, he was almost unable to speak at most times. But he crossed and struck and was struck, and eventually got a stout blow on his left thumb that won some cursing, and he stood shaking his left hand.

Sometimes pain helps.

'I meant to speak to you days ago,' he said. 'I heard what the king did, from de Mézzières.'

I probably shrugged. I was immune to anger as long as I didn't think too much about it. Once I began to think on it, I could get quite angry indeed.

'You have got off very lightly. He did not strip your collar of the Sword – he has not taken your title.' Fra Peter's eyes were terrible – red and puffy and with lines like an old man's. He had aged.

'I don't care,' I said. I didn't; it wasn't adolescent posturing. For once.

He put a hand on my shoulder. 'Lesparre cannot brook a rival of any kind. It is the sort of man he is, although I have never seen this disease in so awful a form.'

'I am no rival—'

'The king spoke of you constantly after you left: of your saving his life; of your devotion;, of the way you and your friends behaved at a certain tournament; even of your devotion to a certain lady.' Fra Peter's eyes were red, but steady. 'Lesparre means to make you small, simply so that he himself can be great.'

'He has succeeded,' I said. 'We are going to Jerusalem, and we will be free of this Hell on earth. God send I never return to Famagusta.'

Fra Peter nodded. 'You show wisdom,' he said. 'Come, and let us exchange some blows.'

'Your thumb is broken,' I said.

'Only mashed. Come.' And indeed, we swaggered sticks for a long time, and we were quite pretty; men came and watched, and a few women, including Sister Marie. Fiore nodded approvingly.

Men heal in odd ways. Fra Peter and I began the healing from Father Pierre Thomas's death in the courtyard of our inn, with sticks.

And the next day, when we trained again, this time on the beach with horses, Ser Peter and I ran an open tilt, and then Fiore and I snapped some lances, which was expensive, but I was having a good day. And then Jean-François appeared with his mesnie, and despite my good work with a lance, he dropped me in the sand. He was always a good lance.

I rose from the sand to the sound of applause, and there, of course,

I suspect what I said was 'Fuck.' I suspect what I thought was *I don't have time for this crap.*

But it was my job, and another man's sins can be a lighter burden than your own, I find.

I remember asking Marc-Antonio if he knew of brothels that catered to men who liked other men, and I remember his face.

I raised an eyebrow. Fra Peter had inculcated me with fairly high standards of obedience; Marc-Antonio swallowed carefully and allowed as how he knew of such.

God. Famagusta. Really, in some ways, worse than Alexandria. But I took Marc-Antonio and Fiore and Nerio with me, and we went to the stews.

Let me say a word or two about Famagusta. In the year of our Lord 1366, it was one of the richest small cities in the world. As the entrepôt for trading to Syria and Egypt from the west, it was a vital port, a superb fortress, and if the streets were not quite paved in gold, there was still an incredible amount of wealth. But unlike, say, Venice, where the wealth seemed to be held, lesser or greater, by everyone, in Famagusta the rich had everything and the poor nothing. Oh, there is poverty in Venice, but mothers do not sell their daughters as whores for bread.

The stews of Famagusta were bad.

The girl-whores looked like children, and the man-whores were more pitiful than any. I've known a good few whores – mostly army women, and a tough clan they are. But tough means fit, and healthy, at least in body, and this lot were ...

Squalid. It is the only word I can offer. And the men who appeared out of unlit alleys to sell me their human wares were perhaps the most pathetic form of life I'd ever seen. Why do we kill Moslems, who are often honourable men, knights, men of honour, when we could exterminate the brothel keepers and pimps of this world? These were men who made a trade of flesh.

And slavery was, of course, legal in Cyprus. Anywhere the Genoese touch, they spread this disease. Bah. I am unfair. The Cypriotes practise slavery, and the Egyptians, so it seems natural. But to an Englishman, slavery is disgusting, and the slavery of prostitutes was ... sordid beyond anything I'd had to endure.

Nonetheless, we found the place Marc-Antonio's enquires had

located. By then, neither Nerio nor Fiore was amused any more, and when the brothel keeper offered us hospitality, I took him by the throat and explained my errand, with my eating knife at his eyeball. I wouldn't have touched de Charny's dagger in that hell.

It would be satisfying to recount a fight, but they cowered before us, four armed men with all the signs of the profession of war: maille shirts, swords. No one showed any fight, and money was put in my hands. Was it my archer's money, or some other poor bastard's?

I took it.

There are worse men than routiers. This pimp wore a small fortune in clothing and gold jewellery. His fortune was made. And in me there burned a small fire; I thought for a moment of killing him for his gold.

And *I myself have been a brothel keeper*.

When the cringing caitiff offered me his wares for nothing, as a sop for my trouble, I kneed him in his privates with as much force and anger as I could muster, and I left him there, puking on his own floor. If I had been alone, I might have burned the wretched place. It was not that he traded in boys. Or children. It was everything about him.

This is the direct touch of Satan, and a few differences of opinion on the value of the Trinity, for example, are *nothing* by comparison.

Bah, I am sermonising. But by all the saints, gentlemen; when they send us men of the sword to fight, I find I am often told that the enemy represents the legions of Hell, and we are standing with angels. And yet, I have fought Tartars and Mamluks and even the Genoese and found good, worthy men and women among them all.

At any rate, by the close of that evening, I won the repute of a man who cared deeply for his archers; and I freely confess that afterwards, I felt a little better. And a little disgusted with my fellow man, as well.

It was the next morning, and I was kneeling at vigil for Father Pierre Thomas, thinking about the brothel keeper, and trying to be sorry that I had hurt him. And thinking unaccustomed thoughts about Anne, my sometime *amis* and sometime whore in Avignon; about prostitution, about the use of other people's bodies and souls. About when Richard and I ran a brothel in Gascony. Kneeling for a long time can be hazardous to your *amour propre*. I was with Nerio, who was, I could tell, bored.

I envied him sometimes; so secure in himself that when I mentioned to him my doubts and worries, over a cup of wine, he'd smile, his eyes would twinkle, and he'd say 'I know a young lady with flaxen hair and a surprising flexibility of both body and mind who could, in an hour or so, lighten your mood.'

At any rate, I knelt and prayed, and Nerio knelt and tried to flirt with pretty parishioners.

We were nearing the end of our watch – the moment when time seems to stand still, or run very, very slowly. And I will tell the truth – it is easy to stand vigil with the corpse of a friend on the first night, and perhaps the second, but by the ninth or tenth it is wearisome and dull. It is possible to think that you are doing permanent injury to your knees and hips and back.

I was aware that Sister Marie was in the church. She came to the edge of my peripheral vision and knelt. I saw her pray; I saw her tears.

I saw the bellringer go past us up the aisle and into the bell tower, and when my eyes followed him, I saw Sister Marie stiffen. I had an inkling immediately that she was waiting for me.

Vespers rang in the bells overhead.

Fra Peter came in with de Mézzières. They knelt, and we, who had now made a ceremony of this, rose as one, and bowed to the bier and the altar, which loosened stiff joints, and then we made a reverence and retired, sheathing our long swords together. De Mézzières looked at me.

But he said nothing. I could tell he had something to say, but the power of the vigil was too much for a man of his piety.

Nerio and I retreated to the side aisle and Sister Marie was there.

'William!' she hissed.

I went to her side.

She handed me a note. There was no light, so I lit a taper from a candle on the Virgin's altar in a side-chapel and read it. I knew Emile's writing well enough.

'They mean to take the queen in adultery,' it said. 'Save her.'

I looked at Sister Marie.

'The queen,' Sister Marie looked around. 'The queen is to meet the marshal. She thinks she is going to ask him for help. Lesparre intends to surround them and take them.'

'De Morphou?' I asked.

She nodded.

'The queen agreed to meet de Morphou at night?' I asked.

Sister Marie made an impatient hand gesture. 'William!' she hissed. By which she meant, 'Judge not, less you be judged.' I took her meaning instantly. In fact, I had the brothel keeper before my eyes, because, of course, *I had been a brothel keeper.*

And committed a fair amount of adultery.

'Show me,' I said quietly.

'I will take you.' She nodded to Nerio, who stood separate. Nerio was a fine man – in many ways my best friend; he was bad with women, and as Sister Marie was not pretty or beddable, she didn't exist as a person, to him. 'And him?' she said with a sniff.

I walked to Nerio. 'I need you,' I said.

He knew I meant violence. He nodded his head. 'At your service.'

'We go to serve a lady,' I said.

'All the better,' he said.

'There will be political repercussions,' I said. 'And a fight, I think.'

'Ah. Lesparre?' he asked. He was perceptive, and he had access to his family sources.

'I assume so,' I said.

He smiled. 'The queen, I expect?' he said, which showed me how far behind the action I was.

'Perhaps,' I said.

He took off his mutton cap, ran his fingers through his hair, pulled his sword four fingers from the scabbard and checked the hang of his round cloak. 'Ready,' he said with his combat smile.

By the risen Christ, I loved him.

Since Marc-Antonio was waiting with Nerio's squire, we sent them for Fiore and Stapleton if they could be found, and Sister Marie whispered to Marc-Antonio. Then we followed Sister Marie into the dark streets of the town. We went uphill, past the abbey and the great nunnery where the queen was housed, and then we came to a city gate. It was open; you could smell horse dung on the air.

'They have already passed,' she said.

'How far?' I asked.

'Right here – the *faubourg*,' she allowed. 'We should wait ...'

I shook my head. 'No,' I said.

Nerio nodded in the gate's torchlight. 'If we hit them now, we can save something,' he said. 'After they take her with the marshal, there's no saving anything.'

'Not that we don't need the others, and horses,' I said. 'Stay here.'

Sister Marie frowned. 'I got you into this,' she said.

I loosed my sword in my scabbard. 'I need this,' I admitted.

'Need what, brother?' Sister Marie asked.

'A fight,' I said. 'Bring the others, they won't be far behind.'

I had Nerio. I had the emperor's sword.

I would not be so bold today, but I thank God I was so bold that night.

Besides, Emile had sent for me.

Then Nerio and I were running, pounding along the drawbridge and onto the cobbles in the dark, but we weren't in armour and we made little enough noise. We came to the street of houses on the far side of the city's deep moat; the first turn, right along the moat, of good stone houses built with pretty wooden balconies out over the cobbled street. Just inside the cover of the street there were four men. Even in the darkness, we could see that they wore maille, and expensive, tight-fitting clothes; one man had a jupon with the latest sleeves.

Courtiers.

They saved us a serious moral quandary by drawing their swords. Now, drawing a sword in the City of Famagusta is a felony. In fact, showing even two fingers of your blade to a potential adversary is the crime of assault in Famagusta, just as in Florence or Bologna or Genoa.

They meant us harm.

Four on two sounds like long odds; add darkness, a need for quick resolution, and our adversaries' firmness of purpose, and I can only claim youth and chivalric love to explain my determination. In retrospect, I wonder if I was off my head.

I roared '*A l'arme!*' at the top of my lungs. You may wonder, but we were, after all, there to warn the queen, not to be silent.

I slowed a few paces before I raced into them. Nerio, may God bless him, was with me stride for stride, and we slowed enough to draw our long swords. I promise you, there is no man born of woman who can draw at a run. The blade's too long.

But we were *very* close, and the nearest man threw a heavy blow from inexperience or the confusion of darkness – or both. His blow was out of distance, and so heavy that his point struck the cobbles in front of me and sparks flew.

I had slowed too much for the length of my stride to reach his blade – stepping on your opponent's blade is a wonderful disarm, and the sole of your boot is the best armour you have when you have no armour. But I got close and cut *down* into his blade and then rotated the sword on its own axis to unlock the edges and flick a small cut straight at him along the centre-line, and he lost control of his sword and gave a sort of scream. I assume I'd cut his left hand, or severed a finger or two. I kept going forward, put my sword arm around his throat, and threw him to the ground.

Fiore liked to tell us, *Just walk through him,* and I did.

Impetus carried me past them. I whirled in time to catch a strike to the crown of my head. It was too dark for cunning. I cut at my opponent hard, then had to change *gardes* and make a cover, and I knew I was taking too long. This was the man in the fitted clothes; he was better than just competent.

He cut at my head again, but it was a feint, to which I was supposed to be conditioned by his first cut. He went from *fendente* to *reverso* in a magnificent hand-cross, and I was with him through both attacks and covered, but I made the mistake of returning my attack in the same line he'd made his, and he covered in turn.

All this in perhaps twenty beats of my heart.

Nerio was fighting both of the others, so that we were reversed; Nerio and I were on either side of our three opponents, who were together in a clump in the middle of the cobbled street.

I had a moment of the clarity that comes to you when you have some *fortuna* in a fight and I took a long gliding step to my left, my feet feeling for the irregularity of the cobblestones. I was in luck, my footing held, and I made a feint thrust from a low *garde* against my adversary and then, having got my blade up, cut into the meat of the thigh of one of Nerio's opponents from behind.

And then, as fast as a man could draw breath—

My own opponent thrust at me and I cut into his blade—

Nerio killed him with a straight thrust to his temple—

I cut back out of my parry at Nerio's second opponent. My blade *ticked* into his, the edges caught, and something failed – perhaps his parry was weak, or perhaps he had intended to make a feint and not a cover ... I have seen all these things happen. My blade kept going even though he'd made his cover, and bit into his chest across his hands because of his weak parry. He gave a sort of squeak and fell to his knees. I kicked him as hard as I could before the fire of the combat left me, and he collapsed.

'*A l'arme!*' I roared again.

'Kill them!' shouted a voice in Gascon French. 'Get it done. Now!'

And a volley of orders in French and another language.

The houses around us seemed to vomit men. It was a flood, and many had torches; the light inside open doors threw light into the narrow street.

A crossbow bolt whispered past my face, a reminder of mortality, and buried itself in the first man I'd thrown to the ground. I would like to say it killed him instantly but the result was the opposite; it struck his groin and he screamed. There were other sounds, and all of it became the utter confusion of a fight.

I think I'm the one who decided to fight all these new men. A door opened, a man was silhouetted against the light, and I stabbed him. In retrospect, I might have killed an innocent townsman.

But I didn't.

'*A l'arme!*' I called again. I had no idea where the queen might be, or the marshal, or really, even how many opponents I had.

I kept moving, and so did Nerio, and from the habit of fighting together we ended up together, moving east along the moat. The hidden crossbowmen were still loosing bolts, but we were not in their sights. The men running down the street, and there seemed no end of them, were still unaware of us.

Best of all, men in the area we fled began fighting each other.

It was dark.

I was trying *not* to kill. I knew at least one of our opponents was dead; the man screaming was in a bad way, and the first man leaving a house got a foot of the emperor's sword in his abdomen before I gave the matter much thought. Enough killing to swing for it or face the headsman's axe, and yet I was still trying not to kill.

Nerio was not nearly as fastidious. He had his blade at mid-sword with his gloved left hand, and he used it like a two-handed dagger in the dark, and he was killing. And as one of the commanding voices mastered the panic of the mob and rallied them against us, I too began to kill or maim; thrusts, because they were less likely to catch in bone and often drop your opponent faster, and because thrusts can be deceptive in the darkness. And some of my blows were near to assassinations, against men who scarce knew I was there.

We cut, thrust, and ducked; broke down a gate, hopped a wall, and were hemmed into a small square, no bigger than the fountain in the centre and room to swing a sword, with tall stone houses all around us and four alleys leading away. I got my back to the fountain.

They had torches all around us.

'Why don't you throw down your swords,' said a man. He had his thumbs in his sword belt and seemed very much at ease. His accent was odd. I knew it ...

'And what?' I asked. Someone didn't believe in truces; a sword flickered like a flame in the torchlight. Nerio slapped it up with a rising parry and then cut back down and something warm struck my cheek. A man bleated 'Christ, my hand!' and another fell back, leaving several feet of space between me and the next bastard.

'And I'll have you dragged to death over the cobbles by our horses,' the man said. He laughed. 'Stay back, you fools. Let the crossbows knock them down and then you can all avenge your friends. Make way there.'

He was a dozen feet from me, and in the dark, that was a mile. I still wasn't placing that accent and I couldn't see his face.

'I want you to know who I am,' he said loudly. 'Guillaume Gold! Do you know me?' he called out.

A man grunted. Nerio was ignoring the talking too. He'd just stabbed someone who fell to his knees.

I got low and then stepped up on the lip of the basin of the fountain and leapt across the open water. It wasn't far, and I was on the other side of the fountain, by Nerio.

'It's me,' I said as I landed, hoping not to get skewered by Nerio, and I thrust. When my man parried, I won the crossing of the swords and stepped past him, took the hilt of his sword between his hands, pounded my pommel into his face so he dropped, and cut with his sword – now in my left fist – at the man behind him, whose sword was trapped by the press at waist height. I cut him hard.

Nerio was, I know now, down at knee height, stabbing in the dark at feet. It's unchivalrous, but so are odds of twenty to two.

'You curs!' shouted our talkative adversary. I didn't know whether he meant us or his own men.

I left the borrowed long sword in a man, grappled an arm and broke it at the elbow, used my pommel and quillons as viciously as Fiore might ever have wanted, and broke out of the press like a drowning man coming up for air on a beach. I was perhaps ten paces down one of the alleys, and Nerio cursed in Italian hard by me.

Together we moved along the alley. But instead of carrying us to freedom, it led us back into the street from which we'd started, still full of men. The first man I'd dropped was still screeching, his arms and legs slamming the cobbles with a fury that seemed impossible from a dying man, and his own mates made no attempt to help him. He was perhaps forty paces to my left.

'Moat,' Nerio said.

It was a brilliant idea, and he suited his action to his word, and leaped for the nearest balcony, a beautiful painted wooden affair at head height and a little. As he jumped, I had time to note that there was light through the shutters. I knew, in that instant, that this was the one house we should avoid, but it was too late.

He got himself up and got the shutter open one-handed – the advantages of a life lived in heavy armour. The men in the street were all coming at me, and I didn't await their onset like a true knight; I leaped too, and got one of the cross members and swung my legs up and got pinked in the buttock for my pains. But Nerio got his hands under my armpits and raised me from the swords below me, and we went into the house, me rubbing my arse and my hand coming away wet with blood.

There was a bed, carefully made, and lights. In a house like this one, the upper floor was the main living floor; we were in the only bedchamber, where master and mistress and servants all slept, most nights, and there'd be a second room, and then probably steps down on the moat side.

I went to the door and opened it to the blaze of a well-lit room; a fire in the hearth, and two good wax candles. And the queen of Cyprus, her face as white as parchment, and the marshal with his sword drawn. I can say, although no one cares any more, that both were fully dressed, and that each had a servant in attendance.

The marshal's sword came to my throat. I crossed it.

He didn't look like my idea of Lancelot, even if he was playing the part.

'Friend!' I said.

We all knew each other well enough, despite the hour and bad lighting.

The queen put a hand to her breast. 'Ser Guillaume,' she said.

The marshal let me in. 'How many out there?' he asked. He was a soldier, and he knew the odds well enough.

'Fifty?' I said.

'More like a hundred,' Nerio said. 'Let's try for the moat. Your Grace,' he said to the queen with a very courtly bow, 'can you swim?'

The queen of Cyprus was surprisingly collected. 'All my life,' she said.

Nerio spoke rapidly. 'It will be horrid – full of dead cats and worse.' He made a face. 'If you will strip and jump for the moat, Your Grace, and Marshal, I believe you will win clear.'

I agreed instantly. 'No one will expect the queen of Cyprus to swim for it,' I said.

The queen thought for a moment.

I was thinking too. 'They don't know which house you are in,' I guessed.

'We are not in the house we were supposed to be,' the marshal said with a smile. 'I smelled a rat. A Gascon rat.'

A stone came through the window. Nerio shook his head. 'If they didn't know where you were before, they can guess now,' he said. 'Or they'll just follow us.'

'If I strip to swim and am caught,' she said clearly, 'all will take my undress as a sign of my guilt.'

There was a roar from outside.

'If they take you here, Your Grace,' I said, 'I would expect the worst, and the state of your dress will not protect you.'

She was quite a lady, the queen of Cyprus. She nodded. 'Well,' she said, 'I have always admired Guinevere. I must try and do a little better than she, messires, and help save myself, I think.' She passed me and went behind the cloth screen with her lady-in-waiting.

We were now in the back of the house, by the moat.

I poked my head out. No crossbow bolt flew. It was dark, but not full dark; moonlight and some background light from the citadel lit the walls of the moat, which, of course, smelled.

Each house had a back balcony, and some had landings closer to the canal.

~~There~~ was no miraculous path to safety. I could see three balconies, and then, at the angle of the moat, there was a gap we would never have managed to cross.

'Where do they swim to?' I asked Nerio.

I could hear men breaking into houses to the north. That must be what we'd interrupted, up the street, when I first called the alarm. That's why they came at us out of the houses. And despite their numbers, they were finite. They couldn't be everywhere – they had to fear us by then, and we'd dropped at least ten of them. Fear makes your foes innumerable, but ten breaths in peace and my head was working, and I couldn't imagine that any faction could find more than fifty thugs to carry out rough work.

Nerio was shaking his head. 'Damn,' he said.

As far as I could see, the canal's walls were smooth, hard masonry. The queen could die in that cesspool, unable to climb out.

The marshal was stripped to his shirt and hose. The queen appeared in a shift, a small woman suddenly anonymous without her jewels.

Men were banging on our door down below.

'I have a better idea,' I said. 'Follow me.'

I didn't see a path to safety, but I did see a plan – a fox's plan. The queen's waiting woman had also stripped to her shift, and I gave her a smile and took her kirtle and gown and dropped them artfully by the back balcony, and the marshal's doublet too. Then Nerio and I stripped two mattresses of straw off the bed and hurled them into the moat with very loud and satisfying splashes. By then the marshal was on to us. He gave me a crisp nod and followed my pointing hand. He took the queen and went from our balcony to the next, and then, without hesitation, to the next but one. The queen's lady scooped up the queen's gown and jewels. The queen was bold, and jumped every jump with the marshal, and her lady jumped like Atlantae herself at her heels. The marshal's squire drew his dagger and made the first leap just as the men searching the next house burst onto the back balcony. I was last; Nerio made the jump into a mêlée, and ended it with his

59

arrival, but the squire was badly wounded in the play and when I arrived, it was clear he'd never make the next jump.

He was very young, and he'd just taken his death wound. He lay in an angle of the balcony. The last rush of attackers had brought torches, and one burned on the wooden floor; I snatched it up.

The squire was coughing blood, as you do, when you have two feet of steel in your lungs. I left it there; he was not going to be long.

Perhaps we should have cut his throat and thrown him into the moat. But we didn't. And there was a sudden roar in the street outside, and a man's voice asking what we'd found.

'They jumped into the moat!' I called in my ready Gascon-French.

'Where?' asked the man at the base of the stairs. He was below me in the dark.

'Next house!' I shouted. 'They are in the next house! Go south!'

'Let me see!' said another man, and he pushed up the steps. I let him past me onto the landing, and Nerio put a rondel dagger under his chin and up into his brainpan. *His* body went into the canal.

'There goes another!' I shouted.

'Get them!' said the men below me. Some said it in Greek, too. And then I heard the sound of shouting, and the clash and click of metal, the unmistakable music of sword on sword.

I looked back at the squire. He managed a smile – which, to me, put him with the Worthies.

'Bridge of Swords,' he said, quite clearly.

Nerio leaned over the boy and pulled the sword out of the boy's side, and he was dead in seconds.

I ran from the back of this house to the front – perhaps three strides, the houses were so narrow – and pushed open the balcony lattice.

From my height, I could see a dozen men in the alley and a swirl of them were fighting.

Another half a dozen men were frozen in indecision.

'King's men!' I shouted from my balcony. Many heads turned.

'Run!' I called, and jumped for the street. I hoped to provoke them to panic, but the same darkness that was keeping us alive was keeping our adversaries from running. I thought that if they saw me fleeing the house, they'd break. Mayhap, a foolish plan.

At least I was intelligent enough, or lucky enough, to catch the sill of the balcony with my hand and drop to the street, and the drop still hurt the soles of my feet. I rolled across some horse manure and got up on one knee with my sword in my right hand. Again, Fiore made us practise these things – leaping, rolling, even running.

The people fighting against the thugs were Fiore and Miles Stapleton, The Marie and Marc-Antonio, and suddenly the odds were perfect. I knew them even in the darkness; I knew their breathing and their focus and the economy of their movements, and even as I moved my attention along the street I knew that the third figure weaving behind her sword was Sister Marie and the fourth, less elegant, my squire. I rose from my roll and stabbed Fiore's opponent in the back, perhaps unnecessarily. Moving to the right across the street, I pulled my blade free and pommeled Sister Marie's man in the temple. She used her left hand to turn Marc-Antonio's opponent; Marc-Antonio went close, seized his sword, and kicked him viciously between the legs.

'Friends!' I called in Italian.

In my peripheral vision I saw Nerio jump from the balcony.

Now the dozen men in the alley had to face the six of us. I do not remember exactly what I did, but I remember the spirit, the feeling that every move of my body was in rhythm to my friends'. I remember Nerio making a low parry and Sister Marie kicking his opponent in the back, knocking him flat; I remember Fiore making a cover over his head against a falling blow, pommeling one opponent and then stabbing the man behind him with a smooth turn of his body on the balls of his feet.

It was beautiful, for a few beats of my heart. It was not a contest; nor did ten breaths pass before the survivors broke.

One unlucky fellow lay under Fiore's boot. Fiore's sword was at his throat. All his friends had fled.

If such men have friends.

Sister Marie knelt by one of the dead men and began to pray.

'Friends!' I said.

'What?' Fiore asked, panting. He glanced at the man under his foot and then killed him.

'Where?' Stapleton asked. His eyes almost glowed.

'I called the watch,' Sister Marie said, with her usual good sense. She was off her knees and moving. She made the sign of the cross over Fiore's man and then looked at him. 'Was that necessary?' she asked.

Fiore was looking at a balcony. 'What?' he asked.

She glared at him in the torchlight.

Marc-Antonio wiped his short sword on a dead man's cloak and began taking purses.

Nerio looked at me. 'Run? Or stay?' he asked.

It was our quandary. I knew that the marshal and the queen must now be hiding in one of the houses that had already been ransacked, but that, a plan born of desperation, was full of holes. Even while I paused, listening for the return of our foes, I heard a woman screaming that there were thieves ... in Greek.

Sister Marie solved our puzzle by calling to the queen. In a minute, the marshal came out of the second house door, and the four of us became a rearguard, covering the queen's retreat. Marc-Antonio had a sack full of purses. Achille, Nerio's squire, ran ahead.

Sister Marie became the captain. She knew the street grid very well – she knew the convent where the queen was staying. We four were but swordsmen, and we backed through the gate, our swords in our hands. There was a half-hearted pursuit; twice, our opponents tried a rush at corners, but when we came to the gate, they vanished.

There were still no soldiers there, which showed us that someone had been bought. I knelt once I was clear of the portcullis; I had to rest, and I had three wounds, as I discovered only then: a long cut on my right arm, a stab wound on my hip, and another on my lower left leg. To say nothing of the annoying wound in my posterior.

Nerio had a gash across his left hand that had gone deep over the back of his thumb.

He was looking at it, and I was trying to make sense of the whole thing, and Fiore took a little bit of linen out of his belt pouch and began wiping his blade. 'That was ... fascinating,' he said.

Nerio's eyes met mine.

And there, under the arch, our laughter echoed and rebounded, banishing terror and pain.

Fiore was looking at his good gloves in disgust, because in the dark he'd got someone else's blood on them.

'Why are you laughing?' he demanded.

The next day we expected to be arrested. The town was hushed; my wounds were stiff and painful, and Nerio's thumb was infected.

Sister Marie told all to Fra Peter before I rose to face him. He met me in our inn's main room by the fire, and put a hand on my shoulder.

'The rumour is that Lesparre and his retinue were set on by assassins,' he said.

'The marshal?' I asked. I was sensible enough not to say the queen's name or title in public.

'Has a head cold,' Fra Peter said. 'They bury Father Pierre Thomas tomorrow. If the wind is fair …'

'Thank God,' I said. I wanted free of Famagusta.

Fra Peter frowned at me. 'There are more than a dozen corpses. Two of them are gentlemen,' he said. He shook his head. 'One is a Cypriote lord. The king is furious.' He looked at me.

I did not shrug. One did not shrug with Fra Peter.

'Fifteen dead men for one foolish woman—' Fra Peter began.

I was stiff and in the black mood that usually took me after a fight. 'Foolish?' I said. 'A woman who is blameless, and a vicious bastard trying to ruin her?' I paused. 'Sir?' I said, as if a little courtesy would ease my hard words.

Fra Peter rubbed his beard. 'Are you sure she is blameless, William?'

I thought of her very small figure, slim and strong in just a shift – as brave as Emile.

'Yes,' I said, meeting his eye.

Fra Peter's face cleared. 'Ah,' he said. 'That puts a different face on it.' He sat heavily. 'I will apologise if you like, Ser William.'

Fra Peter never called me Sir William. It was odd – brought tears to my eyes.

I met Nerio's squire Achille, who had a note that said that he and Fiore were in the market, shopping. Nerio knew no dark nights, or his code never admitted to it and he quietly slaked his fears with smooth skin and bright eyes. And Fiore – fighting for him was business, and passion. He was the epitome of the ordo of chivalry – fighting was what he did.

I was the weak one. In the fight, I was a good knight, but afterwards, I saw them all – the men I'd hurt, and the men I'd killed.

In other times, I'd have found a lass, and lost my darkness in her. But, while I knew which house Emile was in, I could hardly go to her while the court gossiped about her wayward ways and Turenne campaigned to have her stripped of her lands.

I suppose I thought all these things often, but when I walked towards the city market with Marc-Antonio at my shoulder, carrying my sword, I admit that I walked past her house apurpose, and waved to Ser Jason in the courtyard. He gave me a little salute; he was wearing his jupon, and I could guess that he was training with his friends.

I looked up.

There was Emile at the balcony. She was hanging linen veils on a small line, like any matron. She looked down, caught my eye, her face brightened, and she vanished into the house.

I kept walking, my day a little brighter.

In the market, I found Nerio at the stall of a glover, with Fiore trying gloves and a small pile of them in front of him – chamois, stag, and some eastern leather.

'I got blood on my best gloves,' Fiore said. So much for conscience.

I waved at my friends and went along to the old Genoese. Marc-Antonio stood close to me, my long sword in his arms. I was taking no chances. The law, which I was scrupulously obeying, said I could not wear a sword by day – but it didn't say someone could not carry it for me.

Messire Giancarlo bowed. 'Ah,' he said. 'You have returned for your plume.'

'I would like to see the book again,' I said. 'The Vegetius.'

Messire Giancarlo nodded. He sent a boy to fetch the book and offered me a cup of sweet wine, which I accepted. It was warm and spiced – even better. I sipped it and flipped through the book. For some reason, my sister came again to my mind; I had been thinking of her a great deal of late, mostly because of Sister Marie. I had also been thinking of Janet. Of women, and men.

Well.

'How much today?' I asked.

The Genoese sat back. He took the book from me, and flipped through it.

'I have something else to sell you,' he said. He met my eyes. 'A little information.'

I probably smiled. 'Yes?' he asked.

Giancarlo nodded at Marc-Antonio, standing close with my sword. 'There is a large sum of money offered for your death,' he said. 'And there is a man in this town who kills for money, or so they say.'

I thought of my invasion of the stews on behalf of my archer. 'There must be quite a few of them,' I said.

'This one is extraordinary,' the Genoese said. 'And very expensive. I can tell you more. How much is it worth to you?'

I shook my head, and it wasn't bravado. 'Nothing,' I said. 'A dozen men attacked me last night, and most of them are dead.' I moved stiffly; any fighting man could see I'd been in a fight, and the way I sat must have told any *homme armee* that I'd been stabbed in the buttock. Don't laugh! It's bloody annoying. 'How much for the book?'

'I think I suggested sixty ducats?' the Genoese said, obviously displeased.

I rose. 'You said florins. And sixty was too high,' I said. 'I thought you'd have seen sense since then.'

The Genoese held the book in his hand. 'I ordered this book from home because I thought that an army of professional soldiers would provide me a customer,' he said with some bitterness. 'All summer and autumn this book has sat in a trunk, and you are the second man to look at it. And the first was the man they are paying to kill you.' He raised an eyebrow. 'I can name him.'

'Fifty ducats,' I said.

The Genoese shook his head. 'My price is sixty,' he said. 'You and I both know that a book like this represents hundreds of hours of labour by an educated man. This is a book on the making of war, full of secrets. Full of knowledge. And knowledge is power, my English friend.'

'Marc-Antonio?' I called.

He stepped forward with my purse, and counted down sixty florins and some local silver change to make up the difference. Of course, if you are a strict moralist and you have paid attention, you know that about thirty of those pieces of silver came from the corpses of my foes.

The Genoese watched it, weighed two of the local coins on a balance, and after some discussion, received another clipped coin to make up for the lack.

'They call him László, or Ladislav. He comes from the east – his surname sounds like a curse: Makkrow.' Giancarlo shrugged.

'Why tell me this?' I said.

'My friend tells me that this man was paid to kill the legate,' the Genoese said. 'I am only a merchant – but I loved the legate. And everyone says you are the legate's man.'

I shook his hand as if he was a knight. 'If you hear more ...'

'He was in my stall two days ago, with the Count of Turenne.' The Genoese shrugged. 'They mean you harm, and the lady.' He looked away.

I collected my book, and with a flourish, he produced the fine red plume. 'Wear this in your helmet, and think a little better of merchants,' he said.

I carried the book back across the market to where Nerio and Fiore seemed to be buying every pair of gloves in the south end of the fair; a dozen glovers stood around them.

'I'll take a pair as well,' I said. 'Two pairs,' I added.

I was showing Nerio my book.

'You read Latin all of a sudden?' he asked.

I laughed. 'A little. And I'll learn more.'

He shook his head, but Fiore took the book and began to flip through. 'A book on war,' he said. He smiled at me as if I had done something clever. 'What a fine idea,' he said. He flipped through and came to a diagram, a sort of illustration I hadn't ever seen, and while glovers circled us like horseflies in a summer pasture, the three of us tried to puzzle out the Latin.

It took me time to realise this was not even Vegetius. I flipped back and forth and found a new title page. 'By the saints!' I laughed. 'I got a free book! This is someone called "Onasander".'

'An illustrated book would be better,' Fiore said. He had his faraway, not-with-you look. 'Now, if I drew the pictures myself ...'

Then, our squires and John the Turk carrying stacks of new gloves and other purchases, we swaggered to the tavern at the south corner of the market and sat. From there we could see everything. The wine was terrible – sour, stale, and old. But the position was excellent and so were the sausages, and we sat back, and my burdens eased a bit.

We began to talk, guardedly, of the fighting. I was describing the first part of the fight, with Nerio adding his own details – the only reason I can recall it for you now – when I suddenly realised where I knew the foreign voice in the darkness, and I stopped and swore.

'What?' Fiore snapped.

'The bastard in the dark, telling us he'd have us pulled to pieces,' I said.

John leaned forward, fascinated.

'Was that Lesparre?' Nerio asked. 'Didn't sound like him. Too high-pitched. And an odd accent.' Nerio shrugged as if it was of no moment. 'I knew it, however.'

'That's the Hungarian,' I said.

'Sweet Christ,' Nerio said. 'What are we into?'

'He was paid to kill the legate in Alexandria, and now, I believe, he's been paid to kill me.' I was watching the market more attentively.

Fiore scratched his hairline. 'I have seen the Hungarian fight,' he said. 'He is quite brilliant. I hope I can meet him.'

John looked at me. 'George and Maurice have very much respect – hate – for this man,' he said.

Miles, who usually sat silently, managed a smile. 'Unless your Hungarian has a ship,' he said, 'he won't be much danger. Fra Peter says we bury the legate tomorrow. And weigh anchor as soon as we can get aboard.'

'Three cheers,' I said, and we all agreed.

The legate's burial was like a great, solemn festival. The king participated, and so did most of his court; all the knights on the island, including the knights of my Order. The Brother Knights guarded the bier; the donats, in surcoats, came next, carrying our swords point upright in our hands. And behind us, the Carmelites and the Franciscans and some nuns – Sister Marie – then a great concourse of priests and bishops; then more knights; the Order of the Sword all together, and the king and queen, who rode together in what appeared to be amity, and then the court.

I chose to walk with the Order of Saint John, as I said before – with my friends, and close to the man I loved. I had watched over his body for days, and I can attest as well as any the sweet, uncorrupt smell that came off him, which was the more remarkable as my poor Father Pierre Thomas, in life, seldom washed and often submitted to the harshest asceticism, so that he was never the sweetest smelling man. I will also say that in eight or ten days of standing watch, I saw three miracles that I attribute to his intervention ... Ahh, but I'll leave this aside – you wish for deeds of arms and not a canonisation trial.

At any rate, I walked with Miles Stapleton, and Fiore and Nerio were close at our heels, and all our squires, and John the Turk, and some of our archers, and we walked from the Carmelite Priory to the cathedral in a hard rain. We heard a solemn funeral service, and women wept, and mayhap my own face was damp. I own it.

And when we emerged into the great square in front of the cathedral, the sun had burst through the clouds, and men smiled, and women peeked out from under their veils.

I had been aware all through the long service of Emile standing not so very far behind me. I'd taken the time to address a writer – one of those letter-writers you see in any public square – he had a narrow stall and a set of quills and a bottle of ink.

'I need a note,' I said. 'Quickly.' I was watching Emile. I could have found her in total darkness; it was as if I had a lodestone that pointed to her. And her people were gathered around her.

I dictated a note to Bernard, and my writer dutifully took it all down while I watched the squire. Marc-Antonio paid the man and I walked back to where I had been standing with Fra Peter and the other knights of the Order.

She had been standing by the doors, and now she came down the cathedral steps. She had a veil of black silk and she let it flutter in the breeze, leaning on Jean-François as she walked.

I excused myself from the older knights and sent Nerio's Davide – no, of course, Davide died at Alexandria. I sent Achille with my note for Ser Bernard. He delivered it under my eye and came back, almost running, and I looked beyond him to see if Bernard was looking at the note – he could read. I was just turning to John, who had my sword, when …

Just beyond Bernard, I saw the Hungarian. He had his thumbs in his belt. He did not look overtly threatening, but he wanted me to see him, and his close proximity to Emile.

He smiled. And nodded. And then, as bold as a street-strumpet, he began to walk towards me.

'That's him,' Fiore said, or something equally useless. 'The Hungarian.' John seemed as eager as a terrier.

The Hungarian looked different – his hair was cut short, and he wore a well-cut doublet and the sort of over-doublet just then coming into fashion.

I walked to him. I was not going to show any fear to this monster, this assassin who had tried to kill Father Pierre Thomas in the flame-shot inferno of Alexandria.

'Now he is beyond your reach,' I said, as we drew close. We were surrounded by the rich and powerful – by priests and nuns. There were even Jews and a handful of Moslems.

The Hungarian smiled. 'What makes you think so?' he asked with good humour. 'Doesn't it seem to you that he is dead?'

It had not occurred to me unto that moment that the Hungarian had killed him, and I felt a total fool.

'Eh, Sire Gold, you bested me the other evening,' the Hungarian said. 'Although I confess that I am mortified that you did not know me.'

Fiore came up on one side of me and Stapleton on the other.

The Hungarian smiled with his excellent teeth at all of us. 'Please do not get ideas, gentlemen,' he said. 'I have people here in the square. And while I know who you are, you do not know who my people are.'

'You mean, those that are left,' Nerio said. 'What have you got – two cripples and a blind man?'

Just for a moment, the Hungarian's mask dropped, and his anger showed. 'Enough,' he said.

Nerio, bolder, I think, than I, shook his head. 'No, my dear man. I won't have it. I imagine we're supposed to live in fear of you, but really ...' He shrugged. 'I suspect your people shit themselves when they think of facing us.'

The mask was coming off. The Hungarian was not used to being bullied. 'Listen—'

'No,' Nerio said. 'You listen.' He grinned his mad Italianate grin. 'I am quite rich – you know this?'

The Hungarian unhooked a hand from his belt.

'How much would you charge me to kill your employer, eh?' Nerio said, smiling. 'For anything that Turenne can pay you, I can probably put down ten times as much.'

The Hungarian took a breath, mastering himself, and set his face. 'I don't want to kill the Count of Turenne,' he said. 'He is not my employer anyway.'

'Bah, the Bishop of Cambrai, then,' Nerio said.

'I look forward to killing you gentlemen,' the Hungarian said. 'I will do my best to humble you first, for my entertainment and that of my employer.' He had his smile back now. 'And this lady,' he said, nodding towards Emile, 'will be—'

I kneed him in the groin. One thing I have learned from Fiore is to never show preparation. When you mean to strike, strike. Two nuns passed behind me and pushed me a little towards him; the thing was there, I did it.

He fell to his knees on the cobbles.

Nerio laughed.

The Hungarian had a dagger in his hand for a moment, but Fiore took it and Stapleton, of all people, put his own at the man's neck. We were in armour, and he was not.

'If I see you again, I'll kill you,' I said. I hope I sounded careless.

His eyes held pure hate.

I'm quite proud that I smiled. 'Unless you'd like to join us on the road to Jerusalem?' I asked. 'We can expiate our sins together.'

A few people were paying attention. Not many. I could see three men whose attention was focused on us, and I noted them. They were close by Emile, but Jason was watching them. John pressed close behind me; I didn't know, but he had my sword drawn, hilt out, for me to take.

I swept the square. The three men Jason was watching were all tall, with Slavic faces I'd seen out on the Steppes – one blonde, two dark, and the dark men both thin and pie-faced, as we say in London.

There was another on the church steps, I thought. That is, his clothes were out of place, and his attention was on us. He had an odd, Italian hat.

All this in one *coupe d'oeil*.

Nerio spoke quite clearly. 'If you harm my friend,' he said, 'or any of my friends, really, I'll arrange to have you pulled to death by horses.' He put a gloved finger on the Hungarian's forehead. '*And you know I can.*' He nodded, as if they were just meeting. 'Just walk away, eh?'

Nerio straightened up. I thought for a moment what a bad enemy he'd make. He cared very little for what we might call conventional morality. He had almost unlimited wealth, an extensive network of business contacts, and superb fighting skills. He might have been the Devil incarnate, but he was ferociously loyal to his friends, and we were his friends.

But the Hungarian was no weeping virgin. He got to his feet as we stepped away. I would still have been puking, from the blow I'd given him; he was already standing straight.

'I will kill you all,' he said, very clearly. 'The woman first. I will humiliate you all.'

Nerio shrugged. 'You know how it will end, then,' he said.

My hands were shaking. I was thinking of putting him down on the spot.

I should have.

And that night, when John and I were currying horses, he turned to me.

'Christian men make enemies, they not kill them?' he asked.

I wrestled with that a bit. 'Sometimes,' I said.

'Stupid,' John said. 'Hungarian hard, bad man. Next time, no words. Sword.' He shrugged. 'Man Jesus not know about this bad men, this *mann khul*. But Mongol know.'

The next morning, after a night of almost no sleep and constant worry, we loaded our ships off the beach in front of the town, and small boats rowed us out to them. Absolutely nothing happened; my good warhorse was loaded smoothly, and my two riding horses; I saw Emile onto a separate vessel, with Nerio and Fiore and all her knights. We'd agreed that it could not be me close to her, protecting her, because of the gossip.

But indeed, Nerio derided the Hungarian. 'He no more killed the legate than Satan did,' Nerio said. 'He's a cock of the walk, but he has nothing between his legs but a noodle. If I had another day or two I'd pay some bravos to beat him to death.'

Nerio said this with a casual brutality that made my head turn.

'Nerio!' I said cautiously.

He smiled. 'You really are too good to live,' Nerio said. 'This isn't a chivalric contest. Weren't you a routier? This is a hired killer. We deal with him the way we deal with a thug. We pay people to kill him.' Nerio smiled.

Nerio wasn't a bad man, by his own standards. But, while I watched Emile's house all night, Nerio was with his courtesan, whom he threatened to bring to Jerusalem. Just for example.

But never mind Nerio.

We boarded our ships, and before the sun was a hand's breadth over the rim of the sea, we lowered our sails on a fine stiff breeze and we were already moving at what, under oars, would have been a good cruising speed before we passed the harbour mole and turned very slightly for the open sea.

Miles and I were leaning over the stern rail. I was watching our sister ship, another great galley of Venice, a pilgrim galley, for Emile, and sure enough, as I watched she came to the rail. I had given her a note via Nerio, and now she found me and waved.

And blew a kiss.

By God, my heart soared.

And Miles laughed. 'We are going to Jerusalem!' he said.

JERUSALEM

February – May 1366

Crusaders and pilgrims have landed in the squalid port of Jaffa since the Moslem Conquest and mayhap before that. When Outremer was a proper kingdom and pilgrims could travel in peace, they often went from Venice to Acre; Acre was a fine port, or so the Knights of Saint John report.

But despite the town's appearance, we cheered onboard our galleys when the Holy Land came in sight, not so very long after we quit Famagusta. We were still well off the port when a small sailing boat, well handled, closed us from the north; I had been aboard that boat many days before the landings at Alexandria, and I knew her well enough when she was hull up, and I was unsurprised when Nicolas Sabraham, and his apostles George and Maurice, came up the sides of our Venetian merchant and joined our party.

'No doubt Sabraham has already been to the Holy Sepulchre and back a dozen times,' Fra Peter said.

But Sabraham shook his head when he came aboard. 'I had another errand for the king,' he said. 'But I mean to go to the Holy City with you. And I thought you'd appreciate knowing that Jaffa is empty. The garrison is withdrawn.'

Ser Peter nodded. 'That was the news in Famagusta,' he said. 'It should make this simple. We are fortunate.'

Sabraham shook his head. 'Or very difficult,' he said.

Despite his long face, we cheered again when the *capitano*, a Venetian gentleman, a cousin of Zeno's named Gentile Bembo, made the difficult harbour entrance look easy. I could see over the side how badly silted the entrance was, and the great Venetian galley seemed to pass within a hand's breadth of the banks on either hand. Indeed, the third transport touched; we saw her mast vibrate, but no damage was done.

Veterans have told me that the Mamluks destroyed Jaffa and razed the walls so no Christian army could ever use it again. The great stone quay was a ruin like most of the town, and unloading was difficult even for five hundred Christians. No real army could even fit inside the tiny port, which was more like a notch in the coast than a bay.

It is no light matter to unload ships on a beach. Pilgrims are not soldiers, and while I had our two hundred men-at-arms formed on the beach in an hour, the knights and brother sergeants were still trying to land the pilgrims and their baggage.

Sabraham and I, with a dozen men-at-arms, went into Jaffa. It was not deserted, although the Islamic population was afraid of us, and most doors were shut. Sabraham convinced a rabbi to tell another man to open a stable, and we paid cash for horses that had probably been the spares of the former garrison. Of course, they'd gone off by ship. But it netted us sixty decent mounts, and the various caravan sheds, used to serving pilgrims, furnished donkeys and mules and another thirty horses.

We paid for what we took. That was the Order's way, and they had a small hospital at Jaffa. In fact, Maurice rode away, fetched coin from the hospital, and returned, which added a certain dream-like quality to the whole thing.

Or nightmare quality. In late afternoon, a Mamluk official, an Egyptian with red-blond hair and a great belly, arrived with a Franciscan priest. The Egyptian was obviously enraged by our arms, but it was the Franciscan who surprised us.

He was Italian, and he spoke to Fra Peter in Italian. His name was Father Angelo, and he was tall, built more like a soldier than a priest, with a heavy dark beard and thick eyebrows. He rode a mule.

I was involved in the tedious business of mounting the men-at-arms. Our two Greek knights had just taken a dozen of the best horses, beautiful Arab mares with the nostrils slit so that they could run longer and breathe better, for their stradiotes. Because Fra Peter understood the value of scouts, I let this happen, but in so doing lost the confidence of the Gascons, who were demanding better horses and using foul language. My mood was not of the best. Fra Peter had just ridden up and was, I could tell, trying to decide if I needed his support when the Franciscan accosted him.

'Are you the leader of this horrible injustice?' he roared.

His Italian was fluent, but slow, and many of the English and French men-at-arms could follow him. His angry tone was obvious.

'I am the leader of this caravan,' Fra Peter said.

The priest raised a cross as if it was a sword. 'You have no right. The Order of Saint John no longer exists here! You are allowed a small hospital on our sufferance. You are banned here by the authorities. Only a pilgrimage guided by the Order of Saint Francis may visit the Holy City. And by your blasphemous presence with arms, you threaten the entire future of Christian pilgrimage. Be gone!'

I confess that I had rather expected to be greeted, at least by Christians, as a sort of conquering hero.

The dragoman, or whatever rank he might have had, raised a document that was heavily written in a language I didn't know. Arabic? Hebrew? He waved it, and shouted at us.

'Without a charter from the sultan, you cannot come to Jaffa, you cannot land here, and you certainly may not bear arms,' the priest proclaimed.

Now, I tend to harp on Gascons because they are loud and excitable and I have often had to fight them. This is unfair; Gascons are the most like the English of all the people I know, except perhaps Venetians, and I have loved a good many Gascons. Just then young Etienne l'Angars, one of the most quarrelsome of the whole lot, said, *sotto voce*, 'Someone put an arrow in the priest.'

I laughed. I confess it – the same thought had occurred to me.

'You sons of Belial!' the priest shouted. I guess he spoke some French.

Fra Peter tried to remonstrate.

'Back on your ships, or I will excommunicate you all,' the priest shouted.

Sabraham was close by me, and gave a shrug that said 'I told you so.' He had not, in fact, told me so, but he had suggested that this was not going to be as easy or glorious as we all expected. 'Pay the dragoman,' he said. 'Let him quiet the priest.'

Fra Peter was, with commendable patience, attempting to show the priest our *passim Generale* from the pope, and the bull supporting it, which, to my surprise, he had copies of ready to hand. I suppose he had heeded Sabraham's hints.

For me, I took a role I did not fancy, and motioned to John. Fra

Peter looked at me, saw me with John, and nodded – a compliment, in a way, that he expected me to behave with sense.

Some of the Gascons and English thought I was about to use my sword, and they pressed in behind me.

'Tell the Egyptian that we mean no harm – that we know the garrison is gone – that we will pay the tax but we will go armed.' I was making this up, but I knew that the sultan charged a tax per head, and short of killing the infidel officer on the spot, I wasn't sure. Were we in a state of war, or peace? Was this part of the taking of Alexandria? Or were we on pilgrimage?

In fact, I was taking a great deal on my own head. Paying the tax rankled. We had just defeated these people. On the other hand, I was learning things about war. And one was, you only fight when you must. Buying off an enemy …

The Egyptian was no soldier – he was clearly terrified of my angry archers and Gascons. He was surprised to be addressed in passable Arabic.

Sabraham came up with me, on horseback. He made a long speech in Arabic; he was perfectly calm. I turned and winked at the archers. I got smiles from them. I turned to the Gascons. 'Ready for anything?' I said.

I got a good growl.

'Don't draw unless I do, *mes braves*,' I said. 'This is a small man, but he can make as much trouble as a petit bourgeois in a land deal.'

L'Angars laughed. 'With you, Sir William!' he said, and the others followed him.

I turned back to the conversation. Now the Egyptian was shouting at Sabraham, spittle flying. He waved his documents again.

'Gut him and stuff a pig in his arse,' said Ewan the Scot.

I turned and gave him my evil eye.

He was unrepentant. 'We can sack this town in a heartbeat, eh, mates?' he asked.

'Then where do we stay?' I asked. 'Or the *capitano* land his cargo? Eh?'

I hadn't convinced Ewan, I could tell, and the Gascons were all for a little violence.

John gave a little twitch of his lips that I knew meant distaste. 'This son of many whores says we must pay two silver *soldi* for every head and no weapons or armour. He says he has many troops, and we will be massacred. Ser Nicolas says, no, you have no troops, and we go anyway. We pay one *soldo* per two men, none for women or children, in respect to the sultan. Whoreson says hard words – Sabraham says that you and these others ache to kill your first Saracen.'

I almost laughed aloud. The dragoman was such a pitiful specimen it really hadn't occurred to me to kill him.

The conversation went back and forth – bargaining with shouting. The Gascons grew bored and the dragoman grew insistent, and I sent Marc-Antonio for the *capitano*.

The priest continued to demand that we all re-embark.

Master Bembo came through the crowd with his manifests under his arm, and I intercepted him before he reached the Egyptian official.

'You have the silver to pay the head tax?' I asked. Every pilgrim had paid the tax on embarkation at Famagusta. I suspected that Bembo thought it was pure profit, as we'd never pay the very Mamluks we were fighting.

Of course I'm laughing. The world is never simple, and the Holy Land is the least simple place I've ever been.

Two separate negotiations with two very different men conducted simultaneously; to get the Venetian to let go the silver he thought was profit, and to get the Egyptian to accept what we would pay. He was a fool, and a greedy fool. He had no swords to back him, and we were offering a tithe of the real tax to save his face, as they say – to allow him to feel we had not humiliated him. Neither I, nor Sabraham, nor Fra Peter thought it at all likely that he had access to soldiers; but it seemed foolish to alienate the entire Egyptian governmental bureaucracy for a few *soldi*, even if we were nominally at war.

We'd burned the biggest city in the world. I'd have expected the fat bureaucrat to be a little more respectful. I've met his kind in England and in the papal chancery. I'm glad to say that Islam is as badly afflicted, or worse.

This went on for so long that our new horses began to fret for food; the Gascons got bored, and l'Angars suggested that we burn some houses to make our point; long enough, in fact, that my carefully nurtured patience slipped away, and l'Angars's suggestions began to make sense.

John turned to me. 'Give him gold. For his own. Right now.' He shrugged. 'Or kill him.'

I reached into my purse, but I had nothing but some small silver sequins. 'Nerio?' I called.

By God. He was at my shoulder. 'Yes, my lord?' he asked. By which he meant, *Really, you summon me? You arrogant Englishman.*

'We need some gold,' I said.

Nerio held out his gloved hand to his squire without a word. Achille put two fat gold florins, minted on Cyprus, into his hand and he passed them to me. I closed them in my fist.

Fiore looked disgusted, as did Miles.

'We're crusaders,' Miles said. 'Why pay anything?'

I ignored him, because I trusted Sabraham.

'Tell the son of a whore we must finish this and make friends,' I said. 'Tell him my men are restless and want to burn the town.' That was true. I pressed close to him and stuck out my hand. When he closed his grip on mine, I gave him the two gold coins. I saw his eyes change. I saw that here was a man for whom greed outweighed physical fear.

He looked down into his hand. Took a coin and bit it.

And then he gave in suddenly on all fronts – grinned, and demanded to be paid one silver *soldi* for each two men. Which the Venetian paid with an ill grace.

Suddenly, as fast as a wind whispers over the sea, the *capitano*'s manifests were signed, and the dragoman provided Fra Peter with a pass from the sultan, and another permitting us to bear arms. His scribes wrote furiously, and then, in a cloud of ill-smelling ink, they were gone, and we were left with fewer coins and the same horses.

The priest did not budge. Fra Peter had occupied this man for the whole of our negotiation with the dragoman, and now I looked significantly at Sabraham. He shook his head. 'Oh, no,' he said. 'I'm good with the natives. Not with the church.'

Still, he followed me across the ruin of the square to where the priest was still threatening excommunication. I saw Emile; I confess I made it my business to pass within a few feet of her, where she stood looking very pretty with her children and a fine grey penitent's gown, in a crowd of other pilgrims. These were not fighting people; they were genuine pilgrims, and the threat of any interdict from the church worked heavily on them.

'We have spent fifty years arriving at the current partnership with the government,' the priest explained in a very condescending voice. 'We will not thank you for ruining it.'

'The Holy Father has declared a crusade and ordered all Christians—' Fra Peter began.

The priest raised his cross. 'So you say! But there is no Holy Father here—'

I stepped between them. 'Father,' I said, and held up the dragoman's documents, 'I have a licence for every man, woman, and child – I have a second that permits us to ride abroad, armed.' I paused.

Fra Peter gave me one of the warmest smiles I've ever seen.

'While,' I went on, 'in fact, the Papal Legate has directly ordered this expedition, and he is, in fact, your direct spiritual superior—'

'Don't tell me, you bloody-handed—'

I am very loud when I want to be, and I just spoke over him. '… we will ignore your arrogance and accept that you must work every day with the infidel government. For which purpose, I have these licences.'

He fell silent at the same time I did.

He seized both pieces of parchment and read them. While he read, I feared that we'd been taken by the dragomen, but apparently corruption had limits. Both documents were as pronounced.

The priest handed them back to me. 'On your head be it,' he said. 'I will accompany your pilgrims at all times.'

Fra Peter opened both eyes very wide at this volte face. He took a deep breath, mastered himself, and nodded.

'Excellent, Father. Perhaps you'd like to say Mass?'

Miles Stapleton still didn't understand why we'd paid for horses, much less paid the dragoman.

Sabraham nodded in the direction of Jerusalem and raised both eyebrows. Quietly, to the dozen of us standing there, he said, 'Here in the Holy Land, there are as many bad men and fools as anywhere else. But those who are not wholly evil have learned to look past the surface and help their neighbours. Any invader who comes will eventually leave – today's conqueror is tomorrow's victim. So we pay.' He smiled grimly. 'There used to be old men – sergeants of the Order from before the fall of Acre – who said that it was Crusaders from Europe who destroyed us, and not the Moslems. A little tolerance goes a long way here.'

Miles shook his head.

'They are different from us,' Sabraham said. 'Accept it.'

Stapleton didn't.

I had no trouble paying for horses, and with the Order's funds I paid for more, and by Vespers, our little company looked more like an army than I expected. In addition to our two hundred archers and men-at-arms we had Emile's knights and followers, as well as the two Greek knights whom I have mentioned, Syr Giannis Lascaris Calophernes, of middle height, with a thicker black beard than a Latin might have, who had been with us at Alexandria, and his friend Syr Giorgios Dimitri Angelus, who was tall, ascetic, and looked like one of their Byzantine saints. Both were followers of Father Pierre Thomas; both had marched in his procession at Famagusta. Syr Giannis was married to a niece of the Emperor, and was yet a very humble man. The two of them had a dozen horsemen apiece, in light saddles; they came in a military galley that they owned.

And there was Lord Grey and his retinue, which, of course, included Sir Steven Scrope. I had no time for the young gentleman, but he was in good harness, and they had their own horses as we had ours. All told, then, when we mustered in late afternoon after stripping the hostels and stables of horseflesh, we had almost all of our pilgrims mounted, at least on donkeys, and all our men-at-arms and archers were mounted on horses, although we had damn few remounts.

And on the beach, Syr Giannis unfurled the legate's banner and gave it to Lord Grey.

Fra Peter, who, as a celibate, never wore a favour on his harness, took a plain square of cloth from a pack and pinned it to his surcoat. It was old, threadbare and brown – Father Pierre Thomas's Carmelite robe.

'I promised to take it to Jerusalem,' he said.

Sister Marie had a good palfrey, and I was disturbed to see her by Emile d'Herblay. They were both friends to me, and yet perhaps I feared what they might say to each other. And we also had Father Pierre Thomas's confessor, and now we had the Franciscan priest named Angelo, an Italian of good breeding from Vicenza who knew the della Scala and Cavalli and other men there I knew. He had climbed down from his high horse very successfully, by then.

At any rate, we said a prayer on the beach, and then dispersed to the various hospitals and inn and hostels of Jaffa. The town was built, or rather, once had been built, to take pilgrims; there was no need to use our small store of hard bread and sausage on the first day. But it was a difficult town, half down on the beach, half up high by the citadel, mostly in ruins, with good buildings on old foundations and terrible hovels built up against the ruins of old walls. And the walls themselves were not good for much.

Sabraham and Syr Giannis borrowed John and rode off into the evening sun of the Holy Land, determined to find more remounts in the open country to the north.

I walked out in my arming coat, equally determined to find Nerio and Fiore. And even more determined to have a few words with my lady-love, for whom I was as parched as a shipwrecked man on the salty sea. I had a good story to tell myself, too, as you shall hear; I had a reason to prowl the inns of Jaffa. I was protecting pilgrims. But in truth ...

I understand that Sir Galahad was pure of his body like a nun all his days, and that this gave him strength, but I confess that I am a lovesome man and chastity has rather the opposite effect on me.

At any rate, I walked out into the pleasant air. The Holy Land in winter can be cold and rainy, but nothing like London, I promise you. Indeed, I landed expecting a desert and found a great many flowers in bloom, and the fragrance of Jaffa stays with me to this day – flowers I knew only in stories, like jasmine.

And there was filth.

I passed through the market, which had marvels, for such a small, decayed place: good silk, cheaper than Cyprus; saffron, which was worth more than gold at home. I bought a packet said to come from Cilicia, from the very cave of Tartarus, which sounded wonderful to me and still does. I suppose it is worth mentioning that there was still a Christian king in Cilicia then – Constantine, and he was an ally of Peter of Cyprus. The saffron seller told me a rumour – in French as good as my own – that the Cilician Armenians and the Turks were already fighting over the hills of Lebanon to the north, and around Antioch, because the Mamluks had abandoned all their garrisons.

And further along, I bought a lump of lapis lazuli for no better reason than that I fancied the colour. The blue is superb – the very blue you see in the best manuscripts and paintings. I suppose I had some notion of getting it carved, or having a clasp belt made for my lady. The stuff was rare even in the Holy Land, and considered almost magical. I parted with the whole of a Cypriote gold coin for the chunk. I dropped it into my purse and walked on in the beautiful light, looking for something with which to woo my lady.

I found Bernard and Jason playing cards with Fiore, and looking the way men always look when facing him at cards. His memory was formidable, and he could sometimes find you near the bottom of the pack, saying things like, 'Whichever one of us gets the ten of swans will make his point,' while someone like you or I would still be trying to remember what makes a score and how the rules work.

Nerio, may I add, only ever played with Fiore as a means of giving the poverty-stricken Friulian some silver.

Emile and her people had a hostel that was considerably grander than ours, with a fine open room painted white, and a courtyard with a fountain and lemon trees, probably the best building in the town. I sat in the good white room until the oil lamps were lighted, very different from the candle-and-tallow stink of home. I had olives, which I didn't like but have since learned to love, and some not very good cheese. The bread was odd, and there was no butter, and you had to dip your bread in oil – I'd done it in Italy, but everything was a little different in the Holy Land, and had a sort of magical air about it.

I had written out a watch schedule on my wax tablet, just the way the Order and Sir John Hawkwood arrange watches in hostile billets. It was difficult, sitting comfortably in a good inn, drinking bad wine in a city manifestly at peace, to be practising the art of war, but I was damned if I was going to be surprised here, and Fra Peter was very much of the same mind, and we'd written a watch schedule for two days. We'd had a difficult conversation dividing the knights of our little army into those we considered reliable and those we did not. At any rate, Ser Jason was commanding a watch, and he affected to grumble a great deal, pretending that he had not the skill of arms or the name to lead a contingent of knights and archers. But he did, of course, and he did so right well.

And Bernard, of course, merely accepted the tablet and copied his times onto his own tablet.

Jean-François was feeling poorly, so I took his name off the list for the day.

I had saved Emile's inn for last, after a long round of watch assignments, and I sat drinking wine, hoping that she might appear. I suspect I was tolerably transparent to my friends, but at the same time, there were, and are, rules to be maintained. I knew that to flagrantly visit my love would offend her men-at-arms. Not to mention fuelling certain rumours.

Nerio strolled in after me with his squire Achille, and he joined us. He and Jason engaged in a ritual of mocking each other that seemed odd to me and always made me fear they would reach for weapons, but no one else seemed uncomfortable.

'I think we should eat here,' Nerio said, glancing at me. His expression suggested that he knew exactly why I was sitting there.

'Perhaps my lady would care to dine with us today,' Jason said. He raised an eyebrow.

I longed to jump to my feet and shout 'I'll go and ask her!' but I did not. Nor was a messenger needed, because just then, as a reward for my waiting, Emile appeared with both her children in tow. The young nun who acted as her governess had Edouard by the hand, and he came into the room and made a reverence, a bow on one knee, to the knights.

The Savoyards rose and bowed in their turn, and Nerio and I joined them. Fiore never raised his eyes from his cards.

Little Magdalena was six months older than when I'd last spent any time with her, but she remembered me, which pleased me, and she came and made a deep curtsy, and smiled shyly. She was a little more like a sausage in a casing than a child – pudgy and very jolly, with deep dimples and a desire to laugh. Edouard was a solemn sprite by contrast, and it was very difficult to make him laugh.

Sister Anne – I think that was her name – took both children to the garden, and Emile followed her. But she stopped.

'Sir William,' she said, happily enough, 'won't you walk with me in the garden?'

'Watch out, or he'll assign you a watch,' Nerio said, *sotto voce*, and all the gentlemen laughed. If I have not done Nerio justice, let me say that he was very good at this sort of thing – a laugh or a jape to cover any little social stress.

At any rate, I rose, perhaps a little too eagerly, and followed Emile into the inn's little garden, which had a tiny fountain and a bed of flowers. The courtyard garden reminded me of pretty convents and priories I'd seen in England, and it occurred to me that the Holy Land might have exerted some effect on the rest of Europe in this manner, because flowers were so common in the Holy Land.

At any rate, I made some banter with Emile and then played a little with Edouard, but he was still afraid of me. I found him a small stick, though, and he began to fight one of the columns with all the energy of a knight practising on a pell, and that made his mother smile.

'Do you think you will teach Edouard to be a knight?' she asked me suddenly.

'Perhaps,' I said. And then, because there would never be a better moment, I said, 'It would be certain, if you would marry me.'

'Marry you?' she asked. Her eyes flashed a moment. She was a countess, and I a sort of jumped up hedge-knight. I had once been an under-cook. And she knew it all.

But it was she who smiled. 'Marry me?' she asked. 'Most men do not marry their lemans.'

I knew that tone. I knew her sudden desire to hurt herself.

And, because I'm not quite a fool, I realised in that moment that the japes and insults *hurt her*. Because she feared that they were true – that she was a bad woman.

I was suddenly ashamed that I had not challenged Scrope. What kind of knight was I, to accept an insult against my lady, an insult of the most vulgar kind?

Had she heard of it? I had to assume she had. That was like swallowing a knife, I promise you. And never, never had the Order's rules and the world of arms been more at odds.

All these thoughts, and some others, passed in one beat of my heart. I had time to take a breath. There was no good answer – there never was, when Emile was bent on causing herself pain. But I loved her, and there was nothing to be gained from denial.

'Marry me,' I said. 'I love you.' I might have said, 'We can put an end to gossip,' and I might have said, 'We can lawfully enjoy one another,' but those were not the arguments for that moment.

Emile had an odd smile on her face, and just for a moment, she looked down at her feet. 'Do you know,' she said, 'how rich an heiress I am?'

In truth, I had some notion, as she could maintain six knights and a dozen other retainers, wait months in Venice, sail to Rhodes, and then to Jerusalem. Her husband had led quite a tail of routiers. She had to be very rich.

'I do not want your riches,' I said.

Emile put a hand on my arm. 'William. Would you marry me if I told you that every estate I own is entailed to my son, and you will own none of them?'

I laughed. By God, that was a good laugh. Oh, I can put myself in her place easily enough – the up-and-coming landless knight, the entailed estate, the hated husband. Now dead. She must have thought ...

I didn't need to care. I suspect I grinned. 'Good,' I said. 'Then no man can say I love you for your lands.'

'Truly?' she asked. Sister Anne was scowling. Each of us had just touched the other; this was not a court of love, but the courtyard of an inn.

'Truly,' I said.

Edouard chose that moment to assault Sister Anne, and she was, despite her strong ideas of rules for her betters, a fine young woman with a vigorous touch, and she tussled with the boy and he screamed with pleasure. Magdalena began to pummel her governess with her small fists to support her brother, and Emile's hand found mine and pulled sharply. It was sometimes easy to forget that Emile had a will of her own. As she tugged, she stepped back, between the columns that supported the stable roof, and before I was inside its arch, we were kissing.

That was quite a kiss, for all that it lasted perhaps as long as it takes a governess to tackle a young boy and take away his stick. I confess that the kiss had a moment in it where it seemed completely reasonable to me that I was about to make love to the Countess d'Herblay standing up in a stall with a donkey, but, of course, that was not to happen. She bit my lip, pushed me, and walked away, tugging her kirtle down sharply over her hips.

She looked back at me ...

I had to breathe. The look was as much as the kiss, or more.

I went to look at the horses. I had little choice, being in a state. Such a state.

*

That night, while I stood watch and rode from picket to picket around the town of Jaffa, Emile drank wine with her knights, and broached to them the possibility of marrying me. And bless them, they made no quibbles, save that they feared the gossip of the Gascons and some of the other Savoyards about her honour. I think all of her knights assumed I'd killed d'Herblay. And thought the better of me for it.

At any rate, the next day, short on sleep and cursing Marc-Antonio, who had not curried my warhorse, I was standing in the stable just after daybreak. Marc-Antonio was making some miserable excuse, and John was looking at both of us with a sort of contempt that raised my ire. I'd had little sleep and my mood was not good.

'He always says it is my job to care for you and *he* cares for your horses,' Marc-Antonio whined.

'Lie,' spat John. 'I went on scout, Lord leads. You do work. We agreed.'

Marc-Antonio was miserable with the knowledge of having failed, and, like many young men, chose to vent his anger at me. 'It's not fair,' he said.

I hit him. I hadn't hit him often in our year together, but I'd had enough of his whining and I knocked him down.

John gave me a funny look.

'Get up,' I said. 'That was for lying. And whining.'

Marc-Antonio was so angry he could barely contain himself. He pushed past me and John frowned. 'He say …' he began, but Emile, dressed for riding in her pilgrim clothes, pushed into the stall.

'I am interrupting something,' she said. 'Why is your Marc-Antonio looking all blotchy?'

'I hit him,' I said.

John made a little bobbing motion of his head and slipped under my warhorse's belly and began currying, the brush going very fast.

Emile looked interested. 'My pater always said not to hit people who couldn't hit you back,' she said. 'Servants, slaves, monks, nuns. He could be a hard man, but he had some good rules.'

A hot answer came to my lips and I spat it out rather than speak it. I looked away. And back. She was interested.

It occurred to me that she was offering me good advice, and quite possibly assessing my willingness to accept it. You see? I have my moments.

'Your father was a wise man,' I said. 'I'm not happy I hit him.'

She smiled.

John's curry brush went *whisk, whisk, whisk*.

'I would like to accept your offer of marriage,' she said.

I did not whoop. But I did get an arm behind her, and a willing embrace that had every bit of the same potency that our brief engagement the day before had had. My knees went weak. It was quite remarkable.

John never stopped currying my horse, and otherwise, the big stall was as private as a castle.

'I would like to be wed in Jerusalem,' she said.

I floated through the morning after that, and it is probably a miracle that I had my warhorse tacked up, and was astride my good riding horse, was wearing my brigantine and maille, and carrying a pair of javelins in a case and my long sword. If you have not lived the life of arms, it might be possible to imagine that a knight rides abroad every day *cap à pied* in gleaming harness and carrying a heavy lance for jousting, but the Knights of Saint John had long experience in the Holy Land and tended to lighter harness and weapons more suited to fighting bandits than to tournaments. A heavy lance can be a very valuable tool on a close-packed battlefield, but in the open ground between settlements around Jerusalem, you'll never catch the bandit who shot your horse, much less get to wield a heavy lance.

Most of the English and French knights nonetheless wore their harnesses and carried such lances, as the only weapons they had; we had almost a hundred former routiers, most of whom had light lances or spears, and a few had crossbows; and finally, we had our own professional archers, as well as the Romanian stradiotes. We also had a handful of 'turcopoles', local men on good horses with bows, and John rode with them, although he muttered that not one of them was a true son of the plains, and as he watched them ride, he pulled at his long moustaches, with something akin to amusement.

At any rate, I rode along in a haze of happiness, apologised to Marc-Antonio, and managed a civil word with Sir Steven Scrope despite my earlier intention to kill him when next we met.

It is interesting, the effect of happiness. First, because it makes you calm, and increases your self-possession, so that you become a pillar of good humour for your friends. Second, because it can render you more, rather then less, observant. Possibly fretting, and worry, are bad for observational skills, but I have noted on a number of occasions that a well-rested man on a good horse and in a fine fettle sees things that his angrier cousin misses.

We rode north and east. We were told there was a great deal of bandit activity in the hills around Jerusalem, because the Mamluks were gone. Fra Peter had few fears; with two hundred fighting men, no bandit was likely to dispute our path.

Our first day's ride was utterly uneventful; we climbed the first ridge above Jaffa and rode east across a broad plain that alternated between dusty desert and fertile fields. At the edge of the rough ground which rose across our path, we came to a fine village with a pair of churches, a mosque and an inn. It had a Jewish temple too, or so I understood. That is the Holy Land for you.

I was tired from two patrols and a day in the saddle, and I was rolled in my cloak before the sun was down; up for a watch, and then asleep again until the cold tail of the night.

The next day we made a better start, because everyone was getting used to the discipline; the pilgrims were up earlier, and I helped Emile to mount. She gave my hand a squeeze and flashed me a smile that might almost have been lascivious, but that was our only contact, yet still it was enough to make my heart jump.

The rough ground rose almost at the very eastern edge of the village, and we began to climb steep hills – not large, but sharp, with water gullies in all directions and scrubby plant life that seemed determined to attack the traveller. It was cold and a little wet, and I misdoubt I noticed, I was so happy.

A few hours out of Jaffa, on a winding trail that could in no way be called a road, with the pilgrims in the centre guarded by the archers, the best-armed knights as the rearguard, and the rest of us out in a cloud in front, we were hit.

I was riding with John. We were almost a hundred feet higher than the pilgrims, and John was crossing a broken hillside on a track that I would not have dared to take on a horse except that I was coming along behind him. But, due to the complexion of my day, I was the friend to all the world; my head was up, and I was looking in the right direction when I saw the dazzle of sun on metal.

'John,' I called. I was still new enough to the world of war in the east that I raised a hand and pointed.

Instantly, half a dozen arrows came back at me from further up the slope. My pointing hand foolishly told the ambushers that they were detected, and since they were discovered, they were quick enough to shoot. My riding horse went down with three shafts in her, and gave a sort of snorting scream. I got off the right side, got my leg over my dying horse, and then fell ... There was no footing on the slope anyway, and I stumbled, rolled, and came up again, completely uninjured but another ten paces down slope, and too far from John. He turned back, didn't see me, drew his bow, and gave a sharp *yip* and his Arab leapt forward. John already had an arrow on the string and another half a dozen arrows were inbound, but he was no longer where the arrows were going, and they all struck within a horse-length of where he had been.

John drew and loosed, and then he was gone, over a little hump, and there was a gentle shower of dust to mark his passage.

I had no bow. I wished for a crossbow, or something with which to bombard my adversaries. But I had nothing but the javelins, which I saved from the collapse of my horse, who was already gone, rolling over the next small precipice and plummeting towards the road below.

The bandits had caught a lion. Their ambush had closed on the very tip of our advance guard, probably on the assumption we were a small armed party, and now, in a few breaths, the whole of our little army was unfolding below me. The Romanians were riding along the slope below me at a gallop, and about a third of the mounted men-at-arms were moving forward in a body to cover the front of the pilgrims.

It was all very competent and martial, and it looked to me as if Syr Giorgios Angelus and the Romanians were about to counter-ambush the bandits. All fine, except that I was alone on a steep slope, and my horse was dead, and except for John, who'd vanished, I was the closest to the ambushers.

They were no fools. They saw all the dust and made the right decisions too.

More arrows came my way, and some flight arrows – really, light cane arrows with reduced fletching – were launched in the direction of the pilgrims. A good Tartar bow or a Turk bow can reach two hundred paces or more; when they shoot with their lightest arrows, they can shoot even further, all the way out to four hundred paces, or so I'm told. At any rate, shafts started dropping past me.

And I started uphill. I had some cover from the dust, and going *down* with the bandits shooting at my back held no charm for me at all. So I climbed. All I could think of was that those light flight arrows might have hit Emile. It made no sense – I could not honestly imagine that such a thing would happen – but I was far more in fear for her than for myself.

It was not so very dangerous – I was on foot and could use the cover – and once I went up a rock, safe as if I was in a castle due to the sight lines.

I suppose that the two men I found had been left to occupy the pilgrims while the rest escaped. I'm quite sure they'd missed me in my climb, and so much time had passed since they shot my horse that the sun had started to drop – at least, it felt like a lot of time to me, sweating inside my maille and brigantine; hill climbing is hard enough without additional weight. My basinet was an unwelcome encumbrance, but I was unwilling to have it off.

I reached the top of the ridge and saw them. Unfortunately, both men saw me at the same time. They were grizzled, old in evil, wearing dirty kaftans over good maille and carrying swords – one a straight-bladed Mamluk sword, the other a curving Turkish sabre.

But they didn't use them. They both shot at me. The range was per-haps thirty paces, and I managed to knock an arrow down with a cut of my javelin and I got a few paces towards them. Both men nocked again.

There is something uncanny, more than merely frightening, about seeing the archer's eye over the arrowhead. The first man loosed, and my javelin snapped up from a low *garde* to high, but the arrow missed, hissing by my leg to splinter in the gravel. And when his partner loosed, his shaft skipped down my spear, clanged off the bell of the cuff of my left gauntlet, and vanished into the dust.

I ran three or four paces forward and lofted my first javelin. We'd all played with them; the Mamluks and the Turks loved them for close combat on horseback, and they are great fun to throw. The good ones are like big arrows, with fine, chiselled heads. Sometimes they are worked in gold and silver, like fancy swords.

But I was no expert, and my javelin stuck in the ground a few paces short of my foes.

But it had its effect. I have noted this many times – there is a world of difference between shooting at a man who cannot shoot back, and shooting at a man who shoots at you, however ineptly. Both men were slower getting their arrows on their bows, and the one on the left loosed too quickly.

The one on the right looked surprised, and fell to the ground like a sack of grain dropped from a barn. He lay on his face, an arrow in his back.

The first man, the nearer, reached for another arrow and tried to nock it, and I threw my second javelin. It was a terrible throw, and instead of a clean high arc, it tumbled in the air. The head struck a rock at an odd angle, and the shaft twisted away and struck my bandit in the shin, and he dropped his bow. He was trying to look behind him …

John appeared from behind him. He flicked his whip – his riding whip, which he was holding by the thong – and the handle hit my bandit behind the ear and the man pitched forward, unconscious despite his helmet.

John waved, as if this was something we did every day, and rode away into the swirl of dust he'd raised. I ran forward, but there was nothing to fear – one man dead, the other out, and no more enemies in sight. I found the nearly impregnable position the two men had occupied and sat down out of the wind, and pulled off my basinet. It was chilly, and the wind cut through my maille and made my sweat cold. I was suddenly very tired, and very aware that death had once again passed me by, and I prayed for a while. Then I stripped the dead man of equipment; he had an excellent bow, a fine steel cap with maille better than most of my own maille, and a good sword, as well as two quivers full of fine arrows. I took it all, and his purse; I closed his eyes, and began piling rocks atop him, which I did until he was invisible.

John returned with four good horses – the mounts and remounts of our foes. I was very tired by then, and the sun was descending, and our pilgrims were long gone from the valley below us. But with the dead man's horses, I made good time, and we took the unconscious man with us.

John pointed a booted toe at the man. His outer garment was dirty, it was true, but under the dust it was a green silk kaftan with fur edging. His turban was of dirty white silk embroidered with a verse of the Koran.

'That's a Turk,' John said. 'I don't know what kind. But a Turk. Both of them.' He shrugged. 'Of Rhum, I think. Rich.'

'What are they doing here?' I asked.

John shrugged. And rode away. I followed him, because night-time in the high country north and west of Jerusalem is not a good place for a lone Christian, even with a Kipchak to sustain him.

The two of us rode warily, high on the hillside. The captured horses were fine, with small, light saddles that put a premium on the rider's legs and skill, but probably allowed the smaller horse to bear weight all day. I was amazed at the animal's endurance, as good as the horse I'd just lost, or better. Arabs are famous for reasons – a superb breed.

The sun began to sink in the west, and our choices were limited. We were alone on our hillside; there were goats or sheep somewhere, announcing themselves by the sound of their bells, and dogs were barking on the ridge opposite us, where I was confident I had seen men, and probably shepherds.

I didn't really know where I was, and neither did John. When the sun was well down, and we still hadn't found tracks or anything to reveal our friends, we slowed down, found a big overhanging rock high on the hillside, and made a rough camp.

I had got soft in a year with a squire. I didn't have my usual pack on the back of my saddle: a malle with a razor, a clean shirt, a spare cloak and a fire kit. I'd always had some such in routier days, but now it sat behind Marc-Antonio's saddle, not mine.

I was just considering some well-chosen curses when a voice called out from the rocks in pretty fair Latin. You can imagine that we both whirled; John produced both a bow and an arrow on his string in record time, and I drew a dagger, but our potential adversary proved to be a very old man with red cheeks and white hair and a magnificent white beard.

'Blessings! In the name of the Holy Trinity!' said the old man. 'The gentle Jesus knows I am no threat to you. Now put up your weapons and come.' He looked at our wounded man, the Turk, still stretched over a saddle. He lifted an eyelid, and nodded.

In truth, he was a hermit. I have no idea if he was from some Order – I do not think so. His Latin was very good and his Italian was Tuscan. He lived in a small cave, the walls of which were dark with smoke and yet bore some remarkable painting – a scene of Christ's passion as good as you'd see in most Italian churches, much bismotered with smoke and ash, and an Annunciation. He was grinding pigment himself, and there were little clay pots and vessels full of ochre and such stuff in a niche along one wall.

He talked, as much to himself as to us. He was making a stew of chickpeas, very common in those parts, and somewhat bland, but we were both hungry and it was clear he was guesting us. He laid out three bowls and three cups, and three simple wooden spoons, at a low table.

'You are a Frank?' he asked me. He kept a wary eye on John and on our prisoner.

'I am,' I said. 'I was born in England.'

He smiled softly. 'I don't suppose you can be more of a Frank than that,' he said. 'I was born in Ancona.' He went and stirred his pot, which was a good one of bronze – he was not a destitute peasant.

'Can I help?' I asked.

'Tell me of your friend?' he said.

'John was born a Tartar,' I said. 'He serves me, but he is as good a Christian as me.' *Or better*, I thought.

'Ahh,' the hermit said, and he relaxed visibly. 'Tartars are fine men,' he said, and turning to John, he said something like 'Holugui' and John brightened and replied in kind. But that was our host's only word in John's tongue.

We had laid the captured Turk on the ground, and we made him comfortable. I spent a few moments going over his scalp with my hand. There was bruising and mushy blood where John had hit him, but he was otherwise unwounded. His cap of steel had been unpadded, and the blow had hit him as hard as a mace.

John couldn't tear his eyes from the pictures on the walls. Our host lit some oil lamps, and the pictures became clearer. Finally, he said 'This is Jesus?' and pointed at the man on the Cross.

'*Certes*,' our Anconan said.

John knelt. 'Very holy,' he said.

I noted that the men gathered around the foot of the Cross were not Romans, but crusaders. There were some Mamluks among them, but in the foreground were knights and men-at-arms. I was looking at their armour, which was very modern, when the hermit coughed.

'Dinner,' he said.

We prayed; our hermit did not seem to be a priest, as he prayed in Italian. Then we ate, and the stew was delicious, and he served us a little wine and cups of water from his spring at the back of his cave.

John rose with his bowl in his hand and continued to look at the crucifixion. It fascinated him, and the hermit moved to his side and took charcoal and began to sketch on the wall. In a few moments I realised that he was sketching John at the foot of the Cross.

I think I sputtered. 'He doesn't deserve that!' I said.

The hermit turned, charcoal in hand. 'Is he not a sinner? And do not our sins crucify Christ every day?' When he said Christ's name, he bowed his head.

'You say that knights crucify Christ?' I asked. I suppose I was annoyed at the painting.

He made a little motion, not a smile, more like a twitch. 'Did Jesus say anything about killing his enemies?' he asked.

'Who will protect pilgrims, then?' I asked.

'I only ask questions,' the hermit said with a wry smile. 'I never answer them. But ... perhaps God will protect pilgrims?'

John followed what we said well enough. Now he twirled his moustache. 'Bandits,' he said.

'Bandits attacked us today,' I said.

The hermit frowned. 'I doubt it,' he said. 'I think perhaps you were attacked by Uthman Bey.' He looked at the unconscious man. 'That is Uthman Bey's cousin. I have fed him, too.'

'Uthman Bey?' I asked.

'Uthman is a Karamanid prince.' My hermit seemed more worldly than I expected.

'Karamanid?' I asked.

John was looking at the figure the hermit had just drawn, and grinning. 'Just Turks,' he said, 'not people.'

'You know that the Holy Land belongs to the Mamluk Sultan?' the old man said. 'Well, the border is north of Syria, and there the Mamluk empire borders on the Christians of Cilicia and the Karamanid Turks. There are a dozen Turkish dynasties – perhaps twice that. Uthman Bey began raiding us as soon as the Mamluks looked weak.'

'You were once a knight,' I said. 'No one but a knight would follow all this.'

Our host smiled slowly. 'Of course,' he said. 'I came as a pilgrim and found my Saviour here. I will probably never leave.'

I might have asked him more, but our prisoner began to twitch and called out. And then, suddenly, his eyes opened and he rolled to his feet with a shout ...

And collapsed. I had drawn my baselard, meaning to stab him, but when he fell forward and threw up, I felt for him. I have taken some blows to the head; a swift rise is a sure way to lose your dinner.

The hermit and I cleaned up after him while John watched him.

I feel I need to remind you that we called John, 'the Turk,' yet indeed, he was not a Turk at all, but a Kipchak, a Tartar from the high steppe north of the Black Sea. And he had briefly served the Mamluks, been captured, and in turn become a *ghulam*, a sort of slave-soldier, for the Turks in Greece. I suppose I say this too often, but most Latins can't tell one from another and I grow annoyed.

As soon as our prisoner's eyes fluttered open, John spoke to him in what I assumed was Turkish, a fluid, lovely language full of 'olou' and 'argai' and 'ay'.

It took two cups of water and some time, but our prisoner began to talk, at first single words, and then whole sentences.

'He think we invade, thousand men,' John said. 'I not tell him.'

Slowly, John discovered as much as the hermit already knew – that they were Turks from the north, and that they were testing to see if the Mamluks would react. And gathering some loot. And, of course, visiting Jerusalem, the third most holy city in Islam.

I laughed bitterly. 'Looting, murdering, *and* visiting their holy sites.'

The hermit just looked at me.

In the morning, having slept well and eaten, I reached into my purse to pay the holy man. He shook his head.

'I feed any traveller who finds me,' he said. 'If they climb this high, why then, *Deus vult*, God wills it so.'

My hand closed on the lump of lapis I had purchased in Jaffa. I withdrew it, and my host's eyes widened like a child presented with a toy. 'Likewise,' I said. 'I found this in a market, and bought it with no idea in my head but a love of the colour. God wills it so.'

The old man accepted my gift right willingly, and when I asked his blessing, he gave it to all three of us.

Our Turk was looking better. He was a handsome man, much given to sneers, and with the richest, blackest beard I think I've ever seen. As we rode away, he said something aside to John. John nodded and looked at me.

'He says, a true holy one's blessings are good whatever his faith.' The Turk nodded and rubbed his head. His wrists were bound.

John nodded back where the hermit was kneeling, already grinding my lapis for his colour pots. 'I think so too,' he added.

I smiled at the prisoner. 'Tell him I agree,' I said.

Daylight made navigation much easier, and the hills seemed smaller and less fearsome, although the maze of little valleys was confusing enough. But the rising sun gave us east, and the hermit had given some directions with his blessings – very clear directions, may I add. So we crested two ridges, passed a tall standing stone, and had a glimpse of what had to be the earthly Jerusalem on the high ridge to the east and south. Then we descended a short gully, and emerged from a narrow defile to find horse tracks, which we followed. It was almost impossible to pick out a single horse, the tracks were so dense.

We followed them down a valley beneath a village with walls on a height, and I began to think that Jerusalem should become visible again soon. Twice we saw people in the distance, on foot, and both times they vanished. The sun began to climb in the sky, and our Turk made a comment to John. John frowned and looked at me.

'He asks, what is our intention with him?'

I shrugged and offered him a drink from my canteen. 'I'll exchange him for one of ours,' I said. 'Or just let him go back to his uncle.'

John said something, and the Turk laughed. And gave a great shout.

I drew my sword, and John had his bow up. But we were a little late, as there were thirty Turks around us in a few seconds, galloping out of the rocks, or so it seemed. They had arrows on their bows, and they closed very quickly indeed.

There is a moment in these situations where you can die. Or kill, and then die. I had my sword at the Turk's head, and his reins in my hand. John dismounted at the first sign of ambush and was behind his horse, an arrow on his bow.

Our Turk spoke up.

'He say, "My brothers might try to kill you with arrows, just to show they can", and he say too, "And maybe not care if they hit me, bastards."' John sounded almost completely calm. 'So he say.'

They were in behind me already; they could shoot me in the back with little danger to the Turk, although really, my good brigantine might give me time to kill the prisoner. But on balance, there were thirty or forty of them and two of us, and no force on earth was going to save us.

I sheathed my sword. I did it with a little flourish, without looking, to show I was not afraid. Well, of course I *was* afraid. But I got my blade put away, and my Turk began to talk to his friends even as John followed my lead and dropped his bow back in the quiver.

After some jostling, our Turk separated from us and rode away into the throng, and was embraced by a big, heavyset man with wide-set, intelligent eyes and a henna-dyed beard in bright scarlet. His kaftan was as red as his beard, and his sword hilt was gold. His horse was a milk-white Arab with a pretty head and a good size – a magnificent horse. They exchanged a few words, and meanwhile one of the Turks tried to take my horse's bridle.

I was not sure we were prisoners. My attacker had different views, and wanted my horse. He grabbed for the reins, and when I pulled them away from him, he slashed at me with his riding whip. Of course, I had steel arms and gauntlets, so I took his lash on my left forearm and dragged him off his saddle in one move.

Some men laughed, and other men scowled.

The man with the scarlet beard pressed forward and all of them fell back. He was feared, and obeyed.

'Oi, Frank!' he called. His turban was silk, and he had a stone in it that was worth my harness.

I gave him my best mounted bow.

John remounted by my side and said something that was long, and I suspect, elaborate – a ritual greeting.

Uthman Bey – it must be he – nodded. 'A Frank with courtesy! Now Allah be praised, a miracle has come to us in the Holy Land.'

Despite his fair words, he ordered us to dismount. We did, and stood by our horses.

He rode in close, and spoke to John.

'I leave you your lives, as I am no ghazi, and you spared my worthless nephew. I might kill you for Salim, who you killed – but your

Franks have taken others of my men, and I hope we can arrange an exchange. If you give me your word, I will leave you your weapons, but you will ride with us to Ramalie.'

I didn't see much choice. It rankled to be taken so easily, but taken I was.

He left us our weapons, but as he pointed out to John, we were riding his horses. John didn't argue that one of the horses was John's own, and in a moment we were riding away north on the dusty road, and the Turks were all around us. Their laughter was painful, but not nearly as painful as being dead, and as John said when we started our weary ride to the north, he was an apostate and they might have killed him even if they had taken me for ransom. We had, by our own standards, nothing to complain about.

We rode for a few miles, always north. I had never been in the Holy Land, but I knew Ramalie – a Christian town much used by pilgrims landing at Acre or Tyre and coming to Jerusalem.

Uthman Bey's band was larger than I had thought; there were at least a hundred of them, and perhaps more; he had a cloud of scouts out to the south and to the west, and a dozen more men made dust ahead of us. They were all superb horsemen, a pleasure to watch. None of them troubled me, but when they caught a pedlar, they pulled him out of his hiding place, stripped his pack and looted it, and then killed him and left his corpse by the road. I could not tell if the man was Moslem or Christian.

Uthman saw my distaste and he shrugged. Through John, he said, 'I am a raider. I show the peasants that their Mamluk lords cannot protect them. Maybe later I will come back with an army and they will know that *I* can protect them.' He smiled, and that smile held much of the evil of the world.

Of course, this is war as we practised it in France – the *chevauchée*. To hear it said, just this way, by a paynim bandit, as if it was a matter of high policy and not a matter of greed and evil, was like a slap in the face. Because, of course, I have been such a raider. God's judgement on my sins, but I have led such raids.

'Ask him if he has ever seen this work. Have peasants and farmers ever come over to his banner for these reasons?' I tried to look mild.

Uthman laughed. 'It always works,' he said. 'Farmers are all cowards. They do whatever will keep their worthless hides on their carcasses.'

He shrugged. 'Why do you wear your stirrups so long? It looks silly. You should learn to ride like a man.'

'So you kill their sons, and they love you for it?' I asked. This trick of not giving way to anger had all sorts of benefits. It makes you much harder to move in argument, for example.

He frowned. He made an angry comment and John raised an eyebrow. Then his face closed; Kipchaks do not give anything away in conversation. Their faces are as well-disciplined as their cavalry.

'He says, "Why care? Why care what a peasant thinks?" He says, "Kill their sons, take their daughters, spend their gold. That's why God made peasants and farmers and merchants." He asks me if you are – weak. Or some priest.' John's lips twitched. I think he found the idea of my being a priest funny, even when we were plainly captives of a dangerous man.

I nodded. 'Tell him that long stirrups and a high-backed saddle make a man much more dangerous on horseback than a woman's saddle like he rides.'

John reined in his horse.

'He can kill us,' John said.

Well, he had a point there, and so much for reining in my temper. I nodded.

'He asks what you say, and I said you spoke of God.' John raised an eyebrow, and rode away, so that he could not translate any more.

I rode with Uthman Bey. I was happy that he didn't kill any more innocents; I'm not sure I'd have survived the experience. Although I was aware that I had his dead man's – Salim's – coins in my purse. And his javelins with my own under my knee. I too killed and robbed.

Ramalie is another mixed village. There's a Christian hostel, and a dozen Islamic inns and caravanserai, and a big walled pen for herds and caravans. Uthman sent a force into the town to scout, and when we rode in, the streets were completely empty, save for a Greek patriarch who waited, unattended, with the Moslem priest, or imam, as they call them.

John was back with me by then, and he translated. 'Uthman Bey says I am of great value, because I can talk like a Frank and like a Hellene, too. He asks me to join him.' He smiled and said something in his own tongue.

'John, you have always done well by me,' I said stiffly. 'You do what you must. This is a spot, and no mistake.'

John looked at me, considering. 'Among Tartars, it is permitted to lie and deceive to defeat an enemy. How does Christ feel?'

That made me writhe. I was still thinking of the hermit's words. We were in the land where Christ walked. But ...

'We deceive enemies all the time,' I said. That was truth, whatever the Saviour intended.

John nodded.

He rode forward with Uthman Bey and spoke to the Greek priest. They spoke back and forth for a while, and the priest relaxed. The imam seemed, if anything, the more terrified of the two men. But eventually he knelt in the dust and touched his head to the ground in front of the Turk's horse.

Then I was taken to the Christian hostel. When I dismounted, I saw that they took my horse away, and two Turks remained. And no John.

The hostel was run by the same Franciscan Order that had sent Father Angelo to threaten us with excommunication. Nearby was an Orthodox Greek hostel.

There followed a tiresome repetition of the scene in Jaffa. My two Turks stared open-mouthed as the Franciscan lay brothers refused to house me and ordered me out of their inn.

I could tell from their angry sputterings that they didn't understand the complexities of the situation – or that we'd defeated the Mamluks, or even that my two guards were Turks, not Mamluks.

There was nothing to be done. I had no Turkish, but with gestures, I convinced my guards to take me to the Greeks.

Orthodox, or Greek. Of course the Greeks have their own rite, and are schismatics. Let it be said that they say it is we who are schismatics, and that they read the Gospels in the language in which they were written: Greek. At any rate, they were good to me, and their priest came and spoke to me in slow Greek, and I understood almost nothing, but I began to learn it then. I mean, I had heard some phrases from Colophernes; that's Syr Giannis; and Syr Giorgios Angelus, and I learned simple things from the priest – 'yes' and 'no', and 'perhaps', and 'I am good', and phrases like that.

A whole day passed. I had wine and bread, but no company. I

practised with my sword in the courtyard, mostly to feel alive; several of my captors watched me. I borrowed a javelin and threw it for a while; I made a target by stuffing an old linen sack with straw, and then my Turks joined me. I learned a fair amount about throwing a javelin that day, although the Turks throw with a little wrist flick because they think of it as a cavalry weapon to be used very close. I tried some longer throws, and I was just negotiating a trip outside the hostel's yard with my captor, in sign language, when a dozen Turks rode into the yard. They had four captive knights, and a sort of horse-mounted palanquin balanced on two horses.

The knights were tied, hand and foot. They wore maille, but had been stripped of their weapons. And they were not Franks – I could tell looking at them. They had the same silky black hair as my captors, and they spoke a language I had never heard: Armenian.

One of them spoke up as they entered the hostel yard.

One of the Turks struck him with his whip.

It was the same boy who'd tried to lash me the day before. I had a javelin in my hand, and I was close. I stepped in so I was at his side, passed my javelin into the keyhole of his arm and shoulder, and pulled him from the saddle.

Perhaps not my best considered action. In a moment, they were all on me – two men with whips, and my two guards. But no one's heart was in killing me – well, perhaps my young foe from the day before, but not the rest of them. I got a lash across the face that hurt like ice and fire, and then stopped, even though my right hand was on my baselard. Which was wise. I had a spear tip at my throat. And two men holding me.

A great deal was said in Turkish. The man I'd pulled from the saddle spat and punched me in the face.

Then one of my guards shoved him. He said something angry.

Uthman Bey arrived in the yard with another dozen of his best armed warriors, including John. He growled orders in all direction, fingered his red beard, and frowned.

'Oi, Frank? Where is thy courtesy?' he asked via John.

I was lying on my back with a broken nose, a flood of blood over my chest, and a whip lash across my face. No one else was moving.

One of my guards passed me a cotton towel. Cotton is a marvellous cloth, and I may say more of it; I had certainly seen it in Venice, but in the Holy Land the stuff was everywhere. I got the towel up to my face and stopped the flow of blood. I coughed once, to clear my throat, and then pulled on my nose as hard as I could and the pain blinded me, and I felt the bones grate against each other, and then the pain eased. And the flow of blood eased as well. I had set my own broken nose before, but never with an audience.

'This man is a coward,' I said. 'He likes to strike prisoners.' I pointed at my assailant. Then I bowed. 'For my part, however, I apologise for disturbing the peace.'

John translated rapidly, in Turkish. My assailant spat in the dust.

Uthman Bey looked annoyed. He spoke in Turkish, and the man – the knight – who'd been struck answered in the same tongue. The two looked like … old enemies. Both smiled thinly when they spoke.

Uthman came up to me, leaned down from his horse and took my chin in his right hand, the way you might examine a slave or a pretty girl. He spoke angrily. My guards both murmured – obviously apologising.

'He says, "You idiots",' John put in. 'He says, "Now you look like all the men of Allah have beaten you, and your Christian brothers will never agree to a trade."'

I had to breathe through my mouth, and it was very uncomfortable.

'He orders all of you kept together. He makes point – tells me to tell you that you may still keep your weapons. Says he wishes this not happening.' John gave me a little wave, and a slight twitch of the eyebrow.

And turned when Uthman turned his horse.

I'd like to say my trust in my Kipchak groom never wavered, but seeing him at Uthman's right hand, it was obvious that the Turks valued his skills. And he had been a convert to Islam once before – spoke their language fluently.

I thought of every coarse word I'd used to him, and every time I'd sent him to curry my horse.

And other things. Like the fact that Emile was in Jerusalem, and I was a prisoner, or nearly so. Mayhap to die.

I am probably lucky I could not see my face. *Certes*, my nose swelled up like a peach, and the cut from the whip swelled too, and burned.

But the Armenians were solicitous, and three of them spoke French.

And they were so low with being captured that I felt I was needed to rally them.

They were travelling with a woman, a sort of princess from Cilicia, on pilgrimage. They had a dozen followers who had been killed. And they were not prisoners for exchange. They had no idea what fate awaited them.

I learned this as soon as Uthman Bey rode out of the yard and left us with just my two guards. Both of them made a great show of lounging against the stalls in the shade of the stable block, leaving us some privacy. The man who had been whipped – and who had spoken to Uthman as a peer – nodded to me. In good French, he said, 'Thanks for your – intent.'

I put a cautious finger to my nose. 'I was a fool,' I said.

The man shrugged. 'Nonetheless, you took all their attention. I need to get my sister under cover, before the Turks see her and get … ideas.'

His sister was not dark-haired at all, and even in a double veil of fine linen, I could see that her hair was red-gold and she was terrified, almost sick with it.

My new Armenian friend shook his head. 'A bloody day. And many good people dead. We have a treaty with the Sultan in Egypt, of course, but nothing with this Turkish thief.'

'You know him?' I asked.

'How do you come to wear a sword?' he asked. 'Franks are forbidden weapons.'

I was no longer so young as to answer all the questions put to me by my elders. He was a strong, capable man of forty or so, and he'd seen some fighting; his long nose had been broken, he had scars on his hands and face, and he moved like a fighter.

'I take it you know this Turkish thief?' I asked again.

'Uthman Bey? Everyone knows him, from here to Izmir. His first cousin is a sort of sultan among the Turks. Uthman has nothing but what passes under the hooves of his horses. But he is always plotting to rule something – a town, a city, all Outremer.' My new friend smiled bitterly. 'He and I have crossed swords before, and it is pure ill luck that he was here to take me.' He blew air out of his cheeks. 'And my sister. Look, Frank, we told the Turks that the woman was my mother. They don't rape old women.'

'Will he ransom you?' I asked.

The Armenian shrugged. 'If he does, it will only be after I've been held a long time and properly toyed with,' he said. 'This little turn of ill-fortune will make his reputation, the bastard.'

I introduced myself. He was Arnaud, and his surname was like a bowl of lemons, something like 'Hasnus.' All of them had old-fashioned French names, and they were all intermarried with the Lusignans and other crusader lords. It was somewhat remarkable; they wore French fashions; one of the men had a pourpointe cut and stuffed just like mine, with tight sleeves and a tiny waist, but they were swarthy as Saracens, three of them. Only Arnaud's sister and the smallest of the knights were sandy haired.

They kept me well away from the woman, as well, protecting her, it was clear.

The Greek fathers – who I now discovered to be Greeks and Armenians, of course – served us food, and there were hours of con-versation between the Armenian knights and the local priest, all in their own tongue. I couldn't read their books and my nose hurt, and I went and slept, woke to eat, and slept again.

The next day, after a good bath in the yard, I paid a woman to wash my clothes, and another to stitch me up a shirt and braes so that I would have a change and be not quite so foul. About the middle of the day, to my immense surprise, the Franciscan priest, Father Angelo, appeared. He exchanged a stiff greeting with my host in Greek, and then came and sat by me.

'I am relieved to find you here,' he said. 'Your officer is concerned for you. Brother Marco sent me word that a Frank was here as a prisoner.' He leaned forward. 'You see what comes of fighting?'

I touched my nose. 'I did no fighting at all, Father. If I had, I would be dead. Does Fra Peter have some prisoners of his own?'

Father Angelo nodded. 'Yes, my son. The Greek knights captured six men.'

'Were there any … people … injured? Any pilgrims?' I asked.

'Your question does you credit,' he said. 'But no. A few arrows fell near us, but you and your man drove them off.'

I remember blushing. You'd think a hardened killer like me would stop blushing; it's the red hair, I swear it. Of course, I cared no whit for the pilgrims. Or perhaps I do myself an injustice. I cared that they lived or died, but until then I had lived with the notion that one of those slim cane arrows had struck Emile.

I laughed. 'Don't you think that knights are of some value now, Father?' I asked.

He did not give a pat answer. Instead, he looked ... troubled.

'Indeed, Sir William,' he said. 'It is fifty years and more since we lost Acre, and a hundred since Christians governed this city. My Order has had no choice but to develop other means of contesting the truth and acting as Christians than by the sword. You have a reputation as a man who thinks – surely you know what Jesus said about violence.'

'Live by the sword, die by the sword,' I said. I believe I touched mine. 'It is the role of my ordo, and if I die by the sword, so be it.'

He shook his head. 'I do not think that Jesus meant that it was good for some men to choose to die by the sword.'

Knowing that Emile was well restored me as water does a man in the desert.

'I should know better than to dispute theology with a Franciscan,' I said. 'But the brothers who taught me to read taught me that one of the earliest of Jesus's disciples was the centurion, nor is there a word of censure against his profession in all the Gospels.' I held up my hand. 'I do not mean to dispute with you, Father. We had a poor start. I will certainly listen to your sermons, but there are pressing matters. I am not the only prisoner here.' I explained, and Father Angelo rose, troubled.

When I was done, Father Angelo went to the Orthodox priest, and the two had words. I don't think it was a pleasant conversation; it was clear enough to me that the two men scarcely tolerated each other.

Father Angelo sat with me again. 'I would like to move you across the road, to the Franciscan house,' he said.

'I think that I should stay here,' I replied. It was my fancy that, because the Turks had been ordered to treat me well, they were more careful of the Armenians, and that if I left, things could go worse for them. I didn't want to explain this notion.

'They have beaten you,' the Franciscan said.

'We had ... a misunderstanding,' I said. 'You note I am allowed to keep my weapons.'

'I do not pretend to understand why,' he said.

However, despite the way he'd treated us in Jaffa, the priest was trying to be helpful. I rather liked the way he disputed. He was respectful of my views. Most priests treat knights and men-at-arms as beasts of burden.

And I confess that I was aware of how often Father Pierre Thomas had hinted at similar beliefs about violence. I was troubled. By the Saviour, I am still troubled.

At any rate, he was a better man than I had expected, and he agreed to let me stay in the Greek hostel, and even went so far as to send across the road for a small, un-illustrated book of sermons.

I never did read it.

That night, the Greek priest brought minstrels and dancers into his inn yard; most of them were Moslems, and I never did learn whether they were local, or travellers, or professionals. The dancing was difficult to understand at times and very easy at others; a woman took off some clothing in a blatant display of sensuality that was ... too broad for me, and I am a soldier. Two men and a woman did feats of tumbling that I found very wonderful – at one point, when both men had their arms linked, the woman leaped up *onto* their arms and then somersaulted to the ground. I have seldom seen anything so good, and they might have made their fortunes in England. And I wished for Fiore to see the men; they were flexible beyond anything I have ever seen.

Some time after the tumblers, I realised that the Armenian lady had joined us. She hid in a shadow under the eaves of the inn, wearing a long dark robe as many women wore there, but I saw her hair in a little lamplight. Perhaps it was the Holy Land, or my feeling for Emile, but her slim ankles and lovely hair did not fire me to do anything but help her.

I went and stood by Arnaud. He laughed from time to time, but his mood was still grim. I could guess why.

'I asked the priest to tell my captain to negotiate for you,' I said. 'And the girl.'

He frowned. 'You mean well, Frank. But ... Uthman Bey will not give me up unless I give him a castle. Or perhaps my sister to be his wife or concubine.'

I must have winced.

Arnaud frowned. 'It happens. There are more brides across the borders than you might think. My grandmother was born and raised in a Turkish camp.' He looked at the ground. 'Uthman and I are, in fact, cousins.'

'Ah,' I said. Well, anyone who has fought in Gascony and the Dordogne understands this sort of thing.

Anyway, that evening wore on. The players seemed to have an infinite repertoire of tricks and shows; one of the men made a bean grow out of his nose, and we all laughed. It was during that trick when one of my guards accosted me. He ran a hand over my belly and muttered something.

I had no notion of what he wanted, and I didn't like his manner. I stepped back, hand on sword.

Arnaud put his hand on mine. 'Hold hard,' he said. 'He only wants wine.'

Moslems are forbidden wine. And they love it. Well, fair enough, says I; Christians are forbidden adultery, and I've known men and women to make quite a practice of it, aye, and be in church for Mass. To each their own. I was down to my last silver sequin, but I went and fetched a pitcher of the passable red swill that the inn served, and I placed it carefully where the two Turks could see it. I smiled at the smaller man, who'd been kind enough to me, for a guard.

They put the wine away before the dancing girl could writhe under a stick. And now the big man was back, touching me.

'He thinks you have a pilgrim flask on you,' Arnaud said. 'Most Franks have some wine on them, all the time.'

These are the odd things foreigners believe about you. I have never, that I can remember, had a flask of wine on me when I travelled. Easier to carry it inside me, ha ha! The Turk's breath smelled of wine, and he was as annoying as a horsefly.

But the Greek priest put another pitcher of wine in his hands and blessed him.

I'd had a fair amount of wine myself, by then. But as I watched my two guards make arses of themselves – pawing at the dancing girl, mocking the tumblers, and beginning to sway – it occurred to me that we could simply escape.

'We could knock their heads together,' I said, 'steal horses, and ride for Jerusalem.'

Arnaud looked at me as if a bolt of lightning had struck me. 'We'd be caught,' he said, but he was already weighing different odds: long imprisonment, the humiliation of his sister ...

As I've heard better men than me say, these things have to be taken at a gallop or carefully planned. I was at a gallop. 'They change the guards when the paynim priest calls them to prayer at full sunset,' I said. 'Now or never.'

Arnaud was still working it out when I walked up to my two Turks and pulled their turbans off their heads. It is a mortal insult, and indeed, both had shaved heads with only a single lock dangling. Both of them rose, sputtering, and I slammed a fist into one head and then put a knee into the other's nose. They fell to the floor, and I measured their pulses and felt their skulls and congratulated myself that they were not dead.

If this failed, I wanted a chance at being forgiven. And the Franciscan's words were at work on me, as were Father Pierre Thomas's. I began to think about violence. I began to think of it the way a cook uses spice – use only what you need.

Despite my care, the Greek priest was horrified. I think he gave serious consideration to sounding the alarm. Not that he was some infamous collaborator; he had his own people to think of.

I did not. The inn yard gate was open for the players, and I went out as if I had every right to go out. Ramalie is not a big town, and I could smell the horses.

They were picketed in ten or twelve long rows, a dozen or so mounts to each long rope, pinned deep in the ground at either end, in the flat open ground just north of the old town. Very close to my inn, in fact.

There were guards – three of them. But these were bandits, not soldiers, and they were much like bandits in France. I tripped over one guard in the dark, and he cursed and rolled over, drunk and insensible. The other two sat by a fire, looking into it, too far gone to hear anything. I think they were sober; certainly they were deep in talk. I left them to it.

I found the horse on which I'd ridden easily enough, and a dozen more, by the simple expedient of pulling a picket peg, carrying it into the darkness until I found the other end by touch, and pulling that one as well, giving me the whole horse line, if you see what I mean; every horse picketed on that line was now in my hand.

Whoever had picketed the horses did slipshod work. Picket pegs need to be sunk deep. But their bad discipline was my lifeline.

I had no idea what guards there were in the town. Uthman had a hundred men or more; he might have thirty men on duty. Or just the three.

I cut the picket lines on the other horses. Horses are strange beasts; when you want them to stay put, they wander off; when you want them to run, they stand in the dark and chew on their grass. I chose the biggest by walking up and down and looking at them against the moon. It was that dark.

Then I stabbed the big bastard in the haunch with my dagger. I didn't stab deeply, but I drew blood, and the horse screamed in outraged innocence and bolted. His scream got the herd moving, and as their pickets were already pulled or cut, they began to move, first a dozen and then more, and the picket pins bouncing on the ground annoyed them, and struck the hooves and fetlocks of other horses.

I was a bit too aggressive. I shouted and yipped like a Turk, and drew arrows – the two men at the fire were alert enough, by then. An arrow struck a horse, and it gave a long neigh of anger and snorted and tore off into the darkness, and the horses in my fist made fair to drag me to death along with the rest of the herd.

Once again, I wished I had a bow, just to put the proverbial cat among the pigeons; a few arrows into that campfire and my Turks might have run into the darkness themselves. As it was, they thought they were under attack.

The panicked horses raised an incredible dust cloud. Dust is the very devil at night; it is already dark, and you cannot see. Only smoke is worse. And I could not stay still; my little herd of stolen horses kept moving, and I kept having to go with them, because once I let them go they'd run free. One of my first lessons as a horseman – the horse is always stronger than you.

I ran beside them, and ran beside them, and after a miserable mile of stubbed toes and full-out falls, I got a moment, caught my breath when a deep gully blocked my horses, and, with some luck, got both picket pins and managed to get them into the dirt. Any horse, with a little determination, could have pulled those pins, but I was out of options, and they were calming, and I walked among them for what seemed an eternity, whispering the sort of sweet nothings most men save for their lemans.

I got up on the bare back of the Arab mare who'd carried me three days before. I cut her loose, and with only a single rope as a halter and guide rein, I rode back, cross-country, towards Ramalie.

It was another hard decision – to stay, or ride. But my lack of plan was working so far; I had horses, and I had surprise. And a good sword, and in darkness, the best chance against archers. And no one was dead yet.

I have noticed that in war, as in cards and dice, each success tempts you to risk again.

The moon was bright enough to make out the white buildings, and the Greek inn still had lights in the yard. I left my little mare tied to an old stone column and crept in to find the town full of shouting. Arrows whispered in the darkness. I have no notion who they expected to shoot at. I expect that the Turks thought there were Mamluks out in the night, or simply other bandits.

I climbed the back wall of the Greek inn and dropped from the red tile roof, thick with fungus, to the ground. My sword almost eviscerated me for my stealthy pains, catching between my legs and the naked point scoring the inside of my thigh. I'd lost the scabbard's tip in the darkness. That's what comes of wearing a gentleman's weapon on a horse raid.

The Armenians were there, by the gate, in a furious argument, and the woman was with them. I ran up to them, noting that the players had left, probably frightened, and the two guards were still lying like the dead. I hoped they weren't dead, but that was not my first concern.

'Come,' I said in French.

They followed me without argument. Perhaps they were fools, but they got the gate open. Arnaud threw his sister over his shoulder like a Yule log, and we ran. There were shouts, and more arrows, but the Turks clearly thought that they were under attack; we were the last of their worries.

We got the woman on the horse. I didn't know her name, but I boosted her up, and far from being the useless thing I imagined, she got a leg over, astride, and clicked her tongue at my mount and rode away.

Arnaud laughed.

I was not laughing. The night was full of horses and arrows and now, Turks; they were emerging from their camp at the south edge of the village. Perhaps fifteen minutes had passed since I had stabbed the stallion. Uthman's voice could be heard, roaring orders.

I was lost. That is, I knew where the town was; but somehow, between climbing the back wall of the inn and coming out of the gate ... And all the gullies seemed the same, and I was very tired.

In a Chanson de Geste, everything just happens: you steal the horse, save the girl, kill the villain and ride. Well, my villain was organising a search just a bowshot away, and I'd lost my horses, and my sense of direction, and everything.

There follows a singularly ugly period: I ran to and fro, and found nothing in the dust; a horse knocked Arnaud down when he tried to catch it, and broke his hand; the Armenians began to tell me that I had got them all killed. My nose hurt, my fingers and shoulder burned from other wounds and I could scarcely breathe, I was so tired.

And then the girl rode out of the night. She sort of flowed out of the blackness on a dark horse, and her girl's voice was clearly not Turkish, and she shouted for her brother. I knew his name, anyway.

'*Arnaud! Arnaud!*'

She cantered through us, and called something in Armenian. We all followed her.

She had found the picketed horses. Of course she had. The smart little mare took her there. And she was smart enough herself; even in the middle of fear and darkness, she reasoned out that we needed the horses.

Bah. I got myself up on another Arab, who didn't love me. She didn't make a real effort to be rid of me, though, and before my aching lungs had dragged in twenty more breaths, we were cantering across the flat plain by Ramalie, under the moon.

By the sweet Lord, and with the help of a slip of a girl, we had escaped.

Dawn found us waiting at Montjoie, the first sight a traveller has of the Holy City. Some of the stones there are worn smooth by the knees of ten thousand Christians dismounting to pray, and I added my knees to the multitude. And I must say, after captivity, however mild, and the theft of the horses and fatigue of the night, the city rising above us on the great ridge was like a heavenly vision. We all dismounted, and knelt; the Armenians were pilgrims as much as I, and we prayed, each in his own tongue. As soon as it was light enough to see, I found that the Armenians were smiling, and that the girl was taller and older than I had imagined – not a slip of a girl at all, but a full-grown woman, perhaps twenty, with a heart-shaped face, slanted green eyes and a smile that would have made goodwives in England speak of elves and fairies. In truth, she was almost too much – beautiful in an exotic way, and never more so, I suspect, than covered in dust, wearing a man's gown, and kneeling with her face towards God's city.

She was, however, a mortal woman. When her brother told her, in French, to cover her face, she stuck out her tongue.

Then we rode cautiously, because as the light came up we were exposed, but we were in sight of Jerusalem and my spirits rose, and in fact we made it to the Jaffa Gate without any incident except Arnaud's growing exasperation with his sister, who I gathered from his repeated admonitions was Eugenia, a Greek name.

The last bit of raillery brought two guards to the gate – both of them men-at-arms. They called for a knight of the Order, and before the red ball of the sun crested the far horizon, we were in the city.

Fra Daniele was younger than Fra Peter – Italian and easy to talk to, for a knight of the Order. We were lucky he was on the gate; twice lucky, in that he knew all the men and knew I'd been taken. He sent us straight on to Fra Peter, and before Matins was sung we'd told him our tale.

We went and prayed in the Franciscan church together with the other knights; I was still dusty and probably smelled, but I was warmed to the very core by my reception.

But Fra Peter believed in the same maxims I did – at the gallop, or with planning, or not at all. In this case, he mounted me and Arnaud as guides, gathered about half our total force and remounts, and before the sun was high, we were moving back down the great ridge on which Jerusalem sits, across a dozen deep valleys. A dozen of our English archers were in the van with our Greek cavalry, and we spread out to avoid making a dust cloud – the Holy Land requires all kinds of discipline that you do not have to practise in the green fields of Provence.

I rode in front, with Syr Giorgios and Ewan, and Marc-Antonio close behind me. I had embraced that boy when I saw him, and, rare for me in those days, apologised for striking him in front of a dozen other gentleman. It is a small thing, an apology, but he flushed, stammered – and perhaps loved me better than if I had never struck him.

Because men are odd beasts.

We caught the Turks gathering horses. It was clear they'd been at it all day; half of them were still afoot, in the valleys east of Ramalie, and we caught them afoot, many without arms, and killed them. So much for my attempts of the night before; Fra Peter meant to break the bandits.

It is odd – a thing of war. They had treated me well enough; indeed, they might have killed me, and didn't. I didn't like killing them. But I did – although I begged the stradiotes and the archers to keep an eye out for John, and I managed to take a pair of prisoners and handed them to Marc-Antonio: young men.

I rode from small fight to small fight, looking for John, and Ewan, bless him, did the same, but I needn't have bothered. After our initial surprise, the Turks ran, and even on foot they were hard men to catch. And we were spread over a mile of broken country. The Turks were not fully routed; Uthman led those in the town in a sally to buy his men time, like a good leader; the sunset saw a dozen of our saddles emptied by their terrible, fierce archery, and then we charged them, rather than lose more men and horses.

That caused one of the most confusing fights I can remember: a red sunset, dust everywhere on the plain of Ramalie, and two hundred men milling in utter chaos, arrows, dying horses, and no notion of 'sides' or 'order'. I might say it reminded me of mounted tournament mêlées, except, to be honest, at the time it reminded me of *nothing*, because I had no thought in my head except to stay alive. I had no maille, no brigantine, no helmet, no bow and no javelins. I had a fine long sword, which, despite being my favourite weapon, is probably the worst weapon I can imagine in a swirling mêlée with horse archers.

Or perhaps not – it is still deadly. But the encounters I remember: a young Turk who made his horse rear and shot me from perhaps five paces – he missed; another who rode by me, out of a wall of dust, as surprised as I was, and past me, and put an arrow into the rump of my mount in the two breaths he had to shoot. I cut at him and was so late that I almost fell off.

My poor mare slumped down, spent, and with blood pouring from her back off leg – something vital cut, and nothing to be done. I'm sure if I had an astrologer, he'd have told me that my star was in a bad house for horses.

I ran to a rock. I got my back against it and tried to breathe. For perhaps the first time in my adult life, I considered hiding in the midst of a mêlée.

The next man out of the haze of battle was John. He had an arrow on his bow, a sabre back over his right hand and back along his draw arm, and he cantered up, arrow aimed at the centre of my chest. He nodded, perhaps ten paces out.

I thought he was going to kill me. I'm ashamed to own it, but that smile seemed to say I was done with this world and should say my prayers.

But he turned his little horse on her front feet and cantered away into the gathering gloom, leaving me feeling more and more like a spectator. But he was back in no time, with a big mare's reins in his fist and, with a little help, I got up on her.

Then I drew my sword.

'Thank you, John,' I said.

He grinned. 'Always my pleasure,' he said in passable French – clearly a phrase of Jean-François's that he had memorised. 'Turks,' he said with contempt.

For the rest of that fight, he was the knight, and I was the squire. By which I mean, he rode, and shot, and killed Turks, if any of those bandits were truly Turks and not just the broken men of three faiths. He did miss; I can remember two arrows he loosed that went awry, and both times, regardless of the danger, he cursed as if we were in some archery match and not a desperate cavalry fight. I followed him, and collected the horses of the men he shot. If they had arrows, I passed their quivers to John. Once, he threw the entire quiver on the ground in disgust.

I will amuse you, I hope, to say that our third horse had a bow in an open holster, and several quivers of arrows, and I took the strung bow, got an arrow on it ...

And almost fell from my mount. The bow was incredibly difficult to draw – as heavy as Ewan's, and I had never tried drawing a bow on horseback.

But the dead man had a case of javelins, as well. And late in the fight, as the sun finally set, and Uthman rallied his best men around him on the Damascus road, I came up with him. He had perhaps twenty riders around him; one of them was the angry boy I'd dismounted twice. The road was stonier than the countryside, and there was less dust – we rode into them. That may sound foolish, but in a fight like that, every man for himself, fought at the best speed of your horse, no order and no orders either – well, you either turn turtle and wait for other men to do the fighting, or you fight anything that comes under your horse's nose.

Everyone was equally surprised, and I flicked a javelin into the man who'd broken my nose. He crumpled around it like a crushed doll, and I was in the middle of Uthman's rearguard. I cut with my long sword, two handed, made a cover, lost my reins, guided my stolen horse with my knees, took a blow in the back and was out – galloping free, my mount still fresh between my legs. The one advantage of getting your mount killed and replaced.

John threaded through the enemy perhaps ten paces away. Without any plan but a single glance, we split. I rode north, and my mare jumped the roadside ditch I hadn't seen – I was shocked, and almost lost my seat again, and bit my tongue of all things, and then we were turning wide at a canter.

John went the other way, south. I will never forget one sight. There was a ditch on his side of the road, and I was looking back, or perhaps jolted from my own jump, and there was John, his horse at full jump, front feet high, like some mythical flying man-horse, shooting back over his shoulder at the men on the road.

I turned into the heavier dust apurpose – I had no armour, and any arrow was the end for me. But I saw Uthman, and he saw me, and waved his fist at me.

That was the end of the fight, for me. I probably went too wide, trying to stay alive, and then darkness fell, more suddenly than I expected.

I imagine that Chaucer has heard about this fight from Scrope and Stapleton. I know that, ever since, I've heard how every one of them killed a dozen Saracens – the greatest triumph of the crusade. I know that no one who tells this mentions that they were bandits – that Uthman was a Turk and not a Mamluk – and I promise you that no one mentions that the next day, when we scoured the fields around Ramalie for our own wounded and dead, we saw a great many Turks with arrows in them, but hardly a one killed with a lance. The men-at-arms did well in rounding up and massacring the dismounted bandits, I suppose. But the archers and Greeks did most of the fighting. I know that when I rode back to find Fra Peter, he had most of the knights together, ready to charge, and they were two full bowshots behind the action.

And in truth, I suspect that one lone Kipchak put about half the Turks down.

For me, it left a bad taste in my mouth. I wanted them to be Saracens – cruel, hard, bad men. In fact, they struck me as nothing but Moslem routiers – more of the same. I was glad that my first captive, Salim, was not among the dead.

And yet, when I found that Turkish boy who'd broken my nose, lying with a bad wound and both his legs broken, I cut his throat without a qualm.

And then I collected my light harness from the corpses of the men wearing it, took my share of the loot and horses, and rode back to Jerusalem, to worship at the Holy Sepulchre.

That's the life of arms.

The Franciscans try to control everything you do or see in the Holy City. I would like to rail against them, but with a hundred former routiers, swollen with pride, full of the release from fear of the day after a sharp fight, and rich with the gold and silver of dead bandits, I saw why the Franciscans wanted us kept separate from the people of Jerusalem.

To most of our soldiers, all the people were 'infidels' and they could not tell the difference between Armenians, Franks, Jews and Moslems. They wanted wine, and women, and while I suppose that both could be had somewhere in the Holy City, their manner of looking for either was offensive and dangerous.

Controlling your people, off duty, can be as difficult and draining as combat itself. We'd lost almost a dozen men – heavy losses for such a small fight. I've seen this enough to know that losses like that make men angry and afraid; even in victory, they can be violent. For the whole of the next day, from stabling our horses until I fell, exhausted, on a pallet in the Orthodox bishop's house, I did nothing but chase down men-at-arms and archers.

One encounter I remember better than the others – it was Sir Steven Scrope. He was drunk, slurring his words, in a Jewish wine shop. He was threatening the owner.

Thanks to God, I had Nerio and Fiore at my heels. Fiore stripped his sword out of his hand while he was arguing with me and the poor wine shopkeeper's wife screamed.

'Fucking paynim! Worms of infidels!' Scrope shouted.

'Jews,' I commented. I was tired and Scrope annoyed me.

'Doesn't matter. All heretics.' Scrope did not add to his theological argument, but stopped to throw up.

Nerio paid his bill.

Fiore shook his head. 'No, none of them are heretics,' he said. 'The Greeks are heretics – they do not hold orthodox views about the words of our Saviour. The Jews are Jews. They don't believe in our Saviour at all. Moslems, by contrast, believe that Jesus was a great prophet – not quite so great as their Mahomet, but a fine man.'

'Whatever,' Scrope spat.

Fiore arched an eyebrow. 'Not *whatever* at all. These distinctions matter and it is you, sir, who are ignorant. To a good Moslem, we are the heretics – we invest our Jesus with godhood, and that is against the will of God.'

'Just shut up,' Scrope said. 'They're all the same – the enemy. They make me sick.'

He said many such things as we manoeuvred him through the narrow streets. I was going to ignore him; Fiore, of course, debated his every comment with precision and brilliance and sobriety – possibly enough punishment for anyone, really.

But finally Scrope whirled on me. 'Make this stupid foreign clerk shut up, Gold! I hate them all. I don't want to know about them, or their evil religions, or their satanic rituals. I just want to kill them.'

'You might learn something by listening,' I said.

'*I don't want to learn anything! I don't want them to be people!*' Scrope spat the words, but his voice caught on the second sentence.

'They are, though,' I said. Poor bastard. I understood his disease, then. He didn't like the killing. It was eating him.

'How do you do it, Gold?' he asked. 'You like everybody, and you kill them anyway. You think I'm wode? Look at yourself!'

Scrope shook Fiore's arms off. 'Let me go,' he said.

'Only if you give me your word not to kill anyone,' I said.

'How do you do it, Gold?' he asked again.

'Swear, and I'll tell you,' I said.

So he swore, on Saint George.

I nodded, accepting his oath. 'It's war,' I said. 'It is my profession. Like farming, or being a priest. No need for hate or anger.'

Nerio, of all people, nodded. 'Strictly business,' he said.

I shook my head. 'Killing is never business,' I said. 'I imagine that perhaps, someday, maybe in the kingdom of Heaven, there will be no killing. Until then – if you must be a butcher, be a good butcher. Learn your trade, do an honest job, and never trouble to hate the cow.'

Scrope was shaking.

I wanted to say, *This is not for you. You should be a priest.* But you cannot tell a knight this.

When we walked away from him, Nerio put a hand on my shoulder. 'Sometimes,' he said, 'I think maybe you are a great man.'

Fiore nodded. 'That was a good speech, about the butcher and the cow,' he said.

'Sir Steven's problem is that he is afraid,' I said.

Nerio nodded. 'And he thinks that you and I are not afraid. He thinks his fears justify his actions.'

It might have become a great discussion on chivalry, but then a 'woman' screamed, and we found a pair of Gascons trying to buy, or beat, a man-whore. I find life is often like this – from flights of God-sent thought to the most sordid in a single tangle. But that man screaming was a signpost from God.

My friends were my salvation. Stapleton had ridden with us, although I never saw him once the fighting started; Fiore and Nerio had stayed with the 'garrison', if a city of fifty thousand could be garrisoned by seventy men. But they all three stayed with me that night, and when we came upon the man-whore, or boy, two of our 'pilgrims' were trying to force him. Fiore dropped one, and Miles tripped the second.

I was behind them in the alley. The pathetic boy had been beaten, and he was kneeling, blood flowing from his mouth. I knelt by him, feeling squalid, and as I knelt, a crossbow bolt passed over my head. By the will of God it passed the length of that stinking alley without touching Marc-Antonio or Achille and struck the wall of a stable and exploded in fragments.

It was dark. It took me a long moment to realise what had just happened.

'Crossbow,' shouted Marc-Antonio.

I shot to my feet. A heavy crossbow takes a bit to span; whether you use a belt hook, a lever, or your hands, it's a process. I ran forward down the alley. It was narrow – the path of the bolt down the alley ...

In one glance I had it; I saw the window and light behind it. Jerusalem is full of towers; many houses are three storeys and look like keeps in Scotland. This one was a little different, but I could see the man backlit against the lamplight of the room behind. He raised his weapon, the bolt flashed out, and struck me. But I was wearing my reclaimed brigantine over maille; the bolt cracked a rib, but it didn't penetrate.

You don't feel pain in these moment. You feel it later.

The building entrance wasn't off our alley. So I tried to climb the building – easier in Jerusalem than most places – but the same brigantine that had just saved my life was now too bulky for climbing, and I slid ignominiously off the wall and into the dust.

Fiore was ahead of me all the way. He passed me, bounced off the alley-corner, and ran for the front of the building. The assassin had, by then, decided that his plan wasn't going to work, and he'd vanished from the lit window.

I followed Fiore.

We missed him.

Then we went into the tower, which was owned by a Moslem family. I tried to be polite, and John the Kipchak came and helped me, but if they knew anything of the man who'd hired their room, they didn't say. Mayhap there was nothing to know.

He left nothing but a linen bag that had probably covered his crossbow, and the weapon itself. It was a plain military weapon, Italian, with a yew bow and a steel stirrup for loading.

Nerio questioned the two Gascons. He wasn't nice about it. But the boy said they'd been hired to have an 'incident' and the Gascons eventually admitted to it, trying to pass it off as a bit of fun. I handed them over to l'Angars and we – that is, the four of us – assumed it was one of the Hungarian's men. We tightened our watch.

But we had to stay in the streets, and we moved from fight to fight to attempted rape, breaking men up when they fought each other, attempting to patch up relations when an archer ripped the veil off a Moslem woman. It made it harder, wondering if there was an assassin waiting in the shadows. We sent Marc-Antonio to Ser Jason with our suspicions. And then we went back to policing our people.

L'Angars impressed me by doing the same. Perhaps two days in the most sacred shrines had changed him; perhaps I had misunderstood the Gascon. But he, too, rallied some knights and patrolled the streets. I'd like to think we paid a little penance for Alexandria. We rode our own people hard. I knocked a man out with my pommel; Fiore choked another with his sword blade, when a tiny twist of his wrists would have killed the man.

At any rate, at the end of each of those days I collapsed. I slept the clock around, and Fra Peter was in the streets in my place, battering our men into their barracks and then into the churches and shrines.

On our fifth or sixth day, Fra Daniele was shot with a crossbow. He was walking to the Holy Sepulchre, unarmoured. The bolt went into his gut, and he died.

We were the same height. And he had red hair.

So much for the Holy City.

And yet ... it was the Holy City. Most of our people had been almost a week in the Holy City before I began to visit the shrines, but murder and mayhem could not keep me from the greatest sights in Christendom. I meekly joined one of Father Angelo's groups for three glorious days, and in the company of men I might ordinarily have despised – routiers as bad as I had ever been, including the very lout I'd knocked flat with my pommel. I went to the Garden of Gethsemane, and there stood vigil. And although it's probably a sin to say it, the Apostles may have been good men, but they were poor knights; with forty men on that hillside, murderers, thieves, and reivers every one, not a one fell asleep all night, and the Gospels say that all the Apostles slept, even Saint Peter. The man I'd knocked out with my pommel was kneeling by me. It was a long night, with your knees feeling the weight of all your sins.

We were not commanded to be silent, and my companions were quite voluble – griping, like all soldiers. The lout was a small, ferret-faced Gascon named Pierre Lapot, and he seemed to bear me no ill-will at all; indeed, I thought he was seeking my favour.

'I am a bad man,' he said in his lisping Gascon-French, about halfway through the night. 'But by the Christ, monsieur, had I been with Sir Jesus here, the Romans and Jews would have had a fight to take my captain.'

I suppose it is bad theology, but I agreed with him, and so did the other voices in the darkness, even John; I was surprised to hear him there, and I could not see him, for it was full dark. They lock you in; there's no light but a pair of tapers on one of the side altars, and there's a great deal of incense – or was that at the Sepulchre? In truth, I can't remember. I was tired, and yet utterly happy. And the men I stood that vigil with, and the next night, at the Holy Sepulchre – they became my companions for many years, as you will hear.

The next day we bathed, and were given white garments by the Order, and those of us who were knights renewed our vows. And Lord Grey knighted a few men. Then we did the Stations inside the Holy Sepulchre. Even though a man might see that the church had once been mightier and more noble, even though it was plain to me that the Church of the Holy Sepulchre was not itself as grand as churches in Verona or Venice, it mattered not. What was inside was glorious, and the weight of sin that was lifted …

Bah, you all want tales of fighting. Not of my pilgrimage.

But I will tell you one story, and that's about the darkness of the Holy Sepulchre, which is a different and more profound black than the Garden. We knelt, almost a hundred of us, in our plain white gowns. Men shifted, men farted or belched or coughed – we are all sinful mortals, and human. But the silence was great, and the smell of frankincense was everywhere, and it was possible to imagine a great deal, and despite your companions all around you, every man was alone with his conscience. And that wears; the long night, the total darkness, and your thoughts, going like a stampede of horses, or slowly in meditation; some men chanted from time to time, and one repeated the Paternoster over and over and over, as if a talisman.

It was l'Angars who spoke up first. 'Oh God,' he said, 'I did it. I killed the nun, and took the gold paten from her. Oh, Jesu, save me. I killed a nun for what she carried, and I sold the paten.'

And another voice said, 'I killed a babe, and the mother. Christ, I killed the mother ...'

And I heard my voice say 'I killed a boy, in Bohemia.'

The horrors we voiced – and they were not a few, once l'Angars started us on that road. A hundred bad men have a tale of sins it would be hard for any other hundred to match; and men told stories to the darkness that I would hesitate to recount even now, and I hoped that they were lying. And the voices went on, so that it was possible to grow tired of listening to the atrocities we had committed – this one for the English, that one for the king of France, or the Holy Roman Emperor.

Eventually, our voices trailed off, and we returned to silence, and I prayed. I prayed fervently; I imagined myself at the very cradle of the newborn child, and I imagined myself as a man-at-arms of the Wise Men, as I often did. The world of the Gospels was so *imminent* in the Holy Land, it made my meditations somehow practical; I could now imagine a stable, horses, the colour of the earth and the shape of the buildings in the Holy Land.

When they came and unlocked the doors, we were all searched, because so many Christians attempted to use tools to pry bits of the walls, the floor, the old mosaics, the wooden beams that supported recent damage. The Holy Sepulchre was gradually being pulled to pieces by pilgrims, which seemed to me to be a rare allegory of the Christian condition. Regardless, I left the hall in a state of exultation – the night had been glorious, and I truly felt lightened of my sins. I crossed eyes with l'Angars and I could see he felt the same. And outside, we embraced, or clasped hands – oh, a few damned souls slunk away, but for most of us, it was like rebirth.

And you might ask if I was not beside myself with fear, for myself, for my lady love, with assassins abroad. But Jerusalem is ... Jerusalem. I took what precautions I could and trusted to God and Ser Jason. I was not going to cower indoors while I had a chance to visit the place where my Saviour suffered his passion, or preached.

On my fourth or fifth day in the city, men began to speak of leaving. Syr Giannis returned from a long scout to the south, with a rumour that the Mamluks were sending a large force. Our Venetian *capitano*, who, by the way, had arranged for me to have the fine lodging I had with the bishop – it *was* a fine lodging: a clean straw pallet and space to lay out my leather trunk and change my clothes, in a hallway, with Marc-Antonio and Fiore by me. Nerio had a room—

I digress. The Capitano was afraid for his cargo already, and wanted us gone to the coast.

I must mention, to make you smile, that Jerusalem defied even Nerio's lechery. He was very pious while he was there, it's true, but if there was a woman to be had inside the Holy City, I never saw her and neither did Nerio.

At any rate, I rose from my knees after my second straight night of vigil to spend a frustrating morning dodging irate archers – and Franciscans too – to find Emile. She and her household had toured the shrines as a group, as great lords and ladies do. And no one knew where they had gone.

It turned out that she had taken a party outside the city, to see what pilgrims call 'The Saint George'. Lydda was a hamlet not far from Ramalie, where Saint George had been martyred. There were guides, and Emile had taken her people there. I never saw it. I was delighted to hear that both Greek knights had ridden out with her, and jealous, too.

There was nothing I could do to catch them up. Some of 'my' men-at-arms, my new comrades of the long, dark vigils in the Sepulchre, wanted me to lead them to Bethlehem. The Franciscans were against it; Bethlehem and the towns around had many Moslems, and I think that Father Angelo quite rightly feared that former routiers might simply massacre Moslems for sport or profit.

Fra Peter said that they were gathering forage and information for the trip back to the coast, and ordered me to bed. I obeyed. I hadn't slept a night through in three days.

I dreamed of angels. I will never forget that dream – angels that flew into my eyes. I do not know if it was a dream from God – if perhaps something blessed me in the darkness of Jerusalem. But I awoke to joy – joy doubled and redoubled, as I was informed as soon as I was awake that Fra Peter was awaiting me with Emile.

I washed, threw on my arming clothes, and ran to the bishop's hall. I pushed past an ugly spat between an Armenian priest and a Greek one; it was one of the enduring small humiliations of the Holy City to watch all the kinds of Christians at odds. Throw in worldly politics and an assassin and the holiness should have been sensibly diminished.

In this case, some of the Armenians and a few Greeks had accepted various forms of 'union' with the church in Rome; most abhorred 'union', and all of us, more than they hated the Turks or the Mamluks. I leave this to priests.

But when I went to the hall, I found Fra Peter, and Emile, and Arnaud and Eugenia and Sister Marie too – a surprising collection of my friends.

But sometimes things happen when you are asleep. And, of course, there were not so very many Christian women in Jerusalem, nor noble ones. Arnaud's sister had been put in the same convent where Emile stayed, and Bernard and Jean-François had become fast friends with Arnaud, who had led them to Saint George.

I wondered if I had been caught in one of my many sins. All of them were seated on stools, except Fra Peter, who looked for once, like a great lord and not a military hermit. The Venetian *capitano*, Bembo, was seated with them, as was the Franciscan priest and the Orthodox bishop.

I looked at Emile. She looked straight back at me, without dissimulation. I know we both grinned like fools; I know that any person in the hall would have known in that moment that we were lovers.

Fra Peter cleared his throat. 'Sir William,' he said.

I bowed.

Marc-Antonio appeared with a stool, and suddenly it was less like a tribunal. My back hurt. I had, in fact, taken a wound in the fighting at Ramalie – a cut to my back, right through my arming coat. Sitting slightly hunched on a stool was the very worst thing after a night's sleep.

Fra Peter stroked his beard. 'I understand you intend to wed this lady, and she has accepted you,' he said. If I mentioned that his eyes burned into mine, I would do him no injustice. He wasn't angry, but he wanted answers. But he was a good man, and kept his questions for a more private time.

'It is my most fervent desire,' I said.

Fra Peter winced. 'In Jerusalem?' he asked.

The Franciscan looked embarrassed, and the Venetian, amused.

Fra Peter shook his head, as if dismissing my human frailty. 'Ser Bembo wants to start for the coast,' he said.

I assumed they were delaying my wedding – to which, let's be honest, I had given no thought whatsoever in the last three days. 'Yes?' I asked.

Fra Peter shook his head. 'I am going about this badly,' he said. 'Ser Arnaud and his people require an escort to return to their own lands. Lord Bembo has declined to take them by ship.'

Bembo shook his head. 'I have not declined,' he said, a trifle pettishly. 'The wind declines. It is early spring. I could wait weeks for a wind to take me north, and another set of weeks for an east wind to take me back to Cyprus, much less to Venice.'

Fra Peter could fight from the deck of a galley, but he was not one of the Order's sea captains. So he shrugged. 'I mean no slight on your honour,' he said. 'But they must go home.' He looked at me. 'Your lady has suggested that you might volunteer to escort them home to Cilicia.'

'With me,' Emile said. Her smile said more. 'And my knights.'

Fra Peter looked at her a moment. He was never easy with women, and somehow, I had the feeling that Emile frightened him. 'Yes,' he said. 'And any of the … hmmm … Crusaders who would care to accompany you.'

Ser Arnaud nodded. 'We would, of course, pay wages. And be deeply grateful.'

Well, there it was – a military expedition, through enemy country, in the Holy Land, over uncharted roads, with my lady love at my side? I laughed aloud.

'*Certes, gentilhommes et mesdames*, but you have chosen the right man.' I rose and bowed. 'I would be delighted.' I looked at Arnaud. 'There must be serious issues of food, fodder, water, and routes.'

Arnaud's smile was broad; he meant it. 'You are a soldier,' he said. 'Many of you Franks are … Never mind. Yes, I will discuss all these things. Bless you. I will see you well paid.'

Emile nodded graciously, the great lady every inch of her. 'We will have our own little crusade,' she said. 'I will see this splendid maiden to her home, and Sister Marie and I will see all the places in Syria we've talked of.' She rose, and all the men rose; she curtsied, and we all bowed, and she swept out of the hall with Eugenia and Sister Marie, pausing only to say a few words to Jean-François.

Fra Peter didn't follow her with his eyes, and neither did Father Angelo; all the other men did.

'This will be very dangerous, William,' Fra Peter said, 'but essential. If you will get us a report of the coastline, we will be better prepared for the spring season. Sabraham will be with you.'

I confess that as soon as Emile swept from the hall, the weight of the idea fell on my shoulders, and as soon as Fra Peter said 'Sabraham' some of the weight lifted.

Fra Peter proceeded to give me exact orders, and some advice as to my route, and Lord Bembo spoke to me about the ports – especially Acre and Tyre. The near-collapse of Mamluk authority changed everything, of course, and what Arnaud brought to the conversation was the possibility of active support from Cilicia, which was already a close ally of Cyprus.

'I must caution you against too much … enthusiasm,' Fra Peter said, at the end. 'There is a rumour up from the coast that the Green Count is in Venice, and his expedition is *not* going to Cyprus, but to Turkey or even to Constantinople. It is being said in Europe that we failed – that we lost Alexandria through cowardice.'

At that moment, I cared nothing for the Green Count, or the king of France, or even the king of England. I probably shrugged.

'In late spring, the voyage from Cilicia to Cyprus is nothing,' Fra Peter said. 'But you have my permission to go to Rhodes directly if that speeds your purpose. It is a tall order, Sir William. And I will not hide from you that none of my brother knights wants the job. Only Fra Daniele would have been—'

The Venetian captain favoured me with a smile full of nuance. 'Perhaps, as humble men, they recognise that Sir William is the correct man for a role that requires … some thought. Perhaps some … dissimulation.'

Fra Peter spread his hands. 'I feel like a parent sending a small boy into the world,' he said. 'I realise that must seem unfair. And I have never been a father. But, William, this is a very difficult *empris*. If I could dissuade the countess, I would. But she is set on it. And she has her own people – passports signed by every crowned head in Europe. And indeed, should you run across the Green Count, she is our best ally – one of his own Savoyards, who is dedicated to the Cross and the Crusade and knows what King Peter seeks to do. I know you will protect her with your life; I say, protect her with your head, and not your heart.'

I nodded.

'Very well. William,' and here Fra Peter looked at the other men, as if willing them to leave the room, 'I had hoped to speak a few words to you in private.'

Bembo was a man of good manners; he rose, smiled, shook my hand and Fra Peter's, and congratulated me. He told me to pay him a visit in his room before we quit Jerusalem.

Father Angelo nodded. He rose and walked from the hall.

The Orthodox bishop had yet to speak a word. I bowed to him, and Fra Peter and I walked from the hall to a close room, where I leaned against a chalk-white wall and Fra Peter fidgeted with a wall hanging.

'You know, William,' he said, after a time. He looked at me seriously, neither smiling nor frowning. 'You know, I never really understood how deep you were with the countess until just now. And I deceived myself, I think. I had rather hoped that tonight or tomorrow, on the altar of the Holy Sepulchre, I would make you a Knight of Saint John – the first knighted here in an hundred years.'

There are too many moments like this in life – the moment where two paths separate, one going one way, and the other another way.

But there was never a choice, for me. Celibacy would have been a hard road for me, at any time; nor, I think, could I have been like de Heredia, with a mistress or three, and bastards learning to be bishops and knights. I can be a fool and a hypocrite, but I like to be so by error and not with grim determination.

But I was not being offered the choice between the Order and fornication; I was being offered the choice between the Order and Emile.

It was never a choice.

Fra Peter smiled then. 'I know,' he said. 'I saw you look at each other. Forgive me – I loved a woman once. She died, and I am here, with no regrets. But I have known love; I knew what passed between you. So tell me – did you kill her husband?'

'No,' I said. Sometimes the truth is simple. But the blood rushed to my face; of all men, he should have known I was innocent of this.

Fra Peter nodded and took a deep breath. 'Then I shall come to your wedding,' he said. 'And defend you as best I can, although, you must know, you will win only hatred for this.'

The word 'wedding' made me smile.

'The lady's estate is entirely entailed. All goes to young Edouard.'

I shrugged. 'I will still be pinching my sequins and counting silver pennies.'

Fra Peter nodded. 'Well – I will hope that I have your services, perhaps at your wife's expense, for the balance of the Crusade. If we have just a little luck – if Venice will not make peace with the Sultan, and if King Peter keeps his nerve – we will have Jerusalem and Acre too, in the spring. *Deus vult.*'

We both crossed ourselves, and Fra Peter embraced me.

'You have become a good knight,' he said. 'I would like to say I always knew, but *par Dieu*, I have doubted you many times.'

In the goldsmith's guild they used to say, no praise is as sweet as the praise of your own master. And Fra Peter was that.

I burst into tears.

Make of it what you will. *Honi soit qui mal y pense.*

And then I went out to arrange to be married in the Holy Sepulchre.

Well, I confess it, we were not married in the Holy Sepulchre. It only took me an hour of argument to discover that the price was ruinous, the number of priests needing to be bribed probably outnumbers the Host of Angels, and that in fact, Father Angelo, the Franciscan, who had gone from enemy to ally by some subtle process, was happy to host my wedding in the Franciscan chapel. For nothing, and performing the service himself.

Ah, you men of blood do not want to hear the details of my wedding, but perhaps Aemilie, if she will stop her blushes, will care to hear. I was well dressed, through no fault of my own, but because Nerio insisted on dressing me from head to toe. Achille, the former tailor, with access to the silks of the Holy Land, produced for me in about fifteen hours a slightly padded silk doublet that would have been acceptable anywhere in Italy, and a pair of silk hose to match – all red and white and black, like my arms. And Emile and her ladies, and Eugenia and *her* ladies, contrived a marvellous kirtle in silk, with an overdress, sleeveless, in my lady's arms, and trimmed in fur. And I'll add, by way of reminiscence, that the fur on her gown came from my own scapegrace squire; Marc-Antonio produced a board of ermine skins as if he performed this sort of miracle every day, and was insufferable for ... Well, really, he was always insufferable.

We were wed. Fra Peter was there, and Sister Marie, and all the

Armenians and the two Greek knights who had served Father Pierre Thomas, and of course there was Nerio, and Fiore, and Miles. Lord Grey attended, as did even Sir Steven Scrope, and really, the little chapel was packed, all the way out of the doors and into the Franciscan hostel, and when we were wed, several tuns of wine were rolled out, paid for by my rich wife, and trestles were laid, and every one of our men-at-arms and archers were served. In fact, Emile and I served them ourselves for the first cup of wine – a Savoyard tradition, and a noble one.

No other part of the meal bore any resemblance to anything that had ever happened in Savoy, or in England. We had olives, and olive oil, and sheep in a saffron paste with raisins, and a dozen other dishes that were so different from the food of home. But we ate our fill and drank well, and I was pleased, even through a haze of happiness and gentle lust, to see that our company had drawn together. They'd had a sea voyage and a little adventure, and some loot; I speak no ill of mankind when I say that these things usually suffice to create a body of men, especially with a little victory.

And then there were toasts – so many I thought we might spoil the wine trade – and my lady was smiling at me in a particular way, and I touched her hands far more often than I needed, and we laughed together, publicly. Bah, I see you want me to go on to war and fighting.

So I rose, when I was sure that we'd all taken enough wine on board, and bowed to our Armenians. 'My friends,' I said, 'These fine gentlemen of Armenia have asked for an escort to see them home along the coast – a little more than three hundred miles, and all of it through hostile territory. I'd be most pleased if a few of you would consider taking on this *empris* with me.'

I probably said some other things, about my lady's beauty and high nobility and my own unworthiness. But I'll pass on such things, although I meant them.

Afterwards, l'Angars and Pierre Lapot both asked to be taken to Cilicia. So did all the archers, when I assured them there would be pay. I spent an hour that I confess I'd rather have spent attending to other matters, sitting at a table like a recruiter in the Low Countries, offering wages and signing men on. Some were no surprise; the two Greek knights were keen to go home, and they knew far more about the terrain than I did. And between them and *Capitano* Bembo, we sketched out an itinerary that would get us back to Rhodes and then to Constantinople. By then the evening was well advanced; there was some music, and I danced with Emile, and then, with a long parade of raucous men-at-arms behind me, I carried her out into the street and to my lodgings for one night. The Orthodox bishop had, for reasons never explained to me, surrendered his whole house.

I carried Emile up the narrow stairs – the house might be called a palace, but it was three storeys on a very narrow house front. And Emile was no small woman; she was perhaps three fingers shorter than I am myself. I got her to the bed and threw her on it.

'I borrowed this veil,' she said. 'Let's have a care getting it off.'

It was the most remarkable piece of silk, and I was not so far gone in lust or wine to refuse, so we fiddled for some very pleasant time with the veil and various other things, and my lady love smiled at me.

'William,' she said, 'I never dreamed that my wedding would be the start of the chivalric *empris.* I feel like the heroine in a romance.'

'My love,' I said, 'You *are* the heroine in a romance.'

She laughed. I was trying to unlace her, and she was not ready to be unlaced. Well, I'm not quite a fool, and I left off.

'I want to go on with this pilgrimage forever,' she said. She pulled the bed hangings closed. 'I want to be a bandit queen, and you a bandit king. I don't ever want to go back to court, to Geneva, to wagging tongues. Oh, sweet Christ, William. What have we done?'

I kissed her hands, and held her. 'We've done the right thing. The thing that should have been true always.'

She shook her head. I had seen her moods change like this for some years, but on our wedding night, I was not prepared.

'You say that, but William, by the Risen Christ, they will hound us, now that we are wed.' Still, her arms were tight around me. 'I know of the assassin, William. Who has paid this insect?'

I kissed her face a few dozen times. And then I told her about the Hungarian, László.

'He intends to kill us,' I said. 'What I mean is, my love, that world is there, and it would be there even if you ordered me to go away. They want you for your chattels. You would, in time, have to give yourself to some man of their choosing, if only to protect your children.'

'How very grim,' she said. 'And true.'

We had a beeswax candle burning, and I had expected to make love to her by its light, seeing her body, for once. Instead, its light revealed to me all the emotions in her face. 'Do you know how tiring it all is, my William? To be a body and an estate, and never a person?'

I rested on an elbow. 'I probably do not,' I said. 'I come to you with no fortune, and no great birth, my love, but I do have this – my sword, and three friends. I very much doubt, and I beg you pardon my boast, that you could do better for a man to protect you and your children from your enemies. Save perhaps Nerio.'

She was trying to be angry. I could see it. I could even guess what she'd bridle at – that she needed protection.

'I?' She began to laugh, her old laugh. 'Marry Nerio?' she sat up. 'My sweet,' she said, 'I could not bear the endless competition.' She sat up. 'Yes,' she said after a moment. 'You are likely the best protector I could find, and I know you will protect the children. So why do I feel this … this …'

'Hesitation?' I asked. It was hurting me, because it *was* hesitation.

'Yes,' she said.

I laughed. 'I have no idea. But I love you, and we are wed, and unless you want to discuss the fodder costs for the horses we're riding to Cilicia, I feel that I could unlace your gown.'

I say all this because some people want all wedding nights to be simple. Nothing is ever simple – not war, not dalliance, and especially not marriage.

She hopped off the bed and out of the hangings.

I heard a sigh, and wondered what I had said, and then she was back, naked.

I had several days to learn more about my wife's clothes, and her body, and how to take care of them – how to lace and unlace, and when to make love and when not to make love. I owe the Orthodox bishop greatly for that time. I wonder if he knew the uses to which his bed was put, but I suppose he did – he had a wife, who was in the Sinai on a pilgrimage of her own.

During those three days, Emile and I got to know each other in a way we never had; it was a delight, and I think that we began to feel as if we really were married. For you bachelors, there is more to marriage than your wife's pretty eyes and what lies under her shift; you can waste an entire day by making an insensitive comment in the first hour, or really, at any time. And mostly, marriage is like leading men; you must listen, or you fail.

On the second day of our marriage, we went to Bethlehem. Everyone wanted to go, and we made a procession – it was almost as good as a Maying, although there were not enough ladies.

I did note that Nerio had begun to pay his most ferociously well-groomed attentions to Eugenia of Cilicia. She rode in a veil, and Nerio rode with Arnaud, her brother, chatting about hawks, and hawking like the great nobles they were, but when we dined in the ruins of a Greek temple, she unpinned her veil like a church opening its doors and Nerio fed her, and Arnaud affected to be charmed.

In fact, I knew he was not best pleased.

And Bethlehem was a bit of a shock, by which I mean that unlike ancient, glorious, dirty and venerable Jerusalem, Bethlehem was like a Passion Play brought to life. Generations of Christian pilgrims had conditioned the locals to cater to us, and so, for example, there was a stable; in the stable a crèche full of straw, and in the straw a quite genuine human baby, tended by a very attractive and very demure young girl, playing the Virgin.

Now, you needn't show any shock, *mes amis*; we do the same ourselves when we have the prettiest of the Alderman's daughters to play the Virgin at Clerkenwell, when the guilds and the Hospitallers put on the cycle about the Annunciation. But it was a bit of a surprise to find it all so nicely arranged in Bethlehem – and to be charged hard silver for the privilege of seeing it.

Pierre Lapot grew quite angry. He asked hard questions; and he reacted with flat disbelief when the Orthodox priest said that yes, this was the very stable shed in which Our Saviour had been born.

'*Par Dieu!*' Lapot spat. 'If he was a man of the sword I'd give him the lie on the spot.'

Nerio was taking to the angry little Gascon; the two got along, and Nerio put a hand on the routier's shoulder. 'They do no harm,' he said. 'But *certo* they edge towards blasphemy.'

There were other things to admire, or mock, in Bethlehem. We were only there a few hours, and it came to me that the inhabitants had generations of Christian pilgrims to accommodate and almost no actual artifacts of the time of Christ. Hence the acting and the stable and a rather unsavoury parade of relics – rusty nails, bits of wood, and so on.

One young urchin tried to sell me a bit of the true Cross, and I grinned at him.

'I can buy one more cheaply and as fine as that on London Bridge from your English cousins,' I said, and Emile had to pull up her veil to cover her laughter.

And I was glad I could amuse her.

She for her part was delighted to amuse my friends, and again she proved to be, in every way, the woman of my dreams. She could exchange barbs with Nerio and laugh with him; she could sit reading the 'Golden Legend' with Miles and delight him; and with Fiore, she simply counselled him in plain language. I mention this because in Bethlehem, he was explaining to a trio of our archers how this or that thing had been reproduced, and was not at all authentic, and she smiled at him.

'Really, messire,' she said. 'Must you tell us all how clever you are?'

He bridled. 'I am not trying to *seem* clever. I *am* clever. These men need to ...' He paused.

She smiled. 'It remains, my dear Fiore, that you appear to be showing off.'

Nerio was clever enough not to speak his thoughts aloud, or laugh, and we all escaped alive.

But later, in the streets of Jerusalem, a *soi-disant* guide attempted to point out the very stone in the road on which Our Saviour stumbled while carrying the Cross. I saw Fiore glance at Emile and then, accepting her smile as permission, he commented, in the sing-song voice he kept for total contempt, 'Not possible.'

The man standing in the road, a Frank in a stained jerkin, snapped his head around. 'That's nigh on blasphemy, that is,' he said.

Fiore glanced at Emile again and shrugged.

'Oh, my dear Fiore,' she said. 'I *want* to know why it is not possible.'

Fiore snapped his fingers. 'Simple, my lady. You recall the palace of Herod?'

Emile nodded.

Fiore pointed in that direction. 'How far beneath street level?' he asked, and Emile nodded. 'Almost ten feet,' she said.

He nodded as if she was a bright pupil. 'And the floor of the Holy Sepulchre?' he asked.

'Ten feet below street level ...' Emile said dreamily. 'I see it.' She snapped upright. '*Eh bien. Je comprends tout.*'

Fiore bowed in his saddle. 'The street on which our Saviour walked must have been ten feet below this one,' he said.

The 'guide' looked stunned.

Fiore rode on.

The next morning, after distributing almost all the hard currency that we had as alms, the 'Crusader Army' marched away. I remember Jerusalem as a place of healing, as a source of both earthly and heavenly bliss that seems at odds with other memories of fear and stress, but there it is. I have seldom been so happy. And indeed, that time lives in my memory in a kind of golden glow, with my friends, my wife, and my Saviour all together.

The trip down to Jaffa was easier than the trip up, mostly because, having shattered the Karamanid Turk bandits, we had no opposition and a certain amount of grudging respect from the peasants. We rode down to the coast in much the same festive atmosphere as we had ridden to Bethlehem, and the weather was beautiful – almost too good to be believed, so that ladies put on great straw hats and wore no veils, or let their veils trail over this shoulders.

Nerio rode by Lady Eugenia.

Arnaud began to show signs of real annoyance, while Eugenia began to show the signs of a convent-bred girl exposed to a young, handsome man who attended to her every need. Nerio was the perfect courtier; he was like the hero of a romance, and she had no defence.

I was in a cleft stick of my own devising. He was my close friend. He was one of the pillars of my life; he had made every effort to see that I wed my lady. And yet, now, what he did was a danger to us all, especially if we were all going to ride together to Cilicia.

So the night we rode into Jaffa, as *Capitano* Bembo's face lit up with relief to see his great galley snugly anchored in the little harbour, I caught Nerio coming out of our stable.

'I'd prize a moment of your conversation,' I said.

He nodded. 'I am always at your service,' he said.

I drew him into the stall with Gawain, my charger, and I began to curry him, merely to pass the time. Nerio withdrew into the far corner, rather fastidiously.

'I'm wondering if you plan to grace us with your company on the road to Cilicia,' I said.

He gave a half-smile. 'I suspect that I will,' he said.

'Even with the news of your ...' I paused, because the great Niccolò was reputed his father, but the world sometimes affected to believe otherwise. 'Esteemed relative.'

Nerio smiled at my attempt at discretion. 'He will be buried by now. In fact, no matter how I hurried, he would be buried.'

He had a dreamy look to him, and I wanted to keep him talking.

'Where will he be buried?' I asked.

'Ah, we maintain a charterhouse in Florence, and he will be buried there. I have seen his coffin and his funerary statue – indeed, I was there when he reviewed the statue with his sculptor. He'll wear the armour he wore when he fought in Greece.' He played with his beard. 'How he would have loved this *empris.*'

'Yes,' I agreed.

'And the squabbles of all his nephews and his bastards will be over by now,' Nerio said. I could tell by the way he said it that he knew more than he was telling.

'You think perhaps ...' I paused. This was a gambit I had learned from my wife; you allow the other person to develop their thought. You don't have to do anything.

'I imagine many things,' Nerio said, with a smile that suggested that he saw through me. He shrugged. 'I confess that I have a little breath of a plan. Tell me, William – if I were to need a little military force, would you back me?'

'In Italy?' I said. It was an interesting moment. Riding down the escarpment south of Jerusalem, Emile had asked me what I planned to do with myself, now that I was rich.

And with my new-found maturity, I knew that it was a real question, but also a test. In truth I was not rich; and while I had learned to take money from Nerio without a qualm, I also had the intelligence to see that touching my wife for money, constantly, was going to erode any fellow feeling between us.

And so now, in the stable, I realised that I *wanted* to keep fighting. I was a fighting knight; I had a decent retinue, and another one with Hawkwood, if they were still alive, and it occurred to me that while Emile might resent handing me gold for fripperies, she might not resent helping me establish myself as a captain.

'I would be delighted,' I said.

'I'll pay, of course,' Nerio said. 'Stapleton will be going home with Lord Grey, but if you will lead a company for me, I believe we could …' He glanced at me. 'I believe that my father meant me to have his estates in Achaea, and if I act soon, I can have them all. The other "nephews" don't want the dirty work or the travel. I do.'

I nodded. I gave Gawain a pat and he leaned into my curry brush with enough force to stagger me against the wall of the stable.

'So you won't be taking the Venetian galley home,' I said.

Nerio gave me a twisted smile. 'No,' he said. 'I have another beast in view.'

I used my shoulder to put my horse back in the middle of the stall. 'Just what I wanted to talk to you about,' I said.

'*Dannazione, Guglielmo*! Huckstering with Arabs has given you a fine sense of controlling a conversation,' Nerio commented. 'Did that horse bathe in dust?'

'Arnaud is going to plunge a dagger into you,' I said.

Nerio fiddled with his dagger hilt.

'I'm perfectly serious,' he said.

'She's a princess,' I commented.

Nerio shrugged. 'I'm a prince. I'm probably richer than her entire family – by the gracious God, they've lost most of their lands to the Turks in the last twenty years, and King Peter is taking the rest. And denying them their trade.'

'So …'

He shrugged, reached in his purse and produced an ivory toothpick. 'She is beautifully well-born, related to everyone, and she speaks Greek.' He picked his teeth and I changed sides and curried my horse's off side.

'And she's beautiful,' I commented.

'And that,' said Nerio. 'Intelligent too – much more so than most Italian girls. She can ride, and hawk. She's like … a person.'

'So you love her,' I asked.

'Bah. Love. For children. I think she and I might make good babies and a good alliance, and if I come to be Prince of Achaea, she would be my – how can I say? My *bona fides* with the Greeks.'

'So you don't,' I paused, but this was a case of in for a penny, in for a pound. 'You don't plan to bed her and then get killed by Arnaud?'

Nerio shrugged again. 'I admit, the thought has occurred to me.

They've kept her in seclusion so long, there's more fire to her than just red hair. Give me five minutes alone with her and the deed is done.'

It's an interesting slant on friendship that you can, very thoroughly, hate your friends from time to time.

'You would force yourself on a virgin?' I hissed.

Nerio smiled in his most self-assured, asinine manner. 'No force would be required, I promise you. I might have to fight her off.' He laughed. 'You have not always been such a prude. Is this an effect of marriage?'

The curry brush made the only sound in the stall for a while. I was mastering my temper and trying to imagine what to say.

But Nerio knew he'd gone too far. He straightened his doublet, brushed some straw from his shoulder, and shook his head. 'I speak too broadly, I find,' he said.

I let the silence continue.

'I find her almost ... irresistible,' Nerio said, as hesitantly as another man would confess some terrible weakness.

I smiled. 'I know a pretty blonde chit in Famagusta, as elastic of mind as she is of body,' I said, quoting him.

Nerio winced. But he nodded. 'If I could have found a willing companion, even for a little silver, in Jerusalem, I most certainly would have tried to cure myself of this ... disease.'

I laughed. Not my best move, but I couldn't help myself. Nerio, the inveterate womaniser, was infatuated.

'You want to wed her?' I asked.

'I'd like to know if she's on the market,' Nerio said.

'Shall I ask Arnaud?' I asked. 'And if you ride to Cilicia with me, my good friend, will you swear on the Virgin that you will not trifle with her?'

'You are right on the edge of making me really angry,' Nerio said.

I came out from under my horse, who, I'm proud to say, didn't even flinch. He was really a fine horse.

'Listen, Nerio,' I said. 'Why do you want to hire me to lead mercenaries? Because I am your friend. But also because I do it well, yes? And the reason I lead well is that I pay attention—'

'When you are not besotted with a certain Savoyard.' He nodded. 'Bah, I like her too.'

'That's exactly true,' I said. 'So, to command, you must be ...

aware. And I am aware of you, and Arnaud, and Eugenia.' I paused. 'Even while besotted,' I said.

Nerio cursed. In Italian. Eventually he sighed. 'I'm quite sure you are correct,' he admitted. 'Now we should go drink wine with Miles, who is leaving us.'

'I don't think he is,' I put in.

And it proved that I was correct. Men betray their true intentions in many ways, and while Lord Grey and Sir Steven Scrope and all their men-at-arms sold their horses, I was aware that Miles and his squire had not sold theirs.

So in an uncomfortable evening, he finally admitted to his uncle that he would not be sailing home via Venice. 'I mean to help Sir William get the Lady Eugenia back to Armenia,' he said with his usual pauses and starts.

Lord Grey took me aside and offered me money – first to insist to Miles that he go home, and then to support him.

I knew Lord Grey pretty well by then. We had been together on and off for two years. He was the kind of nobleman who genuinely believed he was better than me; he also was inclined to treat me as a good dog. And not a particularly bright one. For my part, I found him honourable, a fine man of his hands, a good knight, and no worse than a great many of his class, and often better; his servants loved him, for good reason. Nerio held him in some contempt, and Fiore looked through him as if he didn't exist. He ruled Miles Stapleton's life and in many ways, it seemed to me that because of him, Miles was never going to grow up.

'I think the purse should go to the young man directly,' I said. 'He is one of my closest friends, my lord. I'll see him home.'

'It would be very much to your profit,' Lord Grey said. 'I would think he'd had enough errantry for three lifetimes.'

But give him his due; Lord Grey seemed to understand that Miles needed to do something by himself. He went off and found Sir Miles, and whatever words they had, they left Miles with a smile and a purse of two hundred byzants, florins and ducats in gold.

And Fiore – I found him outside in the pleasant evening air, waving a shepherd's stick at a pole and muttering to himself.

'Messire?' I said softly, because from time to time, when in a state, Fiore would simply strike you in the head if you interrupted him.

He made a *fendente* blow with the stick. 'Yes, William?' he asked.

'I wonder if you will join us on the road to Cilicia, or whether—'

'Yes, yes,' he said impatiently. 'Have I sold my horses? And why would I return to Italy?' He looked at me. 'Do you think that your lady would like to learn to use a sword?'

And so it was done.

And I went into our inn, and spent the rest of my evening with Fra Peter Mortimer, who was going back to Famagusta, and thence to Rhodes. And I'll confess that when he boarded the great Venetian galley, something within me cried out. I had become accustomed to being his lieutenant. I liked being second or third or fourth. As soon as the drums on the galley began to beat, I was alone.

In the end, we had twenty men-at-arms and more than a dozen archers. Ewan stayed with me, and his friends as well, and Pierre Lapot and l'Angars and all their people. Sir Miles had his squire, fully armed, and a servant, and I had Marc-Antonio, fully armed, and John. I had stopped calling him 'the Turk' now that I knew the difference between a Kipchak and a Turk. Ser Nerio had Achille, who was more a servant than a fighting squire, and Fiore finally had a squire. One of the turcopoles, a Christianised Arab named, of all things, Jesus-Maria, was so fascinated by Fiore's theories on fighting that he put his hands between the Friulian's and swore. He was an older man, in his late thirties, and he had the most horrible scar on his face, but he spoke Arabic and Turkish and a little Greek, and he was a remarkable man.

In fact, he proved a godsend, but I will not get too far ahead of myself except to say that in the Holy Land, goodness and evil came in many different guises, and that I met good men who followed the Prophet and very bad men who professed Jesus.

Of course, we also had six fine men-at-arms who served my lady, led by Ser Jason and Ser Bernard; and we had in addition the two Greek knights and their retinues of 'stradiotes' or turcopoles.

Also, we had Ser Arnaud and his cousins, the Cilicians. We armed them from our spares and weapons and harness provided by men sailing home to Venice.

So all told, we were a little more than fifty armed men and five women. My lady had two servants whom she shared with Lady Eugenia. And then we had Sister Marie.

Sabraham and I spent the next day, after the galley left us, purchasing provisions. Sabraham wanted to be moving; we were no longer an army of two hundred men, and we were all painfully aware that a large bandit band could take us. Sabraham's notion was that we needed to be a moving target.

I concurred.

But it took us an entire day to arrange the food and pack animals to make the journey, and without Jesus-Maria and John the Kipchak, we'd have been in a state. Even as it was, we only had food for three days; we had one tent for the women, and that was a Berber tent which smelled powerfully of camel.

Regardless, Emile was delighted by everything. She was happy, and that made me happy, and we set off on the second morning since the galley departed with high hearts.

We made our way up the coast at a good pace. Most of the coast was empty, and that was a curse with many roots. John and Jesus-Maria explained as we rode, and I learned a good deal about the recent history of the Holy Land. In short, the Mongols and the Mamluks had both sacked every town on the coast, with a few exceptions, and the population had been killed or sold into slavery.

Twice.

The emptiness of the countryside was suddenly explained.

At one point, looking at the ruins of a walled town, John shrugged. 'The old Mongols. They were not Moslem, not Christian, not anything but Mongol.' He looked at me. 'They destroy all cities and farms, and make all the world grass for horses.'

That was quite a picture.

But our stradiotes could range far ahead, and they brought us news that, just as the innkeepers in Jaffa claimed, there was an inn and stable at Caesarea. We pressed on to the edge of darkness and saw the welcome lights twinkling in the distance across the near desert that fifty years of war had created.

The inn was small and had bugs, and despite having my wife just a few paces away, I slept in my cloak in the stable, pressed between Marc-Antonio and Nerio, while Emile slept with Lady Eugenia.

Nerio winked at me before Achille put out the last candle. 'I have you, and Eugenia has Emile, and there is no justice,' he quipped.

I prayed that Arnaud did not hear him, as he was sleeping in the straw above us.

Caesarea was a squalid settlement, a squatter in the ruins of a great town, and we were not sorry to leave her behind the next day. I knew we had a long way to go, and I was a difficult husband, all but hauling my love from her bed to get us on the road at first light. She was not always cheerful in the first light of dawn, and Lady Eugenia all but screeched to find me beside her bed.

But we had saddles on the beasts by the time the sun rose. It was a good company; no one but Nerio was above a little work, and when the Gascons saw the rest of us tacking up horses, they pitched in. They're good people, Gascons, when treated fairly. Like most people.

But the ride to Acre was hard – most difficult for the servants, who did not live in the saddle. Emile and Lady Eugenia had probably ridden as far and as fast as most knights, and it was clear to me that Lady Eugenia preferred life on horseback to life behind gauze. She raced Ser Arnaud, she dropped back in the column and rode with my wife, and as she spoke French, she began to flirt with Ser Bernard and Jean-François.

Nerio's French was painful and slow, and Lady Eugenia's French, while courtly and school-learned, was fluid, and she and Emile began to chatter at a great rate. And my new wife, whose ability to flirt was legendary, had found an apt pupil.

Nerio writhed.

And my estimation of the lady's intelligence went up and up. It is fascinating to watch love from a distance; I could tell that she returned Nerio's feelings with interest, but I could tell also that she was not a slave to her feelings, and she didn't mean to fall into his arms, which cheered me.

Ser Arnaud watched all this with something approaching fury, and despite the demands on my skills of command during the ride to Haifa – encouraging, speeding, demanding, wheedling, up and down our column – I found time to ride with him.

He wanted to see my sword, like any normal man, and hear the story of how I got her, and we had a long conversation about swords.

I was worried that we were spreading out too far, and wondering if I needed to ride to the rearguard under Sir Miles, and urge him forward, when I sensed that Ser Arnaud was coming to his point, and *certes* he did.

'What kind of man is Monsieur Nerio?' he asked in French.

I smiled warmly, without dissimulation. 'One of my closest friends, monsieur,' I said. 'A man of great breeding and immense wealth.'

'And yet he plays the knight errant in the Holy Land,' he said.

'The same might be said of a certain Prince of Armenia,' I answered, with what I hoped was a winning smile.

We rode on a bit.

'I do not like his address to my sister,' he said.

'Tell me,' I said. 'Is your sister promised?'

He looked at me, and his horse started; my question surprised him enough that his spurs touched his mount's flanks.

'She was promised,' he said, 'but he died.'

'I'm sorry,' I said.

He laughed. 'You know, the game of ruling Little Armenia is a cruel one for siblings,' he said. 'My father intended her for the Khan. She would have had a difficult life, and perhaps been converted to Islam. But my little country needs allies.'

I nodded. 'Nerio may yet be Prince of Achaea in Greece,' I said.

I left Ser Arnaud thoughtful, and cantered to the back of the column on my little Arab mare. When I passed Gawain, he neighed. He wanted exercise, so I switched horses and rode him.

'I'm tired of eating dust,' Miles said.

'You want the advance guard?' I said.

Miles laughed. 'Do you think I could get work as a mercenary?' he asked.

'Always,' I said. 'A belted knight with your fighting skills?'

'I'm not sure I want to go home,' he said.

I knew that I should ask him then and there what the hell was going on, but I didn't. I was worried about my column, and having prodded Miles to push the rear forward, I got Gawain up to his lumbering gallop and rode all the way forward to where we could see the sea to our left, and slowed the front of the column. There, Syr Giorgios Angelus, the Greek knight, had the vanguard with Fiore to back him, and he was concerned about a cloud of dust well off to our right, in the higher ground back from the coast.

That was midday. I didn't allow them to stop, and like a chevauchée, we went on, men eating sausage in the saddle or chewing on bread.

Ayie! Bread in the Holy Land. A sore subject. They have no notion of bread – it's all flat, and the wheat is poor and ill-ground. I've had better bread in Scotland.

At any rate, I rode back to the main battle and moved all the soldiers to the right of the road, because unless a sea monster were to rise from the beach, our left flank was secure, and we kept moving.

The sun started to go down, and we were alone on the coast road. It looked to me as if there was a Roman road under our horses' hooves, but where we crossed the marshes north of Caesarea, the road was unrepaired, and twice the vanguard had to dismount, cut reeds and brush and fill the salt-swamp with a temporary road of fascines to join two sections. It was clear from the other fascines, rotting or simply reduced to dry twigs, that we were not the first travellers to be reduced to that expedient, but it slowed us down. It showed me, too, that while the Mamluks might claim ownership of this territory, it was more like a no-man's-land between the rival empires.

The sun was setting on a spring night when the scouts reported that we were within five miles of Haifa, and that there was a watch on the walls and a garrison and a Mamluk officer.

'Despotes, he says he will open the gates when we arrive,' one of the stradiotes, Giorgios, reported.

I had worried about this; we were, after all, at war with Egypt, and I had to worry that we would be taken. Set against that, the dust cloud over the ridge was almost certainly pacing us. I didn't want to spend the night outside walls, unless I was certain that there was no other choice.

Sabraham was with me, or perhaps I was with him. He left the arrangement of the column to me, but I often had the feeling that he, and not I, was in command of the column, and that did not rankle, really.

I reined in by him. 'One of us should go with Giorgios and determine whether we will be admitted,' I said. *And run the risk of being taken prisoner*, I left unsaid.

He nodded. 'I'll go,' he said. 'I speak Arabic and if he takes me, the Order will ransom me. If he takes you, your best course would be to confess Islam and become a Mamluk.' He grinned.

I grinned back. 'I'd be a terrible Mamluk,' I said.

We both laughed.

As it proved, the military governor of Acre was, in fact, an Italian

Mamluk. Or rather, a half-African, half-Italian Mamluk. His mother had been a Genoese, and he spoke Italian better than he spoke Arabic, and he welcomed us with a dozen well-equipped cavalrymen on horseback, carrying torches so that we could more easily find the gate. He put most of us in two hostels, but he took Sabraham and Ser Arnaud to his castle, and feasted them. Sabraham cautioned me against showing that I was an officer; he was still concerned that we were in danger.

In fact, we took every precaution. We had watches – just as if we were in a camp – and a constant flow of our men went back and forth to the citadel, so that Sabraham and Arnaud were visited all the time. We kept our watch both armed and hidden from prying eyes.

Acre was still a prosperous town, and they were in daily expectation of a pair of Genoese traders who were overdue. I met the Genoese bailli the next morning, and he begged to be introduced to 'The Countess,' whose pilgrimage was already being talked of in Jerusalem. It was in Acre that he discovered that we were quite famous – both for being wed in the Holy City, and for defeating Uthman Bey.

The bailli was named Giovanni Doria, a small member of a very important clan, and on his way to riches, I thought. He owned a warehouse and he and the Mamluk governor were on a first name basis. He came and made his bow to my lady, who received him right graciously, and he sat with the two of us in a good inn and shared wine and olives, spitting the pits in a way that would not have been acceptable in England. And later he returned with his own wife, a scion of one of the Pisan families that have traded on the Levantine coast for four hundred years, and Nerio joined us, and the three of them needed only a Venetian to represent every alliance and every rivalry Italians had ever had in the Holy Land.

Domina Angelina, the Pisan lady, told Emile that her husband said Uthman Bey was hunting us in the hills.

We stayed two days, waiting for the Genoese ships. With Uthman Bey hovering, and with the richness of the prizes at hand, Sabraham and I became very wary, and thought we'd just take a ship to Cilicia, especially as the bailli assured us that the Genoese itinerary would be either up the coast to Tyre if the wind was favourable, or over to Famagusta. I was not fond of the idea of returning to Famagusta, but it was better, I felt, than risking my own lady or the Lady Eugenia.

But two days didn't reveal so much as the nick of a sail on the horizon, and I thought about what the Venetian captain, Bembo, had said about sailing in early spring and trying to go north.

So on the third day, I walked up to the citadel. The Mamluks on duty were half-breeds – the 'sons of Mamluks' who were used as auxiliary cavalry. I was learning all about fighting in the Holy Land.

Mind you, they were a likely lot of men: all tall, all well-muscled, in silk and leather, with magnificent weapons, and they themselves in every colour of the rainbow from Mongol yellow to dark African black. And they were not suspicious of us, and in fact were, as far as I could see, better behaved and better disciplined than most of our knights.

I knew no Arabic beyond 'friend' and 'thank you' but I employed both, looked them all in the eye, and got some smiles, and Jesus-Maria passed their questions to me; most of them were about my sword, which they all handled and admired, and then I was admitted and given a pass. I still have it; it describes me as the Mamluk of the Emir Sabraham, which is tolerably accurate and rather flattering, all things taken together.

When I was alone with Sabraham, we talked in platitudes. I made the sign we had for asking if we were private, and he shook his head 'no'. So we went for a walk on the castle's battlements, which might as well have been French, and in fact, once were, and then out through the gate and into the lower town. We visited the tower with the arms of the Knights of Saint John, now occupied by a family of Christian Arabs on the first floor and another family of Jews on the second floor.

'Do you think it is possible that the bailli and the governor are trying to hold us here?' I asked him.

He cursed. I'd never heard Sabraham blaspheme before, and I was a trifle shocked.

'Of course you are right, Sir William,' he said. 'By the grace of God ...'

I told him of what the Venetian captain had said of the sailing season. He pulled at his beard.

'I should have known,' he said. 'And it is a long ride to Tyre.' He shook his head. 'We'll have to leave. And that will cause trouble.'

'And we can expect to get hit by Uthman Bey,' I said. 'Who has no doubt been gathering troops. But I take heart in knowing that we must be expected to enjoy the hospitality here for a week or two before getting angry. I propose we simply leave tomorrow and eat dates. I'll buy food in the market today and give no reason – we'll load the mules in the dark and leave by the main gate at dawn.'

Sabraham was looking at the young woman on the first storey of the tower, who was hanging her laundry where once the Grand Master had said his prayers. 'It could get nasty at the gate,' he said. 'And what of Uthman Bey?'

I looked out to sea. 'I may be dead wrong,' I said, 'but as long as they try to hold us here, I assume Uthman Bey either has no troops or is off in the north gathering Turcomans.'

Sabraham laughed. 'You are very good at life in the Holy Land, Sir William,' he said.

'I've had all the best teachers,' I said.

By late afternoon, I'd bought a lot of dates and biscuit in the market, and tried to do it in small lots and pass it into the stables. And George, one of Sabraham's 'angels', reported to me that he'd gone for a pleasure ride along the beach and happened to take a detour into the hills, and that there was no dust to the east.

There's courage, my friends. A Christian, riding *alone*.

You'd think that the bailli and the governor would have guessed it all, but the first, apparently, that they knew was in the morning when our column, including my not-so-very pleased wife, appeared at the gate. And since we had a pass, the gate guards let us go. Too easily, I feared – but before Sabraham, who had the rearguard, cleared the gate, an alarm bell rang and the Mamluks appeared on horseback.

They were brave men, and the more so because we outnumbered them. Almost all the professional soldiers had been withdrawn; it was clear to me that the half-Italian 'governor' of Acre was self-appointed, possibly almost as much a bandit as Uthman Bey.

He came down to the gate in person, and his guise of helpful servant vanished in two tirades about our ingratitude, the danger of the desert, and the likelihood of the advent of the Genoese ships. But Sabraham had played this game before, and I listened to them through the gate while John the Kipchak fingered his bow and my Greek knights looked thoughtfully at possible handholds in the wall by the gate. But the gate opened, grudgingly, and we were free, and riding, before the sun was three fingers above the horizon.

And if Emile thought I pushed the column hard on the ride to Acre, the ride to Tyre was harsher, and I knew we would have to camp. When the sun was high in the sky, I left Sabraham in command and took John and Jesus-Maria, and five of the stradiotes and Syr Giannis, and we all took a spare horse and rode quickly, cantering and trotting, until we reached the forested heights that mark the border of the country we Franks call Lebanon.

There was water, although it wasn't abundant. It was a chilly day, and was going to be a cold night, but we marked a campsite, and I sent John back to push the column along while we set up the tent we'd brought. I made a fire, and we began to build little shelters with a roof and no sides. We built them the English way, which none of the Greeks had ever seen, because their climate is so kind – two shelters facing each other, with a fire in the middle. We built six of them, and I was standing stripped to my shirt and hose in the cool air, so hot that steam all but came off me like an overworked horse, when my beloved rode up with the main body. She laughed, slid off the horse, and said. 'Show me' in a tone of wonder.

I took her into one of the little low shelters, and we were kissing like ... Well, like lovers.

She patted the cedar boughs. 'I will not lie down in the cedar,' she said. 'because of what I'm quite sure would happen.' She licked her lips. 'But I will mention that my Lady Eugenia is a heavy sleeper, and perhaps ...'

It was delicious playing at illicit love in a camp of soldiers, when in fact, we were wed.

And as the fates would have it, I drew the middle watch, so that I rose from my blankets and tended the fire with John and Marc-Antonio. We went well out into the darkness, two at a time with the third man keeping the fire, and watched the hills and the road. The moonlight was strong, and made strange shadows, but any veteran knows that moonlight plays strange tricks.

But when we were done with our duty and had carefully awakened our relief, I went quietly to the wall of the Berber tent and scratched, and almost immediately my wife came and took my hand.

We walked into the cedar trees a way, in the moonlight, and we kissed from time to time.

And we found a place where someone had made a pallet of cedar boughs. She laughed. I thought her the most wonderful woman who'd ever lived. I still do.

All my life I've heard of the wonders of moonlight, and really, it is all true.

The next morning, I was little the worse for wear, and my lady was as bright as a songbird. I helped her to mount, and she smiled through her riding veil.

'You are very beautiful this morning,' I said.

'I had the most pleasant dreams,' she said.

It was as well that she was in a fine fettle, for we had almost forty English miles to ride, and we had two horses who were the worse for a night in the cold air, and Maurice was sure he'd seen movement on the next ridge, and went to scout.

If the salt swamps before Acre had been challenging and the causeway unrepaired, the road over the Heights of Lebanon was worse. After the old road split to go down to Krak de Chevaliers to the east, the coast road became a track that was often blocked with fallen trees – some small, a few giants that were as long as a ship and could not be crossed, even on horseback – and all day we cleared the trail. In a way it reassured me; no one was laying an ambush ahead of me, and there was no one on my flanks.

But we were not going to make Tyre, and again we had to camp. We were very low on food, and unlike a forest in England, there were no king's deer to poach. In fact, Ewan had that very thought and walked off with his friends to see what he could bring home. The results of all their efforts were two rabbits that made a very delicious-smelling dinner for my lady and Lady Eugenia, while the rest of us ate old bread and dates and contemplated which horse we'd eat first.

We rose, hungry and very glad it hadn't rained, and moved off again. That day we were riding downhill all the way, and had occasional glimpses of the coast and the sea, and by evening we made Tyre.

On the causeway, Sabraham pointed at the ground. 'Alexander built this,' he said.

That's the Holy Land for you – in all of Outremer, history is waiting under every rock, and sometimes in the rocks themselves.

I remember that night passing well, mostly because that was the night that Emile discovered that I didn't read Latin and wanted to learn; or rather, that I read Latin very badly – I had, after all, read the Gospel at Rhodes, and in fact I had been a reader in London. But years of blows to my head had driven much of my Latin out, if very much had ever entered in.

And Sister Marie and my wife immediately determined to improve my Latin, and they began, that very night, in the courtyard of the best inn we'd found in Outremer – although, being Moslem, it had no wine – to teach me better Latin by reading the Vegetius I had purchased in Famagusta, what seemed like a lifetime before.

And very quickly, the verbs began to return to me, and in fact, Messire Vegetius was not so very difficult. And that made a pleasant way for me to have an hour each evening with Emile, and a rest from the cares of command.

And Sister Marie enjoyed it thoroughly, almost as thoroughly as she enjoyed swaggering sticks with Fiore, which the two of them did almost every evening, to the delight of many of our men-at-arms and the mortification of Lady Eugenia, whose ideas of womanly behaviour did not encompass hiking one's skirts with one hand and fighting with the other.

Tyre was no one's city; it had about three thousand inhabitants, and they were as surprising a mixture of refugees as you might find anywhere in the world, with Greeks and Franks and Arabs and Turks and Mongols all together in one town. Tyre had been sacked twice, and was almost exactly on the border between the Mamluk empire and that of the Turks, if fifty squabbling princes can be called an empire.

But they were perfectly happy to receive us when we offered a peace bond and some money, and we used a market outside the walls to buy food. I did not blame a town of three thousand from refusing fifty Franks with weapons the right to enter altogether, and instead we stayed at an inn outside the wall, a caravanserai, and we were only allowed in the town unarmed, five at a time.

We kept men armed and by their horses all the time, but we needed the sleep – the good sleep – and the plentiful food, and we took two days to rest. Sabraham took his two angels and rode off headed east, and I feared for him – and I wanted a glass of wine. And Lent began, and so there was neither wine nor fornication, and I admit that I wished that Sister Marie had not accompanied us. And Nerio grew frustrated, because apparently Lady Eugenia had given *him* up for Lent; she stayed by Sister Marie and they prayed together a great deal, and Fiore's sword practices grew more sustained and more ferocious as various tempers frayed.

I had a great deal to look after. And this, mind you, was only fifty men, and those of good heart.

But on the third day we mounted, gathered all our donkeys and a few new we'd purchased, and we rode for Beirut. The Tyrians had helped us, but at exorbitant prices, and we could not afford to stay another day, or to anger them. Sabraham returned to say that the hills seemed empty.

'I think we're lucky,' he said. 'Uthman Bey should be back by now.'

'Or we were seeing ghosts in Acre and there was no threat,' I said.

Sabraham had the good grace to smile. 'Always possible,' he admitted. 'Perhaps you are merely infecting me with your fears, young sir.'

The journey from Tyre to Beirut was very easy compared to what we'd just endured. It was a bigger town, and claimed a certain independence; they had, in fact, had an Egyptian garrison until just a month before.

They did not want to admit us, and so we camped under the ruined walls, all of Crusader work – good French and Italian stonework. It was Lenten, indeed – we ate a porridge made of lentils because that's all we could buy, and it rained, and most of us were wet.

On the other hand, our horses were mostly under cover and we got grain for the chargers, so we were, as a party, stronger and not weaker.

At Beirut we heard, again, the rumour of two Genoese ships coming along the coastline, but no one knew very much, and there was no Genoese bailli, although several people claimed there was such a man at Ladiquiya.

And we were warned, and well warned, even by Moslems, that there were Turks everywhere, since the Mamluk garrison was withdrawn, and one middle-aged man admitted to me that he didn't dare even ride out to his farm.

Thus began a small adventure in my path to knighthood.

The old man sold us chickpeas, two days running, and seemed an honest man, and Sabraham and I had just decided to spend one more night and then go for Ladiquiya. He was one al-Haji'Abdalah ibn Abu Bakr, which, let me tell you, seems to be the name of every older gentleman in Arabia. And Hajj, or Haji, I had already learned, was their name for a pilgrim who had made the sacred voyages, usually to Mecca, their Jerusalem – although most of them, except some Sufis, hold Jerusalem holy as well.

Don't try me, Chaucer, or I will bore you with my fascination by all the sects of Islam – Ismailis; Sufi mystics; Shia looking for their missing imams; Sunnis discoursing endlessly on their Sharia. John and Sabraham and Jesus-Maria (who proved to have an Arabic name as well) were not precisely 'teaching me Arabic' but it was all around me, and I'll tell you a strange thing – with Sister Marie teaching me Latin, it was almost as if I was being trained to learn Arabic, or that's how it felt. And Sister Marie, I'll add, was as interested in learning Arabic as I was.

But I have gone far from my path. As I said, Monsieur Abu Bakr complained to me that he couldn't even ride out to his farm, and I asked him, without thinking, if he'd like me to take him. And he would have kissed my leather boots, which I found a little difficult to accept.

I knew it might be a trifle dangerous, so I took John and Marc-Antonio, and at the last moment, Maurice joined us with his crossbow cocked.

'Boss says if you want to do the evening scout, I'm to bring you back alive,' he said. He didn't smile.

I went and kissed my wife, a familiarity she allowed. She touched my face. 'Where are you going?' she asked.

'To help the Arab gentleman,' I said.

She nodded. 'Very chivalrous,' she said.

I didn't think much about that comment, at the time.

We put him up on a mule and we rode out in mid-afternoon. I had my light harness on – brigantine and maille and leg harness. Marc-Antonio wore the same, and John wore a kaftan and a shirt of maille he now prized, taken from a corpse after the Ramalie fight, much different from ours.

I wasn't particularly suspicious of the old man. I imagined myself a good judge of character, although I was occasionally surprised, but if he was a dissimulating bandit, he was a marvellous actor.

We rode east, and a little north, into the hills behind Beirut, and up into the high ground.

Late afternoon, we found tracks – more horses than I could count, and Maurice began to look serious.

Abu Bakr nodded and told John we were very close to his farm. So we turned south at a place where two tracks crossed with an ancient roadside marker, or perhaps a shrine to some pagan god, and Abu Bakr pointed and we saw a very small stone house.

We moved carefully across his fields to the house. I knew he'd come for something, and I assumed it was money.

It was money, but it was also the old man's wife. The poor woman had spent ten days terrified of Turks, as we learned later, and no one in Beirut would take him out to fetch her in.

But the old man was no fool at all. He got his wife on the mule, and put a sack across the saddle, and John said we should ride.

I was already eyeing ground for a fight. It's difficult to explain if you haven't fought in open country, but I could feel them out there; I didn't think there were many of them. Little spurts of dust, and a glitter of metal.

'I want to fight on our terms and not theirs,' I said.

Maurice gave me a cool nod.

John raised an eyebrow.

I reined in behind a stand of trees that was almost the only cover for an English mile. 'What should we do?' I asked.

Maurice looked at John.

I'll mention in passing that when you are an English boy from Cheapside 'leading' a fight in Syria, you are a fool if you don't get advice, and follow it. Eh?

John sniffed. I mean that; he smelled the air.

'You ride with old man,' he said to me. Lucky me; I was in command, and I got to be the bait.

He nodded to Maurice. 'Left, or right?' he asked with his hands.

Maurice frowned. 'Left,' he said, as if asking to have a tooth pulled. He loosened off the tension on his crossbow and re-cocked it, and put a bolt between his fingers.

I went forward with the old man, who was plainly terrified, and his wife, who was cheerful; I think she thought she'd been rescued.

Little did she know …

We emerged from the trees and they were right there – six of them, far more than I'd expected.

I turned the mule around.

An arrow hit the middle of my brigantine. The steel held.

I had a little trouble talking.

I didn't want to lose Gawain.

I got the old couple back into the trees and turned Gawain again. The Turks – and they were certainly Turks – were circling us; two had gone east, and two west.

That left two in the middle.

I backed in further among the tall cedar trees.

'Go back!' I called and gestured, and Abu Bakr and his wife turned and fled.

I backed Gawain again and again. There was crashing to the west, and a high-pitched yip.

Then I took Gawain off the road. I went west, downhill; not very far, but there I found what you always find in deep woods – another old roadbed. Gawain and I slipped along it like a thief in the night, and I rode perhaps a hundred paces to the north, at a trot, and then I turned my mount back towards the road. I could see light through the trees, and a heartbeat later I saw my quarry; the two of them were thirty paces away, having quite intelligently halted their horses at the very edge of the woods.

By the time they saw me, I was at them at the gallop, with the emperor's sword in my hand. Now, I freely confess that Gawain's gallop is not much better than an Arab's canter, for speed, but they were on a road with trees all around them, and they waited far too long to turn. In fact, the nearer of the two raised his bow and loosed.

It was a fine shot. It took me on the snout of my basinet and vanished with a screech of metal and some sparks. He was reaching for a second arrow when I sang my war cry, and he flinched, reached for his sabre, and died, a second or two behind the action. I cut two handed, a rising cut from my bridle hand side; Gawain needed no hand of mine on his reins, not in combat.

His friend used him as cover and turned his horse.

I let go of my sword with my right hand and reached for the javelin I had under my left leg, pinned to the saddle by my weight; I got it free and threw it, a clean miss, and he was gone.

I went and fetched the javelin. I only had two.

As I dismounted to fetch it, my opponent burst from the tree line. Now he threw a javelin, and I think that at the last moment he couldn't decide between hitting me and hitting Gawain, because that javelin went just between us, and without thinking, I threw the emperor's sword.

I hit him; the thrown sword went into his chest just above the gut and he bled out. It was all luck, and he tumbled from his saddle. I thought I had a prisoner, but he was dead.

I fetched his mount, and his mate's, and I took their bows and swords and their gold.

There is always a little routier in me.

None of us took a prisoner. All our foes were Turcomans – nomads from Anatolia. It was possible that they served Uthman Bey and possible that they'd never heard of him. They were poorer than his men had been; two men hadn't even had swords, and they were all very young.

And dead.

And John noted that they had no remounts, which either meant that they were very poor indeed, or that their friends were very close with the horse herd.

It took us a surprising amount of time to recover the old couple who were our ostensible reason for venturing so far up the ridge above the coast. But there was no time to linger; there were horsemen to the east, and we moved down the ridge. I had the old gentleman behind me on Gawain, and Gawain, after a fight, was less than enthusiastic about the extra weight.

But we moved across the ridge, slipping from scrub to tree stand, to hiding behind a rickety old barn of stone and mud brick and weathered timber. The fields of this farm had been fallow so long that the ground looked like a plain of wild grass except where you could see a rough shoulder of what had once been a stone wall, or a gate.

Abu Bakr shook his head. 'Bad place,' he said. 'No one live here.'

At least, I think that's what he said. I was curiously like a passenger, as my 'men' were doing all the planning. They moved from cover to cover without a word, and I followed them. As afternoon wore into evening, I figured out what they were doing; John, who quite frankly, looked like a Turcoman, went ahead, moving rapidly, and scouted the next cover. Then Maurice would move, often flanking him, covering him from a distance. Finally, I would be waved to follow, taking the old couple into the safety of the newly scouted cover, where we'd sit waiting for the next move. And the whole time we moved north and west down the ridge, but further north of Beirut.

But before evening turned to night, we cut back along another low ridge. Now we were in a valley, wooded on both sides; Maurice was still keyed up, but John was not, and we made good time, jogging along as if we hadn't a care in the world.

And we had six extra horses. They weren't safe for untrained riders, and they all six had tempers – John loved them. Once we were clear of danger, he rode all six in turn.

'This is *Monghul* horse,' he said. The bay was not particularly re-markable except for her piebald colour and her ugly head. But she had a dignity the other five lacked, and John started to show off, riding circles around us.

The sun was a ball on the horizon when we trotted back into camp beneath the walls.

Emile was waiting.

I could see the storm in her face as I approached. And sure enough, as soon as I slipped off Gawain, she first threw her arms around me, in public, and then spat, 'What was I to think?'

I had not expected her display of anger.

I had blood on my gauntlets and on one knee, and I was worried that it was etching my harness, and my horse, my faithful Gawain, needed immediate attention. The plain above Beirut was not a desert, but the water was not good or plentiful. And I freely confess that, in that moment, the needs of my harness and my horse came before my lady's – the more so as I could make nothing of her complaints. I was well; I had never, by my lights, been in serious danger.

'You love that horse more than you love me,' Emile spat at me. I was standing in my arming clothes, currying, while Marc-Antonio used ash and rottenstone to take the blood off the steel. John had worked harder than I and wanted to curry the six horses, and Maurice and George and Jesus-Maria had all joined him. Beyond them, Sabraham hovered; he clearly wanted to talk to me, but would not interfere while Emile was by me.

I kept currying. 'My sweet, Gawain bore me all afternoon in the heat and a sharp fight—'

'A fight you rode to of your own will!' Emile said. 'You are a baron, a lord, my husband! Why not send our men? Pierre Lapot? Or Jean Francois?'

'Because ...' I paused. It was not that I was going to make an angry retort. It was that I had not simple answer. 'Abu Bakr needed the service of a knight—'

'Abu Bakr is an infidel!' Emile said. 'What care you or I for him or his wife or their brood? They are not our people! We owe them no loyalty, no service. They are not even servants of Christ! You could have died!'

'Abu Bakr has sold us food the last two days,' I said.

'You scared me,' she suddenly said, and there were tears in her eyes. 'You frightened me. Sabraham was worried that you were late, and I ...' She took a breath. 'I will apologise. This is why men think women are weak.'

I put a grimy hand on her face. 'I am sorry to have scared you,' I said. 'I admit I rode out without ... a thought. I ... fight.' I snatched a breath, because I had been working up to a fight, almost like a physical confrontation, and her capitulation left me shaken.

'Your hand stinks of blood,' she said, moving it away from her face. She looked away, and back. 'William. I have dreamed of you. Your face kept me sane in dark times. Don't go and get killed before I enjoy you a little.' She smiled. 'And wash your hands. And the rest of you.'

She leaned over and kissed me. 'And your Fiore is a godsend,' she added. 'I love the way he thinks. He should be a poet.'

'Really?' I asked.

She slipped away. I had trouble thinking of Fiore as a poet.

I went back to currying Gawain.

Sabraham came next. The area under the wall where we worked the horses had become my office, and now Nerio and Miles were in the anteroom. Out beyond them, Fiore was teaching Marc-Antonio in the twilight while Sister Marie watched.

Sabraham crossed his arms and raised an eyebrow.

I looked at him, and went back to currying.

'I've heard Maurice's report,' he said. 'He thinks the hills are full of Turks.'

'John calls them Turcomans,' I said.

Sabraham nodded. 'So does Maurice. Did you think they belong to Uthman Bey?'

'No,' I said. 'No. But … It's bad out there. I don't think this is Uthman Bey and us. I think that the Turcomans to the north know that the Mamluks are gone, and they are moving in. I think we've chosen a very interesting time to ride up the coast.'

Sabraham nodded. 'I would like to try for Ladiquiya,' he said. 'I think we can make it in three days. He cocked an eye. 'There's a rumour here that the King of Cyprus is raiding the coast behind us, and another rumour that a Geneoese ship took a merchant bound for Alexandria. We could be very unpopular here. Or be in the midst of a five-sided war.'

'Have you done this before?' I asked.

'Once, with just George. Never with a party this large – and I had a *furman* from the emir permitting me to ride abroad armed. And not while the Genoese and the King of Cyprus were making war.' He shrugged, as if a knight-donat of the Order of Saint John could regularly be expected to get an official military pass from the Mamluk military governor of Syria.

On the other hand, I was a relative newcomer to Outremer, and I could already see that by hurting the Mamluks we'd unleashed various lions and tigers and not necessarily improved the situation for anyone. And I could see that further military action by King Peter would only hurt us.

And I thought of the ruined fields. 'This whole area …'

He nodded. 'Devastated. In another fifty years, these cities won't be able to feed themselves,' he said. 'Still, if we move fast …'

I shrugged. 'I agree. Let's get an early start.'

'Goes without saying,' he smiled. 'This will be remembered as a great *empris*, William. And it will count as your caravan.'

Caravans were trips to the Holy Land, and knights and knights-donat often had their service measured by the number of caravans; I understood better why that was now.

Sabraham moved off, meaning to tell all our non-combatants to be ready to move, and Nerio and Miles approached me.

'We're moving tomorrow?' Nero said.

I nodded.

'Only, one of the Syrian merchants says that the Genoese ships won't stop here, but at Ladiquiya,' Nerio said. 'And if they come to make war, they will not stop at all.'

'He'd like to join us with forty camels,' Miles said.

Midday. There were flowers on the heights above the Bekaa Valley, and the trees were very green to the east. It was a beautiful day. It was the last day of April, and spring was everywhere, and despite my worries, I rode by my lady and wished her the joy of Beltane as our Syrian merchant followed us with his forty camels and his six men-at-arms, all looking like Mamluks in turbans and splinted maille.

Sister Marie turned her head away and made a sour-milk face. Lady Eugenia clapped her hands together and asked me what Beltane might be.

'It is a holiday, my lady. A festival.' I smiled.

'A saint's day?' she asked with her elven face.

I had to laugh.

Sister Marie shook her head. 'Pah! A pagan festival of fornication, drunkenness, and other sins.'

Emile smiled at them both. 'Ah, Sister, be kind to we poor women who are not brides of Christ. It is a festival where women are allowed to dance and sing – where you sit all night by a fire and welcome in the spring for the first of May. I have known a priest to compare it to Easter.'

'To the peril of his immortal soul – the waxing of the sun is not an event comparable to the birth of the Son!' Sister Marie said hotly. 'Sir William, I am surprised that you would tolerate this paganism. I thought better of you.'

Now she sparked my anger. I was growing tired of being lectured – by Emile, by Sabraham, by Sister Marie.

'I've known priests and nuns who felt differently about Beltane, in England,' I said.

'Oh, England,' Sister Marie said, her blood up. 'A land of heretics.'

Emile put a hand on Sister Marie. 'I think my husband means only to allow his soldiers an evening of fun after many hard days,' she said, and I loved her for it. Especially the word 'husband'.

Sister Marie sniffed audibly. 'I am no prude,' she said. 'I am not intolerant. But Beltaine is a Devil's feast. Not for Christian men and women.'

I rode away and found Sabraham, by passing down the column. 'Does the Order allow the celebration of Beltane?' I asked.

He laughed. 'Allow?' he asked. 'Well, brother. Let's say that in the English *langue* tonight, the Irish and the Scots and most of the English will be unusually merry, and there may be bowls of milk in the yard, but nary, nary a maypole to be found. And no green maidens.'

That lightened my mood. Sometime before Vespers, while Syr Giannis tried to find us a campsite by the coast, as far from the lowering ridge and the Turcomans as we could get, I rode up beside Sister Marie.

'Sister,' I said. 'I will be allowing a Beltane fire tonight. As there's not much wine, the festival won't be very riotous.' I raised a hand to forestall her argument. 'I'd have a mutiny if I refused them this, and I have asked Sabraham – this is within the Order's military rule.'

She sniffed.

You know, when you are young, and see a knight, or an officer of the king, you imagine that this man is instantly obeyed; indeed, you see it happen. And you think, *By the Saints, that's power. That's who I want to be.*

And then when you are 'in command' it turns out that you are in a web of relationships, and they are not unlike marriage. The Bible bids the man to command the woman. *Certes*, I'll wager those admonitions were written by men who'd never loved a woman.

My point is that Sister Marie's sniff was the best I was going to manage. And as we rode into our camp, I had the further pleasure of being addressed by our Syrian merchant, who respectfully requested to understand the religious dispute we were having, in fair Italian.

I almost snapped a short answer.

'In my party there is travelling a very learned man,' he said. 'He speaks Persian,' the Syrian added, as if this was the very highest guarantee of learning. His name is Hafiz-i Abun – he has travelled far, and he can perhaps resolve your dilemma. He has read all the Christian books.'

'I would be pleased to meet him, my friend,' I said. 'For the moment, I have to see to the camp.'

I thought no more about it; Ewan and Ned Cooper had built a bonfire.

Ned stood by the pile of wood, leaning on his axe, with which he made fires, built shelters, and killed his enemies.

'Proper job,' he said. It was his cant phrase. I think Ned had taken too many blows in his days; he tended to snap 'proper job' in answer to almost any situation.

I dismounted, because their work deserved a little attention and praise.

'That's a bonfire,' I said.

Rob Stone grinned. 'It ain't a good fire unless it scares ye a bit,' he said. 'All this 'ere cedar will go like torches at home.'

Nerio was trotting out into the setting sun with John and Syr Giorgios and half a dozen stradiotes, and I saluted them as they went by and then made my way to the tent to see that it had been well pitched, but there was no threat of rain at all. I found the ladies and their maids sitting in the last of the sun with a cloak full of flowers at their feet.

'Lord Renerio brought them!' Eugenia proclaimed happily, and Arnaud, her brother, met my eye in a way that said 'You see what I put up with.'

It took me time to understand that 'Lord Renerio' was Nerio. You can't be everywhere; things were happening without me.

There wasn't enough wine in camp to threaten hard heads in the morning, but I confess that while our maids danced around the bonfire, I watched the hills and twice visited my posts, which were doubled. A bonfire can perhaps hold back the night, and perhaps invite the faeries, but it may invite other, more mortal, foes.

Still, I loved my wife with her hair down and a chaplet of daisies, and I knew a poem or two, courtly poems, and I told her she was the purest flower, and she kissed me and said I would always be a leaf.

I was dancing when the Syrian came to the bonfire. He had with him a handsome older man in Turkish dress – a silk kaftan, tall leather boots with curled toes. The two of them watched us; Arnaud was not yet moved to allow his sister to dance with Nerio, and instead he danced with her himself, and Nerio threw flowers and compliments.

Emile leaned over and breathed in my ear, 'Don't let those two alone, or they will bring in the May.'

I laughed, and suggested we could do the 'work' ourselves, purely as a service to others.

She sighed. 'I don't think the small folk have ever been here,' she said.

When we had danced, with Rob and l'Angars and John the Kipchak, who was always eager to try anything new, John took me aside and I made a good bow to the Islamic scholar. And he was clearly more than a man of words; he wore a fine sword and a matching curved dagger. He had white in his beard, but he was hale and strong. I think he was no more than forty.

He bowed with his hands together, like a monk praying. 'I had wanted to give you my thanks in person, Emir of this host,' he said, in very passable Italian.

I made a good bow in return. 'Good scholarship is welcome anywhere,' I said, a tag I'd heard from Fra Peter.

The man smiled in pleasure. 'This is courteous talk,' he said. 'So many Christians are mere brutes.'

What do you say to that? *So many Moslems are misguided infidels?*

'May I ask you a question?' the man said, with another bow. 'My friend tells me that your soldiers say this is a pagan festival. And yet, as a soldier of your tripartite god, you allow it.'

I should have gone to an astrologer, who could have warned me of this thread in my life.

'My beliefs are my own,' I said. 'My responsibility is that my company – all of you who travel with me – are safe and happy. I will not force my tripartite God on you, my friend. Nor will I refuse my people a small joy.'

'There is only Allah,' he said. 'And while your care for all of us does you credit, your unwillingness to press the truth of your religion only shows me how weak your belief is.'

He smiled, exactly as a superior Roman priest would smile – he clearly thought that I'd be as glib as a beast of burden.

I thought of Ramón Llull, that great knight, who wrote the 'Livre de Chivalrie' and who died a martyr for the faith, not sword in hand, but disputing in Algiers.

So I made myself take a breath.

He was going to go on, taking my stupefied silence for granted. John was shuffling, a little embarrassed that the man was so rude, and yet wanting me to dispute with him.

Let me remind you that all this happened while my wife was breathing the fragrance of love five paces away, and we had real fears for our outposts and a Turcoman raid.

I raised my hand for silence.

'Have you ever seen a boy who parades his bravery and his prowess?' I asked. 'While an older man, a proven warrior or an experienced hajj watched in amusement?'

Hafiz-i Abun shrugged. 'I suppose I have,' he said. 'Young men are given to such things.'

'Are they braver and better for prating and preening, do you think, then the older, wiser men who tolerate them?' I asked.

Our eyes locked.

'Well said, Frank,' he said. And he grinned. 'You are like an expert swordsman – you lure me, and then the subtle allegory slips through my defence.' He laughed aloud, and offered me his hand.

Now, there are many reactions a man may make when he is beaten in a contest like this: he can grow angry; he can make excuses; or he can admit defeat – and the last is best done with humour. This man, this infidel, shocked me with the ease of his conciliation.

'So you would maintain that al-Islam is like a younger brother?' he asked.

I shrugged. 'I would only maintain that those who speak loudest are not always best, and as gentlemen, we both know that sometimes we should speak softly.'

'Now, Allah be praised, this is wisdom indeed,' he said. 'And this is your wife, and you allow her to dance without a veil?' he asked.

'She is a great lady,' I said, 'greater than I, so I would not order her in any way.' I shrugged. 'But you must know that we Franks do not always cover women's faces.'

'Nor do the Turks nor the Mongols nor the Persians,' Hafiz-i Abun said. 'Women themselves are not united that this is good or bad.' He smiled at Emile, who took his hand, and through John they managed a few exchanges. I could see that the scholar was charmed.

I thought no more of it. I went out into the darkness and checked my outposts; I enjoyed a single sip of wine from Sabraham's canteen to mark the night, and took another mouthful in my horn cup to Emile. I found her by the tent; she'd just put Eugenia to bed.

'If ever a maid wanted a festival of love,' she said, and rolled her eyes.

'Not you, though,' I said. 'I brought you wine.'

'Ah,' she said. 'I have found my festival of love.'

Well. You can't let a line like that pass.

We were up with the dawn; some old hands had indeed waited out the whole night to welcome the sun. I know Ewan got no sleep.

And our ladies wore their crowns of flowers all day, and when I saw Sister Marie in a crown of roses, I said nothing, because I am not utterly a fool.

But an hour into our day, we saw dust to the north and east, and the next hour only deepened my apprehension.

Sabraham felt the same. 'Sixty men,' he said. 'And perhaps three times that.'

I began to eye the country for a place to fight.

But morning dragged on until Nones, and we were still riding. The dust was out there, and I was tempted to aggression; my enemy was hanging back.

'Not Uthman Bey,' Sabraham said.

'Because whoever it is doesn't know what we have and is very cautious,' I guessed.

'You are a good student,' Sabraham said.

Afternoon. The sun beat down on us on the first of May, and it felt like summer along the coast of Syria. We were making excellent time, and I was beginning to wonder if we could simply outrun our Turcoman bandits.

Or buy them.

'Can we offer them money to leave us alone?' I asked.

'You really are thinking like a Hospitaller,' he said. He smiled. 'Most knights have to fight everything.'

'Perhaps my wife makes me cautious,' I said. 'But we cannot fight three hundred Turcomans.'

Sabraham nodded.

'My current thought is to locate our camp on one of these little points of land flanked by the sea – easy to guard. And then, as soon as the animals are unloaded, we take all the soldiers out on a sweep.' I pulled my basinet off and wiped my brow. I remember doing that all day. My helmet liner smelled bad. I wanted a wash. Or five.

'We can't catch them,' Sabraham said.

'We'll see,' I said.

And as it happened, George and Maurice found us a fine camp – an ancient site with two good fireplaces and a broad, flat place with stone walls for animals; quite clearly, other caravans had stopped there. In digging out one of the fire pits, Ned found a coin, and he brought it to me and dropped it in my hand.

'Proper job,' he said with a grin.

I took it to Sister Marie. It was copper, and had the head of a Caesar on one side and an inscription in Latin, but all in abbreviations like clerks use.

She looked at it in wonder.

It was twilight, and the tent was going up, and the horse herd was in one enclosure and the camels in another. Horses don't love camels, but they were growing better. Fires were lit; smoke began to climb to heaven.

'I don't like it,' Sabraham said. 'Best to sit tight. They won't attack us here.'

'There's not much water in this camp,' I said critically. 'And if they moved down from the heights and penned us in here, we'd have to surrender pretty quickly. I want to be sure we can ride away in the morning.'

'I think it's too . . . aggressive. You could lose a dozen men.' Sabraham shrugged. 'You are the commander here. Ser Peter was specific.' Then he looked at the ground. 'I'll stay and watch.'

I nodded. 'I'm sure I can do this,' I said.

Sabraham nodded. 'You probably can,' he replied.

That felt good.

I led all the stradiotes and all the archers out of camp. We were all afoot with our horses, riding and spares, by the reins, and we went along the beach quite a way, almost two miles. Then we rode up to the high ground, and I hoped we'd been invisible to our adversaries.

We swept east first, moving fast; every man had two horses. We moved through the rough ground at the edge of the wooded ridge, often single file until we found a good track.

It was just like hunting.

The light was failing too fast and I'd probably ridden too far along the beach, or so I thought.

And then, there they were.

The range was very close. Our surprise was complete.

So was theirs.

We didn't run head on to their scout party, either, but brushed the edge of it, so that what I saw was Ned suddenly dismount, and Rob take his reins. Ewan was already moving in some reeds to the north, his horse standing, ears pricked, head up, and reins down.

An arrow came out of the rough ground to the east.

John rose in his stirrups and loosed.

Three men yipped and broke our files, emerging from the rough ground. They were obviously shocked at how many of us there were, and the first man went down with Ned's heavy war bow arrow through him.

Ned's bow came up again, but Ewan took another man, and then Rob, mounted, nonetheless got an arrow off his bow, shooting east at a target I couldn't see.

I got a javelin in my right hand and gave a high-pitched yip of my own. Syr Giorgios looked at me and turned his horse, and his stradiotes followed him. Behind me, Ser Bernard's horse turned on her front feet and we all burst through the reeds together.

We'd caught a tiger.

There were a hundred men there, just a few paces away.

I threw my javelin into the first man I saw and fetched my second one, already sawing at my reins. Bows were coming up, but our adversaries were in shock, and the stradiotes threaded their column, bursting through.

I remember parrying sword blows with my javelin, jabbing overhand with very little result, and then Gawain did all the work. I threw one of the Turcomans to the ground with my javelin around his neck, and threw it at another man and hit him in the middle of the chest.

I went for my sword, got a scimitar on the head for my pains, and then I was out the other side.

I had taken a stout blow, and I shook my head repeatedly to clear it, and got Gawain around. The way home was through the column again.

Syr Giorgios thought the same, and we went in together, a horse-length apart, and I saw a man who seemed covered in gold, and a woman in a silk kaftan; I saw her in time to pull my blow. Then I crossed swords with another Turcoman, and I let his light sword turn my heavy one so that I could put the pommel into his teeth, and use the pommel as a lever to throw him from his horse.

His horse followed me out of the mêlée. Or ambush. It was all very fast – faster than I tell it. One of the stradiotes was probably done for, with a cut across his face that went through an eye, and blood everywhere; but it seemed he was the only man hit.

My three archers had all dismounted, and they were *pouring* heavy arrows into the column at forty or fifty paces range. The fringe of brush that had allowed this mutual surprise was now full of dust, rising into the last red sunlight, and the archers weren't aiming.

'Let's get out of here, gentlemen,' I said. I admit, I may actually have said something cruder, with the word 'run' in it.

I got my archers up and moving, Rob complaining about replacing war arrows in 'this 'ere 'owling wilderness' or words to that effect.

The stradiotes were gone; when they burst back through the column, they rode straight for camp. Ser Bernard was the last of us out of the column; he'd had the enormous pleasure, as a knight, of being mounted on a warhorse, in armour, in the midst of a tide of foes on lighter horses, and he'd put down half a dozen before riding clear.

We cleared the next old field, and we all changed horses at my insistence. And then we flew along the open ground, and the Turcomans who emerged from the brush line behind us were minutes late, and had not changed horses, so that, for once, it was a case of the biter bit.

I halted my little party, and John cantered up. The Turcomans were coming on very cautiously, a bowshot away.

Ewan slipped from his saddle and took an arrow from his quiver. It was not a war bow livery arrow, but a long cane arrow of the kind the Mamluks used for long shooting.

'Wanted to have a go,' he said, and loosed.

I couldn't even follow the arrow, it went so far.

He pulled another.

And another.

Night was coming on. John was watching under his hand, and he kept shaking his head.

The cane arrows would leap into the air like fireflies and simply vanish, they were going so far. Two of them flexed so much at launch that they lost power and fell close to us.

One exploded off the bow. That was exciting.

'That's a heavy bow,' John said.

Ned smiled. 'Proper job,' he said.

Ewan launched his last Mamluk arrow and got up on his little horse, and John shook his head.

'Too fuck dark,' he said. 'But they gone.'

It was true. There was no further pursuit.

We rode back into our camp in the small headland facing the sea; the fires were banked, and the whole camp was standing to arms – my wife had a spear in her fist, and so did Lady Eugenia.

Fiore had been giving them lessons. I wondered what Arnaud had thought about that, but I had other concerns.

'I want to move before first light,' I said.

Sabraham came and held my stirrup while I dismounted.

'You were successful?' he asked.

I'd have shrugged, but most of my body hurt. I didn't feel like raising the weight of my maille and brigantine with my shoulder muscles. 'We lost one man. They must have lost ten. But I fear they'll come for us in the morning.'

Sabraham nodded in the firelight. 'Hard to guess,' he agreed.

'I'm guessing that we can be ten miles away before they're ready to attack, and then we're a moving target,' I said. 'If we find a place, we leave an ambush.'

Sabraham nodded slowly. 'This is more like war than pilgrimage,' he said.

I lay down in Emile's arms for a moment of peace, and was awakened by her hand on my cheek. Outside, Ewan was clearing his throat, and Marc-Antonio was asking people if they'd seen me.

I kissed my wife, damning the fate that this was our life together. I slithered out from under the tent and walked off to use the cat-hole that we'd dug, and then sauntered back to get armed.

'Where were you?' Marc-Antonio hissed as he laid my harness out on the sandy ground by a campfire.

'Sleeping,' I said.

John rolled his eyes.

Our little pilgrim convoy was getting good at moving. We were all in our places while the moon was still up, and Syr Giannis rode out into the plain, moving carefully, and reported our area free of Turks.

I had learned something from John's tactics. I sent John with a dozen archers to move fast along the road to Ladiquiya. When he'd selected a good resting spot, he halted and sent us a rider.

Then the column moved with all the women and camels and a strong military escort – all the knights. We moved very fast, alternating a trot and a canter for the horses, and the camels were moved along smartly. By the time the sun rose we had made ten English miles, and I was waiting in a stand of scrubby oak trees, my reins in my hand and Marc-Antonio beside me cursing the midges, watching our back trail. We had Ewan the Scot, Rob Stone, Bill Vane and Ned Cooper, and all of Emile's men-at-arms, and we stood or knelt, waiting to see the sparkle of weapons and the sheen of horseflesh in the new light, or dust on the horizon.

Nor were we disappointed. Before my knees could cramp, the earth shook a little, and we could hear shouts along the coast to the south. A rising column of dust showed us – well, I think it showed us – that our Turks had tried for revenge, attacking our empty camp at dawn.

But I'll never know, because whatever they decided in the first light, it did not include pursuit. This is the thing I learned fighting Turks – they are very, very good at war. And because of that, you never get to use the same trick twice; nor do they fall into ambushes.

On the other hand, when the sun rose towards mid-day and there was no pursuit, Ned took off his basinet, wiped his face with a rag, and laughed.

'Proper job,' he said.

By which he meant that the English are also very, very good at war.

We each had three horses to catch the column, and we still didn't catch them until the edge of darkness. Sabraham and Nerio pushed them along, and after almost twenty days in the saddle, we were all hard and our horses were just as hard. Horses get in and out of shape as well as men; sea voyages and stable life are no better for horses than they are for men, and the ride from Jaffa to Jerusalem and then along the coast had trained our horses as well as it had trained us.

And it did train us. In the fullness of time, if I'm still telling you tales, you'll hear of my days fighting under Hawkwood in Italy, and then the War of Chioggia. L'Angars, Pierre Lapot, Ewan and I learned something on the road to Ladiquiya. I can't define it – it's about how everything counts from the moment you rise in the morning; how the trade of soldiering involves measuring the grain for the horses and seeing to it that your slowest man learns to ride better, rather than just being punished for riding badly. It's harder to teach in Italy, which is rich, and has no Turks. Nor the holiness that somehow focused me, and did as much, I think, for Miles and Bernard, but not for – say – Nerio, or Jason.

At any rate, we caught the column at sunset, and the lights of Ladiquiya were visible, twinkling in the evening air on the next headland, and our pace picked up. I remember riding towards the rear of the column, gathering men as I went, to form a rearguard for the last light, just in case the Turks had shadowed us. What I remember was the professional joy of riding along through the dust, pointing at a man, and having him silently turn his horse and fall in, so that we formed a skirmish line, two deep and ten horses wide, and then spread out, and all done without a word said. We learned from John, from Jesus-Maria, from the Greeks, and from the Turks who faced us, and the way I remember it, we were as disciplined a body of light horse as I have ever had the pleasure to command.

Our caravan trotted into Ladiquiya untouched. We'd lost one man.

I was the last man through the gates. Sabraham was waiting there with the emir of the town. It proved that our Persian scholar had won us entry in a few sentences, backed by our Syrian merchant.

It brings tears to my eyes to relate, but after I handed over my absolutely useless pass from the dragoman at Jaffa, and the emir read it, and we exchanged some compliments, he smiled and invited me to dinner through Sabraham. And then we entered by the Jerusalem Gate, and there was my little army, all formed by lances, standing by their horses as if we were going to be mustered by Hawkwood for our pay.

The emir of Ladiquiya rode over and walked his horse along their front. He smiled at me, made a comment to Sabraham, and rode off into the evening.

'He says, your *ghulams* are as good as his own,' he said. 'I think that's a compliment.'

I gave the lads a little speech. By then, I knew there was a pair of Genoese cogs in the harbour, and that we were safe.

Then I kissed Emile and went off to dine with an emir.

It was interesting, and a very great honour, I have no doubt. I sat between *ulema*, that is, their priest-scholars. Sabraham and I were the only two soldiers there, except the emir and a man I took to be his lieutenant. The Syrian merchant was not invited, but his passenger, the worthy Hafiz-i Abun, was, and held forth at great length. I was treated to a tale of his cleverness in solving a Christian religious question, which he told as if Sabraham and I were not there; the question was about the celebration of Beltane.

I smiled. I assume I'd sound the same if I attempted to lecture about a point of Sharia law and Ramadan.

And if I'm allowed a digression – later, when I met more Turks at Adalia, I discovered through Hafiz-i Abun that Islam has the same division on points of law that concern 'old' practices; some see such things with toleration, and others view them as heresies or straying. There are, in fact, many wisdoms.

I had my first sherbet, too. Delicious – like flavoured, pounded ice, but more clever. Mine was coloured and flavoured with honey and saffron, which might have been an astrologer's way of warning me that my next two weeks were to be intimately tied to saffron.

An advantage of dining with Moslems is that they drink no wine – or rather, Arabs do not – and so you awake with a clear head and strong purpose for the day. But, in fact, my exuberance was wasted. In the morning, I found that Emile and Jason had done all the work with the Genoese. It was all luck; they had no cargo, and the near annihilation of government in Syria since the sack of Alexandria meant that they were having a difficult time assembling any cargo at all. They took all the Syrian's carpets and all his glassware and then, with delight, accepted our entire little army as passengers for Corcyra at a very good rate. Corcyra was, and is, one of the best fortresses on the coast of Anatolia; the fortress is a small island off the coast, and the town is on the coast, an open beach, sheltered by the rock, and with access to one of the richest sources of saffron in the world.

It is also one of the principal ports of the Armenian Kingdom.

Arnaud made no secret of his joy, and I was repeatedly embraced.

The Genoese were as friendly as I'd ever encountered; it was clear to me that our money for passage was probably saving them from penury.

Nerio was particularly amused. He went into the bazaar and got us both money on a draft on his bank. 'You think we're a long way from Florence,' he said. 'But in fact, I was only charged eight per cent on this, and that's almost the same as our rate in Genoa or Venice – so that, in fact, we are very close to home indeed.'

The Genoese could only carry so many horses. At the same time, I could see that I had the nucleus of a company here, and the horses were veterans, just like the men. I was loath to part with such good horseflesh, and in the end, the Genoese, eager to increase their profits, agreed to take two horses a man. We took all the best, the Arabs and the best Turkish ponies, horses we could not easily replace; in fact; with John coaching me, I bought a dozen more Arabs in the market, and we left them the plugs that the stradiotes had ridden, and sailed away the next morning.

Messire Parmenio, the *capitano*, and his mate, Messire Doria, tried to explain to me why the wind was so fair for Corcyra; I'm not a sailor. Apparently we'd come so far along the coast that the prevailing winds were different from what they had been at Jaffa.

Not my business.

Arnaud leaned over the stern rail and told me of the country as we passed. Perhaps I should say, the ship was a type you never see in northern seas – very Italian: a two-masted ship with very round, low bows and a tall stern with a fighting castle. She was as round as a sow, really, and could clearly hold an immense cargo, so that Parmenio said that they often took passengers for free. We all slept on deck; there were no cabins, and we made a tent for the women of our horse-cloaks.

The country we were passing went from low and fertile to parched mountains very quickly as we passed from Syria to Anatolia, although Cilicia has deep, fertile valleys that stretch away from the sea, and you can see vineyards and olive groves on every seaside hill, and white-washed buildings.

The sea was far easier on us that it had been in the passage from Cyprus to Jaffa. And the two Genoese kept easy company in a fine breeze, their great lateen sails filled with wind.

Hafiz-i Abun was fascinated with all of it, pointing into the rigging and trying, through John or Sabraham, to explain Persian ships and how different they were.

We also taught him to play cards. That led to trouble; as soon as we'd taught him to play, Nerio introduced money, and Hafiz-i Abun rose angrily and stalked off.

Sabraham shrugged. 'Apparently the Prophet—' he began.

'Peace be upon him,' we all said together, in Arabic. It was becoming habit.

'... was against gambling,' Sabraham said.

John rather pointedly looked out to sea.

'And wine?' Ewan asked. 'Damn me. I know the sort.' He looked at Sister Marie.

She smiled. 'I have absolutely nothing against wine,' she said, and wrinkled her nose. 'I feel the Prophet—'

'Peace be upon him,' five of us said together.

'... may have had the right idea about gambling.' Sister Marie sighed, and began to say her beads.

But Hafiz-i Abun returned to cards, and eventually began to play for money with a ferocious determination that was fuelled, I suddenly understood, by his desire to defeat Fiore, whom he viewed, perhaps alone among us, as a member of his own caste.

We landed behind the castle at Corcyra, and when Arnaud went ashore, he knelt and kissed the sand. One by one his people did the same, except Lady Eugenia, who had told my Emile the night before that she wished that the voyage would never end. I was troubled for her, because no sooner were we ashore than she was enveloped in women, and veiled as she had not been for many days, and taken off in seclusion. In fact, I didn't see her again on that *empris*, and neither did Nerio.

I confess I was not there to support my friend in his moment of loss. Ser Arnaud wanted to take us to see every part of the country, and I was aware of the campaign season proceeding, of spring and even summer on the coast, and the Genoese were only staying three days to chaffer for saffron. But I agreed with Arnaud that we would make a party to go up country, to see the source of the saffron at the Valley of Corcyra. Emile and I went, attended only by Marc-Antonio and her maid Helen, who spoke Greek and had dressed as a groom through the whole of the pilgrimage.

We rode up into the cool hills, and again there was the smell of jasmine, this time augmented with oregano and fifty other herbs. And when we reached the caves we were astonished. There are two deep valleys, which the local people call 'heaven' and 'hell' and which, according to Ser Arnaud, were once thought to lead to those very places.

And there is a monastery built into the mouth of the cave of 'heaven', with forty monks of the Armenian rite. We heard Mass there, and Emile and I walked among the crocus flowers that grew like a riot, a forest of orange and yellow, a living fire.

We walked hand in hand, and spoke of the pilgrimage, of the life around us, of my plans for Marc-Antonio. It was in many ways the first time we had talked as man and wife. Eventually we reached a small spring above the carpet of flowers, with a stunted olive tree growing from it, and then above the pool of the spring, a great holly oak perhaps a thousand years old, or older, so big around that we could not, together, get our arms around it. And caught in its trunk there is a stone, clearly cut by the hand of man, with square edges, so that we wondered, and after a little digging, I found that the pool of the spring had been made of stone, laid up carefully with no mortar, and was very ancient.

We found a little patch of grass, and we lay on it.

'This is how I imagined life might be, if I were a man,' Emile said.

Now, I was used to her mercurial direction changes, but I was not prepared for this. 'If you were a man?' I asked.

She was looking at the clouds overhead. 'When I was a little girl, I dreamed of being a man. So free – to vent your anger when you wish, to kill your enemies, to ride about and see things, participate in things.' She looked at me. 'As opposed, my love, to sitting quietly with my hands in my lap while some arse slanders me; to calming the arguments with a husband who hit me; to sitting at home when the meanest churl with men's parts could walk into the mountains, giving no one a reason. Try being a woman, William. Try telling your father you intend to go for a walk.'

Aye. Well, I had thought these things, and more than once. I thought them about girls and women, about my sister, about Annie in Avignon and Janet, trying to live as a man in a company of mercenaries.

'I hate what they are doing with Eugenia,' she said. 'I hate how we all just let it happen. As if it is right that her brother shut her up with a dozen other women to live out her life waiting for some man to come and make babies with her – some man appointed by her brother. In a romance, we'd call a monster who did such a thing an ogre.'

I lay on the grass and looked at the bright summer sky. The flower smell was staggering in the high-sided valley, like a perfume given off by the earth.

'Women must be protected . . .' I began.

She rolled over. She was fast, and strong, and she got my hands faster than many men would have done, threw her hip atop me.

She was smiling. 'Must we?' she asked. 'Am I the worse for having lain with you out of wedlock, in a certain castle in *la belle* France?'

She was fast. She knelt on my right wrist, and used both hands on my left. Short of using actual violence, I had no chance of escape, and she was not light, my Emile. She was only three fingers shorter than me, and she had the muscles of a woman who rode and hunted; indeed, she'd ridden just as hard for twenty days.

'Are you saying I should not have told Nerio to behave himself?' I asked. I was a little uncomfortable, but not so uncomfortable as to fail to notice her scent, her slightly tanned neck, the strong muscles of her shoulders, the way her hair was slipping out of its net.

'I have no idea what I'm saying,' she said. 'I want to overthrow the order of the world and make everything new. Mostly, like Eugenia, I want the pilgrimage to go on and on. With you, my glorious knight, despite the ease with which you ride off and abandon me.'

She leaned down and kissed me.

Her hair fell around me, a smell of citrus and healthy woman.

'This has been the very best time of my whole life – all the way from Venice to now. I don't want to go home. I just want to wander the world. You can command our escort – that seems to please you. You remind me of my mother. She gloried in her housekeeping, and by the Saints, she was the best housekeeper I have even known, and she would fuss to make sure that the jellies were made on the right day, that the right cake was baked for the saint's day – things a steward and a head cook might do.'

While she made this little speech, she pulled her skirts up to her hips, which freed her legs so that she could sit on my arms, her lap on my chest.

'You enjoy all the details of war like no man I've ever met,' she said, pulling her overgown over her head.

I couldn't pretend to be anything but elated with the afternoon's developments. 'I do,' I said. 'There are few delights, for me, as wonderful as seeing a well-ordered company—'

'Of course,' she whispered in my ear. 'A well-ordered company.'

She unlaced her kirtle. 'Tell me,' she asked breathily. 'Tell me what delights might equal a well-ordered company?'

Emile was no blushing maid. She was a strong woman of almost thirty years with children. The sight of her – the lush skin where her breasts rose from her chest, the place where her neck met her shoulder, and she was tanned, and then suddenly her skin was soft and white, the muscles of her arms ...

Who can really describe the person they love? But she freed her side-lace and crossed her arms and pulled her kirtle up over her breasts, and she was naked from head to toe. In daylight.

'I can't think of any,' I said.

She leaned over and kissed me. It was a long, long, provocative kiss, and she let her tongue play inside my mouth.

She sat up. 'No pleasure at all?' she asked.

'None,' I said.

Her hands began to play behind her hips, and then suddenly she jabbed her thumbs into my side and I writhed, giggling; I am ticklish.

'None?' she asked.

And then, when the laughter died away, she kissed me again, her clever fingers at all my laces. And she released my arms and lay full length on me.

'Let's make a baby' she said. 'A pretty one to remind us of this day and hour, when we are in some draughty castle in France, awaiting the good pleasure of some old bastard.'

'But ... People?' I said, with the cowardice of the public man.

She laughed. 'Helen and Marc-Antonio have their orders,' she said.

And there on the grass in Cilicia, she showed me that there was at least one thing much, much sweeter than a well-arrayed company. But in truth, I already knew it.

We dallied there for hours; we swam in the cold, cold water of the spring, and made love again, to get warm.

Truth be told, I learned a great deal that day.

And ever since, I have loved saffron above all other seasonings.

Back at Corcyra, we were feasted by the Cilicians, and Emile tried to arrange for Eugenia to dine with us, or at least to visit us, and that's when we discovered that she had already gone north, to the capital.

And I felt some of Emile's anger. I understood her brother; if my sister was as beautiful as an exotic angel, I'd have been wary of Nerio, too. That is a man's part; but Emile had me questioning even that protection.

At any rate, we ate with the Persian, Hafiz-i Abun, in our company. He was sailing west with us again, at least to the next port, which was Alayie, one of the Turkish emirates of the coast.

'Karamanid,' said Sabraham. 'Held, in fact, by Uthman Bey's nephew. Or cousin. They are all related.'

'Dangerous?' I asked, looking at my love.

Parmenio shook his head. 'I have all the safe conducts,' he said.

'We are knights of the Order,' I said. 'I am not sure ...'

Messire Doria shook his head. 'They need our money,' he said. 'Fear nothing. We'll touch at Alayie and Adalia and then we're off to Rhodes. But we need a cargo.'

That night, in a sort of Christian caravanserai, a fine travellers' inn – we could, at last, lie in the same bed, although not in glorious sunlight – Emile asked me if I thought she could pass as a man.

I tried to use my hands to show some things that she had that might give her away; but she was insistent.

I had found that my love was whimsical, and that it took time and energy to satisfy her whims; but also that she was deeply thoughtful, and it was often worth the effort. I leapt out of bed, naked, and rummaged in my malle, pulling out a threadbare but perfectly clean linen shirt, a pair of linen hose I kept for when all else was filthy, and a pair of long braes more fit to wear on a cold day in Scotland.

'Let's try,' I said.

She produced a long linen scarf – quite possibly someone's white turban. By then, every one of our men-at-arms had a turban, and some atop their helmets; the women had them, too.

We wrapped her torso tightly. I admit there was some play, but the wrapping gave her the chest of a muscular young man. She put on the braes, hose, and shirt, and I laced her into my sweaty doublet.

I piled her hair under an arming cap. She practised walking like a man; I slapped my thighs and laughed.

She picked up my sword belt and put the emperor's blade on her hip.

She had strong hands for a woman; she had the heavy leg muscle of a horseman, and her legs were almost as long as mine.

'Not bad,' I admitted.

'I'm going down to buy wine,' she said. 'Let's see. Give me your purse belt and dagger – I'll die on the stairs if the sword catches on something. How do you wear this thing all the time?' she asked stripping off the sword. 'My hip hurts just thinking about it.'

In a purse and dagger, she looked like a handsome squire.

'All the girls are going to want you,' I said.

She blew me a kiss. 'I'll bring a couple back,' she said.

She was only gone a few minutes, and then she came back, red in the face, with a jug of wine.

'Well, no one took me for a woman,' she said.

'But?' I asked.

'Madonna, you were right about the girls,' she said. 'I could get used to being a man.'

So the next day when I was going to the souk, the market of the town, Emile would insist on coming, and as a man. This presented all sorts of problems, but to me, the most pressing was that if she was with me, she'd be more easily recognised. Also that I didn't really have many clothes.

But Emile had an answer ready, and I was fitted for two suits – simple stuff, in brown and gold wool. And then Emile and Helen unpicked them, shortened the hose, and re-cut the doublets.

I left her to it and went to the souk with Miles. Nerio was sulking, and Fiore was in the caravanserai yard, practising. Sister Marie had been watching Fiore, but she joined us, tucking in her veils to cover most of her face.

Miles and Sister Marie and I walked with Marc-Antonio carrying my purse. It wasn't far; the whole purpose of the caravanserai was to allow foreign merchants easy access to the market. I had some notion, having summoned a tailor, of buying fabric; I had seen superb silks in Jaffa.

I was lucky enough to find both Parmenio and Doria in the souk. They stood in the center of a huddle of local merchants – Greeks, Arabs, Turks, Jews. They were bidding on lots of saffron.

Parmenio waved us over, and we were served a sweet drink I'd had in Jerusalem – sugar cane and spices, delicious. The merchants all fawned on us, briefly and perfunctorily.

Parmenio grinned. 'I think I've just made a fortune,' he said. 'They're bringing in the second harvest of saffron, and I'm taking as much of it as I can buy. Worth more than gold, by weight. It's not cheap here, but it is cheaper here than anywhere else.'

Sister Marie nodded. 'Might I purchase a little, *Capitano*? For my friends in Venice?'

At the name 'Venice' Parmenio made a face. 'I suppose there are good people, even in Venice,' he said. He shrugged. 'Yes. Perhaps you would like to buy one of the smaller parcels I'm not taking – half a pound.'

'Goodness, how much is half a pound?' she asked me.

Miles blinked. '*Bonne Soeur*, an ounce is enough for a feast of many people, in the rice, or on the goose.' He blushed – Miles was delightfully like a maiden at times – and tilted his head. 'My mother loved to cook. And she loved to entertain Father's friends.'

Messire Doria and Parmenio were paying in silver for their purchases, and they had perhaps forty pounds of saffron, an enormous amount. It made a sizeable bundle, too, I can tell you, and yet a small bundle to represent so much potential profit.

With Messire Doria's permission, I too thought to buy some, and I approached the disappointed huddle of saffron sellers who had not managed to sell to Captain Parmenio.

Parmenio caught my arm. 'How much money do you have?' he asked.

'I have two hundred gold florins,' I said. 'I could perhaps triple that.'

Parmenio scratched under his chin. 'Listen, friend,' he said. 'I've spent all my capital, and you won't sell yours in Genoa anyway, will you? If I had two hundred gold florins, I'd spend every silver soldi on saffron. I'd borrow more, if anyone in this blighted town would accept a note of hand. Indeed, my brother captain is actually considering tacking back to Ladiquiya because there are better banks there.'

I turned to Marc-Antonio. 'Would you be kind enough to run back to the inn and fetch Lady Emile?' I asked.

He bowed. I took the purse and he walked off into the market.

There were other wonders in the souk. I looked at fine horses, and some curved swords, and some very fine maille, and some silk, but Parmenio told me that Adalia would have better silk and for less. The saffron merchants were patient, and I wandered a little, and then a young man leaned past me, fondled a piece of velvet, and frowned. 'I've seen better at Bruges,' he said.

My first thought was that he was insolent, for someone's page boy, and then, of course, I knew it was Emile.

'Mistress wasn't available,' s/he said. 'She sent me.'

I took 'him' at face value. 'Come along then,' I said. I led the 'young man' to the merchants. 'I'm considering buying a parcel of saffron, to sell at a profit in Europe. What do you think?'

'I love the stuff,' Emile said.

She gave me the most marvellous look, redolent with memory; saffron, and the hot sun by the spring.

I bought almost ten pounds, and then, taking a risk, I bought another parcel almost as large for Nerio. And as we carried it back to our inn, I began to think of the unaccustomed wonders of being able to walk out with my wife in public. I wondered if we had fooled anyone, but she went unchallenged.

I knocked on Nerio's door.

'Your saffron,' I said.

'Go away,' he said.

'Open the door,' I said.

'No,' he said.

'I spent all my money and I need yours,' I said.

He opened the door. 'How on earth could you spend two hundred gold florins in this shithole,' he said.

Then he smelled the saffron. 'Ah,' he said. 'You cornered the market?'

'No,' I admitted. He'd explained the concept. 'The Genoese have twice as much or more.'

Nerio had been crying. I could see it – face blotchy, eyes red. And there was a wax tablet open, and it looked as if it had been savaged by badgers – deep score marks through and through the wax.

He opened a small parcel and took the saffron out. It was a brilliant orange, even in the dingy light of his room.

'Ah,' he said. 'That's very good.' He looked at Emile. 'Where's Marc-Antonio?' he asked.

Fiore came in. I didn't even know they were sharing a room, as they were often unfriendly, to say the least. But Emile and I had the only really good room, and Nerio, who could be an arse, had quietly resigned himself to being cooped up with Fiore.

Fiore glanced at Emile. 'Very suitable,' he said. 'You'll find lessons much more agreeable that way.'

Her face fell.

Fiore went straight on into the room.

'Lessons?' Nerio asked.

'I'm teaching the women to fight,' Fiore said. 'It's fascinating.'

'What women?' Nerio asked.

Fiore laughed. It happened seldom, and it was never nice when Fiore found something funny; it was usually because someone had done something stupid.

'Imagine!' Fiore said. 'A beautiful woman that Nerio can't see!'

Nerio frowned. '*Dannazione!*' he spat. 'What bullshit is this?'

Fiore fell on his bed laughing. He was really convulsed.

I ignored him. 'This is your saffron,' I said. 'I spent your money.'

Nerio smelled it again. He allowed himself a small smile. 'Bless you,' he said, glancing at Fiore. 'I am distracted. I should buy all I can. I may land in Rhodes to find that I have nothing. This has all taken too long – I should never have played pilgrim so long.'

Emile sat down on his bed. 'Say rather that you miss your lady and that colours all your thoughts.'

'And who in the Devil's name are you to be so free with my lady?' asked Nerio.

His hand was on his knife. He was in a state; the state where men like a fight.

'Nerio,' I said, 'That's Emile.'

Fiore snorted so hard that snot came out of his nose.

Nerio's head shot around.

Just for a moment, I feared we'd gone too far. His nostrils were white, and his forehead flushed an angry red.

But then he began to laugh.

A little later, when Nerio had gone out with Miles and John the Kipchak to buy more saffron, I flipped over his wax tablet. Love poetry. I turned to Fiore. 'How'd you know?' I asked. 'About Emile?'

He looked at me with what might well have been pity in a man with any empathy at all. 'How could I not know? Shoulders, hip musculature, pelvic tilt, cheekbones. Ears.' He shrugged. 'What's saffron, then?'

*

We sailed in the morning. I tried to convince Nerio to ask Arnaud for Eugenia's hand in marriage, or permission to address her. He set his face and waded out to the longboat.

We wafted along the coast as if on a cruise for pleasure. Even the sailors were relaxed; we apparently had the perfect wind to get to our next port. Our consort stayed just to seaward of us, and men called back and forth. Sister Marie said her prayers on deck, and then read sermons aloud from a book she had, and then I had a Latin lesson and worked on Vegetius – fascinating stuff on scouts and spies. And words you never hear in Mass, like *exploratio*.

We spent the night at sea, on the deck, and late the next morning we were inspected by a Turkish customs boat manned, as Parmenio explained to me, by men who twenty years before had been Byzantine customs officials. Some of the Greeks had converted to Islam, and some had not; the border between the two was not as clear-cut as you might think. The inspector himself was Christian, in a gown that would have been at home in Pisa or Florence. He went through our bills very carefully. After some consultation with Messire Doria, he summoned me and Nerio.

'You are merchants?' he asked. 'With wares you are not landing in my master's lands?'

I opened my mouth, and Nerio trod carefully on my foot.

'Yes,' Nerio said.

'Excellent,' the inspector said. 'Will you go ashore?'

I said I would.

Nerio said he would not.

The inspector bowed to me. 'Here is a pass for you and one servant. Enjoy our poor little town of Alayie, Frank.'

Indeed, from the ship, it looked like a veritable garden of earthly delights. Unlike the towns of Syria, it was rich, vibrant with life and business, and thirty minarets rose over it. The call to prayer, when it rang out, was startling; all the muezzins seemed to compete at discord and disharmony, and yet the sound was haunting and oddly beautiful.

My palms itched with my eagerness to go ashore and see it.

I was unsurprised to find Emile in men's clothes.

'I need a name to call you,' I said. I had fears, very real fears, about taking her ashore. But I could tell that this was important to her, and that, perhaps, it was this kind of adventure that she'd wanted when she fixed her eyes on me in the first place. You see, I *can* see through a stone wall, in time. I could tell that if I craved adventure, so did she; that perhaps this was what tied us to each other.

So Marc-Antonio sulked with Achille on the ship, and 'Edouard' came with me. When she chose the name, tears came to her eyes.

'I miss my children,' she said. 'This is longer than I expected.'

'Even though it is the best time of your life,' I said.

'I can be both people at once,' she said.

Well, I understood that all too well.

Once ashore, we found we were to be guarded by half a dozen *ghulami*, good men-at-arms, all Turcomans, with heavy dark beards and long coats of maille over their kaftans. I had a few words of Arabic by then, but these were men of the steppe, and all they spoke was Turkish, and not even John's version of Turkish, although I greeted them correctly and made them smile, a promising start.

We walked the market, the souk, and then, with the help of our escort, we went to a mosque. 'Edouard' had always wanted to see one, and we took off our shoes, washed our feet, and went in.

When I came out, one of our *ghulami* pointed at 'Edouard's' feet and said, in French, 'Woman.' But he shrugged. And smiled.

I'm going to guess he was a Bektashi, or one of the other Sufi orders; I've met more of the steppe peoples now, and their Islam is more … elastic than the Arabs'. I think we were very lucky; we might, indeed, have caused a terrible incident, or even been killed. Instead, we had a pleasant adventure, bought some coral and some carnelian from far to the east, and returned to our ship.

Our consort, however, had found a cargo – the results of the overland trade. I feel I need to explain.

Out east, somewhere, is India. And beyond that, China, if that is not just a name, and the Venetians assure me China is real, far across the ocean to the east.

But the goods of India and China only reach Syria and the Holy Land by camel train across the high steppe. There is no ship that goes from China to Syria, and Samarkand, the centre of the silk trade, is in a desert.

But in the Inner Sea … Listen, we lost the Holy Land to the Mongols and the Mamluks before I was born, but the Italians and the

Aragonese never lost the sea. Not a Moslem ship sails much outside sight of land along the coast from Egypt to Anatolia, and while the coastal emirs all have galleys, the Italians hunt them. About the time I was born, the Turkish emirs began to fight back, with the help of their recently conquered Greek ship builders; that's when the Order took Rhodes, and it became a base for Christian ships.

I mention this lest you find it odd that a Genoese ship was welcome in a Turkish port. The truth was, without our trade, they'd have had no way of shipping their goods, because pirates of all races and faiths, or none, attacked any small merchant. Only big, heavy ships could sail that coast.

There's another truth, an ugly one; Parmenio was delighted to have us aboard because we were donats of the knights. The knights were reputed the most dangerous pirates in those seas, and Parmenio claimed that the Order was not above taking a rich ship and butchering the crew. I wasn't sure I believed it, but it seemed possible.

So when the other *capitano*, Messire Florico, found a cargo of spices and ivory from Africa and Yemen, it was not so unnatural. A Moslem merchant would move his goods as far west as he could, and then hope to find an Italian ship to carry them to a buyer in Europe. I didn't know any of this before I went out to Rhodes; by the time we were in the market of Alayie, I had began to understand why veteran knights of the Order all seemed to know everything about being a Levantine merchant.

And knights are supposed to have contempt for merchants, but I found it fascinating; not just the possibility of profit, but the adventure of seeking out a cargo in an alien land and then getting it home undamaged.

So, that afternoon, we learned that the second Genoese ship would stay another day or perhaps two. Messire Florico attempted to convince Parmenio to stay with him, but we all wanted to be on Rhodes.

So we sailed the next morning – another perfect day, with a blue sky and lovely white clouds.

I was on the deck with Sister Marie, doing my *hic, haec, hoc* while Emile and Helen used sword and buckler under Fiore's watchful eye – and Sister Marie's. I enjoyed watching them, and I enjoyed the Latin, and I was not paying any attention to the world outside the deck of the *Magdalena* until Messire Doria let out a volley of curses.

'Arm!' he shouted, and men raced in every direction.

I closed my Vegetius on a bit of tape that Emile had woven for me, and as soon as I rose to my feet I saw them – a pair of predatory shapes close in with the coast, but coming hard under oars.

I looked at the helm, and at Parmenio.

He nodded. 'Arm yourself. I can edge away, but I can't outrun them. On this wind, the best I can do is make them wait an hour.' He smiled thinly. 'You gentlemen will have to earn your passage after all.'

'Mayhap they are Christian ships?' I asked.

Parmenio gave me a pitying glance. 'Pirates,' he said. 'Don't imagine a cross, or a crescent, makes much difference to them. Dogs. Scum.'

Marc-Antonio had my brigantine on deck, and my arms and legs; I pulled maille over my arming coat, and watched the galleys.

Our Persian passenger came on deck, took one look, and went below.

Parmenio had no marines. His deck crew were well enough armed, and every man of them had a crossbow. We had a dozen fully armed men, and John, Ewan, Rob and Ned as well as Bill Vane, and they were already on deck.

'Are they worth anything if we take them?' I asked.

Parmenio gave me a hard look. 'I'll be happy to save my cargo,' he said.

Bernard was by me, looking under his hand. 'Not much armour,' he said in French.

Ser Jason had a heavy poleaxe in his fist. He was smiling.

'Have you ever fought at sea?' Parmenio asked.

I nodded. 'With Venetians,' I said.

'Oh, yes, I have fought the Venetians many times,' Parmenio said.

We all laughed. When you are going into action, everything and nothing is funny.

'The archers can begin shooting as soon as they can reach the pirates,' Parmenio said to Ewan.

'On the contrary,' I said. 'They should get below the gunwales. We should not show them the glitter of harness, either.'

I was looking at the low bows.

'I have fought this ship for ten years,' Parmenio said stiffly.

'Then you should enjoy this,' I said. 'If we do it right, we should take both of them.'

'They'll be packed with men,' Parmenio said, but he was looking at Fiore and Stapleton donning their harness. 'It's true, by the Saints, I've never had so many men-at-arms aboard in all my life.'

'Will their rowers fight?' I asked.

He shrugged. 'I doubt it. The rowers are all the crews of the ships they've taken.'

Fiore was serving out spears to men who only had swords. Pierre Lapot grinned at me.

'Shares?' he asked.

I nodded. 'Equal shares, men-at-arms and archers,' I said.

Parmenio looked at me.

I shrugged. 'Business,' I said.

Half an hour later, I lay at the edge of the deck, hard against the bulwark, in full harness, and my legs, out in the full Mediterranean sun, were bloody hot, I can tell you. I was looking out through a little hole in the bulwark that was really there for seawater and crap to run out in a storm. But I could see one of the pirate galleys framed perfectly in the little hole, and she was an elegant, predatory craft, all raked forward with a high ram spur like a fighting cock's beak.

The captain was Greek, in a long hauberk of maille; I could see him on his little command deck astern, and he was waving at something. Then his well-handled little ship shot alongside, and he called in Italian as the rowers pulled in their oars.

He was demanding that Parmenio ransom his ship. He called it a 'toll'.

He asked for two hundred ducats of gold. I could see Parmenio in our stern, high above me, and I could see he was thinking about it. I understood his doubts; battle was never certain, and my wife was sitting in the captain's cabin with my arming sword across her knees. The stakes are very high at sea – imprisonment, ransom, rape, life as a galley slave or worse for anyone, man or woman.

And the decks of that pirate ship were *packed*. Every criminal and routier in Anatolia seemed to be standing on the gangway, perhaps sixty men packed onto the half deck of a ship smaller than our own, and of course, there was another the same.

But in the end, they offered us no choice, and the first pair of pirates leaped onto the bows. They had no intention of letting us ransom ourselves, and they ran, as mad as ghazis, over the little foredeck, and a dozen grim bastards came after them.

'Up!' I roared, and we all got to our feet.

The pirate captain was the very first man to die. He was still looking up, grinning like a madman, which perhaps he was, and John's arrow went into his open mouth.

In the bows, we had a low, very solid bulwark in front of us, and all of us had spears save Ser Jason, who had a poleaxe. It was surprisingly like fighting at barriers; I was covered waist high. The difference was that none of my adversaries had any harness to speak of, and I was surrounded by the best knights a man could want as companions.

The sea rats rushed us in waves. Later, I heard from Ewan that they'd intended to board aft, into the stern windows, but a dozen expert bowmen had shot their boarding party to pieces before the first man could get across.

The Genoese sailors began to work their way down the side of our ship, shooting into the rear of the men trying to get aboard us. Their captain was dead; there was no one to tell them to pole off. The pressure on us at the bulwark lessened and then fell away; there were perhaps half a dozen men, all wounded, standing on our bow, but they had no fight in them. When I climbed over our bulwark, one of them jumped into the sea and the others jumped back onto their own ship to avoid me.

That's when a crossbow bolt hit me. Luck, or God's hand, saved my life; the bolt hit my left pauldron, skipped across my aventail and slammed into my helmet with half its force spent, but I was knocked flat, and only a mailled hand saved me from going over the side.

The second ship. It was coming, bow to bow, and their bow was packed with bowmen.

On the other hand, our bowmen were higher, and the sailors dropped the mainsail so that the archers in the castle could drop arrows forward. And meanwhile I was on the wrong side of the bulwark, and the man who'd just pulled me to my feet was the Persian scholar, now in a coat of maille.

But as our archers began to drop arrows into their archers, their bow slammed into us. I was driven to my knees, and a hundred men came for me, all screaming, or so it seemed.

I owe my life to my friends. Nerio and Fiore and Jean-François came over the barrier; I got to my feet, and there we were, helmet to helmet on the bow of a sailing ship, with fifty fathoms of deep water ready to swallow anyone who went over the side in armour.

We formed a sort of wedge; I was at the head of it because of where I'd fallen, and the Persian was on my left and Nerio on my right, with Jean-François almost against the bulwark to my left. Fiore in the same position to my right, and Jason towering behind him, his poleaxe up over his head.

I only remember the end. I was fighting with my baselard. I had broken my spear, and I had no time to go for a sword, and men were trying to wrestle me over the side, and many of them had some armour, or shields, and they all had helmets. And Ser Jason killed them. Mostly the rest of us stayed alive, and used our armoured bodies as shields; we pushed, clawed with our gauntlets. It was close, as close as any fight I can remember, and they screamed.

But between men in plate harness and men without armour on their hands and arms, in a close fight, breast to breast, there is no contest. I could rip a man's face off with the flange on my elbow, and as he cringed away from the loss of an eye, kill him with a dagger and go for the next.

It was like Poitiers, for a few dozen breaths.

And then the archers flayed them.

The men in front of us began to flinch away. Fiore did his *volte stabile*, throwing one man into two more, and all three went over the side. Ser Jason's hammer hit another helmet so hard that a piece of bone, or perhaps a tooth, rang against my helmet. Nerio, who was using his long sword with one hand on the blade and one on the hilt like a long dagger, put his point into a distracted man's eye; he did it with the care of a good workman, withdrew the killing point, and used his pommel to help the falling corpse over the side.

The Genoese, above us, shot a volley of crossbow bolts *down* into the boarders, and they broke.

I went to one knee to breathe.

Something tapped me on the helmet. Hard.

I turned my head, and Ser Jason leaned over. In his Norman French, he said, 'Next time, stay on our side of the barriers.'

They all laughed.

And then we all got to our feet and went over into the second galley. The first had clawed off; some bright lad had the spark to get away, and he forced the rowers to pull away.

Our more recent attacker simply made a poor decision – to stay and fight. It was a terrible decision; our archers had decisively outshot his, and we had fifteen men-at-arms who had not yet used their weapons, due to my foolishness.

They did now. I'd like to tell you that I stormed the pirate galley alone, but honestly, I stood in the bows of the pirate while Pierre Lapot and Etienne l'Angars earned their shares, killing their way down the gangway with Fiore and Ser Bernard behind them with spears.

As soon as we had a fair lodgment on their deck, their slaves rose against them. I'm told that this seldom happens, but it must have been plain to all which side was going to win, and suddenly the surviving pirates were being clubbed with broken oars, and stolen knives were thrust into bare feet.

Two hundred paces to landward, the second galley paused to consider rowing in to rescue her consort, and our archers cleared their command deck. Again.

That was the end of the fight. It should never have been a contest, except for my stupidity in leaving my barricade too early, for which I was rightly mocked. And the women in the closed quarters hugged most of us, and we started the systematic looting of the pirates.

The second pirate galley lay just to landward of us.

'We can take him,' I said to Parmenio.

He didn't look at me. It was only later that Emile said I looked like a monster.

But he gave the orders and we dropped down on the unmoving galley.

It was a charnel house. Aboard the second galley, the slaves had risen, and they had not won or lost. They had fought what was left of the crew to exhaustion; I went over the bow and five surviving pirates all jumped into the sea.

We stripped every shirt of maille, every decent weapon, but it was like stripping scarecrow routiers in Auvergne. These men were poor.

And dead. I think there were a hundred dead men in the first galley and as many again in the second and on our deck; two hundred men dead in less than an hour.

Sea fights are incredibly bloody. There's nowhere to run, nowhere to hide.

We pushed their bodies into the water, took the two galleys in tow, put half a dozen men-at-arms in each one, and Parmenio raised the sails for Adalia.

In Adalia we discovered that we'd just killed the notorious corsair 'Tête de Mal', who was reputed to be French or perhaps Algerian; that should give you an idea of the international nature of piracy. The Genoese handed over the wounded pirates to the justice of the Karamanids, and the governor ordered them killed.

They were killed on the spot. The *ghulami* killed them efficiently, without fuss; some of the pirates begged for mercy or for a priest, and others simply sat and waited for the spear or sword blow.

It rather put a pall on our feelings of victory. And in truth, there's no reason; I'd killed a number of them in the fight, and never given it a thought. But I didn't like that slaughter on the docks, and I still don't, although I cannot see a cure for it; they were bad men, and they were unlikely to come suddenly to righteousness. On the other hand, I know what Father Pierre Thomas would have said – that God was the judge of that, and not man; that in the eyes of Jesus, all our sins were about the same.

Any road, we landed, and were taken to a caravanserai for foreigners, which served wine; quite good wine. Most of the population was Greek, and the rest were Turks. Turkish women do not wear veils; they ride horses astride, and hit men who annoy them with riding whips – I saw this the first day.

And John found some of his own tribe, or nation, serving the emir as *ghulami*. So he went off with them, taking Jesus-Maria along, and leaving us with no interpreter, because Sabraham was in the other ship with our Greeks.

But among the Greeks, many merchants spoke Italian, and at our inn, most of the staff spoke Italian and some spoke French, so we could get wine and food well enough. Maestro Parmenio said that we'd be some days in port, as he had business up country, or he hoped that he did; he was trying to buy silk, and it sounded as if we were too early. And there was war up country, although none of us could make head nor tail of who was making war on whom. It sounded as if one of the Turkish beys, Orhan, or perhaps Urthan, was making war on the Karamanid bey on the high plains. Different from my Uthman, obviously. The Turks were all Uthman, really, or Suleiman. Or Ortan or Orthan.

I had a good look at two galliots building on the beach. There were six shipyards, all Greek, but it was clear that they were building a navy for the bey.

The second day, when Emile and I had walked out in the town – and tried, and failed, to meet any Turks – we were sitting out the heat of the afternoon in the cool of the inn's hall. Helen was fanning us, and herself, while playing at flirting with Marc-Antonio, who was sewing up a long rent in his arming coat.

There was a fuss in the courtyard, and Marc-Antonio, with every sign of a young man's impatience with doing work, rose and went out to see what was happening, and he came back.

'Some Moslem beggar asking to see the Christian lord,' he said. 'The inn's people say he's not a beggar,' he added.

'Well?' I asked. 'Which is it?'

Marc-Antonio looked a little ashamed, and the innkeeper's wife, a fat Greek woman, bobbed a sketchy bow. 'So, *Despotes*, he is a good man. A ... cobbler.'

She had trouble with the word, so that I still wasn't sure of the man's status. But one of the inn's boys brought him in by the hand, as the Arabs and Turks do with a person of consequence, and in truth, I've seen as much in Italy; if someone takes you by the hand, it is a sign of gratitude or close friendship, and if someone leads you by the hand, it is a sign that you have nothing to fear, and that you are greatly prized.

So the boy led this man, and he was fairly ragged, but in the manner of a working man and not a beggar. He was a Turk or an Arab; he wore slippers and an apron over a robe.

He bowed.

I rose and bowed.

'You are the Christian lord?' he asked. His Italian was excellent.

'I am a Christian. This lady is a noblewoman.' I shrugged. 'I am not.'

'Ahh!' he said and I thought he said it in consternation. 'She is the emira, and you are her *ghulam*?'

'Yes,' I said, smiling at Emile.

He bowed again. 'This I understand. I am one of ... some men. We ... serve. Food.' He shook his head. 'I have been chosen because I can speak in the tongue of the Franks.'

The innkeeper's wife, Anne, put a cup of cold water by the young man and smiled at us. 'They are a society for ... hmm. Entertaining travellers. It is part of their religion.'

The young man beamed his thanks at Despoina Anne.

'I am not sure we have served a woman before,' he said with another bow. He drank some water. 'But I come to invite you and your companions to our ... place.'

That night they came to the inn. There were sixty or seventy young men, all dressed in long robes with outlandish hats on their heads – tall hats of white felt with plumes. Some wore workmen's clothes underneath, and others had fine silk kaftans. And we went down to meet them: Emile wore a silk kirtle with a stiff overgown, and three veils, so that the Despoina Anne said no Moslem man could take exception; Helen dressed in the same manner, and Sister Marie wore her habit; all the knights and men-at-arms wore their best, which in most cases was a good wool doublet without bloodstains, but Bernard had a fine pourpointe covered in silk. And the archers were quite creditable in good cotes; Ned might have been mistaken for a gentleman until he spoke.

But the same might have been said of me.

We went unarmed, except wearing daggers or eating knives. It was an adventure, if you like, but we'd taken the feared pirates, we had seen the emir, and we didn't think we had anything to fear.

Nor did we. The men were all young, as I have said, and their association is called a *Fityan*. Hafiz-i Abun, dressed very soberly, was delighted.

'This is as good as home!' he said. 'In Persia, every town has two or three of these. Sometimes they are rivals, and they fight for the honour of receiving an important guest.'

And indeed, although they paid Emile every courtesy, they were most attentive to Hafiz-i Abun. He sat at the head of the table, and his opinion was asked on almost every matter. And he told stories, the way I'm telling you now, and they were delightful, and I wish I could remember one; there was a nightingale in one, and another was about a clever dancing girl winning her freedom, and another about a man who farted and farted; excellent stuff, and Emile was trying not to roll off her pillow, she was laughing so hard under her veils.

I was close to Hafiz-i Abun, and he smiled at Emile and nodded to me. In Italian, he said, 'We are lucky. These are fine young men, and also Ismailis. Almost heretics, really, but the tribal Turks believe many odd things. However, their sects do not distance women from men. There are places, even in my own country, where men would not sit with women to eat.'

So I explained that there were people of similar belief in France and Spain, but that in England and Italy we rather preferred to have women at our dinner tables.

Then he turned and spoke to the two Turks closest to him, at length, about a point of the Koran, which is their Bible. And I was surprised at how much I understood, with a little help from Sister Marie, who was a quicker study.

And then one of the young men danced, with a sword – stirring stuff – and then they asked Sister Marie to explain the Trinity.

Well, she knew her theology well enough, but thanks to Sabraham we also knew that this is, to most Moslems, the sticking point of Christianity. To them, 'There is no other God but God.' This simple statement cannot be glossed. There is one god.

And for us, we have the three who are one. The mere mention of three makes some Moslems say you are a heathen, an idolater, a pagan, and others hold us strangely deluded. They, of course, deny Christ's divinity. Nor, to be fair, any divinity for Mohamed, their favourite prophet, or Elijah. Instead, they believe that only God is divine.

And while I'm quite sure that old Mohamed was wrong, and probably some hot-eyed desperado in the desert, still I have to wonder, after fighting against and alongside Moslems half my life, whether they, who follow most if not all of the precepts of the Sermon on the Mount as well as any Christian, or better, are such bad men. We say they are deluded, and they say the same of us, and I wonder about what Father Pierre Thomas would have said about the pirates on the dock; that to Jesus, all of our sins might appear about the same.

But I am a soldier and not a priest. No one pays me to speak on these matters, and I suspect I'm a sad heretic at times.

Regardless, Sister Marie feigned a demure reserve that she seldom practised with us. But the Turks pressed her, and said, in effect, that they never got to speak to any kind of Christian holy person, and they were most respectful, but insistent. And when one of the young men referred to the inviolate virginity of the Queen of Heaven as 'a stupid myth', Sister Marie flushed so hot that I could see it through a white linen veil.

She rose to her feet.

The Turks clapped their approval. They were not mocking her. They wanted to see her fight.

Emile was worried, and she motioned to me and I went to her. Let me add that we were seated on pillows, whose tops were magnificent with silk, or brocade, and whose bases were leather; beneath them were layers and layers of *Rumi* carpets, which in England now you call Turkey work. In that one fine hall there were perhaps three or four hundred carpets, four deep all along the floors and more hanging on the walls, where in England, John of Gaunt might have five.

Which is to say we were very comfortable indeed. And rising to go to my lady's side was harder than you might imagine after a few days of wearing harness.

I think she was afraid for Sister Marie. But I could see they wanted to see Sister Marie in disputation with Hafiz-i Abun, and they wanted him to win. And this is natural enough.

When she rose, they clapped, because they were going to have some sport.

'You need to stop this,' Emile said.

'Sister Marie can handle herself,' I said.

Emile raised her veil slightly. 'And how well do you think Hafiz-i Abun will deal with being bested by a woman?' she asked quietly.

That was an excellent point which I had not considered, but by then, Sister Marie had gathered her thoughts, and raised her head and spoke.

'Master Hafiz-i Abun,' she said. 'May I beg for you to translate my words?'

He was not best pleased, but he nodded. 'I will,' he said.

She nodded. 'I would do the same for you,' she said.

He managed a smile. 'I may hold you to that, Good Sister. Now speak of your Virgin Mother, and I will hold my revulsion in the back of my head and be your advocate.'

She swept back her veils. It was a bold gesture, and some of the younger men looked away. Interesting.

Sister Marie was a strong-faced woman of perhaps forty years. She was not pretty, and yet I liked her face; it had so much written on it, and it had a beauty of its own. Not an ascetic beauty, either; the face of a woman who had managed a farm for twenty years would have the same character and the same power.

She smiled at all of them. 'I must, to defend the Virgin, first speak of Our Saviour Jesus Christ. I recognise that you see him as a prophet, and not as the Son of God – as a form of the godhead himself. But to understand why we speak of the virginity of Mary, you must also accept that for us, Jesus was not a prophet but the Messiah, and God, incarnate, which is a Latin word that implies—'

'Stop, stop!' cried Hafiz-i Abun. 'So much heresy and so many words!' But he smiled. 'Truly, most of these men will never have heard any of this. Let me explain.'

Sixty Turks sat, spellbound, as a doctor of Sharia law expounded to them the basic tenets of Christian doctrine. I loved him for it – not because he was one of us, but because he was *not* one of us and he was, as far as I could see, doing an honest job for Sister Marie.

Several of them asked questions, and he answered them.

'Go on,' he said at last.

'What did they ask?' she said.

'Foolish things. Ignorant things. Honestly, I wonder at their religious instruction if they ask these things.' He shrugged.

She went on to explain, in the simplest terms, the Trinity; I was delighted, as I will admit, to my own embarrassment, that the Trinity has often puzzled me.

At one point, Hafiz-i Abun interrupted her to say, 'But this is marvellous. I had never heard this so succinctly put.' he smiled. 'Full of error, but internally consistent.'

She finished her allegory of the Trinity as inter-nested globes of glass, which caused some of the younger Turks to clap their hands in delight.

She drew breath. 'So, if you will accept that this is what we believe . . .' she said.

Hafiz-i Abun raised a hand. 'A moment,' he said, and spoke rapidly. I could not follow him, but many of the Turks nodded. A sherbet was served, and some wonderful nuts in honey, and bowls of rosewater for us to wash off the honey.

Jean-François looked at me and raised an eyebrow. Not the most pious, I think he found the disputation interminable.

'Let's ask them about *their* beliefs,' he said. 'Every man likes to talk about himself.'

That might have been a good notion, but we were in their hall, eating their marvellous iced sherbet, and they were still asking the questions.

But Hafiz-i Abun glanced at me. 'What does our companion say?' he asked.

'He wishes that you would speak of your own beliefs,' I said.

Hafiz-i Abun nodded. 'Let Sister Marie answer concerning the virginity of the mother, a point that has always puzzled me. And then I will refute her point by point. Not, let me add, because I mean any harm to your belief, but so that these young men of *my* faith may not fall into error.'

Listen, you are all Christians. Here we sit in Calais, and I doubt you give your faith a thought, but in the Holy Land, sitting in a hall surrounded by Saracens ... I was becoming afraid, and I could not tell you why. Sister Marie was making them uneasy; I was fairly certain that Hafiz-i Abun was making an honest job of it, but at the same time, he was not one of us.

I wondered if we could all be murdered for being different.

And I suppose I was ill at ease at the notion that he was going to refute my religion, point by point.

Sister Marie began her explanation of the life and role of the Virgin. She talked about the Virgin's early life, and that she was a handmaiden of the Temple, and many of the Turks nodded. And then she reached the Annunciation.

I knew where she was going; I'd heard Father Pierre Thomas give the sermon on the Virgin's perfect obedience to God's will fifty times if I'd heard it once. But when she reached the point of the Annunciation itself; when the Holy Spirit came to Mary as a dove, one of the Turks stood up and shouted.

Every head turned.

He spoke rapidly in Turkish, very excited. And another of the Turks agreed, and raised his arms, and he rose and bowed deeply to Sister Marie.

Hafiz-i Abun frowned. His face darkened.

He was angry.

He was also our only interpreter. And now he was being bombarded with questions; it seemed that every man at the table had one. He began to answer one and another would be asked, and finally, he shot to his feet, and bowed stiffly to Sister Marie.

'This disputation is at an end,' he said. 'I would like to go.'

I took his sleeve. 'Have we offended you?' I asked.

He looked at me for a moment and his eyes narrowed. He was considering an angry retort, but he was a thoughtful man, when he didn't have his armour on. 'I am offended,' he said slowly. 'I would like to go.'

I didn't know what was happening, but I didn't need to know. He was unhappy, and he was our interpreter.

One of the Turks was shouting, now. He seemed happy, elevated, and it occurred to me that he was drunk.

He was seated next to Bernard, and Bernard was drinking from a pitcher, laughing.

'They have wine,' I said to Emile. 'Hafiz-i Abun is angry and wants to leave.'

'Let us not offend our hosts,' my wife said. She stood.

That brought instant silence, as she was 'Emira' and sat in the place of power.

She nodded to Hafiz-i Abun. 'I would like you to translate for me,' she said.

He nodded.

She parted her veils. I have seen Moslem women do this, and she did it very fetchingly, offering the men a glimpse of her face without leaving her veils open. There is a complex language to veils, and she appeared only to adjust them, but she also sent a message about power, and she had the attention of every man.

She proceeded to thank them for their hospitality and the wonder of their food and the comfort of their hall, and she wished them every felicity, and begged their forgiveness that she, a poor, weak woman, was overcome with fatigue.

And the shoemaker, who had first invited us, rose and thanked her in terms of abject servitude.

I rose to my feet, and all our people rose; a few were unsteady, but for the most part, we were sober enough. And twenty young men gathered with torches of resin and wood, very sweet smelling, and they lit them at braziers and escorted us out and into the streets. They sang a sort of hymn as they walked us back to the inn, and I began to see how silly my fears had been. But I walked by Hafiz-i Abun, because he was very angry. Not, I thought, at me.

The shoemaker came with us. He took me by the hand – an important gesture, as I have said. 'I had hoped you would sit with us longer, and perhaps make smoke together,' he said.

I was unsure what he meant by the last. When in doubt, smile.

'Why is the Hajj so angry? We only told him what we believe.' He was very earnest. I was probably only a year or two older than he, and I tried to imagine his life. He was an infidel cobbler from an alien world; his people had only just conquered the local Greeks; his father had probably been a nomad on the steppes. Yet there was something familiar about him. The Turks look just as we do, maybe that's all there is. He had blue eyes and a red-brown beard, and he could have been from Kent or Surrey.

I just grinned at him. 'Thanks for a fine evening,' I said. 'In England, where I'm from, we have a saying: never discuss the king or religion at meals.'

He nodded, his face serious in the flickering light of the torch.

'Perhaps this is true,' he said, as if I'd quoted a verse of the Bible or his Koran. 'But we talk always of religion.'

They sang for us at the gate to the inn's courtyard, and we sang them a hymn to the Virgin; it only seemed fair. Sister Marie's voice was very fine.

They cheered us and went off into the night.

Hafiz-i Abun stood in the main room of the inn, pulling at his beard. '*Guluww*,' he said.

I didn't know the word.

He shrugged. 'Heretics,' he said. 'Many of the Turks are ... very strange.'

It wasn't my place to tell him that all Islam seemed strange to me.

The next day, the local governor, himself an emir, sent for Hafiz-i Abun, and for me. We went together, and thus I got the next chapter in the story. Hafiz-i Abun lodged a complaint about the young men and their beliefs, and translated it for me.

The emir was amused.

Hafiz-i Abun kept using a phrase I didn't know, and finally the emir laughed.

'You know this word?' he asked, and repeated it.

I admitted my Turkish was rudimentary or worse.

'He wants one of these young fools flayed alive,' he said.

It turned out that when Sister Marie discussed the Annunciation, the Turks all cheered her because they believed that one of their Khans, Chingiz, had been born of a woman who was impregnated by a beam of light.

The emir grinned. 'I have heard this all my life,' he said. 'Many of the Saints are so born pure, from God.'

Hafiz-i Abun spluttered. 'Detestable heresy!' he spat.

I thanked the emir for his hospitality, and he beamed at me. 'You are a knight of the Hospital?' he asked.

I explained, through Hafiz-i Abun, that I was a volunteer with the Order and not an avowed knight.

'You serve the Order,' he said. 'And you are a *mamluk*.' He waved his hand dismissively. 'We have the same enemies, your masters and mine.'

'We do?' I asked, or something equally inane. I am not always at my best in the morning.

He went on to tell me a story that I wish I'd understood better. But I got the gist: that his master was at war with Orthman, or Ortan: that Othman had been the ally of the Emperor of Byzantium but was now dead, and was replaced by Ortan who in turn died and was replaced by his son Murad, who was now at war with the emperor who had been his grandfather's friend. It sounded to me like life on the Scottish Border, except with infidels. At any rate, the emperor was trying to find allies *against* the sons of Othman – the Ottomanids, I guess I'll call them.

'The emperor in Constantinople has gone to Hungary to beg for help against Murad,' he said. 'And because he is tired of being a puppet where his father was master.' The emir shrugged and waved for us to be served more sherbet. 'My master would be happy to ally with the knights and the emperor against Murad,' he said in the end.

'But you are at war with the Armenians,' I said.

He shrugged.

I suppose that when I was young, I imagined that war was simple – the English fought the Scots, the English fought the French, and it all made a sort of sense. But in Anatolia, the Karamanids could fight the Armenians for territory and at the same time try to ally themselves with the knights and the emperor against the Ottomanids. But both Ottomanids and Karamanids were in a state of open war with the Mamluks of Egypt *and* with King Peter of Cyprus. Concepts of 'infidel' and 'heretic' became blurry.

Italy seemed simple by comparison.

I promised to bring his words to my 'masters' in the Order, and he dismissed me with two magnificent gifts: a fine kaftan and a superb Arab stallion. The horse was very fine, and my eyes practically watered at the gift.

But to Hafiz-i Abun he gave a female slave – a Greek Christian – as well as a silk kaftan and another fine horse, as good or better than mine.

He pointed at the Greek girl. 'You are of the knights and have no use for woman,' he said with a smile.

Now, I knew in that moment that he was perfectly aware that I was married; that my wife was an 'emira', and that the slave girl and I were of a common religion. It was an insult nested in the gifts.

I bowed. 'Do you know Uthman Bey?' I asked.

'That rascal,' he said. He laughed. 'A son of Satan if ever there was one. What do you know of him?'

'We had a little tangle,' I said in Italian, and Hafiz-i Abun laughed and translated.

The emir slapped his thighs. 'You are a fine man for a Frank,' he said. 'You killed Tête de Mal – why did you not kill my brother Uthman?' He laughed.

And that was Adalia.

Our consort rejoined us the day before we sailed, and Sabraham had a long conversation with Hafiz-i Abun. And John reappeared, and I was invited to dine with his friends. And again, Emile dressed as a man – this time with John's full knowledge. We went to another caravanserai, outside the walls, and there we sat with Turks. But these were another kind of Turks altogether; smaller, and all the colours of the rainbow, but most had deeply creased faces, windblown to a fine red-brown like John, with Asian eyes and high cheekbones, although what could look squat and fearsome on a man with long moustaches and a scraggly beard could be hauntingly beautiful on a woman, and there were a dozen women in trousers and kaftans, sitting on rugs and smoking hasheesh with the men.

I had been warned against hasheesh by both Sabraham and Hafiz-i Abun; but Emile tried it, and Fiore tried it, and Nerio. They had tried it in Jerusalem, too, or so I heard.

But there was laughter, and wine. It was quite a good party, even though I understood little of what was said. Men rose and danced, and then women. The dancing was very fluid, very fast, acrobatic; any of the dancers of either sex could have made a living in Italy, I promise you, and yet, according to John, these were nomads, mercenaries. In fact, they were routiers; just as hard, very different.

And there, in the smoky, incense-filled caravanserai, I heard why my Persian friend had to be angry at the local Turks; it was because the steppe peoples believed so many different things, and smoked hasheesh and drank wine, and all of it had angered him. I had to smile, because what I learned from his anger was that he and Sister Marie probably had more in common than they thought.

Sabraham was on one side of me, and Emile on the other. Sabraham was chuckling as John explained.

'I'm sorry I missed Sister Marie defending the Queen of Heaven,' he said. 'But no doubt most of these people believe that the greatest of the Khans are themselves descended from God, just like Jesus. It's very hard on Islamic theologians.'

Later, when my eyes were trying to close from lack of sleep and someone else's hasheesh, a line of men and woman began to dance, and Emile rose and joined them and I had, perforce, to do so too. And we snaked through the wooden columns of the place, and no doubt I made a fool of myself, but then, so did everyone else, and John danced, his boots seeming to fly through the air, and many men clapped.

And then Emile vanished. I was with her one moment, and then she was gone, and Sabraham laughed and told me not to worry, so I didn't. She came back, and she had changed. She had kohl on her eyes, and wore the clothes of one of the Turkish women, who now wore her European men's clothes. But Emile, who was tall, looked magnificent as a Turk, with all her hair in two long braids.

John was drunk. He came and lay down – we were all on rugs and pillows, and it was very late, or very early.

'This, sir, a very fine woman,' he said. 'And many here would have her as wife.' He laughed, but I looked around in worry.

Sabraham shook his head. 'It is a compliment,' he said. 'These are wild people. They do not live as we live, and they only speak truth.'

'You admire them,' I said.

Sabraham's eyes sparkled. 'If I could be anyone,' he said, 'I would ride away with these people, and be a Kipchak on the great plain. They are free.'

'They are infidels!' I said, or something equally inane.

He laughed. 'They are Mongols,' he said. 'They are themselves.'

And later still, by moonlight, we were riding. I confess I can't remember whose idea it was to race on horseback in the dark with torches, but we did, out into the hills.

And Emile was on the stallion I'd just received from the emir. She rode beautifully, and though she had not ridden much with the short stirrups the locals used, she was up to the challenge. She was a light, expert rider on a big horse, and she and another women outdistanced us all, their torches vanishing into a valley and up the other side, and John laughed.

'Oh, she will win,' he complained.

And she did. She stood in the caravanserai's courtyard, flushed, and magnificent; her smile went from ear to ear, and her eyes sparkled like jewels by the light of a hundred torches.

By then the gates were locked, and we were outside the town, and Sabraham said he was going to find some straw and sleep. He stumbled off, and so did the Turks, one by one and two by two.

'You are magnificent,' I said to Emile. I could not think of anything else to say. She was like some pagan goddess, and in her triumph, I saw a different woman – the woman she might have been with the Turks, perhaps. Would she have been a war leader? Or just a good chieftain, an Amira. *Certes*, I saw in her the huntress; I had only seen her like this once before, and that was hawking with Nerio.

'Magnificent?' she asked.

In fact, she seemed to glow; the kohl made her eyes huge, even a little smudged from riding fast.

'I don't want this ever to end,' she said.

And then we wandered, hand in hand, until we found enough privacy to make love, and then ...

Well. There was no sleep at all.

And that was also Adalia.

I was barely alive when we sailed, and neither was Emile, and if I did anything to get my people on board, I don't remember it. Marc-Antonio was difficult, and John was mocking, and it was later afternoon before I realised that perhaps I should be surprised that my Kipchak was still with me.

'You didn't want to stay with your friends?' I asked.

'You are my friend,' he said, and clasped my hand. 'And Emile,' he said, calling her by name. 'She my friend, you my friend, even Marc Anton a friend, for a boy. We go and make good war. I go home rich.' He nodded. 'All good.'

Adalia was a dividing line in my marriage, as well. Before it, we were lovers. After, we were one. I cannot say it better. I came to know her, and she came to trust me.

Which was good.

The third day out of Adalia, we saw the castle of Rhodes break the horizon, and Emile took my hand and kissed me.

'I'm pregnant,' she said. 'And we have been to Jerusalem.'

CONSTANTINOPLE

May 1366 – September 1366

I f our pilgrimage was a dream of going to Jerusalem, Rhodes was the rude awakening.

Or perhaps not so rude, at first. But our first three days were full of the hard realities that had never worried us when we were riding across the Holy Land and in fear for our lives, or worshipping at shrines.

Within two hours of landing, Sabraham and I appeared before the Grand Master Raymond Berenger, whose Catalan French I found difficult to understand. He lisped.

It might have been adversarial, but the Grand Master put us at ease by going to the window of his solar and looking out over the harbour. There, riding alongside a stone pier, were our two captured galliots, towed all the way to Rhodes by the Genoese. The Order was buying them both, as apparently Maestro Parmenio had expected.

'A good *empris*,' the Grand Master said.

Come, said I to myself, *that's a good start*. I was still thrilled that I would be a father; thrilled that I was married.

Then Sabraham described the caravan from beginning to end as I sat silent, fidgeting with my sword hilt. But when Sabraham was done, Grand Master Berenger began to question me, and his questions were uncomfortable.

'You married the Comtesse d'Herblay?' he asked.

'Yes, My Lord,' I said. I heard the ice in his tone.

'With whose permission?' he asked. 'Did you have the permission of her sovereign lord, the Green Count of Savoy?'

I shook my head. 'No, My Lord.'

He nodded. 'And Peter de Mortimer gave his consent for *you* to wed, I take it?' he asked.

Oh, I do not like to burn a friend.

Sabraham spoke up. 'Yes, Fra Peter gave his consent after a tribunal.'

I had forgotten the tribunal. It had, indeed, been quite friendly.

Berenger nodded and steepled his hands. 'So. There was a tribunal.' He looked at me. 'You intend to continue to serve the Order, young man?'

I was, in fact, uncertain. 'I must consult my lady wife,' I said. 'And I have promised Ser Renerio Acciaioli to serve him in the Morea when he asks.'

Berenger ran his fingers through his beard. One does not get to be Grand Master of the Hospitallers without enormous political sense. He raised a hand and Fra Robert Hales came in. The Englishman frowned at me – not a good sign – and went and listened to the Grand Master, and then whispered in his ear.

Then he smiled at me.

In English, he said, 'You will do the Order good service in Greece.' He bowed, and left the room.

Berenger watched him go. 'Fra Robert reminds me that the Acciaioli clan are our allies in the Morea, and that his brother the Bishop of Patras has our writ for our lands in the south.' He nodded. 'So – you are a brave young man, and your caravan to Jerusalem will be accepted. Sabraham, you are, as usual, indispensable.'

'I make every effort,' he said. 'But Sir William was in command.'

'I have no doubt,' Berenger said.

The Grand Master leaned back. I could see that he had high boots and spurs on under his brown gown; a clash of cultures, the man of the church and the man of war.

'Tell me of Adalia, Sir William,' he said.

I had the feeling that this, and nothing else, was the real reason we'd been summoned on such short notice.

I told him everything I remembered, which did not include the name of the emir, so that I worried I sounded a fool, but Sabraham had all the names at his fingertips, and he laughed when I called Murad Bey's men 'Ottomanids.'

'Well put,' he said. 'You are getting the hang of this.'

The Grand Master frowned. 'Murad Bey is surely Murad Sultan, now?'

'And owner of a third of Europe,' Fra Robert said, returning with a basket of parchment scrolls. He handed two to the Grand Master and then kicked a stool over from the wall. 'I had not heard that the emperor had gone to Hungary. I begin to fear that Amadeus of Savoy, the Green Count, has made a separate agreement to lead a very different crusade. Sir William, are you certain that this emir was offering you an alliance against Murad?'

I looked at Sabraham for support. Sabraham looked at his scabbard.

'I wish I had been there,' Sabraham said.

'I'm sure,' I said.

'Maybe he was just playing Sir William,' Hales said.

Berenger frowned. 'We must know. I'd be delighted to have an alliance with Damat Ali Bey against his brother-in-law.'

'I could go back,' I said.

Sabraham nodded. 'I'll go back,' he said, quite happily. 'I speak the language.'

Well, that was that, and it was ten years and more before I went back myself, but that's another story.

The Grand Master dismissed us, and then, as we rose, said, 'Who is this infidel scholar you have in your train, Sir William?'

It was true; Hafiz-i Abun had sailed with us. He was going on to Constantinople and thence across the Black Sea to his home in Persia, and the Genoese offered him passage at least as far as Lesvos and possibly Galata.

'A harmless man, My Lord. A scholar – and a fine man-at-arms. We fought pirates together.' I tried a smile.

No one else was smiling. 'We are not friends with infidels, Sir William,' the Grand Master cautioned. 'He has a Christian slave on board that ship.'

Almost, I snapped a retort about Damat Ali Bey and the Karamanids. It was in my mouth and in my head to speak.

Sabraham nodded. 'We understand, My Lord, but the Persian gentleman opened many doors and was an ally.'

'See to it that he gains no information about the Order during his visit. Where is he to lodge?' the Grand Master asked in his lisping voice. 'Offer to purchase his Christian slave. Do not accept "no" as an answer.'

I bowed and looked at Fra Robert Hales, who was, next to the Prior of England, the next most senior Englishman in the Order. 'I'd hoped to bring him to our *langue*,' I said. 'His master is in Persia.'

Have I mentioned this before? The *langues* are the Order's houses, so that the knights and brothers have the comfort of living with men who speak the same language. This can be odd; the English *langue* includes the Irish, for example – trust me, we don't speak the same language.

That's beside the point. The English *langue* is the finest on Rhodes and has the best rooms, and the best wine and beer, as well.

Fra Robert nodded. 'Yes. The shahs and the khans. Persia is a very complicated place. I would love a word with this worthy gentleman, and with a scribe to hand. The English *langue* will do very well.'

We all bowed, and I thought my troubles were over.

Certainly, in the next day, it appeared so. Having made a pilgrimage, armed, and had it 'counted' as a caravan, I was able to put a gold border on my arms, and I noted that knights of the Order spoke to me with a little less condescension. I happened to meet my former nemesis, Fra Daniele, with the admiral, Ferlino di Airasca, at Matins, and he bowed to me – an unheard-of courtesy – and when he passed me, whispered, 'Two galliots for the fleet?'

And Fra Ferlino grinned. 'I'm in your debt, Englishman. We need every ship this summer.'

For the rest, though, it was complication on complication. Nothing in Rhodes is done for the convenience of a married knight. My wife could only stay with the nuns without me; indeed, one of the senior sisters protested that, as a married woman whose husband was nearby, she threatened to involve them all in carnal sin, and the good sister did not know how nearly correct she was.

And men-at-arms cost money at the best of times, but now, they were no longer layabout crusaders. They were, in every way, my retinue. That meant inns, and food, and money.

And Nerio, the endless source of my false wealth, was suddenly a dry well. It hurt him; he seemed to shrink.

The moneylenders all refused him any advance, nor would anyone on the island cash a bill.

'I have no idea what this is about,' he said. He threw himself into a chair in the English *langue*. 'I'd go to the Grand Master if I thought he could alter the situation. Something has happened somewhere, and I do not know what it is. And no one will tell me. Has our bank suspended payment? Impossible. My brothers have cut me out of the will? Absurd, but even if true, I have my own funds, my own estates.' He put a hand over his face, a thing I had never seen him do before.

That was the first bad sign.

The second appeared on our second night, when Emile was hosted by the English knights. It was a very kind gesture; the Grand Master had let it be known that my nuptials had his blessing, and that was no small thing, as you will hear.

We were sitting in our inn, and the great hall of the inn was full of men and a few women; servants bustled with food.

I was just hearing that Sir Robert Hales – Fra Robert, that is – was going home to England. He was to take the news of the victory and raise more money. He would be collecting Lord Grey at Venice. I also heard that Fra Peter Mortimer, my own knight, was either in Famagusta or had already sailed for Venice.

'Ah, Venice,' I said, or something like, because if I had not been born an Englishman, I'd have wanted to be a Venetian.

'Do you know Tamworth or Lord Hereford, Sir William?' he asked.

I did not. 'I'm sorry, My Lord,' I said. 'Lord Hereford is but a name to me.'

Hales nodded. He had a long beard, split in the middle and combed to two spikes; it made him look a little like the Devil. 'I hear they will be in Venice,' he said, 'with a party of Englishmen. Fra Peter and I are to meet them and escort them to Milan.' He showed me a scroll with the royal seal of England.

I probably shrugged.

'Read it,' he said.

So I did.

Your name, Master Chaucer, jumped to my eye. So did the style of Prince Lionel, and the purpose – a marriage. And the mention of John Hawkwood. The letter was, in fact, far too candid. It laid out a policy and requested, or rather, demanded, Fra Robert's support for the mission, as he was returning to England as an officer of the crown, et cetera.

'I seem to remember that you know Sir John Hawkwood,' he said.

I handed him back the scroll. 'I do,' I admitted.

Hales shook his head. 'I wish you were at leisure,' he said, shaking his head. 'An Englishman who knows Hawkwood could be a good friend in this game. However, we need you in Greece, and there's another matter. So I'll ask you to write a letter to your friend Hawkwood, if you will,'

Emile could not quite hear us, and she handed me a cup of wine and raised an eyebrow.

'Of course,' I said. 'And Fra Peter knows Hawkwood well and will be welcome in his camp.'

Hales smiled. 'That's good news,' he said.

'What is the other matter, Fra Robert?' I asked.

He looked at Emile. 'Your sovereign lord, Count Amadeus, is in Venice right now,' he said.

She nodded. 'That is not unexpected. He is only a year late.'

Hales played with his beard. 'I think you both need to know that the Count de Turenne left Famagusta twenty days ago. His ship touched here, and he was en route to Venice.' He leaned over. 'My lady, his expressed purpose is to see the Green Count and deprive you of your lands.' He looked at me. 'He has heard of your marriage – a pity. If Lord Grey had been a few days slower, Turenne would have left Famagusta none the wiser, although tongues were wagging.' He leaned back and looked at us both.

I said nothing.

Emile's voice was harsh with strain. 'What does this mean, Sir Robert?'

He pursed his lips. 'The Count de Turenne is going to allege to the Count of Savoy that you were unfaithful to your husband; that your children are bastards; that you paid this rascal to kill your husband, and he did so; he can produce witnesses to all these things. How he found these witnesses in Famagusta beggars the imagination, but he has an affidavit from the King of Cyprus, although our notary ...' He fingered his beard and looked away. '... thinks it a forgery.'

'A forgery?' I said.

Hales shrugged. 'Listen, my lady. It is not that we in the Order are so very good, but only that you, my lady, are a pilgrim under our protection, and you, Sir William, whatever your sins, are an excellent soldier and one of our very sons.'

We'd been joined by the turcopolier, Fra William de Midelton, another Englishman; in fact, the head of the English *langue* and commander of the Order's mercenaries.

'Telling the happy couple all of the good news?' he muttered. He smiled at me. 'God will provide, my son,' he said.

Fra Robert nodded. 'So he will. Twenty knights of the Order saw that you did not kill the Comte d'Herblay, my son. On the other hand, a dozen of them saw that Nerio did.' He spread his hands and nodded at Nerio. 'And all of them saw what d'Herblay had become, and what he was doing. We will back you. But you two are in for an uncomfortable time anywhere that Turenne has friends.' He shook his head. 'And all of this becomes Church politics. The Order wants the Green Count to come here – to help us solidify our gains, to save Cilicia, mayhap even to take Jerusalem. The Comte de Turenne, Archbishop Robert of Geneva, and a dozen more I can name have other plans. And the Pope is appointing a new legate. I don't even know who it will be.'

Emile had played the game of courts her whole life. 'So my marriage and my possession of my lands will be a hostage to the Crusade?' she asked.

Fra Robert looked at his hands and didn't meet her eye. 'Yes,' he said.

That threw rather a pall over the evening, and it was worse when I saw that my lady was keeping back tears of anger only with her will; all I could do was touch her hand and wish her good even. She rose, gave me a troubled smile, and pleaded her need to see her children, which was perfectly true; they had both grown amazingly in four short weeks, and Emile could not stop embracing them.

But she was angry.

Sister Marie knew by then, the whole mess, and she went and walked behind my lady and gave me a nod and what might have been a wink.

Fra Robert went on as soon as she was gone. 'Listen, Sir William – and you, Nerio, and you, Ser Fiore, and you, Sir Miles. The Order is spread very thin. Most of our knights have already gone home to their commanderies in France or Germany or England or Italy – it would require another *passim generale* to get them back to the Holy Land. Of the men who are here, more than half are on Cyprus, preparing to support the King. Our little fleet is at sea.'

This was palpably true. There was no one with whom to joust, no one training at the pells, and the English *langue* seemed full only because we all preferred it. There were probably fewer than fifty knights on the whole island, and as many brother sergeants.

Fra Robert turned to Nerio. 'You know that the Princess of Achaea has threatened war with your brother?' he asked.

Nerio shrugged. 'I'm five weeks behind on news,' he said. 'And all my cash is stopped.'

Fra Robert nodded. 'I heard,' he agreed. 'I believe you will find that the word is in Venice that you are dead.'

Nerio slapped his forehead. 'Of course!' he said.

I tugged at my beard. 'Turenne. Or the Hungarian.' I could see it. A very easy matter.

Fra Robert shook his head. 'What Hungarian?' he asked.

I looked at Nerio. 'An assassin hired by Robert of Geneva to kill the legate,' I said.

That brought on silence.

'I don't suppose you can prove that?' Fra Robert asked.

'No,' I admitted.

He sighed. 'Tell me everything about this man,' he said.

We provided a description, and I told him that Fra Peter would know him.

Hales frowned. 'That makes what I'm going to ask even harder,' he said. 'I want you to go to Morea and help Nerio, but most of all I want you to go to Count Amadeus.'

'I think I will be the wrong ambassador,' I protested. 'He has no love for me.'

Fra Robert shrugged. 'My hands are tied. I have no one else. And in truth, you will benefit from the Order's protection; and perhaps Nerio's as well. The Green Count has a great reputation, a sovereign preux, and a name for justice. See if you can sway him to come here to Rhodes.'

Miles narrowed his eyes. 'I had intended to go home to England,' he said.

'And Venice is en route,' Fra Peter said.

Fiore was looking at the candle, as he often did. He could stare at candles for hours, and he said they focused his thoughts.

I was thinking about many things at once: the Hungarian; my wife; how tired I was, suddenly, of the Holy Land.

'If you are going, I'll need you to go very soon. I've held the Genoese two days – could you sail tomorrow?' Fra Robert was pressing.

The turcopolier pretended to be somewhere else. Hales was well known for his political skills; almost as well known as Fra Juan di Heredia.

'I need to bespeak my lady wife,' I said.

'I am rather counting on her to accompany you,' Fra Robert said. 'She, at least, is a favourite of the Green Count.'

I nodded. I was sick of the whole thing.

But I had forgotten my Persian friend, and of course, the evening had been laid on for him. So when he arrived with Sabraham, I had to put on a good face and pretend to be fascinated by the tales of his travels, which were sometimes amazing and sometimes unbelievable. When he saw his listeners beginning to doubt him, Hafiz-i Abun had a tendency to add detail and unbelievable action which made us doubt him the more. And yet, he really had seen an incredible amount of the world, and he was witty and courteous and absolutely unafraid, even though he was, by Moslem standards, in the very epicentre of armed Christianity.

Indeed, he passed his arm through mine and bent close to whisper, 'No one in Persia will ever imagine I came here, or believe me.'

But he could also tell a great tale, and his tale of having diarrhoea while attempting to perform his religious devotions at Mecca was touching, funny, and very human. All of us have had the experience of having something interfere with the very highest motives; we laughed and laughed.

Fra Robert asked him to sell his Christian slave, and Hafiz-i Abun bowed. 'I give her to you,' he said. 'She has been ill-used, and I would not ... abuse her. Tell me, what life will she have here?' The Moslem traveller looked around. 'I have seen Moslem slaves working in the streets, here.'

Fra Robert fingered his beard. 'You make a good argument, my friend. True – our prisoners are put to work. But most are ransomed – indeed, we often handle prisoner exchanges for other – ahem – Franks.' Then he said something in Arabic, very fast, and I only caught the word for 'God.' But Hafiz-i Abun raised an eyebrow and smiled.

'So it is,' he said in Italian.

And later still, Fra William de Midelton turned the subject to Persia, and we heard Hafiz-i Abun describe his home, and the near constant state of war that engulfed much of it, and the Mongol 'rulers' who held it *en fief*, and again I was struck by how very complex the world was. I had thought all Persia to be rich, and fabulous, fantastic, mythological, and so very Islamic; instead, our traveller revealed a patchwork of beliefs and tribes and polities, and many of them were beyond my understanding.

So I lay, later, with Nerio and Fiore and Stapleton in our four beds, staring into the darkness.

'It could be worse,' Stapleton said.

'How?' Nerio asked. 'We've no money.'

'It is a good *empris*,' Miles said. 'We go to the Morea, help Nerio, find this Green Count, and deliver the Order's messages, and we're done. Then we travel to Venice. And then ...'

There was silence.

'Then we part,' Fiore said calmly. 'I have not seen my mother or father in more than a year.'

'I will probably stay in Morea,' Nerio said.

'I will go back to England,' Miles said, 'and be married.'

There was an explosion of comment and laughter, and someone struck Miles with a bolster.

'No, I'm to wed!' he said.

'You've never said a word!' I said.

'You never asked!' he said, like men the world over, and then he laughed himself. 'I've never met her, but there's a letter here from my da, and another from Lord Grey.'

'You should probably go with Fra Robert,' I said.

Somewhere in the darkness, Miles laughed. 'I probably should,' he said. 'But I want ... another adventure.'

Nerio chuckled. 'Miles. You should beware. You can grow too fond of adventure. Look at William.'

Fiore snorted so hard I thought he might be snoring, but it was laughter. 'For myself,' he said, 'I still want to meet a really good Saracen swordsman.' He sighed. ' Hafiz-i Abun is the merest butcher.'

In the morning, I found Emile at the earliest opportunity, and she agreed to sail with the Genoese. We got ourselves and our horses back aboard; Messire Parmenio scowled at me a great deal, and we were both aware that I was directly responsible for his delay in sailing. But our men-at-arms had become veterans at ships, and we had everyone aboard in two hours.

Parmenio glanced at me from his stern castle. His glare softened.

'Always a pleasure to have a hold full of knights,' he admitted. 'In these waters, any road.'

We touched twice on our route north. Despite the Order's need for haste, the Genoese had a route, and he had no intention of deviating, so we sailed to Samos, and then north to Chios, where Emile bought mastic and I bought some as well. Our retinue had begun to grumble about payment, which I could well understand. And at Chios, Hafiz-i Abun was not allowed off the ship.

I had about sixty gold florins to my name, and Emile's purse had about the same, and the merchants of Chios were no more interested in extending credit to us or Nerio than the merchants of Rhodes.

You can see Lesvos from the deck of your ship as you leave harbour on Chios; it is very close. But out of a clear blue sky we had a sudden, explosive storm; our ship was thrown on her beam ends, and she rolled out her mainmast.

I'm not sure I've ever been so terrified. All of us were bruised, and Emile broke a bone in her hand, and her maid, Helen, broke her nose when she was thrown off her bunk and was inconsolable for two days, although at the time she rather stoically continued to hold Edouard.

As for me, I was in the hold with the horses. Nerio and John and Marc-Antonio and I made them lie down, and as the others could reach us – Bernard and Jason and Jean-François and Pierre – they got their chargers down and then helped with other horses. But it was pitch-black down there, with panicked horses and the knowledge that if the ship foundered, we were going with it, and I prayed a great deal and cursed as much or more. And it seemed unending – at one point Fiore got a candle lit, and then it went out; lightning flashes came through the great grating amidships, to show us that one or another of our behemoths had decided to get to its idiot feet and kick something. And yet, when the ship rolled, and the crew did something marvellous and heroic which saved us, I only fell on Gawain, who bit me. As I was wearing an old arming doublet, all I got was a wicked bruise on my arm.

But in the fifteen or so heartbeats where we lay on our side, water pouring in, I thought we were done, and instead of prayer, I cursed that I would drown and not die with a sword in my hand, and cursed again that I was not with Emile, but with my horse.

I swear it almost seemed funny.

And then the ship began to right itself. Actually, Maestro Parmenio had cut away the mainmast with an axe, but I had no way of knowing that, and the inrush of water ceased, and in fact, it was only a little above our ankles. And of course all the horses panicked again.

John performed miracles of horse ministry, and Marc-Antonio was as brave as could be asked, and the rest of us, sodden and stinking, simply hung on to a couple of them and tried to say calming things, and in an hour, there was sunshine flooding the hold.

I went on deck and my wife threw her arms around me, which, considering what is in the bilge of a ship, was very loving of her.

And we didn't sail into Mytiline, the capital of the princes of Lesvos, but rather landed in a great bay on the south side of the island called 'Beautiful' in Greek. And Hafiz-i Abun fell on his knees on the beach and prayed, and so did most of the rest of us.

Lesvos is a great island, the size of an English county – or even two – with four fine cities the size of Lincoln: Mytiline is the ancient capital, with a fine fortress that dates back to the time of the Romans; Eressos, where Sappho the poetess had her school, as my wife hurried to tell me; Methymna, as fine a town as any I've seen, with a castle that Achilles once sacked, above a superb small harbour; and Antissa, a Genoese walled town within signalling distance of Methymna. The Gatelussi family rule the island and several others. They were merchant adventurers about the time I was born, and the emperor – the Greek one – granted them Lesvos for military service. I have been back many times, as you shall hear if we're trapped here a few more nights, but suffice it to say it is a fine place, well ruled and very rich.

You see, Master Chaucer? I can say good things about the Genoese.

At any rate, by the power of the divine intercession of the Virgin, we were saved and had not sunk in sight of land, and Maestro Parmenio had to admit that it would be days before his ship was fit for travel. And our horses were shockingly knocked about; those horses were the livelihood of most of us, and so we landed them, right over the side, and we swam them ashore in the Arab manner. John was instrumental in this, but it is the finest technique – so much better than trying to land them, and injuring them in a crane. I remember seeing the men powering a crane lose their pace, and a fine warhorse go smashing to the surface of a stone pier, breaking all four legs and having to be put down, screaming its noble heart out on a dock at Calais. This is something the Mamluks and Mongols do much better than we do; perhaps because their water is warmer.

At any rate, we got them all ashore, all except one fine stallion, Hafiz-i Abun's gift from the emir, who had to be put down.

Nerio got us guides, and we gathered our horse herd and rode cross-country to Mytilene, which was great fun. We got wondrously lost because we didn't know the shape of the island, and our guides were clearly guilty of wanting to visit a sacred shrine; but we were as happy to worship at a noble church high on a mountain as they were themselves. There we saw an icon donated by the Greek Emperor Alexis, he who was at war so often with the great Bohemund in the days of the First Crusade and the taking of Jerusalem. We stayed there, in the town with the fine church and the ancient icon, called 'Hagios' or just 'Holy' in Greek.

It is a little thing, but as we rode across Lesvos, I rode with Emile and her children, and we began to play at being a family. It was fascinating, and Sister Marie was my best ally, but I did get Edouard to be a little less sullen by letting him ride the smallest Arab. Magdalene was never sullen at any time, and Isabelle was always easy; I think she always liked me. And the second evening, the horses were much better and we came down a great ridge after we passed a magnificent aqueduct built by the Romans.

And there was Mytilene. It was the start of sunset, and the town's red tile roofs were like a foretaste of Constantinople, as were the many churches and the ringing of bells for service.

'Why must you infidels raise such an infernal clamour,' Hafiz-i Abun asked Fiore.

The two of them had begun to be friends, over chess. And the Persian was allowing the Italian to teach him his theories of fencing. They were two exceptionally proud men, but they seemed to have some way of communicating that went beyond language, especially when they played chess.

Fiore laughed. 'Why must you heretics have men shriek from towers?' he asked.

Hafiz-i Abun looked down at the town and then laughed. 'I suppose there is something to what you say,' he said.

'There usually is,' Fiore replied.

Mytilene was like the aftermath of our noble dream of Jerusalem. By the time we crested the hill, forty brilliantly equipped men-at-arms from the palace came out to escort us, and we were taken directly to rooms – sumptuous rooms. The palace was so new that you could smell the plaster and the stucco everywhere – the painted wall, brilliantly frescoed, in our solar was still cool and a little damp to the touch. We had a spectacular view out over the walls and across to the Turkish coast. It was a beautiful place.

By then, the children had decided to be delighted by Lesvos. As it was, technically, Outremer, I'd told Edouard that he was now a crusader, and nothing could make him happier than being a crusader. We had a balcony high above the sea, and I found him there, waving his dagger – de Charny's dagger, in fact – at the Turks four miles away.

Well. He had spirit, that boy.

The Prince himself was there to receive us, and after we'd stabled our horse herd and our still-damp belongings, we were invited to his hall for food, which proved almost impossibly sumptuous, especially as the meal was for thirty travellers who had arrived late.

The captain of the Prince's company of lances was English; a Northumbrian and a Percy – Sir Richard Percy. It was a pleasure to hear English spoken, and my archers all but fell into his arms. He had a dozen English men-at-arms and as many English archers, almost all northern men, burned brown so that they looked more like paynim than Hafiz-i Abun, especially as they all wore turbans on their helmets.

I asked him what a Borders man was doing in Outremer and he laughed. 'Were you at Poitiers?' he asked.

I smiled. It's always unsure ground, when you admit you aren't well-born. 'I was a squire,' I said.

He nodded sharply. 'Thought I knew you. John Hawkwood was knighted on the field. You were there.'

'I was, too,' I admitted.

'I was in the Earl of Oxford's household,' he said. He shrugged. 'When the Peace was signed, I thought I'd go to Avignon and make my fortune.' He shrugged again. 'An agent for the Gatelussi hired me there and I *have* made my fortune. I was going to Italy to follow Hawkwood, but now …' He grinned. 'The Prince is the best pay-master in the world, except mayhap the Sultan in Cairo.'

I told him a little of my story and he nodded.

'You served with yon knights?' he asked, surprised. 'At yer own expense?' he asked.

'Yes,' I said.

'You must be rich,' he said. 'I could take some pointers. Nay, I mean no offence. They say it's a hard school, and *certes* the Order knights who come here are hard, proud men. Right bastards, too.'

I admitted that many were.

'I've learned a mort of soldiering from them,' I said.

'Oh, aye,' Sir Richard agreed. 'There's nothing like fightin' out here to teach you soldierin'. I can't wait to ha' a go at the Scots.' He shook his head. 'Fightin' Turks is the best trainin' there is, for cattle raiding or people raidin'.' He looked at me and poured more wine. 'Mayhap we could run a course or two tomorrow and strike our swords together? Eh? Your Cap'n Parmenio will be here a week – his warehouses are here.'

That night I slept in a bed with my own wife; a pleasure, and a restful one. And the next day she helped me dress in my arming clothes, and Edouard, proud as Lucifer, followed me to the wooden lists in the castle's enormous courtyard with my gauntlets and helmet, which were almost too much for him to carry.

Prince Francesco was there, sitting on an ivory chair with his sons around him; he introduced me, very seriously, to his sons Andronico, who was just ten, and Domenico who was eight – closer to Edouard's age, and clearly jealous that my step-son was carrying my helmet.

I was also surprised to find Nerio sitting in a fine chair like a great lord. It's odd, when I tell these tales, I suppose it always sounds as if I'm the focus, because ... Well, because I am me. But at Mytilene, Nerio was very much the great lord, and I was merely a knight, possibly in his train.

I knew that Nerio was working to establish his credentials so that he could raise money. I was worried, really worried, that I was going to lose all my fine men-at-arms and all my good horseflesh for lack of means to pay them. I had got used to spending Nerio's money.

But fighting, especially fighting with an audience, always does wonders to focus the mind. My opponent, Sir Richard, was already armed. And my lady came with Helen and sat with the prince's lady, an Orsini of Rome, and her ladies. For an impromptu tilt in a castle tiltyard, it had all the trappings of a deed of arms, and I could see that Sir Richard was a serious jouster.

Well, you've all heard my experiences with jousting. I've never been as good a lance as Jean-François or Fiore. On the other hand, as soon as Gawain came out, we all knew that I had a better horse.

Sir Richard came over while I was arming, and pointed at Gawain.

'When I'm lyin' on my back,' he said, 'I guess I'll see yer girth. What a horse!'

I probably beamed with pleasure. This is something I have often noted with men; that before a fight, they will often proclaim their weaknesses – a poor horse, a bad shoulder. I've done it myself. It's not cowardice; you may, in fact, believe that you will triumph, but you admit to these problems in some sort of attempt to establish rapport with a man you'll try to kill or maim.

Perhaps. Men are as complicated as nations and tribes. I can't tell you why men are as they are, although I often lose sleep pondering it.

Marc-Antonio had me in my harness in record time, and I could see rust on my arms, and he shook his head.

'No blame,' I said. 'We've been at sea for days.'

He shook his head. 'I've tried tallow and I've tried olive oil,' he said. 'There was no pork fat to be had in Adalia. I'm out of whale oil.'

'We'll get it out,' I said. 'Edouard will help us.'

Edouard didn't immediately agree. 'Will you kill him?' the boy asked, pointing at Sir Richard.

'Avert!' I said. 'I hope not, young man. He seems a good knight and a worthy man.'

'Then why will you fight him?' Edouard asked. 'Is he one of the bad men who insults *maman*?'

Oh, that hurt. That a mere boy should hear that men insulted his mother?

I knelt by him. 'Nay, lad. Sir Richard is a good knight and serves this prince,' I said. 'We fight only for sport.'

Edouard sighed. 'I want you to fight the men who insult *maman*,' he said. 'And kill them all.'

I suspect I was supposed to give him a lecture on Christian virtue and how many of his *maman*'s enemies were merely misguided, but instead I gave him a steel embrace and said, 'I will, Edouard.'

And then Marc-Antonio got my aventail over my face and my

cervelleur on my head and I mounted, and then I donned my great helm, which slipped into place with a satisfying click.

And then the world was the horse between my legs, the heat, and my eye-slit vision of the lists. The Gatelussi didn't have a barricade in the middle of the lists, and so we were forced to make a lot more decisions about riding at the start of a pass. Sir Richard saluted me by waving his lance tip and I did the same, and then we were running, and my whole world became my lance tip. I got my lance down nicely, but my attempt to pick the pauldron off his shoulder failed, and he splintered his lance on my shield. I kept my seat well enough, but that was his pass all the way.

Then Miles rode a pass with one of the local knights, an Italian, Ser Giovanni, and they rocked each other, a brilliant pass, and now we had hundreds of people watching – most of the garrison, and all the castle servants, and many of the people from the town below the walls. Fiore rode against Nerio, and their lances seemed to explode at the same instant.

I remember that pass. It was one of the most perfect I have ever seen; it is emblematic of that summer. After it, they embraced each other, and the Orsini princess, Beatrice, threw flowers at them.

Then Sir Richard and I were ready again. This time, Gawain was on his mettle; he was smoother somehow – I find it difficult to describe, but he was himself. I seemed to float down the lists, and my strike took Sir Richard's visor off his helmet even as his lance splintered on my shield.

Fiore took my unbroken lance. 'You think you are a poor jouster,' he said. 'But in fact, I have made you a very good jouster. Your only foe is your own head. Look at this. Beautiful.'

Then Nerio exchanged splinters with Ser Giovanni. Fiore unhorsed a knight in a fine harness, the newest Brescian style; a tall young man who was not as good as he thought, and sought to do something fancy – against Fiore. I was just having my helmet put on when it happened; I put my hand on Marc-Antonio's arm and sent him running out into the lists because the young knight wasn't moving.

Luckily for all of us, he was only stunned, and he rose after a moment and Marc-Antonio helped him off the course. He was none too pleased with the result and snarled at Marc-Antonio. I was proud of my squire, who was a Venetian among Genoese and nonetheless remained courteous.

Sir Richard's squire appeared and asked if I might be willing to try an exchange of sword blows next, on foot. I bowed and changed helmets to my basinet, a new one just purchased on Rhodes, with a very fine aventail in very small links and a better visor. The eyes were barred but the brow heavily pierced; I had better vision in it than in any helmet I'd ever worn.

Sir Richard emerged in a basinet with no visor. It was still common enough back then; indeed, most of our men-at-arms never wore them.

Jean-François was dropped by Ser Bernard. I had never seen it happen; Jean-François was accounted our best lance, or perhaps Fiore, but one cannot win every day, and down he went. He was a big man, and slow to rise, and then I walked out across the dirt and the crowd roared.

Sir Richard and I were a fair match for size. He had a very long sword and mine was almost a handspan shorter, and we were otherwise a match for reach. We saluted and I put my sword behind me, so that he could not measure its length; Fiore called that *garde* 'long tail'. I like it when I face a new man; it gives nothing away and allows the opponent no play on your weapon.

We circled for so long that a woman laughed and men called advice.

By that time, I knew that Sir Richard was canny, well-trained, and patient.

He had his sword half-on his right shoulder, almost like what Fiore calls the 'posta di donna or the *garde* of the woman'. He moved smoothly, his weight was always centred, and he looked as capable as Fiore.

So I was very careful.

But I can be affected by crowds, and when people began to mock us, I lost my battle with impatience and moved. Still, I moved with purpose. I didn't change *gardes*. Instead, I closed the distance to try to force him to strike.

And he struck.

He was fast, and strong.

Luckily, I am also fast and strong.

Our blades met, the edges bit into one another, and as fast as the strike of a falcon, he moved his hips, stepping off my line to my left and cutting for my arms. I felt he left the bind too early, and I thrust at his face ...

And pulled it. Christ, that was close. His blow missed, and mine fell short, and then we were circling. My heart was pounding; I had almost killed him.

He didn't seem to know what had happened.

I was in another low *garde*, this one called 'gates of iron'. He cut again, from his high *garde*, and I snapped a rising cut into his cut; we met in a rare high-low bind, and we both counter-cut, snapping blows into each other's helmets. I stepped in, reaching to take my sword at the mid-part of the blade for half-swording. He got a hand on my right arm and my pommel clipped the side of his helmet, and we were apart, both cutting back one-handed as if we'd ridden past one another.

Then he whirled and came at me with four blows. He was fast enough that all I could do was cover; I could tell that he was trying to rock me so that he could enter for a grapple. I got my weight down, and rose off his fourth blow with a thrust at his armpit, which he covered.

And then we were circling again, by this time breathing as if we were powered by a blacksmith's bellows.

I won't say he was the best swordsman I ever faced. But he was fine; and he wasn't easy, and nothing especial was coming to me, except that Emile was watching me. I wore her favour.

He did seem to favour cutting into a crossing of the blades and then whipping his sword to one side or another. I understood that; I just didn't have an immediate answer.

But I had a guess. I can't even tell you that I thought this, con-sciously. I just decided what I was going to do and how I would do it, and it all required him to throw another heavy descending blow.

Which, as if he could read my mind, he refused to do. There fol-lowed an excruciating passage where he tried thrusts and rising cuts, and I covered them. Perhaps better swordsmen will mock me, but I can rarely keep more than one strategy in my head while I fight. I wanted that hard downward cut as my set-up.

Meanwhile, I parried.

And then he pressed me, taking his own sword at the half and thrusting fast from up close. I matched him, and we ended up pressed together, weight low, jabbing at each other while our armoured forearms touched or slammed into each other. I was trying for his underarm, and he for my visor.

I deceived his weapon and thrust, but I missed over his shoulder and I backed away. I slipped my weapon up over my helmet, changing to the 'woman's' *garde*.

I think he echoed me unconsciously, and seeing me retreat, he cut – a heavy, powerful descending blow.

I powered forward into his blow and met him, using the weight of my step to push his blade off line to my right, opening his centre. We were close, and I slammed my pommel forward into his unprotected face. I was now a heartbeat ahead of him; it sounds odd, but I knew I had him, and I had time to put my armoured arm under his chin, instead of putting my pommel in his teeth, and I dropped him with a little lift-and-push, stepped on his sword blade, and saluted the prince.

'You bastard!' spat my opponent. He was laughing, so there was no insult. I stepped off his blade and he rose smoothly. He threw his arms around me. 'Well struck, Sir William!'

The crowd roared.

Emile leaned down from the stands and kissed me.

Really, the life of arms is very satisfying, at times.

Back at my pavilion, I told the herald I was done for the day. Marc-Antonio was just unlacing my arms when Fiore came in. I had heard the roar; I assumed he'd unhorsed another victim.

I was full of myself. I admit it. I grinned at him. 'Did you see that?' I said, or something equally braggy.

'Yes,' Fiore said. 'Perfectly competent, although your weight was overcommitted.' He picked up his sword and went back out into the sunlight.

Really, he could be a very difficult friend.

I went out in my arming clothes and was invited to sit with the prince. I met my recent adversary as I approached, and we bowed; I was glad to see no rancour.

He caught my arm. 'See yon sprite in the white harness?' he asked me. It was the young knight in the brilliant Brescian harness whom Fiore had dropped like a sack of grain. 'Prince's son. Well, wrong side o' the blanket, mayhap. Apple of his eye.' Sir Richard touched the side of his nose with his finger.

We approached the ivory chair together.

'You are a brilliant fighter,' the young knight said as we knelt.

Prince Francesco waved at the man in the Brescian harness. 'This young devil is my son, Francesco.'

At the word 'son', the faces of both of the younger boys behind his chair grew very grave. Or rather, all expression left them. I gave the young man a good bow anyway before kneeling in a *reverencia* before the prince.

The prince either didn't notice or didn't care what his two legitimate sons thought. He nodded to me. 'Nicely done, although perhaps on your next visit you could leave us all some shreds of our pride, eh?'

'My Lord, if you mean my fight with Sir Richard, an Englishman would have won, any road.' I was kneeling, so I bowed my head.

'Fair enough,' the prince said. 'But your *preux* is well known here,' he added.

What do you say to that?

'Where did you learn all these tricks?' the prince's by-blow asked.

I might have bridled at the term 'trick' but princes are princes. I bowed. 'Ser Fiore there is the best lance and the best sword I have ever met,' I said. 'I practise with him constantly.'

Prince Francesco nodded at his son. 'Ah, my son. Sir William Gold, the best knight in this castle, says that he practises constantly. Does that say anything to you, my son?'

I winced.

The young man shrugged. 'Pater, there are so many things that I ought to practise. Which one is paramount? Statecraft? Fencing? Hawking? Sailing? I understand that it takes much study to understand religion. How about shoemaking?' He laughed. Several young men around us laughed as well.

The elder Prince Francesco's nose had been broken several times, I could tell. He had a look; he'd seen many things. He had the skin of a man who'd spent a lot of time out in the weather.

His son's skin was as smooth as Emile's; his eyes were bright. He wanted to sound wicked and worldly.

I thought of Richard Musard. And of me, of course.

'But if you fail in a real fight, you are killed or taken.' His father steepled his hands, even as Ser Jason threw one of the castle men-at-arms in a wrestling match behind us.

'I can pay people to fight for me,' the boy said. 'I can pay them to write my letters, I can pay them to train my hawks.' He shrugged.

His father frowned in, I think, disgust. I knew perfectly well that the lad was speaking to annoy his father.

A servant handed me wine. Emile was shaking her head, 'no' from left to right and back, but I essayed the *empris* anyway.

'Ah, but My Lord,' I said to the young man, 'if you fight well, the men you pay will fight better – they will love you better. If you know a little about how to make shoes, you will never be cheated by a shoemaker. If you know a little about God, you will be all the wiser, and the harder to deceive.' I shrugged. 'And I confess that I know nothing of hawking, and only wish I did, as my lady wife loves it.'

The young man was not offended. He turned his head a little to one side, like a dog; he wanted to listen. That was interesting for itself. 'But why?' he asked. 'Why do you know nothing of hawking?'

I shrugged. 'I have never put in the time,' I admitted.

'Sir William was too busy mastering the arts of war,' Prince Francesco said.

Now it was my turn to shrug. '*Eh bien*, but perhaps not,' I said. 'I have wasted a great deal of time in garrison and elsewhere. Wine. Dalliance. I suppose I might, at some point, have learned to go hawking. I regret it now, but at the time, I thought it would never be part of my life.'

I thought of all the hawking that the Black Prince's household did, and how I almost never went.

There was a moment's silence.

The young man nodded. 'I see what you are saying,' he said. 'But you did choose to master your ... weapons.'

I shrugged. 'And even that, although perhaps it is not the example your father would choose, is because I love this man Fiore, over there.' I waved at Fiore, who was giving another Italian knight an education in fighting on foot with a long sword. 'Because of my friendship for him ...' I shrugged. 'I have to learn.'

Prince Francesco smiled. It was a thin smile of an old corsair, and yet held some warmth. 'Now this is a true thing,' he said. 'Yes! What my son needs is to follow someone he admires.'

The young prince shrugged. 'Perhaps,' he said with disdain. 'I don't tend to admire much.'

Now Emile was smiling, so I knew I hadn't done so badly. The wine was delicious, and I enjoyed the plaudits of the courtiers. I watched another hour of fighting – some excellent wrestling. Fiore wrestled, and so did Nerio, which surprised me. He was thrown early, but rose to fight again, and he made a brilliant throw against a bigger man, with a hip feint and a tackle, putting his man down, rolling him over and forcing his surrender.

Fiore shook his hand. It was almost the best feat of arms of the day, although Miles's fight on foot with a poleaxe rivalled it. He was against Sir Richard's lieutenant, Ser Giovanni, and at the drop of the wand, Miles stepped forward, thrust with the head of his axe, pulled, and threw his opponent to the ground. It happened so fast I didn't see the whole of it; I was just turning my head from whispering to my wife, who was just saying something about 'the mild-mannered Miles'.

And he struck, and threw his man. Fiore pounded his back. I went down on the sand and did the same.

It was a fine day. A triumph for us.

Our Persian friend watched it all as the Prince's guest. At the end, he said to Fiore, 'Almost as good as watching my master's *ghulami*. But of course, they are slaves.'

Prince Francesco had another feast for us that night, and although there had been nothing formal about the deed of arms, he did hand a crown of gold to Miles. Miles had never won anything in his life, and he was transported. Pretty women fawned on him, and he was unable to decide what to do about it.

I shook my head. I still do; this was a man who'd fought his way into Alexandria and stood his ground in a dozen actions, but the attention of three Italian maids flustered him so badly that he was speechless. One had on a sideless surcoat and under it her kirtle, which laced up her side. But the laces were very tight and she showed a fine stretch of flesh from hip to underarm – the very 'gates of Hell' referred to so often by priests in sermons. Even Miles took notice.

Nerio went and stood with him a moment, and made all three young maidens smile. One of them blushed. Nerio whispered in Miles's ear and walked back to me.

He rolled his eyes.

'He's afraid of them,' Nerio said.

"And you told him?' I asked.

'To flatter their intelligence,' he said. 'Women want to be told how smart they are.'

'Fie, Ser Nerio,' my wife said, at his elbow. 'All the romances say women want to hear of their beauty.'

Nerio shrugged, smiling at her. 'Most women are perfectly aware of their beauty,' he said. 'They are less sure of their brilliance.'

'And this is the key to your success with women, Ser Nerio?' my wife asked.

'Yes,' Nerio said.

'And you tell foolish, empty-headed girls how intelligent they are?' she asked.

'Oh, yes,' Nerio said. 'Especially them.'

Emile told me later that it took all her matronly wisdom not to strike his masculine self-assurance.

'I was one of those girls,' she said to my chest. 'It is their age, not their lack of wit. And he preys on them.'

Yes. And so had I. Perhaps this is the age-old war between men and women. Which is mostly, I suspect, about youth, and innocence, and age, and experience.

Bah. I sound so old.

The next day I slept late, and so did my people. I woke late, left my lady abed to sleep even later, and went down to the courtyard, where, with the help of a borrowed wooden sword, I inflicted a little damage on a pell. It felt good, and I was growing old enough that the day after fighting I needed to loosen up my muscles.

Then Marc-Antonio and I sat in the yard with a fascinated Edouard, and also with Fiore and Achille and all of Emile's people, and we worked on our harness. It was the perfect day – not too hot, but with a good full sun above us to dry our arming coats. We started on my arm harnesses, which had rust on them, and worked our way through, patching a cut in the fabric covering of my brigantine, stitching the gloves of my gauntlets back together where they had opened along the stitch lines, as they always do; oiling, polishing, mending.

Will you think less of me if I say that I love to do this? Perhaps it is because I grew up so poor, and never imagined I would own such a fine harness; or perhaps I just like to fondle fine things. And it is a pleasure, too, to help another man – to have the right needle, the right wax, the right thread, or a rivet to make a repair.

The young prince appeared early, with his friends, all dressed in silk doublets. I could tell he'd been awake all night, and I could also tell that he wanted me to be aware of that.

I wasn't born yesterday, or even the day before. I ignored him unless he spoke to me, and kept sewing on Jean-François's arming coat, which was in a shocking state.

Miles appeared, looking far too bright. Possibly even brittle. He almost seemed to float along the ground.

Not like our Miles at all.

'Ah,' said one of the young courtiers. 'Brave Sir Miles. Which of the prince's mares did you ride last night? Was it a good ride, Signor?'

The three courtiers laughed, and young Francesco smiled.

I got up, dumping Jean-François's doublet in the sand.

Miles was aware enough that they meant mischief. But he was gently born and not used to rough wordplay. And I admit that we'd been with the knights of the Order a long time, and on pilgrimage. I hadn't heard a broad joke about dalliance in three months unless I went to Ewan's fire.

Miles looked at the three of them. 'I don't think that I understand,' he said. 'Perhaps my poor Italian.'

'He means that the ladies would be whores if they had the brains to charge,' said another of the courtiers. 'But as they lack the brains, they provide what is in their nests for free.'

He laughed.

They all laughed.

I noted that Miles had a small square of green silk pinned with a long and rather elegant silver pin to his shoulder. It was on the back of his shoulder; I hadn't seen it, but I knew what it was.

A favour.

I wore one myself.

And Miles took everything seriously.

He had turned bright red. So bright, it was almost painful to watch.

I was moving.

So was Nerio, who, of course, was not doing any work.

My thought was to prevent violence.

Nerio had a different thought. He got between the most recent speaker, who had a hat entirely of peacock plumes and I still think of as 'Peacock', and Miles, who had relaxed into a fighting stance and had his right hand on his rondel dagger.

Nerio put a hand on Peacock's shoulder. 'He'll kill you,' he said. 'You soft children probably say such things about women, and laugh. But in an army camp ... You do not call even a whore, a whore. Understand me, child?'

The boy spluttered. He cursed. He blasphemed. But he moved further from Nerio.

I smiled a nice, insulting, condescending smile at him. While pinning Miles's arm against his side.

'I would be happy to meet you,' Miles said through clenched teeth, in terrible Italian. 'On horseback or foot, with any weapon you choose, if only you will allow me to kill you.'

Peacock stepped back again.

Nerio shrugged. 'If you run away,' he said, 'I'll be sure to tell everyone I meet that you are a coward.' Nerio had this terrible power – his insults were more telling than anyone I had ever met. His sneer was so much more effective.

Peacock was so afraid that he was afraid even to run away. He stopped.

'Best just apologise,' I said.

Prince Francesco came over. In a way, I approved of his standing up for his friend, even if the man was an arse.

'Papay,' he said gently; some local nickname. 'You know what my pater says of speaking ill of a woman.'

Peacock was trembling. 'I ... misspoke. I ... Do I have to do this?' he asked, looking at the young Francesco.

The young man looked at me, and for a moment, we were peers. It was odd. We were almost adversaries, but he was asking me how to play this.

So I changed roles, drew myself up, and walked over to stand with the prince.

'Sometimes men make broad jests about things,' I said. 'Farting, pissing, fucking.' I shrugged. 'Sometimes these japes are ill-timed. We are rougher men than your father's men, My Lord. If Miles loves a lady *par amours*, he is in his rights as a man-at-arms to defend her honour. That is *our* way.' I turned and looked at Peacock. 'And as a matter of course, young sir, it is sometimes funny to make a joke about mares and stallions, but it is always in bad taste to put a name to any. Killing bad taste.'

He was shaking.

I think he took me seriously.

'I beg your pardon, Sir Miles,' he said.

Fiore kicked Miles in the shin.

Miles coughed. 'Yes,' he said tightly. 'I'm sure you misspoke,' he said.

Young men and young women.

Very complicated.

Like Anatolia.

I found that my hands were shaking when I went back to sewing; I suppose I'd been ready to fight. Miles was sitting alone, and when Nerio tried to talk to him, he shook Nerio off.

I was just getting back to work, hoping that the sun would clear away the air, when Sir Richard appeared.

I rose to my feet, worried about the consequences of our confrontation of the morning, and his face was clouded – anger, fury, confusion.

He looked around and then at me.

'Can you come with me?' he asked tightly.

By then I was on Achille's gauntlets, that had once been Davide's gauntlets. I set them down and followed him.

'The prince would like to see you,' he said.

'I'm wearing a linen peasant's cote besmottered with rust,' I said.

He glanced at me. 'Prince Francesco will not care,' he said.

'Nothing happened,' I offered. 'We prevented—'

He shook his head. 'No idea what you are talking about,' he said. 'Come on.'

I had not, until then, been in the prince's apartments. We went through the great hall where dinner had been, and where a dozen men in livery were building a dais. We went up broad stairs and into an antechamber panelled in dark wood. There were two ancient statues against one wall – both naked. Not my taste.

Up another flight of stairs. These were very narrow, and guarded by a fully armed man. If they arrested me, I was helpless.

Up and up, the stairs turning. We were in the wall of a tower, a round tower.

We emerged high above the sea, to find the older prince sitting in a big, heavy chair on the top deck of the tower. Asia all but glowed green across the narrow sea in the ferocious sunlight.

'Sir William Gold,' Sir Richard said.

Prince Francesco turned his head. 'Ah,' he said.

'My apologies, My Lord,' I began.

He shook his head. 'The affairs of my son are not my business,' he said. 'Or rather, not worth my breath. One of my son's useless boys was chastised? It might do him a world of good.'

He sighed.

'I thought your son behaved well,' I said.

That got his attention. 'Why?' he asked.

I remember that I looked out to sea for a little while before I answered. 'He stood up for his people, but he was almost looking for ... a way out.'

His father nodded. 'Interesting. People do not generally stand up for my bastard son.' He made a hand motion dismissing the entire matter. 'I have other news.'

A servant brought a stool.

I sat. Wine was put in my hand.

'The emperor has been taken,' he said.

'Taken?' I repeated, or something equally foolish.

'Somewhere in Hungary or Bulgaria,' Prince Francesco said. 'You know that my wife is his sister?'

I nodded. 'Yes, Your Grace,' I said.

He turned his entire attention on me. 'Your wife is a Savoyard, and you yourself are en route to visit the Green Count, is this not true?' he asked.

There was no need to prevaricate. He was exceptionally well informed. He still is.

'Yes,' I said.

'Count Amadeus is the emperor's cousin,' he said, steepling his hands. 'Will you take him a letter from me?'

I took a breath.

Sometimes, it would be easy to be a plain, fighting knight.

I knew what the Order wanted; they wanted Nerio in Greece, and the Green Count on his way to Rhodes. Not on his way to Constantinople, which would not help the Kingdom of Cyprus or the Order.

On the other hand …

'You think that the King of Hungary has taken the emperor?' I asked.

Prince Francesco shook his head. 'I cannot fathom it,' he admitted. 'Unless Hungary has determined to try and seize the Empire for himself, and I would say he lacks either the reach or the ambition. Eh, perhaps not the ambition. More likely that the Bulgarians seized the emperor. They were at war just last year.'

'Could the Bulgarians be working with the Turks?' I asked.

He looked at me … I remember thinking, *Ho, Your Grace, I'm not made of wood.* Until then, I think he'd thought me a sword-swinger.

'Murad,' he said softly. 'Very clever.' He sipped wine and then looked out to sea. After a few moments, he looked back at me. 'If one of the Bulgarian princes has invited the Turks in to the north …'

I had no idea what he was talking about. I bowed. 'Bulgarian princes?' I asked.

'There are three. Their father, Alexander, died last year, and divided their kingdom in three. The eldest, John Sisman, has the bulk of the country. The other two – I cannot remember their names …' He looked at his councillors.

A swarthy man in a long robe bowed. 'Your Grace may mean the second son, Stracimir, and the third son, and weakest, Dobrotich.'

The prince nodded. 'As you say, Isaac.'

I realised when he spoke that the man in the long robe was a Jew. He was the most elegantly dressed Jew I'd ever seen, and wore a fine, ivory-hilted baselard. He saw my attention and inclined his head, and I returned the courtesy.

Then he turned his attention to the prince. 'May I suggest that we need more information?' he asked. 'I cannot help but notice that the emperor has been taken, and leaves his son Andronicus …'

'Christ Risen,' cursed the old pirate, sounding considerably less princely. 'Damn me to Hell.'

He looked at me. 'Well?' he asked.

This has happened to me a few times – but this was the first. It was the first time that I was the point of the spear. The first time I had to make a decision that would affect many men, and the policy of the Order. Not a battlefield decision, but a life decision.

I suspect I tugged my beard. I don't remember, but I usually do in such moments.

It was a fine balance. I had been listening when Fra Robert spoke. But I couldn't imagine that the loss of the emperor and all Northern Greece would be a fair trade for some raids on the coast of Anatolia. Nor, really, was I fit to make such a decision.

'Your Grace, could you send word of these developments to Rhodes?' I vouchsafed.

'Done,' he said. 'Sir Richard, see to it.'

My new English friend nodded.

'I'll take your letter, Your Grace,' I said.

'I'll be in your debt, Sir William,' he said. 'Let me tell you the contents. No. Come back in two hours. You have given me food for thought. Amadeus is at the very least at Corfu. You can reach him in three days by galley.'

I bowed. 'Your Grace, I must confess to you that I may not be the perfect ambassador. The Green Count may mislike me.'

'Your marriage?' Francesco Gatelussi raised an eyebrow. 'I made one too,' he said. He smiled. 'Amadeus of Savoy is a man of the world.'

'The Count of Turenne has sworn to take my wife's lands,' I said.

'Never heard of him,' Francesco said. It sounded like a death sentence. 'With fair winds, you could be up with the count in three days. Perhaps four. He has to land at Naxos. He might land … Bah. I'll send you in one of my galleys. Will you sell me your *condotta*?'

'My *condotta*?' I asked.

'Will you serve me against the Turks and Bulgarians, Sir William? I am going to rescue the emperor.' He leaned forward.

May I say that, despite his age, the Prince of Lesvos was a man I could follow very easily. I loved the speed with which he decided. I liked his Jew. I liked the way men spoke to him – neither servile, nor pretend peers, but men who spoke their minds. I liked Sir Richard. And he stirred me. I wanted to follow him to rescue the emperor.

I bowed. 'I may owe knight service to the Green Count,' I said. 'Barring that, I am at your service.'

Prince Francesco rose; a signal honour. 'Good. Because I will put you with my son, and you will help him be a man.' He nodded to me. 'In return, I will pay you well and help make Amadeus accept your marriage. Is that agreeable?'

I bowed. I was, in fact, in over my head. I was still trying to imagine that the emperor was taken. I couldn't even imagine what that meant, as I hadn't ever heard of a Byzantine emperor being taken before.

I walked down, out of the tower, to find my wife and tell her. Sir Richard walked with me. He was behind me on the twisting stairs, and he took my shoulder at a landing.

'You are nae after me job?' he asked. 'Ye ken I'm his captain?'

I remember pausing and looking up at him, and Isaac, the Jew, was right behind him. He raised an eyebrow.

'I have another contract, with my friend Nerio, when this is over,' I said carefully. 'And I can follow your lead, Sir Richard.'

He held out his hand and we clasped. 'Good, then. Imagine a pair o' sons of Saint George saving the heathen Romanians fra' the Turks.' He laughed.

I went to find Emile. When I told her all, she made a face.

'He is a good lord,' she said practically. 'And I rather like it here. Get him to give you a fief.'

Very practical woman, Emile.

Then I went to find my friends. They were still in the courtyard.

'Gentlemen,' I said, and they all looked up. Nerio was sitting on a stool, rolling dice in a bowl; Fiore was polishing a sword; Miles was cleaning his poleaxe. L'Angars was lying on his back with a broad hat over his eyes; Hafiz-i Abun, who, by then, spent all his time with us, was watching Nerio roll the dice, and making notes on a tablet.

'The Bulgarians have taken the Emperor of the East,' I said. 'Prince Francesco has asked us to join him in the rescue.'

Nerio glanced at me. A slow smile started in the middle of his mouth, and spread.

'Of course,' Nerio said.

Fiore raised an eyebrow. 'Of course,' he said.

And Miles shot to his feet. 'Of course!' he said.

Hafiz-i Abun smiled. 'May I come?' he asked. 'I have always wanted to see Constantinople, although I admit your emperor is nothing to me. But I can go home that way – to Tanais.'

L'Angars raised his head. 'What's the pay?' he asked.

The next hours were a whirlwind; I couldn't remember the order of my actions if my life depended on it. In the end, Emile and her retinue stayed on Lesvos; she was a great lady, and the emperor's daughter and the prince were delighted to have her. She kept her knights by her.

Our little company could not all fit on a tiny Genoese galliot – it was almost a racing shell. In fact, they couldn't take a single horse.

So I left Miles in command. Fiore was a fine man, the best sword I ever knew, but his gifts did not run to people and their management. His tendency to say exactly what he observed could be a gift from God in training, but it was deeply painful when dealing with archers and their little ways. Miles, despite his pious ways, or perhaps because of them, liked people, and mostly, people liked him back.

It is more complicated than that, though. Look – most of the men at this table have led companies. What is the most essential prerequisite of leadership? I ask you. And I leave aside money, Master Chaucer, although I agree that money makes a leader better and easier in every way.

I want to say that it is the ability to praise. Praise is the gold that glues men together. Oh, discipline is all very well, but sullen discipline won't get a pack of curs to bite the enemy, nor to stand up to better men and die, if that's what is required.

But love will. Be a man never so humble, never so squalid, never so ill-used, praise and love will make him fight better than shouts and blows. The praise must be accurate; the love must be genuine. There must be punishment for transgression, with justice; and the punished man must know that having been punished, he is once again a member of the company.

Really, it's not different from how you raise a child. Sir Jesus would have made a fine captain; look at how he managed his useless pack of disciples, and not a good man amongst them, unless maybe it was Saint Peter or his own brother James. But he led them well, and in the end, they changed the world after he was dead – the very best thing you can say about a captain.

You think I'm far from my mark, eh, lass? But Fiore had no praise in him. Or not much. He wanted to be perfect, in himself; thus he only saw flaws in folk, including his own self. Men in our little company worshipped him for his skills that could keep them alive, but they feared him, and none of them wanted to follow him across an alley, much less into battle.

Nerio and I had a complex little negotiation in those hours, too. He had his own needs in Romania, which is what we called all that was left of the old Eastern Empire. But he agreed that the taking of the emperor outweighed his immediate needs. Still, we signed a contract; I had the captaincy of twenty lances, dated from the first week after the rescue of the emperor or my release by the Prince of Lesvos.

You may think that odd, between men who owed each other their lives ten times, but good walls make good neighbours, and like Sir Richard telling me straight that he was the prince's captain and I was not, I didn't want Nerio fretting. At the same time, I now had two contracts, one after another; my little company's future was assured. Twenty lances meant twenty knights, twenty squires in harness, twenty archers and twenty pages. As of that morning, I had the archers, was only a few short on the pages, but I lacked the knights or squires.

So while Emile and Marc-Antonio packed me a pair of bags and a wicker basket of armour, I approached our two Greek knights, Syr Giannis and Syr Giorgios. As they had converted, they were in a difficult place; to be honest, I think that they had expected to be taken on by the knights at Rhodes, but the Grand Master was not fond of Greeks. Any road, they agreed to serve with their stradiotes at least until the emperor was rescued.

And so, I had a sort of *compagnia*. I was too new to being a captain to realise that it was always like this – makeshift, with men coming and going. Let me tell you, gentles, that you no sooner bring any body of men to perfection than you fight someone, your best archer is killed, another is wounded and turns to drink, your best lance finds a lass and chases her to France, and you have to start again. That, too, is the life of arms.

Bah. Leave it there.

In a few hours, I had two signed contracts, both for sizeable amounts of money, and I arranged that Miles would collect our advance from the Prince and pay it out in wages. I borrowed money against my own part of the contract and handed Nerio half.

He still couldn't get money.

I had never, in all our time together, loaned him a copper. He took my little bag of gold and silver as if it was full of dung, and he shook his head, his demeanour downcast.

'I will repay this!' he swore.

'Why bother?' I asked. 'It's less than a tenth of what I owe you.'

That shut him up.

And there I was kissing Emile, shaking hands gravely with Edouard, kissing Isabelle, and bouncing Magdalena on my knee.

Emile took me aside. 'I won't ask you to be safe,' she said. 'Or brave. You won't be the first, you will be the second, will ye, nill ye.' She smiled. 'But I will ask you to do your very best to win peace with my lord, the Count of Savoy. If he values you, my love, our lives become ... possible.'

The Count of Savoy. The Green Count. Robert of Geneva's cousin.

I kissed her again. 'I will win his love,' I said.

'For me,' she said with a kiss. 'When you want to hate him, think of me. Or we'll be exiles all our lives. And we cannot always be going to Jerusalem.'

We kissed again, and she did not cry, and neither did I. Just.

And then we were at sea.

The galliot was very small, as I have said. It was so light I thought perhaps a man might have lifted her; she had benches for fifty men, and the rowers were professional, local fisherman and their sons, paid in silver. The master was a Genoese, Andrea Carne, with a gold ring in his ear and a curved Turkish sword in his belt. He never had his maille shirt off his back, and as we rowed like fury along the north coast of the island and raised our sails on what he called the 'Deep Blue', Nerio and I came to understand that we were on a very well-run pirate ship.

Carne was not talkative. He'd lost all four of his front teeth some-where, and he spoke in a sibilant whisper, and his men clearly feared him. Nor was he any too happy with our present commission. When, on our second day out, a small Venetian cog passed us on the other tack, with the red lion of Saint Mark bravely at her masthead, Carne watched her with an attentiveness not unlike the lust of a sailor who has been too long at sea and sees a young woman walking by.

His left hand played obscenely on the hilt of his scimitar. It was somewhat troubling to watch, especially as it often seemed to give away the turn of his mind; harder when he was angry, softer when he was pleased.

Not a pretty man at all. And he didn't like John the Kipchak; when John was by us, his hand went up and down his sword hilt like … Well, too much alike a certain action.

Achille, Nerio's squire, avoided him as if he had a disease. And they were both Genoese.

But by all the Saints, he was a superb sailor. And the crew, whatever their own little ways, were professional; the ship was as clean as work could make her, and the oars were served day and night in shifts; all the metal was bright and clean, and no one shit in the bilge, pardon my language. And mayhap there are other ways to lead men – Carne scarcely spoke an order, but he was obeyed. The barest smile had to suffice for praise, and I could tell that even his Greek helmsman, a swarthy man who might have been African and had a name longer than my sword, feared Carne.

I am not a great sailor like some I have known, although my skills were better then they had been when I'd embarked at Venice, but the navigation of our trip was beyond me. Nerio drew it on the deck with his dagger, so I remember it: we threaded the hundreds of islands in the Aegean and touched at the Venetian fortress of Negroponte, but we only took water there and stretched our legs; I ate octopus in the Venetian manner and Marc-Antonio looked homesick. Nerio had expected the Green Count to be there, and we were all disappointed, the more so as I really did not particularly want to sail any further with Maestro Carne.

But sail we did, and then we rowed, because the wind was against us; south along the shores of Attica, and then I knew the waters well enough, having fought there the year before. Athens, but only for an hour, and we were away. By then the rowers were surly, bathed in sweat, stinking; Carne's hand was moving constantly on his sword hilt, and I wanted to leave the ship and her pirate crew as soon as ever I could. It was so hot that it was hard to sleep on deck, and I had a hard time imagining what it was like to pull an oar for twelve hours.

But Carne got news at Athens and we ran south past Aegina and then across the sea and around the southern tip of the Peloponnese; past the great rock of Monemvasia, and then we had the summer wind at our backs. The rowers groaned and lay over their oars and slept, and the heat followed us like an enemy. Somewhere, summer had overtaken us, and it was high summer at sea. The sky was clear, and the stars hung at night like a woman's hairnet of jewels, so that I stared up at them in wonder, and almost couldn't sleep for watching them. I had never seen so many stars, and I swear there are more stars in the Inner Sea than England ever knows.

Two days out of Athens we fetched Modon, a port that Nerio knew well, and we landed for water. We hadn't even closed the beach before we knew that the Green Count lay just up the coast, and that Nerio's cousin had Marie de Bourbon, the self-styled Princess of Achaea, under siege at Jonc.

Carne grunted.

'I won't loossse my ssship for your convenienccce, gentles,' he spat. 'Venessshians and Sssavoyards and a nessst of viperss.'

'We are surely the Green Count's allies,' I said.

Carne glared at me.

I've been glared at.

'Kindly land me wherever the Green Count actually is,' I said. 'I believe those are your orders.'

Carne's eyes narrowed. His hand was all but spasming on his sword hilt.

We just stood there.

'This is my ship,' he said.

I shrugged. 'Of course,' I said, or something simple like that.

He grunted, and in a few minutes, we were away.

We rowed.

I was not well-beloved of the rowers. But Carne would not raise the sail, even in a fair wind, because he didn't want to be seen, the pirate. Still, it was only a few miles, and while we rowed north, Nerio enthralled me with a tale of a great battle fought just to the west, on the long, low island, where the Spartans were defeated by the Athenians.

We saw the Green Count's fleet from well off the coast; fifteen heavy galleys with the white cross on a red field, and one great galley flying a huge green silk banner and another from the stern with Saint Maurice.

I had brought clothes for this moment, and so had Nerio.

'Lay us under his stern, or close enough that you can row us over,' I said to Carne.

'Do not presume to give me orders on my own ship,' he snapped.

Nonetheless, he folded the wings of his oars in fine fashion and we coasted in. I could see men standing to arms on the galleys, but they had no picket ship and I wondered at their unreadiness in these waters.

The anchor was let go into the shallow water of the Bay of Navarino with a splash and no command given – that was the way with Carne – and the little galliot fetched up against her hawser and stopped a half a ship's length from the command galley. A dozen sweating oarsmen paid out cable until I could leap aboard the ship, with Saint Maurice in the stern.

My heart was beating a hundred to the minute or more. In fact, I was terrified. I own it. But it was like storming a breach – best done on the fly, and not overthought. In fact, it was fear of the Count and of Richard Musard that had kept me up the night before, not the stars. I should own that, too.

I could be facing Musard and Turenne, and perhaps the Hungarian, too, all in one ship. And I had to go unarmed, except de Charny's dagger.

Nerio was as calm as a sleeping cat.

I walked to the bow, put a hand on my dagger, and leaped.

I was still in the air when I saw Richard Musard for the first time in three years. He was easy to spot – the only black man on the deck. But he was dressed with a quiet magnificence that he had never managed when we owned an inn; he wore a fine green doublet and black hose, a gold belt on his hips, and the collar of an Order around his neck, and he looked more like a prince than a knight.

I wore, by careful choice, a good red velvet arming coat, recently completed by my wife's maid Helen; my brigantine, which was very pretty, and over it, my surcoat of the Order, which, just by happenstance, looked remarkably like the arms of Savoy – scarlet, with a white cross, and my own arms in a gold border in the upper left quadrant. I left my head bare and wore red hose to match my arming cote and red fighting shoes. I was trying to find clothes that would send a message – *I'm not just William Gold the routier.*

I didn't see the Green Count – that is, Amadeus of Savoy – on the main deck, but the whole stern was shrouded in a great, green silk awning, richly worked in gold embroidery, with the arms of Savoy in red and white, and roses, daisies, and laurels, and a magnificent image of the Virgin with our Saviour in her arms, all done in silk thread, the size of a house. It was a staggering display of wealth; that awning was worth as much as everything I had ever owned.

I saw Richard Musard turn his head, pass his eyes over me, look at Nerio as he landed behind me, and then ...

Then his eyes came back to me and fixed.

I didn't see Turenne or the Hungarian. But by God, gentles, in that moment I was fit to puke in terror. When you are fighting, you never have to fear much; after all, you are fighting. When you go to fight, there's death, of course. But not humiliation and depravity.

Musard met my eye. So I walked towards him.

I guess that people got out of my way. The deck of a galley, even at anchor, is a busy place, but all I remember is Musard.

I walked up to him. Bowed. 'Richard,' I said.

'William,' he said, 'why have you come?'

A natural question, but a slight emphasis on 'you' suggested everything.

'I am here on behalf of the Prince of Lesvos,' I said. 'I have news of immediate import for the Count of Savoy.'

'Ah!' said Richard. Clearly not what he'd expected.

'This gentleman is Ser Nerio Acciaioli,' I said.

Nerio inclined his head.

Richard bowed. 'I was informed that you were dead,' he said with a start. 'Is your cousin the Bishop of Patras?'

'Archbishop,' Nerio said, with his killing smile. 'I am not dead. The Count of Turenne is a liar and a thief.'

Richard took a half-step back from Nerio's anger. 'That is a dangerous accusation to make,' he said.

Nerio shrugged. 'I don't think so,' he said, 'as I am alive. Please take us to your master.'

I winced at the arrogance of Nerio's tone.

Richard was getting his back up. How little a few years change a person; I knew the language of his body so well.

'Richard,' I said quietly, 'we are here to help, not harm.'

'When have you ever done anything but harm?' Richard asked quietly. 'You bring evil with you.'

I shook my head. 'You have been misinformed,' I said. 'I will be happy to explain, but our news is immediate.'

Richard took a breath. 'I have been misinformed?' he asked. 'That you stole my wife and discarded her, and now have raped and forced marriage on the Countess d'Herblay after murdering her husband?'

Nerio snapped his fingers. 'All lies,' he said. 'Could we dispense with this and see the count, please, Sir Richard?'

'I never stole Janet, Richard,' I said. I stepped forward.

He stepped back, a hand on his sword hilt.

'Richard!' I said, as urgently as if I was calling to him to save me in a fight – and I was. 'Richard! *I never stole Janet. She left you.* She is serving John Hawkwood right now. Ask any soldier in Italy – there are not so many women in harness.'

Under his dark skin, Richard was pale – almost grey. 'I will take you to the count,' he said, and he was choking. 'And God have mercy on your soul.'

So we followed him under the awning. The deck was silent. Every man on it had stopped moving and was watching us.

Amadeus of Savoy was of middle height. He was a very handsome man with dark hair and green eyes, and he was vain. His vanity was as palpable as his love of the colour green. He was dressed from head to toe in that colour, a sort of emerald flame in silk that shone with rich under-threads, so that the green awning compounded the green of the clothes.

He had the collar of his Order around his neck and a belt of gold plaques, all round, and each one enamelled with his arms. The enamel showed that it was all gold, and that meant the belt itself was worth as much as a small town or castle.

He wore green silk hose, and green leather boots.

He did not rise. 'Who is this, Monsieur Musard?' he asked in his Savoyard French.

'My Lord, this is Sir William Gold,' Richard said. And bless him, he added no content. He said my name as if it was a name – any worthy name.

The Green Count's raised eyebrow vanished to be replaced by a raptor-like attentiveness.

'And Ser Nerio Acciaioli,' Richard added.

Now we had the count's complete attention.

He leaned forward, ignoring me completely. 'Really?' he asked.

Nerio's smile was as catlike as his languor. 'As far as I know,' he said.

The Green Count leaned back. 'So you won't mind meeting your cousin the bishop this afternoon,' he said.

'Archbishop,' said Nerio. 'No, I will not mind seeing Angelo at all.'

The silence was as thick as the green light under the awning. I was on one knee before the count, as custom demanded. Nerio was not.

Nerio was behaving as if he was the count's equal.

The game for Achaea had begun. I knew it, Nerio knew it, and the Green Count was beginning to understand the ramifications. He had clearly been told that Nerio was dead.

Now Nerio was on his deck.

The silence went on and on.

'My gracious Lord, I have a message from the Prince of Lesvos that bears no delay,' I said. I reached inside my brigantine and handed over Francesco's letter.

Richard took it from me and handed it to the count.

He took Richard's baselard out of its sheath – a gesture of curious, military intimacy, and used it to open the seal.

'Now, *par dieu*!' he exclaimed.

He looked at me. 'This is true?' he asked.

'Yes, My Lord.' I was still kneeling. It was my year to kneel.

'How old is this?' he asked.

'My Lord, I sailed on the fifteenth of July from Mytilene.' He was reading. I chose not to speak more.

He allowed the parchment to snap closed, and tapped his teeth with it. 'Do you bear any verbal message, Sir William?' he asked.

'My Lord, I was sent to you by my Order, the Knights of the Hospital, with a very different message, begging you and your force to attend the Grand Master in the harbour of Rhodes and join King Peter of Cyprus in his *empris*.' I took a breath.

He sat up. 'We hear that Alexandria is abandoned, and that King Peter is a broken reed,' he said.

It was like walking on quicksand; I had no idea what he had heard, and from what source. Fra Peter? Turenne? Some routier?

'My Lord, the Order is still strong and acting for the Faith in the East, and as for King Peter, I saw him two months ago in Famagusta and he was not a broken reed.' I could not say more, and I could sense the hostility around me. Indeed, it occurred to me then and now that I was happier eating sherbet with a Turkish emir than meeting the great Green Count.

He nodded. 'I see we have much to discuss. But these matters are for later – this letter has the precedence.' He tapped his teeth again. 'I assume you really are Nerio Acciaioli?' he asked.

Nerio raised an eyebrow. 'I suppose I could be mistaken,' he said. 'But it seems unlikely.'

Amadeus of Savoy let out what can only be described as a heartfelt sigh. 'Well,' he said. 'That certainly simplifies matters.' He looked back at me. 'Do you know the contents of this letter?' he asked me.

'We both know,' I said.

He nodded. 'Sir Richard. Arrange an immediate meeting with the Archbishop of Patras – I will even go as far as to meet him in his camp, if he will not come here. Tell my niece, too, that I have arrived at a verdict, and not, I fear, one in her favour.'

Something passed between him and Nerio. Some amusement, some disappointment. No words.

Nerio had read the whole situation in a glance. He was a better politician than I. He understood that his father had left him a good portion of the old Duchy of Achaea in his will, and that someone of the Savoyards – and I won't push you too hard to guess who it was – had spread the word of his death so that Amadeus could claim the lands for his sister's niece, Marie de Bourbon.

I confess, it was a brilliant gambit. If the emperor had not been taken; if we had not been sent as messengers ...

But we were.

I admired the way the Count of Savoy accepted the change of fortune. He nodded, looking at Nerio, and as I say, something passed between them.

'You will support us in our attempt to rescue the emperor,' he said to Nerio.

Nerio smiled. 'Of course, My Lord,' he said, using the count's style for the first time.

He looked back at me. 'You will attend us ashore, Sir William,' he said.

I had time to thank God that Robert of Geneva was not there, and that Nerio was.

We landed on a beautiful beach that seemed to extend to the horizon to the south, and to the north wound around into an estuary, or so it appeared. Jonc was a castle perched on a rock, like every castle in the Inner Sea. It was held by a Frenchman, Guillaume de Talay, for Marie de Bourbon. Nerio's cousin was laying siege to it, at least in part because it was part of Niccolò Acciaioli's patrimony. In fact, I had begun to suspect it now belonged to Nerio. Remember, we didn't know; the wheels were turning inside other wheels.

We landed with wet feet because the wind was rising, and it was only as I leaped from the bow of a longboat onto the beach, trying to preserve my fighting shoes from salt, that I saw our Genoese galliot already well out to sea, and running south, the bastard.

Nerio narrowed his eyes.

'We've been in worse spots,' he said. Which, from him, indicated we were in a very tight spot indeed.

However, we walked up the beach to where a large company was drawn up – routiers and mercenaries – and the Count of Savoy's lips curled back from his teeth in a sneer.

'Your cousins, Sir William,' he said, the first indication he gave that he remembered me, or that he disliked me.

There is no good answer to make to one of the greatest princes in the Christian world and his dislike of you.

And they really did look like the worst of our breed – rusty haubergeons, old brigantines of heavy, square plates, aventails of cloth, painted helmets. Their discipline was fair; they didn't talk, and the men-at-arms stood with their spears in their hands upright, and formed a sort of road for the count. An officer with a baton of dirty white greeted the count and bowed.

The count walked right past him towards the red pavilion in the distance, up on the grass above the beach.

He rose to the insult, angrily. 'You have brought more than the agreed number of men, My Lord,' he said.

Amadeus turned his green eyes on the man. 'Spare me your pettifogging,' he said. 'I mean no harm to your master and in fact, only good. Do not seek to delay me, or it will be the worse for you.'

The life of the routier does not, in fact, prepare you to deal with the power of a prince.

On the other hand, I was there at Brignais when we smashed the Savoyards and the King of France's marshal, too. And we were routiers. I had the oddest feeling that I was more one of these men in their rusting maille than I was a follower of the count's. His arrogance made the worst men in my Order seem ... merely pleasantly arrogant, like Fiore or Nerio.

He walked up the beach. At the edge of the sheep-cropped grass, his servant opened a folding stool and he sat, two men took off his shoes, dumped the sand, and then laced the shoes back on. It was a performance, if you like.

Then we walked to the great red pavilion.

The Archbishop of Patras was a handsome man, and his Acciaioli blood was obvious; he and Nerio shared a nose and forehead. He was dressed for war, in an arming coat, and he had a small Turkish mace in his hand. He was surrounded by courtiers and officers of his household, but he came and bowed to the Green Count as was proper, and when he saw Nerio, he started in astonishment, pressed past the count and took his cousin's hands.

'I thought you were dead!' he said, and threw his arms around Nerio.

Nerio smiled at me over his cousin's shoulder.

'*Sic transit gloria mundi*,' sighed the count. 'This is your missing cousin?' he asked.

'It is,' the archbishop said.

Amadeus knelt and kissed his episcopal ring, as did Richard Musard and I and even Nerio.

In the next hour, the Green Count played the great man to perfection. He had an army at his back, and more, as I heard, on the way; the Savoyards expected a Genoese fleet any day. The archbishop was rich, and had a good company of routiers, but they were not going to be a match for four thousand professional men-at-arms. I had only been with the count a few hours and I had already had time to marvel at the quality of his army: he had Savoyard knights, hundreds of them; he had Picard and English and Scots archers; engineers, siege machines, horse transports, food and water. His army was superb, and a shockingly better force than that which the legate had led to Alexandria.

I mention this because he could have had any peace he wanted, but he was scrupulously fair. He dictated the terms, but they were very favourable to the archbishop, and thus to Nerio. I know the count spoke briefly to Nerio on the ship, but Nerio said the conversation was meaningless – a mere exchange of pleasantries – except, I discovered later, that the count asked, quite baldly, for a loan from the Acciaioli bank, and Nerio agreed to see to it that such a loan was made, to the sum of ten thousand ducats – a staggering sum.

Nerio had in his purse about eighty ducats, if that. He was not used to counting his coppers or his gold florins either. But he guaranteed a very powerful man a huge loan.

I'm glad I didn't know.

So the count sat in the archbishop's tent and made a treaty between his wife's cousin and Nerio's cousin. Marie de Bourbon was forced to renounce all her claims to Corinth and all of the lands held by the Acciaioli throughout the Morea, and in exchange, the archbishop released her steward from captivity and received back his own bailli, who was handed over that very afternoon.

He did it without arrogance; I mean, beyond the incredible arrogance of abrogating to himself the right to force a treaty on his wife's cousin and an archbishop. And I confess that the treaty he made was fair enough.

We were given a place to sleep in another galley, and we ate a dinner with a dozen English men-at-arms in Savoyard service that was pleasant enough. I found the food without taste, because I was still afraid.

As we lay waiting for sleep, Nerio spoke aloud my thought.

'Why did Turenne tell them we were dead?' he asked.

I had no idea. 'Is it possible they thought we *were* dead?' I asked.

I fell asleep wondering.

Morning and old bread and watered wine, and a summons to attend the count – just for me.

Well. It had to come. As I dressed, I saw that the Genoese had come, and their dozen galleys were anchored out by the island where the Spartans had lost to the Athenians. It occurred to me in my trouble of spirit that had we the army of King Peter and all the Order's galleys, we'd have been a far, far better Crusade than the one that went against Alexandria.

Nerio was up with me. 'You want me to come?' he said. 'He can't kill you with me there. He needs me.'

I shook my head. 'I think . . .' I said. 'I think I have to do this alone, win or lose.'

Nerio spat over the side. 'So do I,' he admitted. 'But if he kills you, by God, I'll break him.'

That made me smile; my friend Nerio versus a prince of the West. 'Remind me never to make you angry,' I said.

And then I put on my dagger and went with the squire who had come to fetch me.

When I went aboard his great galley, he was alone under the green awning with Richard Musard.

'Sir William Gold,' he said.

'My Lord,' I said with my best bow, a full *reverencia* on one knee.

'You have pretty manners for a routier. Richard tells me that you have been at my court in Geneva.' He didn't smile.

'Yes, My Lord,' I said. I was stiff, unshaven, and feeling ill-used.

'You are married to my cousin Emile,' he said. His green eyes were on me. 'She holds several important fiefs in my county, Sir William, and she may not wed without my permission.' He raised an eyebrow. 'Yet you dared to wed her. And then you dare to come into my presence, as if your red coat will protect you.'

I wasn't going to shrug. 'Yes, My Lord,' I said.

'Yes My Lord, what?' he shot back. 'Do you know the charges against you?'

'Yes, My Lord,' I said. 'The Grand Master of my Order informed me.'

That took him aback.

'I assume, My Lord is referring to the charges levelled by the Count of Turenne,' I said. I'm sure my voice wavered; I'm a great deal better at fighting with swords than words.

'Interesting,' he said, looking at Richard. 'You know the charges, and you came anyway.'

'There was no one else to send,' I said. 'Rhodes is virtually empty of knights, My Lord.'

'It didn't occur to you or your Grand Master that I might just find you guilty of treason, *lèse-majesté*, a dozen other crimes, and string you up by the neck at the end of my main yard?' he asked.

'I'm sure it did occur,' I said. 'Your Grace must know that I was aware of it. My wife told me as much.'

He was served wine. I was there on one knee, and Richard would not meet my eye, and I thought, *Dearest Jesu, if this is it, let me be debonair and a good knight.*

'And why should I not string you up?' he asked. He didn't smile.

'I might say that as I am a belted knight, I would at least like to have my head cut off with a sword,' I said.

Not a glimmer of a smile.

'But rather like the report of Nerio Acciaioli's death, My Lord, the whole thing is a tissue of lies, excepting only that I had no idea that my lady wife was such a powerful vassal that her marriage was entailed.' I looked him in the face. Met his odd green eyes.

'You did not kill the Comte d'Herblay?' he asked.

'No, My Lord. And a dozen knights of the Order were present.' I was breathing better by then. Truly, it is like fighting. Once you are in it, most of the fear falls away.

The Count looked at Musard. 'Really?' he asked. 'Name one.'

I named five.

We looked at each other.

'Why would the Count of Turenne fabricate such a ridiculous charge if it was so easily disproved?' he asked.

The phrase *Because he's a lying, cowardly sack of shit* came to my head, and I had to work not to say it. 'I have no idea what goes on inside the count's head,' I said.

'Interesting,' the Green Count said. 'You dare to sneer at the Count of Turenne. You, a former routier, a killer, sneer at my cousin, whose birth is so far above yours as to merit your instant death on his word alone.'

Sometimes, it really is better to be hanged for a lion. If he was going to hang me, I was damned if I was going to be nice.

'My sneer is for his cowardice,' I said, and I added sneer to sneer. 'He was among the first to demand we retreat from Alexandria. Indeed, he never wanted to land in the first place. I know nothing of his birth, My Lord. I speak as the merest fighting man, as you say.' I continued to kneel, but my back was straight. 'D'Herblay was roaming the streets killing women and children.'

Count Amadeus shook his head gently. 'What a spotless Christian knight you sound,' he said. '*Par dieu*, Richard, is this Lancelot or Percival before me? I can scarcely tell.' He looked at me. 'You are a bold rogue, William Gold. This man, who has been my squire and is now my best knight – he begged me for your life this morning on bended knee.'

I doubt I've ever been so shocked in all my life.

'Interesting,' he said, observing my reaction. 'Richard has begged your life and I give it you. I would be a fool to hang you and bear the wrath of your Order. And my cousin Turenne is a fool, I'll give you that.' He pursed his lips. 'Monsieur Musard, take Sir William with you, if he is agreeable. If he dies, so much the better.'

He looked at me. 'The Turks have closed the Dardanelles, or so the Genoese just arrived have told me. You and Richard will investigate this, and then fetch your Prince of Lesvos to the new fleet rendezvous at Negroponte,' he said. He smiled, or rather, the corners of his mouth twitched. 'If you are not a false traitor, Sir William, then in fact you owe me a dozen knights' service for sixty days for your wife's lands. Either way, frankly, I have the power of high justice, middle justice and low justice over you, and I command you to attend Sir Richard Musard to Gallipoli. Serve, or be declared miscreant.'

'I will go gladly,' I said. I doubt I sounded glad.

'Die in service, then, or return with a better repute,' he said. 'I will be just as happy, either way.' He looked at me. A servant handed him a document, and he kept me waiting, on my knee, while he read it and signed it. 'Where is my cousin Emile?' he asked.

'At the court of the Prince of Lesvos,' I said.

'Interesting,' he said. He waved his hand.

I was dismissed.

Richard walked down the deck with me.

'We are not friends,' he said. 'But I couldn't see you killed.' He shrugged. 'And Turenne is an arse. Even the count knows it. Your knight, Fra Peter, spoke to the count at Corfu.'

I was still having a little trouble breathing.

'And we are going to Gallipoli together?' I asked.

He nodded.

'It's a long swim,' I said. 'Do you have a boat?'

Richard looked at me. 'You haven't changed much,' he said. 'This is an insane mission, William.'

'No it isn't,' I said. 'Mayhap not a picnic. But not insane.'

'Under the walls of an infidel city?' he asked.

'I walked around Alexandria five days before the army landed,' I said. 'And my man speaks Turkish.'

'Damn,' Richard said with his old smile. 'Damn.'

'We need a boat,' I said.

Richard nodded. 'No problem there.'

Nerio didn't exactly decline to come. But he wanted to establish himself, if even a little, in his patrimony. And he had guaranteed the count a loan – a loan which may or may not have played a major role in the preservation of my skin.

I left him.

We lost the whole day looking for a boat. It was evening; Richard was trying to convince any of the Venetian captains to run us to Negroponte, at least, and I was hiring.

I know that sounds odd, but remember I had a contract with the Prince of Lesvos. Western men-at-arms are not so common in the East, in Outremer. And the Archbishop of Patras no longer needed his army.

It seemed too good to pass up, even though I had no idea how to transport them to Lesvos, but Nerio said he'd see to it, and so I hired a dozen men-at-arms and as many armed squires. They were routiers, but so was l'Angars and so was Pierre Lapot. They had no horses; I was willing to bet I could get them horses.

It was all risk, like business. On the other hand, I got to pick and choose, and I did, taking only the best men with the best kit: some Scots or Irish, all Islesmen led by Hector Lachlan, a very big man indeed in an old-fashioned long haubergeon; a little *famiglia* of five Italians from Vicenza, all exiles, all named Cavalli, led by Maurizio di Cavalli, a good knight and a fine lance; and some Englishmen, led by Diccon Crewel. I admit that I prefer Englishmen. So even if their harness wasn't as good, I took them. Oh, and I mustn't forget my Welsh – three archers, all named David, and a man-at-arms with hair as red as my own, William Chetwyn, known to his mates as Red Bill.

I had no time to get to know them, so I left them with Nerio, because I was just clasping hands with the leader of the English I'd just signed, Diccon Crewel, a small man and too gentle to not be very dangerous, and I was laughing because Gospel Mark, an archer I'd known at Poitiers, was right there, and he knew Ned Cooper and Ewan too. And over his shoulder I saw Nerio, and with him, a familiar face.

Carlo Zeno.

I'd last seen him in the fighting at Alexandria. He was still the same, handsome, with a scar on his face and an almost perpetual sneer, dark-haired and dark-bearded. We hadn't started as friends, but we'd done well enough in the end.

'Messire Zeno has a ship,' Nerio said. 'I believe he's the man to take you.'

Zeno has since told me that the voyage from Jonc to Gallipoli was one of the least pleasant experiences of his life. It's probably a wonder we remained friends.

And the reason was Richard Musard. Or, to be precise, me and Richard.

For a day, it was smooth sailing, both really and metaphorically, and Richard and I kept our distance, but off the Hand, south of Mistra's vale, we hit bad weather. We were driven from the deck of Zeno's little galliot and into the tiny stern cabin, and there we were, two men who had once been friends, with Zeno, literally, between us.

Many galleys do not have a full stern cabin, but Zeno was both wealthy and militarily active and he'd had his purpose-built for long voyages. He had a swinging bed that hung by chains at night and was roped up to the slanted ceiling by day, and two great stern windows, the first I ever saw, with a bench that ran along the windows as if they were *loggia* in some great *Ca'* of Venice, and the bench had a red velvet cushion and was very comfortable. There was a table that almost filled the little room – although it, too, folded away – and five determined people could sit around it, but we were just three. John preferred to be out in the rain rather than listen; Richard's squire was a very young Cornishman named Robin, and he stayed out as well.

We sat and stared at each other for half a glass.

I found that I hated him. I had let it go; it all seemed long ago. But when the smug bastard was one seat away from me, so close I could reach out and choke him, all I could think of was that this particular blackheart had betrayed me to be tortured and hanged by the Bourc Camus, or at the very least to be taken as a criminal by Jean le Maigre.

And of course, if you recall, he thought I was the engine of depriving him of his lady love.

So we sat and glared.

Zeno drank, and tried to make various forms of small talk; he discussed fights he had seen, he asked me to tell him about Jerusalem, he told entertaining tales of serving various Turkish emirs as a mercenary. He had known old Orhan, the father of the current Ottamanid sultan, Murad. And he spoke Turkish.

And none of that moved either of us as we sat in the cabin and hated each other.

It only took a couple of hours of rain, and Zeno had had enough. He rose to his feet, fought past me for the door, and paused there, the brass handle in his hand. 'I'll go and make sure the deck is still there,' he said. 'If one of you kills the other, just fling the body out the windows and clean up, eh?'

He slammed the door.

I looked at Richard. 'So,' I said, 'why did you beg the count for my life?'

He looked away. 'Because it isn't fair. I know you didn't do any of those things. So does he. Turenne is a fool, and he knows it, and he would only blacken his repute by killing you.'

'Not because you've already tried to have me killed once, and that didn't work out?' I asked.

'Why don't you just fuck yourself?' he said.

'I couldn't do it as thoroughly as you did it to me, brother,' I said. 'Taken by the Bourc Camus. You fucking *set me up* to die at the hands of the *Bourc Camus*.'

'No, I did not,' Richard said calmly. And then, much more quietly, 'I just let it happen.'

'You just let it happen?' I asked.

'Like you just happened to start fucking my woman?' he asked. 'While we're spewing obscenities like brigands, let's get that right.'

'Never touched her,' I said.

'Bullshit,' Richard said. 'I saw you in her tent, and she told me herself.'

He crossed his arms.

Well, here's the thorn amidst the roses. I've never known Janet to lie, but she wasn't there right then and I really hadn't ever put a finger on her. I hadn't even particularly fancied her, although she was both beautiful, in a French way, and a fine swordsman. Swordswoman. Horsewoman. Everything I knew about hawking, which, as I have said, is little enough, and chess and table manners I learned from her.

I shrugged. 'Never touched her, before or since,' I said.

Richard glared.

'And while we're on that, I doubt she was ever "your woman".' I don't know what imp drove me to say it ... Probably because I was Janet's friend. I knew what she thought of being owned.

'What the fuck does that mean?' he asked, and his hand went to his dagger. 'She was *mine*.'

'I think she was her own,' I said.

'Her own what?' Richard asked.

'Her own woman. Listen, Richard. Listen to me. When she came to us in sixty-two— '

'When you stole her from me,' Richard said. 'Christ, why am I sitting here listening to you spew lies? You know what, William? I volunteered for this stupid mission because I thought I could *redeem* you. Once upon a time you believed in chivalry, in knighthood. You were better than just a routier. I saw it. I thought you could be ... saved.'

I had a moment of nearly white-hot anger. I was unused to being thought a bad knight. The pain was particularly sharp from Richard. He had his hand on his dagger, and I had mine on my rondel – not my baselard. For whatever reason, I had de Charny's dagger on my hip, and I could feel the steel cap under my thumb.

I had the oddest sensation, as if the world was not all I thought it to be. I saw de Charny's corpse at Poitiers. I heard his voice say, *Those who do most are worth most.*

I heard it so clearly that he might have been at the table, sitting between us.

I let go of my dagger.

I took a breath.

And another.

And another.

'Richard,' I said slowly. 'I am a knight-donat of the Order of Saint John of Jerusalem. I have just been to Jerusalem, Richard. I served at Alexandria at my own expense.' I took another breath. 'When I left Italy, Janet was serving in armour in John Hawkwood's company of lances – the White Company or whatever they were calling themselves. I assume she still is. Somewhere in Venice I have a letter from her in which she tells my wife – the woman who is now my wife – that she was never my leman.' I shrugged. 'I am not, perhaps, the mirror of chivalry, but I do as much as I can, every day, to be a good knight. I did not take Janet from you.'

'Then why would she leave me?' Richard asked.

Now, friends … What do you tell a friend, when you know the truth will cut like a heavy sword? What do you tell a man you both love and hate?

'Because she didn't want to live as your wife,' I said. 'And you know that, Richard. She told you over and over.'

He turned his face away, set hard. 'She never meant that. That's crap.'

'No, Richard. It's because—'

'She was *mine*. I saved her, and she was *mine*.' Richard's voice all but hissed.

'You cannot own a person,' I said. I thought I was being reasonable.

'You can own a person!' he shouted. 'I was fucking owned. I was a slave! Is that it? Because I'm black, swarthy, whatever you want to call it? Is that what it is? Because I was a slave?'

Truly, I hadn't ever thought of Richard's slavery before. I mean, I had. But let's be frank, back when he talked about his life, we were running a brothel and trying to be knights, which is a difficult enough balancing act without over-thinking your friend's birth and upbringing.

I was honest enough, in the moment, to shrug and say no more, and Richard slid out of the bench and left the cabin, slamming the door.

That was round one.

We had our second joust later in the day. We were served dinner in the cabin, of course. Zeno crammed all four of his gentleman marines around our table, and he was *capitano* – very much so. He sat at the head of the little table and talked. I think he talked relentlessly to prevent another outburst; he described how he had come into possession of the galliot, and how he'd ordered her rebuilt, and the rise in his fortunes since the taking of Alexandria.

Richard fussed with his food. We had good food – chickpea soup full of spices, and cold chicken, and barley rolls that were apparently re-warmed, but tasted fresh baked.

Zeno nodded to me. 'I have a wonderful man. I bought him in a Genoese slave market. He can cook anything, anywhere.'

'I didn't think Venice allowed slavery,' I said.

Zeno shrugged and made a face. 'Oh, I'm sure he's not a slave aboard this ship. But really – are any of us free? I serve Venice; he serves me.'

I had some doubts. But like the Genoese, Carne, who might have been Zeno's brother, Zeno did not feel himself constrained by mere ethics or notions of morality. I have noticed this a good deal among captains of ships, and kings and princes; when men reach the epitome of power, they are free to ignore the strictures of their homes, and the laws.

Knighthood, to me, is nothing more or less than this – the training to avoid this pitfall. To remain beholden, if you will – to a lady, to the Church, to your lord – despite the power of your right hand and the protection of your armour.

Nor do I mean that Zeno was a bad man. I liked him. But at sea he was a tyrant, and his will was the will of all men on his vessel. Perhaps I am naturally servile, although I doubt it, but I had no trouble obeying his strictures. I could understand that he wanted no more friction; harsh words carry on shipboard, and anger breeds anger, as any soldier knows.

But Richard began to speak of Count Amadeus in the terms most used to describe God, and he very quickly got under my skin, as he no doubt meant. He spoke of Amadeus's victories over the 'routiers' – by which he meant my friends; he spoke of the infinite superiority of the Green Count's army to that hired by the Church; and he openly said that Europe was cleaner for the many thousand routiers taken out of it by the 'crusade'. It was only then that I learned how many of the 'crusaders' died of Plague then raging in Venice.

And I confess that he said aloud many things I'd thought, or even said, or heard said by cynical souls like Nerio. But it is like the old German saying; I can speak ill of my sister, but you cannot. In his mouth, it was the worst hypocrisy, and I found it difficult to listen to him when we had, together, and by force of arms, run a stable of French girls from an inn whose owner we terrified.

Twice, we did that.

Damn me, friends. I'm *far* from proud of being a whoremaster. But I did it, and it helps me appreciate what drives other men. Bad places make bad men.

So I sat and fretted. But I kept my temper; if you are paying attention, you know that I was better and better at this, and as I hadn't killed Scrope, I was unlikely to fly out at Musard. I kept my peace, pasted a smile on my face, and this drove Richard to drive the spurs in more recklessly.

The Venetian marines were all gentlemen; they tried to make small talk in Italian, and when Richard drove on in his Savoyard-Anglic French, they gave up, poured white wine from a skin, and chattered in Veneziano, a language I could not really understand. I was pretty sure that they were talking about us.

Zeno had also had enough, and after dinner he wiped his eating knife with a cloth and looked at me.

'What is your plan for scouting the town?' he asked.

I shrugged. 'First I think we want to know whether the Turks have actually attempted to close the Dardanelles,' I said.

Zeno nodded, wiping his moustache. 'My thought exactly. I'll pick up a fishing boat off Tenedos – that's the fastest way to get news.'

Tenedos, the jewel of the Straits, and a perpetual source of contention between the Genoese, the Venetians and the Byzantines.

'Why do you address him?' Richard asked. 'I am the leader of this expedition.'

Zeno raised an eyebrow. 'I know him,' he said. 'I know he's done this sort of thing before. I do not have the honour of knowing you particularly, sir.' Zeno bowed.

'I will tell you my will in this,' Richard began.

Zeno put his eating knife down and shook his head. 'This is my ship, and I'll decide what happens to her and aboard her. I asked the opinion of a comrade, Sir Richard. I do not take orders, except from the doge and the thirty.'

Richard sat up. 'Then you can take us back to the count and see how you are rewarded,' he said.

He got up and left the table without the *capitano*'s permission. Zeno frowned.

I put a hand on his sleeve. 'I'll talk to him. We were friends once.'

'And then what?' Zeno said.

'He thinks I stole his wife,' I said.

Zeno laughed, a short, almost demonic bark. 'And did you?' he asked.

'No,' I said.

'Too bad,' Zeno said. 'If you had …' He shrugged. 'Men do these things. You could pretend to be contrite and he could pretend to believe you.'

I fingered my beard. 'But I didn't,' I said.

Zeno looked at the four marines chattering in Veneziano. 'That's bad, because that means she left him for another reason. I'm guessing she left him because he was an arse.'

I shrugged. 'A complicated woman,' I said.

'He who says woman says all,' Zeno said.

I shook my head. I disliked the tendency of men to dismiss women as alien and incomprehensible. Men seem to learn to understand horses – horses are far more alien. And as Emile once said to me, that's because men spend more time and effort on horses.

But here, again, I'm cutting away from the pell.

'I'll speak to him,' I said again.

Zeno waved. 'Be my guest. But I'm going to Tenedos – we'll have a look at Gallipoli, will he, nill he. He seems to think that the sun shines out of this count's arsehole – for my money, he's another Frank with a better retinue.'

I went on deck. John was cleaning my armour; I hunkered down with him while he did my arms, and I drew the emperor's sword and looked it over. The sea was never a friend to steel, and there it was; a slight tug in drawing, and a little haze of rust at the top of the blade. I went to work on it, forgetting Richard for a few moments in the work, and then I saw him in the bow. I walked out along the catwalk amidships and then up onto the forward fighting platform, which even a little ship like this had to have.

He turned. 'I knew it was a mistake sailing with one of your many friends,' he said.

I considered a number of replies and let them all go. 'Richard,' I said.

He shrugged. 'I know. I'm being difficult.' He looked at me. 'You know that they call me "the Moor" behind my back?'

'No,' I said. 'I don't understand their Veneziano.'

'Nor I, but I know the word for Moor,' he said. 'Among the Savoyards, I am a famous knight. I have my own retinue. I wear the collar of an Order. On this deck, I am a Moor.'

I leaned on the rail beside him. Sometimes, when you talk to a man, or a woman, for that matter, eye contact is the wrong approach; too intimate. Too close. Side by side, looking at the sea …

'And I am here,' I said softly. 'Reminding you that once we were not knights. We were hired muscle at best.'

'Yes,' he said, very softly.

'It is too close, is it not?' I said.

The bow cut the water. If he said anything, I didn't hear it. I wanted to speak. I wanted to tell him that he made *me* into a monster in his mind, and that monster hurt me, because I had been that man …

I didn't. I talk too much at the best of times, but sometimes, I can hold my tongue. I wanted him to speak.

But he said nothing. So I changed tack.

'Zeno was sent by their *admirale*, Contarini, because of Tenedos,' I said. 'That is, he was sent to help us, but also to test the waters, so to speak, rather than allow the count to choose one of the Genoese captains, who would have been unacceptable operating in these waters. To Venice.'

'Fucking Venetians,' Musard said. 'They have no graces, no aristocrats, no natural leaders. They live for money and petty politics – so fucking petty compared to the Genoese.'

'The slavers?' I spat.

It's odd how, when you try to hold your temper, letting go is so sudden and so subtle. You don't even notice, and it is not on the subject you expected. 'You started your life as a *slave* and you think the Genoese are superior to the Venetians?'

'Now you tax me with being a slave?' he snarled, stepping away from the rail.

'No!' I said. 'Use your fool head, Dick! I'm telling you that—'

He swung a fist at me, and I blocked it, as Fiore taught me, but Richard was far too fast for me to catch his wrist.

I backed a step, and Richard spat, 'Is that what you and Janet talked about?'

I shook my head. Useless, at twilight. 'We never discussed you, Richard, damn it—'

'You lie,' he said. 'I can see it in your whole body.'

'Richard,' I said.

But he turned and clambered down the ladder to the midships catwalk.

I stood there, watching the bow cut the water. Just below me, one of the oarsmen laughed ruefully. I had forgotten they were even there.

'Take his woman, did ye?' he said in accented Italian.

Another oarsmen below me laughed. 'Mayhap she'd had eno' of his temper.'

Well. You forget that there are men all around you, servants and soldiers. But they know things.

Eventually I curled up by John. The deck hurt my hip.

I lay there, thinking about how right Richard was about one thing; that I was somehow a different man on board Zeno's little ship than I was leading a company in the presence of my wife. I thought some dark thoughts, too, about who I was; routier, knight, soldier of Christ, mercenary. Husband, lover. I thought of Anne, in Avignon. I said a prayer for her; for the girls who'd been our whores in France.

I thought of de Charny, dying – making a great death. Is it that we respect the manner of death so much because it shows us the true inner man, stripped of all the trappings of status and family and wealth?

And it seemed to me that Richard wanted me to be the monster of his dreams; a mad routier. The Bourc Camus, in fact.

And that led me to wonder if my hatred for Camus wasn't in some part my recognition of what we had in common.

Uncomfortable thoughts for an uncomfortable deck.

The third day we raised Tenedos, and just as he said he would, Zeno snapped up not one but two fishing boats in the dawn of the fourth day out of Jonc, and we questioned them separately, but they were small men, terrified, and yet happy enough to tell us the news. Yes, the Turks had closed the Straits. They had turned back a Genoese cargo vessel which was in the port of Tenedos that moment, and they had seized a Catalonian trader.

The fishermen knew nothing of the politics, although they said that there was a 'great army' at Gallipoli, and that the Turks were ferrying men every day from Asia to Europe.

Zeno consulted me openly, and didn't invite Richard. But I insisted, gently, and was rewarded with Zeno's cautious acceptance.

Richard must have slept better than I, both nights, and he came with a bounce in his step. Zeno outlined the problem; Richard listened attentively, like the good soldier I knew he was.

'So sailing up the channel is not an option?' he said.

Zeno picked his teeth. 'I don't think so,' he admitted. I knew it was the sort of adventure he'd enjoy telling about in Saint Mark's Square.

'Let me have one of these fishing boats and a handful of oarsmen,' I said. 'John can speak all the Turk for us.'

'I speak Turkish,' Zeno said. 'And Sir Richard, if I may beg his pardon, looks like any jihadi or ghazi from North Africa.'

I expected an explosion from Richard. But he just shrugged. 'I do, at that,' he said.

'I know a little Turkish,' I said.

'And you can pass for a Turk with that red hair,' Zeno said. 'We'll be fine.' He bought us all Turkish clothing, or rather, nondescript clothing – soft trousers, bare feet like any sailor, kaftans belted with old leather belts, soft felt hats.

Fine, it turned out, was eight men in a tiny open boat, tacking out of Tenedos into a stiff wind, soaking wet all the time. I learned more of small boat-handling in those two days than I had learned from Contarini in six weeks; the tiller was alive under my hand, the spray was annoying, the salt got into everything, and when I referred to the weather as a storm, Zeno laughed.

'This is just rain with a little wind,' he said. 'You really are a lubber.'

Two days. Even the bread was wet; the water was as bad as water in a city under siege, and I got to know our oarsmen as well as I knew Zeno. Richard and I had no way of avoiding each other. John gave us all lessons in Turkish as we rowed, and my hands bled, but then, so did Zeno's, and he laughed his evil laugh.

'I'm out of shape,' he said.

'How do you get used to this?' I asked.

He was rowing, so he didn't shrug. 'Musard! Keep the tiller straight!' Then he glanced at me. 'I was a galley slave for the fucking Aragonese for two years,' he said. 'I hate them. And the Genoese.'

'That's a lot of hate,' I said.

Zeno's eyes were slits. 'I have plenty,' he said.

The wind was always against us. It varied between so directly against us that we could only row into it, and lightly against us, so we could tack. Zeno showed us all how there was a counter-current at the shores of the Dardanelles.

Perhaps I need to explain. The Dardanelles are more like a great salt river than like a sea. There is a flow to the whole body, from the Euxine, the Dark Sea to the north where the Russe live and the steppes begin, down past Constantinople, through the Sea of Marmara, and out into the Mediterranean. The current runs about two knots and sometimes a little more, but close inshore on either bank there is a little bit of a counter-current. With skilful boat handling – only Zeno could do it, and one of the oarsmen – we could coast, creeping along, without doing any work.

But a change in the wind, or a steering error, and we were out of the counter-current and rowing, or tacking in a long, long reach across the whole strait. I got to know those looming ridges pretty well, and then towards late afternoon we came to the great bend in the strait. As we crossed from east to west, we opened the next arm of the Dardanelles, and there we saw six galleys, low to the water, clustered on the Asian shore by Carnak. They were well hidden there, and no merchant ship would be able to flee them once committed to the tack.

They saw us, right enough. And despite our best efforts, we were alone; there was no other shipping in the great dark river of salt water – no fishing boats, no pleasure boats.

Two galleys crossed their lateens.

'Shit,' Zeno said. 'I wanted to do this in the darkness,' he added.

It was true. We'd made better time than he expected, despite the stiff breeze, and we'd all lost track of the sun in the haze of fatigue.

I was rowing, so I could see every part of the drama play out. 'Run for the bank?' I asked.

Zeno spat over the side. 'Let them board us,' he said. 'We're a boat full of bad men, and we were trying a little piracy down towards Tenedos. And we are lying – we pretend first we want to go fishing.'

John nodded. 'I like this,' he said. 'Many tents on the Asian bank. No Turkish emir can know all the men.'

'Our oarsmen are obviously Venetian,' Musard said.

'You haven't been out in Outremer very long, have you?' Zeno said. 'Plenty of Italians in that host. Aye, and Franks and Berbers, too. Greed and violence have no borders, eh?' he laughed.

John said, 'I must be in command.'

We all looked at him.

He shrugged.

Zeno nodded. 'He's right. By Christ's beard, Turk. You take the helm.'

John skipped along the benches. He took the tiller from Musard, who took the oar John had abandoned, the one next to me.

And then John turned our little boat to meet the oncoming galleys.

They were alongside us in ten minutes. We never had a chance, running. They knew their business, and were sprightly and well-handled, full of men.

A Turk hailed us, and John roared back. There was laughter.

The nearer galley took in her oars and the farther crossed our bow. It was almost laughable; there were nigh on five hundred men to our eight.

They'd had a dull day, I could tell.

But John was unsinkable. He roared out his answers, and men on the galleys laughed.

Zeno translated.

'He says we are fishermen, and the galley asks, where are our nets? And he says, they got lost over the side. And the galley asks, what are we fishing for? And your man says, gold. And everyone laughs. A good answer. And John says there is a Venetian galley at Tenedos, too big for these cowards. And the galley's master says, almost anything is too big for that cockleshell. And he tells John to get his wet arse back to his unit.

'And your John says, all he wants on earth, with Allah's help, is to put his wet arse on the rump of a horse and never touch an oar again.

'All the Turks laugh.'

Musard coughed.

I turned and looked over my shoulder, and the galley off our bow was already under way, her oars going.

'Oh, fuck,' Zeno said.

There was a stir on the nearer galley.

'Look up at me, number four oar!' called a strong voice in Italian.

I had no idea who was number four. I looked up.

'Not you, you Judas! The bugger next to you. Look at me, whore-son!'

'Fuck,' Zeno said.

He looked up.

John cursed.

In twenty heartbeats, our little boat was chained fore and aft to the Turkish galley, and we were taken, sitting placidly under the stares of a hundred archers.

'Carlo Zeno,' said a voice above us. 'What a pleasure.'

'Fuck,' said Zeno.

They stripped us. They still didn't know what to make of us; John was obviously a Kipchak, and they took Musard for a Mamluk or a Moor, and I growled in Turkish and was taken for a Turk.

As soon as they got Zeno up the side, the bastard who had identi-fied him tripped him, put him down, and kicked him in the guts.

'There you are, messire,' he said with satisfaction. 'How's that? And that?'

He cocked back his leg for another kick and I caught his foot and dropped him.

One of the archers slammed me in the head with his bow. It was almost casual; I saw the staff coming ...

The advantage of being knocked unconscious was that I was taken for a Turk. Red hair and bad manners, I suppose. I never went all the way out; I was aware of a good deal, but I wasn't going anywhere on an enemy galley, and I didn't want to be made to talk. And my act had, in fact, changed the situation; the galley's *capitano* came down amidships and began yelling in Turkish that Zeno was his prisoner, and valuable. And that Sultan Murad was not at war with Venice.

God works in mysterious ways.

They carried me to the bow and dropped me; that was John and Richard carrying me. And one of our oarsmen was called Aldo, and he turned out to have a fine turn of Arabic, and he apparently professed to love Allah and was put with the three of us in the bow.

You may laugh, but when my head stopped hurting, I relaxed. I'd taken some blows to the head in my time, and I was more interested in avoiding sleep than in worrying about captivity. I've been taken before; I didn't see this as any worse, so far.

John growled at our captors from time to time, and then alternated between an obsequious humility and a brash arrogance, and one of the galley's under-officers told him to shut up, he'd be sent back to his Ordo.

That had to do for us. The galley rowed across the strait to the Asian shore, near Carnak, and there we were disembarked. I saw Zeno taken ashore, surrounded by Turks, and our other two oarsmen were already at oars. In chains.

The four of us, who were taken for locals, weren't even questioned. An agha, or officer, came and took us in charge. He asked John one question, and John said something like 'Fucking Turks' in Turkish, and the officer laughed. He had the same wrinkled face as John.

He ordered us to follow him.

He asked John a dozen questions. John answered him readily enough. We passed some tents, and Musard almost had to carry me as a wave of nausea hit me; I had trouble walking. The agha snapped a question – asking, I thought, if I was sick. I mumbled 'Yes, Lord' and 'No, Lord' which must have been acceptable.

John barked a laugh and said a long, monotonous speech in a language that was *not* Turkish.

The agha nodded. The two men clasped hands, and the officer waved us to a wagon and walked away.

As soon as he was out of earshot, John turned.

'He is ... of my people. Listen. I tell pack of lies. He know I lie. He hates Turks but needs horses. So it is with my people. So I say, we criminals maybe, maybe *muu khün*. But he help me. Yes?' John spread his hands. 'Work, do what I say, what he say, what any Turk say. Maybe tomorrow we walk, or run. Yes?'

No one was offering a better deal.

I spent the next two days with a raging headache, currying horses, shovelling horse manure, and carrying fodder and feed. I was astonished at the level of organisation among the Turks. This was not a tribal horde; this was a better army than most I'd served in, and most of the administration and logistics was supplied by Greeks. Nor were they slaves.

I thought of Adalia.

My Turkish was tested to its limits every hour, but the commander of the baggage was not that bright himself – somebody's second son, I'll guess, and he thought me a fool and said so. Red hair is always humorous, at least to those who do not have it, and they mocked me. They mocked Musard, too for his dark skin. We worked side by side, and said nothing to each other. Richard knew a little bit of Berber from his childhood, and a little Arabic, and no Turkish, so I did my best to cover for him.

But frankly, no one was looking for spies on the eastern shore of the Dardanelles. No one quizzed us, and no one watched us work, either. In fact, on the second day, one of the other horse boys told me to do less work, and John punched him in the head, and an hour later, John was head horse boy.

By my count it was the first of August. We were prisoners, or slaves; I found myself working to make a little steppe pony's flanks shine for some Turkish *ghulam* who would ride about burning monasteries, like as not.

And Richard and I worked together as if we'd never been apart. There was no place for whispered denunciations or anger.

We worked.

The morning of the third day in camp, a pair of Turkish *ghulami* came to choose remounts. One dropped his quiver and his sword, all on the same belt, and went to do his business with one of the Greek whores who were everywhere with their children in the baggage train – the flotsam and misery of war. He pointed at one and was stripping his trousers before he got to her tent.

John snapped up his quiver belt as if it was his own and waved to me, and the four of us trotted on to the far horse lines, where other baggage men were working. It was that easy. And later that day, I got a quiver with a good knife on it; it was lying in the grass.

I was hungry all the time. They didn't really feed us – they expected us to 'forage', by which our officer clearly meant that we should steal food from the same Greek families who were supporting his expedition with taxes. By that time, I probably knew as much about Murad's plans as his inner council. I knew that he intended to keep the Venetians from reinforcing Constantinople, and he intended to take it while the emperor was a hostage in Hungary or Bulgaria, thus betraying the emperor's son Andronicus, who all the Turks thought was a fool.

I want you to think of me and Richard, arguing on the foredeck while a hundred rowers were within six feet. The Turkish officers talked about everything. John got most of it, but I heard some too. And I saw Zeno; his nose looked bad, but he was upright, walking between two guards at nightfall. I nodded to John, and John raised an eyebrow.

'Foraging' gave us a chance to talk. We went well out from the army. Their transports were late – very late. They were expecting Genoese merchant ships to carry them over from Carnak to Gallipoli so that they could take Constantinople.

The Genoese were apparently sending a fleet to support the Ottamanids, even while they supported the Green Count. Make of that what you will.

Or so I had heard. At any rate, we roamed up into Asia, maybe four leagues out of camp, on borrowed horses. We were, to all effects, free. I doubted that anyone would look for us. Various refugees poured into the camp looking for work.

'I want to rescue Zeno,' I said. 'We know what we need to know, otherwise.'

Richard looked wistfully at Gallipoli on the far shore. 'We should go there,' he said. 'At least scout the gates and approaches.'

I looked at John. 'Richard is correct, John,' I said.

John shrugged. 'Take Zeno and ride,' he said. 'Ride east a little and then south. Find fisherfolk, take boat. Or ride to Karamanids peoples. Ten days.'

I tried to look at this as a sailor would. The current ran south. 'The Turks can't keep the fishing boats here tied up for weeks, can they?' I asked.

Our oarsman shrugged. 'Venice couldn't,' he said. 'Arsenali would down tools. Don't know about fuckin' Turks.' He was Aldo Bendetti, and he looked more Moorish than Richard. He was also the only sailor with three cavalrymen. He sucked his teeth for a while and then pointed north. 'Must be boats up north,' he said. 'Stands to reason. We could float down in the dark.'

'How do we rescue Maestro Zeno?' I asked.

No one had an answer.

'Genoa sent the Green Count a dozen heavy galleys,' I said. 'Would they also send transports to move a Turkish army?'

Bendetti spat. 'Only God and Christ know what a Genoese would do,' he said.

'The Genoese are better servants of Christ than you godless Venetians,' Richard said.

I suspect I rolled my eyes. But we found some sausage and a small pig, and we cooked them in secret – the worst Moslems who ever lived – and drank some stolen wine.

'Like old times,' I said to Richard over the fire.

He smiled, and his teeth glinted. 'I was just thinking the same,' he said.

We walked back to camp, and made our preparations. We meant to go the next night, taking Zeno from his guards, and we chose horses and an escape route into the hills.

But while I was standing, looking at a horse, a pair of Turks grabbed me and threw me to the ground.

Just bad luck. It was the man who'd gone to have the whore, and he remembered my red hair, even under a prayer cap.

He struck me several times with his fists, and his two friends held me. They opened my kaftan and searched me, and found nothing. Then an ulema came with John – a sort of holy lawyer, among the Turks. A man who knew the religious law. They are not like our judges; they hold the law in their heads, and they pronounce judgement on the spot.

John argued with the man. But John had brought him.

I had been hit again in the head, and on top of the earlier blow, my brains were rattled, but I acted worse than I was, to avoid talking – slurring my speech at every phrase. My accuser rattled off his accusation, which I didn't understand a word of, aside from the word 'thief', and John managed to slip in what the man was doing with his belt off, so that the ulema snapped something at the Turk and he turned bright red ... and kicked me.

And then they took me under the arms and carried me away. I was tied to a heavy post, and John came.

'I am sorry, Lord,' he said quietly. 'You are to be whipped. And made to work. But not killed.'

And so I was. They left me tied there all night. I know that Richard pleaded with John to cut me loose; it would have been easy. But it would have given everything away. John was a good captain, although my back is still sometimes sore when the weather changes.

And there was one tiny blessing. While I was tied to the post in the middle of the camp, occasionally taunted by small Greek boys but otherwise alone to meditate, pray, and be afraid, I saw Zeno led out of a well-lit tent. He did some exercises, not fifty feet from my post, and he stretched, and asked his guards in Turkish to let his hands free so that he could exercise his arms, but they only grinned.

'Do you think we are fools?' asked one.

Zeno walked past me when he was done jumping like an antic. He didn't show any interest, but I managed a wink, and he returned it. He had to turn his head to hide a smile.

'What has this man done?' he asked.

'A thief,' the Turk said. 'Or not. Perhaps he will be flayed alive, as an example.' He looked at me.

I tried to breathe.

In the morning a dozen Turks came, led by the bastard who accused me of stealing his sword. The ulema asked me, very slowly, what I had done with the sword.

'I do not have it,' I said. 'Never had it!'

Want to cost a man a night's sleep?

Use the phrase 'flayed alive' in a sentence.

He shook his head. One man passed a rope between my tied hands, and pulled so hard I almost cracked my head on the post, and I gasped, and the first whip blow hit my back.

The man behind the whip knew his business. He struck fast, and high on my back. Fifteen blows, and after the fifth I could not stop myself crying out, the pain was so intense. And the wait between blows, even though it was no more than a heartbeat or two … Oh, how I think of the agony of Christ when I think of that moment. I took only fifteen blows, and I was almost entirely unmanned.

And then the man in front of me let go, and I fell. Almost the end of me, I admit it. But the ulema came and murmured something, and two men began to rub some salve into my back.

I screamed.

It was aloe.

It hurt like ...

I have no description for what it hurt like. I hurt. I hurt. I curled up, and that hurt. Having your back flayed betrays you in many ways, and the worst of them is that curling up hurts, because it stretches your back muscles.

But the aloe had an almost instant effect.

They put oil on it, olive oil, and the ulema, who seemed a decent fellow, snapped his fingers and a slave handed me a plain, clean kaftan. They put a clean cotton bandage around my torso, and then they helped me into the kaftan, and then I was taken back to work.

Turkish women sometimes give birth and go back to work, tending flocks. I've known French peasants to take a beating and go back to the fields. They must be made of sterner stuff than me; I sat by a horse, very suddenly, and almost got kicked for my pains.

But the other three covered for me. They curried my horses and moved my picket lines and I just wandered, barely able to breathe and wanting only to lie down and sleep, except that was one thing our masters did not allow baggage people to do.

'Can you ride?' Richard asked me.

'Yes,' I said.

John came later. He gave me something to eat. It tasted like flowers. And the smell of jasmine mixed with something like old soap of Castile. Even that doesn't really capture the scent. I ate it, and was instantly ...

Away.

'Opium,' John said with a soft smile. 'Make all better. For a little while, eh? Come along, Lord.'

The shadows were getting long, and John had separated our horses, moving them to the end of the last picket line as if they were the last to be fed, watered, and perhaps cleaned that day. He had a small fire going, which was not uncommon. It was hot as Hell; my skin prickled, and there was something oozing through my bandages. The colours of the fire held me entranced, though, and my friends were there, and that was enough for me.

Then I watched some ants. They were fascinating, in the haze of pain and opium, and I wondered if they had souls. If they all existed in a web of friendships and obligations. If some were soldiers and some, priests.

I wondered if I had an analogue as an ant.

It was all very curious. Everything seemed to pass very slowly, and in fact, I began to wonder about time, something I'd never even considered before.

Richard appeared next to me.

'William,' he said. 'Wake up.'

'Not asleep,' I said.

'Zeno didn't come out for exercise,' Richard said.

I thought about that. I was still thinking about ants, and men, and the futility of endeavour, but at the same time, my mind seemed to be very fluid, very quick, and – you won't credit this – I thought that I could see in the dark.

'He is in a tent,' I said.

John was on the other side of me, but I was curled around the anthill and didn't see him.

'Do you know what tent, Lord?' John asked.

'Yes,' I said. 'By the stake.'

In the end, they had to take me.

Perhaps it was the worst plan ever made. But I couldn't explain, through the opium, where the tent was compared to the stake, and so they carried me, a wounded slave, through the enemy camp, to the very stake where I had been flogged.

I turned in a little circle. 'That one,' I said, pointing with my head at a red silk pavilion.

'Can you fight?' Richard asked.

'I don't think so,' I said.

'Me neither,' John agreed.

'We spend too much time fighting,' I said, or words to that effect. 'The world is too rich to waste it on fighting. We can be stepped on, like ants. And then what are we?'

'Good point,' John muttered. Look, I don't actually remember any of this. But I've been told it quite a number of times. It won't surprise any of you that my friends enjoy mocking me.

So I was handed over to Aldo, who hobbled along with me back to the horses. We walked past dozens of Turks, ghazis, and various *akinjis* and other soldiers, and no one troubled us at all. In fact, I'll go as far as to say that I got a kind look or two, perhaps from Turks who had been flogged themselves. And then, many of them were sick, too;

some fever or grippe was passing through the camp.

We sat and sweated in the insect-filled dark. I played with colours in my head.

Richard ran out of the darkness with a turban on his head. 'We have him,' he said. 'Mount!'

I don't remember much after that. My horse was good enough – a big steppe horse, sort of like a very large, slightly vicious hill pony. He was perhaps fifteen hands, if you were generous, and his square head would not have recommended him anywhere. Despite which, he ran and ran, out into the darkness beyond the horse lines.

I know we went north, because that's what John and Richard told me later, but at the time, I was somewhere between abject misery and opium-induced euphoria, and my clearest memory is impossible – that of riding on a cloud, moonlit from below. I'll assume that didn't happen.

There's a lesson there, though, because that moment, riding across the tendrils of cloud illuminated in an ivory gold, is my clearest memory of the whole escapade. And if that memory is false, than what is memory?

Bah.

There was pursuit. Once we halted in some scrubby trees, and I watched the moonlight play on the ground; moonlight so strong that there were crisp shadows across my hand. And the sound of men in armour trotting by, and Richard with his hand over my horse's nose while I played like a child.

And later, we were high on a ridge watching three parties below us, all headed in the wrong direction. John said later that we threw them by going north, deeper into Ottomanid territory.

The day that followed was one of total misery – blazing hot, and I had a pounding head like a man who has drunk wine all night, and I began to vomit at midday and was too weak to move around much. John carried me to a small stream, which gurgled down the ridge – just a trickle where, in spring and autumn, it was no doubt a flood. I lay there, bitten by invisible insects, sweating profusely, and vomiting bile.

Delightful. I had no idea where my comrades might be; nor was my head working well enough to worry overmuch. I lay, and was miserable. I slept and dreamed dark dreams, woke, and vomited.

Eventually I slept, and then I was over the back of a horse, and a new kind of misery overtook me. We were moving fast, and I was bouncing like a sack of grain. Indeed, a sack of grain would have been more useful.

But we'd ridden over the high ground and we were coming down to the coast; I remember seeing the sea. Twice, they had to stop in the high country so that I could relieve myself. I won't dwell on it, but John saw to my back, too, rubbing in some liniment or some salve that made the fire less.

I have since imagined that a high fever on a hot day in Asia, a flayed back, and some wicked disease of the camp, wringing out my intestines, was as close to a glimpse of Hell as ever I need have. Time seemed to cease; I couldn't see that we moved, and I couldn't ride.

No one ever suggested leaving me. And on the second day, when we were coming down out of the high country towards the Sea of Marmara (although I could not have said so at the time) Zeno began to be sick, and by the end of the day, everyone but John was down, and John did nothing but clean us and curry, water and watch the horses.

But in that night, I had a clear dream of Saint Michael and Saint George and Saint Mary Magdalene, praying for me, and I awoke from chills to find my head clear for the first time in four days. My back hurt, and hurt worse because I was lying on the red dirt with no bedding, but I could think.

I groaned for a while, I suspect, and then I got up, fetched myself water, and then began, without too many words, to help John. I did the best I could. Richard's sickness was different from mine – he was freezing cold where I had been boiling hot – and I built up our small fire and did my best to make it burn hot and without smoke.

We couldn't move. Aldo was so sick that cleaning him was a full-time job. Richard was sick enough, for all love, but he spewed more infrequently and he never completely succumbed to the fever. Zeno was the worst, though, and I thought at one point that he was dead.

Indeed, it was as bad as the Plague, in the filth and the bile, but not anywhere near as mortal. Still, we lost another day, and then John, who had been proof against the disease for so long, caught the fever.

By then I was in my right wits, and my back was healing. I got everyone mounted, and took us about a mile – mostly to get them all out of the rank odour of our own disease. John had found a tiny valley, a sort of rivulet with well-wooded sides, and I moved us there and built a new camp, and as Richard recovered, he helped me.

And I know that we lost a day there, somewhere. Because when we finally had John fit to travel, and we headed back down the ridge towards the sea, I would have had it Sunday, but it was more like Tuesday, as we found later.

Regardless, we found ourselves in a small Greek town on the Sea of Marmara, looking at a crop of little islands. It was a fishing village, and Zeno got them to send out the Orthodox priest, whom we kept a horse-length away because of the disease. In two hours we had ourselves a fishing boat – a big one, about twenty feet long or maybe a couple of feet longer, and painted a sky blue long before, so that it showed more weathered wood than paint. Still, she was all the boat we had, and after filling her full of water at the edge of the sea, Zeno pronounced her seaworthy, if foul – years of throwing dead fish and their guts into the bilge made the boat smell as if the five of us had all had our disease in the boat.

Still, she was a weatherly little boat, and after some practice in by the little beach, we gave the priest our horses with a suggestion that he not tell the Turks where they came from, piled our very few belongings into the little vessel, and raised the threadbare sail.

We sailed out into the Sea of Marmara and made the nearest island in one tack. It has a monastery on it; the monks didn't trouble us, but sold us bread and salt fish, which we paid for with money John had stolen. I cooked, and Richard Musard gathered firewood and made our usual fire; that is, the fire the two of us had lived at for several years – a deep end full of coals for baking and boiling water, and a shallow end with a hot fire of small wood for cooking and drying clothes.

John was at the height of the disease, and I poured water down him, stripped him naked, washed his clothes in a tub loaned by the monks, and they gave me an herb which I put into his fish stew. He drank it greedily enough, and his fever broke, but whether that was from the goodness of the monks or because he was due to heal, I do not know.

And I would like to say that Richard and I fell into each other's arms. But it wasn't like that at all. It was as if we'd passed straight

273

through reconciliation without having to reconcile; disease and danger made us comrades, and that night on the island, as we ate together from one borrowed pot, he was by my side as he had been across most of France.

That night, instead of discussing our lives, or our friendship, or Janet, we talked instead about our mission. Richard and I were allies; we were the only two who believed that we had to actually touch the walls of Gallipoli to do our work.

Zeno cursed. 'You two are incorrigible!' he said. 'It is only by the grace of Our Lady that I am a free man. Paolo Dormi must be tearing what little hair he has out of his scalp,' he said with relish.

'He certainly hates you,' I said.

'He will have reason, the black-hearted traitor. Ah, I wish Dante's Hell were real, that I might put him there.' Zeno shook his head.

'Traitor?' I asked.

'He who says "Genoese" says "Traitor",' Zeno said.

Richard bridled. 'There are many good men among the Genoese,' he said. 'Good and gentle men.'

Zeno laughed. 'So people assure me,' he said. 'And yet I have never met a one.'

Aldo, a mere oarsman, laughed. '*Il Capitano* spent a few years rowing for the Genoese and it has poisoned his views of their hospitality,' he said.

'True for you, Aldo,' Zeno said. 'By Satan's prick, Ser Guillaume, you make a fine fish stew, and if you were not so interested in war, I would suggest that you open a little place in Venice. I could supply the wine.'

'And we could kill people for spare cash?' I asked.

'He's always been a fine cook,' Richard said with amusement.

John ate more stew, hunched over the iron pot as if we might take it from him.

'So, you two insist we visit this infernal town, yes?' Zeno asked.

'In a word, yes,' I said.

Zeno sighed. 'Well,' he said, 'I suppose we can assay it again. With the current in our favour, I imagine we'll have more luck – best of all, we can touch in the darkness. But I know of no landing on the European side – they may be there, but I've never used one. If I say I cannot land, will you allow us to sail on?'

Richard was stubborn. 'I saw beaches,' he said.

'That may be, Ser Knight. But all beaches are not alike, and there are currents, and you are no sailor – not even as much as Ser Guillaume here, who has at least had a little instruction. I will make every effort, but you must accept my word as final.' He looked at me for support.

'I accept,' I said. 'We will need a full day.'

Richard looked at me across the fire.

'Very well,' Zeno said. 'I'll put you ashore at midnight and return for you at the same time. If we can put you ashore at all.'

'We can swim,' I said.

Richard looked at me as if I'd grown an extra head. 'You can't swim?' I asked.

'How long have you known me, William Gold?' he asked.

We spent the whole next day on the island, cooking, eating, and restoring our strength. My back was surprisingly good; John was recovered, or nearly so. And Zeno went to the point and threw chips of wood in to measure the current, or so he said. I don't think he learned anything very important.

Just before nightfall, we returned the cook pot and washtub to the monks, donned clean clothes, and boarded our boat. Considering I'd only been on the little island two days, I found that it was like leaving home – so quickly had I fallen into the comfortable routines of work, washing, cooking, making fires.

We sailed south and west, and the sun set magnificently in the west. Constantinople, the greatest city in the world, was that way, but we could not see her.

We rowed a while, and my back hurt all over again; sweat is no comforter of scars. After rowing, when it was fully dark, we raised the sail. I had quite a frisson of fear, out there on the great waters, alone in the dark in a small boat, but Zeno was elated, and sang Italian songs as he played with the sail until he liked the speed of the boat. We had a nice little wind – too much wind for my comfort – and when I was at the tiller I found it a little too thrilling. Zeno questioned me about my sea-knowledge, and I told him what I felt I had learned from Contarini and then again from Brother Robert.

'Aren't we moving too fast?' I said.

Zeno nodded. 'Yes,' he said. 'But that gives us more time for decision. We need to be clear of the gut by dawn. Not a lot of extra time.' He smiled. 'This is sailing, eh?'

We did well enough. The others slept, and Aldo and Zeno and I took turns sailing along the ever-narrowing Sea of Marmara until it turned into the Dardanelles. And there we had our first fright – before we really saw them, we were in among a trio of armed galleys. But they were anchored out, and a line of campfires showed us that their crews were ashore. If we'd had a dozen soldiers and some oarsmen, we could have taken them all.

But we swept by, as silent as seabirds, and then we turned to port and Zeno adjusted the rig and we were running down the strait itself. After less than an hour, he turned the bow almost due west, and we ran across the strait from the Asian side to the European side. No alarm was sounded, and if anyone saw us at all, no one called out, and then we were close inshore and the breeze was lighter and the inshore current slowed us, which was fine.

The whole European coast was a beach. It was obvious we could land, and not long after midnight, we could see Gallipoli, and Carnak on the opposite shore, the narrowest point in the whole channel. Some men say that when the Great King, Xerxes, attacked Greece five hundred years before our Saviour came, he built his bridge of boats right there. I don't know if that's true or not.

But we could see the masts of the squadron against the opposite shore, and see the pinpricks of light that were their watch fires.

'You two determined to try this?' Zeno asked quietly. Richard was asleep.

'Yes,' I said.

Zeno nodded. 'Very well, then,' he said. 'I'll land you along here and meet you below the town tomorrow at midnight.'

'How will I find you?' I asked.

'I'll run a lantern up the mast,' he said. 'If I can find a lantern. You do the same. Wake your friend, now.'

John was awake. It's curious to me now that it never occurred to me to distrust him. He was a Turk; we were going ashore in land held by his people. Yet I also had learned that this was more appearance then reality; an Englishman might very well prefer to fight the French alongside a Moor than to join the French against the Moors.

I'd learned an enormous amount from the Order, and from

Sabraham. 'If you will be guided by me in this,' I said as humbly as possible, to avoid sparking Richard's resentment, 'I would say, swim ashore with our clothes on our heads. Less danger to the boat. The current may make swimming difficult.'

Richard nodded, muzzy with sleep. 'Fine,' he said, and began to strip. We all had Saracen dress, of course, and authentically dirty. In fact, what we looked like was three escaped slaves, which was problematic. We took only daggers.

The water was far colder than I expected, but it helped to wake me, and by the time I got my feet on the gravel, after a swim of less than two hundred paces, I was tired, and my back hurt all over again – salt in wounds. But our clothes were mostly dry, or dry-ish, and we began walking south and east along the shore; soon we were trotting to keep warm. Zeno was just visible out in the strait, and he'd already come hard around and was running upstream for Marmara.

I wished I was returning to our little island.

As soon as we saw fishermen net-mending, we were more cautious, and we walked inland, climbing through olive groves and barked at by guard dogs, but by the grace of Saint George, we were into the gardens of the suburbs easily enough. The inhabitants were Greeks, and early risers looked at me with a mixture of hostility and fear. As Christian Greeks, they had every right to be afraid of low caste Arabs and Turks, who were as rapacious as brigands. However, a good Samaritan, a matron drawing water at a well, was delighted when Richard and I hauled her buckets up, and gave us some to drink, and then offered us, in passable Turkish, some warm flatbread and honey, and we hauled the rest of her water willingly, I promise you. She had a crucifix hung just inside the portico of her little home, and it took all my attention not to cross myself.

She also served us a drink which was new to me; it was hot, and very bitter, sweetened with honey, and it put fire in my muscles. She called it *quaveh*. I have since had it many times, as a drug and as a drink; I'm very partial to it. But the good matron was my introduction to it, on the shores of the Dardanelles.

When the sun was up we emerged from her house, and she gave us a little food to carry and an old bag like a pilgrim's scrip to carry it. As soon as we were away from her I prayed she might be preserved from the coming assault and sack.

We were going against the flow of people as we walked up to the gates; mostly it was poor men, which is what we were disguised as, going out to work in fields or tend animals. But there were a few dozen going in – dock workers, probably – and we went with them, and aside from a few muttered comments, we were let along until the gate itself. I had just time to be afraid, really afraid, and then we were in the line. There, a dozen Turkish *ghulami* in full armour, splint and maille, stood guard, two on horseback, the rest on foot, and they examined every man and every woman entering. Nor did they trouble any unduly; a modest young woman in a headscarf was examined but neither mocked nor harassed; a Turkish woman on horseback was also examined, and her voice, a little shrill, suggested that the guards were less polite to her than to the slaves and Christians.

When it was our turn, I was afraid, but it proved that John was the man they found suspicious. Remember – I'd had some days to improve my Turkish. I could grunt with the best of them, and when the *ghulam* took my chin between his fingers and looked at my face, he asked, 'And where are you from, boy?'

'Frankesi,' I said with a false smile.

He nodded and his fingers closed on my bicep. 'Strong,' he said, in Turkish. 'You fight?'

I smiled. 'Maybe,' I said, a fine word that covers many ambiguities.

He pointed at himself. 'If you turn away from unbelief, brother, and look to Mecca, and accept Mohamed as the prophet, you could wear armour like me, and not shovel shit for some merchant.'

I cast my eyes down. 'I am a slave,' I said.

'Ah,' he said, and let me go. 'We are all slaves, brother,' he said.

Richard Musard didn't even get a glance – which was good; he didn't have ten words of Turkish, and his little African Arabic would have made him seem far too educated.

But they held John. There was a fast flow of Turkish; only then did I fully understand that they had been careful with me, identifying me easily as a foreigner. John spread his hands, and the man who had questioned me called an officer.

John shot me a glance. I understood in a moment, and I took Richard by the sleeve.

'What?' he asked, in English, and then flushed.

But, by the grace of God, no one noticed.

I looked back at John. There were six *ghulami* around him, and I knew he was taken. I was pretty sure that I understood a little of their jabber; he was taken as a foreign Turk, not as a spy. Or perhaps as a spy. We hadn't done anything in the line to make ourselves appear as three men together – something else I'd learned from Sabraham.

Richard and I were in Gallipoli.

It quickly became apparent that Gallipoli was more of a military transit camp than a fortress. There were a dozen major gaps in the walls; it looked as if an enormous siege machine had hurtled huge rocks and collapsed sections of wall twenty paces long, but a Greek told us that an earthquake had collapsed the walls some years before. The Turks, who were not precisely masters of engineering, had never paid to replace them, and had only repaired the gates and a few towers in strategic locations. The citadel was in better repair; it had four tall towers in the Greek style, and a good garrison. We went right in, carrying water with other slaves, walked out again to get more, and kept going.

The citadel's water supply was outside the walls of the citadel. I noted that.

But what I really noted was that the gates of the citadel were chained open – and that the gatehouse had a stairwell on the interior. I have led a few *coups de main*, and if you ask me, no gatehouse should ever have an interior stairwell. I won't explain. You'll see.

West of the walls was an entrenched camp. Towards afternoon, we left the citadel and slipped out of the city through one of the gaping holes in the walls, cursing our ill luck; if we'd known they were there, we need never have lost John. We stood on a mound of rubble – or rather, crouched – and watched the camp. Then we joined a big pack of slaves or servants washing pots, and with them we went into the camp. I carried a great iron kettle with Richard, and I was glad to set it down where an agha ordered me.

Then he gave me a piece of silver for my troubles, and patted my head as if I were a small child. I'll probably say this again, but in that moment it struck me how odd it was that you can be a great knight to one man and a childlike slave to another in the space of a few days.

When we emerged from the mess tent – for so I'm sure it was – I saw John. He was with twenty other squint-eyed Turks, being harangued by an officer as blond as my sister.

'What is he saying?' Richard demanded.

I shook my head. It wasn't even the Turkish that I knew. I assumed that this language was Kipchak; I'd heard it often enough, but I knew no words at all. It sounded Turkish, but then, French and English no doubt sound similar to infidels.

I began scheming to free John. But there were a great many *ghulami* in the camp, and there were a dozen of them guarding his twenty companions.

Still, we followed them.

'There are a lot of empty tents,' Richard commented.

He was correct; two-thirds of the tents were empty, and only one end of the camp was busy. Further, as we looked – and sniffed – we could see that there was sickness here; I knew the smell, having had it myself for days.

'Fever,' I said, and Richard agreed. We tried to give the latrines a wide berth, and we did various tasks to look busy. But before I could make contact with John, an overseer came and shouted at us that we were late, and we turned and ran.

Again, the task was carrying water, and this time it came from a well to the west, almost half a mile. I carried a yoke of buckets, and Richard carried a very European-looking cask. That took us almost an hour; the sun was setting, and no one offered to feed us, and the widow's bread and honey were a long way away. On the other hand, I saw a fine way of approaching the empty corner of the camp from the scrubby ground to the west; a depression, almost a gully, probably created by the earthquake. In fact, one of the slaves led us back on the 'short way' and his trail went right over the corner of the wall, which I could see was completely unguarded.

But after we poured our water into the cistern at the centre of the camp, we slipped back to the empty end of the camp and there was John, with more like fifty companions, all sitting cross-legged in the dust. Now they were being lectured by a tall man with a long beard – in Arabic.

Richard looked away. 'This is an open-air *madrasah*, and these men are receiving religious instruction,' he hissed. 'Your friend has changed sides.'

'I doubt it,' I said. John had sworn to me for two years and two days, and he had a year to run on his time. Besides, what I saw from the men sitting was resignation. One scratched his arse; one rolled his eyes; several were asleep, or simply looked out at the setting sun. 'If he's changed sides, why not do it a week ago, in the other camp?' I asked.

I moved cautiously from tent to tent. They were empty, and it was easy to move. Richard hissed at me, and finally said that if I was determined to be captured, he was not, and he walked off.

I let him go.

I moved until the little square in which the Turks were receiving their lessons was opposite me, and I was behind the teacher.

I moved very slowly out from the cover of my tent, a low wedge of white canvas. Then I waved, and John finally looked, saw me, looked away, and looked back.

He smiled, and looked away.

Then he looked back at me. He pointed at the ground.

The teacher snapped something in Arabic.

In Turkish, John said, 'This unworthy one stays here. He will learn much, and then perhaps go against the enemies of the Faith.'

The teacher then chastised him, in Turkish, for speaking in Turkish.

I noted a number of things.

I noted that when John spoke, every one of his companions looked at him. And then looked away.

At least a dozen of his companions saw me, but none of them spoke.

Finally, John winked.

I rolled into a tent, and when the ulema turned his head, I was gone. I had no idea what John's game was, but he was with his own kind – Kipchaks to a man, I suspected – and he didn't need me. But he was glad I was there, and so were his companions.

I suspected that meant he had promised them a rescue by the Franks.

I waited until full dark, lifted an earthenware oil lamp and some oil, watched the sentries on the earthwork walls, and when two of them began a dispute in Turkish about horses, I slipped past them, jumped the low wall, and made my way along it, noting where it could be climbed with ease. Then I made the mile-long walk to the beach.

I was worried for Richard, and annoyed with him, but I needn't have worried. He was a skilled man, and I found him on a point of rocks that jutted out into the sea, sitting cross-legged.

'So?' he asked.

'I think John is planning a little insurrection,' I said, and explained.

Richard shook his head. 'Just enough loyalty to you not to sell you to the Turks,' he said.

I shrugged.

'People are like that,' Richard insisted. 'Most men would sell their own sisters.'

I turned and looked at him. The sky was still pink; there was a little light from the new moon.

He realised what he had just said. 'I didn't sell you!' he said.

I rolled that around.

'William!' he said urgently. 'I didn't sell you. I just ...' He paused. 'I remained silent.'

I looked out into the darkness.

'You had such a bad ... way ... with Janet.' He frowned. 'I knew you would take her side. I feared ... that she loved you better.'

'They took me to hang me,' I said. 'As a routier.'

'Which you were,' Richard spat.

'I was,' I admitted.

'Damn it!' Richard spat. 'I hate your false humility worse than your fucking arrogance.'

'Hmmm,' I said. Now, I confess that I think I'm a better man for not needing to debate every foolish point made by my fellow man, but in this case, I knew Richard better than he knew me. I knew that my silence would infuriate him more than my arguments, because he loved to debate. To argue. To make his will felt by others.

'Admit that you were seducing Janet,' he said. 'Admit it.'

I looked at him. 'I forgive you, you know,' I said. 'I never touched Janet. I won't say she doesn't appeal to me. Merely that she didn't want me, and that was plain. And whatever you meant, Richard, it's past. Father Pierre Thomas rescued me. If I hadn't been taken, who knows who, or what, I'd be today.'

'So you think you are different?' he said. 'I find you the same.'

I shrugged. 'I try to be different,' I said.

'Men do not change,' he said, as if it was an article of faith.

'Yes they do,' I said. 'If they do not, then penance is a lie, and all Christianity is a mockery.'

'So you married this great countess for her pious good works?' Richard mocked.

That got me. 'Richard, you knew Emile—'

'This is the great Emile?' he asked. 'Ah, I understand better.' He thought a moment. 'Of course, I see it now. D'Herblay. Emile.'

And pause. Stars winked in the sky.

'Oh, sweet Christ, William. I see it.' He hung his head.

It is difficult to see the world through another's eyes. I had always taken for granted that Richard knew all about my love for Emile, but of course, he was largely gone those years; he wasn't always with me, and I was very, very careful of her name. On the other hand, I was not sure I fully believed him.

And, of course, he served with the Savoyards at Brignais, so he was already in the Green Count's *mesne* and routiers were the very devil to those Savoyards, and I was one of the fallen angels in the Pantheon of routier Hell.

I didn't say so, but I also knew that as Richard had begun as one of us, so he must have had to distance himself from us to become one of the Savoyards.

At some point, you can forgive, or you cannot allow yourself to forgive.

And as Father Pierre Thomas had told me a dozen times when I confessed to him, the result of Richard's betrayal, if it was a betrayal, had been a new life for me.

And, as I sat with him in the darkness, I knew why he needed me to confess to seducing Janet. That would make us even. An ugly even, but even nonetheless.

Perhaps I should have said something. But I did not. We sat on the rocks, and no *ghulami* came for us, and some time deep in the second watch, I saw a pinprick of light out on the water.

I used my tinderbox to strike a light and got my little lamp lit on our fourth or fifth try. We were down to one piece of char cloth, and I thought that the damp tow would never catch, but Richard made a little tent of his hands and blew through it and I got the wick lit.

Almost instantly the little light went out. I kept ours going until the boat was in close enough to see, and then we slipped into the cold water and swam.

We were at Tenedos that evening, with wind and current behind us, and the change couldn't have been more sudden. As the boat ran down towards the harbour of Tenedos, Aldo and I were chatting away amicably, and he was asking me how exactly I'd spiced my fish stew. But not much later, we went up the side of the Venetian galley, and in a moment I was Sir William Gold and he was Aldo the oarsman.

I marvelled at it, though. In the space of a few days, I'd been a baggage slave, an escapee, and now, a knight. It is interesting, is it not, that as much as we prize who we are, we also remain the results of other men's thoughts? When I was a slave, I spake as a slave ... Richard thought me a mere routier still, I could tell; it was essential to his image of himself that I was a routier.

I suppose that all those years, I assumed that when Richard and I were together, we'd make it up.

We prepared to sail for Negroponte, and I was afraid for John, but I also felt that some part of me had died. Richard could not let me be myself. He could not change his views of who I had to be. Would he, in the end, make me a routier?

We never made Negroponte, however. The first morning, on a little beach on the coast of Thrace, we exchanged greetings with a fishing boat that sold us some clams, warily, and they told us that the 'Great Frankish Fleet' had sailed for Lesvos.

Lesvos. Where my wife was.

Something prickled in my head, and I was afraid.

The fear was with me for the next two days. Maybe it was only that without my friends about me, I began to fear the Hungarian, the Count of Turenne, and the distant Robert of Geneva. Mayhap even the Bourc Camus.

Being a prisoner of the Turks was almost a comfort by comparison.

And I worried about John. I was sailing away from him, and it went clean against my notions of what was fitting. I wanted to rescue him on the spot, with fire and sword; especially now that I had braes and hose and a cote-hardie on, and felt like a knight.

Two difficult days. I remember fencing with Zeno on the catwalk, with sharps. He was a good swordsman, well trained, and yet he formed his parries so late and so suddenly that he could never make a play from the crossing, a habit I have seen in many men who imagine themselves slow. I offered to improve his covers, and he bridled, looked down his long nose, and told me that he knew enough about fighting with a sword to write a book.

Richard watched for a while and then went aft. Later he frowned at me.

'Why do you imagine that you know more about fighting with a sword than other men?' he asked.

'I do,' I said. 'I practise. I think about it. I have studied with Fiore.'

Richard shrugged. 'I do not see that you are any better than the *capitano*.'

This all seemed very petty to me. Richard seemed angrier and more distant every day, at sea; I had no idea why. But it contributed to my growing sense of distance.

I note that men, in general, all believe that they are born knowing how to impress women, chop firewood with an axe, and use a sword. Most men were quite wrong about the first, and I have noticed that almost all men were wrong about the second. Fiore had opened my eyes to an entire philosophy of swordsmanship, an entire way of imagining the sword and its use – the body, direction, motion, all of it. Thanks to him, I was to other swordsman the way a priest is with theology to a flock of his parishioners.

At any rate, on the third day we raised Lesvos, and we were racing along the north coast for Mytiline when the lookout hailed to say that the harbour of Methymna was full of shipping, and he could see a *galia grosse* on the beach. We were almost past the town, and the sailors were standing to the sheets and halyards to take in the sail for our turn into the strait between Asia and Lesvos, Zeno cursed in Veneziano, spat once over the side in a thoughtful way, and issued a volley of orders which, thanks to my time with Contarini and my lessons with Fra Robert, I was mostly able to comprehend. Then the sails came down, and the oars came out, and we turned in perhaps twice our own length to creep back into the wind. Closer in, we could see the ten miles or so to Antissa, a Genoese trading town along the coast, and the harbour there was also full of masts.

Zeno looked at me and raised an eyebrow.

'You know,' he said, 'my whole life, we have done nothing to fight the Turks or the Hagarenes in Egypt. And now, in just two years, we show them our teeth.' He grinned – a feral, pirate's grin. 'They must be shitting their braes from Alexandria to Gallipoli.'

'*Certes*, they cannot face us at sea,' I said.

Zeno nodded. 'All the Turkish emirs and sultans together might have seventy galleys – and they hate each other almost as much as they fear us. The Egyptians just lost their fleet to us last autumn – perhaps they have twenty more galleys laid up in ordinary, or up the Nile, but I doubt it.' He nodded to his timoneer. 'It will be rich pickings on these coasts for years to come.'

'While we hold the sea,' I said.

And then he spat over the side again. 'Can you imagine if Genoa and Venice were to combine?' he asked. 'Throw in Sicily and Aragon, and the Christian fleet might be three hundred galleys and that again in round ships.' He shrugged. 'You know why we don't own Jerusalem, Guillaume? Because no one gives a shit, that's why.'

I looked out at the bright summer sunshine and the breathtaking sight – a Venetian fleet at Methymna and a Genoese fleet at Antissa; probably, between them, more ships than the whole might of the infidel in the world.

No one gives a shit.

Those words bit deep.

Listen, when you are in something – a fight, a war, a romance, a friendship – you take if for granted; it is the totality of experience, it is what you are.

Take a step back …

It is a very dangerous step.

'These ships are not going to Jerusalem,' Zeno said. 'They never were. They're going to rescue the emperor, now, but they were only, ever, going to fight on the count's behalf in the East. Rumour is that the emperor has offered to renounce his schismatic ways and join the Latin Rite, if the Green Count will clear the Asian shore of Turks and push back the Bulgarians for him.'

'Christ,' I blasphemed, and bowed my head.

'Yes,' Zeno said. He spat again, looked at his masthead, watched his rowers, and then turned. 'Yes. The Pope is more interested in forcing the emperor to obey him than in taking Jerusalem.' He looked at me.

I watched the harbour. I was thinking about Robert of Geneva; about Richard Musard; the Hungarian; Nerio, Venice, Genoa, the Pope. All of it.

The sun was all around me, and the day was dark, and Father Pierre

Thomas was dead. For years, he had been my anchor. Sometimes, now, my prayers took the form of talking to him.

No one gives a shit.

Indeed.

We landed on the superb beach at Methymna – one of my favourite places. I still own a house there. I went ashore fearing everything, and found that my wife could protect herself; she'd ridden around from Mytilene with the Gatelussi entourage, and made her bow to her feudal lord with her three children. Edouard had already sworn his fealty to Count Amadeus. Emile was seated with him in the hall of the castle of Methymna when I climbed the seven hundred steps from the harbour to render my report with Richard and Carlos Zeno. Up on the castle gates hung two bodies, eviscerated and left to be pecked by gulls. I wondered who they were. But my eyes were only for my lady.

She gave me a brilliant smile. I returned it, but bent my knee to Count Amadeus. He was dressed like a great lord, in emerald silk, lined in fur, and his face was sheened in sweat. It was hot in the hall – not as hot as it was outside in the summer sun, but hot. And his face was burned.

Richard reported all our adventures. The only mention of me he made was that I had been sick. At one point I turned my head to look at him, I was so amazed at his telling. He left out John; he left out Zeno, except to note that he had been captured and rescued; the story was about him.

He also left out the existence of a military camp – the pestilence in it – and the strength of the Turkish army at Carnak. And he neglected to mention the daily expectation of a Genoese transport fleet by the Turks.

When Richard was finished, the Count uncrossed his legs and looked at Zeno. 'And milord *Capitano*?' he asked.

Zeno smiled. It was not a nice smile. 'I am not sure that Sir Richard and I were on the same *empris*,' he said.

Zeno's manner of recitation was very different from Richard's. Where Richard had spoken – fluently – the language of chivalry, speaking always in terms of honour and prowess, Zeno spoke a different language, although in good French. He spoke of distances and petty difficulties and discoveries; so many Turks at this camp, so many at this other; difficulties in landing or anchoring. It was like listening to a shipwright explain how a ship was built – very professional and very dull, and ten sentences in, he'd lost his audience. The count smiled at my wife and offered her a cup of wine on bent knee, in one of his many extravagant displays of chivalry.

Emile was trying to say something with her eyes.

I assumed she was saying *Do not react*.

So I did not. I let the count ask a few languid questions of Zeno and dismiss him with thanks, waiting my turn, but my turn did not come. When Zeno was dismissed, the count waved at Richard.

'My thanks, Sir Richard. Bravely done. We could not perform these actions without you.' He rose, and embraced Richard a few feet from me, and the two of them walked off down the hall together.

I won't lie.

I was angry.

But Emile was there, and I was wise enough to remind myself that as she was not murdered by the Hungarian or arrested by her lord, the count, I had little to worry about and a great deal for which to be thankful. I embraced her, smelled her hair, kissed Magdalene and Isabel, and exchanged bows with Edouard, who was standing with Domenico, the Prince of Lesvos's younger son. Both of them had hawks on their fists and they looked like what they were.

'You look like a fine young lord, Edouard. And you, Prince Domenico.' I nodded.

'I am a lord, now,' he said. 'I am the Count d'Herblay!'

I bowed to him.

'People say you killed my father,' he said suddenly.

He said it quite spontaneously. There were a hundred people watching and listening.

I was kneeling, so I was at eye height. 'No,' I said, 'I did not.'

He nodded. 'That's good. I didn't believe them. But ... people keep saying it!'

'What people?' I asked.

'The count's confessor, his secretary, and his esquire,' Emile said. 'So one can guess where this might arise.'

'My father would never say such a foul thing,' Prince Domenico put in.

Quite without thought, I put my arms around Edouard and hugged him. He grinned.

'I didn't kill your father,' I said. 'And if I had, My Lord, I would tell you, man to man.'

'Because you are a knight,' he said, nodding.

We were not even clear of the hall when a page in the Gatelussi colours came and tugged at my sleeve.

'Prince Francesco requests the honour of your presence,' he said.

'Tell him I will attend him directly,' I said. I kissed Emile. 'I may yet kill someone,' I said with what I thought was humour.

'I fear, my love, that we are now at the point where that may be required.' She sighed.

You look surprised, Chaucer. Listen; this is the world of arms, the law of Chivalry. I could not allow my own repute and my wife's to be assaulted forever.

Then I bowed deeply to her and followed the page to a big solar with a fine window, almost as good as a church window, with two knights fighting. There were coals in the hearth, and the room was cool despite them – cool, while outside the summer sun grilled the island.

I found the Prince with not one but two of his captains; Sir Richard Percy, and the captain of Eressos, another Englishman I'd met the year before, Sir John Partner. We all bowed.

Prince Francesco sat in a big, carved chair. He wore a simple linen cote-hardie worked with flowers in fine embroidery, and his hawkish face wore a wry smile.

'You had a cool welcome from my cousin-in-law,' he said.

'That I did,' I admitted, allowing a little of my annoyance to surface.

'For whatever reason, I was not invited to hear Sir Richard's report,' he said. 'I expect I'll do as well to hear yours.'

I bowed and rattled off the report I'd prepared while listening to Richard.

Prince Francesco fingered his beard. 'Disease, eh?' He looked at his captains. 'You think there are ten thousand *ghulami* at Carnal?'

'Yes, My Lord,' I answered.

'As many again at this camp behind the town?' he asked.

'No, My Lord. Perhaps three thousand, and many of them sick. May I intrude a personal comment?'

'Be my guest, Sir William.' He leaned back and waved to the page, who brought me a big cup of iced sherbet. It was made with lemon and almonds, and was perhaps the most delicious thing I'd ever tasted.

'My man-at-arms, John, is a Kipchak,' I began. Percy raised a finger, as if to say *the man about whom I told you.*

The Prince nodded that I should continue.

'We were dependent on him every day, and he kept us alive. However, on the last day he was taken, right in the gate of Gallipoli. He was not taken for being a crusader, but for being a Kipchak, and I saw him in the camp with two dozen of his fellows. I would very much like to rescue him. I imagine that his friends would also be grateful.'

The Prince nodded. 'And the citadel?' he asked.

'Difficult to storm,' I said. 'Quick enough with trebuchets.'

'But the walls of the town are breached,' he said, confirming my suspicion that even though he had not been invited to Richard's report, he knew its contents.

'Yes, My Lord,' I said.

He reached into a basket by his side and withdrew a scroll in a wooden tube. 'For you,' he said.

It was from the Order; it bore the seal of de Midelton. I bowed and cracked the seal and read it.

It confirmed what I already suspected – that the Order accepted that the capture of the emperor trumped operations on the coast of Cilicia. But it bore the thanks of the Grand Master, and the news that the admiral would join the count with two galleys.

I read it aloud to the prince, who nodded.

'Have you considered my offer, Sir William?' he asked.

'My Lord, saving any feudal duties I prove to owe to the count, saving my faith to the King of England, and saving my contract with Nerio Acciaioli, I am at your service.' I bowed. And I had no interest in serving the Green Count. Paragon of chivalry that he was, I disliked him. Somehow, my disappointment with Peter of Cyprus attached itself to Count Amadeus; they were both brilliant knights, and probably good men, but they both had enough vanity for a hundred pretty women, and they both lived by their favourites.

Prince Francesco, by contrast, reminded me enormously of someone. I couldn't place it, exactly, at our first few meetings, and then I hit on it; he reminded me of John Hawkwood. He was like a slightly older and more refined Hawkwood.

When I think of the leaders I have admired most, they were none of them the greatest knights. The Black Prince and the Green Count and King Peter all come to mind – fine lances, all. The best leaders, the men I loved to follow, were Juan di Heredia, for all his scheming, and John Hawkwood; Prince Francesco; Pisani, the Venetian. Well, and Father Pierre Thomas, but he was a saint from God, and not a war leader at all, really. But even Father Pierre Thomas, for all his saintliness, played no favourites, was unstinting of praise, and careful and accurate with censure.

The Prince smiled at me. 'Well, I will ask the count directly,' he said. 'I assume, from the venom he allows to spread about you, that he has no intention of requiring your service.' He met my eye. 'Gentlemen, give me a moment with this good knight,' he said, and the other Englishmen bowed and took their leave.

'You seem a careful man, Sir William,' he said to me when we were alone. 'My wife tells me that the count has made not one but two attempts to seduce your wife. A nun attends her – not the nun with the children, but the one who writes so well.'

'Sister Marie,' I snarled.

'My wife has arranged that Sister Marie is with your wife at all times.' His eyes met mine. 'There is *absolutely* nothing you can do. He is an amorous man, as my wife's maids can attest. However, I can protect you and your wife.'

I was, thank God, clear-headed. And it was like talking to Hawkwood.

'From the count?' I asked.

'You have quite a variety of enemies, for so young a man,' Gatelussi said, with a thin smile. 'May I be frank? You need a good lord who will protect you. I would be happy to be that man, and my hand is not light. I will be even more direct – not only will I protect you, but I would be happy to see your friend Nerio prosper, as well. I am Genoese, but I need friends in Florence and Venice. It is summer now – the flood tide is on us, and my harbours are full of Christian ships. But when I look out from my battlements, I see Asia, and when the wind blows, I know that winter will come.'

I knew he told me about the count to make me more malleable;

I knew him, in a way. But I also recognised that I was in over my head; I could not afford to face the Count of Savoy and the Count of Turenne on my own resources, much less the Bourc Camus and Robert of Geneva.

And he brought that home. 'There was an attempt on your wife and her son,' he said. He smiled, a malevolent smile, the smile of a plotter who has out-thought his rivals. 'The assassins underestimated me.' He waved out the window. From his solar, you could just see the two dead men hanging from the gate.

I needed a protector.

I knelt and put my hands between his, and swore my oath.

He didn't smile. 'I wish I could have all four of you,' he said. 'But it is sufficient for now that you will help me rescue the emperor, my brother-in-law. We will speak again.' He picked up a small bell and rang it. 'There is one other small thing. Perhaps not so small. I'd like you to take my oldest son with you – Francesco.'

I nodded. It was not unexpected.

'He is a knight?' I asked.

'Not yet,' the Prince said. 'I think perhaps we will see if he deserves that honour during the campaign. See what you make of him. Try and keep him alive.'

I tried not to choke on that.

'I will find you a good holding here,' he said. 'One house here, in Methymna, and another in Mytiline, and a country town for income. But only after we find the emperor.'

A page came for me. But as I made to leave the room, the prince held up his hand.

He turned to the page. 'Go fetch me some wine,' he said with a smile. As soon as the boy was gone, he raised an eyebrow to me. 'I want to say more of my son,' he said.

I nodded.

He hesitated. I have seen this other times; truly powerful men are at a loss when dealing with the rare moments wherein they are powerless.

He opened and closed his mouth. Then he rose and looked out of his beautiful window. The sun was bright, and the jewel colours stained him – his face a lapis blue, and his hands scarlet, as if there was blood on them.

'I loved his mother,' he said. 'It is very difficult being a bastard.'

I didn't really need to be told that.

He was going to add something, and then he shrugged. 'Treat him like any other man-at-arms,' he said. 'But keep him alive.'

He waved me away.

I should have said something about the dangers of the life or arms, but the prince was a veteran of a hundred fights and had, according to repute, been a notorious pirate.

I bowed myself out of the solar.

'The count is making advances?' I asked carefully, when I was alone with Emile.

She raised an eyebrow. 'You could say that,' she said. 'He never ceases. I have sent back all his gifts, and Sister Marie is with me all the time and sleeps with me at night.' She frowned, and Sister Marie emerged from the bed hangings.

I hugged her fiercely. Somehow she had become one of 'us'. With Nerio and Fiore and Miles and Emile – my inner friends. And she and I shared Father Pierre Thomas in a way that the others didn't.

'I think it is his nature,' Sister Marie said, 'to possess.'

My wife threw her hands in the air. 'It is also my fault,' she said. 'I was not always ...'

It is odd, is it not, how we say different things to different people? Or rather, in some cases, the same things to different people, but not, perhaps, to two of them at once?

I knew that Emile, who often berated herself for her wantonness as a young woman, meant to say 'chaste'. She intended to say that she was not always chaste. She would say that to me – because we were honest with each other about our many flaws. And she would say it to Sister Marie, I guessed, because the nun had become her confessor and protector and friend.

But not to both of us together.

'He's an arse,' I said. 'A popinjay and a courtier. It is *not* your fault.'

'You cannot fight him,' Emile said.

'I won't,' I said.

'Fiore challenged his esquire, and the count demanded that the challenge be withdrawn.' Sister Marie smiled. 'No one wants to fight Fiore.'

*

And when we were alone in bed, and we had had our joy of one another, my wife rolled atop me and buried her head in my chest. 'He wants me to be the woman I was,' she said bitterly. 'He won't let me be the woman I am.'

I thought of my life with Richard. 'I know that feeling,' I assured her. 'I swore fealty to the prince,' I said, changing the subject.

Emile sat up, suddenly, her hair all about her. The summer night was beautiful, and the windows were open. I could see her by starlight. She kissed my hand. 'Brilliant,' she said. 'I hoped you would.'

'You are very beautiful,' I told her.

'Hasn't Nerio taught you to tell me how brilliant and witty I am?' she said.

'I have my own theories,' I said.

The next day I mustered my little company. All my newly recruited routiers from Jonc had arrived and been provided with surcoats by Miles Stapleton, and for the first time, I had twenty lances, as well as my two Greek knights and their men-at-arms, who were, to all intents, a separate company – sub-contractors, if you will. And now I had young Francesco. who called himself 'Francesco Orsini'. He had his own armed squire, a big, dangerous-looking German or Dane named Holger. I gave him his choice of our new archers and he took Bill Vane. He bought Vane a new horse and new clothes. His lance looked splendid.

They were all looking good; there was new equipment throughout the ranks, and our horses were probably the best on the island, thanks to the various horse markets of Anatolia and some small prowess. Fiore didn't have a squire, being too poor. I had a notion that Aldo, the oarsman, would make a good man-at-arms, and I begged him of Carlos Zeno.

'You'll all be Venetians at this rate,' he said. 'Yes, I saw he was a good man while we were out in the boat. He deserves ... Yes. It is good.'

It is always a pleasure giving a man his step up in life. Zeno, Fiore and I took him for a cup of wine, Zeno leading the way and warning us about what an oarsman's taverna was like.

It wasn't so much squalid as densely packed, and it smelled very strongly of octopus and male sweat. There were benches, and at least eight men to a bench. Women served the wine and fish stew – tough-looking women, most with knives in their kirtle belts.

Aldo was stunned to be visited by 'gentlemen' and attempted to seat us so that we wouldn't see the two whores working the far side of the room while men chanted and waited their turns. Fiore looked him over while we exchanged stilted comments, and Aldo introduced us to his silent companions. The whole taverna was falling silent. I doubt two knights had ever graced its doors.

One of the whores said, into the silence, 'I need a break anyway,' in Italian, and she pulled a cover over her and took a cup of wine. Men laughed, but there were some nasty looks.

Zeno glanced at me. 'Not for the gentry,' he said. 'Be quick.'

I'd been a cook in an army camp. Not only was I not surprised, but I appreciated that these men didn't appreciate my presence for reasons. I smiled genially, pulled a trio of golden florins from my purse, and put them in front of my slattern, who was old enough to know her way around and had a simple kitchen knife in her belt – big enough to behead a chicken – a little grey in her hair, and a ready smile.

'Sister,' I said in Greek.

She smiled.

'This trinity is to buy wine for every man here, and every woman,' I said.

She put her hand over the coins, and when she lifted it, they were gone. She flicked me the hint of a smile. In the purest Veneziano, she called out, 'The *cavalari* buy you all wine.'

Some men nodded. One spat. But there was a cheer.

An old man in a smock was introduced to me as 'Neptune'. I shook his hand, which was curled, as if around an oar. He had a grip like an armourer's vice.

'You saved this young scamp, My Lord,' he said. 'He is my brother's son. Useless for work, except at an oar.' He smiled.

He was an interesting old man – completely unafraid to speak to us, the gentry.

Zeno nodded to him as if they were old friends. 'He's a damn good oar,' he said.

'Not much of a carpenter, though,' Neptune said.

Zeno nodded at me. 'When I was fitting out, I tried to get some men of the arsenal as crew. We all do it. They are the best fighters because they are citizens.'

Yeomen, I thought. *Yes, we are the best fighters.*

Fiore glanced at me and gave me what was, for him, a warm nod.

'He is strong, and for a man of his class, intelligent,' Fiore said aloud, with his usual assurance.

I winced. But I gave Zeno the nod.

'These gentlemen have a proposal for you,' Zeno said. 'Know that you have my permission.'

'I would offer to sign you into my company,' I said. 'As a squire-at-arms to this gentleman, the noble knight Fiore of Udine.'

Aldo the oarsman sat speechless.

Neptune grabbed him by the shoulders and shook him.

'He accepts, by God and Saint Mark,' the old man said. 'Christ and the saints, boy! You can be a gent!'

The burly oarsman on the other side of me raised his wine cup. 'Must be hard-up for men-at-arms is all I can say,' he said, genially.

'Fuckin' useless oarsman,' said another, raising his cup.

A dozen more of his mates praised him in similar terms.

'Really?' he asked Fiore.

Fiore shrugged. 'You think I would come to a place like this to play a joke?' he asked.

Sometime in the morning, the prince and the count had a meeting. By all accounts it was perfectly amicable – the count agreed that Gallipoli must be taken immediately, and was surprised to find that there was a military camp behind the town; the prince proposed a plan of campaign, which the count accepted.

At some point, the prince apparently asked whether the count intended to ask for my knight service.

'No,' the count answered.

'Excellent,' the prince said. 'I will have him with me, then,' he said, with sixty knights listening. 'My son has entered his company.'

I saw the count look at me; a considering look. And I thought that the prince was a damned good lord. His son was suddenly under my protection.

But while I reviewed my company, the great lords had made their plan. The plan was simple, like all good plans. The count would enter the Dardanelles at dawn, drive up the strait and land on the beaches below Gallipoli – landing all his ships simultaneously on the long beach.

The prince would sail up the west side of the peninsula and land on the Thrace coast, and cross the ridge in the darkness. As soon as the count's ships were in sight, the prince would attack the military camp behind the town, and from it, the open breaches in the damaged walls.

'Don't be too quick,' the prince insisted when they met, in armour, the next morning, with their armour reflecting the first magnificent rays of the sun. 'It will be the work of an entire night to get my people over the ridge. And the landings may be delayed.'

The count smiled. 'We will wait,' he said. 'Although I'm quite sure that with such knights as I have about me, I can do it without you.'

So it came to pass, as the chronicles say, that I kissed my wife and her children, donned my armour and surcoat, and led my people aboard ships that belonged neither to my liege, the King of England, nor my liege by marriage, the Count of Savoy, nor my commanderie in the Order to which I was sworn, but rather boarded a round ship and a pair of galleys belonging to the Prince of Lesvos.

I remember little of the voyage. I was not with my men, which I regretted; I had barely seen Fiore, had only exchanged somewhat formal military words with Miles, and no one knew quite what had become of Nerio. Hafiz-i Abun, whom I now counted as a comrade, was on my ship; he had no qualms about fighting Turks, or so he said, and he wanted to observe a Christian army. I will say again, that in England we imagine that the divide between Christian and Moslem is a cliff – but out in the Holy Land, there are Italians and Spaniards serving emirs; there are Italian Mamluks, as I have related. And the Mongols have no love for the Turks, as I may someday have a chance to tell you – nor the Persians, not the Arabs, any more than Englishmen love Frenchmen, or Florentines love Siennese. Eh?

I have left my road again.

The prince wanted me to be present for his councils, and I knew that was the way of my professions; indeed, I had just received a lesson in the politics of command. One must not just serve well, but be seen to do so.

The prince's galley was curiously spartan. It lacked any amenities – no gold lamp shone in the stern cabin, and the cabin itself was only

297

a tent of canvas; it was not silk, nor was the deck polished or overlaid with canvas. As the Gatelussi were bywords for riches, I attributed this to the prince's former life as a Genoese pirate.

His whole armed force was about eight hundred men, exclusive of his rowers, who were almost all Greeks – fishermen and sailors. They had their own weapons, and enough of them had brigantines or coats of maille so as to lead me to believe that I was looking at another species of successful routier; gold earrings abounded, as did smiles.

'We will land at Portefino,' the prince said. To me, he said, 'I raided it five years ago. Two beaches, a small harbour, and no real defences. The Turks didn't have a garrison the last time I visited.' His smile was ferocious. 'As soon as we're ashore, I'd like your light horse to get on the road and move as quickly as possible to seal off the town from the landward side. I don't need a courier going over the ridge to the Turks. I brought my Orthodox patriarch to speak to the locals.'

'Is there a road?' Percy asked.

The prince smiled. 'More of a track, but it's enough. We'll pick up guides in the town, but I know the ground well enough, and Syr Giorgios and Syr Giannis will help. It is all a matter of timing. I will wager that the count will try to land early – the kind of glory he seeks is not to be shared.'

Partner shrugged. 'All one to me, My Lord.'

Percy grinned. 'Or me. He can do all the fighting, if that pleases him.'

They all three looked at me. I laughed. 'Do I have a reputation as a fire breather?' I asked. 'I got enough at Alexandria to last me the rest of my life.'

Then they asked me some questions about the attack, and the sack, and about Father Pierre Thomas.

Afterwards, it was all fresh in my mind, and I lay on the deck under the stars and thought about Alexandria; about the horse dragging its innards through the streets, and the naked woman with her jaw ripped away.

Marc-Antonio shook me awake. 'You screamed,' he said, 'my Lord.'

Aye. I suppose I did. I had ugly dreams.

The sun rose, and Marc-Antonio armed me.

'Do you think we'll ever go home?' he asked me.

I had a powerful image, then, of my uncle's house in Cheapside;

of Nan's father's house. Of London Bridge, and London. My sister, about whom, to be honest, I almost never thought, in those days. It's odd; when I was a brigand, I thought of my sister all the time. As a pious soldier of Christ, I thought of her less often. No idea what that means.

'Yes,' I said. I also thought of his father's house in Chioggia, and how comfortable and happy I was there. I realised then that I had had enough of crusade. It was an odd thing to think, while arming to fight the Turks, but in truth, I rather liked the Turks, and I wasn't so very fond of many of my fellow crusaders.

I had my orders, and I understood them; I got armed, watched two of the Gatelussi pages arm Marc-Antonio, and then we were running in with the land. The Lesbian galleys were experts; they ran right along the coast, very close in, so that they were virtually invisible to the town until they rounded the last point, and the steep terrain of the peninsula protected them. Indeed, the terrain was terrible and beautiful by day – towering cliffs and long ridges crowned in stone, like natural castles and long walls. In a few places, there was a narrow ribbon of beach at the base of the ridge, but until we rounded the last point, there was no place to land a flock of goats, much less an army.

And then we shot clear of the point. The prince's galley was in the lead, with his little fleet in two columns behind us, and as we opened the twin bays I could see the beaches, a small forest on the headland, and a village. On the headland, a shepherd was screaming at the top of his lungs, but the prince's galley was too fast for him.

'No rape, no theft,' the prince said. He looked around at his officers. 'If you catch a man doing either, kill him. That is my law. I need these people more loyal to me than to their Turkish lords.'

We all bent our knees.

Richard Percy was the first man ashore, and he landed twenty fully armed knights. Then the pages landed a dozen horses. By then a round ship was coming up, full of crossbowmen, and they landed behind the knights and formed in close order, and the landing was uncontested.

Both of my horses were on the third ship, with all the stradiotes and Syr Giorgios. Marc-Antonio took charge of Gawain and I mounted my brave Arab stallion, and then I found both Giorgios and Giannis collecting their men.

'Gentlemen,' I said.

We clasped hands, and Hafiz-i Abun came up, and vaulted onto his own Arabian, as pretty as mine and carrying less weight.

'I have never made war with Franks,' he said. 'You wear a lot of armour. But this manner of covering your landing is very good.' He pointed to a round ship with two tall castles, bristling with another company of crossbowmen; they were fifty paces offshore, and every man had his crossbow laid to the rail, ready to loose.

I thought of the sheer chaos of the Frankish landing at Alexandria.

Fiore came ashore as Giorgios rode up the beach at the head of his men. They clattered into the little town square and I saw them bespeak the village priest, a brave man who came out to greet them. Every man doffed his cap or helmet, and they saluted him before riding on, and he blessed them.

By then, my archers were ashore, and there was a sort of riot as the horses came ashore in the wrong order, so that a dozen annoyed archers stood on the beach holding the horses of a dozen absent knights. By then, Giannis had come back, and he led the company of crossbowmen into the town.

I had nothing to do. It was, in almost every way, the most competent army in which I'd ever served, and no one needed me. So I rode about, praising men for their speed and efficiency, and then I directed a party to fill canteens.

Glory.

Miles Stapleton did all the things I'd have done, under other circumstances. He'd turned l'Angars into his lieutenant in my absence, and they worked marvellously together, and I did not need to interfere. And Fiore fussed over details, and did it well; I noted that every one of our men-at-arms had every buckle fastened, every belt tight, and their horse harness was as well-fastened as their armour.

Now, friends, I must confess that I love to command. And I felt that something had been taken from me; there was nothing for me to do but watch.

Well, and praise. When there is nothing for the leader to do, there is always praise.

We were ashore in about an hour. That may seem like a long time to land eight hundred men and three hundred horses, but I promise you, friends, it was like lightning, and I was startled by the speed. We approached at sunset, and we held the whole town and all its gates before night fell, and as far as we knew, no one had run ahead of us to carry tales.

Then Hafiz rode up to me, in the sunset. 'There is ... an incident,' he said.

He raised an eyebrow.

'You want me to come?' I asked.

'The prince gave a command about crime,' he said carefully. 'I believe his ... son ... intends to flout him.'

Of course he did, the useless lout. Nay, not useless. He had a fine head on his shoulders and enough mother wit to know how to anger his father. He'd already referred to his service with me as 'exile with my father's brigands'. Mostly, as I was not his parent, I ignored his japes.

This time I gathered my horse under me and galloped heavily across the sand towards Portefino, Marc-Antonio at my shoulder and Hafiz trailing along.

I rode up the steep street, my horse's hooves sounding like thunder. There were armed men in the town, and there should not have been – mostly crossbowmen. They were in the narrow streets, and no one had opened a door that I could see, but many of them looked guilty as I rode by in the red light, and I made them cringe; one warhorse is about all you can get into the street of a Greek town.

Bill Vane was standing in a tiny square surrounded by tall stone houses like little towers.

Behind him was a church, and the doors were open.

'I tried to stop 'im,' Vane said.

I nodded and dismounted. I made as much noise as I could, and then I went straight into the church.

There was Francesco, who called himself Orsini, with two of his scapegrace friends. They had an Orthodox priest by the ear – literally.

'Let him go,' I said.

All three of them looked angry. And ashamed.

But Peacock, the boy who'd insulted Miles's young lady, didn't let go of the priest's ear.

I broke his nose.

Then he let go.

I was very careful with that blow, as I was in my fighting gauntlets.

Francesco went for me, as I wanted him to. I plucked his dagger hand out of the air with my left, tugged him off balance and threw him. He was in his armour, and he hit hard. I had his dagger in my hand.

'Fucking bastard!' he said in Italian.

'Get up and go out of the town,' I said. 'Keep your childish antics for your father. Or next time, someone will kill you.'

'You wouldn't dare,' he spat.

I was dusting off the priest and wishing I had more Greek.

It is interesting, when you've been a routier, and you know exactly how evil you can be. Even more interesting to try and harness all that … for good.

I knelt by the lad. 'Sure, I could slit your nostrils and maybe cut one hamstring,' I said. 'Just so your father knew I'd kept you alive.'

'Christ!' he muttered. 'You are all horrors!'

I shrugged. 'You want to be bad?' I asked. 'In the next few days, you will see what bad is like.' I got up. 'Right now, you are merely young and angry.'

Sir Richard Percy and Sir John Partner drew lots to see who stayed to be captain of the town, and Partner lost – or won, depending on how you see it. He took command of the crossbowmen.

The rest of us ate a cold meal with our reins in our hands, and marched east and south. My little company was in the van. We had the prince with us, and two Greek guides, local shepherds.

'If the Turks get word we're coming,' Gatelussi said, 'a dozen archers could hold us all day up there.' He pointed to the high ground behind the town.

But the stradiotes occupied the high ground without opposition, and our march was not interrupted. I understood that we had about twenty-five miles to go, and after the laborious climb up the ridge, we moved quickly, free of the imagined terror of plunging fire from the heights.

We might have been riding through a desert. Here and there, some industrious peasant had attempted to plant olive trees; some were visibly more successful, even in the darkness, but mostly there was little vegetation beyond scrub.

The prince was silent. It wasn't my place to badger him, and he and the guides agreed on all the choices on the roads, which seemed to come every five minutes. For a deserted peninsula, it was a web of tracks and paths, and ancient stone walls and sheepfolds, and once we passed a small citadel of enormous stones.

'That was probably here when Achilles stormed Troy,' Prince Francesco said. 'The old people built in those huge stones. They fit together perfectly. Look at them.'

We rode off the track to examine the citadel in the moonlight, and I thought with a chill how easily it could have been held against us.

Later, as the stars moved like a wheel and dawn grew closer, the prince began to fret a little about how far behind the main body had fallen, and he ordered me to halt and rode back. I had my people dismount, and drink water and piss it away if they needed.

I put a hand on Stapleton's shoulder. 'You have done marvels,' I said, or something equally trite, and true.

I'm going to imagine that he flushed at my praise, because that was Miles. But I couldn't see him.

Fiore came over and handed me an apple. I love apples, especially when my mouth is full of dust, and I ate it.

'Why do people say, *Live by the sword, die by the sword?*' he asked.

I loved him in these moods. So focused, so unaware. He suffered pre-battle jitters; he just showed them differently.

'Jesus said that,' I said. 'When Peter drew his sword.'

'I *know* that,' Fiore said, with the whole patronising force of his disdain. 'But surely he knew that those who truly live by the sword do not die by it. Not if they practise.'

Miles Stapleton laughed aloud, and then shook his head. 'You are the limit,' he said. 'I don't think our Saviour meant sword masters, Messire di Liberi. I think he meant killers.'

'Why didn't he say so, then?' Fiore said. 'I very much doubt that I will die by the sword.' He paused. 'And if I do, it will certainly mean that I had not, in fact, lived by the sword. Or not well enough.'

I spat a mouthful of wine and then shared the flask with both of them.

'Where's Nerio?' Fiore asked.

'Somewhere in Romania,' I said. 'He promised to rejoin, but I don't think he even has a ship.'

Fiore nodded. 'It is odd without him,' he said. 'And I have no money.'

I laughed.

Then the prince returned with word that the column was close behind, and we should march.

We reached the flat ground behind the town a little before false dawn. Then passed an anxious time when Rob Stone and Ned Cooper slept, but I was awake, in a sort of fog of fears – noise, discovery, horseflesh, paths, Turkish patrols. It was surprisingly unhelpful to have my new employer remain with us.

But, say what I might about the Savoyards, their Venetian and Genoese captains were expert seamen, and as the light began to dawn over the straits, there was the Christian fleet. It appeared huge, coming up with the dawn from the east, and of course, I saw it long before any Turk would. I was four hundred feet higher. I suppose I even saw the sun first.

'Bide,' Prince Francesco said, when I was restless. 'Let them land.'

They made a fine show in the red dawn, with the great banner of Our Lady floating on the morning breeze, and all the red flags with white crosses for Savoy, so like the flag of my Order. And indeed, there were a pair of Order galleys with them, and they landed first, putting a dozen knights and forty men-at-arms ashore very quickly, at least in part because the Order practised landings relentlessly.

Alarms were sounding in the citadel. The camp began to boil; I could see men going for horse lines, and other men wriggling – probably putting on armour.

And the Turks must have had conflicting orders. A company of *ghulami* rode out of the citadel to charge the Order's men-at-arms on the beach, took a volley of crossbow fire from one of the galleys, and only then woke up to the sheer size of the Christian fleet, even as another company of *ghulami* formed in the town's gate, where John had been taken, and then vanished – recalled, I assume, to the walls.

'You will let them assault the walls without our support?' I asked.

Prince Francesco smiled. '*I can do it without you,*' he said, mimicking the count's French. 'Listen, Gold. My family have been in Outremer for ten generations. Let me tell you a secret about these crusaders. They come and go. They don't stay. We live here. They can give the Turks some target practice for a while. If they get into the town without us, so much the better. If they get into trouble, we will ride, I promise.' He smiled in the half-light. 'You think I'm hard-hearted. But I am not on a crusade. I am not at war with Murad Sultan. I want to rescue my brother-in-law before something worse happens. The last vestige of the Roman Empire is tottering, Sir William. I have chosen to keep it alive. That is my crusade.'

I saluted, and sat down. I watched ants for a while. I meditated a little, prayed, thinking of Father Pierre Thomas, and lost myself sufficiently that Prince Francesco had to call my name.

The Savoyards were ashore. They were well formed, and they were headed for the town, ignoring the suburbs to the north, which pleased me. I thought of the woman who'd given us bread and honey.

The prince seemed amenable, so I described the incident.

'Yes,' he said. 'Well thought. I will want to protect the Greeks. And you want to rescue your friend.'

'I do, My Lord,' I said.

Prince Francesco watched for a while. A Christian army, smaller than ants, crawled to the walls.

'What will you do?' he asked.

'I expect you will use us to storm the camp,' I said. 'I thought that as soon as I went over the walls—'

'Why don't you go over the walls *before* I storm the camp,' he said. 'We only have three hundred men, Sir William. I think you should go and create chaos inside the camp – free your friend, if you can. I'll come along in a few minutes and give them something else to think about. Leave me your Greek knights ... I'll send them to the suburb.'

I had a brief moment of real fear.

Would he leave me to die, as a distraction?

He did seem capable of it.

But he met my eye and smiled, as if he could read my thoughts.

'Yes, My Lord,' I said.

I might have liked to spend all day crawling my way to the edge of the camp with my sixty men, but we didn't have time. So I separated my people, the way the Turks do, so we wouldn't raise dust, and I showed them which corner of the great camp I wanted them to gather at. The archers had a ladder we'd brought from Lesvos, the kind routiers use, that can be bolted together in sections.

We rode in a long, open column, down a gully with a sheep path at the bottom. If anyone sounded an alarm, I didn't hear it. Then, at a walk, an impossibly long ride across the flat ground behind the town; it is only five hundred paces, as I know now, but at the time it seemed a day's ride.

Inside the earthworks, the *ghulami* – those who were not sick – were forming their ranks. Despite this, and as I learned soon after, our surprise was nearly complete. The Turkish emir in charge of Gallipoli did not even know that there was a Christian fleet in his waters; reports had reached the sultan at Adrianopolis, which the Turks call Edirne, but somehow word never got to the target.

And the fever in the camp was terrible.

Worst of all, they had no infantry. All their vassals who supplied infantry were across the straits, at Çardak, dying in the other camp, waiting for the Genoese.

Well. It's good to know that it is not only Christian armies that suffer unnecessary disasters.

Given how unprepared they were, and the near state of war existing between the Agha of the Orta of *ghulami* in the camp and the emir of the city, it should have been an easy conquest.

Except that the Turks fight well all the time.

As we were about to find out.

I was one of the first dozen men to the south-western corner of the earthworks. The ditch was only about four feet deep – the result of slaves working in sandy, stony soil – but the upcast, where they threw the loose sand, dirt, and rocks excavated from the ditch, was almost six feet tall and topped with two rows of palisades. One pointed out like spikes at a would-be attacker, and a second pointed up, making a shelter against archery.

It wasn't much. But it would have been deadly if held by determined men.

Instead, it was completely empty.

I went up the face of the upcast almost alone. I slid on the loose earth, and filled my fighting shoes with gravel, which annoyed me for the next hour. But at the top, I could see down into the camp. It stretched away to the north and east, with space for ten thousand men and horses, and a large parade off to the north where the *ghulami* were forming ranks.

Closer to me was a smaller open square. I guessed that this was the *madrasah* where the Kipchaks were receiving religious instruction. At the head of the square was the stockade that I'd seen a week before, and that I guessed was where the Kipchaks were held.

To my left there were a dozen men – slaves, baggage men. They looked at me with more curiosity than apprehension, until Ned Cooper came up next to me in his velvet covered brigantine and turbaned basinet.

'Proper job,' he said.

Then, as the rest of the archers followed him, the baggage men ran. But they didn't run far; seventy paces away, two of them stopped and came back towards us – hesitant. But eager for freedom.

I had all the archers on the wall by then. Pages were holding the horses, and most of my men-at-arms were gathered at the edge of the ditch.

'Listen to me,' I called. 'We're here to rescue some friends, who are going to look just like Turks to you, so don't kill everything you see in a turban. The baggage slaves are mostly unredeemed Christian captives – let's rescue them, too. Eh, *mes amis?* As far as I can see, the only enemy are all *ghulami* – mounted men in armour. There's going to be plenty of loot – don't even take any now. We'll collect our loot when we're done fighting. Any questions?'

Ned Cooper looked at his strung bow. 'What do we shoot, then?'

'Shoot when I tell you. Or any mounted infidels that aren't Hafiz-i Abun.' Heads turned. Our Persian laughed.

'Don't shoot me,' he said in Italian.

Cooper nodded, looked at his archers and back at me.

So much for speeches.

'Miles, I have an inglorious job for you,' I said. 'Watch our progress. If we make the side gate, bring up the horses.'

He flicked his arming sword in a salute.

'Over the wall now, and form like lightning.' I scrambled down the far side, ran a few paces clear into the open ground between the wall and the first row of tents, and turned.

L'Angars was the first man over the wall, and he ran to his place, and the other knights and men-at-arms fell in on him, forming a line twenty men wide. The squires fell in behind, and then the archers, who, having climbed the wall first, obeyed the biblical injunction and were last.

Then I led them off from the right, and we moved cautiously north, through the maze of tents. There were baggage slaves, now – a few dozens – and we sent them to the rear, to the armed pages with the horses. Most were Christians; a few were Jews. I made it plain to the Jews that they were rescued too.

Or I tried.

My back burned like fire, my shoes were full of sand and gravel, and none of that mattered. I moved my people along two parallel streets, and just as we entered the square of the *madrasah* we encountered a company of Turks, all on foot but wearing maille. I had a minute's warning, as I saw them move on a cross street; I think that if they saw us, they assumed we were friends.

Right at the edge of the square, I halted, and my files formed to the left across the square.

I nodded at Cooper and slammed my visor down. The Turks still had their bows in quivers. They were there, I suspect, to guard the prisoners, not to fight us.

We only had twenty archers, but our first volley went through maille and man. They were caught completely by surprise.

Listen. You think we were in white surcoats with red crosses? We were sixty men in brigantines and leg harness, with turbans on our helmets against the sun. It was dawn. The Turkish officer made a bad assumption.

They charged us. They gave a long scream, and on they came, drawing their curved swords or using spears. They were recklessly brave; they took one man in ten as casualties and came on.

Our archers loosed again.

I'd been moving with my long sword reversed, held by the blade against Marc-Antonio's long spear. This is how we practised in Italy; it is the way the Order fought on foot. Now, as the Turks came on, I let go of Marc-Antonio's spear and it came up, over my shoulder. I took my sword in both hands – one hand on the hilt, and one in the middle of the blade.

Without any command, the whole company pressed from the flanks towards the centre, closing the alleys down which the archers loosed. Most of the archers tossed their bows backwards over their shoulders and drew their swords or their axes, and all of them leaned forward against the men in front.

My Turk had an axe; a small head on a long haft. He swung it up three or four paces out; it's virtually the only thing I remember from the first fight of the day.

I made the cover from the *garde* Fiore calls *vera croce*, the true cross. It is a true cross in every way. You start with your weight back, your sword hilt forward on your left side, and as your opponent cuts, you sweep the sword forward and parry the enemy weapons between your hands. It is perhaps the easiest cover to make in armour, and that's perfect for dealing with the real world of terror and confusion. Complex swordsmanship is for the tiltyard.

I crossed his haft and killed him – cross, rotate the blade, thrust into his eye socket in the same tempo. It's more like murder than combat, when you know what you are doing.

I don't remember the rest. There was another opponent, and then I ran the emperor's sword through some poor bastard who was already impaled by Marc-Antonio, and then the fighting was over and a couple of dozen survivors broke and ran, mostly from the left end of the line.

Ned Cooper stepped past me – elbowed me out of the way. He had three arrows on his fingers, and as fast as I can tell it, he dropped three of the running men. To my left, Rob did the same, and Bill Vane loosed only one, but dropped a single man running off to the left. Hafiz-i Abun dropped one, as well.

Perhaps six of them got away.

Then we killed all the wounded.

That's how it is, when you are storming an enemy camp.

Francesco Orsini looked sickened. He stood with his visor up, unable to tear his eyes from the scene of hell in front of him.

'John!' I roared, my visor up. 'John the Turk!'

'Here!' he called.

There was a stockade. An arrow came out of the stockade, which slammed into Pierre Lapot's helmet and he fell.

'At 'em!' I roared. These things have to be done; you can't mill about and plan assaults while archers pick off your knights.

Then the gravel in my shoes was forgotten; it was fifty paces across the square, and there were perhaps five archers loosing at us by then.

One arrow *tinged* off my sword and *clanged* off my visor, ripping the visor off the top of my helmet, popping the pins that held it. Bad luck for me. Or good luck; it didn't kill me. My visor was up; two fingers lower ...

But that was the last arrow. There was a sort of strangled roar from within the stockade, and then grunts, and then I was at the gate, which, of course, opened from outside with a simple slide. I slammed it open with the palm of my hand, shoved the gate open, and got my sword over some poor Turkish bastard's head. He was trying to fight a dozen Kipchaks who were attacking him with nothing but their fists and teeth.

I cut his throat.

They'd killed the rest of their guards.

I whirled. 'Cease!' I roared. 'No more arrows!'

Bill Vane was twenty paces away, at full draw, and Rob punched his arm.

John threw his arms around me. 'Knew you come!' he said, his eyes glittering with excitement. 'Knew you come!'

He called something, a long, fluid speech in Kipchak.

And then the whole pack of them broke past me, headed for the square. I had no idea where they were going and I was already sagging; I remember my greatest wish was to get the gravel out of my shoes.

But, of course, they ran to loot the Turks we'd just put down. They took bows and swords; a few took the time to strip maille, which is a difficult, messy job. John paused only to buckle on a quiver.

We were all spread out; despite my admonition, a dozen of my new people were looking inside tents, or staring balefully at the Turks, or looking for coins. There were men over every part of the square, and so, naturally, that's when the mounted *ghulami* hit us.

It wasn't even a fight. It took them too long to figure out that we were the enemy; the Kipchaks began loosing arrows, as did my archers. But these Turks were mounted, and far more ready; they shot back, and two of my new Breton men-at-arms were face down, dead, before I'd taken breath to shout an alarm.

It was not really like any fight I've ever seen, before or since, and I'm not sure I can do it justice. Everyone *moved*. The *ghulami* broke off, in among the tents, shooting as they went, and then appearing between two tents to loose again. But our archers ran along the ground, using tents as cover and loosing in their turn – a brutal shot-storm at point-blank range in thick and blinding dust raised by our movement and the horses.

The Kipchaks threw themselves at the Turks and took losses doing it. I confess I didn't understand their apparently suicidal attack until I saw John loose into a Turk at a range of maybe a dozen feet and then, as the man died, throw him from the saddle – a small leather saddle nothing like ours – and roll into it.

Then John leaned over *all the way to the ground* from horseback and *picked up his bow*. He already had an arrow in his rein hand, and long before he righted himself in the little saddle, he had an arrow on the bow. He seemed to lean out from the horse as he shot across his own leg into an oncoming Turk. The range was perhaps an arm's length, and John's man went down, shot in the middle of his chest through his maille, and John righted himself and vanished among the tents.

More dust.

I had no control over my troops or the mêlée. I could hear l'Angars shouting for the men to rally, in French, but I wasn't sure at all that this was the best answer. I began to run along the palisade, mostly so that I would not be a standing target.

But the mounted Turks were not willing to try the open square, and instead they loosed arrows over the tents. They yipped like hunting wolves, and either there were more of them than I had expected, or more were gathering.

Somewhere to the south and east of me was the camp's south gate. If it was unguarded, I could get to a horse.

That was as much plan as I had. I was painfully aware that my people had been caught out of formation, by cavalry; I'd lost them in the dust, and of course, my young charge, the prince's son, was somewhere in the mêlée. I passed the last of the palisade with the rueful thought that I might simply have stepped into it and been protected from arrows; the things you don't think of when you are afraid are legion. An arrow skipped along the packed sand at my feet, but I had no idea where it had come from.

I felt vulnerable with no visor, my back burned like a sinner's torments, and my company was being crushed.

I plunged into a tent and cut the back with my sword, and I was through into the street behind, headed south. A Turk appeared to my right; he shot, I swung my sword at his horse's nose, and Marc-Antonio speared him out of the saddle, all at the same moment, or so it seemed to me. His shaft shattered on the hardened plates of my brigantine and the force of the blow made me stumble, but he was gaffed like a fish. His horse went right past us.

I hadn't even known that Marc-Antonio was with me. I smiled at him.

He grinned, ear to ear.

Fiore appeared behind him with Aldo, the oarsman, at his back. The four of us filled the street of tents, and we moved carefully down the street, waiting for the thunder of hooves. Off to my left, deeper in the sea of white canvas, one of the Welsh Davids rose from behind a tent and lofted a shaft; I couldn't see where it went.

A pair of Turks appeared at the end of the street and ended my interest in looking around me. They both touched spurs to their mounts and shot, turned and backed their horses, and we had had time to move, and both arrows missed. Archery from long range is not as dangerous as from close – especially when you have room to flinch.

'Forward,' I said, and we trotted down the street.

There was a scream to the left, a flash of movement, and a dozen horsemen erupted from three directions; through, over, and past tents. A horse went down, tripped on a guy rope; a mounted archer loosed at close range into the gut of another, and I could not tell Kipchak from Turk. One horse had a war bow shaft buried in its haunch almost to the fletching.

Ned Cooper stepped out from between two tents, drew, held for one breath, and loosed into a man wearing a conical helmet; a safe bet as one of their 'knights'. His heavy shaft knocked the man forward, and the needlepoint bodkin went all the way through the man's armour and his body, and apparently pricked the horse's neck so that his horse bolted.

Another Turk shot Cooper, his arrow burying itself between two plates of his brigantine. Cooper had his next shaft on the stave and loosed – a broader point that went into the man's open-faced helmet, snapping his head back. He went over the tail of his horse like a tumbler, except that he never rose again.

Cooper slumped to his knees. Blood was *pouring* out of his chest over his thighs. He was heart shot; I knew it in a moment.

He looked at the shaft and then at me and frowned. 'Proper job,' he said aloud, and died.

I pulled off a gauntlet and made sure, but he was gone.

'Come on,' I said to Fiore, Aldo, and my own Marc-Antonio. 'Gate.'

We got to the south end of the street – the cross street of tents – and there was John, with a dozen of his mates, all mounted.

They looked like the very incarnation of depraved barbarity. One man was just taking the head of a dead Turk, and he was covered in blood, and the lot of them were laughing. But John grinned when he saw me, sprang from his mount and offered it to me.

'What's happening?' I asked.

'Turks dead,' he said. Indeed, the dust was settling, and the only sounds were the screams of wounded men.

Then we went back through the tents, finishing their wounded. And most of our own.

'I kill agha,' John said.

I didn't understand what he was saying until some time later, when, as l'Angars directed the gathering of our wounded and I blew his horn to call any stragglers, I saw one of the Kipchaks flourish a horsetail standard. I added that to the gold-mounted sabre John was cleaning.

'John?' I called out. 'You killed the Agha of the Ordo? The officer?'

'The lord. Yes,' he said with pride. 'Broke neck.'

'Christ,' I said, blasphemously. Diccon Crewel had an arrow through one thigh and was down; Red Bill had a broken arm; the Prince of Lesvos's son had blood on his sword. He was upright, his eyes glittered a little, and his German minder looked like a butcher after a long day; Bill Vane was behind the two of them with an arrow on his bow, watching Gospel Mark and Rob Stone arguing over who was head archer; I had eight dead, and Hector Lachlan looked as if he might just die from the sunshine, he was so red. He was weeping; his brother was dead. And he was in some Celtic madness; he wanted blood.

These are the moments when being the captain loses its charm.

I whirled on Mark. 'Shut it,' I snapped. 'White, you are master now.'

They were both silent.

I walked to Hector Lachlan. He was bigger than me, and he had an axe in his hands, and he was, quite literally, foaming at the mouth; there was red in the foam.

His eyes were blank.

'Hector!' I roared, from arm's length. 'Will you follow me?'

His eyes focused. If I say that they focused on me slowly, I won't do justice to the dawn of his thought. He had been an animal for some minutes.

'Hector!' I called.

He shook himself and the axe came up.

I got a hand on one ear and tugged it, almost hugging the big man. 'Hector! Come on, man. We need to storm the town.'

His brother was at my feet. He had four arrows in him. His eyes were open. I knelt, and closed them.

'When we're done,' I called, loud enough to wake the dead, 'we'll come back and bury them all like Christians. I swear it.'

His mad eyes met mine. 'Bury?' he growled. 'Aye.'

L'Angars gave me a look – a good look, as if I'd satisfied him.

Fiore looked past me. 'You think we should go for the town?' he said.

I was watching the dust settle. We had raised a lot of dust. It was brutally hot already, at least in harness; my back was on fire as my sweat soaked into the scars, and I had that bad prickly feeling you have when wounds begin to bleed.

'What do you tell a swordsman of small stature, Maestro?' I asked him.

'Keep inside your distance. Keep advancing, so the big man ...' He paused. 'Yes,' he agreed.

I turned to them all.

'Now we go for the town,' I said. 'I won't order you. I'll only say I think it is the best way.'

No one cheered. But when I headed towards the town wall, they all came. All the ones who were alive, anyway.

If there was anyone alive in that camp, we didn't see them. We had no idea what was going on – what the Count of Savoy was doing, how he was faring, where the Prince of Lesvos was – we knew none of those things. Later, I pieced it together; I'm still not sure I'm right, because it was a very confused fight.

When we entered the camp, the first fight raised the alarm as our movement had not, and the agha went in person to investigate; hence the armoured men on horseback. But John killed him; our archery and the Kipchaks defeated the Turks, and the survivors ran off.

Deprived of their commander, the *ghulami* who had formed on horseback at the head of their camp sat on their horses. And then, when the survivors fled past them, they abandoned the camp, riding out into the plain.

Where they were ambushed by the Prince of Lesvos. The survivors fled, and Prince Francesco then rode south, sent the Greeks into the suburbs, and with his main body, went to help the Savoyards on the beach. He had stayed in the high ground as long as possible – like the canny fox he was, he was the last man to enter the battlefield; he stayed high up to know what his allies and opponents were doing. Hawkwood always speaks of the value of keeping a reserve, even a few men; but I think there is also a sort of reserve of knowledge. The last man thinking and directing has a huge advantage over his adversary who is lost in the fight. Because once you are in the fight, you direct nothing, as I had just learned.

We knew none of these things. We came to the open ground where the Turks had formed their ranks an hour before, and it was empty; the horse dung was fresh, but the men were gone.

I halted my little company. 'Friends,' I said. 'The people of this town are Greeks. The Prince, our employer, says no rape, no theft.' I looked particularly at young Francesco. 'He says he will execute any man who commits either.' I looked them over. 'I won't let him,' I said. 'I'll do it myself. Everyone clear? Fight the Turks. Leave the Greeks alone.'

Hector growled. I think he was actually biting at the inside of his own mouth. I've known men to cut themselves and enjoy the pain, but Hector was something else again.

A good number of my men wouldn't meet my eye.

I was about to lead sixty men into a town with a thousand-man garrison, and I couldn't trust the former routiers not to turn instantly into arsonists, thieves and rapists. And we'd already taken casualties.

I admit it. I hesitated. I didn't trust them, and I was pretty sure they didn't trust me, either.

'On the other hand ...' I said.

Every head turned.

'I'll give one hundred florins to the first man into the citadel,' I said.

Men looked at each other, and one archer spat on his hands and wiped them on his hose.

'We need a priest,' l'Angars said quietly.

I knew what he meant. But the offer of gold was going to have to do. Something moved to the south; of course, Miles Stapleton and my pages had all the horses for us to mount. That was part of another plan, from another day. That plan was blown away on the wings of the wind and the edge of Red Bill's poleaxe.

But I knew that John and his Kipchaks were not going to dismount to storm a town. They didn't have the armour for it. So I grabbed his stirrup and asked him to find Miles, tell him what we were doing, and then help Miles reach the prince. He waved a riding whip.

'Sure,' he said. 'You?'

'The town,' I said. 'I intend to try…' I paused, and realised what I intended. I hadn't even voiced it to myself. 'The citadel.'

John made a face. 'Sure,' he said.

'On me,' I called out, and went forward across the parade ground.

The parade ran right to the edge of the wall. Not a single arrow fell among us, and right in front of us was a section of collapsed wall, almost twenty paces long, with a long slope of collapsed rubble and old fill, crumbled brick and dirt. It looked to me as if the whole town used it as their dump; it was littered with broken crockery, a dead dog inflated with its own rot, a pile of rotting vegetable matter.

But no defenders.

The walking was bad – you could turn an ankle in a missed step; much easier, without enemy archery. I moved too fast, shoulders hunched, expecting the first shaft with every pace.

It was a longer climb than it looked from the base, and I went up and up, angling around the corpse of the dog, and worried that his evil, bony and fanged smile was an omen. The whole stretch stank of urine, and then I was at the top of the collapsed rubble, looking down into the town, and no one stood against me.

The streets were *empty*. Well, the Greeks were not fools; they'd known an attack was coming, and every householder had locked his doors. No Greek had any reason to love or trust the Franks.

I paused at the top of the breach, looking for something – anything.

I had taken a dozen towns by escalade in my routier days, and the tactics yet escaped me. When we went into a town, we looted it to the doors. The garrison would either come down from the citadel and fight us, or sit tight and watch the town destroyed.

This was a different game.

I was going for the citadel. I had been there as a disguised slave; I knew the steps to the gate, having carried water there more than a few times just a week ago. It seemed to me that the gate might be open.

'Follow me,' I said.

I trotted down the slope of destroyed wall, and into the undefended town. I admit freely that part of my plan was to keep moving forward so that the Turks could not take the initiative. Equally, I wanted to keep my people moving and where I could see them, so they couldn't wander off and start looting.

I got lost in the winding streets, no more than two men wide, with shacks and old stone and masonry houses packed tight, and wooden second storeys and balconies that touched above us.

But before I could acknowledge my error I found steps going up, and I took them – stone steps carved into living rock. We turned once, and I looked back, and there was my whole company trailing along behind me.

Then through a narrow tunnel with arrow slits, a turn to the left, and we came out into the brilliant sunshine. It was perhaps the sixth hour of morning; a muezzin was calling in the citadel, and we were on the main street that rose to the citadel with ramps and stairs. Between one breath and the next I knew where I was.

I paused, because I was winded, and I assumed all the men behind me were winded too.

We stood, or bent, and panted.

'One run, all the way to the top,' I said.

L'Angars nodded.

Fiore reached past me and pulled the pins on the pieces of my ruined visor. He showed them to me, complete with the piece of Turkish arrow that had penetrated the right ocular, and then he tossed it down the steps, and it rattled.

'Then what?' Fiore asked.

He was always like that.

No commander likes to be asked 'then what' in public.

But it made me think. 'We take a tower, if we can get one,' I said. 'And hold it. The citadel gate. It's a goodly tower.'

Fiore nodded sharply. 'Good,' he said.

Mark laid an arrow to his bow, and Hector Lachlan and three of his Irish pushed their way to the front. They wore no leg harness, and Lachlan kicked off his shoes and was barefoot and bare-legged. The Davids, only two of them now, kicked off their shoes and hose and got in behind the Irish. They had more plan than I did.

L'Angars looked at his sabatons but left them on. Young Francesco stood and breathed like a bellows. His German squire hefted a big spear.

I grinned at the German. I barely knew him, but he clearly knew how to do this.

In a way, we'd all done this before. This was *escalade*, and if there's one thing at which routiers excel, it is this.

'Everyone ready?' I panted.

I held up my gauntleted hand, and counted down: five, four, three, two, one ...

I turned the corner and did my best to sprint. Did I mention the gravel in my shoes? Now that I was on a cobbled street, the gravel was like walking on knives.

Hector Lachlan shot past me in ten strides, and all his Irish, or Scots, and the Welsh.

It was as well.

Fifty paces away, the gate to the citadel tower yawned like the mouth of Hell.

A horn sounded.

A man on the walls gesticulated.

Another horn, muffled in my helmet. At least I could breathe. My visor was gone.

One arrow in the face and I was a dead man.

An arrow arched out from the walls and vanished over my head.

I was two paces closer to the gate. Hector was in the lead, flying, already ten paces ahead of me.

Another arrow, this one better aimed, plucked an Irishman. He took it in the chest, went down in a tangle, the Welsh leaping over him like salmon in spawn, and then he got to his feet as if the whole thing had been a stunt.

The two great doors of the citadel, solid wood and studded with iron, began to close. But they had no portcullis, and the doors were not on a machine, like one of the king's castles in England, or the lord's in Verona. They had the right door almost closed, and the left yet open about a pace, when Hector's shoulder struck it.

It moved.

The other two Celts hit it, full tilt, and one actually bounced, but again the door moved; a man inside called out in pain.

L'Angars struck the gate, and Marc-Antonio, and Aldo, and all three Welsh; Aldo was as big as Hector. They were all ahead of me, that's how slow I was. Red Bill was one pace behind me, broken arm and all.

I didn't go for the doors.

I went through the gap, and began killing, and Fiore came in behind me, slim and steel-bright, and as if we'd practised storming towers, I went to the right and he to the left, killing the men pushing the doors. Most of them were unarmoured, and at least two were baggage slaves.

The thing I remember best is that they'd pushed a bench across the closing gates, and somehow I managed to jump it, in full harness, and so did Fiore.

And then we killed them.

The doors crashed against their falling bodies and pushed them raggedly over the cobbles, painting the floor in ordure, but I had already turned for the stairs, even as a rush of armoured men came through the other end of the gate.

The old Romans must have been very confident in their soldiers; they put stairs inside the gate tower. In an English fortress, the only stairs to the second level are located elsewhere, to prevent just exactly what I was doing.

Storming the gate.

I left Fiore and the men who had slammed back the doors to fight the sortie, and I went up those wooden stairs. The second level was a barracks room, hung in carpets; there were perhaps six men – two arming, another standing with a bow, the last three fully armed.

I roared a war cry and charged the standing men.

The archer loosed at me and missed. My sword snapped out and his bow exploded into fragments, and I cut back, left to right, very flat. My man missed his cover, or only got a piece of my blade, and I hit his steel cap and he slumped, but I could not finish him, for his mate was on me. I covered his hasty blow and pressed close, my left hand now at mid-blade, what we call 'half-swording'. I saw in his eyes the realisation that he was now dead before I rammed my point home like a pick, and then ripped it out and swung my hilt like an axe at the next man.

I missed and lost my sword as my opponent stumbled back, my quillons caught in his aventail, and my own blade cut my hands. But he was just drawing, and I got my left hand on his wrist, stopped his draw, and my dagger went in under his arm and he was down.

To my left, l'Angars finished the archer, and behind me, Aldo beat another man to the ground with huge sword strokes – heavy, overhand blows.

I went down on one knee.

Fiore bounded up the steps, sword all blood, and went right past us for the curving steps to the third level.

I reached out and grabbed the emperor's sword. The man I'd struck with the hilt was alive, collarbone broken. He went for me while I tried not to kill him, and I got a steel-clad thumb in his eye.

And then I was climbing the last steps to the tower, and Fiore was fighting cautiously, guarding himself from three men. Two more were down. Aldo took a wound, and then they were all dead, and we had the tower.

'That took you longer than I expected,' Fiore said. He didn't even seem tired. He wiped his sword fastidiously and handed me the bit of rag he always carried.

I wiped my sword and my gauntlets. Then I went to the steps. There was a fourth level.

'Why did I just clean my sword?' I asked the world.

The third level had two doors, out to the walls, I assumed, as did the second. The fourth would stick up above the walls.

'Block those doors,' I said. I leaned down into the stairwell. 'Block the doors,' I roared.

Marc-Antonio called something from below.

'Come on,' Fiore said, as if I was holding him back.

'What of the gates?' I called down.

Marc-Antonio answered again.

The whole tower shook.

'They'll close the trap!' Fiore said.

He went up the steps without me. But Aldo was right by him, sword over his knight's shoulder like a spear, and l'Angars went up next.

'Get the bar on the gates!' I roared down the tower. God, how I wanted water. And the gravel out of my shoes.

Then I went up into the last steps.

When I got to the top, no one was fighting.

The two men who'd shot from the top of the tower were un-armoured. One was dead, and one bleeding out, both hands severed at the wrist. Even as I watched, Fiore finished him with a thrust.

The top was roofed, but open. It had hoardings, but they weren't built out, and heavy oak shutters that could be closed.

An arrow struck Fiore in the back and bounced off his back-plate.

'Sweet Christ,' he said.

I cut the rope over my head, and the big shutter crashed into place. There were crescent-shaped loopholes every few feet, but the sun was cut off.

Another arrow struck the heavy shutter.

I looked out of the nearest loophole.

The citadel's yard was full of men. There must have been two hundred men, some armoured, some not.

'Archers!' I called down the stairwell. 'Rob Stone! Get up here, now!'

Aldo, despite the cut to his arm, was throwing the other shutters down.

Fiore sat suddenly. 'I'm fatigued,' he admitted.

I didn't have time to be fatigued. I ran back down the tower, four flights of steps, passing Mark and Rob and all the archers coming up, and the gravel was still there, thanks. All the way to the charnel house of the ground floor, where there were a dozen corpses on the cobbles and the cobbles themselves were sticky. But the gates were closed in both directions, and huge iron bars had been slid across. Hector Lachlan was covered in blood. He'd cuts to his face, his legs, and one arm. But he was standing leaning on his axe behind the closed gate with Red Bill, who, despite a broken arm, was still standing.

On the other side of the gate, I could hear men shouting in Turkish.

'Fuckin' lost it there aweel,' Lachlan said, as if we'd been speaking all morning. 'A mickle bett'r now, thanks.'

I nodded and smiled, as if this was all perfectly normal. Right beside us was a man I'd known since Poitiers time and after, lying with his head half-severed in the near darkness, and every time I looked at him, I thought he might be alive. I couldn't remember his name. Gaston? Arnaud?

The inner gate rang like a bell.

'Found an axe, I reckon,' Lachlan said. 'I ha' one, as weel.' He grinned.

I nodded and left him in the darkness, and went back to the second level.

Pierre Lapot and a dozen men-at-arms and squires were piling corpses, furniture and anything they could lay hands on against the doors. And looting.

I tried to look on the best side of it. We were trapped, but then, none of my people was looting his way through the town, either.

I remember very little of the next hour. The archers emptied the courtyard; ten shafts, and the Turks were gone into the stables and the other towers, leaving new corpses to bleed out on the cobbles. But they had an engine, a mangonel, and they loosed it from the stables at the gate. A pair of very brave men began to try the inner gate with axes, while what seemed like fifty Turks rained shafts on our shutters, but Rob leaned out and feathered one and ducked back before he was feathered in turn.

They turned the mangonel on the fourth floor and shot at our shutters. The first bolt slammed in and ripped the left side of the huge oak frame off its overhead hinge. Mark dropped one of the Turks loading the thing.

The next shaft brought the whole shutter down off its hinges. Immediately Gaspard, one of our Gascon archers, died with two Turkish arrows in him, and Rob ordered the top floor abandoned.

The loopholes in the third and second floor were for crossbowmen. But the better archers could use them, although they had difficulty picking targets.

The axes started again.

'You know what I wish?' I said to Fiore.

He smiled. 'Is this a joke?' he asked.

I laughed, despite everything. 'No,' I said. 'Although I agree that men in our position might wish for a wide variety of things.'

L'Angars laughed and slapped his armoured thigh. Then he pointed at my hands. 'You are bleeding, Monseigneur.'

I had completely forgotten the cut across my hands from my own sword. My gauntlets were soaked.

'What do you wish for?' Fiore asked, while Marc-Antonio helped me get them off.

He made tutting noises, and I noted that he was confident enough in his own survival that he could dread cleaning my harness.

'I wish we had a banner,' I said, 'so that the Green Count and the prince might know we are here.'

Fiore made a face.

L'Angars was a hard man, but a thoughtful one. He looked at me, and then ripped a white linen sheet from one of the Turkish beds, and pulled from the wall a fly whisk hung there by one of the dead occupants, probably because flies were a menace even when there weren't a dozen corpses and a stew of blood and other foul juices on the floor. With the fly whisk as a brush, and with his own hands, he painted a cross on it in blood. The floor was covered in the stuff; some of it was mine.

My knees were shaking. I'd lost a fair amount of blood; I was curiously cold, I remember that.

While l'Angars did the grisly work with the horsetail fly whisk, I sat in a carved chair and ordered Marc-Antonio to get my sabatons and shoes off. The relief was almost miraculous.

Then there were axes coming against the second floor doors. There was little we could do but wait.

I put the bed-sheet on a spear shaft. Marc-Antonio sewed it on, so it wouldn't fall, and I slung a rope from head to iron, knotted through knife-slits in the sheet so that it couldn't fall.

Marc-Antonio got my shoes and sabatons back on. Without stones, thank God.

'Don't wait up for me,' I said, and crawled up the steps to the fourth storey. But I was no fool; I didn't show myself above the parapet, and I tied the ropes I'd secured to the top and bottom of the spear shaft securely, and then dropped it over the wall facing the sea.

I had no way of seeing whether it was visible.

There was no satisfying answering roar.

I crawled back to the stairwell, and slithered down the steps like an armoured snake as a dozen shafts clattered around the oak floor, launched at random.

By then it must have been nones or even later. I really can't tell you.

Later, we'd discover the well in the ground floor; discover, in fact, that there was a whole level under the gatehouse, a cistern I hadn't seen on my first visit and a little room. There were two Turks in the little room – our first prisoners.

Then one of the second floor doors gave way. We had lots of warning, and the iron strapping held. The Turks tried to throw fire through the door, and Mark shot one through the opening the poor bastard had just made.

'You lads still have our ladder?' I asked.

The archers brightened up.

I looked out from the third and second levels, to make sure, but it still appeared that the outside of the citadel was free of Turks. I ordered the outer gate opened – just the left half, which had a portal, or sortie gate in it. I slipped out and waited for death, but none came. I was alone in the town, in broad daylight.

Maurizio di Cavalli, Pierre Lapot, l'Angars and a dozen other routier veterans joined me in the street. Mark and Rob appeared on either side of the now-assembled scaling ladder we'd brought from Lesvos, and it went up to the second level parapet.

In for a penny, in for a pound. I hate heights, and I hate ladders, but the price of captaincy is measured in willingness to go first – at least with men like mine – and I went first up the ladder. It seemed to me the bravest thing I'd done that day, my back burning, my hands flayed, and sweat and blood everywhere.

I went over the wall and onto the catwalk, and I was twenty paces behind the party trying to put fire into the gatehouse.

They had no place to run. Our adversaries in the yard tried to support them with archery; Bill Vane shot down from the fourth floor, perhaps the bravest act of the day, exposed to archery with every shaft. But he put down two Turks and the rest began to flinch, and Cavalli and I cleared the door. But I got pinked in the thigh and my right greave got deformed at the ankle from well-aimed archery. I threw myself into the tower through the remains of the door, and the Devil take the consequence. Then I hauled Cavalli in after me, and below us, in the street, Lapot took the ladder down and came back into the tower.

I hadn't even thought to look up at the tower, but Lapot reported our cross of blood was hanging beautifully in full sun.

'Blood's already brown,' he complained.

Following Bill Vane's lead, the other archers went into the top storey; they drove the Turks off the courtyard again. At the time, I thought it was their superior height and perhaps English marksmanship, but later, when John rejoined us, he told me that their archers were probably out of arrows. They had expended them recklessly in the first hour, and the inner doors of the gatehouse looked like a rich woman's pincushion.

Whichever it was, we drove them out of the yard, and the mangonel only loosed one more time. By then it was noticeably cooler, and there was rain coming in. I could smell it, even above the carrion reek. We were trapped in a hot tower with twenty-five dead men or more, and the smell was bad.

I'll tell you something funny, though.

Sometime after the attack on the second floor, a cat emerged on the third floor. He was a tom, with a big head – scrawny, a feeder on scraps and mice. He purred like a hawser running over a board, and men began to pat him – hardened killers, men who'd just stormed a tower. Every hand seemed to stretch for the cat, and Rob Stone fed it some sausage that every man of us would have fancied, even from his bloody hands.

About sunset, the Turks came in armour. They had a ram; they'd made it out of tables and a roof beam, and they didn't have enough overhead shielding. We dropped roof tiles on them, and our archers shot shaft after shaft.

The ram hit the inner gate.

The whole building shook.

'Fuck,' Hector Lachlan said.

He'd stood there all day, and now I was standing with him, because my sense of the strength of the inner doors was that the axes and mangonel had weakened them enough that they might give. Nor was I wrong.

The archers drove the ram out of the courtyard, but the respite was brief.

The mangonel shot three times in the time a priest gives a sermon. That machine's captain knew his craft; each bolt struck within a palm's breadth of the others, and the iron bar holding the gate together bent, and on the third shot, one of the braces popped right off, all its clenched nails ripped free.

Then the ram was back, flying across the killing zone, and into the gate, and one door ripped free, opening perhaps a hand's breadth.

Marc-Antonio had a spear, and he put it into a man on the other side and lost it; another Turk pulled it out of his hands.

The makeshift ram slammed in again.

The German squire handed Marc-Antonio his big spear.

'Two more,' Pierre Lapot said. 'Bet you five ecus.'

'Done,' l'Angars said. 'I say three.'

Lapot won. On the second blow, the gate snapped back, and there was the yard, red as blood in the sunset. There were ten Turks, but fifty more came out of the shadows, out of the stable and the other towers.

I didn't have the men to hold.

'Back!' I called. I pulled Hector back. Then I leaned past him, crossed with a big Turk in plate and maille, and backed a step, made a wide slash, flicked my blade from low to high, and threw the handful of sand I'd kept in my left hand into the man's eyes.

I needn't have worried. I had Fiore behind me, with a spear. He killed the man with sand in his eyes, and then the tide of the running men broke on us. I got my feet one step up, and the world was narrowed to two men wide.

I retreated another step.

It's odd, but what I remember is not hunger, thirst, nor the pain in my hands. What I remember thinking was that it was all perfect. I was probably the best armoured man – the only man in my company in sabatons. There was nothing for the Turks below me to hit, and Fiore and his spear were as well armoured on the next step. Their sabres were hampered in the bad light and narrow quarters; my sword, held at the half-sword, was ideal.

Our archers began to loose down the stairwell.

Even to this, there is a rule. That is, the men below must *loft* shafts to strike a man higher, and avoid their own; but of course, a lofted shaft strikes the roof of the stairwell and loses all power. But the men above have the pull of the earth on their side, and drop their shafts on their enemies.

When they'd taken some arrows, they charged us. They were brave, and they were desperate. Of course, they had no water but through the gate, and they knew what I did not about the fight on the beach and outside the town.

I can't tell you a thing. I stabbed and covered, I'll guess. I didn't die. Isn't it odd? I remember the cat, but not the fight on the stairwell. It was like a nightmare, I suppose; something bruised my left forearm right through my vambrace, and I have no idea what it was, but I wager it was an axe.

It went on and on.

I remember a spear shaft coming between my feet and skewering some poor bastard two steps down and vanishing in a flash, like a viper's strike.

I remember when the pressure loosed so suddenly that I went down a step, and then again.

And then we were in the gatehouse, and they were running.

I knelt, but not to pray. Or, I did pray, after a bit, but I knelt because my knees would no longer hold me up.

Before darkness fell, Miles came to the outer gate with John. Forty minutes later we were relieved by all the knights of the Order, with Fiore's friend the Admiral of the Order in charge and forty of their red-clad mercenary men-at-arms. He saluted me. I was, for one of the few times in my life, too tired to talk.

We stumbled down the hill or were carried by Savoyard men-at-arms, themselves covered in blood and ash. The Turks had held the outer walls until mid-afternoon after losing the fight on the beach. Two of the Green Count's friends had been killed: Simon of Saint-Amour and Roland de Veissey had both been knights of his Order of the Collar. Two more of his great nobles were also dead, Girard Mareschal and Lord Jehan of Hiverdon, and some hundreds of other men.

The count himself had fought for over an hour, hand to hand. I later heard him say it was the hardest fighting he saw in his entire life. Prince Francesco told me that the fighting at the edge of the beach had been unbelievably savage.

I missed it all. Frankly, I doubt I missed a thing.

They had a Greek church in the lower town set up as a hospital, and the count's own physician and some serving brothers from my Order were all working there. I got Hector Lachlan onto a clean pallet of straw, and a dozen other wounded men. Pierre Lapot had a leg wound, Aldo had a deep puncture in his left arm, and Marc-Antonio was wounded. In fact, I was wounded, l'Angars was wounded; Francesco Orsini had two cuts in the backs of his legs, because he hadn't worn maille below the waist and the sabres got to him. Everyone was hurt somewhere, we were all exhausted, and only Fiore seemed un-hit. Of my little company, I had twelve dead – almost a fifth of our numbers.

A serving brother, one of the many Brother Johns my Order sported, was bandaging my hands with clean linen. He'd sponged my arms and hands clean, or clean-ish.

Fiore sat unmoving on a priest's chair, or perhaps a choir-stall chair. When I say unmoving, I mean he didn't twitch. He was like a corpse.

But just after I told Hector Lachlan that I owed him a hundred florins and he needed to live to collect, Fiore opened one eye. 'Better than Alexandria,' he said.

I had my harness off, and was barefoot in the nave of the church when a page came for me.

'If you are not too sore hurt,' he said with a bow, 'His Grace the Count of Savoy and His Grace the Prince of Lesvos beg your attendance.'

I nodded. And Marc-Antonio came up, despite his wound, with a bowl of warm water and my filthy fighting hose, which he laced back onto my doublet. And then I put my shoes back on my feet. I could walk, if only with a sort of rolling gait. It was a day later before I found I'd broken a toe at some point, and I had a puncture wound right through my greave and into my shin – an arrow from the fight on the catwalk, I guess.

Well, and my hands kept bleeding through the bandages, and the salt in my sweat continued to burn the lacerations on my back.

And I was hardly the worst wounded man. I was merely the only one ordered to attend his lords.

I stumbled and rolled along in the wake of my page, who, I could see, had a wound of his own. He was about fifteen, and blond, and handsome, and he had his left arm held stiffly.

'You are wounded?' I asked.

'Nothing like you, My Lord!' he said, a little breathlessly. 'But it hurts,' he admitted.

'Worse tomorrow,' I said. 'Don't be afraid of it. But keep it clean. Hear me, lad?'

Same advice Master Peter gave me for my first wound, I think.

They were in another Orthodox church – a smaller one, with a beautiful hanging lamp in silver.

Still hanging, I noted.

Not looted. The count might be a popinjay, but he had his Savoyards under command.

I walked down the nave to where they were seated. The Green Count wore his arming coat – green silk velvet, of course – and emerald hose. The Prince of Lesvos wore blue and gold; he had a fine, fur-edged gown over a sweat-stained doublet, and there was blood on his right hand. Richard Musard was waiting on the count as if he were his page, handing him a cup with a deep bow, and the count was drinking from a magnificent cup of crystal.

I made a reverence on one knee.

Count Amadeus looked up. Saw me, wiped his lips with a cloth.

'Wine for Sir William,' he said.

The prince rose from his seat, and with his own hands, fetched me a chair.

I was dumbfounded.

I collapsed into the chair.

'We are sensible that the outcome of today's fighting is largely due to you,' the prince said.

Count Amadeus looked away, as if he wanted to be somewhere else.

The prince went on, 'Your Mongols turned the tide on the beach. And when we saw the cross flying from the citadel tower ...' He looked at me. 'Men cheered you.'

'Your son fought well,' I said. 'He is wounded, but it should be nothing.'

Prince Francesco smiled his rare, genuine smile. 'Ah,' he said, clearly pleased.

'I would like to have that banner,' the count said. He ignored the prince. 'I will have it embroidered, and it will become a standard for Crusaders. Is it true that the cross was painted in blood?'

'The blood of brave men,' I said. Of course, some of it was mine, and some of it was Turkish. But they were all equally brave.

The count nodded. 'I wish I had been there. A great feat of arms.' He looked at Richard. 'I thank you.' He said the words as if they were teeth pulled from a man by a mountebank – they came out so unwillingly.

I rose and bowed, somewhat unsteadily. 'No thanks are required, my liege,' I said. The word 'liege' was like a needle in his flesh, I could tell; even Musard writhed a little. He didn't want me as a vassal.

Good. I still like the scene. I was too tired to give a fart.

The prince nodded and rose and took me by the elbow. 'I'll see Sir William to a pallet of straw,' he said.

The count didn't rise. He gave a nod and drank wine. I still hadn't received any.

I rolled back down the nave of the church with the Prince of Lesvos all but holding me up. He led me out, and we walked – I hobbled – along the street.

The Prince of Lesvos, warlord of the Eastern Aegean and veteran pirate, does not walk you home like a lovelorn girl, for nothing.

'He should have made you governor of this place,' Prince Francesco spat. 'You took the town. Fuck him. He's a fool. And he just wasted his pretty little army on the Turks.' He laughed bitterly.

'Wasted, Your Grace?' I asked.

'He lost more than a hundred men. Three of his own nobles. For nothing. The Turks are not our foes. You know what he should have done?' the prince asked me.

I suddenly knew I was being tested. I was also aware that two large men-at-arms were behind us on the cobbled street.

We came to the hospital and I bought time by entering, crossing myself, genuflecting to the Host at the altar. The Greek Orthodox priest nodded.

I was too tired to be tactically brilliant. 'I suppose he could just have sailed by,' I said. 'Together you have forty galleys. What fight could the Turks have made?'

'None,' Prince Francesco said. He sounded satisfied. 'Fighting ruins armies. His little army is probably ruined.'

'Ruined?' I asked, too tired to follow.

He shrugged. 'Perhaps I speak too harshly. What losses did you take?' he asked.

'My master archer,' I said. 'Seven men-at-arms, a squire, and four archers.'

'Christ risen. Out of how many men?' he asked.

'Sixty-eight,' I said.

He was silent a moment, and the big man-at-arms in the door nodded at me, as if to commiserate.

'How long before they are ready to fight again?' he asked.

'Three days?' I said, and then looked at him. 'Or longer. I take your point, Your Grace. Losses hurt. I will be a long time filling Ned Cooper's shoes, and half my lances will be in chaos.'

'Every manoeuvre that your lad Stapleton taught them will have to be relearned with different men in different vital roles,' he said. The way he said 'Stapleton' would make you laugh. 'And the new men have learned that death is real.'

I'd seldom heard a fighting man speak so candidly. 'You advocate avoiding war?'

Prince Francesco looked at the vigil light for a moment. 'I remember my first crew – my first ship that was *mine*. We took a Venetian, oar to oar and ship to ship. When we were done, most of my officers were dead or wounded. I had to do it all again.' He shrugged. 'To be honest, I'm not sure my second crew was as good as the first. After a while I went for easier marks – took fewer risks. You will too, if you are wise.' He looked at me. 'I'm a weary old man. You were noble today. I am delighted you are one of my captains – Richard Percy is jealous. I am providing the garrison for this town, and yet the count refused to accept you as the captain here – said you cannot be trusted.' He shrugged. 'Be wary of him, Sir William. Perhaps he covets your wife, or her lands, or both. But he is not an honest brigand like the Lord of Lesvos.' He rose. 'I have a good estate in the farmland behind Methymna – a knight's fee that I could deem a barony. I hope you will accept it.'

'Willingly, My Lord.' I made as if to kneel.

He pushed me into my chair. 'Go and sleep. Tell your Stapleton I would do the same for him, if he stayed.'

I had to shrug in my turn. 'Sir Miles is a rich man, and goes home to England to be married.'

'Ah, well,' the prince nodded. 'Sleep, Sir William.'

I saw him walk along the line of beds and bend over his oldest son. He kissed the boy's forehead and looked at him awhile, saying nothing. And then he left.

The next day, we awoke to find the Turks gone. The Savoyards were enraged, and promised to pursue the Turks, but I noticed a certain reticence on the part of the prince. When I met Sir Richard in the narrow streets while looking for a Latin priest to perform funeral rites, he took me aside, congratulated me warmly and without reservation in a way that warmed my heart and raised my estimation of him. Let me pause here to say that the ability of a knight to admire another knight is always worthy. The man who cannot admit admiration of others is weak. When he'd paid me a thousand compliments, I blushed and stammered, I hope, and then I looked up at the citadel. He laughed.

'Our prince arranged it,' he said.

'I thought as much,' I admitted.

'You didn't look as if you were born yesterday,' Sir Richard said. 'The Savoyards don't have to live here, and we do. Now the sultan owes our prince a favour.'

I could only find one Latin prelate, and he was the Savoyard chaplain. I will mention that there was a distinct thaw among the Savoyards after the storming of Gallipoli; several of the Savoyard lords were suddenly cordial to me, and young Antonio Visconti, one of the Lord of Milan's bastards, was effusive in his praise. He it was who helped me engage the count's chaplain for funeral services.

We all rode out – that is, my little band. We rode to the back of the Turkish camp and fetched in our dead, all of whom were bloated and unlovely from the heat. But the Orthodox Metropolitan found us places to bury them all, and a marble carver was hired to put a slab over them; I've been back, and it's still there. The Green Count's chaplain came, and prayed and gave us a service.

As I say, there was a definite warmth, or at least a thaw, from the Savoyards. We all felt it; the respect of other men is a tonic, if you like, and taking the gate tower of the citadel made us something in everyone's eyes. Several of the Savoyard knights attended our service: Visconti came, and the Bastard of Savoy, Humbert, a good knight if a bit slow, bastard son of Giacomo, Prince of Achaea; and Antoine de Savoy, who was one of the count's children, by another woman. The

Count of Savoy and his family clearly had no problem siring children. And they were all big, strong men.

We stood in the sun when the chaplain had said all the words, and I felt as if perhaps I should say something.

In fact, they were all looking at me.

I don't really remember what I said. I said all the names – that's important. And I said some of what the prince had said; that the loss of good men was a loss to everyone, because the company was like a tournament team. And I offered that, as crusaders, every man was likely going to heaven. I'm not sure I believed in my heart, by then, that killing Turks was 'better' than killing Frenchmen, or Germans, or Italians.

The Savoyards shook hands, and young Antoine said some good words about the company's prowess. When they were gone, my people relaxed.

'Ned Cooper going to paradise?' Rob said aloud. 'He'd want the mussulman's paradise, most like. Seventy-two virgins who wouldn't know to tell him his prick was tiny.'

'Proper job,' muttered Bill Vane, and they all laughed.

That afternoon, I was summoned by the prince and Sir Richard handed me a casket bound in iron, which proved to be full of silver coin in bags – fifty-nine bags.

'Well-earned,' he said. 'Double pay, and a share of the value of the town. I'm paying because I suspect that the Count of Savoy is out of money. We'll be off to Constantinople in a week, perhaps less, and then ... I hope we are still rescuing my brother-in law.'

I shared out the wages immediately, in the little square by the hospital-church. I bought a small tun of good wine and had it served, and made sure the Hospitaller brethren all had a cup too.

When every man had his little bag of silver, I gave another speech. This one was about having an employer who paid on the nail. 'No rape, no theft,' I said again. 'I've lost too many of you bastards to want to hang any of you.'

No one laughed, but to the best of my knowledge, no one broke the rules. Soldiers are at their most dangerous with a pocket full of silver.

I walked over to Orsini, as he wanted to be called.

He didn't meet my eye.

'You fought well,' I said. 'I expected no less. Now lead. They will do as you do – that's why I can't have you messing about. Everyone knows who you are. Help me lead.'

'Help you?' he asked.

'Yes,' I said. 'Don't you want to be a knight?'

'I could go over to the Green Count and he'd knight me this moment,' the boy said.

I thought about it. 'Yes,' I said. 'He probably would.' I nodded. 'And then I'd have to raise your pay.'

He didn't get it at first, even with a little sack of silver coins in his fist. But then a smile crinkled the corners of his mouth.

'I see,' he said, in very much his father's tone. Then sulky. 'My father sent all my friends back to the ships.'

I nodded. 'I did that,' I said. 'You could go too. You've seen it – a real fight. You did your bit. There's a thousand knights in England and France that have never been in fights that hard, and wear their spurs and fancy belts every day.'

He nodded. 'I'd like …' He paused. 'It was …' He shook his head. 'I can't remember much, except when all the prisoners were killed.'

I pulled at my beard. 'Yes,' I said. 'That was bad.'

He didn't meet my eye. He seemed to quiver a moment, and then the moment was gone. 'Oh, well,' he said. 'Somewhere in this town is a whore.' He flourished his bag of silver, as if he was not the son of the one of the richest men in the world.

My purse was full of gold, not silver; my little bag from the prince had four hundred gold florins.

I remember praying that afternoon; asking God for more men and less fighting, and a priest, and a little luck with the prince's son. It was a funny prayer, and yet …

The next day emerged out of the darkness in a damp grey dawn. One of the Irishmen, Angus, who had taken what I viewed as a light enough wound, suddenly turned his face to the wall and died. None of the Hospitaller serving brothers could tell me what he died of, and I could tell they were, themselves, lacking spirit.

I went and found the matron who had hidden me and fed me the day I scouted with Richard Musard, which by then seemed to have been a lifetime before. And she was awed and somewhat difficult. I tried to give her money, and she pretended not to understand.

But I thought to ask her help in feeding my company, because I thought that a civilised dinner might help their flagging spirits, and my matron was the right woman to ask. She transformed from confused and bashful – and just possibly resentful – to helpful and eager, and with Syr Giorgios to translate, she produced a menu and a trio of women like herself to cook. I paid them in silver and everyone appeared well satisfied.

Having arranged for a small hall in her *bourg*, I invited the Hospitaller knights and brethren to join us, and we settled to a feast of pork and fish and strong red wines. The fish was not one I could remember having before, and cooked inside out, with the skin turned in and stuffed full of ginger and nutmeg and other costly spices that made the archers wonder.

During dinner, Pierre Lapot surprised me by willingly relating the tale of his experience in the darkness of the Holy Sepulchre, and Fra Daniele pronounced it a 'road to Damascus' conversion. This led to a general conversation about paths of chivalry; I remember it as a noble evening, and I was pleased to see my little company begin to have a tone – an idea of themselves as different, because so many of us had gone to Jerusalem together.

But we were not a legion of angels, and we sat up late and drank a good deal of wine, and I was very late to rise the next day. My pavilion was still on a galley or a round ship twenty miles away. My bed was on a palliasse of straw on the floor of an Orthodox church, and I shared it with the big tom cat from the tower, who seemed to have been adopted by the company.

So it was one of the serving brothers who woke me, and my head hurt, but not for long, for standing behind the serving brother was Nerio Acciaioli. With him, of all people, was Father Angelo, the Franciscan who had been so difficult at Jaffa and Jerusalem.

Nerio laughed at my confusion. 'I found him at Corinth,' he said. 'I thought I'd bring him along and show him a different kind of crusade.' He looked around the church. 'How bad was it?' he asked quietly.

'Fourteen dead. Including Ned Cooper,' I said.

Nerio pulled his beard. 'So you will be glad that I engaged most of the rest of my cousin's brigands,' he said. 'They were going to Mystras to take service, and it occurred to me that they would only end up fighting against us.'

I got up off my little bed of straw and embraced him. He was as elegant as ever, or more so, in blue and rose, with matching gloves. Then I opened my arms to embrace Father Angelo, who flushed, but accepted my embrace and gave me the kiss of peace.

'Be welcome among us, Father. I had hoped to find my company a chaplain, if you are at liberty.' I waved my hand at the nave of the little quincunx church. 'And none of us have heard Mass since we left Rhodes.'

He raised an eyebrow. 'I didn't imagine ...' he began, and thought better of it.

'Where are you bound, Father?' I asked.

He looked at Nerio.

Nerio shrugged. 'I will have the appointment of the new bishop for my lands in Morea,' he said. 'I like him, and he's not a pushover.' He nodded to the Franciscan. 'I would be delighted if you would consider being our chaplain for the balance of this campaign.

Father Angelo made a face. He tried not to; he was, as I have said, a well-bred man, and related to the Cavalli. In fact, he and Maurizio had to embrace twenty times ...

We were right by the doors, and I stepped outside, where one of the younger brothers was stirring a boiling pot full of dirty laundry. I took the huge ladle out of his hands without a word and stepped back inside.

Father Angelo looked at me, bemused.

I handed him the huge wooden utensil. 'For supping with the Devil,' I said in Italian.

His eyes met mine. And he grinned.

Nerio gave me a minute nod of approval.

Then I had to return the ladle.

Nerio had brought us better weather, a priest, and another eighty men. Most of them were Italians – exiled nobles and younger sons. They all had good harness, and Nerio had already offered them land grants in his principality when, as he put it, he 'came into his kingdom'. His arrival was also a godsend for my dealings with Orsini, because suddenly he had twenty young Italians to impress – men not so different from him, and who were impressed that he had helped storm the town.

And I had all the Kipchaks. Which is not to say they followed me; they followed John. John followed me. This seemed a perfectly adequate arrangement, and we didn't question it.

That day or the next, relations between my employer and the count grew more strained – mostly because, as I have said, the count insisted on appointing the captain of the town, a town he now clearly viewed as his own to keep or sell. For twelve hours I feared I would be ordered to attack the count.

At the same time, Nerio's return meant a return to my usual levels of information. Nerio had gathered a great deal of news at Nafplion, a fortified town where he'd gone with his cousin, the Archbishop of Patras – and where he'd rented a Cretan military galley. I learned that the emperor was almost certainly being held in Hungary; that it was possible that Robert of Geneva had played some part in his captivity; that Turenne had declared us all dead; that Nerio's credit was restored in some circles, but not others; and that Andronicus, the crown prince, if you like, of the Eastern Roman Empire, was moving to secure his power in his father's absence.

I listened, because Nerio seldom wasted time – at least with men – and I understood that he was preparing to be a Lord of Achaea; seeking to understand a new chessboard with new pieces. But for me, I was more interested in joining l'Angars and Stapleton and arranging messing groups, so that every man got fed, and so that the new men, who had not been to Jerusalem or stormed Gallipoli might nonetheless feel part of us. They were, for the most part, Italians, who willingly enough took orders from Maurizio di Cavalli, who had been on the stairs behind me when we held the gate tower of Gallipoli; he was one of them, and a scion of one of their greatest military families. Some were Bretons – but they were as stubborn and arrogant as Bretons always are, and l'Angars and Lapot were too Gascon for them. Their leader was a cocky man, as big as a house, named Ranulf Guiscard.

'Why are you in command?' he asked me. 'I have more men than you.'

'No,' I said. Otherwise I ignored him. I came back to him later, when we assigned him to a mess-group.

'I see no reason to take your orders as if I were some lackey,' he said.

I'll wager I sighed.

In the short term, I had all the Bretons serve directly under Nerio. He was paying them; they were unlikely to question his authority.

That evening – or was it the next? Ah well, my friends, you can't honestly expect that I remember every day ... At any rate, that evening or the next, Prince Francesco summoned me, gave me good wine to drink, and informed me that we would ride to Constantinople and our ships would meet us there.

As there were likely to be Turks all along the peninsula, it was no light undertaking, but Prince Francesco was so angry at Count Amadeus that he would be away the next day. We rode all the way back to Portefino, as the Genoese call it, and only there did we rally, gather supplies, and assemble something like a baggage train.

The next morning, in brilliant sunshine, we rode out for the great city – almost a thousand men in a long column, with John's Kipchaks in the van, and Syr Giannis and his stradiotes to talk to any locals. And the weather was fine for two days, as if to lure us onward, and then it turned to high winds and heavy rain, despite the season. The rain poured down onto the rocky ground, and drained away, but starting fires became a sort of test of arms and prowess and will. Then our two Welshmen became heroes, and Ewan the Scot; all three men had been foresters, and had the skill to make dry wood and light fires in any weather, and a thousand men owed them any little comfort they had.

We had no tents. It was August in Thrace; we were moving fast. Men sickened, horses sickened, and the rain fell and fell. And fell. No Turks attacked us because only madmen would have been out in that rain. At every moment, I expected to see old Noah float by in his Ark.

The prince shook his head in disgust, and water fell off his hood and dripped from his liripipe. 'I've never seen weather like this,' he spat. 'August? The world is going to Hell.'

Hector Lachlan, who had been recovering well enough to ride, sickened again. Several men with wounds took fevers.

In a village on the north coast of the Sea of Marmara, we rented two stone barns belonging to the church and got our company warm and dry. Lachlan's fever broke; the red marks around David the Brown's arm wound retreated.

On the other hand, the Greeks were surprisingly hostile. Where at

Gallipoli they had rather liked us, on balance, at Larna the Orthodox priest would have nothing to do with us. I had intended to leave my wounded there, but when the next day dawned clear, I chose to take them, even if they slowed the whole column. I was afraid the Greeks would murder them. And despite being close to Constantinople, we were in debated land; no one seemed to know whether the sultan or the emperor held sway.

And, of course, Franks had conquered the Greeks a hundred and fifty years before, around Magna Carta time. And not gently.

We camped the last night in a gentle rain. Camp is a euphemism; I had horses with hoof rot, and men with inflamed wounds again. My joints were so stiff it hurt to dismount, and both of my hands were infected. No one slept; there was nowhere to sleep, even for veterans, and water flowed over bare rock. Prince Francesco cursed his ill luck and the weather, and Sir Richard Percy rolled his eyes.

'Rather be here than at sea. Those bastards got it bad.' he said, and I had to agree.

We rose the next morning and the day was clear; there were a few clouds off to the west, but the sun was bright and warm. By mid-morning the road was dry and so were the rocks; the sun was hot. My back didn't hurt for the first time in several weeks, and Hector Lachlan rode with his head up. He had the damned cat in his saddle pack, riding along like a small lion, head out of the bag, enjoying everything.

I smelled Constantinople before I saw it, and it was a smell of city, like London or Paris – wood smoke and Man. Constantinople had another smell, like spice, under the scent of smoke; the prince told me it was incense from the forty or more monasteries and seventy or so churches. That may be so.

'You have never been?' the prince asked me.

I shook my head.

'A wonderful, terrible place,' he said. 'I prefer Lesvos.'

We rode along. The ground was mostly flat, and soon enough we could see the walls.

There is nothing on earth like the walls of Constantinople. I gather they were built by the Emperor Theodosius, a Roman emperor.

Indeed, when I speak of Constantinople, you need to remember that the place has never fallen but once – and that was to Franks – and that the emperors of Rome have made it their capital since Constantine.

The walls themselves are superb, and the Greeks keep them in good repair, for the most part. The land walls are over seven miles long; there is a deep ditch, and splendid towers, each as good as a fortress. The walls have so many gates that I never saw them all; the emperor's army guards them in turn, rotating each day to prevent corruption or treachery.

We came up from the Sea of Marmara on the road, and then rode north along the wall, all the way from the south to the north, while my employer regaled us with a description of the wonders to be found inside the mighty walls.

Outside, I noted, were fields, and a few little villages; we passed a fine monastery dedicated to the Virgin, and many of us dismounted there and prayed. But the farming was not very modern – indeed, I saw two young men using a plough that was little more than a stick, not like our big English ploughs; ours take a yoke of oxen. And the soil is sandy.

I could hear singing inside the city, and bells, but it all sounded very distant.

In early afternoon, a unit of cavalrymen rode out of a gate. They were Mongols; by then, I knew a Mongol when I saw one. Their captain rode to the head of our column and exchanged words with John, and then the two of them rode down the column to where the prince was with me. The officer dismounted and bent his head, and handed Prince Francesco a fine scroll in an ivory tube with an eagle inscribed on it in gold leaf.

The prince took it, kissed it, and opened it. He read briefly, nodded, and smiled at Sir Richard. 'I think there has been a mistake,' he said.

The officer of the Mongols attempted to remonstrate, and Prince Francesco cut him off with a peremptory hand motion and summoned me, as well as Sir Richard and Sir John Partner.

'Something is very wrong,' he said. 'Close up. Andronicus, the emperor's son, orders me to turn around and says the gates will be shut against me.'

Then he summoned Nerio, and Syr Giorgios. We all dismounted; most men fell asleep. It was sunny and warm, and we were desperately short of sleep.

I found myself by the Breton knight, Guiscard.

'We going to fight?' he asked in French.

'Only after I have a nap,' I said.

He chuckled and went to sleep.

Marc-Antonio woke me as the sun was sinking. He had a canteen of fresh water; I drank half and poured some on my face and hands, but I still felt heavy and stupid.

Not too stupid to thank him for the water, however. He was beginning to be a good squire; I didn't want to let that slip by unremarked.

No, that's not fair. He was a good squire – an excellent squire, really – and he was growing better by the day. Soon I'd have to knight him, I thought.

The prince was already mounted. 'I believe I have solved our little trouble.' He had Nerio by him, and Nerio raised his eyebrows.

'I dislike this rumour that Andronicus is attempting to unseat his father,' the prince said. 'I do not want to hear it repeated.'

'Yes, Your Grace,' I said. I had a strong feeling that the old pirate was a right bastard when crossed.

'Good. I have arranged quarters in the city. All the Englishmen will go together; I think you will find it quite pleasant to be with people who speak your language, yes? And perhaps hear Mass in English?'

I agreed that this would be a fine thing. You might think that Latin is a universal language, but English Latin tends to be very different from Italian Latin. And some English priests will say a whole Mass in English, if you ask nicely.

I saluted.

'May I ask what happened?' I said.

He raised an eyebrow. I noted that all of our Greeks were gone.

'There was a misunderstanding,' Prince Francesco said. 'Which by now has been dealt with, I hope and pray.'

We rode all the way to the north end of the wall, and there we entered at the Blacharnae Gate, where the emperor has his palace, and we were all alert. I saw Sir Richard loosen his long war sword in its scabbard and I did the same, pulling the emperor's sword a finger's width from the throat of the scabbard to speed the draw. I nodded to l'Angars, and my men-at-arms duplicated the action all the way down the column.

There were men on the gate in plate and maille and red silk surcoats worked in gold, carrying axes – some like Swedish axes, and some like our poleaxes. They were all big men.

'Hey, Syr Christos!' Prince Francesco said to one man with blond hair and a fuller beard than most Franks. 'A chance to practise your father's tongue.'

The man so named made a reverence to Prince Francesco. And then to me, he said 'The sele of the day to you, My Lord,' in London English. Miles Stapleton laughed aloud; there really isn't anything more remarkable than being addressed in English at the gate of the emperor's palace in Romania, is there?

So the emperor's inner guard is English. They have a proud history; their *banda* or company has served the emperors since Charles the Great ruled the Franks and Roland fought the Saracens, or so they say – six hundred years. Some say that they began to be English when Earl Sigurd fled after Harald's defeat at Hastings. And I will say out of place that later, when I stood on the balcony at Hagia Sophia, I saw where Englishmen had carved their names in the railing; by God, it did me good to know that there were bored, blasphemous louts among them even then.

Syr Christos, as he proved to be, was Greek; but his mother was Russian and his father English, and Constantinople was the only home he'd ever known, for all he could sound like a lad from Cheapside if he wished. We clasped hands, and I relaxed, and introduced him to Miles Stapleton and Diccon Crewel and Red Bill, and then we were accused of blocking the gate, and all our men rode in. Syr Christos seemed curiously hesitant, or perhaps taken aback, by us. I found him difficult to read. But any doubts I might have entertained were blown away by the palace.

The Blacharnae palace is probably the finest palace I've ever seen; built of brick and stone and marble, it rises in striped glory to a height as great as Westminster, but it is not a church. The hall is vast, and outside are three churches and a double garden, all walled, with a small monastery and a vast block of stables, and all enclosed in a double wall that is gated in four places. The walls have their own towers, and the whole is as fine a fortress as Caernarvon or the Tower, but the gardens and stables and religious buildings are each more marvellous than the next, and as beautiful inside as out – perhaps, if possible, more beautiful inside. I have heard many men tell me that the Empire is in rude decline – and indeed, I can see the signs myself – but the frescoes and the mosaics are so wonderful, so fresh, that it is difficult to imagine that this is not a people at the very peak of their strength.

The army paraded two regiments for the Prince of Lesvos's arrival: the Varangians, who, as I have said, are mostly axe-bearing Englishmen, and the Vardariotes, who are 'sons of Turks'. In fact, while that might once have been true, most of them are Kipchaks like John, with a sprinkling of Mongols from even further to the east, and a superb and barbaric spectacle they make in red silk kaftans and white turbans.

But I noted there were fewer than two hundred Vardariotes and not even that many Varangians. The emperor's 'army' wasn't as big as John Hawkwood's 'Compagnia di Aventura'.

Mind you, if I could only have four hundred men, I'd take Englishmen and Mongols. I might conquer the world with such an army.

But they saw us to quarters with efficiency and courtesy. I saw the Bretons bedded down in a tower on the outer wall; the Italians rode off under Ser Maurizio to three towers by the Genoese and Venetian Quarter where they could find taverns and friends, taking with them both Francesco Orsini and his German squire. I was hesitant, and told Sir Richard as much; we were being broken up and scattered across a vast city, and I misliked it, and Sir Richard and Sir John liked it no better, but the prince would hear nothing of our suspicions,

Syr Christos took me himself, and led me, as well as most of our English, Scots, Welsh and Irish, into the great small town beyond the palace. All my friends stayed with me, whereas Sir Richard and Sir John stayed at the palace with the prince. First we crossed farm fields, while Syr Christos explained that where once five hundred thousand people had lived in the city, nowadays only seventy thousand lived there, and that the Imperial complex had been moved from the Golden Horn to the Blacharnae district. But the land enclosed by the walls was so vast that we saw fields, and then a village, to the south, and beyond, to the east, another wall, and beyond the wall an endless profusion of tile roofs.

But we didn't go further east, but north around the palace walls and to the very edge of the sea where we found a fine neighbourhood, a proper *bourg*, nestled between the palace and the sea wall. There we found a small church dedicated to Saint Nicholas, where an English priest said Mass for us. And then we went to two big inns and a dozen private homes, and every man and woman in the little *bourg* of the great city spoke some English, and they came out into the street as if it was a holiday. Syr Christos told us that this little quarter had been 'English' since at least the First Crusade and the taking of Jerusalem. He showed me the graves of Englishmen going back to men with Saxon names in the little church of Saint Nicholas and Saint Augustus of Canterbury – a name that was music to my ears so far from home.

I ate beef and drank good dark ale and was content. My hostess, who was Syr Christos's lady mother, was charming, and spoke English with a lovely Russian accent. After we had supped, Syr Giorgios came to the hall, and proved to be a friend of the family, and then he promised to take me on a tour of the city the next day.

Syr Christos gave him a cup of wine, and while he was out of the hall, Giorgios turned to me and Nerio. 'You know what happened, eh?'

'No,' I said.

He looked at Nerio. 'I swear, we caught Andronicus *in flagrante delicto*. About to put on the purple.'

Nerio raised an eyebrow and watched a serving girl. 'We're not supposed to say,' he murmured. 'But there's a rumour at Negroponte that Andronicus intends just that.'

Giorgios muttered some blasphemy in Greek and drank some wine. 'Things are not good here – the city is tense, and the patriarch is not speaking to the caesar.'

'Caesar?' I asked.

'The emperor's son. Caesar Andronicus.' Giorgios glanced at Fiore, who was sneezing. 'Be careful. I'll come tomorrow.'

The next morning, I had no duties, and Syr Giorgios came as he had promised. He was good company, if a trifle long-winded, and took us into the city proper, past the outer farms and the inner wall, walking us up the hills, taking all of us through a ruined gate to avoid the toll, and telling me of each church and its particular saint. Nerio came along, and Miles; Fiore stayed abed, having developed a head cold of staggering proportions in the rain.

Giorgios and Christos spoke Greek, a mile to the minute, as we strolled out into the warm summer day. Mostly they showed us churches, starting with Hagia Sophia, the most staggering sight of the whole day. In the enclosed court outside the magnificent cathedral, Giorgios and Christos had an argument, which I ignored to buy a spiced sausage from a vendor. It might have been London, except for the heat.

Between churches, I had time to see a little of the great city. The streets were miraculously broad – as broad as ten London streets – but the alleys and warrens that led off the fine thoroughfares were as narrow as anything in London, and perhaps worse. They had the same smells: death, rot, urine.

A fine aqueduct runs into the centre of the city like a spine, across the hills in the centre of the peninsula. I find I have not really described anything, which is an old man's reminiscence at work. Constantinople is like a man's left thumb, if his hand is palm down on the table. It is a broad thumb, I confess it – perhaps more like two thumbs side by side. The nail is the old palace and all the imperial gardens; when I looked over the wall, standing on Nerio's shoulders, it looked to me like a tangle of untended trees, but with the walls of the old palace rising like a derelict ship and then the bulk of Hagia Sophia like a mountain constructed by men. Just at the lower edge of the nail is the hippodrome – an incredible place, like a vast theatre built for jousting. The old Romans used it to race horses, or so they told me. West and north of the hippodrome the city proper begins, with the 'Millon' stone, the first milestone of the Roman Empire, from which other roads were measured. I have seen the one in York; imagine! And imagine, too, that Constantine, who built Constantinople, was crowned emperor at York. He was an Englishman, naturally!

At any rate, I stood there at noon, with statues of Roman dukes and counts and knights all around me, and thought of roads that ran from this stone all the way to the Pict Wall, past York Minster. One empire. One faith.

We walked and walked. I ate my highly spiced sausage and listened to the criers; again, they shouted in different languages, but it was not unlike London. The sounds were loud – some in Italian, most in Greek. And in the background, everywhere, the singing of monks.

Summer gives long days, and most of the markets were open. We saw the emperor's spice market, and I bought saffron and split a sweet cake with Nerio. The spice market was full of Italian sailors and merchants buying, but Giorgios admitted that it was unusually quiet. People looked at us oddly. A Pisan asked if it was true that the Count of Savoy was coming to storm the city.

Then we walked back inland, up to the height of the city, where we could see across the strait to the Genoese tower at Pera on the far side, a symbol of the power of that republic within the empire.

I wanted to see the inside of a church, and Giorgios insisted that we go all the way back out to the area between the two walls – almost an English mile. By then we had probably walked a dozen of those miles, and Nerio was willing to stop and drink wine.

'Where are the women?' he asked at one point.

Giorgios shrugged. 'Women do not come out except for religious observance, and fetching water, and gossip,' he said, dismissively.

Nerio sighed. 'Barbaric,' he said.

Giorgios began to explain the beauties of his city while we trudged along what might have been a country road anywhere else in the world, except that in any direction you could see the towers of the great walls, and to the east you could see the roofs of the city.

Christos fell behind with Miles, and Giorgios took my arm. 'That man worries me,' he said, nodding his head at Syr Christos. 'Why is he staying with us all the time?'

I thought Giorgios was being rude, and I said so, and he shrugged. I took his shrug to mean that he was not offended because I was something like a fool.

'You are a fine soldier,' he said. 'But this is Constantinople, and men were hatching plots here when Rome was in the hands of barbarians.'

But he went back to speaking of the wonders of the city. I admit that I wasn't as impressed as I might have been. Constantinople is old and magnificent, but like an old knight, you can see all the scars; you can guess how strong he once was, but you can see the wrinkles in his skin and the loss of muscle, and so it was with the city of Constantine. Nothing was well-maintained, and almost nothing was new. And the people were, to me, shockingly superstitious; every single thing was explained to me in terms that would have made a Venetian snort or an Englishman from Mary-Le-Bon laugh aloud. They're priest-ridden the way Italians are not; they venerate saint's relics that are themselves slightly too much, if you take my meaning – milk from the Virgin's teat?

Perhaps I am just a doubting Thomas.

And under every glory there was dirt, or over it: many mosaics were dirty; there was trash in all but the broadest streets, and even Giorgios's proud guiding could not conceal empty houses and gloomy streets with no children playing.

There was great beauty too; the Lykos river flowed through much of the town, and we ate grapes along the bank, and I looked upstream and saw trees overhanging the river. Giorgios told me they belonged to an estate of the Komnenos family, and that they were in exile. The stream was beautiful, and the fields on either side beautifully farmed.

However, we crossed the fields, boiling in the sun, and Giorgios interrupted the flow of his lecture to take us to a beautiful church with many frescoes; the 'Church in the Fields'. The priest on duty was no friend of Franks or Englishmen, and he followed us as if he expected us to steal the lamps, but Giorgios spoke a few words to him and he smiled at us.

I stopped under a superb mosaic of Christ Pantokrator – Christ the King, we'd call him. He looked exactly like Giorgios: narrow face, intelligent eyes. I said as much, and Giorgios hushed me with a smile and said this was blasphemy.

'But you are a Latin!' I said.

He winced and looked over his shoulder at the priest. 'Not here, I am not,' he said, with a smile full of irony that suggested to me that he wasn't a Latin anywhere, except perhaps while Father Pierre Thomas was alive.

'You don't like us,' I said.

'Bah,' he said, with a frown and a little shake of his head. 'I am too old to dislike a whole race. Men are men. But the Franks were no friends to us. You are, William. But you are not a typical Frank. Nor Nerio. And it is easy to hate you, when we need you so much.' He glanced at Christos. 'There are many here who loathe all the Franks. Some would rather ally with the Turks.'

We were leaving the Chora church and there was a little rain, and despite the damp I saw a market across the courtyard, full of pottery and saints' images, and I left my friends and crossed the yard.

A man in an Italianate half-cloak ducked away into the portico of the monastery.

If he hadn't moved so fast, I would never have noticed him. But the Italian half-cloak was the odd thing. The Romanians, or Byzantines, have their own styles: men wear small turbans, and woman often wear larger ones; men favour Turkish or Mongol coats or kaftans, and women sometimes wear kirtles like Frankish women, but more often a shapeless overdress and veils. When men wear hose, they are linen, and quilted. The man I glimpsed was in Italian clothes – jupon, tight wool hose, and a half-cloak – and he stood out. In the spice market it would have been nothing. In a small churchyard, he was as alien as I was myself. And his face – flat, and Slavic.

Despite which, it's like seeing a drunkard in the Papal Palace; not your business. I went into the market and bought some fine wares, as good as anything I'd seen in the Damascus Market in Adalia. I bought plates, a few cups, and a big platter which, by God and Saint George, made it to Venice intact, and off which, friends, you may one day eat a meal.

It was not so far back to Blacharnae and beyond it, our little English quarter. But we were tired, and at Giorgios's suggestion, we rented horses and rode, with a boy on a pony to take his father's horses home. As we left the stable, I saw the half-cloak again, this time in the shadows by the stable gate. And I saw him pointing, and the man with his head turned to follow that pointing arm was Greek – nondescript, but he wore a long dagger with a cross hilt. A very workmanlike weapon, in fact.

'I think we're being followed,' I said to Nerio, who had been watching a solitary girl get water at a fine well head.

'Ah,' he said. But his focus changed; the insufferable half-smile left him, and he became a different kind of predator.

'Giorgios,' I said, putting a hand on our guide's shoulder, 'we are followed.'

He raised both eyebrows. 'They could be the emperor's men,' he said. 'We are very careful of ...' He paused.

'Franks?' Miles said.

'Foreigners,' Giorgios said graciously. But he looked at Christos. 'Except ...'

I thought no more of it.

*

Marc-Antonio was waiting for me that evening and gave me a message from the prince, asking my attendance the next day at the palace, dressed for court. Marc-Antonio, with some daring, had gone off with Red Bill and Achille and seen Hagia Sophia, and was full of praise for the church, which he said was far grander than Saint Mark's in Venice.

'I'm sure I should say that Saint Mark's is better,' he said ruefully. 'But in truth, it looks to me as if Saint Mark's is merely the imitation of something vast and great.'

I had seldom seen him so moved. He'd made drawings, which we all admired; indeed, Christos's mother, who was named Anna, asked if she could keep them.

'It is many years since I have worshipped in the great church,' she said. 'They say Justinian built it, with the help of the Archangel Gabriel.

When we were private again, Marc-Antonio told me that they had been followed.

I resolved to protest this to the prince, but in truth, in London, the King would have certain dangerous foreigners followed, and I could well imagine that to the emperor, we English were the very archetype of dangerous foreigners.

And yet, as I told Nerio, the man in the Italian clothes worried me.

'You think too much,' Nerio said. 'Do you think that this city has courtesans?'

'Don't you ever tire of lechery?' Fiore asked. He was somewhat recovered from a day of our hostess's close attention. She had fed him Russian soups, and cosseted him, and he was, in fact, much better.

Nerio looked surprised. 'Never,' he said. 'You may kill me when I tire of women.'

Miles laughed. He had had a cup of wine or two, and his focus was relaxed. 'Why is it that I fear Hell every minute, and yet, I assume God will forgive Nerio because he's Nerio?'

'I'm sure that the Acciaioli have already made a private arrangement with God,' Fiore said. 'Rich men buy what they want, be it flesh or forgiveness.'

Nerio frowned. 'I feel that perhaps I must ask you to retract that,' he said.

Fiore smiled. 'Or what? We'll fight? Shall I list your tells?'

Nerio frowned.

'Did you come up with the funds to loan the count?' I asked, to distract him.

'I love women,' he said. 'I do not treat them as whores.' He paused. 'Even when I pay them.'

Fiore shrugged. 'Tell me you love God,' he said.

'Would you two consider not talking to each other?' Miles said. 'Fiore, you are uncommon snappish. Go visit our hostess and ask for more soup.'

'He was away. I forgot his disgusting ways.' Fiore left the room.

Nerio's hands were clenched.

I put my hand on his arm. 'Nerio,' I said, 'you *love* Fiore and he you. Go and find a nice Greek girl. Return in a better mood.'

Nerio nodded. He took a deep breath. 'Why must he ...' he began, and then shook his head. 'Yes,' he said. 'I borrowed it from the Archbishop of Patras. Until I prove to the Venetians and Florentines that I am alive ...' He paused.

I gave him a gentle push. 'Watch out for followers,' I said. 'Take your sword.'

'In this city?' he asked.

I remember shrugging. 'Or stay in!' I said, more forcefully than I needed to.

'No thank you,' he said. 'Somewhere in this vast city, a woman is crying out for me.'

What do you say to that?

While I was considering various crushing replies, Nerio snapped up his sword and went out into the hall. I heard him stop in the doorway and ask Giorgios something, and the Greek laughed and responded at length. Directions.

Nerio went out into the late summer evening, looking for a willing partner. I didn't see that he had Achille and Marc-Antonio and a couple of archers with him, but it was none of my business.

I was sound asleep when Marc-Antonio roused me. I understood that something was wrong, and I got shoes on my feet and Marc-Antonio handed me my sword belt.

'Nerio's hurt. Red Bill may be dead,' he said. He was shaking. 'Ser Nerio has barricaded a room and said to hurry.' He looked at me, his eyes pleading in the candlelight for understanding. 'He sent me,' he said. 'I didn't run away! I'm not a coward.'

It hadn't occurred to me. People doubt themselves at the oddest times.

I pulled a maille shirt on over my jupon and buckled on my sword. Ewan met me in the front hallway of the house, and Syr Christos.

'You cannot wear armour in the streets or carry a sword,' he said.

'One of my men has been hurt,' I said.

'You cannot ...' he began.

I pushed past him. I didn't like his look, but I was sure that I could drop him. Even more so with Ewan at my back.

Syr Christos buckled his own sword belt and put on his brilliant scarlet surcoat. 'Come then,' he said. He shook his head.

We went out into a very dark street. Listen, London is dark at night, and so is Paris, but Constantinople is black as pitch. Householders don't light cressets at their front doors, and even the thoroughfares are dark unless there is a church or monastery.

Marc-Antonio was tired.

'You were with them?' I asked.

'Yes,' he answered after a hesitation.

'Fight over a woman?' I asked.

'No,' he said.

'Horses,' I said.

Christos looked miserable in the flare of a torch. 'I will get,' he said, and he was as good as his word, back in five minutes, but for those five minutes, all I could do was imagine Nerio dead, captured, abused, humiliated – the Hungarian, or Robert of Geneva, or ...

Imagination is a deadly foe.

Then we were mounted, and riding. It was as well we had a Varangian; we were stopped twice by military patrols.

Then we were jogging along. We rode east and then through the inner gates and downhill, towards the Pera tower on the opposite shore. We came to a cross street and Marc-Antonio stopped.

And I heard footsteps behind us.

Ewan looked at me and drew a long dirk from his belt.

'We'll outpace them, whoever they are,' I said softly.

'Picked us up at the gate,' Ewan spat. 'Didn't expect us to have horses.'

Syr Christos shook his head. 'You cannot just kill who you please in my city,' he said.

'There are men behind us,' I said.

Marc-Antonio was unsure of the way, almost sobbing in desperation, and I began to understand that he'd left Nerio while the fight was still going on. Christos ignored me and pushed ahead.

'I know where they must be,' he said, 'if they went to buy women.' He turned and led us to the right, all the way down the hill, past the spice market again and to the base of the sea wall, where there was a long row of inns.

'Brothels. For foreigners,' he said, wrinkling his nose.

The street was completely empty.

The sound of violence carries wonderfully. Someone was screaming his life away, and there was the sound of that arrhythmic rapid movement that characterises a fight.

I ran for the outside stairs on a long, low building with an overhanging second storey.

'Nerio!' I shouted.

'Stop!' Christos said. 'Let me ...'

I ignored him. 'Nerio!' I shouted again.

'Here!' he called. 'I left some for you.'

I got to the door, an outside door, but not locked, with a simple wooden latch that had been cut through. The door was half open and there was furniture against it inside, and I wrenched it further open to find a big room and enough dead bodies for a storming action. Red Bill was clearly dead, and a woman was also dead, her neck half-severed. She was naked, and so was he. A small man was drumming his heels on the floor, and across him lay one of my Irishmen, bleeding out.

A man came at me from my right. I drew into his attack; my point grazed his face and his head snapped back to avoid my cover as I gathered his sword. My left hand caught his right elbow and I shoved him, hard, turning him, and slashed him on the descending stroke so that I opened the length of this spine as he stumbled one more step and fell across the Irishman.

To my left was Nerio's opponent. I could see Nerio was hurt; he was also naked. He had a dozen cuts, and he was covered in blood. But I had made a plan and I executed it; Nerio's man was over-extended and I went for him. He pivoted quite competently on the balls of his feet, but his blade was behind his body thanks to Nerio's parry, and I stepped right through him, planting my pommel in the centre of his forehead and throwing him to the floor with my sword arm.

There were two more of the rats. One was sword to sword with Marc-Antonio, and he made three mistakes in a row: he crossed at mid-blade against Marc-Antonio's much longer sword; he stayed close; and he tried to remove his sword while his opponent was still on centre. In other words, Marc-Antonio killed him without much thought, and he died, a monument to poor swordsmanship and bad training.

The last man was Half-Cloak, and he was off down the stairs in the middle of the building. I followed, leaping the railing, and I was two steps behind him when I realised that there were other men in the middle of the common room. Half-Cloak was yelling in Greek, and a dozen men were drawing daggers. Others were pushing for the doors.

A girl, no more than fifteen, appeared from my left and I almost killed her. She was naked, and screaming, and I kicked her out of my way without gentility, but she cost me two steps and my man was out of the door of the tavern.

I went across the common room floor without a glance at the dagger-wielding men. It takes a complete fool to attack a man-at-arms carrying a long sword. Not a one of them was such a fool.

I was, though. I went through the brothel door and he hit me.

Some reflection saved me, but not by much; I got a piece of his thrust, he cut the top of my leg, and then I was down in the garbage behind the back door of a brothel.

He kicked at my head. 'László says goodbye,' he said, and cut.

I suppose he thought he'd wounded me.

My left hand flipped something foul at him from the muck; he turned his head and I rolled and came up. 'A pity you won't live to tell him,' I said. I don't like to talk when I fight, but I had Half-Cloak's measure. He was done – he'd fought too long, and now his little ploy had failed and he'd folded.

'I thought I killed you, you fuck,' he spat. He cut and I parried. Like many men, he raised his hands to assure the parry because I am fast, and I kicked him in the crotch.

In that moment I knew him. He was the man from the steps of the cathedral, when we had humbled the Hungarian. But brothels need lanterns, and he was standing with his back to one, holding his balls.

353

He threw his sword.

It was a very good throw. Men usually only throw their swords when desperate; in the dark, it's a good gambit, and as usual, Fiore saved my life – his training, and the red lantern at the door – because I was across the garbage pile from him, in a low *garde*. As I saw his arm move, I guessed and covered with a rising cut, and I caught his sword in the air so that the hilt only clipped my thigh.

And he ran.

I had to let him go. His thrust into my thigh had done damage and he'd just hit it again with the pommel of his thrown sword. I couldn't walk, much less run.

But we had a prisoner, and after a doctor was summoned and damages paid, I tied the man I'd knocked unconscious to a bed.

I spent about an hour moving bodies with the brothel keeper. I didn't want to let my wound cool or seize up. Syr Christos and I went through every purse. The brothel keeper made a long complaint to Syr Christos, who looked at me from time to time and made me wish for a translator.

'He thinks your man started killing his girls,' he said.

I shook my head. I was slow; I was just wondering where Ewan was. He had been with us, and now he was not.

I looked at Christos. 'This was an assassination,' I said. 'These men were paid to kill me, and Ser Nerio. Look at this man,' I said, pointing to poor Red Bill, who was a good deal redder by then.

'I see,' he said. 'Yes.' He shook his head. 'Perhaps,' he said, and he sounded unhappy.

'The man who ran – I know him. He serves a Hungarian mercenary named László Makkrow or Makrov.'

Christos's eyes were blue. They met me across Red Bill's cooling corpse. 'I see,' he said.

And I could see that he did see. He knew something; perhaps a great deal. And he was not telling me. His face closed; he rose to his feet and dusted his hands.

'I have duties at the palace in a few hours,' he said woodenly.

I swear; my first thought was to tackle him, and beat it out of him. I'd almost died; Nerio was hurt.

I drew on what the Order taught – on what Father Pierre Thomas taught.

'Would you care to tell me?' I asked, as mildly as I could. 'You know the name.'

He looked away.

'You are far too honourable a man for lies,' I said.

'Fuck,' he said, in English.

I put my hand on my sword hilt. The brothel keeper backed away, and Marc-Antonio covered him.

Syr Christos didn't unlock his gaze from mine. 'If you draw,' he said, 'it will only be worse.'

'For whom?' I asked.

He looked away and cursed. 'I am not trying to kill you,' he said. 'In fact, I think I have just saved you.'

'So you say. You know who is, though,' I said.

'Look to your prince,' he said. 'Why the fuck did you have to be English?' he added.

Then he turned and clattered down the exterior steps.

I sent Marc-Antonio for more men; he returned an hour later with all the archers. The brothel keeper had sent for the watch, but they stayed well clear of me. We put Nerio in one handcart and the unconscious man in another, and walked them through the early morning streets to Christos's mother's house. I did not believe that she'd allow us to be killed, and I didn't think, somehow, that the Varangian was my enemy.

By Matins I was bandaged and dressed. I took the time to wash carefully with hot water and sweet-smelling soap; I'd rolled in that foul garbage pile, and every laceration on my back was bleeding again, and everything hurt, led by my right thigh. I hate punctures; you never know what's going on in there. I poured wine into it, made it bleed again, pushed some honey in – which felt terrible – and put a good linen bandage made from the hem of my clean shirt on it.

Then I sent Gospel Mark and the Davids out to find Ewan, and had the rest of them guard Nerio and the unconscious man. I saddled my own horse; Marc-Antonio was face down on a bed. Achille was with his master. My only companion was Miles; Fiore stayed to watch.

We clattered across the cobbles and out into the fields, and a few minutes' riding brought us to the palace of Blacharnae.

The Varangians were on guard. I was dressed for court, in a silk pourpointe and chausses and long, absurdly pointed shoes, with my best purse and my tallest hat. The guards ordered me to dismount and then demanded my sword.

I handed it over and gave Miles a nod, and he backed his horse. We'd agreed on this already.

Then I allowed the Varangians to escort me to the nearer church, where the Prince of Lesvos was hearing Matins.

I allowed myself to breathe when I saw Prince Francesco kneeling at prayer. He gave me a nod, and I went to stand with Sir Richard on the cool marble.

'You look like you've been in a fight,' he whispered.

I managed to make all the correct responses as the Latin priest made his way through the service. It was equally clear to me from the magnificent music coming from the next building, another church, that there were two services running side by side, and in the other church, the music sounded like all the choirs of Heaven.

I didn't know the magnificently dressed man kneeling beside Francesco Gatelussi. I raised an eyebrow. *Sotto voce*, Sir Richard nodded at him. 'The Venetian bailli,' he said. 'We've already had the Genoese.'

'Men tried to kill us last night,' I said very softly.

Sir Richard's body stiffened.

'A Varangian told me to "look to my prince",' I said.

Sir Richard rose to his feet with a fluidity I envied. 'Stay,' he said. He slipped out of the service at the back and left me on my knees.

I needed some prayer.

We crossed the magnificent gardens to return to the prince's lodging; I didn't see a rose, I was so focused on possible threats. Sir Richard was back just before we left the church, face closed, walking stiffly.

Just at the corner of the palace hall, where the wall passed the magnificent windows, there was a patch of shadow. Sir Richard drew the prince's attention. There, lying by the window, was a fine gaze-hound, and it was dead.

'Your breakfast,' Sir Richard said, stiffly.

The prince turned to me. 'We didn't eat last night,' he said. 'They all fell into beds. I had wine with the Genoese bailli and the old empress's chaplain and nuns ...' He paused. 'I have it,' he said through clenched teeth. '*Dannazione!*' he spat. 'They tried to poison me. Or all of us.'

His men-at-arms closed in around us; Maurizio di Cavalli was there, close behind me. Young Francesco was there as well, harness well polished.

We got him to his rooms. No one had so much as a sausage.

'Hail Constantinople, queen of cities,' the prince said.

Sir Richard shook his head. 'I need to understand,' he said.

Prince Francesco looked out his window. Below us, a long procession was threading its way across the gardens from the second, larger church to the palace. It was led by two men with swords on their shoulders, and then a long, magnificent gold and purple canopy; from above, I could not see who was within, but the eagle embroidered in gold suggested it was the emperor.

Except that the emperor was five hundred miles away, a prisoner of the Bulgarians or the Hungarians.

Behind the canopy were incense bearers, and then a dozen men with axes on their shoulders.

'He intends to make himself emperor,' Prince Francesco said. 'Or he already has. Christ on the Cross, how very unsettling our arrival must have been!' He looked at the Venetian bailli. 'You were right, of course.'

The Venetian bailli tugged at his beard. 'Do I have the honour of your acquaintance, *Signore*?' he asked.

I bowed. 'I am Sir William Gold,' I said. 'If you were feeling very courteous, you might style me Baron of Μάριον.' Marion in Greece was one of the few words I could pronounce in Greek.

That made the prince smile.

'You trust him?' the Venetian asked. He took my hand. 'I mean no offence – these are difficult times.'

'I trust him,' the prince said.

The bailli nodded. 'Well – so you were attacked,' he said. 'I tried to send you a warning.'

'No warning reached me,' I said. 'Would you have known where to find us?'

'Of course. All the world knows that actual Englishmen, all the way from Thule, are in the *Enkliskvarangan* quarter.' He nodded.

'Who?' I asked. 'Who would attack us?'

'The emperor's scheming son, Andronicus,' Prince Francesco said. 'Damn them for fools. They'll fight among themselves until there's nothing to fight over.'

'Nerio told me that this son may have paid to have his father taken,' I said.

The bailli nodded. 'Ah. Where did the young Florentine hear this?'

'In Ragusa, or some like,' I said.

The Venetian's eyes narrowed. He shook his head. 'I don't understand,' he said.

Prince Francesco was toying with his dagger hilt. He looked at me and indicated the Venetian. 'He told me the same,' he said. 'And I didn't believe him. I'm sorry. But it is the Court of Constantinople, and people say such things all the time.' He looked out at the priests in the procession. 'Sadly, this time it appears to be true.'

'I have a prisoner,' I said.

The prince turned to me, and there was nothing in his eyes but pirate.

'Don't be gentle,' he said. 'This is bad. A great deal is at stake, and I have been blind.'

'Will they let us out of the palace?' I asked.

A number of the men-at-arms exchanged glances.

'Sir Richard, would you be kind enough to recover my sword?' I asked. 'I prize it. But I have a friend waiting with a horse, and I suspect I can go over the wall with no one the wiser.'

'Wait until they change the guard,' he said, with some practicality.

I went over the wall at the same corner where he'd disposed of the dog. It cost me my best silk chausses and some amour-propre, and my wounded thigh screamed at me, and blood flowed over the ruined hose, just to make sure I knew I'd wasted twenty days' pay. and the ditch on the far side was full of mud, so, my pointy shoes were ruined.

And I didn't have an audience with anyone. I could have gone dressed as a servant.

Miles was just where I'd asked him to be, two towers to the south, sitting on a bench by one of the small city parks. His back was to stone, and he could see anyone who approached, and we were away in the time it takes to say the Sanctus.

'Well?' he asked.

When we were well clear of the walls, in the open farmland around the pretty Chora church, I stopped our horses and dismounted.

'I think I understand,' I said. 'Christos is an officer for this

Andronicus, the emperor's son. Andronicus may have paid to have his father taken – and whether or not, he's ready to usurp the throne now that his father is gone. We arrived into this palace revolution. So Christos must have divided loyalties. Christ, they all do – Giorgios too, probably.' I was working it out.

'And the men that attacked us?' Miles asked.

'One of them works for the Hungarian,' I said. 'Damn his eyes and Plague take him. And Christos knew his name when I said it.' I looked at him. 'Which means that Christos knows I'm on to the Hungarian. But he can't decide what loyalty he owes to us – because he thinks of himself as English.'

'We need to make sure he feels English, then,' Miles said – a very perceptive statement, if you consider it.

'I need to go down to the brothel. I assume all the archers are still there. And ...' I glanced at Miles. 'Someone needs to go back and tell Fiore what is going on.'

Miles shrugged. 'I'm not good at brothels,' he agreed with a slow smile.

I rehearsed him once on what I knew, and I took all his cash; between us, I had more than a hundred florins in gold and silver.

I tied the horse to a tree. It was a Varangian military horse, I was sure; the saddle was Greek and the horse was small. I didn't need to be tracked with it.

An hour later I was at the brothel. Ewan was there, and both Davids, and Mark and half a dozen other archers; also Hector Lachlan and both Irishmen or Scots.

'I know where the man is,' Ewan said. It proved he meant Half-Cloak, but we wasted precious time establishing that.

I took the brothel keeper aside and gave him ten gold florins. That was the last trouble I had with him. I told him in Italian that I was taking all my people back to the *Engliskvarangan* and he nodded as if that made sense.

By then, my thigh wound was leaking and my plan didn't make me happy, but we went out into the streets, and stopped in one of the broad forums where there was a market. At my order and with my money, men bought sausages and pies and wine and cider, and a dozen big amphorae of water. I made the sellers have a bite; all of them did. I have never been in such a state of distrust as I was that day. At any rate, when we had some food and full water bottles, I led my people into the darkening streets. I kept them moving, hobbling along and fearing pursuit. But whatever I feared, it didn't come to pass, and as we walked I heard their news.

Ewan knew it all; he'd followed Half-Cloak to an inn in the Pisan quarter and watched the inn for hours. In fact, it was his need for relief that had brought most of our archers out to help; well, that and the use of the brothel, let's be fair.

Rob Stone had spotted Half-Cloak leaving his inn; the Davids had shadowed him, probably too close; he'd been almost to the brothel when he'd spotted Big David and vanished.

Rob and Ewan were convinced he was on his way back to finish what he'd started.

'Alone?' I asked.

'Would you leave your man behind?' Rob asked me.

'What are we doin' now?' Ewan asked.

We were passing through the old walls. There was no gate guard where we crossed; a tower had fallen in an earthquake. The old gate was only wide enough for one man to squeeze through at a time, but Giorgios had brought us that way the day before to avoid a tax, as I have mentioned.

Then I got us lost, in the dark, but eventually I found us the trail through the trees that led to the road; we got off the road when we heard horses coming, and that was twice. And then – very late by the bells, between eleven and twelve – I found the gate I hadn't seen but knew had to be there: the gate to the Komnenos property. I was amused to find that the gate was high and strong, and had a path right around it – just like England. I took my archers down the lane to the banks of the river, which was just a trickle, and we gathered wood and made a little fire, as snug a camp as any band of outlaws have in Sherwood, I'll warrant, except that ours was in the midst of the mightiest city in the world.

Hector had carried the man I'd dropped with a blow from my pommel over his shoulder. He dropped him by the new fire, and the man cried out, so I knew that he was awake.

Ewan saw me looking at him. 'You think 'e knows summit?' Ewan asked.

I nodded.

Ewan looked at Rob. Then they both looked at Gospel Mark, who shrugged.

'Perhaps the sir would like to take a stroll?' Mark asked.

I grinned. 'That was kindly meant,' I said. 'But I won't take a stroll. Let's get this done.'

Mark smiled nastily. 'Let it be done in the morning, then,' he said. 'When you question a man, a peasant about 'is 'idden silver, like, it's better in daylight, like. You can see 'is face.' He raised both eyebrows. 'But if'n the watch might take turns keeping the bastard awake ...' He nodded at me. 'Most men can't stand bein' awake too long.'

I was ready to collapse; I knew what he meant. 'Have it done,' I said. 'Not too rough. Just keep him awake.'

'My pleasure,' Rob said. 'Marc-Antonio says he's the bastard as did Red Billy.'

I have strong ideas of justice. 'Mayhap,' I said. 'But this is no assize.'

'I don't need no fuckin' assize,' Ewan said. 'We'll keep 'im awake right an' proper.'

I assume they did. I went to sleep with the gurgle and whisper of the stream passing me; the water was clean, out here in the fields, and made a clean sound.

In the morning, the sun rose, and so did I. My leg was terribly stiff, and every cut burned. It was the second day after a fight. I was coming to dread these days as much as fights. I drank some wine and some water and was handed a pie, which I ate, delighted.

''E speaks Italian an' a little Greek,' Mark said. ''E tried 'em both on me in the night.'

'You speak Greek?' I asked.

He smiled. 'Been out here four years,' he said. 'Some time you mun speak to a priest or a girl, eh?'

Well, that was true, too.

I took a sausage and my eating knife and sat down on an old pillar which made a fine bench. The cat rubbed against my legs and I gave him sausage.

'The cat?' I asked.

Mark made a face. 'I can't lose him, and neither can 'Ector,' he said.

'Fetch the prisoner,' I said.

By arrangement, none of us said anything after that.

Rob and Mark forced him to sit, and then sat behind him. Hector lounged, looking dangerous and big.

I sat in front of him and ate sausage, cutting the pieces with a knife. Each time he started to nod off, Mark jabbed a sharpened stick into his back. I fed myself and the cat.

We all just sat there. It took an hour for him to start talking. First, he complained, in Italian, of the pain from the jabbing stick, and then he begged to be allowed to sleep.

I'd never done this myself before, but I'd watched John Hawkwood do it often enough with guides and spies.

After a while, he started telling us what the Hungarian would do to us when he caught us.

I took ten gold florins from my purse and tossed them on the ground at his feet. And then I took my baselard out of its sheath and placed it near the coins.

He nodded off.

The stick jabbed him.

'You are all dead men!' he shouted.

We all smiled. He couldn't see Mark or Rob, but they smiled.

'The emperor will hang you all!' the man said.

All in all, it took about three hours – well, that and the whole night before, the pain of his wounds, and the obvious fate that awaited him.

We still hadn't said anything when he said, 'Can you protect me?'

'Yes,' I said.

It came out of him, not in one burst but in evil little snatches; I wondered if this was what priests felt like, taking confession from a bad man, because he made me feel dirty and helpless just in speaking.

What I got from him was a mixture of bragging and confession. He didn't know much; I knew more of his plots than he did, except in two places. But his confession was the key.

So, of course, it was Andronicus's plan. The caesar, as he was known, wanted to be emperor. But his plan was far too complex; he had too many plotters to 'help' him, and he was, himself, a weak and ineffectual man who couldn't make up his mind. Like most people who make complicated plans.

It is clear to me now that the only thing that saved the emperor's life was his son's unwillingness to order his death. And that was of a piece with his plotting. It was, in a way, the worst piece of bungling; any two of my archers could have made better plans. In fact, the only thing that kept me, or the prince, from grasping the 'plot' immediately was its sheer foolishness.

But I could make out the threads. Antonio, the piece of scum sitting at my feet, had been ordered to kill me by Half-Cloak, who was called Bonhomme – with some irony, I think – a steppe nomad who had been made a slave by the Genoese and served the Hungarian. He had ordered the attack on the brothel; he had told Antonio that they would kill me and Fiore and Nerio and Stapleton, our servants, and the Green Count as well. He said they had attacked Red Bill because he thought he was me.

And he thought Nerio was the Green Count. Or so he claimed.

I let him ramble. It was a grandiose plan, full of death, and yet it had not accounted for very basic things, like the loyalty of the guards and the possibility that the Prince of Lesvos would come to visit.

Antonio thought that the Hungarian was close by. But listening to him describe the plot, I had to assume that the Hungarian was somewhere else, possibly guarding the emperor.

Still, I needed to move carefully. Antonio didn't want to tell me how many allies he had, but he told me straight out that the 'young emperor' would act to protect him, and that I needed him to save me. For a man lower than a routier, a hired killer, he was very full of himself.

Back in my days as a routier, I had ransomed any number of men whom I had captured – knights and merchants and others. I knew how to be careful; men who deal in such things need to be careful.

So I sent Mark to find us a Greek boy to run a message. We never let him see our camp, and we sent him, not to the English quarter, but to Syr Giorgios and his house. Our message asked Syr Giorgios to meet me, but not at our little camp. Instead, we had him go to the market opposite the church of the Chora.

This may seem tedious to you, friends, but when you trust no one, you want to watch. I was two hundred paces from the church, and I had two archers with 'borrowed' crossbows covering me when Syr Giorgios cantered into the courtyard and dismounted, with Syr Giannis and Fiore at his shoulders. As soon as I saw Fiore, I knew we were not betrayed; I do not want to say I distrusted my Greeks, merely that when emperors play games, friendship can be … strained.

I gave the 'all safe' signal and walked forward.

'We were worried,' Fiore said. 'By the good God, Guglielmo, even I was worried.'

'I have one of the Hungarian's men,' I said. 'I need to get him to the prince.' I looked up at Syr Giannis, who was still mounted. 'Andronicus is planning to take the throne and kill Amadeus of Savoy, too.'

Giannis rolled his eyes. 'Good God, why?' he asked. 'How rich does a fool need to be?'

Fiore asked where we'd all gone. I explained in general terms, and by the time I was done, Ewan appeared with Antonio the killer mounted on a pony and with a halter around his neck.

'Take him to the prince,' I said. 'I'm going to stay where I am, just for a little while.'

I told them how to reach me, and Fiore told me that Nerio was doing well.

'Watch Syr Christos,' I said.

Fiore made a 'Was I born yesterday?' face.

'Tell Miles …' I paused. 'Tell Miles to make Christos very English indeed.'

'Whatever this means, I'll pass it,' Fiore said. 'Listen – I have a new disarm!'

Syr Giorgios rolled his eyes. 'I tell him there is more to life than fighting.' He looked at me. 'The caesar is looking everywhere for you. If you are taken … it will not go well.'

'I guessed that,' I said.

They turned their horses and rode away.

I left the Davids to watch the church. The signal was a chalk mark on the south-west corner by the entry. But in truth, I wanted to keep the church under observation anyway; to see if Fiore was followed, for example.

And he was.

'Shit,' I said, or words to that effect. But we'd been quick; too quick for a watcher to get help, even from nearby Blacharnae. But David the Big came for me an hour later, while I stared at the stream, and I heard that twenty cavalrymen had come and interrogated the monks.

I was more interested in attacking than defending. I wanted Half-Cloak, and I knew, thanks to Ewan, where he was. I was still trying to puzzle out why the caesar and the Hungarian wanted to kill the Green Count. It made no sense.

I didn't care. At a different level, I knew that when you don't know what's going on, you steal the initiative and attack. Basic swordsmanship.

The problem with attacking was that we stuck out. We were all a foot taller than most of the locals; we had small beards or no beards, and we had red and blond and light brown hair, and we didn't speak much Greek. Now, Constantinople is one of the most polyglot cities I've ever seen. There are lots of blonds and lots of men without beards – Jews, Turks, Mongols, even a pair of Chinese. But ...

But fifteen of us together? And they were looking for us.

And I didn't know the level of co-operation between Andronicus and the Hungarian. But I could guess; I could guess that the emperor's son would try to distance himself from his assassin, and that if Half-Cloak was living in a tavern in the Pisan Quarter, he was not working hand-in-glove with the caesar. The two-mile separation told me a great deal.

So that afternoon, I walked into one of the farming villas along the big road and found the slave quarters. I gave a man three silver *soldi* and took from him a dirty off-white shapeless linen garment, some really awful braes, and a pair of untanned cowhide slippers that stank like dog shit. With Mark's help, I used a little oil to darken my red hair to a lank medium brown, and I went in the late evening towards the centre of the city and the Pisan Quarter.

Disguise can be liberating or confining. It is odd to change your clothes; I cringed when big men stepped near me, and I pulled at my dirty wool cap constantly – a Moslem slave in a Christian city. I was invisible. I needed only to say *signomi* in a guttural accent, the Greek word of apology; no one expected anything of me.

Of course, no one looked at me with admiration, either.

Or hatred, come to think of it. I spent most of the walk thinking about humility. I prayed a little without crossing myself, and I passed the guarded gate to the Pisan quarter without any comment from the two professional soldiers on the gate. They didn't even see me.

I was temporarily paralysed when I found that Half-Cloak's inn didn't have slaves at all – that all their people were Italians. On the other hand, I was able to squat boldly across the inn yard from the front, and several passers-by gave me coins.

I have many talents.

I saw Half-Cloak meet with a man who was clearly a Greek aristocrat. He had a long cloak despite the summer, and it had the embroidered panel that denoted rank at court, and under it a fine silk kaftan in the Mongol style. They shared wine under the grape arbour. I don't read lips and I couldn't understand a word they said, but it was pretty clear anyway; Half-Cloak was worried, and so was Aristocrat.

While they sat outside, I approached the inn from the side street – a narrow alley deep in refuse. I hate to think what touched my feet there, and I'm not fussy; but I came in the old side gate, and was right behind the inn midden and the latrines.

A poor waif was emptying chamber pots; a noisome job, always given to the lowest. She was clearly the lowest; her shoulders slumped forward, she had a bruise on her face, and her face had the vacancy of the abused.

'Should I help you, miss?' I asked in Italian. 'I'm new.'

So clever. Clever enough to get to help empty other men's shit, but in less than a watch I knew which room was Half-Cloak's and the layout of the whole inn.

Little Lise was disturbingly grateful for my help. I hated even to think about her life.

She told me she didn't go to the kitchen because of how men behaved, and she never let me within arm's reach, and she flinched when I spoke. And she knew Half-Cloak by name, and she told me that there were four other men in the inn who went regularly to his room, and that she'd had to service him twice and he was 'bad'.

There aren't enough knights in the world to right all the wrongs.

I left the Pisan Quarter at curfew after scouting a way in through a broken wall and an abandoned house; Constantinople was crumbling, and I could use that to my advantage. Then I went to one of the ancient baths and bathed; no amount of hot water could make me feel clean after the shit I'd touched, and heard. But I made it back to our little camp in the Chora without incident, and all my archers were game.

'Right now,' I said.

They had knives and cudgels. I had my baselard; de Charny's dagger was back at Anna's house.

What I was doing was right. But I was going to do it a fairly rough way, and I wasn't sorry to leave de Charny's dagger out of it.

I left the Davids with their crossbows to hold the abandoned house where we crossed the wall, and we moved carefully through the Pisan Quarter, but it was only six streets and the guards were playing dice.

The inn was locked and shuttered. But then, I knew the back way, although Ewan cursed me and claimed he was knee deep in turds.

Well.

We went in past the midden, and I left Rob and Mark at the kitchen door and went in by the servants' stair where Lise and I had gone to the rooms. The place rambled – several centuries' worth of rebuilding like the English Inn at Rhodes.

I knew the rooms, and I put Hector and the Irish and Roger LeBlanc, another English archer, on the doors.

Then I went to Half-Cloak's door.

He was fucking someone. The noise was plain. And the door was unlatched.

It wasn't Lise, but bless her, she pinned his hands as soon as she saw I meant him harm. I got my baselard to his throat as soon as I had his shoulders, and I hauled him off her.

The girl was terrified and managed a smile anyway.

'Tell the other girls that Satan came for him and dragged him down to Hell,' I said, and left her a gold florin.

She bit it.

He tried to escape. There were two candles; I suspect he knew who I was. I broke his arm, and then a rib, and then I had to hit him in the head because he was shouting. He went down.

Not dead, either.

I searched the room while the girl breathed raggedly under the dirty sheet.

'Satan?' she said.

'Yes?' I said.

'He told me if I ever touched his purse he'd rip my eyes out,' she said. 'It's hanging on the chair.'

Well. God sends the most unlikely helpers. I took the purse and it was heavy.

Then I went out into the hall. All I had to do was nod.

Four men died.

Sorry, Monsieur Froissart. That's how it is, sometimes.

Then we were out of the inn and moving through the darkness. We made it to the abandoned house well enough, and then David the Brown grabbed my shoulder.

'Someone is following ye,' he said in his sing-song voice. 'Like a ghost.'

'Kill him,' I said.

Little David aimed his crossbow.

'Fuckin' girl,' he said. 'Kill 'er?'

I peered back into the darkness.

'No,' I said.

I watched, and saw movement.

'Let's go,' I said. I didn't hear anything – no alarm, no shouting.

'Satan?' said a voice.

Hector looked back. 'Who's that, then?' he asked.

'A girl from the tavern,' I said.

'Like the fewkin' cat,' he muttered. In one grab he had her. She didn't even scream.

'I want out of that place,' she said. 'Whoever you are.'

She was tall, and might, in another life, have been beautiful. She was hard instead – wire-thin, muscular.

Hector had her by the throat.

'Bring her,' I said.

As raids go, it was one of my best. We took Half-Cloak and killed his henchmen and, as far as I know, no one knew until they found the bloody bedding in the morning. I can guess what confusion we sowed.

Katrina was a Slav; a Russian slave who'd worked at the inn for four years or so, and knew a great deal. And she *was* like the cat; she followed us home, and the boys took her in. I had Mark watch her the first day, but when I found her sitting with his head in her lap, I decided maybe he was not the man to be trusted watching her.

When day dawned, I went myself in my slave clothes and posted the chalk signal at the Chora church.

Three hours later, and some coming and going, and I had the Prince of Lesvos sitting beside me on my fallen column, looking at Half-Cloak, who was conscious.

'You are a dead man,' he said to me.

I shrugged. 'You're the one with your hands tied,' I said.

'The emperor is my friend,' he spat.

Prince Francesco laughed. 'You are behind,' he said. 'About an hour ago, the Varangians took Andronicus into custody. He is at the Windy Tower now. The patriarch has command of the city, and I have a warrant for your arrest.' The prince tapped him with the warrant and Half-Cloak flinched.

'Who the fuck are you?' he snapped at Prince Francesco.

The prince smiled. 'Your Hungarian forgot me, but I'm the most important person in this blasted city.' He looked at me. 'You can just kill him. We don't need him.'

I was disappointed. I had performed a great coup, and no one cared.

I emptied the man's purse on the ground. He had about three hundred gold *piseri* or bezants, hence the weight, and a document sealed by the emperor.

In the name of God and His Imperial Majesty, do not impede the bearer of this, it said, in Greek and Italian and Turkish.

Prince Francesco's eyes went to mine. 'Interesting,' he said. He looked at Half-Cloak. 'We have your man Antonio, who has told us a great deal, and we have Andronicus, who is not one of you, and who has told the patriarch almost everything,' he said. 'Is there any reason to keep you alive?'

'You are bluffing,' Half-Cloak said.

'How do you communicate with László?' I asked.

He looked at me as if I was a fool.

Prince Francesco blinked. 'Ah,' he said. He looked at me as if he'd just seen the first sign of intelligence in me.

'That would interest me,' Francesco said to Half-Cloak. 'But not much, and I don't have much time.'

He convinced me. Prince Francesco was a darker man than most, including, I think, John Hawkwood. I suspected he would kill merely to avoid inconvenience. Sometimes I feared Nerio would grow up to be this Gatelussi prince. On the other hand, the world is full of these men, and I was happy enough with the one I had chosen.

Regardless, he had apparently convinced Half-Cloak that he meant business.

'I don't want to die,' he said. 'But ... the Hungarian ...'

Prince Francesco smiled, and it was he who was like Satan. 'I am here now,' he said with a shrug. 'I could make this nice young man go away, and then make you walk around this fine old oak tree until you told me anything I wanted to know.'

'Really?' said Half-Cloak, a little of his cockiness returning.

Prince Francesco smiled at me and blinked. 'You know, he said, 'when I was younger, I used to need to learn things from men.' He shrugged. 'I used to make them walk around trees,' he went on. 'The trick is to make a little cut, just above the groin. Take out a little bit of intestine – cut it. The man is dead from that time, but, of course, he will live a long time – maybe two days or three. Nail the end to the tree.' His smile was unwavering. 'And he can walk around the tree a long time – winding his guts on the tree so that he can see them. His own mortality. Eh?' He moved his eyes from mine to Half-Cloak's. 'Choose,' he said.

He chose.

He told us a series of signals. A recognition signal, and some cut-outs.

'Name all your people in the city,' Francesco said.

Half-Cloak looked trapped. He named some names.

Francesco didn't write them down.

'Give me a moment,' he said. 'Go get me that big man. The Scot.'

I rose.

'And wine,' he said.

When I came back, Half-Cloak was dead.

Prince Francesco was shaking his head. 'If you are going to do evil,' he said to me, 'you should do it for a purpose. Not for nothing. Not because you are an animal, and you like to cause pain.'

'You killed him,' I said stupidly.

'He bored me, and he was lying.' Prince Francesco sighed. 'Ah, wine. I have not killed anyone in a long time.'

I don't remember much of the next three days. We paraded all of the prince's soldiers in the Chora, and then we moved to take control of the palace and the harbours. We were spread thin, and we had to be diplomatic, so that the Varangians and the Vardariotes didn't take offence. John, my Kipchak, was a great help with the Vardariotes. He had his own part in all this; in fact, there were plots in all directions, and really, I am only telling my part. But we struck with more information than Andronicus could have imagined that anyone could gather; we succeeded so well, at least in part, because the prince brought some Englishmen and a Mongol, and we had friends. Language, culture.

At any rate, we struck. The prince wasn't going to allow a counter-attack.

There were arrests. Cavalli and l'Angars took part; I was protecting the prince and the patriarch. I lost more sleep, and I witnessed a dozen beheadings and blindings. Blinding is particularly horrible. They use boiling vinegar and a white-hot nail. I'll say no more.

I came to hate Constantinople.

On the evening of the third day, with the city under curfew and all the foreigners restricted to their quarters, the Green Count's fleet was sighted.

The patriarch went out to meet the count. I was with him as the captain of his guard, with half a dozen Varangians, and Guiscard and some Bretons, and Fiore and our Franciscan, Father Angelo, who spoke Greek and Italian and French. We were taking no chances, and we rode around the patriarch and his dozen priests and acolytes, all across the city and down to the port on the north side by the foreign quarters. Thousands of eyes watched us; it was uncanny.

The patriarch had no particular love for us, I can tell you. But by then I'd been with him two days; he'd heard from a captured killer that he was on Adronicus's list for arrests and executions, and he knew he needed me. And he spoke several times to Father Angelo, which I saw as a good sign.

We were standing on a stone pier in the Port of Theodosius when he turned to me.

'Canst thou read?' he asked in very careful Italian.

'Yes, Eminence,' I said.

He didn't offer me a smile. 'Holy Father,' he said, again in Italian.

'Ah,' I said. Of course, just like the Pope. 'Yes, Holy Father,' I said, waiting to be struck by a bolt of lightning for my temerity. But truly, all the schismatic Greeks seemed to me very holy men. I glanced at Father Angelo, who was amused.

'Thou hast read this Aquinas?' he asked me.

Well, in truth, I had read some of the great scholar's work, and understood very little of what I read. 'A very little, Holy Father.'

He grunted, and our boat came alongside the quay – a thirty-oared boat. The patriarch blessed the oarsmen, who seemed transfixed by his presence. I left most of my knights there on the dock, but took Fiore and the Varangians, and Father Angelo.

I mean no boast, but if they meant the patriarch harm, I was sure Fiore and I could dispatch them. But I was fairly sure of them, even after three days. When pressed, all the Varangians, Greek-born and Scandinavian and English and Russian, had chosen the distant emperor over the traitorous son.

Or so it seemed to me.

Regardless, there were four of them, plus Fiore, and me, all in harness, and polished and pretty, unlike all the other times I'd been to see the Green Count. I had on a red surcoat, borrowed from Christos. So did Fiore.

The Green Count's galley was flying a big banner of the Virgin, and it had seen better days; later I heard they had terrible weather in the usually placid Sea of Marmara and had almost lost a ship. The count himself received the patriarch at the side of the ship, as was due his status. The patriarch had a Greek monk who was fluent in Italian and made introductions.

Amadeus smiled, but did not bend his knee to the patriarch or kiss his ring.

The patriarch expected no better, but was still, I could see, displeased.

Richard Musard was standing by his count, wearing the collar of his Order, and his eyes passed over me a dozen times before he really looked, and saw.

By then, the interpreter was done with the formality.

The patriarch spoke very softly.

The monk glanced at me in surprise, and translated.

The count turned.

I stepped forward. 'Your Grace,' I said, making a reverence.

'You do keep turning up,' the count said. 'I am told,' he said very quietly, 'that the patriarch is merely here as a guarantee that you speak truth.'

'Your Grace,' I said again. 'The Caesar Andronicus apparently

372

intended to usurp the throne and hatched a plot to do so. By God's will and good fortune we have frustrated that plot.'

The count frowned. 'Who is "we"?' he asked.

'Prince Francesco and the patriarch here,' I said.

Behind me, the monk, Sylvester, was translating everything I said.

I handed him a scroll tube from Prince Francesco. He took it, stepped aside with a whispered command to Richard, and we were brought wine. The patriarch was brought a magnificent chair, on which he sat with dignity, and looked around himself with a lively curiosity.

The count read through the prince's letter carefully.

'You think there is a plot against my life,' he said.

'I do, Your Grace,' I said.

He nodded and tapped the scroll against his chin. 'I am not afraid of assassins, thanks to God,' he said. 'I will quarter my army in Pera, as the prince graciously suggests, but I will accept his offer of a house by Blacharnae, so that we can meet and plan our campaign.'

His physician, Master Guy Albin, was to hand, and he copied out the count's reply in a fair hand. While he wrote the count's letter, the count spoke to the Orthodox patriarch through his monk, Sylvester, and introduced the Latin patriarch, whose presence obviously caused the Orthodox patriarch a nearly physical pain.

I stepped aside to take wine with Antonio Visconti and Richard Musard, who seemed again to be my friend. It was hard to guess what Richard thought, but he was cordial, and I smiled at them both as we watched the count fail utterly to charm the Orthodox patriarch.

'The Greek patriarch knows as well as I do myself that the Pope had ordered us to give no support at all to the emperor unless he abjured the "Orthodox" schism and adopts the Latin rite,' Antonio said.

My head almost fell off. 'What?' I snapped, or something equally discourteous.

'You didn't know?' Antonio shrugged and grinned the grin that superior young men grin. 'Everyone knows.'

Richard Musard raised an eyebrow and pretended to know nothing.

The physician, who was right by me at a little table, looked up at me. 'Your Prince of Lesvos had better know that,' he said quietly.

I know I swore. For me, it was the last straw; my interest in crusade died there, for all my loyalty to my Order. Father Pierre

Thomas preached a respect for all religions; tolerance, understanding, leadership by example. When he was legate, we had had a chance of impressing the Greeks with our tolerance.

Now the Pope was sitting far away and dooming any attempt to retake the Holy Land to failure in a petty desire to be primate of the world. I have seen more good fellowship between two brigands arguing over spoils.

My lips set. I remember looking away, and seeing Fiore, who looked at me with something like wonder.

'Are you all right?' he asked, a tribute to his growing powers of human understanding.

Gentilhommes, you might think that my crusader vow would have died in the blood and rape of Alexandria. But it did not. However horrible, that was war, and it was the very war I had been commanded to make.

And Jerusalem had been splendid.

But I stood on the Green Count's foredeck, and all I wanted to do was return to Italy. I am a soldier; arms are my profession. I didn't propose to stop fighting.

I merely proposed to stop fighting for bad men and foolish goals.

The prince, the patriarch, and the count wrangled for days. The Empress Helena, who had been forcibly confined by her son, was released by Sir Richard Percy, and she took up the reins of government. She sent an embassy to Vidin, in Bulgaria, where one of the three candidates for the throne of Bulgaria supposedly had the emperor as a prisoner. The Count of Savoy sent another embassy, under his bastard son, to the King of Hungary, who was, as we heard, approaching with a great army to fight the Turks.

There were more problems than solutions. In providing guards for the patriarch, the prince, the count, and the empress, I gradually came to know too much, as did Sir John Partner, Nerio, Stapleton and Fiore, as we had become the captains of the various guard detachments. We never saw each other – I continued to live at Lady Anna's house, in the English *bourg*, and so did Nerio and Fiore and Stapleton – but I was there perhaps one night in three, and never the same night as my friends. I did take the time to write letters: to Emile; to Hawkwood; to Fra Peter and de Midelton; and finally, in the same cover as the one for Hawkwood, to Janet, asking for a note for Richard. And explaining a good deal too much, I felt. I had time to write, but I never saw my friends; we were on watch too often.

I only mention this so you will understand that there was never a moment that we could pause and compare notes, so to speak. We never could examine the plot, or guess at the main players. We were reacting.

My second day arranging the guard detachments with Syr Christos, I asked the count for the loan of his physician, and was granted him. Master Guy Albin was a polymath, a brilliant mind and a fine scholar, independent of his practical medical knowledge. He was a cautious, careful man, of middle height, and he seemed quite old to me, being the same age I am now. He had white in his beard, but he was quick-witted. He wore a sword and considered himself a gentleman, and all the Savoyards treated him with respect, which is rare for quacks and mountebanks and doctors.

I cadged him to help guard the princes, as we called the lot of them. As they were close to hating each other, and as they were very strongly *not* in agreement on anything, they refused to live in one building and share food, to our endless annoyance.

However, Fra Peter had taught me well, when we were guarding the legate. I knew how to guard a great man, or even three great men and a great woman, and with the doctor's help and a small army of tasters, mongrel dogs, and an ever-increasing army of informants, it almost seemed as if we could relax.

There was a Greek officer; I was allowed to speak to him, although the empress was concerned about his loyalty. His title was logothete; he was a spy, the head spy of the Empire. He was a large man, bald and tall and heavy; he was not my idea of a spy at all, but he gave us the only warning we had to the counter-attack. He seemed to have a legion of thieves and thugs at his service, but in fact, it was a washer-woman, blushing because she was talking to a man – and a foreign man at that – who came to my door.

'They will try and take the caesar,' she said, after giving me the correct sign. 'Now, or very soon.'

'Christ,' I spat. I was in arming clothes. 'Marc-Antonio!' I roared. I was home, off duty. It was the sixth of September, and I had intended to go to Mass after a bath in hot water.

I grabbed the young woman, who was indeed very slight, and pulled her into Lady Anna's house and slammed the door. This terrified her. I pushed her into Lady Anna's arms. Syr Christos was also off duty. He came into the hall.

I hesitated for perhaps ten heartbeats.

'Someone is trying to take Andronicus,' I said. 'It's now.'

He looked at me for the count of three. 'Then they will kill the empress,' he said.

I didn't even think it through. 'I'll cover the empress,' I said. 'You go to the tower. You know … everything.'

He nodded.

I grabbed my sword, long since returned to me, and buckled it on.

And we were out of the doors, Marc-Antonio behind me with a fine brocade napkin still tucked into his black arming coat – he'd been that close to food.

The empress was in the palace proper, of course. She was guarded by Varangians, mixed with some of my people; by then, after almost two weeks, we *were* Varangians. That night, the men on duty were Guiscard's Bretons.

I ran. I didn't bother with a horse.

As soon as I neared the gatehouse, I roared '*A l'arme!*' at the tower, and I heard men move inside.

'It's the captain!' someone called. I waved and saw Mark between crenellations, and the gate opened.

'We are under attack,' I called as soon as I was inside. 'On me. The whole quarter guard.'

'Quarter guard is on rounds,' Mark said apologetically, but in fact, it was their duty. 'It's just the four of us here.'

I cursed. 'No one in or out.'

I ran for the palace hall.

I was just too late.

But then, sometimes, just too late is perfect.

Guiscard was dead, cut down at the entrance doors of the palace, stabbed in the throat with a dagger. Even with a dagger in his throat, he'd killed one with nothing more than his steel gauntlets.

They left the hall doors agape and they had *just* killed him.

I ran in, stepping over his body, and I was *right* behind the pack of them. I didn't even get to count – they had huddled up to pass the doors. The killing had put them in that state – terror, elation, purpose – they were too loud and they moved in jerky, ugly movements.

They were a mixed bag of Greeks and Franks. Hired muscle, for the most part, although I could see two men in silk by the hall's candlelight.

I could see the Empress Helena on her feet on the dais, and thanks to God, two of the Varangians by her, axes coming off their shoulders.

Men at the back of the attackers were turning as I barged into them. The nearest was a sailor in a knit cap, and he had a long knife in his hand, with blood on it; his eyes glittered, as a certain kind of man's eyes shine when killing.

I was too close to him to draw.

I stepped back with my right leg, drew across my body and used my scabbard against his knife hand in one motion, and then ran him through the throat bole. He was dead before the fourth inch of steel went in. I whipped my blade out and made a little turn to the outside, and cut about a hand's breadth of the next bastard's skull off the top of his head.

And then I waded in. I wasn't in harness, but this was what we trained for, and I couldn't let them reach the empress. Odd, isn't it?

I had no fealty to her. And yet, I take to duty quickly. It was my duty.

I turned on the balls of my feet and punched the hilt of my sword into an undefended face without freeing my point from the man I'd killed with the blow to his skull. He slid off the point as my third victim stumbled back with the imprint of my pointed pommel cap in the centre of his forehead, dead or dying.

They were bravos with sticks or daggers.

I was a knight.

I took a blow – thankfully from a cudgel – on the muscle of my left arm and lost my left grip on the sword in the pain. I cut, thrust, and Marc-Antonio killed my man with a nice, economical blow under my right arm. I got my left hand down at mid-blade and stepped in again, parried, and I had six men backing away from three of us.

One of the silk-robes lost his head, literally. The Russian Varangian beheaded him with a sweep of his axe, and the back cut belimbed another one.

Axes are fearsome, and the bravos were not in armour.

377

The other Varangian was hard by the empress, and had his axe across his chest. Waiting.

Good men.

Except I wasn't sure that the nearest Russian knew I was on his side.

'Hrolf!' I roared.

His axe wound and cut again.

A hired sword backed, turned to eye the axe, and fell when Marc-Antonio stabbed him low, in the kidneys. The man screamed on the floor, dark blood *pouring* out, and Marc-Antonio finished him on the floor.

The axeman's cut went down, slashing a man's face almost in half, and then rose, spilling his intestines with a delicacy worthy of Fiore.

There were now only three of them left, and they were broken; one was the Greek nobleman I'd seen with Half-Cloak at the Pisan Tavern.

He was dead before I could stop Hrolf, but in that pass I knew the Russian knew me as an ally, and the last two dropped their weapons.

I shook the blood off the emperor's sword. Hah! The Western Emperor, of course. I took a dozen steps forward and knelt on one knee to the empress. 'Apologies for the interruption of your dinner,' I said in Italian.

She was very pale. She put a hand to her veil and twitched it forward; but then she held out a hand and touched mine.

She was made of stern stuff.

'My thanks,' she said, in very good Italian.

I bobbed my head and motioned to the two Varangians. 'I need to know if there are other ...' I shrugged. 'Conspirators,' I said.

They spoke Russian and Greek. I didn't.

'I can tell them,' the empress said. She rattled off a string of words in Greek.

Hrolf shrugged. 'Guard,' he said, using a dead man to wipe the cutting edge of his axe.

'Aye,' I said.

The empress said a few words, and they bowed – first to her, then to me.

'They understand,' she said. 'Go. I fear ... everything.'

Marc-Antonio didn't even look pale. He was an old soldier by then. And not a mark on him.

'Quarter guard!' I roared.

Ah. Pardon, *mes braves*. When you set a watch of say, twenty men, you keep some in reserve. I'm told the habit originated in guarding a quarter of a town – but for me, it was always a quarter of the men on watch, all together, to overawe an enemy and respond to an emergency.

I found them, quickly enough; four Breton men-at-arms, enraged by the death of their best knight. I led them out into the darkness outside the palace gatehouse, our swords in our fists. We found a group of men outside; they couldn't answer for what they were doing after curfew. One bastard drew his dagger, and then they were dead.

The Bretons were ready to massacre the population of the city, but luckily for everyone, there were only four of them. And we kept them in hand – ran to the house where the prince and his knights were staying.

They hadn't had an attack; instead they had a fire. I saw Percy, made sure the prince was alive, and then we took horses and rode to the Green Count's house, but he was safe.

That left the patriarch, who had steadfastly refused to be kept in the Blacharnae neighbourhood and was being protected that night by Fiore and Maurizio di Cavalli.

I needn't have worried. But I did, and I rode across Constantinople in the dark with Marc-Antonio by my side to find the patriarch saying prayers for the dead, and Francesco Orsini a mirror-bright armoured presence, barely visible in the candlelight and incense.

It was a night of death, but thank God, none of the dead were ours. And in my panic, I forgot that the whole plot would be directed at the rescue of Andronicus. I forgot, but Fiore didn't. When the plotters came for Andronicus, Fiore ambushed them; the survivors were pursued through the streets by Kipchaks.

Over the next four days, they hammered out a plan of campaign while the imperial torturers had a go at the survivors. It didn't really matter any more; I think we knew more about the plot than Andronicus or the Hungarian knew. But the attempt to kill the empress broke her heart, because that was her son, trying to kill his mother. He denied it, and claimed that the palace chamberlain had acted without his permission.

I'm not a follower of the count, nor his greatest admirer, but I confess it was he who convinced the patriarch to move into the palace. When the Prince moved all his crossbowmen into the palace barracks, I finally had all my charges secure and in one place, and I think that I slept the clock around.

When I awoke, I was summoned by the empress, and I was treated to a level of court ceremonial that would have staggered King Edward, or even Prince Lionel. There were perhaps three *hundred* courtiers and functionaries, and as many again in servants present; the occasion was the presentation of a pair of ambassadors from the sultan, who was currently holding court off to the west, at a city called Didymoteichon.

The empress used me to send a little message. You may smile, but here's the wonder of it – the Turks were, of course, spies. I was almost sure they had provided material support to the assassins – perhaps even paid them – and the empress herself said, in private, that she believed they only demanded audience to see if any of the principals had been wounded or killed.

So she made them wait, standing at the very entrance of the magnificent hall, while I came forward with my harness all polished, my maille immaculate as Marc-Antonio and I could make it, my helmet gleaming and wearing a fine scarlet silk surcoat. I knelt where I had been told by the new chamberlain, three times approaching the throne, and then I kissed her shoe, as if she was the Pope.

She put a foot on my shoulder, so that I stayed with my head bent while the chamberlain opened a purple scroll with gold ink, and read from it of my devotion to the Imperial Majesty, and how I had saved the empress from a cowardly attack by paid assassins. And by the order of the emperor, I was made *spartharios*, an officer of the Imperial household, with the right, still mine to this day, to bear the emperor's sword in a procession, and further, to wear my own on all court occasions.

I know she did it to rub the Turk's faces in the failure of their plot. Well – if they were involved at all, which is debatable. But I enjoyed it very much, and the little bag of gold sequins that went with it, and the fine scarlet silk cloak, which, I'm sad to say, I pawned.

The Turks eyed me and listened to the empress, bowed low, and left.

My friends gathered round me and congratulated me, and that

night I dined well, with Lady Anna and her son; Hrolf and his mate Ragnar; Giannis and Giorgios and the Logothete; and, of course, Fiore, Nerio, Miles and Richard Percy. And we had roast boar in the Greek manner, and a variety of other dishes – a wonderful dish of saffroned rice, and some sweets in the Russian manner. After dinner we paid the company from the empress's beneficence, and Sir Richard informed me that we were sailing for Bulgaria.

I watched the cat eat Russian salmon from a plate, and listened to him purr, and wondered if I would ever get home to Emile.

BULGARIA

September 1366 – March 1367

O n the sixth of October in the year of our Lord 1366, we passed the ancient lighthouse at the head of the Bosporus. Just when you think you understand something, you see something else; just when I was comfortable that the Eastern Roman Empire was at the edge of death, I saw this – a magnificent tower with a flame that lit the dull heavens from miles away, towering over the entrance to the straits. It was manned by a garrison and a keeper, and well tended.

But like many things in the empire, this proved to be symbolic, for it was the last vestige of imperial authority, and when we turned west into the Euxine, the Black Sea of the ancients, we immediately picked up fishing boats who reported that the entire coast was in the hands of Prince Dobrotitsa, who styled himself 'Lord of Dobrudja' and had seized all the imperial possessions on the Black Sea coast. We landed at Lorfenal, a mere fishing village which pledged its loyalty to the emperor, and there we disembarked. We heard there of a Turkish force – that is, an Ottomanid force – that was planning to move against Constantinople. The Prince of Lesvos decided to return to Constantinople to help the Savoyard Gaspard de Montmayeur and the empress to hold it. He intended to take with him Sir Richard Percy and all his soldiers.

I met with him on the beach, and he tugged at his beard.

'Walk with me, Monseigneur,' he said.

I suspected he was about to offer me the kingdoms of this world, nor was I disappointed.

'I have had enough of the good count,' he said, with a false smile. 'But he does not have the men to conquer Bulgaria. Even with all my people – even with my levies from Lesvos – I would not be sure we could take it. Bulgaria is strong.' He shrugged. 'It is also an utter waste of time. The count doesn't even appreciate that if he storms these coastal towns, he is only helping the man who holds the emperor to fight his brothers.'

I said nothing.

'He is not a fool,' the prince went on. 'Merely very sure of himself, and utterly wrong.' He shrugged. 'I need you to stay with him. Listen – I have a very good place for you, if you wish it. You have given good service – excellent service.'

I bowed. In fact, I knelt.

'You have already sworn to me for the baronetcy of Methymna,' he said. 'I will hold you to that. I will hold your pay and that of your company at Constantinople – the Pera banker Niccolò di Quarto will have the whole amount to pay out.'

I nodded. He was a good lord, and a good captain – a pleasure to serve. I suspect that perhaps he was a bad man; on the other hand, his goal, of preserving the empire, was worthy. I have no idea how to judge such a man.

But it is God's to judge, not mine.

'However, I will pay your wages from now until the emperor is rescued,' he said. 'And double your wages and add a bonus if you get him. Yourself.' He stopped on the gravel. 'Savoy is a good captain, and he has a fine army. It is possible that he will cut his way to the emperor and rescue him. Well and good.' He smiled a crooked smile, looked away, and then looked at me.

'But I predict he will reach Varna, or perhaps a little higher, and run out of men and money,' he said. 'The King of Hungary is not coming. He was never coming. Your friend Nerio knows all about this. I do not think the King of Hungary is part of this awful plot – but I think that he is happy to benefit from it.'

Still there was nothing for me to say.

'When Savoy has run out of time and money and men, I want you to try and rescue the emperor,' he said. 'It is not worth trying now. They will be ready. But men who are alert in the autumn may be fools in the dead of winter. Understand me?'

'Yes, My Lord,' I said.

'Good man. They may just kill him. A pity – he is my friend, or at least, as close to a friend as I have ever had.' He shrugged. 'But …'

He was silent a while.

'You can preserve the empire without him, but if the Turks take Constantinople, it is over?' I asked.

He nodded. 'You are a deep one,' he said. 'I had not thought of it in just these terms. Come and work for me again.'

'Your Grace will have a care for the countess, my wife?' I asked.

'Of course,' he said. 'And your back.' He paused. 'I will take my son back now.'

I nodded. In truth, I seldom even thought of young Orsini as the Prince's son any more. He was a competent man-at-arms and was growing into Cavalli's lieutenant, but of course he had other things to do with his life.

The next morning, he took his galleys and sailed away. We had two small war galleys from the empress and of course, Giorgios and Giannis were wealthy men with their own galleys. Nerio now had his own, a mercenary galley out of Negroponte whose crew were probably pirates in their spare time, and I was in a heavy Gatelussi galley left for me by the prince, with another one of his gold earring-wearing captains in command. He was Andrea Batussi; he, too, had been an Algerian slave for part of his career, and clearly saw the Bulgarian campaign as a waste of his time. On the other hand, he took to my friends, and he was a gentleman-pirate, and he and Nerio's hired pirate were apparently old comrades in sin.

We sailed west, into the setting sun, and landed the next day at Sozopolis. There was fighting, but the Savoyards and their routiers did it all. We were last in the column of ships, and we tried to land on the flank of the Bulgarians, got tangled in a swamp, and missed the fight altogether.

The Bulgarians fought a careful retreat, but they were outnumbered and they had very little armour compared even to the count's routiers, and the count's magnificent and remade Virgin banner went up over the castle of Sozopolis.

That night was our first night in a military camp since Gallipoli. I walked through my camp, checking my sentries and making sure the latrines were well dug. By then, I had read most of 'The Art of War' and my Latin was stronger, and the campaign served to remind me of how useful many of the instructions were.

I was also a little surprised to see the extent to which my company had grown. We had servants; many former baggage slaves from Gallipoli were now currying horses in my camp. There was the cat, stretched out by a campfire like a small and very relaxed lion; there was Katrina, with a dozen of her kind in their own tents, and hard by, Father Angelo with a tent as a chapel and a man saying confession in the setting sun. Possibly confessing a visit to Katrina in the next tent.

Well, I find it humorous.

I also noted Francesco Orsini, chatting with Father Angelo as if this was a typical day of the week and he had every right to be there.

I raised an eyebrow.

'I like it here,' he said.

'God save you,' said Father Angelo.

I had almost two hundred men, by then. And fifty camp-followers of various sorts.

It was a 'Belle Companie' in every way, and I liked what I saw – men cleaning kit and bitching about the weather.

L'Angars stopped me on my rounds.

'Late in the season,' he said.

I nodded.

'We'll need better cloaks,' he allowed.

I winced, because wool was not going to come cheap out on the frontier of empire, but he was right.

'Best send a man you trust,' he said, 'because the count means to fight all winter, or so he says.' The Gascon shrugged. 'Mayhap he thinks this is the Holy Land.'

The next day we re-embarked and sailed across the gulf in order to land on a beach below the fortress of Mesembria, which surrounded a big, red-tiled town.

It was a year, almost to the day, since we'd taken Alexandria.

The Bulgarians, as it proved, had quite a large army indeed.

And they were waiting.

As usual, the Green Count was the first ashore. But the Bulgarians were no more willing than the Mamluks to let us form our army, and their infantry came down to contest the muddy beach – first men with spears and slings, who did a frightful damage among the count's household, and then the better armed men, *voynuks* with axes and pole arms. But the count and his household knights made short work of them; the Bulgarian prince would have done better to continue pounding the Savoyards with sling stones.

We were still in the rear battle, or main battle, depending. The count's army was well led, but if he was aware of the level of flexibility in tactics and mobility that the routiers had achieved in the last fifteen years, he showed no sign.

I was on my prince's rented pirate galley, staring into the October sun and trying to figure out what our commander intended us to do.

It was disgustingly like Alexandria. All the ships were crowding into the one muddy beach, trying to help the count.

I spoke to Banni, my captain, briefly, and he agreed. He ordered his rowers to warm themselves, and laid me alongside Nerio's galley, and I leaped across – no light matter in harness, I promise you.

I looked at my friends and probably cocked an eyebrow. 'We have two hundred good men,' I said. 'I propose we tack out of the line, go around that headland, and see if there's another beach.'

Fiore looked at me. 'Why would there be another beach?' he asked.

I shrugged. 'Stands to reason,' I said.

'It does?' Fiore asked. It really irked him that he hadn't figured this out; in fact, he wanted me to be wrong.

Nerio nodded. 'Let's do it,' he said. 'I have other business to which these men could be attending. I have had enough of your count.'

'I agree,' I said.

Nerio spoke to his captain, I went back aboard Batussi's galley, and both ships waved banners at Giannis and Giorgios. The Gatelussi captain led our little squadron, and we were off.

Best of all, when we turned into the wind, out of our places in the line, the two Greek galleys sent by the patriarch followed Syr Giorgios, and then the last four galleys in the column, full of routiers, followed them.

We passed Antoine de Savoy, our nominal commander. He shouted something, which I'll pretend was encouragement, and the galley behind him left the column and followed me, cutting in between my ship and Nerio's, so that I was now third in line.

Then came an hour of heart-stopping terror for me and me alone. To me, battle is terrible, but also wonderful. I fear it like any sane man, but it is my work, and I have spoken to enough craftsmen to know that the very work that ignites passion is often the work that causes the most tension.

And so with war. I didn't *know* there was a beach around the headland; I had merely noted that everywhere in the Aegean, cities were built on points of land with a beach *on either side*. Why, you ask? Because if you are in a galley, with a very few points of sail and tired oarsmen, you want choices in landing and launching your ship, and two beaches at ninety degree angles offer the good array of choice.

You see?

Fiore was from mountains. He cared nothing for the sea.

And also, because I ordered the ships out of the column, I was, just possibly, ruining my repute, and might even, if the count was in a mood, be accused of desertion and cowardice. Just two days before, we'd tried to get on the flank of the Bulgarians and had ended in a swamp.

Ah, well.

For an hour, I watched the headland and the hazy ground beyond it with the intensity of a cat for a mouse hole, and then we reached a point, and the bay on the far side began to open, and there was golden sand.

On the other hand, we could also see a big troop of Bulgarian cavalry shadowing us as we moved.

We had no signals – something I promised myself I'd remedy. And I could not move from ship to ship – not in harness, not with oars out. I wanted many things, but most of all, I wanted to be fast.

But the speed I required meant we should land our horses. I thought of Alexandria; I thought of the Captal de Buch at Poitiers.

The problem was that most of our horses were in a round ship, and it wasn't following us. But there were chargers in each ship, and John's men had their horses with them in the lead ship.

Sometimes, there are no tactics, and all you can do is trust your friends and your men to do what they've trained to do. I couldn't alter anything.

'Straight for the beach,' I told Nerio's pirate.

He nodded and grinned. 'Think there's any loot in that town?' he asked, looking at the red tile roofs of Mesembria.

'Yes,' I said.

He sucked on his snaggle tooth a little while. 'I will land my oarsmen,' he said, 'for a full share of the loot.'

'No rape,' I said. 'I'll hang a man I find doing it.'

His earring twinkled and he smiled, all cynicism. 'Sure,' he said.

'I mean it,' I said. 'These are Greeks and Bulgarians.'

'Maybe I won't land my oarsmen,' he said. 'If you are so holy.'

'Suit yourself,' I said.

We went in first. It was a good beach for galleys – deep until just a few paces off shore, and then suddenly very shallow. Our pirate landed us stern first, elegantly, and the Bulgarians were like Turks, loosing arrows at us from horseback, as I led the way down the boarding ramp.

There were a good five hundred Bulgarians awaiting us – all nobles, with maille and some plate, and lances, and bows, all on horseback.

The sand was very different from the beach at Alexandria – deep, and soft. A man's feet sank. A horse went even deeper, and the Bulgarians didn't come down to the water's edge, but stayed up on the firmer ground.

Off to my right, Nerio's galley came in but stopped in deeper water, and Hafiz-i Abun rode his horse off the deck and into the water with a splash. His big Arab swam ashore effortlessly, and John and his Kipchaks were right behind the Persian knight.

Look, when men tell you that the Mongols are born in the saddle or how superior their archery is, they never get at the kernel, the reality. It's not just their riding, which is superb, or their archery, which is legendary. It's that they know how to do things none of our soldiers know how to do. John leaped his horse into the sea from the deck of a ship, and he had his bow, all his strings, and forty arrows waterproofed. Mongols swim rivers and fight. They know how to fight in all weathers, in all conditions.

Well. So do the English. Use makes master, so they tell me.

The Bulgarians were no fools, and the moment Hafiz-i Abun leaped his stallion into the water, they split, and dozens of them rode north along the beach, loosing arrows as they rode.

But even that level of division caused chaos in their ranks. I saw a man in a purple cloak riding along, telling men off in companies, but the whole time he did that, no arrows flew, and I was ashore, and I had my friends by me, and then my Bretons and my Irish, and the beach was filling, and *still* no arrows were flying.

My archers were coming down the ramps. The Greeks were forming to our left; they, too, could put horsemen straight ashore, and
again the Bulgarian commander had to worry about his flanks.

Just to my right, the ship that had cut into my column landed bow
first, a daring and slightly showy move. Antonio di Visconti was the
first man into the water, leaping straight off the bow, and a dozen
Milanese knights came into the dirty water with him.

We were forming the way butter solidifies out of milk in the churn;
suddenly, we were an army, not a mob or a few men.

We still didn't have a banner, but I'd taken a red Saint George's
cross from the Gatelussi galley and put it on my spear, and now I
waved it and started up the beach.

Sand is brutal under your sabatons, and again, my fighting shoes
filled with gravel. An astrologer could doubtless have helped me with
this.

An arrow slammed into my helmet with the sound of mortality,
and I palmed my new visor closed. The Bulgarians were aware that we
were serious.

Off to my right, thirty Kipchaks had a shooting contest with almost
a hundred Bulgarians that lasted less time than it takes me to tell it,
and the Bulgarians broke and rode away, leaving a litter of screaming
horses and dying men.

We got up the beach to the surf line and the deeper sand.

Our archers were running for their places.

I watched the man in the purple cloak. He was trying to decide
what to do, but in fact, this part of the battle was already over. I knew
it, and he didn't. His best choice was to take his force, intact, and ride
away out of our bowshot.

But he didn't know that.

Rob Stone's voice carried all along the beach. 'Nock!' he called. His
voice wasn't as deep as Ned Cooper's, but it carried well, almost like
singing.

I didn't even know the archer at my back; a Picard, I found later,
who'd marched with *les Anglais* for years. He grunted as he pulled,
shoulder and back in the bow, and his arrow rose past my nose and
into the air.

'Loose!' Rob called. It was an eerie sound – his order blended with
the sound of the shafts singing through the air, *loooooose sshhh.*

Fifty Bulgarians died or lost their horses. They had no armour against war bows.

I think every arrow took a man. Listen – our lads had time, and little to fear; the range was chillingly short, perhaps fifty paces, and the Bulgarians were all packed together at the edge of the beach.

My part of the battle was so obviously over that I stepped out of the battle line and walked back to order the horses landed. Archers began loosing as individuals; to the north, Hafiz-i Abun and John began to drop shafts into the milling confusion that was the Bulgarian gentry.

Fiore looked at me over his shoulder. 'We should charge them!' he shouted, and Visconti called the same.

I could see Gawain in the sling. And Marc-Antonio had two chargers in his fist and was leading them down the boarding ramp.

The Bulgarians were melting, like ice when hot water is poured over it. Some died; more ran.

The Kipchaks started hunting them.

I trotted back to Fiore. 'Why?' I asked. 'Why charge them?'

Fiore shook his head in disgust.

The Bulgarians ran.

I hadn't even worked up a sweat.

'It is unknightly!' Visconti said.

I sighed. 'Get your horse,' I said, 'And we will have a chance to demonstrate our prowess. In the meantime, let the archers have their glory.'

The galleys were spewing men. It was clear that all the captains had decided to throw in their oarsmen. Genoese and Venetian oarsmen are as well armed and armoured as brigands – coats-of-plates or maille, spears, swords. The Greek oarsmen were lighter, but had slings.

Visconti was an officer of the count. I grabbed him. 'Would you care to go for the town?' I asked. 'With the oarsmen, and your own knights?'

He nodded. 'Of course!' he said, and strode away.

We mounted all the archers we could on Bulgarian horses, but it was all taking too long, and there were Bulgarians coming around the flank of the town and forming against us – *voynuks* and peasant infantry. The shock of our first onset and our archery was wearing off. It always does.

And landing horses, unless you swim them ashore, is a long, hard job that makes huge demands on your squires and pages.

Finally, I left Miles and Nerio with all the men waiting for horses and I took di Cavalli and all the men who were mounted – maybe fifty men-at-arms and some Greeks and Kipchaks – not a hundred men all told.

But the Bulgarian gentry were game. They formed against us, with their infantry, at a corner of the town. In fact, when they saw the oarsmen going for the open back gate, they charged us.

The Kipchaks rode off to my right, breaking away like starlings fleeing from a hawk. The rest of us closed our visors and lowered our lances and rode through them. I don't remember anything but unhorsing a man with my arm because I couldn't get at my sword. My lance was gone, and then I was rallying men while the peasant levies broke and ran without being charged.

In fact, Syr Giannis was shouting at them, and they ran. They were all Greeks – they owed their Bulgarian overlords *nothing*. Syr Giorgios had a fine banner, a great eagle in gold on red, and some of the peasants simply ran forward and knelt in front of the banner. They thought he was the emperor.

At any rate, their whole wing unravelled. The oarsmen were already in the town, and the *voynuks* were throwing down their weapons. And I still had fewer than one hundred men under my hand.

But the bastards had killed Gawain. I felt him tremble, and I looked down, and saw a shaft in his chest, and he slumped forward, game to the very last. He was, I think, our only casualty that morning, but I missed him sore. I stood by him till his great dark eyes closed, and I wept. I have had great horses; he was among the best, and he was brave and smart, and he loved war. I wasted time trying to get the shaft out, and fighting the obvious truth. Marc-Antonio brought me a fine heavy charger, with a purple housing; the horse fought him, and he almost lost the bastard.

I didn't want another horse. I wanted Gawain. On Gawain, I knew I could take any knight ever born.

His eyes went last; his legs stopped shaking, and a sort of mist came over his eyes, and then they closed, and he was gone. I hope he knew I was there.

Damn it! I'm crying now, and that was twenty years ago.

*

I mounted the purple brute without much thought and used my spurs to keep him in line; he didn't like me and I wanted Gawain back. I don't think I'd touched Gawain with spurs twenty times in all the years I had him, and that Bulgarian half Arab got the spurs twenty times in our first twenty minutes. But we were in similar states, he and I; a Bulgarian had killed my Frankish horse, and a Frank had killed my new mount's Bulgarian master.

But my little Saint George's cross went up, and Fiore and Nerio and Miles were all mounted; we rallied together at the edge of the town.

The count was still fighting under his banner on the mud beach below the town. No one had told the Bulgarians that they'd lost, or perhaps they thought that if they killed the emerald knight, we'd fold.

Odd thoughts go through your mind in a fight. Worse when you have time to think. But that day, in that hour, what I thought was that maybe this was the last time I'd go into action with all my friends around me. I knew we were going our separate ways soon. We all knew.

And yet, in that hour, there we were – the four of us. Maybe five; Hafiz-i Abun had almost become one of us, despite being an infidel. And there we were – all mounted, all in our best, formed together. I was in the middle; Marc-Antonio was behind me with my blood red cross of Saint George, with Prince Francesco's son right next to him on a fine bay. Nerio was on my right, and Fiore on my left; Miles was to Nerio's right, and Cavalli on Fiore's left.

We rode along the headland until we were just above the Bulgarians on the beach. The Savoyards had fought manfully and pushed the Bulgarians, who outnumbered them, back up the beach almost to the grass of the headland.

I remember that I looked right and left.

We were all grinning like fools.

'Come,' said Fiore. 'Let us be knights.'

And we were.

I would love to tell you that the Count of Savoy loved me from that hour, but I'd be lying. Instead, I rather think he felt we stole his glory, because he has never stopped, from that day to this, telling me that he didn't need to be rescued.

Possibly not; he'd cleared the beach.

It didn't matter. We took Mesembria; the Bulgarian prince had been dead for over an hour, and as it proved, I was spurring his horse.

Whatever the count said, his men sacked Mesembria thoroughly, with the help of the oarsmen. I formed my men by our ships and refused to let them join the sack. I lost men that day, but some actions define you, and I also *gained* men. We made camp north of the headland, curried our horses, and listened to the town die.

Two days later, the count began to get his soldiers back under command. When men are let loose to be animals, it is difficult to recall them to discipline. In fact, it takes days; some men never return.

That night, I sat by a fire with my friends – Hafiz-i Abun, l'Angars and di Cavalli, and a few others. We'd set a board across two barrels and paid the men a small amount in silver to prevent mutiny. I noted that the Greeks didn't participate in the sack, and in fact, they protected as many peasants as they could.

L'Angars shook his head. We were avoiding discussing the sack, although you could smell smoke for miles, and then he just shrugged and said it. 'A year ago, I'd have been in the town with them,' he said.

'Three years ago, so would I,' I said.

Nerio smiled grimly. 'You are not widely admired just now, William Gold,' he said.

I was looking at the fire and thinking of Pont-Saint-Esprit, and Janet. 'It's stupid and ugly,' I said. 'It turns soldiers into criminals. How can a man who rapes and robs pretend to be a knight?'

Fiore raised an eyebrow. 'I have little interest in either,' he said. 'But killing is killing, and the dead are dead, whether you kill them finely or meanly.'

'Perhaps the dead are dead,' I answered. 'But I am here, and I have to live with myself.'

Nerio, the hard man of the world, shocked me. 'I agree,' he said. 'Do as little evil as you can. I agree.' He smiled crookedly. 'Perhaps even sometimes do good.'

Fiore shook his head. 'We killed a great many Bulgarians,' he said. 'They are dead. Their lives are over. They too have women, and children.'

The fire crackled. It was cold.

'The count took more losses here,' Nerio said. 'And winter is close. Have you given any thought to rescuing the emperor?'

I nodded. 'Are you all in?' I asked. 'I'll wait until we are in winter quarters. But I assume that the Hungarian has him, at Vidin. Wherever that is. My first thought is to send John and his men to scout the countryside and the route.'

And when men started going to bed, Hafiz-i Abun came and took my hands.

'You are a good man, for a Christian,' he said. 'And I will not pretend that my prince's armies have not sacked cities – aye, and put a pile of skulls to mark their prowess.' He shrugged. 'But I will not travel with you any more. I am not a warrior like you. I will fight at need, but this was sickening. At least, after the first few moments, which were terrifying. It was ... like fighting children.'

I nodded. 'I'll miss you,' I said.

'And I you, my military philosopher. Come and see me in Isfahan and I will show you some hospitality.' He grinned.

'How will you go home?' I asked.

'See the little Genoese round ship in the roadstead?' he asked. 'He will land me at Tanais, as it was called in the ancient world. I will ride across the steppe, and be home in four weeks. Perhaps less, *inshallah*.'

So we embraced, and in the morning, he was gone. I still have letters from him; indeed, I will visit him, someday.

Our next attack was at Varna. If you like political irony, Varna was the first city we attacked that was actually held by our 'enemy', the Bulgarian prince who had the emperor captive, although he kept his captive far to the north.

He was a much cannier warlord; no army met us on the beach, and over the next week, I learned that however excellent my count's little army was, he was woefully short of Italian siege engineers, or even English ones. The Greeks built him two big trebuchets, and we pounded the walls for a few days, and one of the galleys unloaded a heavy *gonne* that threw a thirty pound ball, and it brought down a corner tower before the iron cracked; one of the Italian men-at-arms said that it was too cold for wrought-iron gonnes.

And cold it was. We camped in mud, and then the mud froze, and my *compagnia* spent all day, every day, gathering wood and fighting Bulgarians for it. Nor were we in recently conquered lands with Greek peasants any more; at Varna, we were in Bulgaria proper, and the people hated us. The fighting was vicious; we took losses. Mark took a wound. Fiore got an arrow through his left arm.

I watched the count's army change.

It is difficult to describe, because if I said that they lost their courage, I'd be far too strong. But as days turned to weeks and the snow fell, men ceased to take chances – to be bold or dashing.

Little by little, our foraging grew feeble, and we were increasingly hemmed in. There was no battle; instead, the ropes gave way on our trebuchet and no one found more. The supplies of firewood and food came from down the coast, at Mesembria, and were brought up the coast by our little navy instead of being taken by our soldiers, and we were penned in our camp. It was we who were under siege.

Despite which, and with no reference to my lord the count, I sent John and his Kipchaks out to find Tarnovo and news of the emperor. One of the count's best knights was captured, failing to take a little town down the coast. He led a punitive expedition in person and they sacked the town, which, as far as I could see, merely stiffened the resolve of our Bulgarian adversaries to hold to the very end. And Varna was big, double walled and very strong.

The count held a great council of war in his beautiful green silk pavilion with six braziers burning charcoal. We were warm, and there was much debate, but in the end, Jean de Vienne and Guillaume de Grandison, two of his best knights, were sent to summon the town to surrender and see what terms they would accept. The next morning, before our embassy went forward with a flag of truce, my friends and I went to have breakfast in our frozen trenches, mostly because it seemed like a foolish thing to do. But Marc-Antonio had produced a chicken and some wine, and we went out at dawn, built a fire at the bottom of an icy trench, and shared our chicken with a dozen archers who were on duty. We were opposite the ruins of the tower that the gonne had collapsed before it cracked, and I raised my head a few times to look at it.

There were workmen in it; I could hear them. And whenever we raised our heads, a crossbowman with a heavy arbalest would loose at us. I took to raising a rusty helmet on a stick, because he took so long to reload; I could draw his bolt and then have a long look.

My third time, I was eating an apple; I raised the helmet and he hit it, and the heavy bolt went right through the iron helmet.

My archers cheered.

That's how the siege was going.

My Picard was there – Pierre Lapot. 'Any chance you could get him, when I draw his bolt?' I asked.

'Why?' Pierre asked me.

'I'm planning to have a look at the tower,' I said. I looked at Fiore.

He got to his feet, crouching to avoid the arbalest. 'At your service,' he said.

'I think they're entrenching in the rubble,' I said. 'But I don't think they have any soldiers.'

'So?' Nerio asked.

'So we take the tower,' I said.

'We can't hold it,' Nerio said.

'Of course not. We take it, hold it for a few minutes, drive off their workers and set fire to the wood scaffolding they're building. I can smell the new wood.' I was very sure of myself – a lord of war.

Nerio frowned. 'And then?' he asked.

I shrugged. 'And then we've had a little exercise, covered ourselves in glory, and shown the Savoyards how to conduct a siege.'

Miles Stapleton stretched carefully. 'You mean, so they'll hate us even more than they hate us now?' he said. 'I could be home. Married. A hero of crusade. Why am I here in a frozen trench with you three?'

'I could be killed,' Nerio added. 'I am very fond of me.'

Fiore gazed at him a moment. 'I am fond of you too,' he said. 'But we have been quiet an entire month, since I was wounded. The count must think we are dead.'

'Oh, fine, then,' Nerio said.

I turned to Pierre. He was laughing to himself. 'You ...' he said. 'Never mind, Monseigneur. If I do not hit him, I will at least make him brown his braes.'

Fiore looked at me. 'Perhaps that is better. What have the Bulgarians ever done to me?'

Miles Stapleton laughed bitterly. 'I heard one of the Savoyard knights saying that they were infidels. Are the Savoyards fools?'

'There is a certain element of myth-making to their war effort,' I said. 'Come. Let's see what the Bulgarian gentlemen have to offer in the way of a fight.'

I raised the ruined helmet and drew the man's bolt.

But as soon as he had shot his bolt, the bowmen around me pelted him. Pierre loosed first, and grunted with satisfaction, and then the others; six arrows flew, and I was up and over the end of the trench.

Another crossbow bolt almost ended my military career and rang off the frozen earth.

Just when you think you are so very clever …

A third bolt might have ended this tale, but there were only two, and then I was up and running. Frozen ground may be the devil to sleep on, but it's not bad for wearing armour and moving; there was no actual ice, and I was in the moat before the arbalester could reload. Then Fiore dropped in by me, and Nerio was ahead of me already and starting to climb the rubble of the tower. Miles was next to me, stone for stone, and we scrambled to the edge.

The arbalester rose to loose and one of our archers got him, and then we were in. I fell; I have a tendency to go too fast, and I went down over a charred roof beam. Miles saved my life, because of course there were Bulgarian men-at-arms covering the tower. Really, I was just bored. And probably foolish.

Fiore dispatched my would-be killer, and then I got to my feet in the icy water in the base of collapsed tower, long sword against pole-axe in the hands of a *voynuk*. He hacked at me a few times – heavy, overhand swings – and then I cut his hands, broke some fingers, and got my sword across his throat. He had the good grace to yield, and we had the tower just like that.

Our archers came across with fire, even as the Bulgarians sent a sortie to retake the tower. We were on their out-wall; this wasn't Gallipoli, and the tower didn't even communicate with the inner wall, an excellent design.

I planned to burn it, but it was defensible.

The first enemy sortie came on hesitantly – perhaps twenty men-at-arms in middling armour. My archers cooled their ardour immediately by dropping their captain with a few clothyard shafts right through his coat-of-plates.

'Get me the company banner,' I shouted down to Marc-Antonio, who was standing around with a basket of food. He ran off down our trench. I could see now what the Bulgarians were after, working the collapsed tower; they were raising the level of the rubble so that they could loose bolts and fire down into our trenches. The bastards.

A quarter of an hour passed and they tried to drive us out again. This time they filled the wall opposite us with crossbowmen, but they could not quite clear the rubble edge, and we all cowered in the shadow of the wall with a healthy desire to preserve our own lives.

Then Rob began to pelt the walls with arrows from our trenches.

Crossbowmen are deadly in sieges because they can *wait*. They can cock the damned machine and watch for you to raise your head. But they cannot shoot in volume, and they are no more brave than other men.

Ten archers can outshoot forty crossbows, as our archers proceeded to demonstrate, and more archers came up all the time. Soldiers get bored. They will, at times, risk their lives merely to avoid the boredom.

The second counter-attack came along the space between the walls, and we didn't have enough archers who could fit in the tiny safe space in the rubble to loose at them.

We had to fight.

But they had to climb the rubble, and we had the poleaxe and a spear, and after we wounded three of them, the rest stood in a huddle down in the covered way, a little too long. Two started climbing the 'safe' rubble wall by the inner wall; I went to wait for them.

Rob's archers cleared the city wall above us. I don't think they hit a single man, but the crossbowmen couldn't stand the constant rain of shafts and scrambled off the wall. That left Pierre and his comrades free to get back up on the rubble pile, loosing almost straight down into the milling men-at-arms.

Marc-Antonio came up the outer wall with the banner and l'Angars and twenty more men-at-arms, and then we went down into the covered way and beat the Bulgarians in as sharp a mêlée as I have ever seen – man to man, harness to harness. I captured one of their *boyars* and we dropped a dozen of them; Fiore was almost captured because he went so deep into them, and Nerio had to cut him free.

Nor did they break. They retired step by step. By then, we had Antoine de Savoy and Visconti with us; a dozen great knights in fine harness are worth their weight in gold in such an action, and they were, for all my carping, great knights. We drove the Bulgarians down the covered way, and then crossbow bolts began falling among us, and we had outrun our support, and it was our turn to scramble back.

We didn't take Varna. But we held that tower until darkness, and then we slipped away, leaving the tower rubble afire, and by then we'd scared the Bulgarians into making a truce. They agreed to send to their tsar, and ask for the emperor to be released. The count sent the patriarch and Jean de Vienne with a delegation from the city, and we swore to withdraw under the flag of truce in two weeks.

We received a fair amount of warm praise from some of the Green Count's friends, but none from the great man himself.

But those weeks were very bad for us. The count did not cease military operations – he couldn't. We had to forage for food, and we had to keep the peasants off us. But the men were used up, and wouldn't go out of the camp without knights to lead them.

Listen, let me tell you a thing, Aemilie, and those of you listening who have never made war. Battles happen by day. But campaigns are about the night. If you can cow your enemies and make them sit behind fortifications and roam abroad in the darkness, then you are master of the land. Whichever side wins the night has usually already won, and there does not need to be a battle.

The fight for firewood and food was mostly fought in the darkness.

And as men grow tired and disillusioned, they are fractious. Even my little company, which was, dare I say it, well led – even they needed to have knights and men of note leading them, even on a little cattle raid by starlight.

And the count's fine little army was worse. The Savoyards had to lead every foraging expedition; the routiers and the archers following the Green Count built fires with whatever wood they could scrounge, and were very hard to move. One evening a dozen big brutes tried to steal our firewood.

Rob saw them off.

Lord Guy de Pontailleiur, who, I confess, I thought was a fool, but who was nonetheless Marshal of Burgundy, was taken by the enemy. He was a great lord of France. His ransom was probably worth more than the town of Varna.

Tsar Stratchimir sent a courteous reply to the count, saying that we were making war on him for no reason; that the emperor was his honoured guest, and that if we quit our siege of Varna and withdrew from his lands, he would consider releasing the marshal.

*

The first week of November it snowed, and I led a raid, a chevauchée, out into the snow. Our horses looked like scarecrows, and everyone felt like crap, and it was difficult to get the best men to move, and the slackers lay in their blankets and pretended to be sick. Or they were. We had a lot of sick.

I took my people out into the snow after full darkness. We passed the enemy pickets, if there were any, and we went north, not south, into the fertile country behind Varna. My moonlight sweep netted us a dozen head of beef; we captured two more boyars in a simple ambush, and lost no one. That's not true – one of the Irishmen lost some fingers to frostbite. But we moved fast, in the darkness, guided by a pair of Greeks, and I paid my guides in gold more than the beef was worth. On our way back, we pounced on the enemy sentries and cleared them off about a third of their frozen, shallow trenches, and by the time I had my beeves butchered, the Bulgarians had their entire army standing to arms. We ate hot beef and mocked them.

We were getting to be very good at war. We ought to have been – between the Black Prince, Hawkwood, the Order and the Turks, I'd had the best teachers, and so had my friends.

Nor was it just me. Visconti led a successful raid as well; in fact, he brought in about four times as many head of cattle as I did, although no prisoners. He shared his beef with us, and our men ate well. As we ate that day, we watched the Bulgarians bring forty wagon-loads of wood into their camp – firewood and the sinews of new trenches.

With the knights of the Order and Visconti's Italians, we made a little plan.

The next night, I feinted a raid, got the Bulgarians in their trenches, and then Visconti assaulted the same collapsed tower. Imagine: we were laying siege to Varna, and they were laying siege to us, but they didn't have so many more men than we did that they could protect everything. We retook the tower, took a dozen good prisoners, and when the torches showed them running around their outworks and bringing men into the city, Miles took the real raid out into the darkness. He didn't go north. He went into their camp. He took their wagons full of wood and brought them across the frozen ground to us, and the Bulgarians couldn't do anything to stop us.

Sadly, that was our last salute. The Savoyards didn't relish this kind of war. They called it '*Petit Guerre*', the little war, as if it was a thing of no value.

So, under orders, the next night we piled up all our firewood and set fire to it.

And then we filed silently onto our ships and slipped away, leaving our fires burning. That was the end of the siege of Varna.

We sailed. We sailed down the coast, all the way back to Mesembria. And the town that we'd sacked became our winter quarters; I leave you to imagine how popular we were.

But it got worse.

In early December, the count paid all the galley captains. He had to; they were leaving for ice-free water. They were quite blunt – if he didn't pay, they wouldn't come back.

Antonio di Visconti told me one night, over wine, that the twelve thousand gold *perperi* or byzants had taken all the gold the count had left from his massive loan on Nerio's cousins and Nerio himself.

Nerio just shook his head. 'I feel like a landlord,' he said. 'Watching over a bad tenant and trying to decide when to evict him.'

It was clear that his Genoese bankers felt much the same.

As soon as we settled into winter quarters, I began writing leave chits for my men to visit Constantinople and Pera in shifts. L'Angars thought the idea was insane – and to be fair, it was Stapleton's idea and not mine. But Hawkwood gave leave to his men-at-arms, and to archers if he trusted them. L'Angars said that the men who could easily arrange other employment would desert. Stapleton held the opposite.

But life in Mesembria was brutal and cold. The peasants and people of the town hated us; we didn't even have the usual thin skin of traders and obsequious turncoats to pretend we were saviours. The Greco-Bulgarian population were Orthodox and they hated Franks, and the count responded by giving them lots to hate. He increased taxation, arrested prominent citizens, and imprisoned them pending payment of their taxes.

I was preparing, at the time, to take my first *rota* to Constantinople for leave while also trying to get my archers interested in putting on a Passion Play for Christmas. Miles was writing out the names for the first *rota* and the second in his fine hand; Nerio was casting their accounts so that we could arrange for them to be paid by the prince's

Genoese banker Niccolò di Quarto on arrival in Pera. I was taking steps to see that they didn't leave Pera, or cross the Hellespont to Constantinople. I agreed with Nerio that money would hold them – and daily inspections, and a little support from the authorities in Pera.

Fiore was helping Stapleton copy. He had a good hand.

'I miss the little sister,' he said, and I agreed. I missed Sister Marie; I missed my wife. I had sent her a letter, giving the dates of my projected visit to Pera, but I had no way of knowing whether she'd received it.

'Our employer had better pay,' Nerio said. 'I'd desert if I wasn't paid. It's too cold out there to do anything but huddle and curse.'

All of our people were in barracks built into the walls of the town. We'd knocked down a section of inner wall and replaced it with wood and brick to install six big fireplaces and chimneys. Sheer luck had got the mortar dry – luck, and a little judicious use of fire.

'The people here are on the verge of open rebellion,' Miles said.

Nerio threw down his stylus. 'This count – he hates routiers? And yet he seizes citizens and holds them to ransom? He *is* a routier.'

I agreed, but I kept my views to myself. Richard Musard had been wounded twice, and had a terrible cold, and was no longer attending the count's councils, to which I was, by and large, not invited. Mesembria and Sozopolis were being administered by marginally competent French and Savoyard nobles, who treated the population with all the consideration that they showed to their own people at home.

A great many of the count's mercenaries were English or Scots, and there was a distinct national friction developing. I chose to ignore it, and even l'Angars admitted that the prospect of leave made our veterans far more docile and cautious than the openly mutinous archers in the other contingents.

Rob Stone came to me a day before I was due to sail to Pera.

'A word, Cap'n?' he asked.

Captain. I rather liked being captain.

'I could ha' my pick o' the lads in this camp,' he said. 'Every blessed day, two or three sidle up, like, and ask ...' He shrugged. 'No one's been paid.'

'Including us,' I said.

Rob nodded. 'Lads trust you to get us paid,' he said. 'And we're all paid to September, eh? There's bastards I won't name, in this camp, not been paid since they boarded ship at Venice.'

'I'll talk to Nerio,' I said. Nerio held our next contract, and he was increasingly restless.

That evening, he asked me if I thought John the Kipchak would return.

I shrugged. 'I confess I'm … not well pleased he's been gone so long,' I admitted.

Nerio sat back. We had a fireplace of our own, and six braziers paid for by Nerio. It was still cold. 'I trust him,' he said. 'And I think we need him for the work in Achaea.' He shrugged. 'But at some point, I'll admit there's no reason for me to be here. My patrimony is slipping away on me, out there. And the count is like all bad creditors – he doesn't want to see my face.'

'You want to go to Achaea in winter?' I asked. 'Who'd attack you in winter?'

'Lawyers,' he said.

That had a ring of truth to it.

And increasingly, as the count separated himself from us, it was clear there would be no spring campaign, or if there was, it would be conducted without us. I noted that the count had, quietly, not included any funds for our transport in his spring treasury.

I knew that eventually I would have to take action.

But I was too damned cold and tired to confront him. He disliked me; the feeling was mutual, and I wanted to be done with him. But Emile had said that he was important to her. And I understood that.

And sometimes when you leave a problem, instead of festering, it solves itself.

We sailed to Pera on the heavy galley the prince had left for us. I noted with interest that our captain seemed unafraid of ice; his orders were to obey me, and he did. He was quite content to ferry soldiers from Mesembria to Pera.

We were met on the dock by a pair of notaries and the Genoese banker in person. He had two booths right on the dockside, and men stepped forward, were paid in hard coin, and then led off by garrison soldiers to lodgings pre-prepared and pre-paid out of their wages – inns and taverns. It was like a Christmas miracle. Adding to the miracle was a pair of tables covered in heavy goat-hair cloaks in a sort of dusty gold colour. L'Angars had suggested them, and I had asked the banker to see what he could find.

'Shepherds and outlaws use these,' the banker said, with a smile.

The cloaks were superb – warm and heavy and soft, and full of whatever pungent oil goats give off that resists water. And the men loved them.

But even more like a miracle was Emile, now visibly pregnant, and her three children; Sister Marie and Sister Catherine the governess, and a whole stack of letters and scrolls for me – a trio of missives from the prince, a letter from the turcopolier of the Order, and a letter from Sir John Acudo, or Hawkwood, and even a letter from Hafiz-i Abun in good Italian, and a short scrap of parchment from Parmenio.

I read through them in order of my interest. Hafiz-i Abun was home; his letter rambled to tell me of some legal dispute he'd resolved in Tashkent and his meeting with a warlord who had impressed him, another Mongol named Timur. The prince informed me that my pay was up to date and offered further employment when I was at liberty; the second scroll was a charter guaranteeing my rights to Methymna and the countryside behind it – four hundred farms and a town of five thousand.

Emile smiled. 'I live there,' she said. 'It is very pleasant in winter. We have an orange tree.' She smiled. 'Soon, my love, I must go home to Savoy. I had three times as many letters as you.'

The Genoese captain, Parmenio, wrote to me from Genoa; a short note thanked me for my efforts, sword in hand, very courteous, too. And added to it, a small, sealed packet, which, when opened, turned out to be a bill of credit on Francesco Negrino of Pera for an enormous sum of money – almost two thousand gold florins.

'I sold your saffron,' he said in his note. 'I believe you forgot it.'

I showed this to my wife, who laughed aloud. 'Friends, for you, are better than riches,' she said. I treasure that comment and I always strive to make it true.

I read the missive from Sir John last. He had news that was no news to me: he was to be wed; he was working for the Visconti. He understood that I was with Ser Antonio, and he asked me to watch out for the young knight. He added that I had done a fine job of adding lustre to my repute, but that I should come back to Italy now and cash it in. He offered me employment as commander of my own contingent within his great company.

It all seemed a little fantastical, except that at the end of his missive he included the greetings of a dozen men I loved right well, and for a moment I was there, with the White Company. He had enclosed a note from Janet, too.

Last I read the letter from de Midelton. He wrote to encourage me to support Nerio in Achaea, and then, to consider supporting what he called 'The English Wedding'.

I got a scroll of account from Niccolò di Quarto. I had a fine estate on Lesvos that actually paid. I had more money on account than I had ever had in my life, and my troops were being paid.

Really, it was one of the nicest weeks of my life, that second week of December of the year of our Lord thirteen hundred and sixty-six. We ate and we drank, we walked about. At Emile's excellent suggestion, we took every sober man from the *compagnia* across the water to Constantinople, where we visited eight churches, drank wine with Syr Christos, and my wife had an audience with the empress.

Then I did. The empress asked me to explain to her in detail what the count was doing, and what had been done to rescue her husband.

When I was done explaining, she looked away. We were in the hall of Blacharnae, and we were not alone; my wife was sitting at the foot of the dais, and there were courtiers and servants around us.

'I do not really trust this count,' she said. 'But I do trust my brother-in-law, the Prince of Lesvos. He says you are capable of fetching my husband. Is this true?'

'I'm not sure I'd discuss this here, in the open,' I said.

'I don't mean to discuss it,' she shot back. 'I mean to order you to effect it.'

I looked around. 'Your Highness,' I said – a new title to me, but the form of address for an empress. 'Any attempt I make could result in his death.'

I looked up then, and met her eyes. They were large, and deep and dark. The eyes of a person who has seen much, and survived it. 'God will provide,' she said. 'I can make no other answer. If he is not restored soon, there will be no restoration.' Very quietly, she said, 'The pressure ... to restore my son to his offices ... is immense.'

Her son, who had proposed to kill his mother and father for power.

'I would reward you,' she said, 'as no man has ever been rewarded.'

I won't pretend those words didn't quicken my blood.

'Your Highness,' I said. 'I will try.'

With Emile at my shoulder, I wrote Hawkwood a letter I had never anticipated writing. In it, I told him the size of my *compagnia* and its composition and offered him my services from the first of August, thirteen hundred and sixty-seven. Emile and I thought that was enough time to see Nerio installed in his estates, and to escort her from Venice to Savoy.

Then, a week to the day after arriving, I mustered seventy very hung-over archers and men-at-arms aboard our galley, and sailed for Mesembria. I kissed Emile; she gave me this fine pin, which I still wear for her. I gave her a string of pearls. I sent my greetings to her knights, who claimed to be jealous of missing all the fighting.

We had good weather and in three days we could see men huddled around fires in Mesembria. Except that I had brought tuns of Candian wine, and materials for costumes, and all the makings for Christmas puddings and cakes and some other treats.

Instead of wild cheering, I was greeted with sullen looks. I was slow to note that the Green Count's magnificent banner of the Virgin no longer flew over the fortress.

Miles met me at the water's edge. 'The count has withdrawn to Sozopolis,' he said. 'He left Peter Vibod as captain here. The count's gone. He's left us most of the really bad men, too.'

Miles looked pale and thin-faced and the shrew, never so far from him, was right on the surface.

I shook my head in disgust. But then I listed off the stores I'd brought, and I restored his humour, and we got our own men to unloading them. And the men coming off the boat put heart into the rest of ours; they all knew their turns were coming, except for a few awkward sods who'd forfeited their leave.

I'd spent a fair amount of money in Pera, mostly on clothes. I had fallen for the Tartar kaftan, and I had one in silk but lined in wolf – scarlet and grey. But I'd got several of the sheepskin-lined variety that the Tartars favoured, and I was looking forward to giving presents to my friends.

'And Antonio di Visconti got himself captured,' Miles said bitterly. 'And there is a Turkish army moving to the south-west.'

'In winter?' I asked, appalled. 'And what the hell was Antonio doing?'

'We lost Lavorno,' Miles said. 'Ser Antonio tried to take it back.'

By then Nerio and Fiore were embracing me and cursing my good fortune. 'Coldest week of my life,' Fiore said.

'John is back,' Nerio said, with infinitely more practicality.

John was waiting in our little solar, his boots up on a table. But he rose and embraced me, thumping my back many times while I told him how worried I had been.

He looked embarrassed. 'Rode long way,' he said.

I have since come to understand that he had a mission of his own – his own goals. And he accomplished them, and only attempted to do my bidding on his road home. I think that this is natural – the way of men – and we often imagine ourselves to be heroes, when in another tale, we are only the smallest player on a very full stage.

Regardless, he had found the emperor.

'Emperor is at castle of Aikos, north and north,' he said.

'Aikos?' I asked. Aikos was not on any of our itineraries. It was hundreds of miles north, on the Black Sea. John sketched it out in charcoal on our unpolished tabletop. Listen, this is another thing Steppe people do – they draw pictures of the ground, like those maps of the Heavenly City you can see in monastaries. It is odd that this talent is shared by monks and Turks. But these pictures of the ground are very useful.

'You are sure?' Nerio asked.

'Saw him,' John said. And then, with a grin, 'Spoke with him.'

'Christ!' Nerio said. 'How?'

'Emperor hunts with Bulgarian tsar.' John looked insufferably smug. 'John the Kipchak make good huntsman, yes?'

'But Aikos is where Visconti is held,' Miles said. 'I sent a flag of truce and a trumpeter,' he said.

'Bulgarian tsar say he ready to release emperor,' John said. He shrugged. 'But emperor guard is Hungarian bastard László.'

I think we all stopped whatever else we were doing – writing, talking, buckling on dry boots.

'The Hungarian?' Nerio asked.

'I knew it,' I said.

Fiore smiled and touched his sword. 'We heard the Hungarian was involved, did we not?'

John smiled. 'This time, just kill. Yes?'

I admit I took very little urging. Listen, friends. Men like the Hungarian make threats all the time – threats about death and rape and humiliation. They do not carry them all out. It had been a year since László threatened Emile, and I doubted he even knew where she was.

But I had come to agree with John, nonetheless.

'Well, gentlemen,' I said. 'Shall we rescue the emperor?'

When we debated plans, they came down to two. We could go in very quietly, and try the rescue – just our own people. John knew the castle well enough.

As a side plan, we looked at the possibility of making a winter camp in the area and watching the castle, and grabbing the emperor if he emerged.

But ... Every time we got to that point, I would emerge from the sheer glory of such an attempt to the cold reality that I had almost two hundred men in my employ, and if they were good at one thing, it was *escalade*.

Our second group of leave-takers went to Pera with Miles, and returned. We had had a total of two desertions – both difficult bastards we could live without.

We practised our Christmas pageant, passed out a few sweets to local children and tried to convince their parents to come, and held an inspection which was much derided by the other routiers.

We picked our men. I'll be honest – we told them nothing. We offered triple pay for a three-day raid, and they accepted. I took all the best men, and left l'Angars, who deserved to be with us, to stay and watch the rest. We took ninety men.

John left first, with a horse herd and all of his own men. They already had sheepskin coats, I noticed.

John was making a detour south to look for the Turks. Then he would ride cross country, inland, to Aikos. A long way, but the thing we knew by then is that the Bulgarians were no more fond of making war in winter then we were ourselves.

Nerio took the third *rota* to the ship, and three days before Christmas he set sail for Pera, exactly on schedule, in case anyone was watching. The men left behind continued to practise for the Passion Play of Christ's birth, which I understand was quite well received.

I wasn't there to see it.

It was a fine day; a stiff, cold wind was coming out of the north, but the galley sailed east until Mesembria was lost behind us in the morning haze, and then the captain promised every oarsman three days' double pay and a week of leave in Pera. They groaned, but they accepted, and the galley turned north and rowed, well out of sight of land – rowed all day and all that night too, warmed by wine heated on braziers.

I know.

I was there, in my harness. I'd boarded dressed as an archer with Rob and Mark, helping to carry the folding scaling ladders that every routier knew how to use.

Morning showed us the northern coast of Bulgaria. We were north of Varna already, and we hovered off the mouth of the great Danube – one of the hundreds of mouths – and this was where our expert Genoese pirate was worth his weight in gold. At sunset we turned towards land and raced the sun into the estuary on a light westerly, and if there were herdsmen or guards to see us, that was a chance we had to take. The sunset showed us trees stripped of leaves and some snow, even in the delta.

In truth, when you make a plan like the one we'd made, you usually have no idea what can cause your plan to fail. In my case, I had no notion of the sheer complexity of the estuary of the mighty Danube – so many islets, so many little towns, and havens, fishing villages and mud flats. We spent half the night being lost, and our *capitano* fully knew what he was doing.

But as the dawn star came bright on the horizon, two full mornings after we set sail, and the morning of Christmas Eve, the *timonier* spotted the landmark for which the *capitano* had been looking, a stone cross set in the ground hundreds of years before, and before a priest could say half a Mass, we were ashore in the freezing early morn.

We had six horses, and we used them to find a flock of sheep and two shepherds. We killed and cooked two sheep on the shepherd's own fire, and pressed into their byre to pass the day in frozen misery. The shepherds Nerio and I questioned separately.

We were in the correct place. We were about six miles from the castle. Neither shepherd would admit to ever having seen a patrol from the castle.

Lazy soldiers. Bless them all.

It sounds so bald, told like this. But in a great hazard, a great risk, you are not in control of events. I had counted on an empty, winter countryside. It was thus around Mesembria, and let's be honest, it's just as empty in the countryside of Cumbria or Yorkshire or Wessex, in the dead of winter. Who goes out of their home, whether hovel or castle, when the wind howls?

And rain, freezing rain, is the absolute enemy of armoured men. The cold water finds every joint in your harness, and little by little, the cold wetness seeps into your arming clothes, and once you are soaked, you can never get warm. You could throw yourself into a fire, and before you burn to death you *still wouldn't be warm*.

Armour is good for one thing, in winter. It cuts the wind. If your helmet is well lined and you have a good cloak, you can tolerate some cold. If you have a warm horse between your thighs, and a great cloak that covers both man and horse, your level of warmth goes up.

Thanks to l'Angars and a Genoese banker, we had excellent cloaks. So we huddled in our sheep cots, built fires from other men's cut wood, and tried not to get our feet wet for a long day of freezing rain and snow.

At sunset, we moved off in two columns, with six of us mounted to keep the columns moving together – no torches, and the two shepherds as guides, promised a hundred golden ducats for success and death for failure. And my guide, Ionnis, came very close to death when he marched us into a frozen swamp. But I had terrified him, and he was having a difficult time thinking. And the whole area was swampy.

But from his trembling and confusion I assumed it an honest mistake. Try marching terrifying foreigners over your countryside in the dark.

Midnight, and I knelt to pray. It was the night of our Saviour's birth, and in the Castle of Aikos, the garrison feasted.

We could hear them.

Aikos had a pretty little town with red tile roofs and two churches, both well lit for the birth of the Saviour. The town wrapped around two sides of the walls, and we gave that a wide berth and made for the long curtain wall that faced across a water-meadow towards the estuary.

The Bulgarians were singing in Greek.

Mark was afraid of breaking his bow in the cold, and wanted us to start a fire to warm the bows.

'Even drunk men will note a fire under their walls,' I said.

'Quarter?' Rob said.

Everyone looked at me.

The night of my Saviour's birth.

Escalade.

'No quarter until we have the emperor,' I said. I didn't like it.

But the profession of arms has some dark moments. Every man nodded.

'Take anything you like,' I said. 'But when we have the emperor, we're leaving.'

Every man nodded again.

'Don't get left behind,' I said. 'When we have the emperor, we will leave like snow in the sun.' I looked around in the darkness, but all I could see were ragged turbans on helmets that were now painted or rusted brown. We looked like routiers again.

'Let's go,' I said.

We'd gone over the first ten minutes several times – on the galley, and then in the sheep byre.

We knew who was raising the ladders, and who was going up them, and who was opening the postern gate, and who was racing for the north tower, where the emperor was. We were, in the first moments of Christmas Day, the best organised routiers in history.

I looked to the right and left in the starlight on the snow. We were under the wall, and I thought for a moment of Pont-Saint-Esprit and other times I'd done this. No one gave the alarm.

The wall looked very high.

'Ladders up!' I called.

Forty men raised two ladders that had been meticulously bolted together. Only then did I smell smoke; Mark had lit his fire, despite my orders.

The ladders went up and up.

The walls were tall.

So were the ladders – wide enough for three men to climb together, with a broad base on wheels, all in parts.

With a scraping loud enough to wake the dead, the ladder closest to me struck the wall and bounced. Despite my fears – heights, ladders, archery, the Hungarian – I had a foot on the ladder while it was still moving, and then I was climbing, and thirty men were climbing with me. I had Fiore at my shoulder and Marc-Antonio behind me.

I don't remember the climb, except that it was dark, that the wind coming *up* into my braes was brutal, and I knew better than to look down. My ladder was taller than the crenellations, and I went all the way to the top and jumped down onto the battlements, and I was in the castle.

There was no one on the wall. No one.

Talk about a Christmas miracle.

Fiore was there as soon as I, or even earlier, and we took a moment to get our bearings. There was a door in the next tower. John's description of the interior had not included the intervening tower, or the shape of the courtyard, or the inner bailey. So we'd stormed the outer wall, but the north tower lay off to the right, inside its own smaller fortress, so to speak.

We were in the wrong place. I have said many things about John; he is a wonder. But never ask a Kipchak for advice on a fortification.

I cursed. Men were flooding the wall and they were not quiet.

'Get the ladder up here,' I said. 'Pull it up!'

Try lifting a siege ladder on a freezing cold night; try it in steel gauntlets, with numb fingers and the sound of your enemies singing in the hall beneath your feet. Time passed and we made no progress, and then Miles suggested we pass a rope under the base of the ladder like a sling. It proved, after ten minutes of fruitless pulling, that we needed two slings.

It was incredibly difficult, and every moment I expected to be discovered and attacked.

Moreover, and I add this for those of you who will command, it is tempting in a crisis to make hasty decisions. It was tempting to abandon the *empris*, or to simply storm the hall – anything to avoid discovery. Every beat of my heart, I was presented with different foolish solutions to my predicament.

We got the ladder up and over the wall with a clash and a clatter, and down into the outer yard, where there was a frozen tiltyard and a row of pells for men to practise, and some miserable shacks that leaned against the walls like drunken men.

In the centre of the courtyard was the great hall – a separate building, as it was at Blacharnae and other places in the Greek east. It stood by itself, with a few tall windows and two fine chimneys like those the Venetians build, so much more efficient than the open hearths of home.

I was cold. That hall looked warm.

Now our own training told, because as soon as the ladders were over the out-wall and down in the courtyard, men ran to the base of the ladder in the same order we'd gone over the first wall. Nerio dropped his own part of the initial plan and took command of the archers, whom he stationed opposite both the obvious exits to the great hall.

We were just preparing to go over the second wall when one of the hall doors opened and a man stumbled out, laughing. He shouted something, raised the skirt of his gown, and began to piss in the snow. You could hear it – smell the urine in the cold darkness. Another man mocked him from inside.

One of our archers, over-eager, put a cloth-yard shaft in the pissing man. He died, still unable to believe what had happened; he fell to his knees, and then full length in his yellow snow, now dyed red in the ruddy light of the door behind him, then black as the door closed.

The man who had been laughing stumbled out. And saw the black blood on the white snow. He shouted – and died.

'Go,' I called.

I ran up the ladder. I assumed that the Hungarian had orders to kill the emperor if there was a rescue, but then, I was not sure which side the Hungarian was on, or what purpose he served. It was totally possible he was working for Turenne, or Geneva, or even the Green Count, and had orders to *protect* the emperor.

We'd spent the winter trying to figure out how all the plots worked. Nerio and Fiore each had theories.

It was my plan to cut the Gordian knot. Take the emperor, and to hell with theory.

I didn't think of any of that just then. I just ran up the ladder, got to the top and jumped down onto my second set of battlements, except this time, they were covered in snow and ice, and I fell, slid, and stopped.

But this time we were in.

The steps down from the inner keep wall led to a very small yard, and the closed door of the tower. I took in that door in a moment; looked at all the other levels.

One door.

Well, if I was going to hold the emperor in a tower, I'd want a tower with just one door, too.

The steps down were clogged with snow and ice, and in the end, I sat down and slid on my armoured arse to the small yard below, holding the back of my fauld between my legs like a man with a boy's sled between his legs. It did me well enough, and then I got up the steps of the tower, with Fiore right by me and Cavalli and two Bretons just behind them.

There was no longer time to think, or plan. But I did turn my head enough to catch Fiore's eye.

We might have been terrified of the attack, or perhaps we might have been full of the importance of our mission, but Fiore shot me a look of pure *joy*. Some men gamble, or race horses.

My friends fought. I winked.

I pulled the door and it didn't open. I pushed it – of course it didn't push open.

But when I took pressure off it, someone inside began to push it towards me.

Fiore caught the edge and wrenched it open, and I killed the man who'd opened the door for us; he was in maille, and I hadn't time for mercy.

Sword in the eye. Step over the corpse, and head for the steps. John hadn't known anything about the layout of the tower. I was going on instinct.

I went *up*.

At the head of the steps, my sabatons gave me away, and a man loosed a small crossbow, like a hunting bow, down the curving steps, but he was too hasty and his bolt clattered around, hit my helmet and vanished below. I got up the next three steps on will alone, and there was one of the pie-faced Slavs in a fine leather doublet. He had a short, heavy sword in his hand, and no armour, and he was full of wine, and he still managed to delay me through two parries. I caught my sword edge on his, rotated past his cover on sheer ferocity, and snapped his head back with my pommel. I threw him over my left foot and pinned him to the floorboards with my sword's point while raising my head.

Fiore passed me, with Orsini at his heels and Bill Vane behind him and Marc-Antonio last.

There were two doors out of the tower's guardroom, as it appeared to me.

The leftmost door opened, and Vane put a shaft through the opening, and then, as quick as I can say it, he put another *through* the door. The dying man fell forward, because of the drag of the arrows caught in the pine, and the door fell open. A crossbow bolt killed Vane where he stood, pitching him back into Orsini, and Marc-Antonio went into the open door, with Fiore behind him.

I got the right hand door open. It was a small room with fine furnishings and an icon of the Virgin on the near wall, and standing on the other side of a bed with hangings was a tall, handsome man with a dark beard.

I saluted with my sword. 'Highness?' I asked, in Greek. 'Rescue.' In Greek and Latin.

The flash of a smile was all the recognition I needed, and I turned my back on the emperor and back to the guardroom.

Luck, and ferocity, had got me between the Hungarian and his prey.

'Get him out!' I called to Cavalli and Orsini. 'With your lives!' I said, and then I ran for the first door, jumped the cooling corpse, and went through the door in time to see ...

Marc-Antonio, making a one-handed cover against the Hungarian, and Fiore lying in a pool of blood, a crossbow bolt in his chest through his left bicep and his harness. Marc-Antonio was already wounded, his left arm limp at his side.

He made the cover. He had Fiore under him, and he would not retreat.

I threw my sword. No sword is worth more than your best friend, and I told you – throwing your sword is what you do when you are desperate. Marc-Antonio didn't have another parry in him; even as I threw, he fell to one knee atop Fiore, who lay as if dead.

The Hungarian moved to cover my throw, and I saw the fourth man in the room; he was using a belt to cock his crossbow. I should have known – Fiore had been shot by someone.

Fiore made us practise throwing swords – did I say that? I could throw mine like Jove's thunderbolt.

Still, the Hungarian was a great swordsman; he was in a low *garde* and he snapped his sword up to cover the thrown weapon. Marc-Antonio thought it was an attack and his sword came out, feeble but in time, and tapped against the Hungarian's rising cut, slowing it, but the Hungarian was *so fast* that he got the blade up and covered most of the weapon.

Bad luck, fortuna, fate, or God's will caused the sword to rotate on the parry and the quillons to slash his face.

I was still moving. From the moment I threw, I was going for Fiore's right hand – extended in falling, slightly open, with a sword hilt still in it. Marc-Antonio, still game, fell forward and went for the Hungarian's feet, making the man skip back. He cut at Marc-Antonio but geometry was against him, and his sword merely put a dent into Marc-Antonio's backplate.

I ignored him, scooped Fiore's sword out of his extended hand, and killed the crossbowman with a straight thrust into the middle of the head. His loaded bow discharged into my right foot; a lance of pain shot up my leg. I rotated, the stable turn Fiore taught, removing my point from the dead crossbowman and turning to face the Hungarian on my good left leg. An odd thing – the crossbow bolt broke my foot under my sabaton. Aside from the initial pain, I never felt it until the fight was over.

Marc-Antonio had the Hungarian by one ankle.

Makkrow kicked him. He raised his sword at me. 'I have something you want,' he said.

But the death of the crossbowman changed the balance of terror.

My blade was in the *garde* the Order calls 'the long tail,' way out behind me, dragged there by the dying crossbowman as he fell off the point.

The Hungarian snapped another kick into Marc-Antonio's face, breaking his nose and two teeth.

Marc-Antonio hung on.

I snapped a rising *mezzano* cut at the Hungarian's head. He wasn't in armour and I was, and I didn't need to be as good as he was. All I had to do was get close.

He parried, but his parry brought us close, and he could still only move one foot.

I let his parry push wide, and he accepted and pushed his blade right into my face …

A superb blow …

Against a man without armour. His point scraped across my visor and failed to go in my eye slit.

He was so fast that even after he realised that he had wasted his blow, he got his point back to cover my thrust to his face. I could smell his breath.

I had my sword at the half blade then, and I pried his point aside, cutting his hands. He couldn't move his left foot. He had a long time to know what was coming, and he was very strong.

'Fuck you,' he said, at least twice. 'I'll kill you all.'

I let my sword slide through my left hand just a little, cutting myself in the process, again; his head snapped aside to avoid getting my point in his face, and that wrecked his balance. Suddenly my left wrist was at his throat, my sword a bar of iron to help my throw, and I turned and threw him so hard that I heard his knee joint break, because Marc-Antonio *still* had his leg.

And then he lay at my feet. His left leg was badly broken and my gauntlet had flayed his face.

He screamed.

'William!' Nerio called.

'Here!' I roared.

Nerio came in with Stapleton behind him.

'Fiore's on the floor,' I said. 'Save him. Marc-Antonio …'

'You …!' spat the Hungarian. 'You …'

I got my foot on the Hungarian's sword hand and I stepped with all my weight.

'You can't kill me,' he said grimly. 'I'm worth far more alive. Do you know what Geneva's done, William Gold? I know …'

Two of our Gascons lifted Fiore and he groaned.

Nerio tilted Marc-Antonio's head back. My squire was still alive, although he looked like a revenant with the front of his face removed.

Nerio had slung his heavy winter cloak; the guardroom had spears, and he and Stapleton began to make a little stretcher.

'You have the emperor?' I asked.

Nerio kept wrapping.

Stapleton nodded. 'Already out,' he said.

'Visconti?' I asked.

The Hungarian twitched.

'We will kill everyone you know, and your stupid English prince,' the Hungarian said.

Nerio looked up from folding the cloak. 'What did I tell you?' he snapped, and for a moment he was that very dark man that I could almost fear. He looked at me.

I shook my head.

'You can't kill me!' the Hungarian said with satisfaction. 'I know everything.'

Those were his last words. John the Kipchak is right – there is a place where there is no longer room for mercy. I killed him, as I had not killed the Comte d'Herblay.

Perhaps I should not have killed him. Perhaps he really did know all the terrible things that awaited us. The words 'English prince' certainly resonated for years.

I have never lost an instant's sleep on the subject, my friends.

Nor did I forget to collect the sword I'd thrown. Or to find young Visconti, either.

But if getting in was relatively easy, we still had to get out. Fiore was down, maybe dead; I was not leaving him. Marc-Antonio had, in my estimation, just won his spurs, for all he had half the skin of his face hanging in shreds and several wounds.

'The hall?' I asked Nerio. He was opening every casket and case in the room where the Hungarian lay dying.

'I left it to Master Stone,' Nerio said.

I ran back down the stairs, my foot just beginning to hurt me. Men were looting the tower, which was fine with me. Except that we were leaving.

'Rally!' I roared. I was out of the door and hobbling across the icy ground. I didn't fall, mostly because the edges of my sabatons bit into the snow like the iron ice-creepers my horrible uncle used to wear in winter in London.

The Welsh Davids, who were as responsible a pair of men as I've ever known, had taken the gate of the inner bailey, and instead of looting, they were standing by the gate with lit torches – another Christmas Miracle. With them at my heels, I went out into the main courtyard, where the best men of my *compagnia* were slaughtering the garrison. I could make this sound more knightly if I suggested that it was a desperate struggle, a fair fight, but we'd taken them completely by surprise on Christmas night, and all I can say is that they were brave. They had no armour and most were drunk.

Just as I came into the outer yard, however, a gate opened and more of them poured in; I assume they were the town garrison, alarmed by the fighting.

They came charging in the main gate, which their friends opened for them.

It began to look as if we could not hold the outer bailey. The archers were running low on shafts, and they were forming a good line with swords and bucklers, shuffling back to the gateway, to the ramp up to the inner bailey. The newcomers followed, pushing us back. It was dark, but not dark enough – the light from the hall reflected on the snow. Men in polished armour reflect light in an odd way, so that they can appear to be wraiths in darkness.

My foot had begun to throb.

Then the men who had stormed the tower came at our backs, with the emperor and the wounded. Suddenly we had a dozen fully armoured men. Stapleton gave a shout I didn't know he had, and we were at them, knights in front and archers pressing in behind, and the Bulgarians broke.

That should have been the end, but some idiot had left the main gate open after letting in the town garrison, and so, naturally, John and his Kipchaks came in the gate and began to shoot down any Bulgarian they saw in the yard.

We had the emperor. Nerio had Visconti, who had someone's spare arming sword in his fist and looked like he wanted to kill every man in Bulgaria. The gate was open, and the postern – if we'd wanted, we could have owned the whole castle for the winter; the archers and the Kipchaks were minded to massacre the survivors.

I wasn't. I had what I'd come for. There was no reason for further killing, and Miles Stapleton and I hobbled around the courtyard and demanded our people stop killing.

But all the bells in the town were ringing, and in the next town, audible across the snow. The emperor was probably the most valuable hostage ever taken; I had to assume there would be pursuit.

We took the emperor out of the postern, where John was waiting with a dozen more horsemen and twenty spare horses. This was the most expensive part of the raid, but bless John, he'd stolen most of them; expensive because we only rode back to where we'd left the sheep, and the ship. We left the forty horses for the local peasants or the garrison's survivors, bowed to the emperor of Rome in a sheep byre at the break of Christmas Day, and hunkered down to await our ship.

And then our luck deserted us.

The ship was gone. We had men climb trees, and John rode all the way out the peninsula, and we could not find our ship.

The sky began to grow light; a pretty, salmon pink crept up the eastern sky.

We'd taken a pair of servants who claimed to be with the emperor, and they approached Stapleton with demands for the emperor's comfort. I put him in the sheep byre with the shepherds.

After I set my pickets and sent a strong patrol under Fiore down our back-trail towards the fortress, I went and made my best bow. Up until then I had not spoken to him.

He smiled. 'Is there wine?' he asked, mildly enough for an emperor.

I sent Achille, Nerio's squire, to Ewan, and wine appeared. Some men are natural looters, always capable of finding the right thing; Ewan produced hot hippocras, perhaps the most delicious ambrosia in the history of winter warfare.

The emperor drank his hot wine and then, quite spontaneously, offered me his hand.

'Who sent you, sir knight?' he asked. 'My cousin of Savoy? We heard much of his approach.'

'Your lady wife, Highness,' I said.

He nodded. 'I knew my wife and son would see to me,' he said. 'I will see you richly rewarded.'

I bowed.

He was a very dignified man, and he spoke very little. He may

421

have said other things to me. I do remember that later, as the pink sky became a heavy, rain-swept day with too much wind, he told me a little about his captivity, which had alternated between guest-like comfort and dire confinement.

He also told me that the Hungarian had only taken over the duties of imperial gaoler in the last month or so; before that, there had been a pair of Bulgarian boyars, but they had gone off to serve in the army. But although His Highness knew a little of the Hungarian, yet the man had kept his distance, and the emperor had hardly ever seen him. To me, this was a sign that the Hungarian planned to kill him; you don't get to know a man you have to kill, unless you are a monster. Of course, to me, the Hungarian *was* a monster, but even monsters have limits.

I didn't spend too much time with the emperor. I saw to Fiore; all we could do was keep him warm. He was in shock, his pupils were pinpoints and his arm continued to weep blood.

'Bolt has to come out,' Rob said.

Stapleton came back with no news, and I sent Nerio immediately with another. It was full daylight now, and my beautiful plan was a smoking ruin.

So we cut the head off the bolt's shaft as carefully as we could and took it out. If that changed anything I didn't see it; there was more blood. And then less blood.

Nerio came back before mid-morning. 'There're men on the roads,' he said. 'Luckily the rain is covering tracks, but it's just a matter of time. There's already hundreds of them.'

I am not much of a sailor, but I had a notion that the stiff east wind was the cause of our troubles. I knew that I ought to move my people down the peninsula to the end, where we could hold out another day or two, but we had fires, most men were warm, and Fiore was dying.

I stayed by his side and sent Syr Giannis out with another patrol, and then John and his horsemen.

By that time, I had half my people cutting firewood in the rain, just to keep them moving. If we were taken, I suspected they'd kill the lot of us; my bold plan looked foolish.

Damn the boat.

John came back while the town bells tolled for Nones off to the east. The rain was turning to snow, and the temperature was dropping. He showed me a bow which had burst.

'They saw us,' he said, with a shrug of apology. 'We killed a few. Listen. Give me emperor. I take him far, fast.'

I thought he was right. But John would have to thread through the whole kingdom of Bulgaria with the most wanted man in Christendom on his saddlebow. I didn't like it.

Perhaps a cold winter's day in Bulgaria doesn't sound to you like the epitome of chivalry, but it was my proving ground. As the sun rose higher in the cold heavens behind a towering wall of cloud, I had to keep my people moving. They were exhausted; we had no food and little water and insufficient firewood.

So I moved around a great deal, talking, slapping backs, or just listening. Everyone was afraid. By the risen Saviour, I was afraid. I was afraid I'd bungled the whole thing; I could see the next act – a halter around my neck, approaching some ruthless boyar, asking for mercy for my people, most of whom had killed far too many Bulgarians in the fire-lit darkness of the night before.

But I set myself to be the confident knight; I told them that the east wind was keeping our galley offshore, probably just off the delta of the Danube, and that we'd be warm and dry in two days.

It's odd that two days can seem like nothing when you are on leave or holiday, and an eternity when you are waiting in the freezing rain for a rescue.

Afternoon came. Fiore was still alive; he had half our blankets piled on him. He was not a 'popular' man, but he was a man who'd saved a lot of lives. We had a dozen other wounded men, and we pushed them into the back of the byre with the sheep dung and the emperor, and kept them as warm and dry as we could manage.

At mid-afternoon, I took a patrol up the ridge towards the castle. I was out of people to send. Nerio had dark smudges under his eyes and Stapleton was asleep in the byre. There were four big fires going and the piles of wood were no longer growing; no firewood collection was going to happen unless I led it in person.

We went up the ridge.

On the other side, we avoided the swamp we'd stumbled into less than a day ago. My dozen archers were cursing me by then – the only men who weren't by a fire. But when we found the road, we saw an *army*. There must have been a thousand men clumped up on the road and there were big fires under the trees.

'Good Christ,' muttered Ewan.

We moved along their column, watching them. There were a dozen different bands, and I couldn't understand a word they were saying, but they were not patrolling, and they were not coming over the ridge.

We slunk away without a fight, but I had been reminded of something important – the enemy thinks you are ten feet tall, too. They didn't want to find us.

Back in camp, John begged me to give him the emperor. 'No soldier in hundred miles take us,' he said.

I looked at the emperor, sitting quietly between his two servants in the byre. Tall, ascetic, handsome. 'He can't live in the snow for two weeks,' I said.

John shrugged.

John took his horsemen out again. He disobeyed me and shot up the horse herd of the men on the road over the ridge.

Naturally, this spurred the enemy into action.

But by then, the short winter day was over and darkness was falling. I got forty men moving up the ridge, and we dropped some arrows on our adversaries as they toiled up the ridge past the swamp, and they turned around and went back to the road. It wasn't a fight – I doubt a single man died; our bowstrings were wet. I say 'our', because I was there with a looted crossbow, shooting bolts that mostly struck trees.

I couldn't leave a picket on the ridge, though. It was too wet and too cold, and they would easily be cut off and massacred.

So I brought everyone back, and in the very last light, we cut firewood. We found two fallen oaks, and we dulled our axes cutting them, and then one of our shepherds saved all our lives by producing a big, heavy saw.

Darkness fell on the sound of a few archers and two men-at-arms sawing away with a clumsy, dull saw meant for two men. We were so tired that we used four. Out in the darkness, there were pops and cracks like ice breaking up on the Thames. The Kipchaks didn't use the saw, but merely picked up dead branches and used the crotches in living trees to break them up into arm-length pieces, and our fires grew. A man produced a whole sausage and sold it for an ivory reliquary. Men gambled by firelight for jewels. I had a notion that some of the richest items were the emperor's, and I said nothing.

Sometime late in the night, John and I went and walked all the way up the ridge. We could see the enemy fires in the next valley, a mile away, even through the trees, which was eerie.

Then we went back down to our camp. I didn't go to sleep. I couldn't. I sat with Fiore and Marc-Antonio. At one point I held Fiore's hand.

At another point I thought he was dead.

Ewan boiled water in his copper canteen and brought me hot water, which I fed to Marc-Antonio. I dribbled a little hot water into Fiore.

I thought of all my many sins, and everything I'd done wrong. If we'd ridden south the moment we had the emperor …

Eventually the army in the next valley would scout us, find how few we were, and come.

About an hour before dawn, I hunkered down by Nerio.

'I am considering riding in and surrendering,' I said.

'To save Fiore?' Nerio asked.

I shrugged. 'Yes.'

He nodded. 'Yes,' he said slowly. 'If they do not kill us all out of hand, it is the best plan.' He shrugged. 'Christ, I am cold,' he said.

We were silent for a while. Then he said, 'If I am taken, they will ransom me high.'

I had to agree. 'Even if the Hungarian is dead,' I muttered.

Nerio grunted. 'They will kill the emperor. They all want him gone – have you seen this? If he was not the count's cousin, he'd already be dead. They are all fools, the King of Hungary included – when the Romans are gone, the Turks will turn on Europe like the wolves they are. Your Prince Gatelussi is right.'

I couldn't really follow him; he was tired, and the words ran out of him.

I shrugged. 'Perhaps they will not kill us,' I said.

Nerio smiled his wicked smile in the firelight. 'Given what we have proven we can do,' he said with a grim smile, 'they'd be fools not to kill us.'

'The Bulgarians may not even know who we are.' I looked at the fire.

'The King of Hungary's men are there,' Nerio said.

We let that hang there in the darkness, and then the slight brush of pink began to colour the horizon.

I rose. Everything was stiff, and my feet were soaking wet, and I was so tired that I was *angry* that I could not sleep. But I was damned if I was ready to surrender. I checked on Fiore, and there was life in him yet.

'Getting more sleep than we are,' was Nerio's judgement.

I took Miles and Rob and went out into the dawn. One more time I forced my steel-harnessed legs up the damned hill above the byre. Up and up. I passed little landmarks I'd memorised in the darkness; they were ludicrously close together in daylight.

We crossed the ridgeline before dawn, and looked down into the valley. I could smell their food. My stomach rumbled.

Miles Stapleton laughed.

I turned and he was standing behind me, looking the other way, back towards our camp. The leaves, as I have said, were gone fromt he trees, and you could see, in a hazy way, quite a distance.

Out, past our camp, past the rising smoke that meant we'd be discovered the moment the enemy got one man to the top of this ridge. Past the pyre, past the scrubby trees ...

Into the estuary, where a galley flying the Gatelussi colours was rowing with laboured strokes up our arm of the delta, maybe a mile away.

We watched until there could be no doubt – until we lost the galley's mainmast in the trees.

And then we forgot fatigue and ran back down the ridge to camp.

An hour later we were freezing cold on the catwalk of the heavy galley – ninety damp, cold men huddled like sheep in a biting wind that was driving us out to sea.

But we had the emperor, and Fiore was alive.

Fiore almost died. Indeed, he was months recovering, even though the bolt barely scratched his side. The arm wound was terrible, and turned septic. As you will hear, if you stay another night.

Marc-Antonio's looks were not improved, but he began to recover in a day.

Regardless, we had the emperor. We left forty horses for the local peasants or the garrison's survivors; no great loss. In the end, we had six dead. We delivered the emperor into the hands of his own officers, and the Count of Savoy's, on the first day of January. The weather was dark; there was snow falling, and we were chilled to the bone. No, that doesn't do justice to our level of cold. It makes me cold just to describe it.

The count didn't come down to meet me, or to congratulate us. He and Richard Musard had been shooting crossbows for amusement, and the count went straight into the citadel of Sozopolis with his knights, to greet the emperor and welcome him.

Musard came out to meet me. I was still in the stables, having borrowed horses so that the emperor could ride into what was, after all, *his city*. I had on my new kaftan lined in wolf fur and I was still cold, and my broken foot was like a club tied to my leg.

Richard caught me almost alone. John the Kipchak was an important officer now, and never had time for my horse, and Marc-Antonio was recovering in our barracks with Fiore, surrounded by every brazier that we could afford to buy and feed with charcoal.

Almost alone – Nerio was waiting for me, twitting me for being such a ninny as to curry someone else's horse, while Miles Stapleton helped me.

'You got him,' Musard said.

'We did,' Miles said. He grinned in satisfaction. 'We really did.'

Richard shut the stall behind him. 'I wish I'd been with you,' he said. Then he gave me a wry grin, a look I hadn't seen from him in many year. 'He'll never thank you for it,' he said. 'In my count's creed, you just made him look bad. Again.'

But he had a tenth of a smile on his face.

'You could thank us, for him,' I said.

He laughed. 'I could,' he said, 'But I have to imagine that you have a more tangible reward in mind.'

Nerio had been cleaning his nails with a little tool and now he raised his eyes, and just for a moment, I saw the darkness there. 'Not really,' he said. 'Do you know your precious count is my debtor, and my cousin's, for thirty thousand ducats?'

Richard paused. 'Yes,' he admitted.

'So we don't really need much in the way of material rewards,' Nerio said quietly. 'But you keep insisting we do.'

Miles Stapleton surprised me a great deal. 'Which,' he said, with some intensity, 'might cause us offence.'

Richard nodded. Wisely, he was silent.

'I came here today,' I told Richard, 'To be quits with the count. I'm sorry he sent you. But I am taking my company and leaving. You might mention that we have Antonio di Visconti with us, as well. The count is not my paymaster, or my lord in this, and he declined my homage – I owe him nothing, and I can't say I'm any too fond of him. So please bid him a polite farewell. You might mention that my lady wife will be returning to her estates for a while this summer. I do not expect her to be molested. Indeed, I may accompany her to be sure.'

Richard might have spluttered, but he didn't. 'He's a great man, William,' he said. 'I'm sorry you have not seen him at his best.'

I shrugged. 'I served a great man, Richard. He was truly great, and he was always good to great and small alike.' I shrugged. 'Father Pierre Thomas is dead. I will not expect to find another this side of Heaven, so instead, I think I'll go back to Italy.'

Richard surprised me by embracing me. 'Wait an hour,' he said. 'Do not leave in anger.'

Oh, I was tempted. My foot hurt. But I thought of what my lady had said; that my greatest gift to her would be good relations with the count.

Nerio sneered.

But Miles put a hand on my shoulder. 'Don't be a fool, William,' he said in English.

So I cooled my heels in the count's cold antechamber while he entertained the emperor. Richard went in and out, with wine, with a document, with a pen case, and with a magnificent cloak lined in wolf hide. He smiled at me every time.

I did some praying. I find that when I'm tempted to pettiness, prayer is often the answer.

But I couldn't help thinking of the day I'd spent on my knees with the King of Cyprus.

However, after two hours, Richard came to the anteroom and summoned me. He bowed as if I have never met him and brought me by the hand into the count's borrowed hall.

There he sat in emerald magnificence. The emperor was already gone.

He looked up as I entered. 'I'm sorry, Sir William,' he said. 'I would have seen you sooner.' He didn't rise, or offer his hand, and I knelt. I wasn't going to, but I did.

He gave me his hand, and I clasped it.

'Stay,' he said. 'We have not seen eye to eye, Sir William. Sir Richard has even told me, with some force, that perhaps I owe you an apology.' He smiled, and for a moment I saw a more complex man than the green popinjay. 'Instead, you must settle for my thanks. You may have my thanks – my grateful thanks. For the rescue of the emperor – and my scapegrace cousin Visconti, and some other things.'

I probably smiled.

He nodded. 'I owe your friend Nerio a considerable sum of money. In turn, I need the emperor to pay some of the costs of my expedition, in order to pay Nerio. You understand me, sir?'

'Yes, Your Grace,' I said.

'The emperor has just engaged to cover my debts,' the count said. He looked out the window and shrugged. 'So you and your friends might be said to have saved me from ruin.'

I should have said something gracious, but all I could think of was the words *That's right, mate.*

The count nodded sharply, as if my silence confirmed something.

He reached for a rolled piece of parchment. Richard brought him a magnificent seal.

'This is a legal instrument proclaiming my approval of your marriage,' he said. 'I suspect it will be more valuable to you than anything I could give you.' He took my hand again. 'You are now my vassal for six estates, Sir William. Will you swear to me, putting your hands between mine?'

The wax hissed as the seal bit into it. I could smell the sealing wax. And Richard's smile was dazzling.

Odd. Instead of hating him, I was about to be his vassal. In truth, I could not afford to say no. That was the reality of being a small man in this world; even as a knight of some renown, I could not say 'no'.

The vassal of one of the greatest knights in Europe. A sort of unassailable position, if you like. I was already kneeling.

I swore.

He kissed me on both cheeks. 'Tell Emile that I think perhaps she chose wisely,' he said.

I went out, still unsure whether I'd been cozened or rewarded, and Richard embraced me.

As it turned out, it was good that he did – good that's the way I left him, that time.

'By the way,' I said, producing a scrap of parchment from my purse, 'Janet sends her best regards.'

He flushed. The red suffused his dark skin. He broke open the little note. I don't think he even noticed that it was sealed.

He walked away from me, paused under a narrow archer's window, held the scrap to the light, and read.

I knew more than a moment's qualm. I didn't know what was in it. I knew I'd written to her asking for a note for Richard; that seemed like a lifetime ago.

He shook his head violently, and then, after what must have been two readings, he folded it closed and slapped it against his thigh in irritation.

He glanced at me. Shook his head. 'Fuck,' he said.

I nodded. Hoping this was good.

In the end, we packed all our people into two ships and sailed for Lesvos. Anxious as Nerio was to try for his inheritance, winter is not a good time to ride abroad, even in Greece. And our company was too good to lose to disease; I had the money to keep them and I wanted to see the orange tree, and the woman who sat beneath it.

We touched for two days at Constantinople and Pera. I lost a few men to the fleshpots, but most chose to winter with me in the Aegean and campaign for Nerio, and gold, in the spring. With the promise of Hawkwood in the fall.

But I did have an audience in the Hall of Blacharnae, with the empress and the emperor. Fiore was too badly off to attend; Miles and Nerio came with me, and we knelt to the sovereign we'd rescued, me with my swollen foot like a ball and chain dragged behind me, and heard them tell us that they were bankrupt, and there was no treasure with which to reward us. Indeed, it proved that the emperor had had to promise money he didn't have to get the Green Count to release him, and hand over the port of Gallipoli and the citadel of Sozopolis.

But he did give us all titles; Nerio still uses his in his documents. I have used mine once or twice.

On the way down the steps of the palace, Nerio laughed, pulling on his best gloves.

'I do believe this Green Count is the greatest routier of all,' he said. 'And yet, it appears to me that there's to be no money from this *empris.*'

On the last day of January of thirteen hundred and sixty-seven, we sailed into the little harbour of Methymna, and landed our little army to great rejoicing, at least from three children, a woman grown, two religious sisters and a great many squawking gulls.

And Emile kissed me, although she was so pregnant she was nearly round, which, I'll add, I was clever enough not to mention. Nerio found himself company for the winter, and Fiore was almost immediately better for my wife's ministrations; we had hired one of Guy Albin's assistants with his permission and we had his exact instructions. Young Francesco Orsini went home to his father, willingly enough.

'I want to be a knight,' he said.

That made me smile. 'Soon enough,' I told him. Marc-Antonio was also ready to be a knight; I hoped that the prince would knight them both, in the spring. Then I settled into being a husband, a lord, and soon enough, a father.

We knew the good doctor Albin was looking for a new employer. I sent him a letter, and when he didn't come, we settled for a pair of Greek midwives for the birth of our daughter, Cressida – an event of pure joy, and a joy to me still, the lovely thing. Just fourteen this year; she may yet be taller than I am.

And in the excitement of the birthing, we lost the world outside. We were, instead, a family; we dined together, and Emile began to show me two things I have ever loved since – hawking, and fishing with a rod. She recovered from her birthing so fast I wondered at her, and we roamed about as spring came on, riding, or we'd sit and talk with Nerio and Fiore and Miles.

I was happy. Happiness seldom makes a tale, but there it is. My people were happy; Rob married the wiry lass from Constantinople, Katrina, and he had the whole company as witnesses.

You may think it odd that it took me weeks to remember the document that the Green Count gave me, but it did; we were well on into Lent when I found it in the leather bag where Marc-Antonio stowed my maille when it was clean. I laughed, and took it to my lady, and presented it to her on bended knee.

She began to read it, and Cressida played with the dangling green seal, her pudgy arms waving.

Then she leaned over and kissed me. It was a good long kiss, like her old kisses. I had just learned that the weeks after having a baby are not a woman's most amorous, and that kiss was worth the wait.

'You might have told me sooner,' she said. And my failure to remember the grant (which, I confess it, gave me powers over more land than I had ever imagined) led to a fair amount of mockery from Bernard and Jason and Jean-François, who were annoyingly mock-obsequious, insisting that I was their 'liege-lord' until I wanted to take my sword to them.

Nerio, I remember, was playing cards with his leman, a Greek girl. He looked at me for a moment while Jason, whose humour and loud voice had returned, mocked me. Then he smiled. 'By God, William,' he said. 'you may be richer than I am.'

The thought terrified me.

I took refuge in helping Fiore as he had helped me. He'd never had a bad wound; I saw him every day, and as soon as he was strong enough for food, I made him walk a little on the walls, and every day our walks grew longer, so that by Easter he could sit a horse. We rode across the island to the prince's court for Easter at Mytilene, and Fiore rode with us, as did all of John's Kipchaks, who made enough riot to be English.

John's Kipchaks were all the wonder at Mytilene, and they were all baptised at the great Feast of Easter, and then gave a show of trick riding and archery that I have never seen equalled. And the prince proclaimed a tournament for Ascension Day, to be held in his castle of Mytilene. Young Francesco beamed. I had a quiet word with the prince about Marc-Antonio.

Nerio shook his head. 'I may as well stay and see the young men knighted,' said my aged friend of twenty-five years. 'Indeed,' he said, 'until the Green Count pays me, I'm too poor to field an army to invade Achaea.'

'And we all like a tournament,' Miles said.

It was the word 'tournament' that sparked John's memory, so that after a magnificent Easter feast, he came to me looking troubled and produced a somewhat battered parchment with an Islamic seal.

It turned out that I was not the only man to forget a document.

'You recall,' he said in his vastly improved Italian, 'you sent me to scout before I go rescue the emperor.' He smiled. 'With you. Rescue with you.'

I shrugged. 'You did all the hard work,' I said.

He shrugged. 'Maybe,' he admitted. 'Got the tower wrong, though,' he said, and drank some wine. 'Anyway, you send me – sent me? Sent me scout the Turks.'

'Yes,' I agreed.

He nodded. 'And we steal emperor and everything. And then go the count. To count.' He shrugged. 'You know. Anyway, and regardless, yes? Many thing happen, and then other thing. But before rescue emperor. Before we *went* to meet you,' he said with pride, 'I meet Turk captain. Ottomanid Suleyman. He rides his border, so he says. But he said this was for us.' John looked rueful. 'For Count of Savoy, I am thinking.'

I read it. I had to get help from Prince Francesco's council, and from a Turkish merchant who came in after Easter with a cargo of saffron and hides, escorted for a fee by the prince's galleys. When I had the whole thing, I made a fair copy myself and took it to my lord, riding across the island on a brilliant spring day with a much-recovered Marc-Antonio, leaving Emile, as beautiful as the Queen of Heaven, playing with Cressida under the orange tree.

I knelt to present the document to the prince.

'It's an invitation to a tournament,' I said. 'Your Grace – a Turkish tournament under the walls of Didymoteichon.'

Didymoteichon was one of the cities the Ottomanids used to rule Greece. It was north of Constantinople, and well west into Thrace. A long way away, and yet, not so far, by ship.

The prince read it. 'Well, well,' he said. He looked at the translation. He nodded. 'On the road to Achaea, Renerio. Which reminds me that I have something for you, too.'

Nerio bowed his head.

'I think that the Ottomanids might make good friends for a prince of Achaea,' Gatelussi said. 'I think we should go. We'll have our tourney here, and then we'll visit this Suleyman. I usually take my fleet west in the late spring, just to show the world that the emperor has some teeth.'

The prince sat back in the sunlight, complained about his age, and then nodded at a servant who produced another parchment.

Nerio tore it open, and laughed aloud. He held it up – one single sheet of parchment that I could have covered with the palm of my hand, written very small.

'You see that,' he said. He pointed to the small seal; I knew it. It was the Genoese banker's seal. He laughed again. 'It doesn't look like much, but that is thirty thousand ducats.' He nodded to me. 'Captain Gold, we are in business.'

HISTORICAL NOTE

I am always delighted to return to the world of William Gold. Perhaps that's because this is what I did for my thesis, way back in my university days; perhaps it is because this is what I love to re-enact; perhaps because this world, the world of England, Italy and Outremer in the late fourteenth century, speaks to me in a way that only a few other epochs in history speak to me. All of history interests me, but I confess that William Gold's period seems especially vibrant and especially relevant.

Many of the characters in this series are historical personages, not creations of my pen, although I confess I've chosen to give them life in ways that are fictional. So William Gold himself is an historical character; he was one of Hawkwood's lieutenants, and he really was 'William the Cook'. We don't know a great deal about him, which is convenient for the historical fiction writer. We do know that he was knighted on the battlefield in front of Florence, and that he was one of the captains of Venice (possibly 'the captain') during the 'War of Chioggia', which will be the climactic event of this series and was one of the most important conflicts in Medieval history – certainly the most important war about which most people have never heard. To round out his character, I have given him a lifelong acquaintance with Geoffrey Chaucer, and I have suggested that his (fictional) self might be the basis for Chaucer's Knight in *The Canterbury Tales*.

Fiore Furlano di Liberi was also an historical personage. Fiore is known to us now as the great sword master of the fourteenth century, and author of some of the earliest treatises on fighting, both in and out of armour, with sword, spear, poleaxe and lance, on horse and foot, as well as wrestling and dagger fighting. The most accessible of his manuscripts is in the Getty Museum and is known as MS Ludwig XV 13. From his manuscripts we can understand the whole art of

Armizare, or knightly combat, in ways that had been completely lost. I practice Fiore's art every day. I owe the maestro a huge debt of gratitude.

Rainerio I Acciaioli, Duke of Athens and Corinth (Nerio) is also an historical figure. The cousin, nephew, or just possibly bastard son of the incredibly rich and powerful Florentine banker and knight (a fascinating combination) Niccolò Acciaioli, Nerio carved a magnificent dukedom out of the remnants of Frankish Greece, fought with and against the Turks, and led a life of adventure and warfare that deserves a set of novels of its own. He began from more modest origins; certainly he was always rich, but he virtually sprang from the head of Zeus onto the world stage when he took Corinth sometime between 1367 and 1371 (an event which will feature prominently in *Sword of Justice*). It is my suspicion that rumours of Nerio created the character of Theseus in Chaucer's 'The Knight's Tale'. His presence as one of Gold's friends is a novelistic attempt to explain how Chaucer might have gotten to know so much about Acciaioli and the Duchy of Athens.

Miles Stapleton, the last of Gold's close friends (of whom there are four, as a nod to Dumas and D'Artagnan, Athos, Porthos, and Aramis) is a fictional creation, but a representative one. Outremer was full of Englishmen in the late fourteenth century: there were Englishmen at Alexandria and a company of Englishmen is still remembered on Lesvos as serving the Gatelussi princess. The real-life Miles Stapleton was a generation older and died at Auray in 1364. Our character is (fictionally) his nephew and inheritor, while also being related to Lord Grey. Grey and Scrope and a number of other named Englishmen served at Alexandria and were later acquaintances and friends of Chaucer and Gower at the court of Richard II.

The principle events of *The Green Count* are historical. A party of knights including Englishmen did receive a pass to visit Jerusalem in the chaos after the fall of Alexandria; the Kingdom of Christian Armenia (Cilician Armenia) really did exist, as did the competing Turkish Sultanates, of which only the Ottoman Sultanate survived. Both Prince Francesco Gatelussi of Lesvos, former Genoese pirate and in-law of the emperor John V, and Amadeus, the Green Count of Savoy and also a relative of the Emperor, were real men; I have done my best to be faithful to what is known of them. I have been a little rough on the Green Count; perhaps in *Sword of Justice* the reader will see some evolution in his character, but it remains true that, like many modern politicians, leaders of the fourteenth century were often utterly confused by the realities of Middle Eastern politics, at least at first. But the character of the Green Count's 'crusade', as well as the events surrounding the capture and release of the Emperor of Byzantium, are historical, although still debated, and the impression that the internecine politics of the Papacy, the Emperor of Byzantium, the Holy Roman Emperor, the Ottomans, the Karamanids, the Mamluks, the Venetians, the Genoese, the Milanese, the Florentines, the English and the French all loosely tied into a single international bundle of confusion, woe, war and diplomacy is, at its base, accurate.

I could never have attempted a subject this complex without reading some great scholarship. One man stands above all others in this field, the historian Kenneth Setton, without whose books there would be no William Gold. Setton's magisterial, remarkable, superb work *The Papacy and the Levant* gives almost painless access to the translations of the Papacy concerning all of the crusades and with matters of trade and politics throughout the Latin East.

Almost as vital to my novels as Professor Setton is Professor William Caferro, whose invaluable work *John Hawkwood: An English Mercenary in Fourteenth-Century Italy* remains, to me, the single best primer on the life of Hawkwood, his world, and the finances and politics thereof.

Beyond the bare bones of history it is essential to understand, when examining this world of stark contrasts and incredible passions, that people believed very strongly in ideas – like Islam, like Christianity, like chivalry. Piety – the devotional practice of Christianity – was such an essential part of life that even most 'atheists' practised all the forms of Christianity. Yet there were many flavours of belief. Theology had just passed one of its most important milestones with the works of Thomas Aquinas, but Roman Christianity had so many varieties of practice that it would require the birth of Protestantism and then the Counter-Reformation to establish orthodoxy. I mention all this to say that to describe the fourteenth century without reference to religion would be completely ahistorical. I make no judgement on their beliefs – I merely try to represent them accurately. I confess that I assume that any professional soldier – like Sabraham or Gold – must have developed some knowledge of and respect for their opponents. I see signs of this throughout the work of the Hospitallers – but that may be my modern multiculturalism.

The same care should be paid to all judgements on the past, especially facile judgements about chivalry. It is easy for the modern amoralist to sneer – the Black Prince massacred innocents and burned towns, Henry V ordered prisoners butchered. The period is decorated with hundreds, if not thousands, of moments where the chivalric warriors fell from grace and behaved like monsters. I loveth chivalry, warts and all, and it is my take – and, I think, a considered one – that in chivalry we find the birth of the modern codes of war and of military justice, and that merely to state piously that 'war is hell' and that 'sometimes good men do bad things' is rubbish. War needs rules. Brutality needs limits. These were not amateur enthusiasts, conscripts, or draftees. They were full-time professionals who made for themselves a set of rules so that they could function – in and out of violence – as human beings. If the code of chivalry was abused – well, so are concepts like liberty and democracy abused. Cynicism is easy. Practice of the discipline of chivalry when your own life is in imminent threat is nothing less than heroic – it required then and still requires discipline and moral judgment, confidence in warrior skills and a strong desire to ameliorate the effects of war. I suspect that in addition to helping to control violence (and helping to promote it – a double-edged sword) the code and its reception in society did a great deal to soften the effects of PTSD. My reading of the current scholarship suggests that, on balance, the practice of chivalry may have done more to promote violence than to quell it – but I've always felt that this is a massively ill-considered point of view – as if to suggest that the practice of democracy has been bad for peace based on the casualty rates of the twentieth century.

May I add – as a practitioner – that we as a society have chosen to ignore the reality of violence, and the hellish effect on soldiers and cops – and we have done so with such damning effectiveness that we have left them without any code beyond a clannish self-protection. Chivalry should not be a thing of the past. Chivalry is an ethic needed by every pilot, every drone controller, every beat cop and every SWAT team officer, every clandestine operator, every SpecOps professional. I often hear people say that such and such act of terror or crime justifies this or that atrocity. 'Time to take off the gloves.'

Rubbish. If you take off the gloves, *that's who you are*. Whether you do it with your rondel dagger or your LGB (Laser Guided Bomb) or your night stick. There need to be rules, and the men and women facing fire need to have some.

A word about the martial arts of the period. The world sees knights as illiterate thugs swinging heavy weapons and wearing hundreds of pounds of armour. In fact, the professionals wore armour that fitted the individual like a tailored steel suit, with weight evenly distributed over the body. We have several manuals of arms from this period, the most famous of which is by a character in this series – Fiore di Liberi. The techniques are brutal, elegant and effective. They also pre-date any clear, unambiguous martial manual from the East, and are directly tied to combat, not remote reflections of it. I recommend their study, and the whole of Fiore's MS in the Getty collection is available for your inspection at http://wiktenauer.com/wiki/Fior_di_Battaglia_MS_Ludwig_XV_13. If you'd like to learn more, I recommend the International Armizare Society http://www.armizare.org/.

AUTHOR'S NOTE

My greatest thanks still have to go, first and foremost, to Richard W. Kaeuper of the University of Rochester. The finest professor I ever had – the most passionate, the most clear, the most brilliant – Dr Kaeuper's works on chivalry and the role of violence in society makes him, I think, the pre-eminent medievalist working today, and I have been lucky to be able to get his opinions and the wealth of his know-ledge on many subjects, great and small. Where I have gone astray, the fault is all mine. To Professor Kaeuper's work I must add the works of Professor Steven Muhlberger on chivalry and the minutiae of the joust and tournament, as well as the ethics of chivalry themselves. Several hours of conversations with Steve have not only been delightful but helped me with some of the themes of this book.

Not far behind these two, I need to thank Guy Windsor, who introduced me to the Armizare of Fiore di Liberi and profoundly informed my notions of what late-Medieval warfare was like among the skilled. I'd also like to thank the other two masters with whom I've studied and trained this last year – Sean Hayes of the Northwest Fencing Academy and Greg Mele of the Chicago Swordplay Guild. To these three modern masters this book is dedicated. I'd also like to thank all the people with whom I train and spar – the *Compagnia* mentioned below. Re-enacting the Middle Ages has many faces, and immersion in that world may not ever be a perfectly authentic experi-ence, but inasmuch as I have gotten 'right' – the clothes, the armour, the food or the weapons – it is due to all my re-enacting friends, including Tasha Kelly (of La Cotte Simple, a superb web resource) Chris Verwijmeren, master archer, and Leo Todeschini, JT Pälikkö, Jiri Klepac and Aurora Simmons, master craftspeople. I cannot imagine writing these books without all the help I have received on material culture, and I'm going to add more craftspeople – all worth looking up – Francesca Baldassari and Davide Giuriussini of Italy, and Karl Robinson of England.

Throughout the writing of this series I have used (and will continue to use), as my standard reference to names, dates and events, the works of Jonathan Sumption, whose books are, I think, the best unbiased summation of the causes, events, and consequences of the Hundred Years' War. I've never met him, but I'd like to offer him my thanks by suggesting that anyone who wants to follow the real events should buy Sumption's books!

As Dick Kaeuper once suggested in a seminar, there would have been no Middle Ages as we know them without two things – the horse and Christianity. I owe my horsemanship skills largely to two people – Ridgely and Georgine Davis of Pennsylvania, both of whom are endlessly patient with teaching and with horseflesh in getting me to understand even the basics of mounted combat. And for my understanding of the church, I'd like first to thank all the theologians I know – I'm virtually surrounded by people with degrees in theology – and second, the work of F. C. Copleston, whose work *A History of Medieval Philosophy* was essential to my writing and understanding the period – as essential, in fact, as the writings of Chaucer, Gower, Boccaccio and Dante.

My sister-in-law, Nancy Watt, provided early comments, criticism, and copy-editing while I worked my way through the historical problems – and she worked her way through lung cancer. I value her commitment extremely. As this is her favourite of my series, I've done my best for her. I'm pleased to say that after five years, she is still alive and reading – and working.

And finally, I'd like to thank my friends who support my odd passions, and my wife and child, who are tolerant, mocking, justly puzzled, delighted, and gracious by turns as I drag them from battlefield to castle and as we sew like fiends for a tournament in Italy.

Three years ago, we formed the 'Compagnia della Rosa nel Sole' and we now have 120 members to recreate a company like John Hawkwood's that fought in Italy in the late fourteenth century. Our company has given me (already) an immense amount of material and I thank every member. We're always recruiting. Interested? Contact us at www.boarstooth.net.

William Gold is, I think, my favorite character. I hope you like him.
He has a long way to go.

Christian Cameron
Toronto, 2017

William Gold's adventures continue in

SWORD OF JUSTICE

1367: Europe stands on the brink of total war.

Political alliances are beginning to rupture. No state is immune: England, France, the Holy Roman Empire, Milan, Genoa, Venice, Constantinople . . . Every mercenary knight for hundreds of miles must sharpen his sword and prepare for battle.

But Sir William Gold has other problems. Just to reach Europe, he must capture its most unassailable fortress. He must also protect his liege-lord, the Green Count, from assassins hell-bent on his demise.

The balance of power in the West will change. William Gold must trust to hope, and his men, that he lands on the winning side . . .

Turn over for an extract from the next novel . . .

Available from Orion Books from July 2018

ORION

There I was with an arming sword in my hand, and I was desperately outmatched. A trickle of blood running down my right bicep, my old arming coat cut through all eight layers of linen, and sweat blinding my eyes.

I made a bad, hasty parry, but at least I wasn't deceived by my opponent's devilish deception. From the cross, I pushed, eager to use my size and strength against the little bastard, but he was away like a greased pig. He evaded my winding cut at the face with a wriggle and we were both past, turning, swords back into *gardes*; he in 'the boar's tooth' and me with my sword high ...

He raised his sword, a clear provocation, given he was so damnably fast.

I shook my head to clear the sweat. Backed a step in unfeigned fear.

He glided forward, perfectly controlled. I dropped my sword hesitantly into a point forward *garde*; I couldn't allow his point so close to my heart ...

And then, out of my hesitation, I attacked. My wrist moved; my blade struck his a sharp blow. And I snapped the blade up into a high thrust, right at his face.

He had to parry. And he had to parry high.

I rolled my right wrist off that parry, rotating my heavy arming sword through almost a full circle, from the high cross all the way around, my thumb flat against the blade for control, and my blade just barely outraced his desperate parry to tag him under the arm, where no one has a good defence.

He burst into peals of laughter, spun away with my sword tucked under his arm, and sprawled to the ground in a pantomime of death. My son Edouard flung himself on the prostrate Fiore and pretended to shower him with dagger blows.

Fiore was laughing. 'I just taught you that!' he roared.

And he had. Just the day before.

It was a glorious spring of training, and we were all on the island of Lesvos, in Outremer. In the year of our Lord one thousand, three hundred and sixty-seven, I had reached the end of my desire to go on crusade. I'd be too strong to say I was sick of the whole thing; that came later. But I doubted the very basis of the idea. It was clear to me that the Infidel were neither so very bad, nor so easy to convert. I had, I fear, spent too much time with Sabraham; I began to see the wisdom in the Venetians and the Genoese, who traded with them every day and seemed to know a great deal more about the Infidel than anyone in Avignon or Rome or Paris.

Spring in Outremer is as magnificent as spring in England. Lesvos is the most beautiful of the Greek islands, with magnificent contrasts; steep, waterless valleys like the Holy Land – which is close enough, for all love – and then lush greenery and magnificent fields of flowers, hillsides like a Venetian miniature, roses. Gracious God, it was beautiful. And as Emile recovered from pregnancy, having given us Blanche, we wandered the fields of my new lordship, and we were like sweethearts. The only cloud in the sky was that Sir Miles Stapleton, one of my closest companions, was recalled to England to marry and take up his uncle's lands. His uncle of the same name had been killed at Auray, in '64. We threw him an excellent revel; before he left, we all wrote letters and I sent Hawkwood a long one, as well as another for Messire Petrarcha in Venice and Marc Antonio added a long one for his family. Finally, I wrote a long letter of eight or ten pages to my sister; some of it in the Latin I had laboured too hard to master with Sister Maria. I sent her some saffron and some ambergris and a few other drugs and spices in a packet, and I sent her a bolt of silk.

Losing Miles was hard. The four of us; Miles and Nerio, me and Fiore, had been together a long time. And we had seen a great deal: we'd lost Juan, we'd been to Jerusalem. I knew when Miles left that soon I'd lose Nerio, and eventually, Fiore. On the other hand ...

I had Emile. My life with her remained as fine as a dream.

After Miles left for Venice in February, I was training hard for the Prince of Lesvos's tournament at Mytilene, which was to be given on Ascension Day. Actually, our entire little company was training:

Nerio, my good friend and one of the richest men in the Inner Sea, was hiring us to defend his holdings in Achaea. That is to say, to defend them by conquering them. He did a little training – if by training you mean being fitted for new armour he was having made in far-off Bohemia – while parading around with his magnificently beautiful Greek mistress. Occasionally he deigned to cross swords or lances with my friend Fiore, who was in many ways his foil: poor when Nerio was rich, devoted to training where Nerio was lazy to the point of indolence, chaste where Nerio's pursuit of women had something unhealthy about it. They quarrelled constantly, yet they were the quarrels of an old married couple, and each knew full well how to land a blow on the other, in conversation or in combat. Indeed, it had become impossible for me to touch Fiore on foot, and hard for me to shake his seat on horseback, but Nerio, who to be fair I could strike almost at will with sword or spear afoot, seemed to trouble Fiore a good deal.

At any rate, training for a great tournament is a fine way to pass a spring, in between dalliances with one's lady and playing with children in a pleasant, airy house full of good food and laughter and one's best friends.

It doesn't make much of a tale, though. I remember a perfect, golden sun, not too hot, not too cold. I remember making love with my wife under our lemon tree, giggling lest we be caught by our servants. I remember swaggering swords with Fiore in our courtyard, and jousting with Nerio, day after day.

One of my favorite memories is that of watching Fiore with a wooden waster in his hand, haranguing all of our knights and men-at-arms and a few others – two local Frankish-Greek boys and half a dozen of the Prince's men-at-arms – who had all come to our School of Mars. Or Ares, as the Greeks would say.

He had just effortlessly dispatched three good knights, allowing each just one blow. They made a little line and came at him; one swung a great blow, one thrust, and the third, rather remarkably, threw his sword.

Fiore just laughed. To each blow he responded by a rising cut from a low, left-hand *garde*, the *garde* he called 'the boar's tooth' or 'dente di ciangiare'. The cut came out of the low *garde*, false edge up, crossed the incoming weapon with precision, striking it away, up and left, and then descending like an avenging angel in the same line to strike the knight on the head, arms, or neck. The thrown sword he sent out of the lists like a boy hitting a stick tossed by another boy; same *garde*, same cut.

Oh, no, gentles. There's nothing false about the false edge. Look here; I talk about swords all the time. Let's look at mine. Here she is: four feet of steel, a long hand span of hilt and the cross-guard as wide as the hilt is long. Not one of those new long hilts you see in High Germany; those are for men who never have to fight ahorse, and never have to fight close, either. A good wide blade, too; narrow blades break, and they don't cut.

A true sword has two edges. Saracen swords have but one edge, because they are simpler men than we, perhaps, or less deceptive, or really, just because their smiths use a different temper process and they can only get one edge hard as good steel ought to be. But in Milan they can make a blade that's straight as truth and has two sharp edges that run to a point fine enough to punch through maille. That's the whole point of the weapon, really, the point. It is mightier than the edge. But for all that, we play a lot with edges; and of the two, the true one is the one under your hand when you grip her; put a finger round the guard if it helps you, and there you are. The true edge is the one that it is natural to cut with: raise your arm and drop it, and you are cutting with the true edge. The false edge is the one on the back, and there's no false thing about it but the name. The true is the down stroke and the false is the reverse, and a better philosopher than me would point out that when you change grip, true and false are reversed, and that on a new sword it's impossible to tell the two edges apart.

I have found Truth and Falsity to look very similar in my time.

Regardless, there was Fiore, with a wooden sword. His *falso*, his false edge cut, had opened up his adversary, and then his own cut came down the line that his *falso* had traced with a precision and fluidity that was beautiful to watch.

'That's all I have to teach you,' Fiore insisted. 'The whole of this art is in emerging like a wild animal from the cover of the outside lines to strike the opponent's weapon and win the centre – and then to strike like the leopard.'

Now, this is the part that I always love when Sir Fiore teaches.

Everyone nodded; after all, they were all professional men-at-arms, who at least notionally fought and killed for their livings. But *certes*, not everyone fights the same way, and many good knights are merely brave enough to set their spear and push in the stour or the mêlée. They have no more idea of the art of *armizare* than they have of *tactica* or *logistica*. They put their heads down and they fight manfully and they survive.

A handful practise the art – really practise it. Fewer yet understand it; even fewer have the kind of cold rage that allows them to kill without mercy or passion. They are the most dangerous, but they are bad knights, because a killer without mercy is nothing but a killer: a rabid dog that needs to be put down. I have known a few such, as you will hear.

Bah, I lose my way. My point is that in this huddle of good men-at-arms, every head nodded understanding, and yet I could tell from the confusion of their bodies that not one in ten understood a word he said. They smiled fearfully and hoped he would not call on them to demonstrate anything else.

I still laugh to remember it. Why is it that none of us is really brave enough to step forward and say, 'Aye, master, I have no idea what you just said?' Eh? To swordsmen or priests or even wives, I trow.

And yet we did learn that spring. If Jerusalem hardened us into something a little special, if the Holy Sepulchre made us something other than brutes, it was Fiore who gave us the art, and there were not fifty men-at-arms and archers in God's creation with a better understanding of the principles of fighting with spear or lance, sword or axe. Marc Antonio, my squire, showed every sign of being a fine man-at-arms; Achille, Nerio's squire, who seemed too soft for a life of war, proved to be an incredibly dexterous swordsman. One day he disarmed me and I had to embrace him. And of course Sir Bernard and Sir Jason and Sir Jean-François were the best of knights and yet seemed to learn willingly enough, something I have often noted in the truly excellent. Prince Francesco's son joined us often, sometimes with three or four friends. Only one of his former companions had stuck with him through the changes he was experiencing; he had served as a man-at-arms and his friend Alessio had followed him to war. That spring, both of them worked hard with Fiore, to master the art of arms.

And what Fiore did for the art of arms, Rob White and John the Kipchak tried to do for the archers, honing them at every skill; fletching their own arrows, or long bowls at extreme ranges, or rapidly rolling arrows off their fingers, loosing and loosing again, while they *ran*. John made most of the English at least passable at shooting from horseback with Hungarian bows we bought from a Turk merchant. And Rob White, Gospel Mark and John all spent time making every man, even our Kipchaks and our Greeks, at least passable while dismounted on the flat.

It was all beautiful, if preparation for war can be accounted beautiful.

And I'll bore you for a moment and say that my children, and by then they were mine, were part of the delight. Young Edouard had begun to play with swords, rising eleven years. Fiore said twelve, but the boy wanted a sword, and he'd begun to use rough and tumble too often on his sister, so I made him a waster and sent him, across his mother's tears, to the Prince in Mytilene and to Sir Richard Percy, to be a page and a squire.

It was as well I did, as you shall hear in time.

And I played with my daughters; a little one too young even to hold up her head or focus her eyes, and an older mite for whom there was no doll as perfect as her sister, and she struggled like a saint with her own feelings of sisterly jealousy. The same Turk trader who had the bows had a load of silk, and I bought some and Emile made her a doll like a great lady, and she called it Lady Emma, and Lady Emma lived with her other ladies from Venice and Savoy. And I, the great knight, was betimes a horse, and betimes a huntsman to a princess, and a juggler, and a fool.

Great days.

Ascension Day was nearing, and we were in the very peak of training, and Fiore himself declared that he would do nothing for the last week, so that no man would miss his moment for a sprained wrist or a broken finger. Training hurts; men are covered in bruises and abrasions that shopkeepers never know.

Regardless, it was our first day free of training when the herald came on a small galliote flying a fine banner of the Virgin in a blue cloak, and under it the arms of Savoy. I walked down to the beach to meet him, thinking that perhaps it was the Count himself; some said he would attend the tournament.

The herald bowed deeply, as if I was a great lord. Which, to be fair, I was, at least at a remove; I was lord of my lady wife, and she was a great lord. And I had three small lordships in my own right; one on Cyprus that paid in gold; one on Lesvos, where I lived, and one in the Italian Alps, which I had never seen.

Well. I started my life of arms as a cook's boy; I am never less then delighted by the deference of my peers or my people, as it is new to me every day. I suppose I imagine I'll wake one day and find that I'm turning a spit and it was all a boy's dream, eh?

Ah, the herald. So he hands me a scroll. I still have it. It summoned me with my full knight service for a feudal levy for the Count of Savoy, at Constantinople, three weeks hence.

I was dumbfounded.

Now, in truth, the Count was in his rights, but only just, and in an absurd way. No vassal could actually be summoned under Savoyard law to fight in the Holy Land; that part was absurd. He was stretching a point, because Emile was *in* the Holy Land. But the reality of the situation was immediately obvious when presented: he'd have to pay us all wages, and he couldn't really summon me with all my service – that is, all of Emile's service – yet, despite the absurdity, I had the men to satisfy him, because I had a small company of my own. I actually *had* forty men-at-arms and forty archers; the whole service that Emile would owe if, for example, the Green Count summoned her at Turin.

The herald admitted over dinner that many of the Count's men-at-arms were sick and more had gone home after Mesembria fell apart.

I looked at Nerio.

'I want to go to Didymoteichon, just as we planned at Christmastide,' Nerio said. 'I want to have friends on the Ottomanid side of this game.' He looked out the window. 'But ... he is your lord, and I imagine he'll esteem it a favour.'

'No he will not,' Emile said. 'He will take it as his due. He makes outrageous demands and later pretends it was all a jest.' She shrugged; she was not one for pouting. 'He can be a good lord. But when he is not ...'

The herald looked as if he might explode in defence of his lord.

I nodded. 'Forty days,' I said.

The herald looked at me.

'Marc Antonio,' I summoned my squire. 'Take this fine young man and show him the delights of Mythymna.'

When the herald was gone, I spoke to Emile and Nerio frankly.

'I know the law of arms,' I said. 'He gets forty days from when we respond, travel time included.' I shrugged. 'Two can play the game of loyal retainer. We have to go to Constantinople anyway, and by then, travel alone will have used eight days. Thirty-two days, and we'll end perhaps five days from Didymoteichon. Just in time to meet the Turks. We can send John and half a dozen Kipchaks across the lines to make sure that this Suleyman understands that we are accepting his invitation for, let us say, the first of July.'

Nerio nodded. 'And your feudal lord can pay the cost of transport!' he said.

'My other feudal lord has to accept the condition,' I said, and looked at Emile and drank wine. The Prince of Lesvos *also* had my knight service.

I sent the young herald back with our decision: the Green Count had to pay our transport and my other lord had to agree.

We arrived in the city of Mytilene a few days before the tournament. I wanted to talk to Prince Francesco, and to enjoy the good life of his court. He had jongleurs from Achaea and from Florence, and a singer from Provence; he kept a magnificent table, and, for an old pirate, he was the finest lord I've ever known – as good and bad a man as Hawkwood. And his son had grown on me; a difficult young man but increasingly a good companion.

Prince Francesco was originally a Genoese. He'd come out to Outremer in the fifties with a fleet of warships, and he'd ranged the coast of the Levant, taking prizes and burning and looting; a sort of sea-routier. About the time that the Black Prince was knighting Hawkwood at Poitiers, the Emperor of the Byzantines was marrying his daughter to Gatelussi and granting him a semi-independent principality on Lesvos, Chios, and Lemnos. These are the easternmost portions of Christendom since the fall of Acre; Mythymna, on Lesvos, is only about three sea miles from Asia. Gatelussi got a bride and a fine little kingdom, and in return he provided the emperor with a fine fleet and a very modern armed fist. The Gatelussi were excellent paymasters; they hired the very best mercenaries in Italy – Germans and English and Italians and Bretons and Gascons – and brought them out to the Aegean, where their superior training and armour gave them mastery of the seas around the islands.

I have always expected to retire on my estates there. It's a fine place, and with plenty of fighting. Francesco is an enlightened despot; his taxes are low, because he makes his income off terrorizing the Turkish coast; his men-at-arms are too busy to brutalize the peasants. He is a patron of the arts.

He sat before me on a stool, while a servant fitted him with a sabaton that was slightly too small. He was trying a new harness; he planned to open the tournament himself.

'I have, hmmm, agreements,' and here the old pirate smiled like a fox. 'Hmmm, with most of the Turkish rulers this year,' Francesco said. 'I won't be fighting alongside your Green Count. And anyway, he has no army; most of his men-at-arms are sick.'

'I gather that new lords reached him from Savoy and Cyprus,' I said. 'Crusaders.'

Prince Francesco laughed. 'Fucking crusaders,' he said. 'The most useless . . .' he looked at me. 'I don't mean the Order, or the professionals. But a bunch of Frankish lords with no idea what the conditions are here, no military training, no idea except to kill infidels.' He shook his head. 'Some of my closest allies are infidels. Old Uthman was far more reliable than the Pope.'

Once I might have been shocked. But now I was a veteran of Outremer. I knew, now, the dividing line between Christianity and Islam that had once seemed so stark was, like everything, a matter of shades of grey. I thought of the young men I'd met in one of the Turkish towns, curious, eager to dispute with us about the Trinity; I thought of the Dervishes. About the curious things men believed.

'I can see,' Prince Francesco said, 'that you are now one of us. So I say, another season of your Green Count harrying the Turks will only fragment good alliances. And anyway, he's attacking the wrong Turks.'

'Wrong Turks?' I asked.

'He's attacking the Ottomanids and not the Karamanids. He probably can't tell them apart,' the prince said with contempt. Then he turned, with a sharp intake of breath. 'Careful there,' he said.

The armourer looked rueful.

'I need to open a rivet, lord,' he said.

'Just don't open my foot,' the prince said. 'Although, Ser William, now that I consider it, the emperor might like us to … bluster … in the direction of the Ottomanids. They are dangerous allies.'

I changed tack. 'Will you go to do the deed of arms at Didymoteichon?' I asked.

'I probably won't break a lance,' the Prince said, playing with his beard to hide a smile. 'But I'll be there, making a treaty with the Ottomanids for the emperor. They have too much of our ground behind Constantinople already; your Green Count should have retaken Adrianopolis instead of Mesembria.' He shrugged. 'But … my fleet will be sitting off the coast to make sure everyone knows we mean business.' He nodded at a seat brought by a servant. 'Sit, William. You treat me like a great lord. I'm just an old pirate.'

A very successful pirate …

'The emperor is out of money; he paid thirty thousand ducats for Mesembria and Gallipoli. Now he needs to raise more funds. He needs to settle soldiers in the north, and stop the blood-sucking leech of a Church from taking all his money.' Francesco snapped his fingers and I was given wine. 'We need five years of peace,' Francesco said.

I toyed with my goblet, which was heavy and solid silver. I understood all his points, and he was my other feudal lord. 'So you forbid me from joining the Green Count?' I asked.

He shrugged.

'May I offer a suggestion?' I asked.

He sat back and flicked his beard. 'You're a smart lad, for an Englishman. Tell me.'

'The Green Count is going to make war on the Turks without the emperor's permission,' I said.

'Against the emperor's express request! It's as if he thinks war in Outremer is a fucking sport and he's going to hunt inside the garden,' Francesco spat.

I met his eye. 'What if, instead, the emperor were to appear to be in control of the Green Count's expedition? Would the Turks not have all the more reason to negotiate?'

'Is this Nerio's idea?' the Prince asked.

'No, my lord, all mine,' I said.

'He's rubbing off on you, and you may yet become Italian. So you go to serve the Green Count, and I hover off the coast with my fleet, and the emperor and I pretend we're running the show.'

'Yes, my lord,' I said. 'And the emperor can repeatedly and pointedly state that he "finds the young Crusaders difficult to control" and other such platitudes. The same platitudes that Venice and Genoa make to each other ...' I smiled. 'And then, when we negotiate at Didymoteichon, the Ottomans will know that we have teeth. And you'll get your five year truce with them.'

Francesco was pounding his armoured thigh with his hand, laughing. 'Jesus Christ, the same bullshit that Uthman used to say when he snapped up one of our towns!' he said. 'By God, Englishman, you have a head on your shoulders. I like it. And I have a terrible reputation for duplicity and brutality.' His eye twinkled. 'I'll make use of it.'

The tournament at Mytilene was magnificent as only the very rich can afford magnificence. We all had new pavilions of silk, at the Prince's expense; need I say more? Everyone was in their best and, somewhere in Milan and Bohemia, armourers must have broken their guild rules and stayed up night after night to get so much polished steel into our hands. A galliote arrived two days before the first list was due to open and disgorged a small fortune in finished plate armour, straight from Genoa. There was a fountain by the fortress rigged to give wine and not water, and the wine was delicious. At first peasants and townspeople came in mobs to fill bottles and clay jars, but then the Gatelussi steward began opening casks just to give away, and the fountain ran on.

We ran our first courses in brilliant sunshine, and the good weather held all the way to the last day; it sprinkled rain from time to time but it was not ever actually raining on the lists. The flowers remained in bloom, and the ladies of the town and the court, and my own lady wife, vied with *Natura* for the beauty of their apparel. Long dangling sleeves and high collars were the order of the day in France and Italy and Cyprus, and for the first day the ladies wore magnificent overgowns that might have been seen in Rheims or Ghent or Pavia. But by the second day, when the serious courses were being run a-horse, most of the women were in kirtles alone; the balance of beauty shifted slightly, from the richness of a brocade or a sweltering velvet to the curve of a hip or breast. As the heat of the second day built, so did the heat of the fights: hundreds of beautiful women with only a single layer of silk or linen covering them stitched as tightly as craft and mothers would allow has a certain effect on the fighting spirit, and a surprising number of men were stretched full length on the sand of the lists. The Prince forbade Fiore and Richard Percy from having a third course after each pierced the other's visor with a lance of war; the Prince's son Francesco unhorsed Nerio, and Nerio's rage was quick and hot. Fiore's comment that more practice might have brought him victory did not do anything to cool his anger.

Young Edouard waited on Sir Richard Percy as a page, and bore himself well, even when he had to control an angry horse that lifted him like a doll. I was watching him, even as Francesco dropped Nerio; shoulders set, head high, determined to hold the horse he'd been given.

Marc Antonio rode in arms, the first time I had allowed him. He was not Galahad nor yet Lancelot, but he held himself well and was never unhorsed, although he came close to going down against Percy. Achille, Nerio's squire, was excellent as well, holding his own against wily older knights like me and managing to score a point against Fiore, breaking his lance despite Fiore's attempt to use his lance at the cross, as he taught. Alessio, the young prince's friend, was unhorsed by Percy but kept his seat against Fiore.

I was adequate, but Jean-Francois stretched me across my saddle as he had on Cyprus. I didn't come off. Otherwise I broke most of my lances easily; Sir Bernard and I broke three and received a great many flowers and a long burst of applause.

But it was Fiore's week. Aside from his very dangerous encounter with Percy, he rode perfectly, dropping men left and right, and his score was unassailable by the time I reached him. I was surprised by his fire; he was clearly playing to win. I didn't want to be unhorsed, and I was on the stage of chivalry: Emile was watching. So I went and kissed her, to make the crowd roar, and it was then that I saw a young woman throw her arms around Fiore; not an everyday sight, I promise you.

'Aha,' thinks I. 'That's how the sail is setting.'

Fiore fell in love in odd ways and quirky moments; his last lady love, so to speak, had been Janet. Not that she ever returned his fervour, but he learned a great deal from it; despite his lack of intuition, he understood the art of courtly love surprisingly well. Perhaps because he read books and memorised things.

All this went through my head in a moment. The young woman was unknown to me, and I pointed her out to Emile.

'Goodness!' Emile said. She was delighted. 'Beautiful. I will find out directly.'

Emile had the confidence of the beautiful aristocrat; she had no hesitancy in pronouncing the girl 'beautiful'. And she was. She had brown hair that hung far down her back, a crown of flowers, and a kirtle of golden silk. She was 'somebody'; even her red leather shoes spoke of her station, and her very slim waist was girded with a chain of gold, which she took off and wrapped around Fiore's arm.

Oh, my.

'I think I'm about to be made an object lesson,' I said.

Emile kissed me, and very softly bit my lower lip, something that has always inflamed me. 'I want my knight to be the best knight,' she said.

It was like a shock; the look in her eye, lecherous and demanding. Courtly love need not end with marriage – far from it. My lady made her demand as she had every right to do.

I bowed, and vaulted onto my courser. My lady love had borne three children, and she still stood straight as an arrow, and she wore her kirtle over her naked body on a hot day. Nothing, for me, had changed since the first day on the bridge when I fought the Jaques for her and under her eye.

Prove your worth.

Fiore was, with Nerio, and Richard Mussard, my first and best friend. But by the law of arms, we put that aside when we went into the lists. He was going to attempt to unhorse me for the slim lady in the golden kirtle.

I was going to return the favour, for the slim lady in the blue silk kirtle.

I had a new helmet, of which more later, but I did not feel that it was up to the rigours of jousting, and settled for my old and somewhat dented great helm, newly painted red, and with one of my lady's sleeves floating from the crest. I took a moment to pray; I find that a prayer can put me in the right space for fighting, and after I prayed, I imagined the cross of the lances ...

My horse was in a fine state; fully worked up. I'd practised all spring. I sometimes beat Fiore, even then. Nothing was impossible.

I kept my lance erect as long as I could, so that Fiore would not slam his lance atop mine and void my blow. And I did not aim at his shield; I went for the crest on his helmet, where a fine piece of golden gauze floated.

Fiore's lance slammed into my shield and split it, but the shaft shattered like glass.

My lance had torn the golden veil off his head and I rode down the list with that dainty bit of silk dangling like a brag from my crenellated lance tip.

I was coming to Fiore's end of the lists, so I rode to the golden girl and placed the silk in her hands.

She flushed.

I turned my horse and trotted back, and popped my visor. There was Fiore, and I saluted him, and he gave me a glare of hate.

I suppose I rolled my eyes. The crowd was cheering me, and my wife's eyes were big enough to bathe in, all the way from where she sat by the Princess.

'Ser Fiore requests that you take up a lance of war to engage in the next course,' a herald said to me, as Marc Antonio got water into my mouth.

I spit the water, took a drink, and patted my horse's neck. 'Tell Ser Fiore that such is my love for him that I would never consider using a lance of war against him,' I said.

I picked up a lance with a crenellated tip. So did Fiore; he wasn't lost to reason.

But he was coming for me with blood in his eye.

I decided to go for his visor. He had a new helm, a great helm with a visor in the Italian style. The visor was broad and a little flat for my taste, and I thought I might be able to seat my coronal, the tip of the lance, against his eye slit.

Seventy paces away, Fiore decided that my old helm had enough dents in the front that he could seat his coronal against it.

We charged. Both horses seemed to know that this was the important course; both were tired, but in excellent condition, and we exploded into the lists like bulls into chutes at a fair. I got my lance into the rest under my arm, and my tip came down ...

457

My lance *exploded*. It was the strangest feeling, and my hand hurt for half a day. I had to let go the butt of the lance; my hand was numb. I rode by Fiore and he was untouched; not even rocked, but his lance was gone too.

The crowd was roaring. Almost everyone was on their feet, and I had no idea why. I just rode down the list, empty handed, and I waved at the crown and turned.

This time, when I saluted Fiore, he reached out his hand and we touched our fists together. The crowd roared again.

A herald met me as Marc Antonio handed me water.

'The Prince forbids a third meeting. You have done enough,' he said.

I bowed. There's nothing to be said on these occasions. You can argue later, or whine about it, but when the Lord of the Tourney says you are done, you are done.

I trotted my courser down the list to where the Prince and Princess and my lady were seated and saluted, and the Princess threw me a white rose, which I still have somewhere. And Emile looked as if she was going to eat me right there.

Bless her.

I trotted back to my end of the lists, and Marc Antonio held my stirrup while I dismounted. 'What the hell happened?' I asked, a trifle pettishly.

Marc Antonio made a face and handed me a jug of water. Achille, who was getting Nerio ready, glanced at me, full of obvious admiration.

'You don't know?' Nerio asked. He was already on his charger. 'By the Virgin, it was pretty, Guillermo. Lance head to lance head; a perfect strike to the tip, and both lances shattered.' He shrugged. 'I have never done it. Never even seen it.'

'Five points,' Marc Antonio said. In Mytilene, in accordance with the French fashion, a broken lance was worth one and driving the opponent to the ground was worth three; there were a few other scores. But tip-to-tip counted five.

I laughed. 'I thought I'd hit his horse or something,' I said. Marc Antonio got my breast and back open and off me; suddenly the hot air of Lesvos seemed cool. I finished the water, took another, drank some, and poured the rest over my head.

Fiore appeared, and gave me a nice steel embrace. 'You bastard,' he said. 'Just once, I want to impress a woman, and you try to steal my glory.'

As Fiore had no sense of irony, I knew he was speaking the truth. So I embraced him again. 'I'm sorry,' I said. 'But you cannot expect me to lie down. Not in front of *my* lady.'

'No,' Fiore said. He sighed. 'Well, tip-to-tip was excellent.'

'And anyway, tell her you trained me,' I said.

Fiore brightened. 'I already did,' he said.

You and Hawkwood and Boucicoult and the Order, I thought.

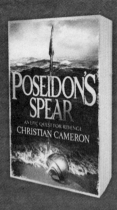

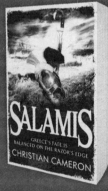